The Lure of Water and Wood

by Helen Lundström Erwin

Copyright Notice

Thanks and Acknowledgements

Swedish institutions and organizations are listed with Swedish names and grammar.

Pelle Johansson, Kulturmagasinet/Helsingborgs museer, for answering my many questions about Helsingborg, Ramlösa, guilds, and history in general.

Markus Henriksson, Kungliga Hovstaterna H.M. Konungens hovstall, for answering questions regarding horses and royal travel in Sweden in the 17th-century.

Inger Olovsson, Livrustkammaren, Skokloster slott, and Hallwylska museet, for answering my many questions regarding clothing and other details.

Sofia Nestor, Livrustkammaren, Skokloster slott, and Hallwylska museet, for providing me with information on King Karl XI's funeral.

Ulrika Torell, Stiftelsen Nordiska museet, for insights into 17th-century communal baking.

Professor Joel Halldorf, Professor Christer Pahlmblad, and Professor Stina Fallberg Sundmark, for answering my many questions regarding Swedish church life and religious tradition.

Martin Markelius, Armémuseum, for answering my questions about royal escorts and Drabant Uniforms.

Torbjörn Sundquist, Myntkabinettet - Ekonomiska museet, for information about 17th and 18th century coins.

Ulf Lindgren, Domkyrkokomminister, Storkyrkan, for answering my questions about the church and its architecture.

Judy Melinek, M.D., for explaining what happens to a body after a hanging and horse cadavers in cold weather.

William Bradley, DVM, and Brendan Furlong, MVD, MRCVS, for explaining how deceased horses may have been removed.

David Christenson, Horological Historian, The American Watchmakers, and Clockmakers Institute, for explaining about watches and clocks in the 17th-century.

Harold Hagopian, Virtuoso Resources, for helping me understand the violin and how to play it.

Thank you to Cari Ellen Hermann for modeling for the cover.

Thank you to Dr. Rolando Masis-Obando for modeling for the cover and for your friendship and support.

Thank you to Ben Erwin for photography and cover production.

Thank you to Mike Young for cover collaboration.

Professor Neil S. Price, for allowing me to use a quote from his book, A History of the Vikings, Children of Ash and Elm.

Christina Carrad LPC. LCAT. ATR-BC. CEDS

Thank you to SWEA New York, for your support and for honoring me and my work with the Mona Johnson Scholarship.

Thank you to my husband, Ben Erwin, for your love and support. And for always changing the music station so I don't get distracted and can stay in the past.

Thank you to David and Shannon Erwin and their children Evelyn, Dylan, and Sebastian.

Thank you to Arthur Vaccarino for your many years of support, invaluable feedback, and friendship.

Thank you to Christine Vaccarino for embracing my work as soon as you met me. And for the title!

Thank you to my Women's Writing Group ladies, Sharon Eccleston, Aurora Tantoco, and Iris Jackson, for your community and friendship.

Thank you to XR Women Co-Founders Julie Smithson, Karen Alexander, and Sophia Moshasha for your support of my book Sour Milk in Sheep's Wool, and its Foremothers Café.

A special thank you to Christi Fenison and Austin Caine of Cause+Christi Immersive XR Design for the above and beyond love and care you put into building The Foremothers Café. I'm looking forward to adding details from The Lure of Water and Wood to my VR World and to our new adventures together.

Thank you to Chris Madsen and everyone at ENGAGE.

Thank you to Juliana Loh, Paige Dansinger, Tom Furness, Tricia Blake, Sarah Barker, Dot Cannon, Michael Bogert, Steve Lewis, and Michelle Deborah Weisblat-Dane for your help and encouragement, and the many more members of the VR Community who have expressed support for my work.

Extra Special Thank you to Marcia Carter
with love and gratitude for your immeasurable support
and belief in my work over the years.

I appreciate you more than I can express.

Praise for The Lure of Water and Wood

"Within Helen Erwin's latest book, we are brought into the panic and fear of sorcery and the influence of malevolent players. She brings humanity and agency not only to the accused but to the supposed masterminds Näcken and Forest Rå. Humanizing this fear can perhaps bring new understanding to the panic that can begin after one fatal rumor." - Grace Beattie creator of Wicked Women: The Podcast

"Helen Lundström Erwin is able to weave the lives of those involved in the 17th and 18th-century Swedish Sorcery trials by taking the perspective of the accused in a world of hushed tones, hierarchy, and confusion. Her attention to detail places you at the heart of a village struck by scandal, where it's hard to know who or what to believe – you may even find that your sympathies change page after page! Erwin brings the reader into a time when magic, faith, and folk tales coursed through the landscape of the Swedish countryside by crafting together historical facts with fantasy storytelling." - Christopher Malone, Curator, American Swedish Historical Museum

For this book, Helen Erwin has combined history with fantasy as she brings to life the sorcery trials that took place in 17th and 18th century Sweden. With her impeccable research, Helen expertly recreates the feeling of the period, but with a twist - she is telling the story from the viewpoint of two enthralling mythological creatures! An intriguing take on the disturbing events of the time. - Judith Thomson, author of Phillip Deville Series

Helen Lundström Erwin's new book weaves a story based on Nordic folklore, combined with Erwin's characteristic thorough historical research based on true stories and court archives. But what is myth, and what really happened? Maria Malmström - Lakewood Memorial Library

"[They] did not *believe* in these things any more than someone today *'believes* in' the sea. Instead they knew about them: all this was as much a natural part of the world as trees and rocks."
\- Neil S. Price

For my mother, Solveig.

Näcken: Male River Entity - A mesmerizing but dangerous musician. Pronounced Neck-en (where 'ä' is similar to the ai in 'air.'

Rå (Forest Rå): Female Forest Entity - A beautiful guardian with a tree trunk or a hole for a back. Pronounced Raw (with a longer rounder a.)

Until the mid-18th century, Näcken and Rå were considered real beings. Having relations with them was illegal.

PART ONE

Chapter 01

Sweden, Anno 1599

Several days ride north of Norrköping

Nikolaos' neighbors pretended to nod pleasantly when they saw him leave, urged to do so by the fear of the sorcery that kept him young. He ignored it, nodding back in the same manner while nudging his horse into a canter. Nikolaos could still see himself in the features of their faces. He had seven children with neighbor Thomas' great, great-grandmother, all gone now, just like her. Nothing bound him to his land anymore; his great-grandchildren's children didn't know who he was and thought him long gone. Taking one last look at the thatched roofs of his farm, he continued south. One hundred and thirty years was long enough.

Nikolaos had been riding through dark, untrampled woods for three days, when after climbing a hill, he spotted an enormous half-timbered castle surrounded by a moat right below him. It took him by such surprise that he halted his horse, staring in disbelief. Green copper roofs and windows were glittering brightly in the sunlight. Two towers cast such long shadows on the ground that, at first, he didn't make out that there was a cluster of cottages and a church surrounding the castle.

But there was a whole town down there, faint movement of smoke above chimneys, pigs and chickens milling about, and people hurrying places. How could he have lived only days from such a large town without knowing of it?

"It's impressive, isn't it?"

Startled, Nikolaos reached for the knife he kept tied to his breeches and turned toward the voice.

A man took a quick step backward, smiling disarmingly. "Pray forgive me. I meant not to frighten you."

Nikolaos' hand relaxed its grip on the knife, and he let out a breath, returning his smile. "No harm done. Good day to you."

The man nodded with relief. "Princess Elisabet and her court stayed there; would you believe it?"

"Truly?"

"Indeed, her royal self. King Vasa's daughter. Three whole years, she graced us with her presence."

Nikolaos resisted a grimace. He had conflicted feelings about the old king. It was he who had forced the removal of their saints from the church and refused to listen to His Holiness the Pope. But he also achieved independence from Kristian, the Danish tyrant. "You don't say? Right down there?"

"Yes. That's Norrköping's House, the pride of our county. Can you guess at how many windows it has?"

Nikolaos leaned forward in the saddle and narrowed his eyes. There were at least forty windows in his direction, and if the towers were the same on all sides, each had at least sixteen. "I can't count them all from here, but there might be more than a hundred from the look of it."

The man smiled, shaking his head. "Three hundred windows. I have counted them myself many times. They're made of real glass, and the roof is copper."

Nikolaos whistled slowly. "Three hundred and all glass?"

"Yes." The man bent down, pulled up a long piece of grass, and started chewing on it. "I know everything about Norrköping's House. I could tell you if you wish. You look like you've been traveling a bit. Care for a meal and some hay for your horse? My woman and I live right down there," he said, gesturing toward a gray cottage with an adjoining barn about thirty paces behind him.

Nikolaos smiled. He hadn't noticed the farm until now. This was a fantastic bit of luck. "I've been riding for eight days." He lied effortlessly. It was safer not to be specific.

"That's a journey for sure. You must be tired then. I'll offer some grain for your horse, too. What do you call the fella?"

"Just the horse," Nikolaos said, swinging himself to the ground. He no longer named his animals. They lived such short lives, and he had lost so many.

"I see. Well, I'm Mats."

"Nikolaos," he said and bowed. "I give thanks for your hospitality."

Mats didn't bow but looked very pleased.

They continued in silence until they reached the edge of Mats' yard. Stacks of wood lined the side of the house, and a gray cat curled up at the far end cast a lazy eye in their direction, then went back to sleep.

"Just go ahead in. I'll put your horse in my stable for a bit and take his saddle off," Mats said and grabbed the bridle.

Nikolaos stared after him as he walked off. All his belongings were tied to that saddle, including his fiddle. He hesitated, wondering if he should run after him, then shrugged and went into the house, deciding to let it be. It would just seem suspicious.

It was dark inside. Only one of the window shutters was open at the end of the room, creating streams of sunlight that made the dust visible. Turning from it, he perceived benches along the wall behind a large rectangular table. It took him a moment to recognize that a pile of fabric in the corner was a woman's skirts and legs. She sat calm and silent, waiting for him to speak.

Nikolaos fixed his gaze on the faint shape of her face, embarrassed. "Your husband, he asked me to go right in, invited me for a bit to eat."

"I heard you outside. We're glad for visitors." She paused, and he could perceive a slight smile on her face. "It's always nice to get news. Where are you from? Do you live in town?"

Just then, the door opened, and Mats came in. "First time it must be. I found him staring at the castle. He wants to hear stories with his meal." He opened the shutters of two more windows, and light flooded the room.

"Sit then," his wife said and stood up, pointing to the benches. "I'm Ingeborg. Pray share our porridge and ale if it suits you?"

"I would give thanks. Bless you," Nikolaos said. He could go a long time without food but had become accustomed to eating regularly. It helped him appear normal.

Ingeborg placed a large bowl on the table, handed Nikolaos and Mats mugs filled with ale, and sat down at the edge of the hearth. In the sunlight, she looked a little younger than he had thought. She was lovely and round, with wrinkles only on her forehead and around her eyes.

Nikolaos pulled his spoon out of his pocket and leaned forward to dip it in the bowl, accidentally banging into Mats' spoon at the same time, causing globs of porridge to splash on the table. "Pray forgive me. I was so hungry that I became impatient," he said, embarrassed again.

Ingeborg just chuckled, left the hearthside, and wiped it off.

"You mentioned that you've been riding for eight days. Where are you from? North of here, is it?" Mats asked, ignoring it altogether.

"Yes."

"Where's your wife? Your children?" Ingeborg asked.

"I've lost my wife." He took a breath and looked her straight in the face. "It felt better to leave."

Ingeborg's eyes widened. "You're so young, already a widower. Was it the winter that took her? She caught a chill?"

"Childbirth, the baby died too." It was a lie, but it wasn't hard to look sad even though it was eighty-three years ago, and Abluna had died of old age, not by giving birth.

Ingeborg crossed herself, and her movements grew heavy when she sat back down.

A shadow of pain crossed Mats' face. Maybe they had lost children recently themselves, or grandchildren more likely. "I was to tell you about the castle, wasn't I?" he said, changing the subject. "What people don't know is that we had another castle here before, but the army had to burn it when the Danes came. It was so it wouldn't fall into enemy hands. Can you imagine? Setting fire to a castle!"

"When was this?"

"I think it was about thirty years ago."

Nikolaos raised an eyebrow in recognition but didn't

respond. The Seven Year War, he remembered it well. His great-grandsons hadn't been forced to fight. He was still thankful for that.

"They rebuilt some twenty years ago. They made it fit enough for Princess Vasa, and we were fortunate to be graced by her presence before she succumbed," Mats added.

"Succumbed?"

"Indeed, her Highness was a kind, sweet soul who died too young, just like your wife. We saw her many a time. She wore such incredible dresses, didn't she, Ingeborg?" Mats threw Ingeborg a quick glance. "Her sleeves were golden, matching the gold cross around her neck. And she wore ruffs, beautiful white ruffs that blinded our eyes."

"Princess Vasa lived here for three years, then had it in her head to travel to Stockholm. Never saw her again. I'm not sure why she saw fit to leave Norrköping, but she must have caught a cold in Stockholm and died. It's very drafty on all those islands," Ingeborg said. She got to her feet, removed the bowl and their mugs, and remained standing.

"I wasn't aware that she died. May she rest in peace," Nikolaos said and crossed himself.

"Yes," Ingeborg said.

"I noticed your fiddle out there behind your saddle," Mats said, changing the subject again. "If you want, you might be able to ask to play at the castle, should you be looking for work? Princess Vasa's court is gone of course, but there are still noblemen. Many of them are from Mecklenburg, like her husband was. Germans, you see."

"Work there?" Nikolaos pursed his lips, considering. Finding work would change everything. And he was far enough from home that no one would recognize him. "Maybe I ought to do that. I thank you for telling me."

Mats smiled. "They're always looking for musicians." He exchanged a look with Ingeborg, but she quickly looked away. "Would you care to play a tune with me? I play as well," he said, looking back at Nikolaos.

He hesitated. It would be stupid to play in such a small

space. Their home wasn't big enough for them to stay unaffected. "Play now?

"Pray yes," Mats said, eyes insisting. "I've not played with others for quite a while. I'd much enjoy it."

"Do say yes, I'll fetch it for you," Ingeborg said. "You men stay here and decide what tune to play." She hurried out, leaving the door ajar.

Nikolaos started to stand. Now would be the time to stop it. If he could get to the barn before she retrieved his fiddle, he could make an excuse that he had to leave. On second thought, the open window shutters let the air in. It might be safe, especially if she also kept the door open.

Mats got his own fiddle from a shelf and pulled out two chairs, placing them in the middle of the floor. "Sit," he said, pointing, then looked up with a smile when Ingeborg came back inside. She closed the door behind her.

"Could you leave it open to get some air?" Nikolaos asked as she handed him his fiddle.

"Air? Then we'd have to close the shutters, or we'd catch a draft. It would be too dark."

"I see, of course," Nikolaos said, suppressing a feeling of dread. It would seem rude to refuse now. He glanced at Mats, who sat looking at him, his bow at the ready. Then he shrugged. It would be what it would be.

When Nikolaos stopped playing, Ingeborg's face was flushed, and her eyes were shining and dazed. Mats stared into space with his fiddle on his lap and his bow on the floor. They didn't notice him leaving.

Chapter 02

Nikolaos stopped in front of Norrköping's House and stared at it. It was massive and incredibly tall. It looked like it was touching the sky. Even though he was on horseback, he had to crane his neck all the way back to see the roof. Birds were circling up there, making him dizzy. A castle of such immense size must have large enough rooms for him to perform in without risking putting the audience into a torpor. He turned toward the town square in front of the castle. It was busy; people were heading in different directions, and there was a small market in the back where a crowd stood around a stall, pointing at things. It seemed a friendly sort of place, a town where he could be accepted again.

Steeling himself, he took a closer look at Norrköping's House. The bridge across the moat led straight to a grand wooden door. It was closed, and there was no wicket door in it, but there was a narrow path between the moat and the castle wall, which may take him to the back or maybe to another entrance. With a quick look over his shoulder, determining that none of the villagers appeared suspicious, he decided to at least ask if they wanted musicians. He crossed the bridge, then positioned the horse so he could reach the door and banged on it with the palm of his hand. It barely made a sound on the thick wood. There was no point. Unless someone was standing right on the other side, there was no way they would hear it. He gave up and steered the horse onto the path along the wall, riding at a slow trot until he came to the corner, immediately followed by a tall wooden fence. Peeking over it, he stopped abruptly, feeling his jaw slack with surprise. There was an enormous garden hidden there. Paths were looping around bushes full of bright blue, yellow, pink, and red flowers. A gardener went from bush to bush, plucking off leaves and placing them in a basket. Behind him were rows of fruit trees surrounded by lush, thick grass covered with tiny blue and white flowers. It was astonishing.

Nikolaos watched the gardener for a moment, enjoying the peaceful scene and the rich scent of flowers. Then he turned the horse around and went back the way he came, this time continuing past the bridge to the other side of the house. He was in luck. There was an open yard in front of another wooden door, smaller than the one by the bridge. It was probably the official side entrance. A good place to ask for work.

Nikolaos' feet had just hit the ground when the door opened a crack, and a portly man with a red nose full of bumps pushed his head out. "Yes, how can I help you? If you come a courtin' the Princess, she's dead already." He laughed raucously and looked at Nikolaos expectantly as if he really thought he had come for Princess Vasa. He was obviously very drunk.

"I've come to see if you'd need a fiddler," Nikolaos said, trying not to laugh.

"Well, come in then, come in. We love fiddling here," he said, letting out a loud burp.

Another man appeared behind him, looking exasperated. "For goodness sake, let him in," he said, pushing the door as wide as it would go. It made a squeaking sound, which made Nikolaos see sharp red flashes at the hinges. The man's shirt was unbuttoned, exposing a dirty chest and an equally dirty undershirt. His hair was greasy and tied with a leather string at the nape of his neck.

"I give thanks. Where can I leave my horse?"

"Bring him in, there's enough room."

"I give thanks," Nikolaos said again, grabbed a steady hold on the bit, and entered, stepping on a cobblestoned floor. There were no windows and only dim torchlight. It must be a carriage room of some sort.

"Put him in the corner over there," the man with the greasy hair said and pointed to a trough and bucket in the corner of the room.

There was a hook attached to the wall, and Nikolaos tied the horse to it, then removed the saddle and his satchel and placed them both on the floor. He was tired, and an overwhelming sense of grief came over him so strongly that he had to stifle a sob. Remaining where he was, he stared at the wall while patting the horse to make it seem like he was still tending to him. He had left his home. The beautiful farm where he had raised his family and loved his wife. Never again would he pay respect at their gravesides. Graves with stones so old, he had visited in secret when no one watched, usually at night. Would Abluna know he still thought of her if he couldn't go anymore?

"Need anything?"

Startled, Nikolaos quickly turned around. The man with the greasy hair had sat down at a table in the corner with a mug of ale in front of him. The drunken man had left. "No, I thank you. I have everything I need."

Gesturing toward an empty chair, the man motioned for Nikolaos to come sit. "You speak German?" he asked, pushing the ale toward Nikolaos.

"No."

The man shrugged. "No matter. So, you're a fiddler? It's how you make a living?" he asked, eyeing Nikolaos' breeches with a slight frown.

"Mostly, yes."

"What manner of work do you do in when you're not playing?"

Nikolaos took a sip of ale. It was delicious. "Well, I used to be a farmer, but I decided to leave and see more of the world, do a bit of exploring."

"Leave? Who sees to your farm? What does your wife say about it?"

"She and our first baby died in childbirth. Her family will take care of it." It wasn't a lie. Their neighbors, most of them his own relations, would surely take over the farm once they realized he had abandoned it. Unless they burned it down.

"I see." He nodded silently, compassion glinting in his eyes. "I'll ask Karl Bagpiper to listen to a tune in a moment. If it's to his liking, you'll get something proper to wear. They like to keep it fancy inside," he said, pointing to a staircase behind him that led up to a closed green door. "If you'd just show me your passport, I'll go and fetch him for you. I'm Gustav, the guard here."

"Of course." Nikolaos reached for his satchel and pulled out his son's passport, praying Gustav wouldn't notice it wasn't his. The pastor would have been as happy as all the rest of the villagers to see him go but would never have vouched for him by writing a traveling passport. The pastor feared him. Afraid when Nikolaos came to church but even more afraid of telling him he wasn't welcome. His son's passport, however, had been tucked away in a drawer. It was so worn that it was impossible to read what it said. He handed it to Gustav, looking him straight in the eye.

He just glanced at it, then returned it and headed up the stairs.

Nikolaos exhaled, put the document back in his satchel, and then finished the ale in one long sip. His throat was dry, he wasn't used to talking this much.

Only a moment later, the door at the top of the stairs opened, and Gustav and Karl the bagpiper appeared. He was completely bald and wore brown knee-length puffy breeches over light brown hose that complimented a pair of muscular legs.

"You're the farmer who plays the fiddle so well that you come here to apply for work?"

Nikolaos stood up and bowed deeply. "Yes, good sir."

"Let's hear it. Get your fiddle for me."

Nikolaos nodded, then went to retrieve it, smiling to himself as he went.

On his return, they were leaning against the wall and had opened the main door to get some light. That was good, the more space and air there was, the less risk there would be for them to become entranced. It was only when he was near water that he lost control completely. If someone got near him then, they drowned. He didn't even need his fiddle.

Taking a breath, he chose a recognizable piece that showed his range and began.

Soon Karl's and Gustav's eyes relaxed, and their breathing deepened. Outside the birdsong stopped, and even the flies ceased their incessant buzzing. But this time, Nikolaos was in control, holding his notes just long enough for them to feel their souls stir with emotion without losing themselves. He smiled as blue and purple flowed from his strings. Colors that only he could see.

When he stopped, both men stood stock still, staring in astonishment.

"Why don't I know of you? I've never heard anything as exquisite," Karl said finally. His voice sounded thick. Gustav was wiping tears from his eyes.

Nikolaos bowed. "I thank you. I play mostly by myself. Not everyone appreciates it as you have."

"They don't appreciate it? They've done you a disservice then and are fools. You shall not hide your talents thus. It's an insult to the gift that God has bestowed upon you," Karl said, waving his hand in the air in front of his face as if to fan himself.

Nikolaos bowed again, not sure what else to do or what to say to such a compliment.

"Get his horse to the stable," Karl said to Gustav. "Brush him and give him the finest oats you have. I'll take this gentleman with me and find him suitable apartments and proper clothes."

They were offering him a place to stay, too? Nikolaos put his hand on Karl's shoulder. "I give deep thanks for your kindness and exceptional hospitality." Now he just had to pray the rooms were large enough.

Karl lifted his eyebrows, "Thank me? Nah, I shall thank you. I'd lose my job if I let you leave, that's for sure."

Nikolaos nodded, hiding a sudden need to weep. It had been a long time since someone had looked at him without a hint of suspicion.

As soon as Nikolaos put his foot on the other side of the green door, he understood that he had entered a completely different world. The floor spreading out in front of him was made of polished stone so shiny it looked like a sheet of ice. Tapestries weaved with warm reds and bright blues lined the walls, making the room seem warm and inviting despite the icy-looking floor. Karl grabbed his arm and pulled him forward as if there were an urgency to what they were about to do. Clearly, he was used to the place and didn't see the need to pay the finery any mind.

Passing room after room, each more incredible than the

next, and with doors so wide they could still walk arm in arm, Nikolaos barely had time to turn his head.

When Karl finally stopped, he pointed into a smaller room with a table and chairs in the center. Fruit, several kinds of cheeses, meats, and soft breads covered the table. Maybe Karl was expecting company. It was an incredible amount of food.

"This is my room," Karl said and went to sit down in one of the chairs. He grabbed a piece of cheese and took a bite. "I'll find you something to wear in a moment. I have several things that might fit. Trunk is right over there," he added, waving his knife at it. "Sit first, have a piece of bread and some of this delicious cheese."

"I give thanks," Nikolaos said and sat down beside him.

"What made you come here to ask? Did someone tell you we need musicians?"

"Yes, I happened upon a man yesterday, lives up that hill behind the castle. He suggested it."

"You don't mean Mats?"

"Yes, that's who it was. Do you know him?"

"I see. That's a bit curious." Karl looked uncomfortable. "I do, yes. Mats performed with me when the Princess stayed with us."

"He performed here?" Nikolaos asked, hand hovering over the cheese.

"Yes, Ingeborg cooked for a while too. She's an excellent cook. We were sorry to see *her* go."

Nikolaos' heart sank. He thought Mats and Ingeborg had just seen the Princess from afar, at a parade or something where she was driven around town to show herself. He should never have come, not after having left them entranced. "How odd. Mats was very eager to tell me about the Princess, but never mentioned that he had played here. Only that I might be able to."

Karl scoffed. "Well... Mats is nice, but he was too infatuated with Princess Vasa. It was becoming bothersome for everyone. He would stop playing and blush like a woman when she came to listen. Asked inappropriate questions of everyone who had contact with her. Seemed to think he was on equal footing with her." He shook his head. "Mats was told to leave. He was probably too embarrassed to tell you. Good of him to offer his old position to you though, I must say."

"Yes, very kind indeed," Nikolaos said slowly. It would be better to leave, but he didn't want to. Living on his music with a place to stay as well, was too much of a godsend to deny. He had to pray that Mats and Ingeborg kept what happened to themselves.

"Well, that's of no matter any longer," Karl said. "You're an exceptionally talented fiddler, much better than Mats. Who taught you?"

"My father."

Karl dipped his fingers in a bowl of water and wiped his hands on the tablecloth. "Your father? He taught you well. Who is he? Do I know of *him?*"

"I doubt it, he died some years ago. He was like me, playing alone or at dances now and then."

"I see," Karl said with an expression of both disbelief and admiration. He stood up and went to open the trunk. Rummaging inside, he pulled out a pair of hose, a red jacket, a ruff for the neck, and a few other items, handing them to Nikolaos. "We'll see if these fit. If not, we'll get the tailor to make you something. Here, take it."

He carefully grabbed the pile and let his hand slide over the fabric. It was impossibly soft.

Karl grinned. "Fine, eh? Come," he said, gesturing. "I'll show you your rooms. You can try it on there and see how it looks."

He led Nikolaos up two flights of stairs and through another series of large rooms, each decorated with paintings of men and women in fanciful clothes. One room was long and narrow, like a hallway. At the far end was a contraption that looked like a chicken coop but was gilded and stood on a fine carved table. It was full of bright yellow birds, large enough for them to fly back and forth in. Nikolaos was so surprised that he gasped.

Karl chuckled. "It's a birdcage. They're canaries from France, some German I believe."

"A birdcage," Nikolaos said, trying the unfamiliar word. What a strange custom.

"I leave you to the birds. Your apartments are right around the corner here. I'll come check on you in a little while, eh?" Karl said and walked off.

Nikolaos nodded, his eyes still on the birdcage. The colorful little birds were chirping pleasantly, jumping back and forth on thin sticks attached to the bars. Small containers with seeds and berries were placed throughout the cage. One bird was picking at the seeds and took no notice of the other birds moving about. Another was looking straight at Nikolaos, cocking its head from side to side. "You're a good little thing, hope you're happy here and don't wish that you could fly away," he whispered to it, then straightened up and crossed the hallway to what was to be his new home.

It consisted of a large room with a smaller one adjoining it. The first room had a table with a candle, a corner cupboard, an identical trunk to Karl's, and a narrow bench along one wall covered with a long, thin pillow. The walls were bare and painted white. The second room had a bed with brown bolsters and a blanket in the same color. They looked worn but clean. There was a water bowl with a carafe for washing on the windowsill and a small chair in the corner. Nikolaos placed the new clothes on it, then sat on the bed, exhausted and overwhelmed. His head was spinning, and words repeated in his mind like an echo. It had been a long time since he had spoken as much as today. Ever since his youngest daughter died, an old unmarried woman by then, and he stayed alive, his neighbors stopped talking with him. It didn't help that he grew his beard long, covering it in soot to make it look gray, or supporting himself on a cane. They were pleasant to him only if there was no way to avoid him and only because they were afraid. That was what hurt the most. He wished they had screamed at him instead so he could at least try to make excuses. But they never did. It made him agitated and grumpy, which only increased his need to spend time in the river.

He lay down on the bed and closed his eyes, imagining water so as not to think of all the hurt.

Nikolaos didn't realize that he had fallen asleep until there was a loud knock on the door.

It was Karl, striding right in without taking any notice of him, then went around and started to touch all the surfaces with his index finger. "Good, they have a better girl now, not much dust," he said, sliding his finger over a candlestick. "I'm glad to see it. Did you try your new outfit yet?"

Nikolaos threw his legs over the side of the bed and yawned. "No, pray forgive me, I fell asleep. The days on horseback must have taken its toll." He reached for the pile on the chair with his right hand.

"It'll do it to you," Karl said and sat on the now empty chair.

Nikolaos pulled his breeches off, feeling embarrassed when he realized how dirty they looked compared to his new hose. They were stained with grass, mud, and something unnamable. He quickly pushed them back behind him with his right foot.

Then, to make matters worse, when he pulled the hose on, his toenails and toes poked the thin fabric, making him feel clumsy as well.

"And these," Karl said when he finally finished, pointing to the same kind of garment he wore, a pair of silky puffy breeches sewn to bubble out on the sides.

They were easy to get into but made his legs look like sticks under their generous shape. He had never seen a musician wear anything like it, but he supposed castle life was different.

"This you put in front to protect your life-hood," Karl added with a smile as he handed him a round, hard object that was hollow inside.

"My what?" Nikolaos turned it this way and that, not understanding until he met Karl's grinning eyes. It was supposed to fit between his legs.

"Your codpiece. It feels odd at first, but it's very convenient. You can store coins there or whatever else you have the need for."

Nikolaos shook his head and laughed. A hiding place for coins? Lord have mercy.

The last pieces of the outfit were the red jacket and the ruff. Nikolaos felt better about them. He had never worn anything as fine, used as he was to farming breeches and linen shirts. Looking down at himself, he felt like someone else. Maybe he would be safe here after all. Hopefully Mats and his wife would stay away from the castle and wouldn't recognize him even if they saw him in town.

"Handsome fella now, eh?" Karl winked and wrapped his arm around his shoulder. "Come on down, bring your fiddle and we'll go play for the Germans," he said and began to walk out of the room with him, slowing down just enough so Nikolaos could grab his instrument. "We have a Venetian looking glass down the hall if you want to see how you look."

"A what?"

Karl removed his arm from his shoulder and stepped away to look at his face. "A Venetian looking glass, you've never seen a looking glass before?"

"No, I haven't. What is it?"

Karl shook his head. "Incredible. Come here. I'll show you." He hurried through the hallway past the bird cage and the chirping canaries and into a room at the far end. Wooden beams spanned the space, anchored to the walls at one end and propped up by a vertical beam on the other. Piles of dresses, hose, and linen shirts were draped over them. In the corner was a large empty frame leaning against the wall. He took Nikolaos' arm again and guided him until he stood directly in front of it. Someone moved inside it and Nikolaos took an involuntary step back. Karl laughed, "You must have seen yourself in something, a still lake or a windowpane, haven't you?"

It was a reflection. Slowly, Nikolaos touched his face, then his hair and chest. He moved forward and almost called out when the man in the frame did the same. It took him several moments to confirm that it really was a reflection and not another man standing there. He flicked an eye at Karl, who laughed again.

Taking a closer look at himself, Nikolaos noticed his cheeks were rounder than he expected and his eyes smaller and browner. He hadn't realized how much his children must have looked like him. It was as if he was looking straight into their eyes, and for a moment he was overcome.

Karl's concerned face met his in the reflection. That too, was disorienting. "Are you unwell?" he asked.

Nikolaos exhaled, pushing the memories and the disorientation away. "No, no. I'm fine. Pray forgive me," he said, looking back at his reflection, touching his bare chin. There was a stubble now, but he could see the paler skin outlining where his long beard had been. His hair was thick and brown, his shoulders broad, muscles visible where the new jacket was open in front under the ruff. His legs were not as scrawny as he thought, but well-built and muscular. There was no denying it, he was handsome. A smile played on his lips, widening into a grin in response to his reflection smiling.

"Takes a bit to get used to, eh? Venetian looking glass is the best kind," said Karl. "The Royal Court had several installed before Princess Elisabet Vasa arrived. They removed most of them when they left, except for this one here and a much larger one in the royal dining hall downstairs. It was too cumbersome to bring back, they said, but never explained how it got here in the first place. This one I think they forgot. It was installed for the Princess and her maids. They dressed her here, you see."

"Ah," Nikolaos said, trying to keep up with Karl's unceasing flow of information.

"We should go. It's already late." Karl looked out the window where the summer sun was setting behind the western tree line.

Nikolaos followed Karl back downstairs. The castle didn't seem quite as big on the way down as it had on the way up now when he recognized where they were going. Instead of turning left to go into the large room with the shiny floor, they made a right and entered a narrow corridor. There was a din of voices at the end of it.

"That's our dining hall. It's not as grand as the royal one that I mentioned earlier," Karl said when he noticed Nikolaos reacting to it. "It suits us just fine, though."

No matter what Karl thought, Nikolaos drew a sigh of relief when they entered. The room was huge. He could safely play there.

"That's my bagpipe," Karl said, discreetly pointing to where it stood leaning against the back wall. Then they made their way across the floor. It wasn't polished and was full of footprints and food scraps. The diners talked and laughed amongst themselves, smiling absently at them as they passed.

"You can start on your own, Nikolaos," said Karl and sat himself down at an empty chair at a table.

Nikolaos nodded, feeling nervous now despite his relief earlier. He took a deep breath to calm himself down. If people became entranced, all he needed to do was to leave. He didn't owe them anything. His heart rate slowed down. Placing the fiddle below his shoulder, he lifted his bow. As soon as he played the first note, the laughing and small talk stopped. Someone said something in German, and there was a scraping sound when someone moved a chair, and then all was quiet.

Playing, he kept a close eye on their reaction. One man looked stunned, but it was probably the wine, or just the fact that he loved his music. Nikolaos finished his piece without trouble. When he looked to Karl to give him his turn, another man hurried to his feet.

"No Bagpipe! Play more. Right now. Play!" the man exclaimed, joined by loud words in German from several tables.

Nikolaos found Karl's eyes and got a nod in response. Well then. He smiled at the audience and chose a piece that was a bit livelier but with undertones of deep emotion. He had composed it when Abluna passed on to the lord. It celebrated the long life they had together, promising he would never forget her. It was his own, but a piece he had played at gatherings without a problem. Deep reds and soft purples floated from the strings, and he relaxed, feeling calm and happy to share his love for his wife again. When he looked back at the audience, a woman was crying openly, and her husband was struggling not to do the same. Nikolaos finished the piece and bowed.

"Who are you? That was extraordinary. Do tell me this isn't the only time you'll perform?" said the husband, then got to his feet and hurried toward him, his jowls wobbling when he walked. He looked important and wealthy enough to have been eating well for a long time.

"I give thanks. I may play again if Karl thinks it's suitable."

Karl sauntered over from the dining table with a piece of meat in his hand. "He isn't leaving here if I have something to say about it. I've already set him up upstairs. This isn't someone we can let loose," Karl said, looking completely serious. "Will you believe Nikolaos is a farmer, played for neighbors and family only? Hiding his talent for us who truly appreciate the finer art of music."

"You don't say?" The man eyed Nikolaos, a scrutinizing look that began at his hose and traveled upward toward his codpiece and jacket. Maybe he thought it looked unfitting for him, a mere farmer. But then he nodded appreciatively and said, "Glad you found yourself here. Our German guests and I have been in sore need for music since the orchestra left with her Royal Highness." At that, he turned on his heels and left, having decided that the conversation was over.

Karl grinned. "I told you they'd be pleased."

Chapter 03

It took some getting used to, but after the first week, Nikolaos felt more at home at Norrköping's House. He felt comfortable in his new clothes and even shaved off all his hair so he was as bald as Karl. It was odd at first, but then the feeling of air on his scalp was pleasant. Life was easy in the castle. He slept well past sunup, not waking until ale was brought to his rooms by a German servant girl named Abela, who was so shy she blushed each time he looked at her.

No one gave him the evil eye or was afraid of him. They thought he was a man in his twenties, not someone who had seen his wife, children, and grandchildren grow old and die.

Nor did they know how affected he was by the proximity of the Motala River flowing through Norrköping. But it was pulling at him, tempting him to unleash his power into its rapids and cause danger to whoever was near. He wouldn't be able to withstand it much longer.

Then, on Thursday of the second week, Nikolaos and Karl headed toward the garden to get some air after performing. As soon as Karl opened the door to the outside, Nikolaos knew he had to go. There had been a sudden rainstorm, and puffs of moisture rose off the ground as the sun warmed it again. Clouds dark with rain sat on the horizon, creating beams of heavy light. Moist light. He needed to be alone. And soon, his blood was already shifting to water within him.

Karl gave him a sidelong glance, holding the palms of both his hands upward to see if it was still raining. "It's a dank evening, isn't it? I think I'll go back inside instead. Care to join me for a nightcap?"

Nikolaos hesitated. If he said yes, there would be no need to make an excuse to stay outside. He could go have a quick drink and then leave. He swallowed hard, shifting his gaze away from Karl's face. Big sheets of fog were rolling in now, obscuring the colorful rhododendron bushes in gray softness. He inhaled deeply. Glorious moisture. He wouldn't handle a nightcap. "I thank you, but I think I'll stay out here a moment and then go to bed. I want to digest a bit before I climb the stairs." Nikolaos kept his face neutral, hoping Karl wouldn't offer to stay.

But Karl smiled, oblivious. "Ah, I hear you. Should you change your mind after, just knock." Then he turned on his heels and went back inside. He probably thought he needed to visit the privy room but didn't want to say so. It would do.

Nikolaos could barely wait until he was out of sight but forced himself to stay where he was until well after Karl had left. When he was sure he had gone upstairs and wasn't coming back outside for some reason, Nikolaos made his way around the moat and left Norrköping's House.

The town was quiet and empty. Windows were still shuttered after having protected glassless windows from the rain, and everything was still. He hurried his steps, feeling the river ahead of him even before he heard it. Only moments later, he turned a corner, and the wind brought the roaring sound of a large body of water just as it appeared before him. It was beautiful! Wide and so alive. Rushing. He ran, feeling the need building within him with each step, and the calmness from knowing he would soon be in his true element.

When he reached the riverbank, he tossed the fiddle to the side and kicked his shoes off, running in without bothering to take his clothes off. It was rapid, and the water filled his lungs easily. Fish followed, curious but not afraid, knowing he belonged.

Afterward, he sat on a boulder at the water's edge with his fiddle. Playing his own melodies, blues, and purples exploded around him, merging with the sparkling sunset on the river's surface.

When he stopped, the short night had come and gone, and the sun was warming him from the opposite direction. A horse neighed, and someone was chopping wood in the distance.

Norrköping was waking up.

The kitchen maids were hauling water from the well when he came back. He smiled at them, feeling relaxed and content.

"Morning, you're up early today. Have yourself a seat, and we'll bring you ale and bread," one of them said and gestured with her elbow at a bench in front of the herbal garden.

"I give thanks, but no, I have to head upstairs." As soon as the words were out of his mouth, he regretted it, mouth watering at the thought of what he hoped was freshly baked bread. Running after her, he caught her arm just before she entered the kitchen, startling her. "Pray forgive me. I didn't mean to frighten you. But I *would* like some of that bread and ale after all. I couldn't sleep and went for a long walk, feeling a bit hungry now. I apologize again," he said and let go of her arm, then gave a quick bow for good measure.

"Of course, Fiddler Nikolaos, I'll get you some." She smiled with noticeable relief and hurried inside. Her skirts caught on a splinter in the door, but she pulled it loose without stopping.

Coming back out, she handed him a loaf wrapped in a blue towel, then pulled out a small tub with butter from a pocket in her apron.

"I give thanks."

"It's my pleasure, Fiddler Nikolaos," she said, blushing as she went back in. She was pretty, with large blue eyes and freckles over her nose, her bosom swelling under her bodice. He wished she had stayed a moment longer.

A few days later, he was awakened early when his maid knocked on the door.

"You're wanted downstairs. Someone has come to ask you something. They're waiting down in the cobble entrance," Abela said when she entered, referring to the carriage room he and his horse had entered through when they first arrived.

"Ask me something? What could that be about?"

Her neck and face reddened in uneven blotches. "I'm not sure, Fiddler Nikolaos, but something is afoot. That much is clear."

He frowned. "I'll go down directly, then."

"Yes, you must, I was told to tell you to hurry."

He got dressed and splashed some water on his face but didn't hurry, annoyed. The sun was still low on the horizon. Why were they calling on him so early?

Gustav and Karl were sitting with a man Nikolaos didn't recognize. He looked up when Nikolaos approached and gave a curt nod in acknowledgment. Karl had a severe expression, and Gustav was staring unseeingly straight ahead. The maid had been right. Something was clearly afoot.

"Sixman Ole here wants to talk to us. Someone saw Näcken in the river some nights ago, and now a woman is dead," Karl said, gesturing for Nikolaos to sit beside him.

"Pardon?" Nikolaos stared at their upturned faces and felt himself go cold. Rusty devils, someone must have seen him the other day. How could he have been so careless? He sat down, trying to swallow the panic and keep his face neutral.

"He drowns them, in league with the Devil he is. Shapeshifting too. He turned into a horse this time. Someone heard him neigh," Sixman Ole said and met Nikolaos' eyes gravely.

Nikolaos swallowed a nervous laugh. He certainly hadn't turned into a horse. That was ridiculous.

"It's very, very dangerous," Sixman Ole continued. "We've seen signs of bad times coming for a while because astronomers have observed comets. Not only that, but some nights ago, I saw shooting stars in the sky." He regarded them intently. It was obvious he was hoping they would ask him to elaborate.

Karl exchanged a glance with Gustav. "I give thanks to you, Sixman Ole. We're very grateful you're here to warn us. We'll be as vigilant as possible. I had a feeling something bad was about to happen when I saw a two-headed toad last spring."

"Who drowned?" Gustav interrupted, ignoring Karl's toad, but Nikolaos saw Sixman Ole's eyes widen in fear before he hid it behind a mask of serious authority.

"A fisherman's daughter. She was promised to a young man who already owns his own fishing boat. His family lives a bit further up the river, but it's certainly not a problem if you have a boat," Sixman Ole said calmly.

"What do you mean by that?" Nikolaos asked, confused.

Sixman Ole glanced around the room and motioned for them to lean in closer, lowering his voice to a whisper even though they were the only ones there. "Well, Pastor Klint is very strict with doing things properly. If the girl didn't want to leave her family, you might suspect she had done away with herself. It's often hard for young brides to live with their husbands' families, leaving their mothers and younger siblings. But with the groom having a boat that could take her back and forth for visits, Pastor Klint thinks there's something more dangerous at work. And you said you saw a two-headed frog?" Sixman Ole shot an eye at Karl, fear shadowing his face again.

"A toad, actually, in the moat right by the big entrance."

"I'll inform Pastor Klint. I give thanks for your information," Sixman Ole said, then turned to Nikolaos. "Have you seen anything? You're recently hired here if I understand correctly? Where are you from? Did you see anything unusual when you arrived? How did you travel? By wagon? By foot?"

"I came…" Nikolaos coughed. His voice was so dry he could barely talk. He hadn't even taken a sip of the ale the maid brought.

"Give the man something to drink," Gustav said and clambered past him in the narrow space between the table and the bench. He went to the shelf in the corner and grabbed an assortment of mugs and a jug of ale. He handed the mugs to Nikolaos, then sat down on the other side of him.

Nikolaos filled their mugs and pushed them toward the middle of the table so everyone could reach, grateful to have a moment to think about how to answer. He sipped, then cleared his throat. "I give thanks. I needed that," he said, nodding at Gustav. "I came by horse from my village eight days from here, northeast. There are just a few farms. We don't call it anything."

"By the coast then, I take it?"

"No." Eight days northeast from here may very well be by the coast, but lies were more believable if they stayed as close to the truth as possible, and he had lived inland.

"And you saw nothing unusual?"

"No."

"I see." Sixman Ole narrowed his eyes as if he could sense there was more to it.

Nikolaos stared back without shifting his gaze. At any moment now, the sixman might recognize him and ask him how he had killed that woman. He didn't remember it but couldn't deny that it might be his fault. He should never have gone in so close to town; he had practically been *in* town. How could he have been so rusty foolish? Sixman Ole finally let go of his eyes. Nikolaos drew a discreet breath of relief.

"I won't speak to the Germans or the women here yet. For now, anyway," Sixman Ole said. "I don't want to start a frenzy. But I wanted to speak with you since you and Karl are the musicians here. I'm sure you're aware that Näcken is known to play fiddle now and then. He might appear when you least expect it. You must be on the highest alert. You wouldn't want Näcken to weasel himself in here in lieu of looking for work."

Nikolaos chortled, then quickly pretended to cough. Karl looked startled.

Sixman Ole got to his feet and gave them a stern look. "This is very dangerous. Pray give care," he said, hurrying out with brisk steps, head held high with importance.

When they couldn't hear his footsteps any longer, Karl whispered, "What do you make of all this? is it really Näcken?"

"Well…" Nikolaos began but stopped when he couldn't think of what to say. How would he get out of this? Of all things, had the sixman really needed to bring up fiddlers looking for work?

"I think so," Gustav said. "She drowned, and someone heard him neigh like a horse. It's probably him."

An oppressive silence followed. Nikolaos forced himself to sit calmly so he wasn't the first to leave. Karl had gone pale.

"Do you know where the woman was found?" Nikolaos asked finally.

"No," Karl said and stood abruptly, followed by Gustav. Then they both walked out. Right at the threshold, Karl looked at Nikolaos over his shoulder. His eyes were wide with panic.

Back at his rooms, Nikolaos went straight to the corner cupboard and pulled out a goblet and a tankard of wine. But his hands were shaking so much he overfilled his goblet. Quickly, he tried to take a large sip, but it just made it worse and spilled all over his shirt, creating an enormous stain on his chest. Rusty devils! He put the goblet down, pulled the wet shirt off with an irritated snap, and threw it in the corner. Then he picked up the wine again and went to stand by the window. Staring at the trees on the horizon, he sipped deeply. His hands had ceased their shaking somewhat, but he felt stupid and embarrassed. How could he have been so careless? Not only should he have gone further away from the town center, but he should have had his water-fill before he applied for work at Norrköping's House. Letting it go for so many weeks, especially after leaving his home and trying something new, was incredibly irresponsible. He always grew restless and irritated if he hadn't been in the river for a while. And careless too, the truth was that he had barely noticed where he went in. Clearly, someone had seen him and then gone to report it to the pastor. Then when the woman drowned, the pastor must have concluded that it was his doing.

For it might be. Even if he never saw her, she could have heard him and gone in. It reminded him of an incident back when Abluna was still young. It was a spring after another long and cold winter where they had run out of food. He had tried to hunt but even the animals were gone, either having frozen to death or moved south. Abluna had to mix the little flour they had left with tree bark to get it to last. Flour from grain that they should have saved for planting. Two of their little boys had died that winter, just three weeks apart. When warmer weather finally came and melted the ice, desperation and grief drove him to get to water. He was in the river when a bear appeared. Normally he would have submerged to hide from it, but with his family starving, he had thrown himself back on shore and grabbed his crossbow, killing the bear before it even noticed him. But someone saw him, another hunter probably. Then the rumors started, accusations that he had drowned one woman and stolen the unborn twins of another, bewitching her to willingly give them to him. They found the newborn little bodies behind a barn and said he had thrown them there when he was done with them. Stories circulated for years and didn't stop until the younger generation passed on. Then people forgot for a while, until they realized that he didn't age.

That look that Karl gave him when he left the cobble entrance. What if he understood who he was?

Chapter 04

Rå was tending her herbs when she felt someone approach. Hurrying inside, she threw a shawl over her back, then returned and continued pruning her hyssop.

Only moments later, she heard whispering. Her visitors were likely hesitating when they glimpsed her home between the trees. Humans were perplexed by it, built as it was in the crevice between two large boulders. A woodcutter had made it for her many years ago, creating a deep cave with several rooms. Despite the common hesitation, women came to her for advice and medicines. They called her Magda and didn't know that she was the same being who lured their men astray in the woods.

The whispers grew louder, then stopped abruptly, as two women pushed themselves through the pine branches to the open space in front of Rå's cave. It was Ingeborg, and a younger woman Rå didn't recognize. She was plump and very pretty, wearing a dove blue dress with a red bodice and a white headscarf that trailed down her back. She was carrying a basket on her right arm. An offering.

"Welcome, goodwives," Rå said, pointing to a shady spot in the grass. "We can talk there."

Ingeborg sat down with her legs folded beneath her, straightening her skirts with her hands. She looked nervous. "We need something to protect ourselves with, something to ward off evil," she said.

"Have you prayed for protection, Ingeborg?" Rå asked and sat down in front of her.

Ingeborg shook her head. "Praying isn't enough. We need something stronger. Näcken is among us! Someone saw him in the river, and then he turned into a horse. I... and I..." She burst into tears.

The younger woman plunked down beside her and reached for Ingeborg's hand, squeezing it for comfort. "Magda, you must help us. Näcken visited Ingeborg and her husband. Even came inside and ate with them and everything!" Her eyes widened. She looked more excited than afraid. "And he played his fiddle, too. Ingeborg says he played so beautifully she forgot the time. Suddenly it was late in the evening, and they didn't even remember him leaving." She threw a glance at Ingeborg and lowered her voice dramatically. "Then he killed someone. That's how it was, wasn't it, Ingeborg?"

"Yes, just so, Karla." Ingeborg wiped her eyes with her sleeve and indicated the young woman with a nod. "This is Karla. She came with me today because I'm scared of walking in the woods by myself now."

"Of course, I understand," Rå said, surprised at their news. She had seen Näcken herself a couple of times, but it was decades ago and not near here. Once, he played his fiddle by the water and was so absorbed in his own music he didn't notice when she tried to talk to him. And one winter many years after that, she saw him swim beneath the ice in a frozen brook. What was he doing going into people's homes? "Have you asked Pastor Klint to give a prayer of protection?"

"See! I told you, you should do that. I told you Ingeborg," Karla said.

"No!" Ingeborg shouted so loud that several birds left their branches and flew off. "I can't tell Pastor Klint. He'd get very angry with me if he found out that I let Näcken inside and even fed him. Never tell anyone, promise me, Magda."

Rå patted Ingeborg's arm. "I won't. I'll go get you something. Wait here."

She went to her herbal garden and picked two small bunches of creeping thyme and some basil leaves. The thyme would give them strength and the basil protection. She felt for Ingeborg. It hadn't been easy for her lately. People said that she and her husband had worked at Norrköping's House but were kicked out because he couldn't keep his fingers off the women, even the Princess had he tried to get to.

When Rå returned, Ingeborg and Karla were standing, talking animatedly in loud tones. "I know he drowned her, I know it," Ingeborg said. "Mats told me someone heard she had marks around her neck. That's where Näcken squeezed her when he pushed her under and killed her. His music is so pretty that you forget where you are, and then he catches you and drowns you. He pushes you deep under the surface until you're dead." She moved her hands downward as if she was pushing someone under, then held her hands there in a display of violence.

Karla stared at her, then shook her head in horror. "Could Näcken talk? Did you see if he had horse hooves?"

Rå looked down to hide a sudden smile. She was quite sure he had regular feet like everyone else.

"No, he looked like an ordinary person, ate normally too," Ingeborg said. "I was just surprised that I had fallen asleep in my chair. Everything else was the same as always. I told you that already…" She trailed off when she noticed Rå approach.

"Sweet Magda, you must be scared living alone here in the forest. You should take care to protect yourself," Karla said, her expression changing from horror to concern.

"I'm not scared. But I'll go to church on Sunday."

"That's wise of you."

Rå smiled. She needed no help from church, but she wanted to learn more about why Näcken was in these parts.

"Don't tell Pastor Klint what we told you. He can't know," Ingeborg repeated.

"I won't. You needn't fear. And this will protect you from danger." Rå handed them the herb bunches and showed them how to hide them within the folds of their clothing. Not that it would actually protect them from him, Näcken was much too strong for that, but it would make them feel better at least.

Ingeborg took a visible breath in and placed her bunch under her blouse. "Should I sleep with it near me?"

Rå nodded. "Yes, it might be wise. You can put it under your pillow or hold it in your hand, just as long as you don't sweat at night? Do you still bleed?"

"No, it's a few years since now. I do sweat some at night," she said, looking worried.

Rå patted her arm and smiled reassuringly. "Don't fear. Place it under your pillow or just at the corner of your bed above your head. It still gives protection, I just don't want the herbs to get wet from sweat, that's all."

"Oh, I see," Ingeborg said, giving Rå a quick smile, but the worry hadn't entirely left her eyes. "I thank you, Magda." She reached for the basket Karla had brought and pulled out a smoked trout and a piece of goat cheese. "Here, Magda, take this here, enjoy it. I give thanks for your counsel."

"I'm glad to help," Rå said, pleased. It had been a long time since she ate cheese. "Don't fret. You're protected now." She reached over to each woman and gave a gentle pat at the spot under which the herbs were hidden. "Go in peace with God's protection."

Rå watched them walk away. Ingeborg moved with lighter steps now. If Näcken was as murderous as they claimed, Rå would get a lot of nervous customers. It would be wise to forage for more herbs. Her little garden didn't have enough.

***

It was clear that this was not to be an ordinary Sunday at church. Rå could see it in their faces, the way they looked at each other, and how they hurried inside instead of tarrying outside for gossip.

Gulla, a girl who frequently came to trade for herbs for her mother's gout, walked closely pressed between her siblings while their parents kept their arms around them from either side. Her father's mouth was set in a thin line.

Rå tried to catch Gulla's eye, but she looked straight ahead and didn't notice her, and Rå sat down in the back row on the women's side. The church smelled of manure from the men's boots and of spices, flour, and fish from the women. And sweat, more pungent than usual. Fear.

Suddenly, a woman marched down the aisle, bumping into arriving congregants, and went straight to Gulla and grabbed her by the arm, pulling her out of her parents' grasp. "You need to come up front so Pastor Klint can speak with you, girl," she said. There was no anger in her voice, but no denying her authority. The woman dragged Gulla through the crowd as people scrambled to their pews, then made her sit in a chair someone had placed in front of the altar.

Pastor Klint strode in, making his way to his podium with rapid, decisive steps, his expression grim. Gulla looked terrified.

Rå couldn't bear it and shifted her attention to the thick beams in the ceiling. A bird was sitting up there, peering down at them. It cocked its head to the side as if it were interested in what was happening below it. Maybe it was. Then it pooped. A large splash fell straight down and landed on the stained-glass window. Rå resisted an urge to get up and wipe it off.

Then Pastor Klint cleared his throat loudly to get the congregation's attention, and the bird flew off and hid in the shadows. "Näcken is among us!" he said in a loud booming voice, which sent a gasp through the church. "Indeed, he is, and Gulla here has seen the creature with her own eyes." Pastor Klint whipped his head around and fixed his eyes on her. "Tell me every detail you can remember. You never know what may be important."

Gulla straightened in her chair and coughed once. "I was walking home and was thinking of the bear with the cubs when..."

"You have seen a bear?" Pastor Klint interrupted.

"No, Pastor, not I. My brother saw it with its cubs, but that wasn't that day."

"You need to tell me everything, Gulla. Animals are known to act strangely if there are demonic forces abound."

Feet shuffling on the church floor and nervous coughs made Pastor Klint throw an irritated glance at his congregation. "Go on, Gulla," he said, turning back to her.

"I had picked berries and saw some more along the path, I was just...."

"How did the berries look? Did they have strange shapes or colors?" Pastor Klint interrupted.

Gulla looked flustered. "I don't think so. But when I bent down to pick them up, I heard him. I mean, I heard his music. It was soft and beautiful. At first, I couldn't see anyone, but when I looked closer, I saw him standing in the middle of it. Right there in Motala River, his hose and all were deep in it."

Pastor Klint looked momentarily taken aback. "This is indeed very, very dangerous. Did he change into a horse?"

"No."

"I see. Describe him for me. It is important. I will write it all down afterward. Everything you say could be of importance. You are the only one who has seen him who has survived."

And Ingeborg and her husband, Rå thought as a collective gasp swept through the congregation. Gulla's mother made a shrill sound of fear. Someone began to sob. It sounded like Ingeborg. Maybe she felt relieved that she wasn't the only one who had seen him and survived, or maybe it just confirmed what she already knew, that Näcken had been the one visiting her.

With a voice that barely carried, Gulla answered Pastor Klint. "He was bald, wore a red jacket and a white ruff around his neck. I couldn't see his fiddle. But I heard it."

Rå raised her eyebrows in surprise. She had never seen him bald. He had long, thick hair, and wore simple clothes, certainly no ruff.

"Did he talk to you?" Pastor Klint asked Gulla.

"No, I got scared and ran home. I only saw him for a short moment."

"That is wise, very wise. Harken this, everyone. Gulla here is alive because she ignored her curiosity and made the sensible choice to run home. I want you all to stay away from the river. And keep a close eye on your animals and meats. If you slaughter a pig and the meat looks odd, you call for me right away. Odd-looking meat might be a sign of demonic forces."

"I saw him too!" someone yelled. It was Sigrid, the wife of one of the merchants. She was approaching unsteadily, leaning on the arm of someone. Her sister, maybe, they looked like each other. Stopping next to the pew where Gulla's mother and sisters sat, she grabbed the armrest and leaned on it as her companion wrapped an arm around her shoulders. "I couldn't sleep and sat and looked out the window when an unnaturally large gray horse walked by our house. It was after that, my younger sister died." Sigrid hid her face in her companion's neck to hide a sob.

Pastor Klint nodded slowly. "He is shapeshifting then."

Rå kept her eyes on him and resisted shaking her head. She would be shocked if Näcken could do that.

"I saw a star fall the same night that Gulla saw the waterman. I saw it!" a man in one of the front pews shouted, interrupting Rå's thoughts. He clambered out and went to stand in the middle of the aisle, pointing at the ceiling with a shaking finger. "To the east, right above the steeple."

Pastor Klint frowned. "The same night? A Thursday then." He spoke as if to himself. The church was silent. The only sound was bees buzzing at a broken pane in the window near the altar. He glanced at it, then gestured in the man's direction. "Describe it."

"I saw something fall from the sky, it looked almost like a tadpole, but it went so fast I couldn't be sure. I think it was a star that fell down."

"If you saw a tail, it was a comet. Then it is much more serious than I thought. Comets are slimy, disgusting things and always bring ill. May the Lord have mercy on us all."

Chapter 05

If it hadn't been for Karl being unusually quiet, everything would have been the same. The sixman seemed to have been true to his word because it didn't appear that the maids or guards knew anything. The Germans didn't seem nervous either and acted like their usual polite selves. But Nikolaos didn't like Karl's silence. He didn't avoid him but kept throwing him furtive glances when he thought Nikolaos didn't notice. After a week of it, he decided to speak with Karl in private to see if he could get him to tell him what was on his mind. Requesting that a meal be sent to his rooms, Nikolaos reminded Karl of a new red wine from Germany, set aside just for them as a thank-you for their performances. It was the perfect excuse to eat alone instead of in the dining hall like they usually did. To his surprise, Karl said yes without hesitation. Maybe he wasn't suspicious of him then, or he would have said no.

He arrived bare-chested, wearing only his hose and breeches.

"It sure is warm, isn't it? Did you visit the kitchen without a shirt?" Nikolaos asked, chuckling. The contours of Karl's muscles looked as if sculpted in stone, he noted.

"Nah, had my shirt on then, but running up and down the stairs got me soaked. There's no air back there," he said as Nikolaos placed two goblets on the table. Karl filled them, and sipped his, smacking his lips with concentration. "This is very nice, it's smooth yet robust with a lot of flavors." He smacked his lips again.

"It is," Nikolaos agreed. The wine was better than anything he had ever tried before. At home, he always drank ale.

Karl drank a bit more, then started drumming his fingers on the table. He seemed nervous all of a sudden.

Nikolaos waited.

"There's something I have been meaning to ask you for a while," Karl said and finally stopped drumming, putting his hands down in his lap.

"Oh, there is?" Nikolaos asked, surprised. Would he actually come right out and ask?

"Yes, and I'm sorry to be so blunt, but are you Catholic?"

"No." That he didn't expect. "What on earth made you think I was?"

Just then, a maid knocked and entered without prompting, only to abruptly stop at the sight of Karl, wobbling her tray so much that Nikolaos had to get up and take it from her. It was Abela.

"I thank you," she whispered as if Karl, even hearing her in his scant clothing, would somehow make them more intimate.

Nikolaos grinned. "There, woman, no need to be embarrassed. He's just warm, is all. Go on now. I'll take it from here. We'll call for you when we're done, and I'll make sure he's dressed for the occasion." He gestured to the bell attached to a string on the wall.

Abela curtsied and then hurried down the corridor so fast that the canaries squeaked as she passed.

"Ah, now she thinks you're promised," Nikolaos said, winking.

Karl gave a one-sided smile. "Eh, Abela is too tall, and now she thinks I'll dress for her. I thought I told you I left my shirt in my room."

"She'll have a time with it then, won't she? Maybe you need to bed her tonight," Nikolaos said with another wink, trying to delay the conversation about his faith. But as soon as he sat back down, Karl brought it up.

"Are you?"

"Catholic? No, of course not." It was a lie. Ever since they changed the church, he had pretended. And it was forbidden now, too. What would Karl have done if he had said yes?

"I see. I was just wondering because you don't go to church. I've never met anyone who doesn't… and I thought maybe…. Well, it's not something that I have a right to ask."

Nikolaos regarded him silently, then shrugged. "Karl… I'm saddened during services. I can't help but think of my wife and how we used to go together. Since the pastor doesn't know me, I decided to wait. I've gone to pray in our chapel here, but only by myself. And I'm keeping my fasts. I don't eat meat either

Wednesday or Friday, you must have noticed, haven't you? I ought to, though. You're right about that."

Truth to be told, Nikolaos found church tedious and boring. It wasn't like it used to be. There were pews inside nowadays, covering the whole floor, where people were made to sit while they listened to the pastors' long and sometimes frightening sermons. He didn't like it anymore. Churches used to be open and spacious. They had all walked around, prayed at the different saint altars, and spoken with each other while the priest did his mass in the background. It felt peaceful, and he felt comforted when he prayed. All that was gone now. It seemed all they cared for was Luther's Catechism.

"I see." Karl sipped some of his wine.

"Pray, were you truly scared that I was Catholic?"

He shrugged. "I've noticed that you have been righteous on fast days. I should've realized. Pray forgive me. It's not for me to ask you these things."

The kitchen never served meat on fast days anyway, but it didn't seem to occur to him. Nikolaos poured them some more wine and decided to change the subject. "Tell me, Karl. Have you no plans for marrying someone even if our beautiful maid here isn't to your liking?"

Karl ripped off a chunk of bread, dipping it in his soup. "Eh, women. They're too much trouble. We'll see. I'm not sure I could house a horde of little ones. Two of my sisters have eight each, and my brothers so many I've lost track. They're darling, but oh so noisy."

"I'm sure," Nikolaos said as a memory of his children shrieking and laughing on their hayloft came over him.

"The maid is a good-looking woman though, I must admit," Karl said with a sideways smile. "Anyway, do you understand enough German to figure what they were saying last night? Did you hear what…. What's his name? The fella with the red beard? He's always fidgeting with it, you know who I mean?"

"Hans?"

"Hans, that's it. Remember when they brought the

sweetmeats, and he kept talking and didn't take any? Did you understand what he said?"

"No, and I wasn't paying much attention."

"He was arguing with the new resident. Don't know his name either, but he was talking about someone who wrote a book that claimed that the sun isn't moving."

Nikolaos laughed. "That's funny. I'd like to read that."

"No, it wasn't a joke. That's what I thought at first too, but my German is too poor to fully understand, so I asked them to explain. You were talking with Jakob, so you didn't hear it. He said the author understands numbers and says it's actually the earth moving, not the sun. How exactly that is, I didn't quite understand, but no, it wasn't a joke."

"Is the fella blind?"

"Blind? No. Why would you ask that?"

"How else could he think that? You only need to be awake for a day to see that the sun isn't in the same place when you wake as when you go to bed." Nikolaos sipped his wine to try to hide a smile. It was plain they had played a trick on him. Either that, or Karl didn't understand as much German as he thought he did.

Karl looked at him for a moment, seeming hurt, but then he chuckled. "Eh, you!" he said, waving his index finger in his direction. "I really thought they were serious."

"You better not tell them you fell for it, or they'll think you a fool."

"Indeed." Karl flushed with embarrassment.

Nikolaos winked and reached for some more food. Abela had brought freshly smoked sausage and salty udder with candied fruit. It was divine. He chewed slowly, enjoying every bite. Karl was only picking at his, casting careful glances Nikolaos' way, seeming nervous again.

"Are you thinking of what Sixman Ole said the other day?" Nikolaos asked. There was no point in skirting around the subject anymore.

"Eh, well I have, of course. It's not something you want to have happen so close to you, hard not to think about it. Especially since they found the second body," Karl said.

"The second body?"

"You didn't hear?"

Nikolaos stared at him. Another one, rusty devils, had he truly been so careless? "No, I didn't. What happened?"

"Sigrid's sister. They found her behind the barn. She was a young woman, her whole life ahead of her."

"She didn't drown then," Nikolaos said and exhaled with relief, hoping it sounded like a sigh of fear.

"No. But they can tell that Näcken did it. She had marks on her neck. He strangled her, you know. She was with child, too. They could tell," he shook his head with disgust, "because there was blood and remains of the baby. It was Näcken who took it. He wants company down there. People have been looking for the baby in the river, but naturally, Näcken is hiding. They'll never find it."

Nikolaos frowned. That was both ridiculous and offensive. "How do you know all this?"

"From Sixman Ole. Pastor Klint was talking about Näcken during service, warning everyone. Then Sixman Ole told me more afterward." His eyes widened dramatically. "In private."

"I see, of course. It's another reason I ought to go back to church. I miss important news."

"Yes, indeed you do." Karl narrowed his eyes. "I also hear Näcken doesn't always live in water but walks around amongst humans." He swallowed visibly. "It's not safe…" He trailed off, swallowing again. "Sixman Ole said we ought to be careful because… because Näcken is a musician like us."

"Yes, I remember." He knew it! The way Karl looked at him that morning. He suspected him but was probably afraid to admit it even to himself, or he wouldn't have dared to be alone with him. Nikolaos' eyes flicked to the fiddle in the corner. If he could get Karl to relax, maybe he could try to make him think there was nothing to his fears. His rooms were small enough that entrancing might work. Casually, as though without thought, he reached over and grabbed the fiddle. "I'm nervous about it too. Did Sixman Ole say anything else about musicians?" He started to play gently and softly. A melody he only played in the river.

Karl's head jerked backward, and his goblet wobbled in his hand. "This song is... it's so gorgeous. What is it? I've never heard it before," he said, forgetting Nikolaos' question. He put the goblet down.

"Thank you." Nikolaos smiled. This was going better than he expected. He sustained each note mournfully slow, keeping an eye on Karl at the same time. When he could see the fine hairs on Karl's arms prickle, Nikolaos lifted his eyes to meet Karl's. They were already losing their focus. He moved his bow a little faster. Karl was breathing deeply and had started to lean back on the bench. Now was the time. "The other day when Sixman Ole came to speak with us in the cobble room, then for a moment you thought that..."

"I thought you were Näcken," Karl said, interrupting.

"Ah, yes. I could see that. Why did you think that of all things?"

Karl didn't hesitate. "It's because Ole... Sixman Ole said we needed to watch for fiddlers because one of them might actually be Näcken."

"I understand. Sixman Ole is scaring people a little too much, but you shouldn't worry. Now you know that I'm not. You know that, don't you?"

"Yes indeed."

"Good." It worked! Nikolaos swallowed a laugh of relief and kept playing. Karl's arms lay still by his side, and his eyes were almost completely closed. He was entranced, open to suggestion. "Karl," Nikolaos said firmly, "I'm a farmer and a fiddle player. That's all there is to know about me."

Karl's eyes twitched, and he gave a slight nod. Then his head lulled to the side, and he slid down on the bench, lying down wholly.

Nikolaos put the bow down on his lap and took one more look at his face. When Karl didn't stir, he tiptoed across the floor, grabbed two apples from the table, and left. Peering inside before closing the door, he noticed how Karl's beautiful bare chest was rising and falling, and that his mouth was halfway open. Kissable.

Chapter 06

When Nikolaos came downstairs the following morning, Karl and Gustav were sitting in the sun by the cobble entrance.

"Good morning, Nikolaos! We were thinking of hunting today. Want to join us? You have your horse here, don't you?" Karl asked, smiling broadly and looking like his old, friendly self.

"Yes, I do," Nikolaos said, returning his smile and feeling almost giddy with relief. It had worked last night, there was no doubt.

"That's what I thought." Karl tilted his head toward Gustav. "He has his own as well, and I can borrow a horse from the stable. We're ready to head out right away. Could you come now?" Karl asked, squinting against the sun, trying to catch Nikolaos' eye.

"But, hunting this late in the morning? Isn't it better to wait until the sun goes *down*?" Nikolaos asked and winked at Karl.

He looked embarrassed but didn't say anything.

"What's this about?" Gustav asked, looking amused but confused.

"You should ask Karl. He knows all about the sun. You could say he's quite the expert," Nikolaos said, grinning.

Karl tried to laugh it off. "Eh, another day. It's silly. Let's talk about hunting instead. I know of a grove where I've caught several deer in the middle of the day. They sleep there, and you can usually get one or two if you startle them."

Gustav shrugged and stood up. "On to hunting then. I'll fetch what we need." He walked off.

"I'll ask the groom to get the horses for us," Karl called after him, then clapped Nikolaos on the shoulder. "Pray forgive me for last night. I must've had too much wine. Woke up on your bench after you'd already gone to bed. I hope I wasn't rude?"

"Not at all." It was precisely what he had hoped for, that Karl would think he was sleeping in the other room, when in fact he had been in the river all night.

***

The same pretty kitchen maid who gave him bread the other morning greeted them when they arrived with the game. She was even lovelier than she had been then. There was something different with her hair, and she wore a different blouse.

"Afternoon, miss," Nikolaos said and smiled at her.

Her eyes flashed to his, then shifted to the does strapped behind the saddles of Karl's and Gustav's horses. "Well done, gentlemen. We'll make something special for you tonight. Bring them in and lay them on the table for me, will you," she said, returning Nikolaos' smile as she held the door open, pointing to a table in the middle of the room.

Nikolaos felt a spike of attraction and smiled at her again, then grabbed hold of the doe's back feet and helped Gustav inside with it. The table was so big that the deer would easily fit side by side. There were two hearths, each with several cauldrons hanging over the smoldering embers. Whatever they were already cooking smelled wonderful. His stomach rumbled, used to eating as it was.

The cooks served them an enormous feast, giving all the credit to their hunt, and thanking them profusely while the maids brought wine and ale. People lingered longer than usual, talking and drinking. Nikolaos was dozing with his back against the wall behind his bench, feeling sated and sleepy, glad he wasn't expected to perform that night.

A sudden clamoring startled him awake. Disoriented, he sat up straight just as two guardsmen rushed in with Sixman Ole. It became eerily quiet. One of the guardsmen gestured to Lord Johan, who immediately hurried over. Nikolaos wasn't sure what Lord Johan did at Norrköping's House other than what Gustav had told him, which was that he was in charge in some way and was well connected to King Sigismund. Sixman Ole took Lord Johan by the arm and pulled him into the shadowy hallway behind the dining hall, leaving the guardsmen standing wide-legged with their hands on their weapons. Nikolaos thought one of them was looking in his direction, but he wasn't sure.

Karl and Gustav exchanged a glance, and then the Germans on the other side of the table started to speak in fast, hushed voices.

"What's going on here?" Nikolaos asked, a bad feeling settling itself in the pit of his stomach.

"I don't know," Gustav whispered, jerking his head toward the hallway. Lord Johan was returning.

As if people weren't already staring at him, Lord Johan banged his knuckles on the doorsill to get people's attention. "Two more people have drowned, and a cow had a dead calf this morning," he said in a loud, shrill voice, his gaze moving across each face in the dining hall, scrutinizing them with his eyes. Then he turned on his heels and hurried away, his heavy boots echoing ominously.

Karl stared straight ahead.

Nikolaos tried to read his expression but couldn't tell what it meant.

Then, everyone began to talk at once. "Why did he tell us and then leave?" Who are the dead?" "Where did it happen?"

"God help us. The Devil is among us," Hans said in perfect Swedish.

Nikolaos looked from face to face, then stood up. "I'll go investigate." He felt their eyes on his back as he pressed himself between the benches and the wall, but no one stopped him.

Once out on the open floor, he resisted the urge to run and walked toward the doorway with what he hoped looked like a determined purpose. The pretty kitchen maid saw him across the room, and for a moment, it looked like she would follow him, but then the other kitchen girl pulled on her sleeve, leaned close, and whispered something in her ear. He kept his eyes on her for another moment, then hurried out of the dining hall and up the stairs to his floor. He was just about to step into the hallway leading to his apartments when he heard voices. He froze, then backed up and hid behind a large cabinet, straining to hear.

"I've had my suspicions a while but didn't want to be a nuisance. I wasn't certain. But he's been acting oddly."

Nikolaos recognized the voice and German accent. It was Abela, the shy maid who brought him ale in the morning. It sounded like there might be another woman there, too. He could hear the faint sound of shallow breathing.

"How? What's odd?" A man's voice.

"The fiddler is keeping to himself, he and the other... the other man, the bagpiper... they won't eat with the others. I had to bring a tray for them just the other night." Abela sounded like she was crying.

Someone mumbled something, another woman. He was right; there were two of them. Then the voice grew louder. "What she's too shamed to tell you is that the bagpiper was naked when she came with the tray. When she didn't go in, on account of him being naked and all, the fiddler came and took the tray from her, laughing at her. They had planned the whole thing and wanted to lure her in to be indecent."

Nikolaos felt a chill, he had been joking about Karl bedding her. Had she heard that? No, she couldn't have. Abela had hurried away so fast, he had taken note of the canaries chirping in fright.

The man said something in response, but too low for Nikolaos to hear.

"Another odd thing..." Abela said, then stopped to blow her nose, "he wants his garments cleaned often. Left a shirt on the floor for me to pick up even though it wasn't washing day. It looked clean to me at first until I saw a stain on the front. I thought nothing of it, but considering what happened last night, I'm sure it was blood. I heard of the woman whose baby was taken into the river, and I think it's him because...." She burst into tears, crying loudly now.

"Slow down," the man said, "slow down. What do you mean 'considering what happened last night'? Aren't we getting ahead of ourselves a bit? Have a seat here." Their clogs clopped on the floor, and then wood creaked. They must have sat down on the cushioned wood sofa in the corner. There was no way to get around them then.

"No, I know it's him because last night, after they had eaten all alone, they were supposed to let me know so I could get the tray. I waited for a long time, but they never called for me. Finally, I couldn't keep my eyes open anymore and went back up." She drew a heaving breath. "As soon as I got to their floor, I heard him play. It made me very tired, but I didn't want to disturb them, so I waited."

"The music made you tired? I thought you said that you couldn't keep your eyes open before you went up."

"Yes, good sir, I did… but…"

"Go on, woman."

"I… when he finally stopped playing, I saw him sneak out. He was about to close the door, but he stood there and stared into the room for a long time, a very long time. I don't know what he was doing or where he was going. But he was probably going home to his river, just pretending to live in that room. I didn't dare to move, but after he left, I finally went in to get the tray. And the bagpiper was sleeping on the bench. Still naked!"

Nikolaos felt panic wash over him. How could he have forgotten to call for her so she could get the tray before he played for Karl? There was a tassel in his room, which attached to a string leading all the way down to where the maids would hear it. All he had needed to do was to pull on it, and she would have come back.

"Well, woman, these are serious accusations. Aren't you getting a bit overexcited here after all? You're sure they didn't just have a bit too much to drink? Was Karl Bagpiper completely naked?" the man asked.

"Well, um, he only had hose and breeches, no shirt. He was completely bare-chested."

The man chuckled. At least it sounded as if he did. "I see. Now I figured that you were feeling panicked, very natural in these situations. I'll take your concerns under advisement, but for now, I want you to go to your room and try to relax. Take Ringborg here with you so you're not alone. I'll go check the grounds, and then I'll stand guard up by your rooms."

"Thank you, good sir, but I know it was blood on his shirt because it was right after he took that woman's baby. The one they've been looking for in the river."

"I see. As I said, I'll take it under advisement."

Nikolaos remained where he was until he heard the women leave, then left his hiding place, feeling both stupid and angry. To think she thought the wine stain was blood. It was ludicrous. Still, it would have been wise of him to bring it to her directly, explaining he had spilled wine on it instead of just tossing it on the floor and leaving it there. Turning the corner, Nikolaos was about to head back into the hallway when he heard boots hitting the floor, loud and fast. Rusty devils, it must be the man. He should have realized he would come this way.

Nikolaos made a quick decision and continued purposefully as if he arrived just then, which he did in a sense. "Evening," he said, looking him square in the face. The fear in the man's eyes was unmistakable.

Chapter 07

It was raining, and Rå had spent the day inside, weaving. Her yarn was beautiful, made from the finest soft wool, dyed green and orange from lichen, which she had traded herbs and salves for. Leaning back on her stool, inspecting her work, the pattern looked like a row of trees in the fall.

Lil' Leaf, one of her hares, looked up from where he was resting on the floor as if he too, were inspecting it. She had taken him and his brother in two springs ago after finding them caught in a hunter's trap. They had been so small, likely newly weaned and on their first outing without their mother. Lil' Leaf had one of his front legs stuck and was gnawing on it to free himself. One Ear's ear was caught and almost torn off when she got to him, just a thin strip of skin still attached. There was nothing to do but to cut it off. It was a cruel world that the humans created. No one ought to have to chew on his own leg or pull off his own ear to be free. She had brought them home in her arms, then nursed them back to health with a poultice and a diet of grasses with some wood sorrel. By then, they had all grown attached to each other, and she let them stay.

The hares came and went as they pleased, running around outside during the day, coming inside with her in the evenings, and even sleeping curled up next to her on her pallet. If she needed to spend time away, they seemed to understand and never followed. They always stayed near the cave and pressed themselves in through the crawlspace at the bottom of the door if they wanted to go in. She loved them.

"Lil' Leaf, let's go outside and see if the rain has let up yet. I ought to go and get some wood for the fire," Rå said. One Ear was lying comfortably in the corner. His ear moved, and his nose twitched as it always did. "You want me to get you some fresh grass and a carrot from the garden?"

At the word carrot he jumped up and stretched out his long back legs on the dirt floor.

She laughed. "I take that as a sign that you're coming with us."

Once outside, she moved her hair aside and opened her back, then closed it as quickly as she had opened it. Something didn't feel right, like a disturbance in the rain. Even Thor had noticed and was ready to take his carriage and hammer across the sky. There was human fear in the air. Panic. She shivered and hurried to get the carrots and the grass, grabbing two dry logs from the bottom of the woodpile as she went back inside. Lil' Leaf and One Ear followed close behind.

Chapter 08

Nikolaos had no choice. Lord Johan and Sixman Ole's words were plain, as were Abela's. It was time to leave Norrköping's House.

He packed his things, moving silently through his rooms, praying that the man, whoever he was, was still standing guard at the maids' door and hadn't yet reported on what he was told. Every sound set Nikolaos on edge, but no footsteps approached his rooms, no startled birds called out suddenly from the birdcage. Karl and Gustav must be waiting for him since he had told them he would investigate, but the mere thought of going back down to look for them made him panic. And he wouldn't be able to bear seeing the truth of who he was on their faces, for surely Karl would remember his suspicions again after what Lord Johan said.

He waited until everyone had gone to sleep, and all he could hear was the wind, then carefully snuck out, tiptoeing past the bird cage and down the stairs to the cobble entrance.

A guard was there, seated on the floor and leaning against the wall, snoring loudly with his mouth wide open and saliva dripping down his chin. It wasn't Gustav.

Nikolaos exhaled with relief and moved past him as quietly as he could. Slowly, he opened the heavy door a crack without taking his eyes off the sleeping guard and squeezed outside, then closed it again. It was raining, making the grass slippery, but he ran as fast as he dared, and made it to the stable without incident.

Pushing the door handle down, he pulled to open the door. It didn't yield. Someone had locked it. Of course they had. The castle had fine, expensive horses owned by German nobles. He almost cursed aloud but managed to stop himself and only gasped. Nervous someone heard even that, he froze, listening for movement, but the only sound was the rain hitting the roof, and grasshoppers in the distance.

The stable was a freestanding building on the south side of

the castle. Built as it was by the moat's edge, it wasn't possible to walk behind it, but there was a narrow space between the castle wall and the stable. If he remembered correctly, there was a window on the other side. He left his satchel and fiddle on the ground and pressed himself into the narrow space between the walls, praying that there was indeed a window, that it was open, and that he could open the stable door from the inside.

The space narrowed the further he got, but he forced his feet sideways, ignoring the pain and suppressing a sudden fear that he might be stuck between the walls. The rain fell steadily and straight down at that, slapping against his bare scalp. The grasshoppers had gone silent. When he finally got through to the other side, he crossed himself and drew a deep sigh of relief. There was a window, and it was open a crack, held in place by a rope attached to a small natural knurl in the window frame. He unhooked the rope, grabbed hold of the windowsill, braced his feet on the foundation, and crawled inside. A white stallion in the stall nearest him turned his head and looked at him as if it were a perfectly normal thing that Nikolaos appeared in the window. Not until he landed on the floor with a thump, did he pin his ears back and snort at him.

Nikolaos chuckled, then hurried through the stable, past the other horses still asleep with their back hooves cocked. The rain made the summer night dark, but there was still some light coming from the window, and he thought he saw a key in the keyhole in the door. Rushing at it, his fingers quickly found the rough edges of the keyhole. It was empty. A surge of disappointment made him break out in a sweat. Naturally, there wouldn't be a key on the inside. The stable master must have locked it when he left for the night. Wiping his forehead with the back of his hand, Nikolaos let his eyes sweep across the dark stable. Maybe there was an extra key that he didn't keep in his rooms.

There was a shelf along the wall next to the door. Nikolaos let his hand slide on the rough surface of the highest shelf, feeling his fingers bump into brushes, hoof cleaners, and what he assumed were pots of saddle oil. Then the tip of his longest finger grazed something cool and smooth. A key! Heart racing, he raced to the keyhole. It fit. He held his breath, scared it wouldn't turn, but it did easily, and he pulled the door open, gasping when he finally let his breath out. Leaving the door ajar, he ran back in to get the horse, and finally retrieved his satchel and fiddle.

Nikolaos had his foot in the stirrup, ready to mount, when he hesitated. What if the guards did rounds at night and would check the lock? If they found it unlocked, they might go in, notice his horse was gone, and chase after him. Maybe it would be better to put the key back on the shelf and hope they would think the stable master forgot. Nikolaos pulled his foot out of the stirrup, staring at the door with its key on the inside. But the stable master was nice and had taken excellent care of his horse. It wouldn't be right to make it seem as if he had been careless. That decided it. He went and opened the door, pulled the key out, and locked it from the outside. Then he threw the key in the moat. It went in with an almost silent splash as if a fish had caught a bug at the surface.

Finally on horseback, Nikolaos made his way around Norrköping's House toward the bridge, hoping none of the guards were waiting out there. Riding on the grass so the hooves wouldn't make too much noise and keeping his feet still to ensure sounds from stirrups or saddle leather didn't betray him, he turned the corner, entering the path between the front wall and the moat. But there they were, appearing like dark shapes on each side of the large entranceway in front of the bridge. Their faces were hidden under heavy broad hats protecting them from the rain, and their crossbows were slung over their shoulders, almost like an afterthought. They were both leaning against the wall with their arms crossed under their coats. For people who were concerned that he would come and steal unborn babies from pregnant women, they looked remarkably relaxed.

But the road from the door to the bridge was muddy and wet. They would surely hear and see him as soon he reached it, if not before. It was dangerously close to them too. He stared at them, willing them to stay asleep, then kicked his heels as hard as he could. The horse leaped forward, galloping toward the bridge, turning into the entrance road with a squelching sound. Moments later they were on the bridge, hooves deafeningly loud as they hit the wood, creating blue streaks in the rain. All at once, the guards jumped to attention and ran toward him, hollering and cursing. Kicking his heels even harder, they flew across the bridge and out to the open square in front of Norrköping's House. Nikolaos flattened himself over the horse's neck, praying he wouldn't get an arrow in his back. He thought he heard arrows whoosh by, but they made it across the square unscathed.

Nikolaos tore past the market stalls, cottages, and larger homes along the Motala River, perceiving flashes of kindling sticks as people were startled out of their beds by the thundering hooves. He kept going, flying past fishing huts, enclosed crops, and farmhouses until the horse stopped on its own, unable to take even one more step at such a pace.

Nikolaos patted the horse's sweaty flanks and dismounted. In the stillness, looking back at Norrköping House's dark shadow against the night sky, the reality that four people had drowned hit him. And old memories of women pulsing through deep water toward him, hot kisses and feverish bodies cooling in the rapids, overwhelmed him with such force he had to grab hold of the horse so as not to sink to the ground. It didn't matter that no one had joined him in the river this time. He might still be responsible. What if they drowned before they reached him? The thought made his heart pound with shame. He was evil; why couldn't he stop? Staring into the darkness, he began to pray as loud as he dared. "Dear Father, who art in heaven, I confess to thee my sins. Sins I cannot confess before a priest for they are too grave. I plead to you," he let out a sob, "hear them here under your heavens, for I confess to you that I cause the death of women." He made the sign of the cross. "I beg you to forgive me."

There was no sign that God had heard him. The night was still as before, no rustling in the leaves nor wind acknowledging that his prayers had been received.

With a resigned shrug, he remounted and gently pressed his heels into the horse's flanks, encouraging him to move at his own pace now, then threw one last glance toward the town behind him. That's when he saw dots of lights moving on the road.

Torches. People were looking for him.

Chapter 09

When Rå arrived for church on Sunday, people were standing outside in tight groups, talking in low, panicked voices.

Gulla and Karla sat together on a bench by the wall, clasping each other's hands. When they spotted Rå, Karla loosened her grasp on Gulla's hand and waved her toward them. "Magda, have you heard what happened?"

Rå shook her head. "No."

"Näcken has murdered several people. And he's stolen a baby, too. Both Gustav and Karl from Norrköping's House will be questioned during service. One of the kitchen maids will be as well."

Rå's back tightened, protecting its hole. "Heavens above, that's terrible. Did he really steal a baby?"

"That's what everyone is saying," Gulla said, leaning across Karla to get closer to Rå and lowering her voice. "They've been looking in the river, but they can't find it."

"What are they looking for?"

"The *baby*," Gulla hissed, sounding like she thought Rå was witless.

"I see," Rå said, ignoring the tone.

Pastor Klint looked pale behind his pulpit, his eyes level and narrow. Rå thought it made him seem mean, but it was probably fear.

Just like last time when Gulla was questioned, Karl and Gustav were told to have a seat on chairs that someone had placed in the chancel.

"I will begin with you, Karl," Pastor Klint said. "Tell me how you know Näcken."

Karl flinched. "I know no one by that name."

Pastor Klint shook his head and scoffed. "You do not? Who is it you have been performing with?"

"A man named Nikolaos."

"A man? Are you saying that the fiddle player you performed with is a *man*? Do men usually murder people and steal newborn babies? You ought to know, Karl. You spent time with him alone… almost naked." A couple of people snickered, stopping abruptly when Pastor Klint threw them an icy stare.

"No, but…" Karl started, looking at Gustav for support. He didn't respond.

"Did you know he got his horse out of a locked stable and past the guardsmen almost unseen?" Pastor Klint asked. "Only one of the guardsmen noticed, and then only barely. When he tried to shoot him, he turned into a horse. That horse of his was Näcken himself. It was never actually a horse."

A look of shock flashed across Karl's face. "How can that horse be Näcken if we've seen them both together and separately?"

"Because he was created by the Devil. The Devil can conjure up whatever he wants. But if, and I repeat if, he is just a man, then we have buried no less than four people in sacred ground who do not belong there." Pastor Klint waved his finger in the air and climbed down from his pulpit. "I will explain," he said when he reached the floor, enunciating his words even more than usual. "If Näcken has not killed them, then it *is* likely suicide. And by burying suicides in holy ground, we have contaminated the graveyard, risking the lives of everyone on Judgment Day." He turned away from the men, eying his congregation.

For a moment, he was looking straight at Rå. She met his gaze. Everyone was silent.

When Pastor Klint spoke again, his voice roared across the church. "It is murder. People who murder even themselves cannot be buried among others. They should have been buried at the gallows. When our community rises on the day of judgment, they will be in league with the Devil and let loose. They may even haunt us while we visit our dead, who we thought were resting peacefully."

At that, Karl leaned forward and retched on the stone floor.

Pastor Klint ignored it. "Our sacred ground where our beloveds are resting would be contaminated by evil! This is dangerous. It is of utmost importance that we find out who this man is, Nikolaos, as he calls himself. We need to learn if Näcken tricked them into death at no fault of their own or if they committed the sin of suicide. Are you still claiming that he is just an ordinary man?" Pastor Klint moved closer. Taking care not to step in the vomit, he whispered something inaudible.

Everyone stayed silent, straining to hear. One of the poorer women who couldn't afford a seat and was standing along the wall fainted and slid straight down with her feet in front of her. No one helped her up. Her sister, or maybe it was her mother, just put a hand on her shoulder and left her slumped where she sat. It reminded Rå that people always gave her space in the pews even though all she had given the church was herbs. They still hung in the sacristy, collecting dust.

Then, a young woman was brought forward through the aisle. Someone had put out a chair for her while Rå looked away.

Pastor Klint regarded her silently when she sat down. She kept her gaze in her lap, crying so much she was shaking. Pastor Klint stood before her, waiting. Suddenly, he slapped her across the cheek. Rå's back pulsated at the humiliation, and she pulled her shawl tighter around herself, afraid that someone would see her trunk even though she wore plenty of layers over her back.

"Now enough with your crying, Maria. Get a hold of yourself so you can answer my questions. Are you able to do that?"

"Yes." It was barely more than a whisper, but Rå could still hear it.

"Now, tell me when you saw him and spoke to him. Did he approach you? Did he try to tempt you to go with him?"

"The first time was..."

"Louder!"

Maria started again, straightening up and looking at Pastor Klint. "It was an early morning. He had been somewhere on the other side of the moat. He wanted some bread, and I gave it to him. He didn't ask me to go with him, but I was very scared of him because he came upon me so fast."

"How fast did he move? Was it an unnatural speed?"

"I... no, I just didn't see him. I'd offered him some bread since it was fresh, and we had a lot. At first, he said no and walked away, but then he changed his mind and went after me. He startled me, but he was polite."

"You offered him bread? So, you approached him?"

"Well, I was just being nice, that's all. We both saw Nikolaos come home, me and the other kitchen maid. We were outside getting water," she said, color spreading across her cheeks.

"I see. Was he wet?"

Maria's face fell. She reached out with her arm as if to steady herself, but the chair didn't have an armrest, and she was just grasping at thin air. "Yes, he was." Her eyes went wide as she said it. "His hose and even his breeches were wet!" She burst into tears again.

A collective gasp swept throughout the church.

Pastor Klint nodded gravely. "Then it is rather clear, I would say. It is Näcken that we have amongst us. May God have Mercy on us. We must pray."

Rå bent her head with the others, but instead of praying, she was thinking about what Pastor Klint said about Judgment Day. She was confused about it and didn't fully understand what it meant. A coal miner she was with many moons ago had explained that God would one day come back from heaven to see how everyone had behaved. Even the dead would be judged and come out of their graves, he said. But she had seen bodies in the woods, rotting corpses with maggots eating them. Surely, people couldn't live after that. When she brought that up with the coal miner, he said humans were different. She didn't believe him. It sounded silly. She preferred the stories about *Valhöll* her mother had told her when she was a child.

Rå carefully glanced at the people around her. Old Anna from Birch Lake was fingering something in her hands, caressing it, and putting it to her heart. Her fingers were shaking. Then she lifted her gaze and looked straight at Rå, fumbling to hide the item under her shawl. A saint, forbidden and banned for its heathen ways.

Rå smiled at her and put her fingers to her lips.

Old Anna nodded gratefully.

When the service was over, Rå left as fast as she could, hurrying back to the comfort of the forest.

She found a secluded place behind a beech tree and pushed her feet into the moist green moss, letting it wrap around her ankles and crawl up her legs. As the chirping birds and the howling wind faded from her ears, her trunk opened.

Chapter 10

Nikolaos was deep in the woods when suddenly, a woman appeared right in front of him. She seemed so out of place that he didn't even react, and it wasn't until the horse veered off to get around her that he understood she was actually there. But by the time he had turned the horse around to apologize for almost colliding with her, she was gone. He laughed, confused. What was going on?

Then he saw her again, standing in a sunbeam under the trees. He blinked to clear his vision. But she was still there. Barefoot, her dress so short he could see halfway up her shins. Her hair was light brown, and incredibly long, and the wind made it wrap around her as if it were a coat. Her skin was pale, and her eyes were startlingly large and green, glowing in the soft light filtering through the trees. She was the most beautiful woman he had ever seen.

"I know who you are and what they say about you. Come with me," she said, then promptly spun around and walked deeper into the trees, her long hair unwrapping itself from her body and scattering sideways with the wind.

Nikolaos opened his mouth to say something but closed it again and just stared after her. Had she been sent by one of the sixmen? It seemed a strange way to get to him. But how else could she know who he was and what they were saying about him? The woman kept walking, seemingly unconcerned if he was coming or not. If someone had sent her, wouldn't she make sure he was following? Nikolaos took a closer look at the surrounding trees. Nothing moved, and it was utterly silent, no sound of shifting horses, hooves, or saddle leather. He relaxed. There was no one else there. He couldn't possibly say no to an invitation from such a beautiful woman. Smiling, he urged his horse into a canter and followed her.

There wasn't much of a path, just a widening between the trees. Riding through it, he expected the border of a village with homes in the distance. But there was nothing, only tall pines with bare lower trunks spreading before him and the sound of a woodpecker somewhere nearby. The woman was gone. This was getting stranger by the moment.

Then one of the pines moved. Just like that, as if it wasn't attached to the ground. The horse reared up and almost bolted. It was the woman, standing still now with her back turned to him, her long hair pulled aside, exposing her back. She was completely naked, and her back was thick and coarse like pine bark.

Nikolaos yelped in surprise, and she turned at the sound. Her breasts were full and had dark large nipples. He felt his jaw drop and closed it again, embarrassed.

"I knew you'd come," she said, completely unfazed that he saw her without clothes. "Follow me. Pray forgive me for scaring your horse. What's his name?" She approached slowly, extending her hand toward the horse, who sniffed it carefully, then lowered his head so she could pet him.

Nikolaos dismounted, dumbfounded. "I just call him the horse. Who are you, and how did you do that? He's usually wary of strangers, especially if they've scared him first."

"I have my ways, I'm a friend of all animals." She reached for her dress, which she had slung over a tree branch, and let it slip over her head and shoulders. "They're still looking for you, but if you stay with me a while, they won't find you. Come."

Nikolaos fell in beside her. He wanted to ask how she knew but couldn't think of how to phrase it. It struck him she might be insane, but for some reason, he didn't think that was it. And her back defied explanation. Maybe he had imagined it.

They went deeper into the pines, then up a steep incline that brought them into a clearing. There were two enormous boulders with a pile of branches stacked between them. When they approached, a pair of hares crawled out from under them and ran right at them, then stopped at their feet, jumping around the woman as if they were dogs happy that their mistress had come home. It was so bizarre that he laughed.

"You must tell me who you are." He gave her a scrutinizing look, and it finally dawned on him. She wasn't human. He felt a spike of excitement. "And *what* you are."

"I'm Rå, though the townspeople call me Magda," she said, reaching down to pet the hares. Then she pushed the pile of branches aside, exposing a wooden door.

"Rå?"

"Yes," she said as if that explained it, then opened the door and went inside, leaving him where he was with the door ajar.

Disappointed, Nikolaos looked after her. Clearly, Rå wasn't just a name but something more. And not only that, but she also expected him to know what it was. He felt ignorant, and intimidated. Tying the horse to a tree, he followed her into the dwelling, trying to look more confident than he felt.

It wasn't as dark in there as he had assumed. There was a lantern on a small table and a burning hearth in the corner. The smoke curved up the rock wall almost like in a chimney. There were rushes on the floor, colorful wall hangings, and an extended bench. It was dark in the back, but it looked like there was at least another room further in.

"Have a seat, just mind my hares. They like to sleep under the table."

"I'll make sure of it." Easing a little, he looked down at his feet, and just like she said, there they lay peering up at him. One was missing an ear, he noticed. "What happened to its ear? And why do you have rabbits here? Hares I mean, they're enormous."

"They were caught in traps, barely weaned from their mother. I took them in to help them, and they stayed. Their names are Lil' Leaf and One Ear."

"Lil' Leaf? Where did you get that from?"

Rå put a bowl of porridge, dried apple slices, and a large chunk of goat cheese in front of him. "He was covered in little leaves when I found him. His leg was wet from gnawing on it as the poor little thing tried to chew it off to free himself. All these tiny leaves were stuck in his wet fur. Cruel, cruel humans!"

"Same story with One Ear?"

She nodded.

He felt for them but knew how it was when your children sat

listless on the floor for lack of food in the winter.

"Eat," Rå said, "get your fill, and then we'll talk. I make no ale, but I have a jug of water from the spring back here. It's safe to drink."

Nikolaos pulled his spoon from his pocket. "Water will be fine."

She reached for a mug and dipped it into a bucket. Handing it to him, she then pulled out a little stool from under the table and sat down opposite him.

"Thank you, Rå. I left in haste and didn't bring anything to eat," he said between bites.

"I know."

"How?" He swallowed, feeling another spike of excitement and intimidation.

She didn't say anything at first, just sat there and looked at him. The fire crackled, and he heard the hares breathe by his feet. The silence felt awkward.

"I have my ways. I can feel disturbances in the forest. Besides, I've been to church and heard what they say about you. People are terrified. They think you've murdered babies and calves and turned into a horse."

He scoffed. "A horse? Where did they get that idea from?" It was what Sixman Ole had said too.

"One of the women explained that a horse was walking past her bedroom window several nights in a row, and then her sister died. Pastor Klint said that you can turn into a horse and that you got yourself out of a locked stable."

He whistled. "I threw away the key. That was stupid, I should've left it unlocked. Though a horse, I'm not."

She laughed.

The hares stirred and moved around under the table.

Nikolaos grabbed an apple slice and chewed on it, feeling more like himself, the laughter and conversation lowering the tension. "How can you go to church with them? Don't they notice?"

"That I'm not human?" She smiled at him. "I cover my back with shawls and try not to get too involved with people there. They come here for help now and then, though, so we must be very quiet in case someone visits so they won't learn you're with me."

He nodded, glancing toward the closed door.

"How do *you* do it?" she asked. "I heard you lived at Norrköping's House. Didn't they realize before all this?"

He stared at her, taken aback. "I'm not... I'm human." He had never said these words before, never explained that he was, when in fact he might not be.

Her large eyes shone with merriment. "You are, are you? How old are you?"

He shrugged. "Older than most."

Rå stood up and pulled off her dress, then turned away from him and grabbed her hair with both hands, folding it over her right shoulder.

What he saw confirmed what he had seen before. Her back was rough like a pine and looked like a tree trunk. But something within it shifted now as if there were waves of water in the bark-like skin. A hole formed, dark and pulsing, pulling at him. He quickly drew back, his heart pounding. Rusty devils, what was happening?

Rå let her hair fall down her back again.

"What *was* that? Who are you?"

"I'll tell you, but first I want you to answer my question. If I trust you to show you my true self, then surely you can tell me how old you are." She put her dress back on and sat down.

He nodded. It was a fair point. "I've lived a long time, Rå, but don't seem to age. It makes it harder to keep track of the years. I think I'm a hundred and fifty or thereabouts."

Rå didn't look surprised. "What about the stories I hear of you?"

"They're not all wrong." Nikolaos paused, uncomfortable. "I have a craving for water, especially rapids. And I see colors. Sounds have color, and when I play in water, I can see my music."

"Ah." She smiled. "That must be lovely."

"Yes, when I play, colors swirl around me, especially in water. It's sometimes why I don't see when..." He stopped.

"I've seen you."

"You have?"

"Yes, more than once. I've heard your music too. It's very beautiful. And once, I saw you with your sons when you were fishing. I could feel the longing in you, how you struggled to focus on your boys instead of the water. The three of you had an argument about why you wouldn't sit at the water's edge with them."

Nikolaos' eyes flashed to hers in surprise. He remembered it well. The boys had begged him to teach them how to fish, and he had finally given in, insisting he stand back and observe, knowing that he couldn't trust himself to keep them safe. They lost them both, but not that day, and not because of him.

Rå's hares left their spot under the table and hopped around on the floor, distracting him. The one-eared one was sniffing something by the door, and he was reminded that the horse was still out there.

Nikolaos shifted his gaze back to Rå. "That was a long time ago. My children are all dead now."

"Yes," she said simply.

Silence followed, and One Ear settled himself under the table again.

"Where can I put my horse?"

"We can put him behind the boulders. There's a crevice at the back that would suit fine. Why have you not named him? He deserves a name."

"I suppose he does, but animals live such short lives, it seems pointless. I miss them more if I know their names."

Rå looked at him without commenting, then got to her feet and opened the door. It had started to drizzle, and the draft brought in a scent of wet grass, pine, and soil. She left it open, and he watched her walk across the damp ground on bare feet, her calves exposed under her short dress. He averted his eyes. The horse sniffed her hair and showed no fear as she grabbed hold of him and walked away with him. The pines and deciduous trees formed a circle around the clearing, giving the appearance of being walled in. It was no wonder he hadn't seen her home, not even when she had led him straight to it.

"Your horse is fed and comfortable," Rå said when she returned. "He's sheltered from the wind, and no one can see him back there. You may stay here for a few days, but then you ought to move on."

"I give thanks," Nikolaos said, but she didn't acknowledge having heard him.

She lit a torch and walked into the darkness on the other side of the hearth, placing it in a hook on the wall. The light exposed a nicely sized room, just like he had thought earlier. There was a loom in there. She sat down at it and began to work as if he were not there.

Nikolaos leaned back against the cliff wall and tried to relax, looking at his surroundings. The cave, if you could call it that, was much larger than it had seemed when he first came in. Just to the right of where Rå sat was a pallet with a blanket spread over it, and beyond that, more space.

"You may ask me anything you wish," Rå said, startling him. She didn't look at him.

Stifling a yawn, he sat up straight. "You must be as old as I, at least, if you saw me and my little boys. It would be about a hundred and twenty-five or a hundred and twenty-eight years or so ago. Pray tell me who you truly are."

"I'm the Forest Rå, I care for the forest." Rå continued weaving, her long hair piled on the floor behind her, moving slightly as her arm slid across the loom.

The Forest Rå of course, the carer of the forest. It made sense now. He smiled. "And your back, I've never seen anything like that before."

"It contains the force of the trees."

He nodded. She had looked like a tree out there; there was no doubt about that, but he still didn't understand. "Do you have human parents?"

"You could say that." Rå finally stopped weaving and turned around to look at him. "I was raised by humans." She narrowed her eyes, and it seemed as if she was going to say something else, but then she shook her head. "Some know of me, but they don't know what I am, thinking they've seen me with a tail or the rump of a horse. Some, like you, thought I was just one of the trees. You must never tell them. In return, I'll protect you. And I'll tell you when it's safe to leave."

Nikolaos nodded again. He wanted to ask her to explain more, but he wasn't sure how to ask without being intrusive and rude. He knew how it was to have to keep parts of oneself hidden. She had her reasons, just as he did.

****

To thank Rå for her hospitality, Nikolaos helped her mend the roof on top of the crevice which formed her cave-like home. They kept a companionable silence, each working on their own chores. He wasn't sure what to make of her. She had an air about her that felt almost holy, as if she was one of the saints come alive. He would do whatever she asked.

On the sixth morning, she told him it was time to leave and to go north.

Chapter 11

Rå followed Näcken, or Nikolaos as he insisted she call him, for days.

One evening, he stopped at a river. It was wide and rapid, full of boulders, creating ripples and whirlpools people could get sucked into if they weren't careful. At first, he turned around and scanned his surroundings to make sure he was alone. He didn't see her. Then he got off his nameless horse, tied it to a tree, and undressed. Nikolaos' body was strong and muscular, larger than it seemed when clothed, and very beautiful. He walked straight into the strong rapids as if they were no more than wisps of smoke from a firepit. Standing out there, staring at something, maybe the colors he had described, he was still as a statue. Then he put his hands forward, fingers touching, and dove straight down like a grebe. Just before he disappeared, his body became transparent like water. It was barely perceivable. An eyeblink only, but she swore she saw it.

Then, when the sun sank below the tree line, Nikolaos' head broke the surface and he stood up, walked back to the beach, dressed, and got back on his horse like an ordinary man.

Rå kept up with him until he reached the coast, and the sea air blew salty wind into her hair. She watched him ride away. Part of her hoped he would turn around and wave, that he had known that she had been behind him the whole time. But his horse trotted steadily forward, and he never looked back.

Nikolaos had surprised her in several ways. She had hoped to meet an equal, someone she could talk to who understood her, someone she didn't need to hide anything from. But he had been incredibly ignorant about the non-human world. He didn't even seem to fully understand who he was. He acted like one of the villagers and was shy and embarrassed, not only when she was naked, but even when she wore her shift. He had pretended not to look, but she caught him staring at her calves several times. She supposed he couldn't help it. He wasn't very old and must have lived his whole life with the prude rules the priests had brought in.

Whatever the reason, she hadn't put her long, cumbersome skirts on for his benefit.

At the end of the week, he had been a little more comfortable with her and had talked more. Just like her, he had lived with a family as a child, but as far as he knew, his mother had given birth to him. Although he had always loved water, his intense need for it, his words, hadn't come until he became a young adult. He hid it, pretending to be like everyone else. That, at least, they had in common. She had wanted to ask him about the drowned, but he gave only vague answers, claiming it was always by accident. It might be, but she had a strong feeling that he wasn't as sweet as he seemed, that there was a fierce power inside him that he hid from even himself.

Rå was almost back home when she heard a woodcutter in the distance. Smiling to herself, she followed the rhythmic sound of his ax against wood. It had rained, and her bare feet were completely silent on the moist ground.

He was alone, working on a felled tree and chopping the logs into smaller pieces. His dark hair was getting thin, but his beard was thick, forming into a point just below his chin, and his arms and thighs were strong from years of hard work in the woods. He wore farmer's breeches, not the annoying hose Nikolaos and other men wore these days. That was good; she couldn't stand hose and puffy short breeches.

An ox stood tied to a wagon in the shade, its large head drooping in sleep. For a moment, the woodcutter stopped as if he had heard her, but then he lifted the ax again, cleaving the next piece in two. One of them flew straight toward Rå. She raised her hand and caught it.

He startled. "Dear lord! Pray forgive me. I didn't see you there. Are you hurt?"

"Not at all. Good day to you," she said, laughing, then studiously sauntered past him, handing him the wood piece. The effect was immediate. He stumbled after her, and she kept walking until she felt his want in her back. Then she turned toward him and waited.

"Who are you? What are you doing out here alone in the woods?" he whispered.

Rå smiled, smelling the scent of sap and sweat from his body. "I have many names. Some call me Forest Wife or Rå. You'll lie with me right here," she said and untied the knot around his breeches.

By the time the woodcutter was snoring beside her, it was getting dark, and stars began to twinkle above them. Freya had a silvery road up there where she walked from one end of the earth to the other. Rå looked for her, hoping to get a glimpse, but she wasn't there. She sent Freya a greeting anyway, then stood silently and made her way back to the woodcutter's pile. The ox turned his head toward her, but when he recognized her, he lowered his head and went back to sleep.

Finding a tree near the woodcutter's pile, she put both hands on its trunk and pushed gently. "Dear child of mine, please uproot and give yourself to this man who gave me his power this night," she said firmly, gave it another pat, and walked away.

When she passed the sleeping form of the woodcutter, the tree fell to the ground. He didn't stir.

Chapter 12

Thousands of islands dotted the coastline, appearing and disappearing as thick fog shifted in the breeze. Stockholm.

Not only was there a lot of water, but it was a town where Nikolaos could hide. Hopefully.

He lined up behind a group of people waiting to cross a bridge to get to a cluster of smaller houses on the other side of a narrow waterway. A woman held a basket overflowing with fish in her arms. It was clear from the smell that some were already rotting. He took a step back to get away from it. The crowd moved forward a moment later, and he had to hurry to pull his son's passport out of his satchel. But no one asked for it, and he followed the others and walked straight into town.

The homes were built so tightly together that the wood almost touched. Men and women, mostly men, he noted, were hurrying back and forth, dodging chickens and pigs that were eating the garbage and refuse people had thrown there. The fog made it damp and it stunk worse than the woman's fish. It was no wonder she could bring rotten food. No one would notice the smell unless they put their noses right in it. He would have to be careful with what he ate here.

Hurrying along, Nikolaos wished he hadn't shaved his head at Norrköping's House. It was growing back but was still just a stubble. Strange custom Karl kept. It wouldn't do here; he looked like a toiler. His hat just served as a reminder that there was no hair escaping from under it.

As if to confirm his thoughts, a gentleman with a fine coat and long hair looked at him suspiciously. Nikolaos thought he would ask if he had stolen the horse, but then the man walked on as if it wasn't worth the trouble. Nikolaos sighed with relief. He wouldn't have had the stamina to be polite if confronted. After almost a week without food, he was hungry and tired, and the constant cacophony of voices, horses, and seagulls made him see erratic colors that seemed to mingle with the awful stench.

He was just about to ask someone for directions to a lodging house when he found an inn.

A portly man with a wisp of thick white hair was sitting on the stoop, waving him in. "Welcome to my inn, come inside and seat yourself at the table. You look as if you could use it. Traveling far?" he asked as a boy no older than nine came running. "My boy will put your horse in the stable for you," he said, smiling broadly.

"I *have* traveled far," Nikolaos said, smiling back. He seemed a friendly sort who wasn't bothered by his short hair. "Now I just want to put my feet up and get my things in order. Do you have rooms available?" Nikolaos dismounted, pulling his saddlebags and bundle off the back of the saddle, nodding in thanks as the boy took the horse by the bit and led him away.

"I sure do. What brings you to our humble town of Stockholm?"

"Humble?" Nikolaos laughed. "I don't know yet to tell you the truth. I'm a fiddler."

"Are you now? My wife will be happy 'bout that. Go in and get settled, tell her I said you should have the blue room."

"I give thanks," Nikolaos said and waited for the innkeeper to move, but he stayed put, his large frame planted just in front of the door. He had to squeeze past him.

The scent of well-cooked fish greeted him inside, fresh and not overly spiced to hide rot. It was a good sign, although he had hoped for meat.

The innkeeper's wife was standing behind a counter in the corner, with wooden plates stacked on it and jugs and mugs. She nodded at him, smiling as broadly as her husband. "Welcome, what can I get you? You look as hungry as a waterman!"

He stiffened. "A waterman?"

"I mean nothing by that young man. Those who work on the ships are usually hungry is all."

Nikolaos cast a quick glance around the room. Most were talking amongst themselves and paid them no mind. "Ah, yes. I'm ravenous." The tension in his shoulders eased. No one knew him here, and come to think about it, people might just think he had shaved his head to get rid of lice.

"Have himself a seat and I'll bring you a plate." She gestured toward a free bench in the corner with her elbow.

The bench was right next to a hearth with a real chimney. It had impressive stonework. Nikolaos had wanted to get one installed at home, but his reputation had made it impossible to find someone to help.

Before long, the innkeeper's wife arrived with a plate of fish and a chunk of hard bread dipped in fat. It looked delicious. Fish was a natural choice this close to the archipelago, he supposed.

"I give thanks," he said, smiling to make up for the awkward moment earlier. "Your husband said I could have the blue room."

"He give you the fancy room, did he now? Well, in that case, hold on a moment." With skirts swishing back and forth, stirring up the dust, she hurried back to the counter and came back with a small bowl filled to the brim with liquor. It didn't look as if she had spilled even a drop.

"How kind! I needed this."

"Yes, I can always tell, finish your meal, and then I'll take you up myself."

Nikolaos wasn't sure what made his room fancy. It was tiny, first of all. There was just enough space for the bed and a small bedside table with a candle, and the blue paint on the wall was scuffed. But it would do. He could afford it too.

***

Nikolaos ventured out at sunrise the next morning. A fresh breeze had dispersed the worst of the stench, and Stockholm lay clear and quiet. Making a left out of the inn, he walked through a myriad of alleyways, passing rows of cottages, pigsties, and yards with chickens and woodpiles. From what he could tell, people were doing well enough to sustain themselves but not much more than that. That was enough. Shelter and food were all one needed. And love. Life was hard without it.

The observation made him think of Rå. Again. It was

impossible to get her out of his mind. She was so calm and kind. And gorgeous, despite that strange hole in her back. It both scared and intrigued him. He had wanted to ask her to explain, but each time he worked up the courage, he lost his nerve. She was so confident and acted as if her not being human was completely normal, a boon, which she enjoyed and took full advantage of. She was surprised that he didn't feel the same about himself, and it embarrassed him. He didn't tell her how often he prayed for forgiveness. Or of the shame he had felt ever since he was a child. The first time he understood he was different was when he was only about four summers old, maybe five. He had been playing in the river like he usually did when suddenly, strong arms grabbed him and pulled him out. Everyone was there, including his mother who was wailing with pain. It was his father who had pulled him out, but his face was so changed from fear he hadn't recognized him at first. Nikolaos' older siblings were on a boat, sticking long poles through the water as if they were searching for something, him. But he hadn't understood that then. Late that evening, when they thought he was asleep, he had heard them whisper. That he had been under for much longer than was possible, much too long. That he should have been dead but that Saint Nikolaos, the seafaring saint, had saved him. A miracle. A thank you for having named their son Nikolaos.

The following morning, Nikolaos told his mother he had just been chasing fish and collecting rocks. She had laughed at him, but her expression said otherwise. She was horrified. Afterward he found her sobbing behind the house, praying for God to keep him safe, and whispering that no one could live that long without breathing. It wasn't until he got older that he understood what she meant by that.

But he hadn't questioned his humanity until Rå pointed it out. Not truly. So, who was he then? And who was she?

The sun was high in the sky when the neighborhood started to change. The streets widened and became cleaner, and soon he was walking down a finer street lined with shops and what looked like a large stable at the end. Turning there, he stopped in his tracks and found himself in front of an enormous castle. He stared as if awestruck.

It was made of stone, shining white in the now strong sunlight, protected by a tall stone wall that circled the whole edifice. It had square bastions in the corners, turrets with ornate roofs, and three golden crowns proudly displayed on a spire over a round keep. It must be Three Crowns, the royal castle. Norrköping's House had been nothing but a homestead by comparison. This was glorious, shining in the sunlight as if illuminated from within. A proper place for a King like in the stories. Only it was likely Duke Erik who was there now instead of King Sigismund. Karl had spoken of it at length, analyzing the situation. Apparently, Duke Erik had been instated as a National Principal of sorts several years ago. It was to monitor the King, verifying he did what he should, specifically that he stuck to proper Lutheranism even though he was Catholic. Then last year, King Sigismund and Duke Erik had warred with each other over it, their armies fighting to the death. Nikolaos didn't understand who had started it, but Duke Erik wanted to prevent the Swedish-Polish King from bringing Catholicism back to the country. According to Lord Johan, Duke Erik had occupied Kalmar Castle and was the cause of an actual bloodbath where several influential men had been executed. Even Johan Sparre, Karl had explained. Nikolaos hadn't admitted that he didn't know who Sparre was. He wasn't sure where Kalmar Castle was either or when it had happened, but if he understood correctly, there were rumors that Duke Erik was already King and Sigismund had been ousted. Maybe it was something he could ask the innkeeper about.

Getting back to the present, he kept walking. A church sat snugly by Three Crown's side, as if protecting the castle with its presence. He laughed aloud, suddenly remembering it must be Saint Nikolaos' Church. Surely there could be no place better fated for him to pray.

Two pastors with their ruffs and capes arrived just as he got to the entrance.

"Reverends," Nikolaos said, bowing deeply. "May I enter to

recite my prayers?"

"By all means," the one closest to him said and held the door open for him. He was older, sixty maybe, with small eyes that became tiny among folds and wrinkles when he smiled.

Nikolaos removed his hat and entered. Rounded arches reached a curved ceiling, large windows let in soft light, and thick columns formed a wide aisle toward the altar. It was breathtaking. He barely noticed when the clergymen hurried past him.

Slowly, Nikolaos made his way through the church until he came upon a giant sculpture. A man sat mounted on a horse, a sword wielded behind his back as a dragon below him bared his teeth, ready to strike. Saint Göran and the Dragon.

Nikolaos shivered. It looked too realistic as if the poor dragon was being slain while he watched. It was what people wished to do with him. In their eyes, he was a creature just like it.

He looked away, then walked over to the altar and kneeled. Crossing himself, he prayed silently that God would keep people safe from him, that he could hide his true self and live among people undisturbed. And that God would accept him and forgive him, even if he wasn't one of them.

***

That evening, the inn was full. A single empty chair across from two men at one of the smaller tables was the only space where he could sit.

One of the men gave him a friendly nod as he made his way over. "First time visiting? You play the fiddle, I heard," he said before Nikolaos' behind had even reached the wood. The man was heavyset, leaning against the wall and cleaning his teeth with a fishbone. The other man also heavyset but more muscular, just glanced at him.

"I do. And yes, it's the first time I'm visiting Stockholm. Might stay a few months or a few years. We'll see."

The friendlier man looked pleased. He put the bone down, leaning forward slightly. "I'm a bagpiper. I'm playing this Thursday down in the meadow below the inn here. Care to join me?"

"I'd be delighted to," Nikolaos said, grateful. God was already answering his prayers.

"You have played with a bagpiper before?"

"Yes, I did so recently as a matter of fact."

"Good, where was that?"

"South, one of the smaller villages near a lake," he lied. "We played together for a few days, and it went well." It sounded plausible. He hoped he could leave it at that.

"Good, then you ought to keep up with me."

"Eh, we shall see," Nikolaos said with a crooked smile, catching the eye of the innkeeper's wife.

She must have thought he was flirting with her and hurried over to refill their mugs, nudging Nikolaos' side with her elbow. Her bosom came so close to his face that he had to move so as not to be indecent.

The man who had asked him to play chuckled. "My name is Björn. This fella here is Anders."

"Nikolaos."

"Just like our beautiful church," Björn said.

Anders acknowledged him with a backward tilt of his head, eyes narrowed and fixed upon him.

"A stunning place, I prayed there just this morning. Three Crowns is as well. I've never seen anything as grand. I'm a man of humble means," Nikolaos said, trying to ignore Anders' scrutinizing gaze.

"It's indeed a place that ought to be fit for a king. Still, Sigmund insisted on staying in Poland all those years. I for one, am happy to be rid of him. Catholic heathen!" Anders spit on the floor. It landed with a faint splat.

Nikolaos made sure to keep his face neutral. "I was just thinking of that this morning. Sigismund *is* out then, is he?"

Björn stretched and got to his feet. "Yes," he let out a disdainful laugh, "Erik is de facto regent now."

"I see," Nikolaos said, but was still confused. De facto regent, so he wasn't King then?

"I have to leave," Björn said. "I'll be by here the day after tomorrow. We'll walk down to the meadow together. Does that suit?"

"Of course. I give thanks."

Björn nodded and was gone, leaving him alone with Anders. It felt awkward. Anders was still looking at him oddly.

"I take it Björn lives in town. What about you?" Nikolaos asked to break the silence.

"Yes, me too... well, usually I do, but my home is gone at present, burnt down, all of it. I'm staying here at the inn now." Anders placed his elbows on the table. His hands had started to shake, and he had to clasp them together to keep them still. "My wife had gone to borrow fire from the neighbor, and a spark from the starter log must have gone to the thatch. I was on my way home when it happened. I saw it take hold from up the street, but by the time I reached the house, the whole roof was alight. I was going to run in, but the door was already collapsing, and I never made it."

Nikolaos instinctively reached out to touch Anders' arm. No wonder he hadn't felt in the mood for friendly greetings. "My sincere condolences. That's awful."

Anders took a swig of his ale, then wiped his mouth on his sleeve. "Stockholm is dangerous. We've had too many fires. Few have chimneys and if it hasn't rained, the roofs burn like they're kindling for the fires of hell. It's why the wealthy are building homes of stone."

Nikolaos looked at him wordlessly. Anders said it so matter of fact that he felt a chill.

"I'm going to take my leave as well. We'll see each other then, both staying here at the inn and all," Anders said and stood up. He gave a nod and walked off, his back rigid. The din from the other patrons had died down, and everyone was looking at him.

"It may be an inappropriate time to ask this, but would you consider playing your fiddle here in the evenings?"

Nikolaos started, turning toward the voice. The innkeeper was standing right behind him. He had clearly overheard.

"The customers would like it," the innkeeper said and sat down where Björn had sat. "You'd live for free and eat. I can't pay you anything. But if people give you something, it would be yours to keep. We'd make good business if it draws customers." He looked nervous and probably didn't think he would say yes, but this was just what he had hoped for.

Nikolaos pretended to hesitate. "Well, I could do that... um... you won't pay me *anything?*"

"Let's just say that if we fill the hall and people buy a lot of ale and wine, then I'd consider giving you a share."

"Done."

The innkeeper grinned, the relief evident. "You start tomorrow night then, and of course, you have Thursday off. Heard you were going to play down at the dance."

They solemnly took each other's hands, each squeezing firmly. It was a deal.

Chapter 13

Seven years later

Nikolaos' prayers had been answered. God kept people safe from him, and no one suspected who he really was.

People appreciated his music, and he did so well for himself that after just a year in Stockholm, he had moved into his own little house on a quiet street.

There was only one problem, the waterways surrounding Stockholm were full of refuse and garbage. People tossed food waste, furniture, carcasses from the slaughterhouse, broken boots, and whatever else they didn't want anymore. It was quite disgusting. But perhaps it was a blessing in disguise because he was forced to leave town for a day or two whenever he needed to get to a river, which meant no one ever saw him in the water.

Then Karl, finally and officially King Karl IX, even though he was not yet coronated, started getting men together for his war campaign. It made Nikolaos nervous, afraid someone would see how strong and fit he was and decide to draft him. It was too risky to ride in and out of town so often. He stayed put, moving only between his home and the inn to avoid exposure. As a result, he was getting agitated and restless, lost his patience at the smallest slight, and was generally in a rancid mood. Even the neighbors noticed and asked if something was bothering him.

Not only that, the other day, he had lost control at the inn, forgetting himself and playing dangerous melodies just to calm down a bit. When he finished, people sat glossy-eyed and dazed with their ale and wine untouched. He was getting sloppy and careless, and it would only be a matter of time before people started to talk. There was no choice. He had to find water in town.

Nikolaos decided to find a spot in Norrström, the river rushing past Three Crowns. It ought to be a little cleaner near the castle where it was more rapid. And if he was lucky, there would be privacy as well.

Waiting until the neighbors had gone inside for the evening, Nikolaos left home and walked through the empty streets, accompanied only by the sound of pigs grunting and poking somewhere in the darkness. Just knowing he would be near water made him feel better, and he started to whistle to himself, swinging his lantern so much the candle went out.

"My good sir, let me give you a bit of kindling for your lantern, you wouldn't want to slip in the mud," said a female voice somewhere to his right. A scantily clad woman was leaning on her doorpost, the door wide open behind her. A prostitute.

"Thank you, mistress."

She smiled approvingly. "You're polite, sir, calling me mistress. I'll give you a good price should you want more than fire. Or another kind of fire altogether, perhaps?"

Nikolaos gave her a half-sided smile. "Not today." He stole a look at her abode when she went inside. It did look comfortable there. She must be one of the sought-after whores. There was a pile of fine green, blue, and orange pillows in the corner, and her walls were covered with red and orange tapestries.

"What are you out here whistling about if you're not looking for a woman to entertain you?" she asked when she came back out, holding up a small lit stick and swaying her hips as she approached.

He laughed, embarrassed. That *had* been stupid, hadn't it? "Well, I have a private errand. It's not as interesting as it seems. An old habit, I'm a fiddler and I guess I was thinking of my music. I should be more careful," Nikolaos said as he unhooked the clasp and opened the lantern so she could light the candle.

She did, then fixed her eyes on him, dramatically dropped the stick on the ground, stepped on it, and walked away. "Musicians are especially welcome," she called out.

Nikolaos chuckled. Water would take care of him, but he couldn't tell her that.

Nikolaos stopped at the riverbank on the opposite side of the castle. People were still awake, hurrying back and forth behind the windows, and he quickly extinguished his lantern to hide himself. He turned away from the windows, letting his eyes adjust to the darkness. It was quiet, just the wind in the trees and a dog barking in the distance. And as he had hoped, no one had fallen asleep drunk, nor were there any carriages with drivers waiting for their patrons at a late-night party nearby. It was deserted and safe.

A breeze brought a scent of Norrström's undercurrents with it, and he shifted his gaze toward the water. From what he could perceive in the dark, it did look cleaner near the castle. Poles were protruding above the surface, the remnants of an old dock. It was perfect. He could jump across them to get to a good spot. Grinning to himself, Nikolaos ran to the water's edge and pulled his shoes off, leaving them on a rock. Then, he carefully put his right foot on the first pole to test its strength. It didn't wobble, and he stepped up with his second foot. It was still sturdy. He paused momentarily to get his balance, then carefully took one big step to the second pole. It, too, felt strong and stable. Then slowly but securely, he made it all the way out to the last pole, which was halfway to Three Crowns, or so it seemed anyway.

When he was sated, dawn had broken. The castle lay dark and quiet, but in one of the windows, there was a silhouette of a man, faint light from a fireplace flickering behind him. The figure stood still. Nikolaos remained where he was. It was probably someone who couldn't sleep. He just had to wait until whoever it was moved away. If he or she didn't, he could silently dive in and swim out of sight.

But as he thought that, something moved, and the window was suddenly flooded with light, illuminating the figure. Rusty devils, it was the King! Nikolaos wobbled and almost lost his balance. The King looked exactly like the likeness on the posters plastered around town, the distinct hairline, bald on top with a ring of hair above his forehead that he combed over his bald spot, creating the illusion of a tonsure with a line in the middle of it.

Nikolaos forced himself upright, but it was too late. The window was flung open, and something long and narrow came out. By pure instinct, Nikolaos threw his right arm over his head, then felt a quick draft of air below his wrist. A bullet? Was the King shooting at him? How dared he? Nikolaos shook his fist at him, then pretended to throw the bullet back at the King.

The King slammed the window shut with a deafening red and blue bang. Then it went silent; the only sound was the soft movement of water and the splash of a large fish up ahead.

Nikolaos stared at the closed window, too shocked to move. Then a door opened somewhere, and he heard hooves on stone. All at once, his heart started thundering and he was drenched with sweat. His pole seemed impossibly small now, but he managed to stand up and jump across the other poles. Going as fast as he dared, he realized swimming would have been better, but he hadn't been thinking clearly. At the bank, he pushed his feet into his shoes, grabbed the lantern, and ran, tearing through the streets until he reached home.

Nikolaos' first thought was to leave, and he grabbed things randomly, tossing them into a bag. Coins, his bundle of horsetail for his bow, a portrait of Abluna that he had commissioned last year. He had paid handsomely for it and thought that the artist got her face almost perfect from his description. Only her ears looked different; they were too small, and her earlobes didn't look right. He loved it anyway. Letting his thumb slide over Abluna's eyes and cheeks, it was as if he could hear her voice. Warning him that fleeing in panic would just make things worse. The best thing to do was to go to sleep. Whatever the King thought, he had been too far away to be recognized as the fiddler from the inn on the poorer side of town. It would be best to pretend that everything was normal. He sighed, put the portrait back on the side of his nightstand, and sat down at the edge of his bed.

When the birds woke him a couple of hours later, the sun was high in the sky, and the bees were buzzing loudly on the flowers growing up the wall outside. Stretching a bit, Nikolaos swung his legs over the edge of the bed and wiggled his feet, feeling content and relaxed as he always did after water visits. Then everything rushed back to him, the King's face in the window, the musket and the bullet almost hitting his wrist. Could the King have thought he was a fisherman? Surely, illegal netting or fishing couldn't justify such a harsh punishment or the need for the King to deal with it himself.

Nikolaos gazed unseeingly at the bees outside, then shook his head. The King must have understood the truth, or he would just have yelled at him. Nikolaos hoped it had been too dark, too far for the King to see his face, and that Stockholm was too large for anyone to understand that *he* was Näcken.

In the first few weeks since the King tried to shoot him, Nikolaos eavesdropped on conversations and scrutinized every news bulletin hammered to doors and walls. Yet, he neither heard nor saw any indication of a warrant out for his arrest. Maybe the King thought he was fishing after all or that he was a painter trying to get a closer view of the castle. It had been prideful, thinking himself so remarkable that even the King himself would recognize him. It made him feel slightly ashamed, and he even laughed at it. Still, he couldn't forget about it, and Stockholm didn't feel the same any longer.

"I'm thinking of leaving Stockholm," Nikolaos said to Björn one evening several months later. They had both been playing at a wedding feast, walking home with Arla, Björn's wife.

"Leaving Stockholm?" Björn cast a glance at Arla half a pace ahead of them. She didn't notice nor seem to have heard him. "Why in the world would you do that?"

Nikolaos put a hand on Björn's shoulder. "I've been feeling restless lately. I miss my family. I'm regretting leaving when my wife and baby died." It was as close to the truth as he could make it.

"Oh, of course, I see." Warmth came into Björn's eyes. "I keep forgetting that you left your farm with relations."

Nikolaos nodded. He could go look now. It had been long enough. See if they had burned it down or had taken it over. "Yes, I have a longing to go see them. Stockholm seems suffocating lately.

It's crowded, and I'm missing the countryside."

"You're not the only one saying that, Nikolaos," Arla said, slowing her steps. "Stockholm is rowdy these days. Hooligans are everywhere. It causes lawlessness and crime, making Stockholm attractive to those from the underworld."

Nikolaos' stomach lurched. "The underworld?"

"Yes, people get distracted and have no time for their prayers. It's how we lose protection from the Lord." She nodded for effect, staring admonishingly at Björn, who looked a little shamefaced. "The baker's wife told me Näcken has been seen in town."

He knew it! "Where?" Nikolaos asked, glancing at Björn, who just shrugged.

Arla lifted an eyebrow, looking more excited to have something to talk about than concerned. "I don't know, somewhere in the archipelago I gather."

Nikolaos let out a breath. He never went out to the islands.

"It's just a rumor, Arla," Björn said, then turned back to Nikolaos. "I'll be sorry to see you leave. I'm going to miss us playing together, but most of all our friendship." He smiled, looking sad at the same time.

Nikolaos squeezed Björn's shoulder and smiled back, feeling disingenuous and guilty. It may be true that his ancestors were family, but the details were still lies, and he would miss Björn too.

But the rumor confirmed his decision. It was time to leave Stockholm. He just felt so alone.

***

His farm was still there.

Nikolaos was so relieved he felt weak, and fell forward in the saddle, slumped over the pommel. He had come in from the back road so as not to have to ride through the village, and from the look of it, not much had changed. It was getting dark, but the shadowy forms of the outbuildings seemed intact, as did the cookhouse and the outhouse. The woodpile looked like the one he had stacked, but it had been too long to be sure. Everything was quiet and still. Perhaps its occupants had gone to sleep already.

He turned around and rode back into the woods behind the outhouse. There was a clear view of his farm, and he would see if someone ran out to use the privy. Pulling his feet from the stirrups, he loosened his grip on the reins, then waited for dawn.

The birds awoke first, then a rooster crowed in the distance, and the scent of cooking fires traveled on the wind from the village. Keeping his eyes trained on his farm, Nikolaos both hoped and feared what he might see. But it remained quiet. There was no movement, nor lights yellowing the oilcloth in the windowpanes, no smoke rising above the smoke hole. He put his feet back in the stirrups and cautiously rode closer, stopping just at the edge of the tree line where the forest ended and his property began. The first sunrays were starting to hit the windows and ought to wake whoever was inside. Staying where he was, he waited a little longer, but there was still no movement, and he moved a little closer still. That was when he realized how overgrown everything was. Grass grew high above the step by the front door, broken branches lay haphazardly on the ground, and the well-trampled paths between the outhouse, the barn, and the house were completely overtaken by ferns and bilberry bushes.

No one had moved into his farm. It lay as he left it. He laughed aloud, but it sounded shrill to his own ears. Shrill and sad.

Urging the horse into a trot, he went up to the house, dismounted, and stepped through the thick grass to pull the door open. It was unlocked. The smell of mouse poop and stale unlived air overwhelmed him, and he swallowed a bitter taste of disappointment. It was silly, but part of him had imagined Abluna inside, the hearth blazing, and the children little again, running to greet him.

Chapter 14

Nikolaos had been traveling aimlessly for several days when he decided to follow the current down a wide stream. There were impenetrable bushes on each side of him, and he could walk in peace, absorbing the healing water. The horse trotted happily behind him, and he kept walking, his melancholy lifting with each watery step. The sun had traveled far across the sky when he became aware of the sound of rushing water ahead. A waterfall! He smiled, telling the horse to wait where it was, then cautiously walked forward and looked over the edge. Breath caught in his throat, and he took a step back. It was enormous, rushing down a steep cliff and pooling into a small lake below, then flowing into a creek beneath the branches of old-growth trees. The forest spread wide in all directions, and there was not a field or steeple in sight. It was so beautiful.

He stood still, feeling the water push past his feet before it fell, staring at the vista before him, absorbing the water into himself. After what must have been a long time, he felt the horse nuzzle his shoulder and neck, and he tore his eyes from the view and waded over to the shore, the horse still with his head on his shoulder. There was a narrow path following the fall. It was steep and wet from the spray, but rocks steadied his feet, and he made his way down until it made a sharp left under a protrusion. The overhang created a corridor of dry space between the cascading water and the cliff wall.

Nikolaos laughed. Rusty devils, it was incredible. Bending his head, he went under it, feeling a rush of chilled air on his skin. The waterfall was like a thick wall beside him, wetting his right shoulder and arm. The sound was glorious, loud, and soothing, soft purple and blue. After only a few steps, he was able to stand fully without getting wet, and he turned toward the horse, grinning. "It's otherworldly, isn't it horse?"

He looked back at him with his big, wet eyes, flicking his ears forward.

Nikolaos' grin broadened. He took hold of the bit, then put

his other hand on the cliff wall for support. It was completely dry to the touch. He kept his hand on it while steadily moving forward to get to the other side. About halfway across the waterfall, the cliff wall suddenly disappeared under his hand. He stumbled, grasping for thin air. It took several moments to get his bearings and for his eyes to adjust. When they did, his heart started beating fast. It was a cave. There was a large cave hidden under the waterfall.

He took a cautious step in, a steady hold on the bridle, listening for the sounds of animals or a bear awakening. But all was silent. The cave opened before him like a ballroom, high-ceilinged and wide. He tilted his head backward. The river was flowing up there, right above him. The thought sent a shiver through his spine.

It wasn't completely dark in the cave, surprisingly. Sunlight trickled in through the thick waterfall and from the sides, and three thin sunbeams shot straight down from what must be holes in the upper cliff wall. A sacred space. And home.

* * *

He lost himself in that cave while the seasons changed around him, lush summers, colorful autumns, and winters that froze the fall into solid ice.

PART TWO

Anno 1653

Chapter 15

Nikolaos was fishing, sitting on a rock by the lake, when a sudden movement caught his attention. At first, he thought it was a deer, and he just glanced at it and looked back at his fishing pole. It was almost upon him when he realized it wasn't a deer, but an old woman on a pale brown horse. Her gray hair had come loose under her head covering, and ragged strands hung over her sagging breasts, barely covered by a thin blouse.

"It *is* you, isn't it? It's going to get me in trouble, but at least I know I'm not a lunatic," the woman said, carefully pulling her right leg over the back of her horse and slowly sliding off, wincing when her feet hit the ground.

He stood up, feeling disoriented. Not a lunatic? It was an odd thing to say. Maybe she was one.

"Don't remember me, do you? Well, I can't blame you. It's been a long time, many years."

"Pray forgive me, I don't." His voice sounded hollow to his own ears. He hadn't spoken to anyone since he lost the horse, and it was long ago now.

"I'm Karin, you helped me when I was sick, remember that?"

He shook his head and jumped off the rock to stand on the ground, away from the lake.

"I had called for you every Tuesday and Thursday. I put money under the bridge for you, and you found me." She caught his eye and broke into a big toothless smile. There *was* something vaguely familiar in that smile.

She walked closer and grabbed his hand, peering up at him. Her eyes were clear and hazel. Startlingly beautiful too. She was right, he had seen her somewhere, but something was different, and he couldn't place her. Then suddenly it came to him, and he almost dropped his fishing pole. She had been praying by the water's edge and told him she had prayed for him to come so she could ask him for help. Gorgeous even though she didn't feel well. That she would ask him to help her had seemed odd to him, and he hadn't known what to do other than to suggest some of the herbs Abluna used when she or the children were sick. It was right after he had checked on his farm after leaving Stockholm. Why was she looking so old? Was she still sick?

"I do remember you! How did you find me? No one ever does," he said, deciding not to comment on how she looked.

"It wasn't hard. And you're wrong. Everyone says you live behind a waterfall. I just followed along the brook, knowing I'd come upon your abode when God willed it."

"They do?"

"Yes."

He was too surprised to respond. An awkward silence followed while she looked at him expectantly. He had to say something. "Why are you here, Karin?"

"I'm in trouble. I need your help," she said in a tone as if it were a daily occurrence he should have expected.

"I see," he said slowly, confused.

She nodded. "Can we go inside? I'm tired and cold. I've ridden for many days to get to you. I'll explain everything if I could just sit down for a bit."

Nikolaos looked at her sharply. No one had ever been inside his cave before, but as long as they didn't stand right at the fall for too long, it ought to be safe. "Very well," he gestured toward his cave with a jerk of his head, "come with me. Can you walk? Or would you rather ride?"

"I'm old and a little stiff, but if we walk slowly, I'm able. You, on the other hand, have not aged. It's obvious now that my friend was right. You can't be human." Karin frowned, eyes sliding up and down the length of his body.

He started, becoming conscious of the crudely made animal skins he was wearing and felt the hairs at the back of his neck stand up. It was quite a while since his clothes had fallen apart, and she truly did look old, but surely it hadn't been that long, had it?

She reached for his arm, squeezing with strong bony fingers. "You're solid and not made of vapor, I see," she said.

Nikolaos scoffed. "Vapor?" There was no end to what people thought of him. He grabbed her horse's bit and started to walk but didn't get far before he heard her slip behind him.

"You were right, it's too steep! Help me mount, will you?" Karin cried.

When he turned around, she looked so sheepish he couldn't help but laugh. Then he went to help her.

When they reached the fall, her mare became scared of the waterfall. She shook her head and stepped sideways, eyes staring in full panic at the water rushing over the cliff.

"Bend your head so you don't get wet," Nikolaos said to Karin, then spoke gently to her horse, patting it under the mane. "Hush, hush, you'll be safe with us."

The mare stared at him, then visibly relaxed and walked in, not even looking at the fall cascading down right next to her. Nikolaos pursed his lips and nodded approvingly. It went better than expected.

"The rumors are true. You do live in a waterfall!" Karin's eyes widened as she took in the high cave ceiling, his bench, table, chair, and shelves. "How did you get all the furniture in here?"

"I brought the wood, then built it inside," Nikolaos said proudly while he gently pulled her horse deeper into his cave and tied her to a protruding rock in the wall. Then without bothering to ask permission, he reached toward Karin and pulled her down.

"Clever." She laughed a pearly laugh, reminding him of that first time they met. It was very disconcerting to see her face so changed.

He held up the salmon he had caught before she arrived and wiggled it in the air. "Tell me why you're here, and then I'll share my fish if you're hungry?" His voice sounded more like itself again, but it still felt odd to talk.

"Yes, a little. And I have something for you as well, bread

and butter if that suits?"

"I give thanks," he said excitedly, the thought of butter and bread making his mouth water.

"I give thanks? You speak like people older than me even," she said and sat down on the bench.

He narrowed his eyes. What an odd comment.

Untying the string from her sack, Karin pulled out a loaf and a small tub of butter, handing both to him. "Like I mentioned, I'm in a bit of trouble because of you, and I'm hoping you'll be able to help me somehow."

"Because of me? How's that?" He put his nose to the bread. It smelled incredible.

"Yes, but the fault is mine. Let me tell you." She paused, distracted by something in the cave ceiling. Then with her eyes still fastened above her, she said, "It's like this, my sister-in-law has always been jealous of me, and though she hides it, I don't think she likes me much. One evening at one of our village dances, she, her friend, and I were sitting on a bench watching. As we sat there, they both started to complain that their stomachs hurt. I offered to go get them some of my own medicine, which I did, but when I came back, they had already left. I thought nothing more of it, thinking it couldn't have been that bad then. But I *was* upset they didn't come by my house to tell me the medicine wasn't needed. What I should have done was to go after them to see if I could help, but I went home and went to bed. It was a mistake."

"How so?"

Karin finally shifted her gaze from the cave ceiling and looked at him. "The next evening, her friend's husband came and asked me what I had done."

"Your sister-in-law's friend's husband?"

"Yes. He said I had put the disease on them and threatened them with poison. I just laughed at him, and he left." She wiped away sudden tears. "The next day, the pastor came with two of the sixmen and formally accused me of putting the disease on my sister-in-law and her friend. They pushed themselves into my house and started questioning me in the rudest manner. Claimed I had gone home to fetch poisonous herbs when I left them on that bench. The sixmen kept pressing me about it, insisting that I had wished them ill no matter how many times I told them I hadn't. I didn't know there were so many ways to ask the same question the way they did that day." She shook her head. "When they finally left, I thought that was that, but they returned a week later. One of the village's cows had died that morning, and they said I had put the disease on the poor animal, too." Karin took a shuddering breath, then leaned forward, grabbing his arms. "Pray forgive me, but I became frightened then and told them that you had taught me which herbs to use. I explained I meant no harm and that the herbs you had recommended had helped me. But it was no use. It made it worse. And I must face a tribunal in ten days. They're going to give me a birching and the water treatment. Thirty-nine lashes with the birch twigs and then water thrown on my back. I won't survive it. I'm an old woman, an old feeble..." Her voice trailed off, ending in a dry sob. Her hands were shaking so hard she was rattling his arms.

Nikolaos gently pulled Karin's hands off his arms and took her hands in his. They were ice cold. Those sixmen were scaring women. How could she have thought it would help to tell them about *him*? Lord have mercy, that was stupid. He patted her right hand, hiding his dismay. "Now, Karin, you sit here and rest yourself. I'll cook the salmon, and then we'll eat it with your bread."

Karin nodded, and he went to get her his only blanket. She wrapped herself in it, then leaned back against the moss he had filled the backrest of his bench with and closed her eyes. A moment later, she was snoring softly.

He made a fire and put the fish on a spit, holding it just so over the open flame to make it cook inside and char on the outside. While it sizzled, he tried to make sense of what Karin told him. It was hard to believe she was the same woman he had met at the river. She looked impossibly old and frail. It scared him.

Karin woke up when he brought the fish over. Then all of a sudden, she pulled a long object with three horns from her skirts. He took a quick step backward, a flicker of fear tickling his spine.

She had brought evil to his cave.

She placed the object on the table, giving him an odd look.

"Why do you carry the Devil's Trident with you?" he asked, crossing himself.

Karin lifted her eyebrows with surprise. It made her forehead wrinkle so much a strand of hair stuck in the folds. "Have you never seen a fork before?" She absently pulled the hair from her wrinkles.

"A what?" He sat down cautiously, ready to spring from the chair if needed.

She chuckled, then cut a piece of fish and stuck the trident into it, holding it out toward him. "Here, you use it to eat with. It's better than your knife and much better than your spoon for some things."

Nikolaos cautiously pulled the fish off the trident with his fingers.

Karin cut a new piece of fish, which she stuck the fork into again. Then she put it to her toothless mouth, grabbing the piece with her lips. "You're right. Some people did think it looked like the Devil's tool, but that's a long time ago now. It's called a fork."

"I see." Nikolaos looked at it, trying not to shudder.

"You must tell me how long you've lived here. And why you look younger than when I saw you last."

"Well," he said, uncertain. Surely he couldn't look younger, but maybe to an old woman, it might seem like he did. "It's been hard to keep track of the seasons. I'm not sure how long I've lived here to tell you the truth." He became acutely aware of his fur vest and skin breaches again, feeling embarrassed.

"You don't? It must be a long time. People speak of you all over the land, and it isn't unknown that you live here. They've seen you but fear you. But they leave you to your own, I suppose."

"The King tried to shoot me in Stockholm once!" he blurted out.

"Gustav the II?"

"No, King Karl IX, I was sitting..."

She interrupted him by waving her fork in his direction. He

tried not to flinch. "Pray pardon me, but don't you even know we have no King?"

He looked at her blankly. Had they ousted him?

"Queen Kristina has been ruling for over twenty years," Karin said.

"Queen Kristina, I see. So, his wife took over the throne then. How did the King die?" He started to feel disoriented. What year was it?

"Dear, you've hidden away for too long. Karl's been dead a long time. His wife did sit on the throne a while, but after him came Gustav II, and now we have a queen, same name, but a different royal. She's odd this one. Some say she's not a lady. She's fond of Catholicism, wears breeches, and rides like a man."

Karin was throwing too much information at him, and he was afraid of her answer, but he had to know. "What year of our lord is this?"

"1653, the pastor reminds us of it every Sunday in church," she said proudly.

Nikolaos' heart started beating fast. It couldn't be. He had left Stockholm just after the turn of the century, 1607 or 1608. He readied himself to contradict her, but something in the back of his mind was nagging him, telling him to think.

"Näcken, what's the matter?"

Ignoring her, the realization hit him all at once and he almost lost his breath. The waterfall had frozen to solid ice, and he and the horse had gone to sleep. Somehow, they had slept all winter, and when they woke up, they were both starving to the point of deliriousness. When he had managed to drag the horse down to the lake, he had noticed that a group of pines were tall and thick when, in the fall, they had been tiny little saplings. He had thought it odd but assumed he was mistaken. But it hadn't been a mistake. He had lost time. Those trees had grown for more than one winter while they slept. It's why Karin was so old now. It had been almost fifty years since he saw her. Grabbing the table with both hands for support, he closed his eyes.

"What is it? What's the matter?" Karin repeated.

"It's nothing. Pray forgive me. I must get some air." Nikolaos got to his feet without looking at her and hurried out, stopping at the stony path beside the fall to look at the pines. They seemed almost defiant, even taller now than they had been back then. It should be impossible. How could he and the horse have survived that long without food? Grabbing the cliff wall, he closed his eyes and listened to the rush of the fall beside him, forcing himself to forget it for now. Then he went back inside.

Karin was licking her fingers, giving him a satisfied smile. Nikolaos sat back down in front of her, suppressing all thoughts on lost time. "Who's the new queen's husband?"

"Queen Kristina is unmarried. They say she doesn't even like men. But pray tell me about when the King tried to shoot you."

He sighed, considering. Then he told Karin everything, including what happened in Norrköping. Telling her that he wasn't sure if someone had come too close to him in the water without him knowing but that he certainly hadn't taken a newborn baby from a pregnant woman. And how insulting it was that people thought that.

Karin reached across the table and patted his hand. "I don't know where they get their ideas from, but I'm sure you had nothing to do with them finding a dead woman and the remains of a baby behind that barn. It's more likely it was a changeling. If you don't carry fire when entering a room where a woman gives birth, a troll could sneak in unseen and exchange the baby for its own. But since she must have given birth out of doors, the baby would've been completely exposed. The family must have realized what had happened and got rid of the baby troll when they found her."

Nikolaos stared at her, stunned. He had never encountered a troll, but changelings he had heard of. Horrific as it sounded. It was a relief that there might be another explanation for it, even if he had never actually thought he was to blame.

"I give thanks for explaining this to me. I never knew."

"Of course, Näcken."

He shook his head. "My name is Nikolaos. I'm named after the seafarer's saint."

"How appropriate."

He smiled.

Karin glanced at the waterfall, and a shadow crossed her face as if she just now realized how close to water they were and what he might do because of it. He ought to tell her that inside the cave, it was perfectly safe. But she surprised him and said, "Poor King, you scared him well that night. You're very fortunate that he missed."

"I am."

"I'd hoped I could ask you to come to the tribunal with me and tell them which herbs you recommended to prove that I tried to help and only had good intentions. I hadn't expected you to look so young. Now I see that it would just make it worse."

She looked away from him again, noticing his glowworms which were starting to glow on the walls as darkness fell. The cave would be full of greenish light soon. He brought glowworms inside whenever he found them so they would light up his world.

Nikolaos smiled at her widening eyes. "Why don't you stay here. You can live with me. I'll be glad for the company. Like you said, I've been alone for too long." His own words surprised him, but it was true; he would enjoy her company.

For a moment she looked happy, but then she shook her head. "Thank you kindly, but I can't. I have chickens and my pig will farrow soon. I have no choice. I'll need to get them to understand that I haven't done anything to hurt anyone."

"Where is the hearing going to be held?"

"Uppvidinge Court."

By the time it was morning, Nikolaos had made up his mind to go with her. Maybe he could talk to the pastor and get him to cancel the hearing. Karin was old and had been riding through the woods all by herself just to find him. He didn't understand how, but she had.

Chapter 16

After much discussion, they decided it would be better if Nikolaos pretended not to know Karin. She was old. Everyone had known her all their lives and knew she didn't have any young relatives who could suddenly show up and speak for her. Instead, Nikolaos would knock on people's doors and ask for work. Hopefully, someone would hire him for something so he had a reason to stay in the area for a little while. If the worst happened and Karin was sentenced to a birching, he could at least help her home afterward. There would be no one else who would do it. So when they neared her village, Karin insisted he stay in the woods while she rode home and fetched some of her dead husband's clothes for him to wear. It was so no one would see him in his animal skins. He was ashamed to admit it hadn't even crossed his mind, but he couldn't enter the village dressed like some kind of wildling.

So, there he was at the border between the forest and the village, wearing a dead man's gray breeches and a stale-smelling linen shirt. Carrying a few belongings in a piece of cloth tied to a stick held over his shoulder and his fiddle in his free hand, he entered the road along the village crop fields. The mound between the wagon tracks was full of grass, bluebells, and pretty yellow flowers he didn't know the name of. And the fence, keeping the furlongs safe from gracing animals was well made, he noticed. He stuck his hands through the bars and reached for the rye on the other side, feeling the smooth yet scratchy grain in his palms. A sudden memory of Abluna grinning with a big pile of freshly cut rye in her round, sun-kissed arms surfaced. He had said something to tease her, and she had thrown the pile at him, pealing with laughter. They had left the other villagers and run off to the woods to make love. He abruptly pulled his hand from the rye, but her laughing face stayed with him anyway.

But shortly after, he became aware of footsteps behind him, and Abluna's face vanished. A man with a large satchel and some kind of horn instrument in his hand was gaining on him. He was walking impossibly fast for some reason, and by the time he was close enough for Nikolaos to see what it was, he had already passed him.

"Pray pardon me," Nikolaos called after him and ran to catch up, surprising the man, then realizing that he was very young, a boy, really.

"Oh, how now? You scared me."

"Pray forgive me. Didn't mean to. I was just curious about your instrument. I'm a musician as well. I play the fiddle."

"Musician?"

Caught off guard, Nikolaos eyed him, bereft of what to say next.

"What caused you to believe such a thing?" the man asked and started walking in the same fast pace. He was probably late for something.

"Pray, pardon me again. I didn't mean to presume, but since you're carrying an instrument, I assumed you were. Is it a hunting horn, then?" Nikolaos asked, noticing that he was in fact also carrying a hunting spear.

Now the young man stopped. "Ah, I see, you must be from the Finnish side. You haven't seen this before? It's a post horn. I have my post plaque here as well." He pointed to a small brass plate on his jacket with an image on it. Nikolaos leaned forward to take a closer look, but the young man set off again before he could make it out. "Well, it was nice to meet you, traveler from Finland. I'll be on my way now, people are waiting on their letters," he cried.

Confused, Nikolaos watched him hurry down the road even faster than before, feeling ignorant. Whatever the young man was doing must be common knowledge, or he wouldn't have assumed he was Finnish.

The road bent slightly, and the farms came into view. The village seemed to be doing well. Every home had a chimney, and several homes had freshly thatched roofs. There were scarecrows guarding herbal gardens, and a swing in a tree. A woman was driving a cowherd into the woods behind the first farm.

Just then, there was a sudden piercing sound, exploding

with red and orange. What in the world was going on? Nikolaos was glad he was on foot. A horse would have panicked and thrown him. Then the sound came again. It was the man. He had stopped in the middle of the road and was blowing his horn. It must be a signal because the village was coming alive with people running in his direction. Even the herding woman left the cows to fend for themselves and ran toward him. He opened his satchel and started to hand things out to some of the people but not all, and then continued walking at the same impossibly fast speed as before. It didn't look as if he had said goodbye even. He just walked away. How bizarre.

When Nikolaos reached the first farm, everyone had gone back inside already, and the road was empty. As he stood there, thinking of what to do next, a young child in a simple dress came running through the front door of the farmhouse, only to run back in again when seeing Nikolaos.

Soon, a woman appeared in the doorway, the child peering out from behind her skirts, looking at him curiously. "How do you fare?" the woman asked.

"Very well, I thank you," Nikolaos said and bowed. "I've just arrived here. I'm hoping for some work. I play the fiddle, and I'm also good with farm work."

"We can always use help once the village gathers for the harvest, but it's too early now. Go to Andreas' farm and ask. He might have something for you to do. But if you want to come here and play the fiddle on Thursday, I'll be glad of it, my sister is coming with her family. I'll talk to my husband about it, but I'm sure he'll say yes."

"I give th...thank you kindly," Nikolaos said, changing his words to what Karin had explained was more appropriate nowadays. "I was curious, I heard the young man blowing that horn. What was he doing?"

She laughed. "Why, he's the post-runner. Came with our letters. Had one from my sister, is how I know she's coming on Thursday."

"Of course, I see," Nikolaos said, pretending to understand.

Clearly, it was a new kind of messaging system. "When should I arrive on Thursday?"

She turned around and pointed west. "See that birch standing on its own back there? When the afternoon sun passes it, it's a good time. We'll be setting up the food about then."

Nikolaos looked in the vicinity behind her outstretched arm. Just like she said, there was an empty spot among the pines with one tall birch. "I'll do so," he said with a nod in thanks.

At the next farm, a man was cutting firewood in the yard. Nikolaos waved, and the man put his ax down and approached. He had a handsome face with a large nose, dark blue eyes, and dark brown hair.

"How do you fare?" he asked, his face widening into an open smile. It made him strikingly attractive.

Nikolaos grinned, feeling something long and forgotten stir within him. "I was hoping to find some work here for a while. Any farm work, I can..."

He shook his head before Nikolaos finished. "There'll be nothing for you here, I can tell you that. The farmer says he barely has enough for me, complains about it all the time. Go on down to the next farm. If they don't need any you can always ask Karin, she lives alone. But watch yourself. She's known for sorcery."

"Sorcery?"

He shrugged. "That's what they say, that she puts the illness on folk."

"I'll be on my watch. I give thanks," Nikolaos said, forgetting to use the newer term. Working for Karin would be a great reason to stay in the village. Why hadn't they thought of that? He gave a quick nod goodbye and kept going.

When Nikolaos came to the last farm, he knew what the answer would be even before asking. Just like the woman at the first farm had said, no one needed help until harvest time.

The owner was leisurely leaning on their fence while his wife was weeding in an herbal garden behind him. They both smiled broadly and waved him over. "Care to play a tune?" the husband asked, gesturing toward Nikolaos' fiddle.

"Gladly." He plucked the strings for show, but the bow was carefully tied up with the rest of his stuff, and he didn't feel like pulling it out. "As a matter of fact, I was hoping for both farm work and performances so I could stay for a while. I'd sleep well in a barn for a night or two."

The farmer seemed to consider it, but then he shook his head apologetically.

"What about the homestead up there?" Nikolaos asked and pointed to where he knew Karin lived.

The friendly expression changed immediately. "I'd be very careful if I were you. She put the sickness on her sister-in-law."

His wife stood up, wiped the dirt off her skirt, and came as close to Nikolaos as she could for the fence. "Karin fornicated with Näcken when she was young," she whispered.

"Did she now?" Nikolaos couldn't quite hide the glint in his eyes.

"Yes." She touched Nikolaos' shoulder and pointed to the farm where the handsome farmhand was still stacking his woodpile. "That's where her brother lives. Her sister-in-law was inside, wasn't she? Still feeling poorly, she is."

"I thank you kindly. But I'm not afraid. I'll go and ask."

Her husband shrugged. "Well, you're young and strong. Do heed the warning though."

His wife opened her mouth to say something, then closed it again, frowning with disapproval.

It was perfect. Now he had witnesses.

Karin's home was set back from the others, hidden behind several old trees. It was a small log house with two outbuildings that were very much in need of repair. Her pregnant sow was penned in along the wall of one of them. The roof was so low she was nibbling on it, making large chunks of thatch come loose and fall around her cloven feet. The chicken house was in better shape and the roof was higher off the ground. Why hadn't Karin swapped them? Maybe he could help her with it. It would make for the perfect excuse for why she hired him.

When he knocked, Karin opened a square peephole in her door, staring at him for a long time as if she didn't recognize him. Then she opened the door a small crack. "What do you want, who are you?" she asked loudly.

"I've come to see if you might need help. I'm looking for work," he said just as loud, catching on. Maybe someone was listening.

"Come in. What are you doing here?" she hissed, quickly stepping aside so he could enter.

"It seems Saint Nikolaos wanted me to be here. I asked everyone. No one had work for me. I was told that you might have some, though." He didn't tell her that he had been warned about her by several people.

Karin sat down heavily on her bed. "Saint Nikolaos. You're Catholic, then. As if I didn't have enough trouble already, I suspected it when you spoke of the sea fairing saint you're named after the other day. My aunt was as well. She was a nun, kicked out of her cloister after forty years when they decided to rid the church of the pope."

"Yes," Nikolaos said. There was no point in denying it. He remembered how they were forced out. The homeless monks and nuns used to come through their village, desperate and shunned. He had given them food in secret.

She nodded. "It's no matter. The sixmen were here again just now, three of them this time. The hearing has been moved, and they want me tried tomorrow already. They said they can prove I've been stealing milk."

"Stealing milk? From whom?"

Karin got up and put a small log on the fire, moved a blackened pot off the direct flame, and placed it on a hook on the side. Straightening her back she said, "I'm not certain, but they want to hurry the process. Since it's so serious, they said. I think there are people out there guarding me. It's why I spoke so loudly when you entered. You ought to go out and do some work in the yard, to make sure it looks like you're working for me." Her chin was quivering from holding back tears. She looked terrified.

Nikolaos went to her and gently guided her to sit on the bed again. He stroked her back. She felt thinner than she had just yesterday. "I can fix the roof for you. That sow of yours is chewing on it. It might be a good idea to move her later. And would you like more chopped wood?"

"I thank you kindly. Yes, that would be helpful. I'll rest a bit here," she said and reached for his hand, squeezing it. She was shaking. Why didn't her brother speak for her?

Nikolaos tore down the thatch so he could replace it. Most of it came down easily, and parts of it were moldy. He was moving it to a pile for burning when two men approached. Karin was right. People were probably spying on her. Both men had something long in their mouths. It looked odd. At first, he couldn't quite make sense of what he saw. Then he realized they were sticks, smooth sticks that were on fire at the end. He tossed the thatch to the ground and straightened up. Were they planning to set Karin's home on fire?

"Who are you? Are you a relation to Karin Persdotter?" one of them asked without so much as an introduction. He kept the burning stick in his mouth as he spoke as if it were a perfectly normal thing to do.

"No. I'm doing some work for her, just passing through here. I'm a fiddler, but that doesn't always feed me." Nikolaos kept a watchful eye on the burning sticks, discreetly moving closer to the house in case he had to run in and save Karin.

Both men were wearing long, narrow brown coats which reached all the way to their knees, not a single button buttoned, and their breeches were narrow, almost skintight. They looked comically similar. If one of them hadn't had red hair, he would barely have been able to tell them apart. Had he worn the clothes he used to wear in Stockholm, he would have looked as out of place as if he wore his skins. At least now, it just looked like he was poor and not as if he had traveled from the past, which in a sense he had.

"You have your passport handy?" The second man said, then

took the stick out of his mouth. There was a little cup at the end, Nikolaos noticed.

"I do inside, if you give me a..."

"No matter. But do you know who it is you're staying with?" the redhaired man asked.

Nikolaos stared at him. Smoke was coming out of his mouth as he spoke, but he didn't pay it any mind at all. Should he warn him?

"Do you know who you're staying with?" the man repeated, now purposely blowing out the smoke.

Nikolaos forced himself to look him in the eye instead of at the smoke. "Yes, I do. Her name is Karin Persdotter like you said. She's old and needs a lot of help," he said, gesturing toward the roof.

"How long will this take you, do you reckon?"

"Well," Nikolaos began, pursing his lips and eying the chopping block across the yard, "at least a few days."

"Young man, you might want to stay somewhere else, at least tonight. She needs to go to court tomorrow for a hearing. We'd rather you come with us. I'll put you up for the night if needed. It might not be safe here, especially not for a young fella such as yourself. If she's not guilty, you can go back."

Nikolaos pretended to hesitate, then shook his head. "I appreciate it, but I'm a man of my word. I promised her to repair the roof. The pig is chewing on it. She needs wood chopped too. Whatever trouble she's in is no concern of mine."

"Very well, suit yourself. Goodbye to you," the man with the red hair said. He was sucking deeply on his stick, making his cheeks look hollow in the process. When he opened his mouth, the smoke billowed out, obscuring his face. It looked so bizarre that Nikolaos laughed, which made both men look at him strangely as they left.

When they reached the road, the redhaired man leaned close to the other and said, "He doesn't know the woman is a witch or realize the danger he's in."

Chapter 17

The tree was small, gnarled, and very old. It had survived harsh winters and wars, seen families give offerings to Thor, Odin, and Freya, and seen the first Christian monks come and instill the fear of hell in people. Rå sat with it every Thursday, absorbing its wisdom and its appearance.

Gulla's granddaughter Mette and her husband, Axel, came every week to check on her and bring her food. Rå usually waited for them on her log outside, pretending to warm herself under her blanket. They were very kind to her, but it took all her strength to appear old. She missed running barefoot through the forest and missed her woodcutters and hunters. But appearing mortal was the price she had to pay for going to church in the village and allowing them to visit her to trade for her herbs and advice.

Now Axel slid off his horse and tied it to a tree, then helped Mette dismount her horse. She was thick with child. Her fifth.

While Axel tied her horse next to his, she hurried unhindered by her belly and sat down beside Rå. Axel had brought the log for Rå a few years ago, flattening it on top and sanding it so it was comfortable to sit on.

"Magda, we have brought you fresh bread. The baking-woman has been in our village for several days. We did well this season, and we have extra. I also brought a pot of lard. You need to eat more. Look at your hands. They're so skinny. We need to fatten you up a bit," Mette said, patting her arm.

"I believe you're the one who needs to eat. I thank you for this though. You're too kind," Rå said, stroking first her cheek and then her round belly.

Axel made himself comfortable on the ground before them, sitting cross-legged. "Magda, please tell me if you need something done. Do you need wood? Should I clean out the smokestack?" he asked, almost shouting. He always spoke too loudly, as though she was hard of hearing.

Rå just shook her head. The baby in Mette's belly reminded

her that if she didn't leave, a younger generation would watch out for her. New people would come and ensure that the old woman living alone in the woods was cared for. She had been here for such a long time. Longer than anyone knew. It was only the last seventy winters or so that she had ventured into the village. The time had come for her to leave, for everyone to think she had entered her final rest, as they were fond of saying. She stroked Mette's cheek again, slowly stood up, and hobbled inside.

Moving easier once she was out of sight, she pulled down one of her wall hangings by her bed. The colors were still bright red and orange and hadn't faded with age. She rolled it up and walked back out, making sure she was shuffling her feet and bending her back.

Axel immediately got to his feet and went to her side. "What are you doing, dear Magda? I could have fetched that for you. Here, sit, sit down," he screamed into her ear. She resisted throwing her hand up to cover it and let him help her back to the bench.

"You shall have it," Rå said, pressing the wall hanging into Mette's hands.

"Oh, Magda, it's beautiful. Why are you giving me this? Look, Axel," she prompted, holding it up for him to see.

He leaned forward and gazed at it carefully. "I thank you kindly for giving Mette such a gift." He smiled, and they exchanged a warm glance. It was evident that they were still in love.

"We ought to be going. We'll see you again in a week's time, Magda," Mette said.

Rå nodded but knew it was not so. She let her hands rest on Mette's belly and felt the baby's strength inside her. She loved Mette and her family and wished she could tell them goodbye, but it would only cause concern, and they would insist on bringing her to the village.

She said nothing and let them leave. Once Alex had helped Mette mount her horse, she turned around and looked at her. Rå's eyes blurred with tears, and she waved one last time, looking after them long after they had gone. Then she went inside to pack her things.

The next morning, Rå went to the brook behind her boulder home. She tipped a basket of wood sorrel on its side and attached a bucket to a branch in the rapids. Then she pulled her shawl off and placed it on the bank, the corner touching the water. Next week Alex and Mette would look for her and find it and think she must have slipped when she was getting water. They would look for her body and tell each other that she was so old, light, and frail that the brook carried her with it. Or perhaps that Näcken had taken her.

Chapter 18

The same men from the day before arrived with a third man the next morning. Nikolaos had already been chopping wood for a while and was stretching his back when he noticed them coming up the hill, driving two separate carriages.

"Good morrow," he said solemnly once they had settled their horses and were walking his way. The men had their sticks in their mouths today, too. They were drinking tobacco, Karin had explained, and the sticks were called pipes. It was the smoke they drank. An odd habit to say the least. The fashion surely wouldn't last long.

"We'll see, might not be such a good morning for her in there. Is she ready? We're taking her now, to Uppvidinge Court," the man with the red hair said.

"I wouldn't know," Nikolaos said, even though she had been ready and on the floor kneeling in prayer since before sunup.

The two from yesterday went inside while the other man stayed outside, nodding politely at Nikolaos. "Are you interested in coming with us? Several of the farmers are going. You can ride with me," he said, gesturing toward the carriages.

Nikolaos glanced upward, pretending to consider. This was better than what they could have hoped for. Maybe he could stop it somehow. "I've nothing else to do. I'm done with what Karin needed help with for the moment, so why not?" he said, meeting the man's eyes.

"I'm Oldrich, what's your name?"

"Nikolaos."

They stood silent after that. It was awkward, but Nikolaos didn't feel like striking up a conversation and shifted his gaze to Karin's door.

When it opened, the men came out with Karin between them, each with what looked like a painful hold on her upper arms. Oldrich gave her a look of such disgust Nikolaos had to look away, or he would have lashed out at him. Karin's eyes were focused firmly on the ground, and she didn't notice. He was glad of it.

***

The courthouse was situated in a small building next to a church. From the look of it, everyone in Uppvidinge and the surrounding villages were present. Some must have slept there since the night before because they were hustling to rise from their blankets when they heard the carriages. No one said a word. They just stood there and watched when the men brought Karin inside, then followed them ominously. Nikolaos couldn't tell if it was fear or anger.

All twelve of the twelvemen were there, sitting in a row behind a large oak table. Eldest Twelveman was in the middle, his quill and ink ready in front of him. This was a proper trial, not just a hearing with gossiping neighbors.

Chairs were placed in rows as if in church, but in a disorderly fashion. Nikolaos found an empty seat in the back. People nodded to acknowledge him, and he recognized the woman who wanted him to play his fiddle when her sister visited. She smiled, then turned to her husband and discreetly gestured in his direction.

Karin was made to sit in an empty chair in front of the twelvemen.

The room was utterly quiet, and there was a sense of anticipation that was almost palpable. As if people were excited, hoping for blood. He should never have brought Karin back home. Then a man pointed into the crowd and two women abruptly stood up, then approached the twelvemen. They were made to stand at an angle so everyone, both the audience and the twelvemen, would see their faces.

"Elonora," the Eldest prompted, looking at one of the women. She was old and skinny, and her head covering barely hid her dirty hair. "You will tell me what happened, and then you, Hildur will describe it as well. I want you to speak clearly and not interrupt each other."

Elonora glanced at her friend and then cleared her throat. "We were watching the dancers on the green, and suddenly we both fell ill. It hurt as if someone took a knife and stuck it in my

119

stomach. A terrible sharp pain. I looked to Hildur to see if she would help me home, and that's when I noticed that she had gone pale and was clutching her stomach. *She*," Elonora pronounced the word, she, as if it tasted bad, "was sitting next to us and claimed she would go home and get medicine for us. And then she walked away. We waited and didn't think anything of it at first. But then we understood that since we were both in pain, but Karin wasn't, she must have put the disease on us. How else would she know what kind of medicine we needed? She didn't ask about our symptoms." Elonora stared accusatorily at Karin who was shaking her head and nervously pulling at her fingers. "We went home and tried to sleep but were in so much pain that we weren't sleeping at all," Elonora added.

"You two live in the same house?" The Eldest asked.

"No."

"How then did you know that Hildur couldn't sleep and was in the same amount of pain as you, Elonora?"

"Our husbands met the next day and spoke of us, and we have spoken about it ourselves since," Hildur answered.

She looked confident and strong, Nikolaos observed. And healthy, not disheveled like Elonora. Whatever illness she claimed to have had couldn't have fared too ill with her.

The Eldest dipped his quill in the ink and wrote something in his notes. "Do you agree with this? Did you, too, have pains in your stomach, Hildur?"

"Yes, it was just like she said. We couldn't sleep and lay bedridden the next day. I couldn't even get out of bed to go to the outhouse."

The Eldest nodded, waving them away without further ado. Then he turned to his twelvemen, gesturing to a man at the end of the table on his right. "Anders, tell me what happened when you questioned her, will you?"

"Certainly. We'd heard how the women got sick, and although it was serious, I didn't think Karin Persdotter would have anything to do with it." Anders stopped to cough, hacking loudly and spitting up in his handkerchief, then continued with a clearer voice. "But I was incorrect. As soon as I stepped inside with the others, I knew Karin was hiding something."

"How did you know that?"

"Karin had a table full of herbs, and then I saw a rune stick. She had tried to hide it under a rag, but I saw it right away. Being so ugly, having all those herbs and a stick like that, made it clear. Wouldn't you say?" He smiled confidentially at the Eldest who nodded but did not return his smile. "We began to question her then. Sat her down and asked her what she had done to Elonora and Hildur, but she refused to say. Said she'd done nothing. But those herbs there, indicated that she's knowledgeable about sickness, so I was convinced. It took many hours but finally she admitted who taught her how to use those herbs." He paused, glancing almost triumphantly at the other twelvemen. "She said that Näcken had given them to her!"

At first no one moved, sitting as if Anders hadn't said anything at all. But then there was a collective gasp and cries from babies suddenly grabbed and pulled close by their mothers. Elonora and Hildur both seemed to grow pale at the same time. And Hildur covered her face with her hands and burst into tears. Evidently, this was the first time they had heard that particular detail.

Anders kept talking. "Karin told us that a wisewoman advised her many years ago when she was sick. The wisewoman told her to call for Näcken by throwing coins under bridges, especially in rivers. Karin followed the wisewoman's advice and did it on Thursdays at sundown, sometimes midday. She also did it on Tuesdays. After a time, Näcken came like a wave in the water and told her what she ought to do. He healed her. You can see so yourselves since she's still among us. A clear sign she's telling the truth." He coughed again, giving Karin a disdainful look.

Nikolaos didn't remember any coins. He found many things on the bottom of rivers, but never coins. It would have been useful if he did.

"You can ask her yourself," Anders added. Then he marched over to Karin and pulled her out of her chair.

The Eldest nodded slowly. He looked stunned, trying to

catch the eyes of the other twelvemen, but they were all staring at Karin and Anders. Karin was shaking visibly as she was made to walk. Anders was right behind her, wide-legged with his arms out to the side as if to prevent her from bolting without touching her.

Nikolaos watched with disbelief. He had to do something. But it was as if Karin knew what he was thinking because just then, she looked straight at him, a piercing look, with a small shake of her head. He leaned back in his seat.

The Eldest studied Karin silently as he tapped the quill on the table. Nikolaos saw sharp green flashes along with tiny droplets of ink splashing across the table. It was distracting. "Tell me about Näcken. How did he look and what did he tell you?"

Karin didn't hesitate. "First, I only saw the water move, but then he stood up and walked out like an ordinary man. He said his wife used these herbs when his family was sick."

The Eldest raised his eyebrows. "His family? Näcken has a wife?" He laughed nervously.

Karin looked confused. "I just wanted to feel better. I had been feeling weak and sick for so long. He told me to eat certain herbs, and it helped. It did."

One of the twelvemen glanced at the Eldest, lifting his hand to ask permission to interrupt, and got a head tilt in response. "Which herbs?"

"I... don't... I, it was long ago."

"He asked which ones," the Eldest thundered.

"I think... I believe it was lemon balm, wormwood, and mint. They're strengthening and help you if you have stomach pains. That's why I offered to help. I had no intention to hurt anyone." Karin's voice was clear, but there was still fear in it.

She had a good memory. Those were in fact the herbs Abluna used to give them all when they felt ill. Nikolaos never did but pretended to sometimes, just to get Abluna to care for him, and to seem more like them. She used to make it into a warm broth and add honey. They had a blue mug just for that. She always warned him not to burn himself when handing it to him.

The Eldest stood, pushing his chair back so quickly it almost toppled over. "Karin, are you admitting that you were going to give them an herb Näcken told you about?"

Karin's head jerked backward.

"Tell the truth. If you lie, I'll be forced to order someone to give you a birching. I won't hesitate to have them give you thirty-nine lashes. And water too. Think on that, Karin Persdotter. It's not a pleasant experience. When the cold water hits the open sores on your back, the pain will be excruciating. Do you understand that?"

She nodded.

"Good, I'm glad you do. You won't have to go through it if you just tell me the truth from the beginning," he said, raising his voice again. The babies who had managed to calm down from the previous disturbance started to wail all at once. The Eldest sighed impatiently and waited for them to quiet down, then he lowered his voice, speaking in an almost caressing tone. "Karin, it's better that you tell us exactly what happened. Don't be afraid, just tell us the truth, and you don't have to fear the lashing."

"I'm telling the truth, I swear it. It was a long time ago. I was young and often felt weak and tired. It was a woman named Wise Klara who told me about Näcken. She was knowledgeable about these things. She said all I needed to do was offer a coin or two in the river for Näcken. I was to do it on Thursdays especially, but I did it on Tuesdays too, a couple of times."

Nikolaos frowned. He didn't remember helping someone named Klara. Maybe Karin made it up.

"And how did you get him to come? How would he know that you put money in the water for him? He could have been anywhere." The Eldest said, sitting down again.

Karin hesitated, her wrinkly old face flushing. "I invoked the Holy Trinity. And…"

"And…what else?"

"I invoked the Holy Trinity and the Devil, but it was to get help not to harm. I did it in good faith and with hope to feel better… and I did."

Nikolaos inhaled sharply and stared at her, thinking of her fork. What utter insanity. Now she was admitting to it. He had been right after all. He couldn't believe it.

The Eldest and the twelvemen exchanged glances of shock, shaking their heads. But one of them waved his hand in the air. "The older folk do this sometimes, an old habit. It's not as bad as it sounds, although the clergy don't recommend it."

"I see," the Eldest said uncertainly.

Nikolaos relaxed. He remembered it now. His aunt had done the same thing. It was to be inclusive of all of God's creation, and the Devil was a fallen angel, she used to say.

The twelvemen spoke quietly amongst themselves.

Then the man who had asked permission to speak earlier turned to Karin. "Did you fornicate with Näcken when he came to you in the water?"

"No."

All the twelvemen except the Eldest snickered. He looked thoughtful, as if there was something he needed to convey but couldn't remember.

This had to end. Nikolaos slid out of his chair just as a man in the front row did the same. He was heavy-set and wore breeches so long they reached halfway down his calves, and he blocked Nikolaos' view.

"She has stolen milk as well," the man said. "We didn't notice at first, just that our cow had died. But yesterday my wife found troll butter in the pasture, so Karin must have milked the cow and put the disease on it."

"Do explain. What's troll butter, and what does it have to do with this?" the Eldest asked, holding his hand up to prevent the others from speaking.

"Troll butter grows where someone spills stolen milk. If someone milks a cow without permission and spills some of it on the way out, the troll butter starts growing in that very spot. It's how you know," the man said. He had an important air about him and went back to his seat, looking satisfied.

The Eldest pushed his quill and book toward the twelveman to his right. "Write that down, will you? The evidence is piling up here." Then he finally noticed Nikolaos standing in the aisle. "Who are you?”

“My name is Nikolaos. I’ve just started to work for Karin. As far as I can see, she’s a kind woman. I haven’t noticed anything sinister at all and would like to speak for her.”

The Eldest cocked his head to the side and looked closely at Nikolaos. “How long have you known her since you’re making an assertion on her kindness?”

“A day,” Nikolaos said, cringing inwardly. Pretending they didn’t know each other had been a stupid idea. But it was too late now.

The Eldest didn’t even react. He just turned to his twelvemen and changed the subject. “This is a serious problem, and I suggest we push this case to Göta Royal Court,” he said, ignoring Nikolaos as if he wasn’t standing there at all.

He tried again anyway. “Truly, Eldest, she’s just an old woman. She’s probably confused.”

The Eldest finally looked at him again. “No, sit down now, or leave. You have no right to disrupt our hearing. You’re not from here. This is a very dangerous and serious matter.”

The other twelvemen nodded in agreement.

Nikolaos tried to catch Karin’s eye, but she was looking at her feet.

The Eldest waved his hands in Nikolaos’ direction as if he were a fly he needed to rid himself of. “I’ll go Göta Royal Court myself tomorrow to explain everything. Have Karin locked up and ready for travel by early morning. You’re all dismissed.” He stood up and waved them away in the same fly-swatting manner.

Things moved quickly after that. Karin was whisked away, and people reluctantly filed out of the building.

Nikolaos’ heart sank. There was nothing he could do to help her then, not if they were locking her up and moving her. Unless he could try to find out where they were going to put her. But from the sound of it, she would likely be heavily guarded. Defeated, he followed the crowd out the door.

When he stepped out, the husband of the woman who wanted him to play fiddle hurried toward him, meeting his eyes with a piercing stare. "I prefer you didn't play on Thursday," he said. "I know my wife invited you, but under the circumstances and you having worked for that woman, we must decline. We understand you were unaware, but we have small children, and we can't take the risk."

"That woman's name is Karin. She's a kind, helpful person. I wouldn't want to play at your house no matter what you offered me," Nikolaos said without hiding his anger.

The husband looked perplexed for a moment, but then he nodded. "Indeed, glad you understand. Do take care of yourself."

Nikolaos scoffed.

The man's eyes narrowed. "Well, go in peace," he said and left to join his wife, shaking his head slowly, once, as he walked off.

Oldrich overheard them and came over. He looked concerned. "I'll go with you, Nikolaos. You shouldn't go back there on your own. I'll drive you again," he said, pointing to his carriage. "You have somewhere to go after you retrieve your belongings?"

"I'll head to the next village. I'm curious to know where Karin will be taken to tell you the truth. Where do you keep prisoners such as she?"

"I wouldn't know. The twelvemen will keep her secure until tomorrow. You should be glad of it. It's not safe having her free after a trial."

"I'm not afraid," Nikolaos said curtly.

Oldrich gave him a pointed look. "Then you're a fool, boy."

Nikolaos raised an eyebrow; a boy seemed a bit of an exaggeration, even though Oldrich looked like he was close to sixty and probably thought he looked young.

"You don't seem to quite understand what we have here," Oldrich added. "Someone admitting to involvement with Näcken is not to be taken lightly. Did you know Näcken is to have been responsible for the Vasa sinking?"

"The Vasa?"

They reached the carriage. Oldrich patted his horse, untied it from the hitching pole, and climbed up without a word. Nikolaos tried to think of what he could have meant. Was he referring to

King Vasa? What did he mean by sinking?

"It was a ship in Stockholm," Oldrich said once Nikolaos had sat down beside him and they were in motion. "A warship, one of the strongest ships ever built. A lot of money was spent on her to get her sea-ready and serve as a symbol of our country's military power. She sunk in the harbor. Some say Näcken was responsible. After today, I wouldn't be surprised if it was true."

Nikolaos laughed, getting a quick look of disapproval from Oldrich. "You're saying that creature can topple a military ship?"

Oldrich looked taken aback for a moment, but then he shrugged. "Perhaps you're right."

Nikolaos smiled. "Probably. Is Göta Court in a town far from here? Could I find work there, you think? Do they need fiddlers?"

Oldrich shrugged. "You could certainly try. It's a bit of a journey though. You have to head north all the way to Wätter Lacus. That's where it is, in Jönköping, just at the south end of the lake." He sounded relieved that Nikolaos had changed the subject.

"I see. How soon do you think they'll take Karin there?"

"You're awfully concerned about her. You shouldn't be. Get her out of your mind so she loses her influence over you," Oldrich said, keeping his eyes straight ahead on the road.

"Yes, sir," Nikolaos said, hiding a smile.

"Good," Oldrich let go of the reins with one hand and reached out and put his other hand on Nikolaos' arm, squeezing gently. "Karin Persdotter will be taken to her new hearing at the same time as when Eldest Twelveman is traveling there. It's for Göta Royal Court to decide what to do with her until trial."

Chapter 19

Nikolaos left the village behind him, praying he would get to Jönköping before the new hearing. It was his fault that they took her, as insane as that was, especially since it was so long ago that he had suggested those herbs. If he could just find someone to talk to, maybe it would be possible to talk them out of trying her. Persuade them that she was a kind, god-fearing woman who meant no harm. The way she had prayed all morning before they arrested her, kneeling on those skinny knees, made his heart ache.

It was foggy but breezy, and the fog shifted constantly. Sometimes it was so dense Nikolaos could barely see his own hand in front of him, only to be swept away by the wind a moment later, creating patches of sunlight framed by fog. It was mesmerizing and incredibly beautiful. From time to time, the wind stilled, and the road became a sea of milky white softness. He slowed down, moving ahead the best he could.

Suddenly, he walked right into something soft and large. Something that quickly turned around to see what had hit it in the back. A bear. Heart pounding, Nikolaos backed away and reached for his knife in his breeches. Just as he felt the cold metal beneath his fingers, the fog cleared again. With his hand still grasping for the knife, the bear dissolved, and his mind slowly understood what he was seeing. It was the young farmhand he had spoken to a couple of days earlier. They stared at each other, then the farmhand screamed and dropped his satchel on the ground.

"Pray forgive me for startling you," Nikolaos said and bent to pick it up. "I thought you were a bear. I couldn't see for the fog."

"And I thought you were Näcken! I too, apologize. I was getting spooked here in this fog by myself."

"Did you now?" Nikolaos said and couldn't help but smile.

"Yes. Would you walk with me?" the farmhand blurted. "I'd feel safer if I wasn't alone."

"Of course. Where are you going?"

"Well... I decided to go see what they're going to do with Karin. She's my employer's sister."

"Yes, so I heard."

"I might not go back. We'll see." He took the satchel from Nikolaos and hoisted it over his right shoulder. It made his muscles strain against his linen shirt. He really was very handsome.
"I'm Johannes. What's yours? I never caught your name."

Thankfully not. "Nikolaos. I'm heading to Jönköping for the same reason myself. By the way, I did get some work up at Karin's place. She showed me nothing but kindness, and I never noticed any sorcery."

Johannes' eyes flashed to his. "Did you? You really didn't notice anything at all?"

"No."

"But it doesn't mean that she didn't hurt those women, just cause you didn't see anything," Johannes said.

"Do you think she did?"

Johannes held his gaze with a serious expression, and then he shrugged. "She's always been kind to me too. But I've seen her bicker with her brother. She's fierce, Karin."

Nikolaos nodded. That was certainly true. "Was he at the hearing?"

"In Uppvidinge? Nah, he hates her guts. He wouldn't lift a finger for her."

"I see," Nikolaos said. That might explain the sister-in-law's accusation, then. It was odd though, that he didn't even go with his wife. She was one of the main witnesses. And Karin, why didn't he try to help her, anyway? It was his own sister. There was more to this than what Karin had told him.

They began to walk. He stole glances at Johannes, noticing now that his brown hair had strands of red in it and that the sun made the moisture in it sparkle in the strange fog-filtered light.

Johannes didn't seem to mind that their hips and arms occasionally bumped into each other. His body was warm, almost hot where it touched his. Nikolaos moved a little closer yet, forgetting his concern for Karin. Pines lined each side of the road, blocking the wind and keeping the fog in place. The moisture strengthened him, filling him with want.

"I'm glad you walked into me," Johannes said, I'd probably have turned back now. I felt afraid, especially hearing about Näcken. Do you think it *was* Näcken who came to her? What if he's still here?" The fog made Johannes' face seem fuzzy.

"I doubt it." Nikolaos put his arm around his shoulder and turned his head in the opposite direction, hiding a grin. He was enjoying this; there was no denying it. If Johannes only knew.

When he was able to look at him again, Johannes' eyes were still upon him, his gaze searching, and so close, his hair tickled Nikolaos' forehead. Then he wrapped his arms around his waist and kissed him on the lips. Nikolaos' stomach flipped, and he felt a need he hadn't felt on land in a very long time. He pulled Johannes closer. It was completely silent except for their breathing, kissing, and the soft crunching of their feet on the road. Johannes' hard, flat stomach pushed into him as the scent of wet human skin tore at him with want.

The sudden sound of hoofs on the road made them freeze, and they tore themselves apart, then started walking as if nothing had happened.

It was a man with an ox, appearing almost ghostlike in the fog. He passed them without so much as a glance and continued in the opposite direction.

Johannes laughed and pinched Nikolaos in the side.

"Stop it!" Nikolaos hissed, laughing, too. It felt so good to be close to someone again. He hadn't since Abluna died, not really. They kept walking, stopping to kiss when they felt sure no one would see.

Suddenly, seemingly out of nowhere Nikolaos felt his blood shift to water within him. There must be water nearby which was enhanced by the fog. Strongly. He stepped back and peeled his eyes from Johannes, forcing himself to stay off of him, keeping his gaze on the bluebells in the grassy middle between the carriage tracks. It didn't help. The fog swept over them like a wave of water, making his own watery blood sing. He had to get away.

"What's the matter?" Johannes sounded hurt.

"Nothing." He took another step away from him.

Johannes followed, reaching for him. "Are you feeling shy? Let's go in here." He grabbed Nikolaos by the arm and led him off the road, through a thicket of dense branches to a meadow.

There was a lake there, just like he suspected. The wind had swept the fog away from it, and waves splashed gently as they hit the beach. It was deafening, and he couldn't bear it anymore.

They started kissing. Johannes' heart thumped so loudly in his chest that Nikolaos could hear it. Grabbing him, he let his bundle slide off his shoulder, then reached for Johannes' satchel and placed it next to his bundle. He pulled at Johannes' breeches, untying the thin rope holding them up. They fell softly around his feet. Then he moved to his own shirt and ripped it off as fast as he could. Johannes stood still and silent. Somewhere in the back of his mind, Nikolaos knew he shouldn't bring Johannes into the water. Still, he couldn't stop. He no longer felt human.

The water was shallow. Nikolaos fell into it with his back to the bottom and Johannes tumbling on top of him. It was glorious, soft, and cool, contrasting with Johannes' hot skin.

It was completely dark now, and the sky was full of stars. They were blinding him with their beauty and their light. When Johannes kissed him, he wrapped his legs around him and rolled him over to escape their brightness.

A comet shot across the night sky.

Chapter 20

Nikolaos was vomiting, holding on to a tree with his right hand, wrecked with such anxiety and guilt he was sobbing between retchings.

It was worse this time because he had pulled Johannes into the water himself. Someone he had talked to, hugged, and kissed, someone he wanted to be with. And on the way to the courthouse where Karin would be tried just for talking to him and for learning about a few herbs. When it was *he* who should be on trial. For murder. Cold-blooded murder.

Words from Luther's Small Catechism kept repeating in his head, along with the image of Johannes' body bobbing in the slow waves. *Thou shalt not kill. What does this mean? We should fear and love God that we may not hurt nor harm our neighbor in his body, but help and befriend him in every bodily need, in every need and danger of life and body. Though shalt not kill.*

He hadn't meant to kill him. His stomach turned over again, but there was nothing left to throw up.

***

When Nikolaos arrived in Jönköping, he fell in behind a group of about fifteen adults with a passel of children hopping back and forth between them. The little ones' dresses were threadbare and their hair so dirty he couldn't see what color it was. The group congregated behind a tall wooden wall. There was a gate and a guard with a long pike in his left hand, addressing each person wanting to get in. Nikolaos opened his bundle and felt around for his son's passport. He had just found it by the time it was his turn.

The guard took one look at it and then burst out laughing. "That takes some guts. You play me for a fool?" his eyes glinted merrily as he winked at the people behind Nikolaos. Several of them laughed.

"What do you mean, sir?" Nikolaos asked, playing it off the best he could. Rusty devils, he was an idiot. His son's passport was really old now.

The guard was laughing so hard that a second guard came over. He was drinking tobacco, and there was so much smoke it made Nikolaos cough. "What's going on here?" he asked with a curious look at Nikolaos.

"This one here is trying one on me," the first guard said and handed the passport to his companion. "It's too old, look." Then he addressed Nikolaos again. "Enough with this nonsense. I admit it was funny. Not many would have the guts to play a joke on us. Now show me your own."

"Pray let me see that. Did I give you the wrong document? I'm not sure I understand," Nikolaos said, heart sinking. Why hadn't he obtained one when he lived in Stockholm? It had never even crossed his mind. The guards there had known him as the fiddler from the inn and never asked.

The guard handed the passport back to him. His mirth was gone, and he shifted the pike into his right hand and shook it threateningly. The crowd behind him was getting larger, some people pressing to get a closer look while others moved back in fear.

Nikolaos swallowed hard, trying to think of an excuse. "Pray pardon me. I might have brought the wrong paper. I may have brought my father's instead. I…"

"Your father's?" The guard shook his head, a look of disdain on his face. "Nobody's father has something like this. What's your real reason for coming here? Do you have ill intent?"

Nikolaos didn't get a chance to reply. The guard whistled, and then everything happened very fast. Two men appeared and grabbed him by the arms. Then they dragged him through the gate and away from the crowd, hurrying along a canal that stunk terribly.

"Where are you taking me?" Nikolaos managed.

"Jail, we have too much happening here right now to have time to deal with charlatans and thieves. You'll get out in a day or two if you can prove yourself," the one to his left said as they turned into a narrow alleyway.

"I'm no thief." Just a murderer. He stopped resisting them. It was no use. This might be God's plan to get rid of him. Hadn't he wished for this earlier anyway?

The guards talked amongst themselves as if they were used to dragging prisoners to and fro every day. They probably were. One of them said that his wife had been so mad at him the night before she had threatened to stop mending his breeches and waistcoats. It prompted the other one to suggest he go find himself a voluptuous seamstress so he wouldn't have to listen to his nagging wife. Both men laughed madly at it.

They kept walking. It was not the nice side of town, so much was clear. Some of the houses they passed were no more than ramshackle sheds. Then the guards finally stopped in front of a large wooden building. This one intact and sturdy-looking.

Someone opened the door before they had time to knock, and Nikolaos was brutally shoved straight into a heavily muscled warden who immediately grabbed him and pulled him inside. The guards gave no word of explanation of why they brought Nikolaos and just handed him off. Shouldn't the prison guard at least know why he was there, to make sure he was let out in a day or two like they had said?

The warden didn't say anything either. He forced Nikolaos through a long dark corridor, holding his arm with a grip so tight that he could feel his nails, stopping by a door at the end. "The jail is full today. I'm afraid I'll have to put you with the Näcken crone. There isn't any room in the men's section." The warden laughed coldly. "She's so old anyway, it won't matter much. But as I mentioned, she's a real crone, so I'd be careful if I were you," he said and kept laughing. It sounded sinister. Then he opened the door with his free hand, pushed Nikolaos inside, and slammed the door behind him.

There was an overwhelming stench of human feces and piss. It made him gag. Vomit reached the back of his throat, and he almost retched.

"It's you isn't it. Have you come to save me?"

Nikolaos started. He hadn't registered what the warden had said until he recognized the voice in the darkness. Karin. He was in the same cell as Karin Persdotter.

"Lord in Heaven, Karin!" he cried, sliding to the floor. It felt sticky, and he put his right hand in a blob of something more unpleasant than he cared to know. He wiped it off on his breeches and forced himself not to gag again. "I wish I were, but it's by sheer coincidence I'm here. In the same cell as you, nonetheless." He groped around to find her hand.

Being used to the darkness, she grabbed it with both of hers and patted it.

"Karin, are you unhurt?"

She didn't answer.

He let her be and told her about the guards at the city gate.

"Have you come to save me?" Karin asked again, ignoring what he told her. Or perhaps she hadn't understood. "You and I could flee and go live behind your waterfall. You were right. I should have stayed with you instead of caring about my piglets."

Nikolaos shook his head slowly.

"I asked if you could get them to release me, then you and I can go live behind your waterfall together, I should have listened to you. You'll do something, won't you?"

"I heard you, I'm thinking," Nikolaos said, realizing that even if her eyes were used to the dark, she couldn't see his head move. Nikolaos felt around for his fiddle. If he could play his melodies, he might be able to get the warden to open the door. But his bundle and instrument weren't there. The warden must have grabbed it when he shoved him in. He suppressed a spike of anger at the thought of the rough man looking through his belongings. Everything he held dear was in that bundle, including his fiddle.

When his eyes adjusted to the darkness, he could see Karin's small shape against the wall. She sat slumped, hugging herself. She was freezing.

"Come here, Karin, sit with me so I can warm you a little."

She struggled to get closer, but it was clear she was so stiff and achy that she could barely move. He got to his feet and resolutely picked her up, careful so as not to hurt her. She was light as an eight-year-old. Seated again, Karin curled up in his lap as if she were a baby and fell asleep.

"Don't let those men get their hands on you. Whatever you do, Nikolaos, never let them," Karin said suddenly, startling him. "They poked and prodded me and already birched my back even though they said they wouldn't until after the hearing here. They insisted that I'd had indecent relations with you. Said that I've communed with the Devil, that you're the Devil. Said that I'm a dangerous, dangerous woman."

"Pray forgive me," he mumbled and instinctively pulled his hand away from her back so as not to hurt it more. He was trying to think of something comforting to say when the door suddenly opened, flooding the cell with lantern light. Nikolaos covered his eyes, blinded.

"Didn't I tell you to watch it? What's she doing on your lap?" the warden shouted, kicking Nikolaos in the side. "Get up! She needs to come with me."

Nikolaos rubbed his side and turned to him, squinting. "Where are you taking her?"

"What's it to you? Be glad to get rid of her. She's already worked her charms on you, lying in your lap like a cat!" The warden spit on the floor. "You get the cell to yourself, should be grateful and thank me," he said, tearing Karin from his lap and dragging her out the door. Her bones crackled as if they were a pile of collapsing kindling wood.

She didn't utter a sound.

The door slammed closed, kicking up a cloud of dirt.

He hadn't even tried to stop him from taking her.

***

Nikolaos lost track of time. There was no light, not even a crack in the door to tell him if time changed at all. It was very cold too. No wonder Karin had been shivering. Searching with his hands across the floor, he hoped to bump into a blanket, but all he felt was sticky hay. The smell told him which corner Karin, and who

136

knew how many others, had used as an outhouse. He curled up in the opposite corner from the pile of excrement. It wasn't far enough; the cell was not larger than a smaller market stall, and it stunk the same everywhere. What if they left him there and forgot about it? What if he stayed alive forever, starving and without access to water or his rapids? The thought sent a wave of such terror through him that he almost peed on himself.

Despite the panic, he fell into a fitful sleep, dreaming he was standing by the cell door, screaming for help. No one came for him, and there were angry voices outside who were annoyed he was still alive, complaining it took too long and that they needed the cell for the Näcken crone. He woke with a pounding heart, feeling his body to make sure he hadn't lost weight, not that he ever did, but relieved it still seemed strong and muscular so he could tell himself it was only hours later, not years.

The second time he woke up, he had been thirsty for so long that his tongue was glued to the roof of his mouth, and he couldn't stave off the panic anymore. His heart started to gallop out of control, so loud, green flicked in front of his face. It scared him which made it pound even harder. Nikolaos quickly closed his eyes, afraid it would make him faint. He had to stop. This was insanity talking, not reality. They wouldn't keep someone for bringing the wrong piece of information through the town border, at least not for that long. Taking a deep breath, he dared to open his eyes. The green was gone, and he managed to relax a little.

Then the door opened. This time he quickly covered his face with his hand before the lantern light blinded him. Something was thrown at his feet with a crash. At first, he was scared to touch it, but thinking it was food or water, he reached for it, even more afraid that whatever they'd given him to drink would spill. But his fingers slid over his own bundle, fiddle protruding from inside it. He was so thirsty it disappointed him.

"Get out! Get your things and get up. You can go, we need the cell. No need for petty frauds like you to occupy it."

Thank God. The relief made him feel weak in the knees, and he had to grab the wall to pull himself up to stand.

The warden grew impatient and grabbed his upper arm and pulled him out. It wasn't the same man who had locked him in, but he acted as unpleasantly as the former, squeezing his arm as if Nikolaos would run back into his cell after being told he could leave. He looked grim, with a small, lipless mouth and greasy hair plastered to his head.

As he was dragged through the prison, Nikolaos looked for Karin, but all he saw were closed jail cells. Then the warded opened the heavy prison door and, ridiculously politely, stepped aside to let him out.

Nikolaos took two cautious steps, then bolted, afraid the warden would change his mind and come after him. He kept running for several blocks but heard no footsteps behind him and finally stopped behind a shed to get his bearings. The air was crisp, and the sun was getting low in the sky. The panic and fear slid off of him as if they were drips of water, leaving just a faint feeling of danger in the back of his mind. He needed to find something to eat and a place to wash the nasty grime off his hands. And something to drink. The thirst was almost painful.

Continuing eastward, he kept walking toward what appeared to be the town center, scanning every house he passed for a place to eat. And as he turned a corner into a town square, he spotted a small tavern on the other side. Relieved, he hurried towards it, dodging a group of women with baskets full of fruit. He was tempted to reach over and steal an apple.

The tavern was empty except for an older man wiping down a table. He left the rag on a chair and approached. "Welcome, have a seat. What can I get you?"

Nikolaos tried to tell him he wanted ale, but his throat was so dry that it sounded more like a craw.

"Thirsty, eh? Sit, I'll get you one, then I'll join you," he said, making his way over to his counter, walking sideways to keep eye contact with Nikolaos. "As you can see, I have no customers today at all. They're all over at the execution. I'm too old for it, don't enjoy them anymore. Getting too close to my own time, I take it."

"I see," Nikolaos said without really listening. He was so

thirsty that he had to fight the urge to tell him to hurry.

When he finally had it in his hand it tasted so good, he swallowed the contents of the jug in what felt like one sip.

"Dear man, you look like you may need another. And something to eat. I have some rabbit and bread with lard should you want it?"

"I give thanks... thank you kindly. Have you a bowl of water? I'm in need to wash."

"Yes, in the corner there. I just filled it," the tavern keeper said, indicating a tall stool with a brown ceramic bowl placed on top.

There was soap too, and Nikolaos rolled up his sleeves and washed as much of himself as he could. He felt better already.

The tavern keeper came around the counter and placed a plate in front of Nikolaos just as he sat down. "Where are you from?"

"Norrköping and Stockholm." It was somewhat true at least. He couldn't well tell him he lived in a cave. Nikolaos grabbed two pieces of meat at once. It tasted heavenly. While chewing, he tore a piece of bread and dipped it in the lard.

"Ah, I take it then you've seen your share of executions and have no need to see one today?"

Nikolaos shrugged. "Who *is* the poor fella?"

"Not a fella this time. An old woman." He raised his eyebrows dramatically and sat down in front of Nikolaos. "She had relations with Näcken some years back."

"What?"

"Indeed, I'm telling you the truth. It's a she. From Uppvidinge, apparently. She learned skills from Näcken and put the disease on both people and cattle over there. They hung her this afternoon, sure she's dead by now."

Nikolaos stared at him, aware that his jaw was dropping. He was too late. He abruptly got to his feet. "How much do I owe you for this?"

"Eh, just give me what you want." The tavern keeper looked disappointed. "I enjoyed the company. I'll have enough guests later.

They all thirst after a hanging."

Nikolaos fished a copper out of his leather pouch and thanked him, hoping it was an acceptable amount, he had no idea what it was worth these days. "Where are the gallows?"

"You'll find them easily, make a left out here, then when you get to the canal, you make a right. You'll see the courthouse from there. The gallows are right behind it."

Nikolaos hurried outside and ran, guilt and shame surging through his body. God had given him an opportunity to try to save Karin by putting him in the same cell as her, but he had squandered it. He could have overtaken that guard when he came in to collect Karin. It would have been easy enough when the guard's hands were busy pulling at her. He could have picked up the lantern and hit him in the head with it, thrown feces in his face, or even just punched him. Instead, he had done nothing. Nothing.

Once he came close enough to see the gallows, it was clear the tavern keeper had been right. Karin was already dead, hanging from the rope for all to see. People were crowding around the structure, shouting and screaming at her, even laughing. Tears blurred his vision. He was the cause of both Karin's and Johannes' deaths. It should be him hanging from that noose.

Disgusted with himself, he pushed forward. In spite of their rude loudness, people seemed afraid and had left a large empty circle of space around the gallows, making it possible for him to go all the way up and take a closer look. It was a horrible sight. Karin's body swayed slowly back and forth, and her head hung at an awkward angle, leaning to the right. The breeze moved her long gray hair across her face and created an illusion that her lips were moving. It was almost as if she were trying to talk to him. He turned away, feeling spooked.

"Don't look as harmless as she wanted us to think she was, not even in death," a man standing off to the side said. He gave a one-sided smile.

Nikolaos ignored the comment. "When are they taking the body down to bury it?"

"She'll be up a while. People need to see what happens

when someone puts the disease on folk. It's for their own good."

"For how long?" Nikolaos resisted an urge to defend her. It was too late anyway.

"Can't say for sure, a couple of days, a week. Or less maybe. I can't say, they haven't dug yet, but they'll bury her right here as usual."

"I see." Nikolaos looked away. Maybe he could bury her in hallowed ground somewhere himself. What would people do if he pulled her down right now and ran? He turned around with renewed energy, looking at the streets and alleyways to seek a clear path out. It was too crowded; all it would do was get him arrested again. His sudden excitement vanished, replaced by panic at the thought of being dragged back to that horrid jail cell. Feeling slightly ashamed of his cowardice, he took one more look at Karin, then crossed himself and prayed God would protect her soul.

***

Even though there wasn't anything Nikolaos could do, he couldn't bear to leave. Walking around aimlessly, he kept his face down to avoid looking into the eyes of anyone who might have seen Karin die or see someone who might speak ill of her.

By the time he finally raised his head enough to notice what was happening around him, it was getting dark, and he was exhausted. A group of people were walking briskly, heading north, and he decided to ask them for a place to stay instead of starting the long journey back to his cave.

"Pray pardon me, are you familiar with this town?" he asked just as they were about to pass him. "I've just decided to find an inn for the night."

"Somewhat," a man walking arm in arm with his wife said. They stopped, letting the rest of the group go on without them. "I'm not sure where the closest inn is though. We came to town for the lecture with Abraham Lövcrantz."

"Who's that?"

"An expert on sorcery and demonology. He studied with

Pastor Prytz," he said, sounding like he assumed Nikolaos would know who Pastor Prytz was.

"After the hanging today, my husband insisted we'd go," his wife interjected, nodding knowingly.

"True enough, I believe it's important to stay informed when the opportunity is given. I'm Merchant Thomas, and this is my wife, Sara. We should hurry. It'll be a full house tonight. First time in town, I take it?"

"Yes, it is," Nikolaos said, then decided to stay as close to the truth as he could. "I had hoped to see them question Karin Persdotter, but I was too late. I helped her fix a roof recently. I admit, I was shocked that they hung her. I had no inkling she was dangerous," he added for good measure, immediately regretting his words, feeling disloyal. She was certainly not dangerous. He, if anyone, knew that.

Merchant Thomas looked taken aback and quickly pulled his wife closer as if to protect her. But she broke herself out of his grip and came closer to Nikolaos, grabbing the lantern her husband was holding and lifting it so she could see Nikolaos' face.

"Oh dear, you must be so afraid. Come with us. You could certainly learn a thing or two from Abraham. If nothing else but to understand that they did right by hanging her."

Nikolaos looked at her uncertainly, feeling torn between her kindness and her approval of Karin's death.

"Yes, why don't you join us? Since you knew Persdotter somewhat, I'm sure Abraham would be interested in speaking with you. They'll provide refreshments as well. Someone there will be able to tell you where to find an inn," Merchant Thomas said, looking comfortable again.

Nikolaos hesitated, but then he nodded. It would be foolish not to. It was better to learn what they were saying about him, no matter how tired he felt. "Why not. It's very kind of you. I'd be glad to."

Merchant Thomas smiled, then took his wife by the arm and set off, walking so briskly that Sara was practically running to keep up.

Nikolaos fell in beside them but kept his distance.

A crowd was already waiting to be let inside when they arrived. Everyone was impeccably dressed, illuminated by a torch in a scone by the entrance. One woman was wearing pearls. And a man with reddish, curly hair long enough to fall below his shoulders wore a fine black coat in some soft, thick material Nikolaos had never seen.

And there he was, wearing Karin's dead husband's attire, after spending God knew how many days in a rank jail cell. Maybe it was better if he didn't go in after all.

Sara smiled at him, oblivious to his discomfort.

A moment later, the front door was opened by a footman. Nikolaos shrugged at his own misgivings and followed Sara and her husband inside.

They were escorted through the hallway to a large room with several tables full of food, brightly lit with real vax candles. It was a fine home, clearly not usually populated by newly released prisoners. Passing an enormous Venetian looking glass, Nikolaos discreetly observed Sara's and Merchant Thomas' reflections. Sara kept her eyes on herself in it, opening her coat and exposing a nice collar which she lifted a bit as she walked by. There was a young man behind her wearing simple clothes, who didn't look like he belonged either. He was also carrying a bundle tied to a stick with a fiddle wrapped up in it. Nikolaos smiled with relief that he wasn't the only person who wasn't rich.

Instantly the man smiled back.

Nikolaos' eyes widened as the man's eyes did the same. He stopped abruptly, disoriented and stunned. The young man was himself, and something was very wrong.

A woman accidentally bumped into him, not expecting Nikolaos to stop right in front of her. "Pray step aside if you need to admire yourself, don't stand here in the middle of the floor. People need to get to their seats," she said angrily, shaking her head and tut-tutting.

Mumbling an excuse, Nikolaos walked closer to the glass, meeting the eyes of a boy. A mere boy, not more than eighteen.

Someone who should have been married for a year or two, not someone who had assumed the role of a man in his early thirties as he had when he lived in Stockholm. Nikolaos felt and saw his skin flush from the shock as people hurried past him.

Merchant Thomas appeared behind him in the glass and put his hands firmly on Nikolaos' shoulders. He looked amused. "Come sit with us. You shouldn't worry if you feel improperly dressed for the occasion. I'll explain to Abraham who you are and that you weren't prepared. He'll be most interested in speaking with you and won't think anything of it. Come sit with us," he repeated. "They're bringing out the ale now."

Nikolaos only managed to nod. He followed Thomas numbly, forcing down his angst. Something had happened when he lived behind the fall all those years. Karin had been right; he did look younger than the first time they met. He had lost more than time in that cave.

***

Nikolaos distracted himself from the shock by devouring a piece of fresh bread smeared with butter, several pieces of salted meat, and dried pears. It helped, it made it easier to breathe and some of the anxiety subsided. Maybe he hadn't looked as young as he thought he had after all.

Abraham Lövcrantz strode across the floor, stopping at the other end of the room and facing all the tables. His hair was long, dark, and curly, and he had a confident air about him while waiting for his audience to adjust themselves so they could see. Some left their tables and went to stand along the walls, leaving Nikolaos with a clear view of him without obstruction.

Abraham Lövcrantz glanced around the room and smiled in recognition at someone in front. "It must have been meant to be that I was scheduled to speak here today. Our lord works in mysterious ways. I know Karin Persdotter is on many people's minds, and I'll be happy to answer all your questions. But before I begin, I'd like to warn you that some things I'm about to describe are frightening, especially for women." He paused, looking calmly over the heads of the audience. "The wife of my host here has graciously offered to take care of every woman who'd prefer to sit down and enjoy a milder conversation suitable for her ears." He bowed, indicating a woman standing to his left.

Sara threw a quick glance at Merchant Thomas but shook her head and stayed put. Several of the other women were escorted toward the hostess by their husbands. The woman was wearing a peach-colored dress which left bare skin wholly exposed all the way down to the tops of her breasts. A string of pearls circled her neck, and she had large pearls in her earlobes. Nikolaos had never seen anything like it.

Abraham was rubbing his chin, calmly waiting until the door closed behind the women, and their husbands were back in their seats. Then he removed his hand from his chin and cleared his throat. "As I said, this is frightening, but important. As a student of Prytz, I'm confident I'll be able to give you enough knowledge to know what to do if necessary." He paused for emphasis. "Creatures such as Näcken, whom you're all familiar with due to the hanging today, as well as the Forest Rå or the Mountain Rå, are actually the Devil himself taking on the shape of these beings. You see, the Devil can't create something out of nothing. He must use what God has already made. As scary as this sounds, it's a comforting thought. You see, in a sense God allows this to happen. These creatures that the Devil embodies cannot be made of flesh unless the Devil decides to embody an already deceased body. And you can tell then by the stench that he isn't human."

Audible gasps were reverberating around the room. Nikolaos felt a chill. What was Abraham talking about? He had been a boy with a mother like everyone else, and his body certainly hadn't been a corpse. Unless his parents found a dead child that somehow… He quickly dismissed the thought.

Abraham nodded knowingly. "The body is cold then as well. That's another way to tell. You ought to be aware though that embodying flesh isn't the only way the Devil tricks us. In fact, it's quite rare for him to use the method. He prefers vapor, moisture in the air like from a fog that he collects for his different forms. In this way, one can say that God allows him to do it since he's using the fog that God created." He held up his hand as if someone had been interrupting even though no one had. "It's why Näcken appeared to Karin in a watery shape, just like a little wave coming toward her at the shore. A perfect example of what I described. In her case, the Devil used what was already there. Water."

Nikolaos laughed nervously, thinking of how the fog had affected him and what he had done to Johannes. Several people turned around and stared disapprovingly.

"This isn't funny, young man," Abraham Lövcrantz said. "Karin Persdotter invoked the Devil when she was looking for Näcken. It's something she admitted in court."

"Yes, sir," Nikolaos managed. That too, and the fork. He threw a sidelong glance at the tables, taking note of the forks and knives lying used and dirtied on the plates. He let out a breath.

"You see, the Devil deceives us," Abraham went on. "He can take on the form of a Rå to steal sperm from men that he inserts into women. On other occasions, he can blow air into a woman to make her think she's expecting. Once the air is released, the Devil returns and places a stolen infant by her feet. This process only takes about four weeks."

Sara let out a high-pitched squeal and collapsed into her husband's lap. Others stared at each other as if they were checking to see if any of the remaining women looked falsely pregnant. Several men looked as if they might get sick. Another was taking notes, writing feverously to keep up.

While Abraham waited for the room to quiet down, he took the opportunity to wipe his forehead and neck with a lace handkerchief, lifting his thick hair to reach his neck. Then he methodically folded the handkerchief into a square and replaced it in his waistcoat pocket. "I understand this is uncomfortable," he said once he had the audience's attention, "but pray let me go on. You can ask whatever you want in just a bit. God, in all his glory, is allowing the Devil to do this to test us. Yes, indeed he is, but remember that he's also giving us signs so we can easily tell." He nodded encouragingly. "Should you come upon one of these creatures, you only need to give them a thorough look over, and you'll see their claws, tails, or hollow backs. Even the stupidest person will notice this. It's not hard. If you just keep this in mind and avoid…"

Nikolaos couldn't listen anymore and got to his feet, waving in Abraham's direction who turned toward him, clearly irritated at the interruption.

"Yes, if you must, what is your question?"

"If Näcken, for example, is made of vapor… like steam, how would he wear clothes? Wouldn't they just fall through the air?"

"Absolutely not. The Devil can transform the vapor to solid. One of our own Kings, Karl IX, tried to shoot Näcken. But the creature caught the bullet and threw it at him. The King almost died!"

Nikolaos startled, loudly bumping into his chair with his right foot. Rusty devils, the King *had* recognized him. He sat back down, breath catching in his throat.

"Indeed, so solid he can catch bullets that would sever the hand of a person. A Dutch diplomat named Anthonis Goetreeis told me this himself." Abraham nodded proudly. "He said the King had told him how Näcken was sitting on a wooden pole in the water by Three Crowns, the royal castle. It was early, early in the morning. The King opened his window and tried to shoot him, but as I mentioned, Näcken caught the bullet in his hand and threw it back at him." Abraham shook his head with an expression of both disgust and fear, and it was so silent you could hear a mouse run across the floor. "It can be perilous. It's how Karin Persdotter learned about the herbs from him. Näcken materialized before her, and then he showed her where the herbs grew."

At that, Nikolaos stood again, and without another look at Abraham Lövcrantz, he walked out, feeling Merchant Thomas' and his wife's eyes on his back and their disappointment that he didn't stay.

Outside was dark and deserted and there were no lanterns

moving about held by people hurrying home. The torch had gone out too.

Nikolaos took a deep breath of the chilly air, trying to clear his head of what had been said inside. Even though he was affected by fog, he wasn't vapor obviously, he knew that. But he could breathe underwater, and when he stayed under for a long time, his body *did* look almost transparent before the water shifted back to blood within him. What if the Devil inhabited him and had kept him alive all these years by his evil power? With a quick glance at the windows behind him, he walked into the darkness and sniffed himself. A whiff of the dank prison cell reached his nostrils, but he didn't smell like death. He exhaled, embarrassed that he had felt the need to check. The notion that he was made of a rotting corpse or vapor was insulting. He had felt that bullet speed past his hand. If it hit, he would have bled like everyone else.

Once many years ago, when he and Abluna were newlyweds, he accidentally hacked his thigh with an ax. It had bled and filled with puss, and streams of death had traveled up his groin, racked him with the only fever he had ever had. But he didn't die. They said it was a miracle. That God had healed him.

Nikolaos kept walking, passing a cluster of low-roofed cottages. Even in the darkness, he sensed that they were gray with time. A single candle caught his eye, and through a tiny window, he saw an old woman knitting by its light. She looked sweet and content, unlike Karin, whose body hung cold and alone in the dark. The thought stopped him in his tracks. He couldn't leave her there.

***

Someone had left a lantern on the ground, making Karin's body visible from a distance. It spun slowly, creating shadows that made it seem like someone was walking around there. It was odd to waste tallow on her, but maybe it was customary. Maybe to protect it from people like him who came to steal the body to bury it.

But as Nikolaos got closer, he realized that someone *was* there. A man was touching her body, standing under it with her left hand in his. He pulled out a knife from his belt, then cut one of Karin's fingers off and put it in a piece of cloth. Nikolaos' eyes widened, and he watched with growing horror as the man pulled a cup from his pocket and placed it under her hand. Blood was dripping from the wound in a steady stream, falling into the cup. The man was calm as if he had not done something odder than slicing a piece of fruit.

Nikolaos finally got out of his stupor and was over there in two long steps. "Rusty devils, what in God's name are you doing?" he screamed, startling the man so the blood splattered all over his arm and face.

"What does it look like? Now you made me spill it! You should pay for this."

"Pay for it?"

With Karin's finger still in his hand, the man wiped his face on his sleeve, glaring at him. "I got here first. Were you planning to take it? No one will buy the blood from you. People need to know that it's from someone they can trust and not from some lying sort who might use pig's blood."

Nikolaos stared at him, at a loss for words. The evening was getting stranger by the moment.

The man shrugged and put the cup underneath the hand again, keeping an eye on Nikolaos as he slowly slipped Karin's finger into his pocket.

Disgusted, Nikolaos walked across to the other side of Karin. The rest of her body looked untouched. He felt for Karin's other hand, reaching fingers that were swollen and cold to the touch. Dead and beyond redemption because of him. Then he stepped back around and picked up the lantern so he could look the man in the eye. "You're selling her blood? I don't understand. Who are you to do this to her? She was a sweet old woman!"

The man snickered. "A sweet old woman? She was a witch who associated with Näcken. I'm the executioner. People pay me a lot of money for blood from regular thieves and murderers for its healing powers. Can you imagine how much they'd give me for this?" He grinned, exposing dirty teeth.

"I don't know what to tell you. But don't you think that Näcken would be here right now trying to stop you if she were a witch?" Nikolaos said.

The executioner cocked his head to the side, and for a moment Nikolaos thought that he had given himself away, but then he laughed. "That, that my friend, is a tale! You're a funny one. Who knows, should he come by here I'd take a good look at him. But for now, I pray you, let me finish my work. Are you interested in the finger? The blood is already spoken for."

"No," Nikolaos said stiffly.

The executioner's face fell. "Why did you come here then? If you aren't interested in any of it, what is it to you?"

Nikolaos looked at him without answering, feeling torn. He wasn't sure if he wanted to bury her anymore. It felt as if things were getting out of his control. Too much had happened and in the span of just two or three days. He wanted to sit in the river and play his fiddle, cleanse himself of all this death. "Did you come here by horse?" he asked, deciding at that exact moment what he should do.

"Yes, it's right down there, behind the oak."

"I thought so. I'll take it. You can keep the body," Nikolaos said, then turned toward Karin, crossed himself, and asked her to forgive him for not burying her.

The executioner was too stunned to stop him, and by the time he reached the horse, it was too late.

Chapter 21

Rå went further south than she ever had, walking through a thick forest with no trampled paths or carriage tracks in any direction. After a while she took off her shawls and shift and continued naked, placing her thick hair over her left shoulder to expose her back to the elements. It felt wonderful. After pretending to be an old woman living with the gnarliness the old tree had gifted her with, it felt as if she were reborn. The fresh air and moisture opened her back hole easily and connected to the trees, their sap crackling softly in greeting.

Rå laughed with pleasure and reached for a trunk, letting her hand rest on its rough bark. She closed her eyes. The tree was strong, supported by a network of roots from its large extended family. Rå felt them reach for her, but she decided not to stick her feet into the roots just now. She let go of the tree and kept walking, feeling its kindness in her back.

Trees were like her, always watching who crossed their path but never getting too attached. Her eyes moistened at the thought. She hadn't always felt like that. It had taken her well over a hundred years before she understood what a blessing it was to live alone, free to do whatever she wanted. The first few years after Rå had been asked to, or forced rather, to leave her mother's village, she had stayed nearby just to watch them. It had hurt so much, especially seeing her mother walking straight-backed between the longhouses. She could still see her thin frame and feel the paralyzing grief when her mother didn't turn around to look at her, even though Rå willed it with all her heart.

When she finally left the area for good, it got easier. She learned to rely on herself, keep her back open and commune with the trees. She was free, free to do whatever she wanted without the ties that bound humans to their tedious rituals.

A few days later, the forest thinned out, opening into a clearing with an enormous ash in the center. The leaves hung thick and low, like a skirt with a circumference larger than a whole farm.

Rå's back buzzed with pleasure. What if it was Yggdrasil herself? If it was, the Norns would be in there, sitting at the foot of the trunk, spinning their yarn of destiny. When Rå was little, she had thought *she* was one of the Norns because of her affinity for trees. Her mother had laughed, thinking Rå was cute. Then she explained that none of the three Norns would be running around like Rå did but were sitting at Urd's well, pouring water on Yggdrasil's roots so she wouldn't dry out, and that Rå was just a little girl. Rå smiled at the memory. She hadn't exactly *just* been a little girl, but they hadn't known that then.

Walking up to the wide leavened skirt, Rå carefully spread the leaves aside, stuck her head through, and looked around. There was so much space it looked like a ballroom with sloping walls made of dark green leaves. Stepping all the way through, she straightened to full height. There was plenty of room above her head, too. The trunk stood like a pillar in the middle of the high ceiling. Further up the trunk were thick branches supporting its enormous width. She held her breath and looked around for a well, but the ground was flat and dry. The Norns weren't there. Disappointed, her back hole closed, but she was also a bit relieved. It would probably have been rude to come empty-handed and without having prepared with a proper blót first.

She went to the trunk and patted its bark, feeling the sap move in response. It was just a tree, after all. A welcoming one. There were crows' nests and squirrels running around in the crown, a good sign. What if she built her home beneath its branches? It would fit easily.

Sitting down to think about it before deciding, Rå removed her shift and rested her back hole against the trunk. Then she placed her hands on the roots, closed her eyes, and let her back open. It only took a moment before the tree pulled her into its trunk. She felt little bird feet and tiny paws tickling what she first thought was her hair but realized were the branches above. There was no way to tell where her eyes were or even if they were open. But she saw everything: the forest, fields and farms, a moose, swarms of birds, and a man with his ax.

Then there was a buzzing, as if bees were surrounding her, and she shrunk back to her own form, sitting at the foot of the tree with the thick leavened skirt in front of her as before. Tears streamed down her cheeks.

"Thank you, beloved," she whispered. "You may not be Yggdrasil, but I bow to you just the same. Thank you for finding someone who'll help me build a home by your roots. I'll be as gentle as possible and will always respect you."

The tree released three large leaves into her lap.

***

Following the tapping sound of the woodcutter's ax, Rå ran all the way there. When she reached him, he had already felled several trees and was in the process of harnessing one of them to his horse, a white stocky mare, who would drag it over to a large pile of them. The woodcutter was bare chested, and Rå could see the muscles shifting in his underarms when he was manipulating the harness. He was handsome, with striking blue eyes, hair thick and blond, and skin ruddy from being outside a lot. She grinned. He would do fine for more than building.

"Good afternoon, woodcutter," she said, grinning wider.

He looked up, startled, but found himself quickly, eyes glinting in response to her grin. "Good lewssa, goofrwssl... alone? You one essbrrr on a day like this."

She frowned. Maybe he had broken teeth. "Pray forgive me?"

"Ah, you're Swedish I hear," he said in a much clearer voice. "Are you sure you want to be here on our side of the woods?"

"On your side?"

"That's right, you've crossed the border. You're in His Majesty's Kristian III's domain now, in Denmark. Border mark is just up there," he said, pointing to a boulder she had passed moments before. Both sides looked exactly the same.

"I see." A new border, humans constantly fought over land. She could never keep track of what was what. "Since when?"

He held up his hands, splaying his fingers. "Some ten summers ago. But I have no ill will toward you Swedes. My family and I have always been on good terms with our neighbors. Most didn't want to fight when Horn attacked us. There were just a few who felt they needed to take a side… or they were forced to. My family fled along with several others. How could we fight with each other after living side by side, celebrating every harvest season, and going to church together?" He looked at her with a raised eyebrow as if he thought she would be able to answer.

Rå shrugged. "The land is its own. We shouldn't own it. I don't understand why one piece of land could be more important than the other. Is this why you spoke so differently? I couldn't understand you at first."

"That's true, goodwife, but it's how most of us speak down here, no matter what side of the border we live on. My good friend from up your parts taught me Swedish. His whole family came down here when I was a boy." He stretched his arm outward, palm down, to indicate a small child.

"I see." She opened her back to draw him in. "What's your name? I'm looking to build a home. Do you do that sort of work?"

"I'm Rasmus, and I'll be delighted to help you. With your new home I mean, I *do* do such work on occasion."

"I thank you kindly." Rå opened her back a bit more.

Rasmus looked disoriented for a moment but went to his mare and untied her. "Would you like to ride?"

She nodded.

He bent down with his fingers entwined so she could use them as a step to mount. His hands felt strong and firm on her bare feet, sending a spike of arousal through her back. Once she was seated, he grabbed hold of the bit and walked alongside.

"Tell me more of why your neighbors had to take sides and why some fled, Rasmus," Rå said when they crossed back over the border, mostly to distract herself from staring at his muscular shoulders. It didn't seem to be an issue to go back and forth.

He threw her a quick sidelong glance. "Not to speak poorly of your countrymen, goodwife, but the truth is that thousands of

Swedish troops attacked us. They wanted our land, still do, I hear."

Rå grimaced with disapproval. She could only imagine how many people, including children and animals, had to suffer for that folly. "A shame."

"Indeed," Rasmus said, sounding surprised. He pointed northward. "They reached a peace deal up in Brömsebo. Denmark got to keep the southern peninsula down here." He moved his arm in the opposite direction and gestured southward, thumb in the air. "It's a large piece of land. We would've lost a lot of landmass had it gone." His voice had a hint of both pride and anger in it.

"I knew nothing of this. I've lived sheltered in a small village near Norrköping." Rå smiled a little. Sheltered sounded good, as if she were a goodwife just like Rasmus had called her.

He didn't reply. They continued in silence after that. When they came to her clearing, she told him to stop, then dismounted on her own.

"Here? The Ash takes up most of the open space. I'd have to cut down several trees to enlarge the area, or you wouldn't fit a house here."

"Yes." She could see the hesitation on his face now. Men always followed her without question at first, intrigued by her beauty and their urge to help. Their misgivings came when the initial enchantment wore off, and they realized it wasn't usual for women to be outside alone like this. That's when she had to allure them further. Rå slowly untied the strings that held her shift in place, and just as it slid down and landed around her feet, she turned away from him, pulled her loose hair over her shoulders, and exposed her back.

He called out in surprise.

She picked up the shift and hurried toward the tree, slipping under the branches without looking back.

Before long, Rasmus came through the branches, eyes glossy and wide as he looked around.

Rå smiled and went to him. "Once you have built what I need, you'll have me. Do you want that?" She pushed herself against his body.

"Yes, I do," he said hoarsely and tried to embrace her.

She laughed and moved away. "Later, first I'd like to show you what I want done. As you can see, I have a lot of space in here. I want you to build my house right in here, connect stairs to the lower branches which should lead to the door and then also to a flat roof, strong enough so that I can sit on it. Do you understand? Can you do that?"

With an expression of deep concern exaggerated by her magic, Rasmus pursed his lips and approached the trunk. Narrowing his eyes, he slapped and pulled at the branches. "Yes, I should be able to do this for you. But where will you cook? It won't be safe to cook in a house built in a tree." He looked nervous as if he thought she would get angry.

"I don't cook often, but when I do, I can just make a fire out there in the clearing," she said, tilting her head toward the place where they had climbed through.

"Good." He looked relieved. "My horse can drag some of my trees over here. It'll take some time to build, several days, even weeks. Can I bring her in here?" he asked, looking nervous again. Her magic was affecting him too much.

"Of course," Rå said, closing her back hole halfway. "You're both welcome to stay with me for as long as it takes. I'm grateful for your help." She reached for him and let him kiss her and touch her for a little while. Then she pulled herself free again and pushed the branches aside. "Go. Get what you need and come back to me when you have it. Go now. I'll wait for you."

He hurried out and got back on his horse, heading in the direction whence they came. That was good. But she opened her back hole fully again, just in case.

***

Later that evening they sat together, eating sweet bread and smoked fish which he had packed for his woodcutting journey. Humans never went anywhere without bringing food with them it seemed. It was another gift from the Gods.

"I've never met someone like you before. Who are you? How is it that a lovely woman like yourself isn't married?" Rasmus asked, handing her another piece of fish.

"I'm Rå. I don't marry."

"Rå?" He threw his head back in recognition. "I've heard tales of you. My Swedish friends spoke of it. They said men sometimes come upon you in the forest. But then when they follow you, your back is suddenly a tree." He widened his eyes dramatically. "They look and look, but all they see are trees, trees, and trees as far as they can see. Then they get lost forever. Clearly, that's not true." He scoffed, eyes glinting.

She laughed.

***

Two weeks later, Rå had a new home, supported on poles reaching halfway up the tree trunk. Rasmus was in the process of adding a platform around the walls, which would serve as a balcony and a place where she could reach the largest and flattest branches to use as storage shelves.

He was standing on it, slick with sweat, wielding his hammer with such force he made her think of Thor. Every muscle on his upper body was visible through his soaked shirt. His hair was held back with a string, a few strands loose and stuck to his face.

"This looks better than I could have ever expected," she said, and meant it.

"I'm glad you like it. I'm surprised too. It's the first time I've made a house such as this." He broke into a broad smile and put his hammer down, fixing his eyes on her.

It couldn't be helped; he was too handsome. Rå climbed up, joining him on the platform, then grabbed his shoulders and kissed him hard on the mouth. She let him wrap his arms around her and kiss her neck. His sweat made her cheek wet. It made her so aroused she could barely resist grabbing his penis and pushing it inside of her, but she stopped, then pulled out of his embrace.

Rasmus stared at her, disappointment and lust making his

eyes shine with more than her magic. She felt sorry for him, but it was best to wait. There was always a risk that the enchantment wore off afterward, and she needed him to finish first.

"I'll make us something to eat. I found chestnuts earlier, I'll roast them for us, and we can eat them with mushrooms."

He looked at her as if he wanted to say something else, probably that he was hungry and longed for bread or meat. Rasmus was not used, as she was, to a diet of mostly acorns, soft tree bark, mushrooms, or berries. His cheeks were getting hollow. She ought to let him have what humans craved.

"Put your hammer down, Rasmus. Get your musket. We're going hunting."

"Really?"

She laughed. "Yes."

"That's a mighty good thought, Rå." He helped her down, and she let him kiss her just a bit more.

***

Rå opened her back and silently asked a deer to give itself to them. And just a moment later, a strong older buck entered their path and stopped right in front of them as if he had been waiting for them to appear. She recognized him. It was a buck she had seen with a herd of younger females earlier in the summer. Now he looked slow and stiff, too old to mate or keep watch over a territory of his own. He wouldn't survive the winter. This would be a faster way to die. The buck looked Rå straight in the eye, and she kept his gaze as he fell, silently thanking him. She would watch over his herd and make sure all the mothers and young ones stayed safe and survived the coming winter.

A week later, Rasmus finished.

The floor of her new home was attached to the thickest bottom tree branch, forming part of the platform surrounding the little house. A staircase with four strong steps and a branch alongside it, led up to it. There were two rooms, a smaller one for sleeping and a larger one for her work and for storing herbs and poultices. Rasmus was concerned she would get cold in the winter and built heating chests, as he called them, for each room in which she would put hot stones. There was a window with shutters in each room and an extra door at the back, leading out to the widest part of the platform. It was extraordinary. The nicest home she had ever had.

Rå grabbed Rasmus by his breeches and pulled him up the stairs. Then she finally took him.

***

Days later, Rå followed him to the edge of the clearing. She pointed to his musket. "Rasmus, pray let me have that for a moment. I almost forgot."

He stared at her, eyes glinting with suspicion and sudden fear. Then he took two steps back. The enchantment was wearing off.

Rå shook her head with a one-sided smile. "Give it to me, I'm not going to shoot you." She reached over and grabbed it straight out of his hand and put it under her arm. Then she pulled a small clay pot from her basket, groped out sticky paste, and smeared it over the barrel. "Here, now you'll never miss your target. From now on you'll have luck with your hunts every time as long as you never pick a mother or a calf. I thank you kindly for all your help. I'll never forget it." Handing it back to him, she leaned into his warmth one last time, then turned away from his astonished and relieved face and ran back to her new home.

Chapter 22

The more Nikolaos thought about how much time he had lost and how young he looked, the more it bothered him. It had to be the waterfall. Likely being in constant proximity to its rushing water was having too much of an effect on him. Not only was it frightening to think about, but he had acted like a fool, not knowing about the Queen or the post-runner with that horn. Even the way he talked was old-fashioned apparently. Both Karin and Johannes had told him he sounded like an old man. He had felt embarrassed. It was time to leave his cave and look for a new place to live.

He had the executioner's horse and could travel easier, too. She was a beautiful mare with a dark brown coat and black mane. He named her Kristina after the Queen and didn't feel the least bit guilty having stolen her. It served that cruel executioner right. A murder for a horse. It was a cheap price to pay. Even so, he felt nervous, worrying that someone would recognize the horse, and thereby him, and throw him back in that awful jail cell. It was probably unfounded, but just to be certain, he waited two more seasons before he finally started looking.

By Nikolaos' calculations there should be a village a couple of days ride eastward from his cave, give or take, he had seen it when he went with Karin. If nothing else, he could start there to see if it might be an appropriate place to settle down for the next few years.

It was closer than he remembered, or maybe Kristina just trotted faster, for he was only about half a morning's ride away when he saw spirals of woodsmoke in the distance. Shortly thereafter a path appeared between the trees. An abandoned wheel lay tossed beside it. The forest itself showed signs of human activity as well. Trees had been cut, and visible footprints appeared in the mud near a puddle, and he heard voices and children laughing. Kristina's ears moved forward at the sound.

Nikolaos patted her neck. "Let's go and see what we can find, darling. Maybe we could trade for some apples, would you like that?”

She responded with a flick of her tail and set off into a trot.

Nikolaos heard laughter again, proceeded by a squeal, and then two children came running from a cluster of pines, and threw themselves on the mossy ground and began to roll around, tumbling around each other. They still wore dresses and didn’t seem older than three or four. And they were almost the same size, looking exactly alike. Maybe they were twins. Boys, it looked like, but he wasn’t sure.

Nikolaos dismounted, and at the sound of squeaking saddle leather, they stopped rolling and immediately got to their feet, standing straight-backed and serious. He chuckled. They were incredibly cute, although their faces were covered with dirt and tears, which had left long clean marks on their cheeks.

Crouching down, he smiled at them. “Good morrow, what are you two doing here by yourselves? Do you have an older brother or sister about?”

The one closest to him shook his head, still with a serious expression. Nikolaos noticed now that he had larger eyes than the other, and his hair was just a little darker.

“Mama!” The other child exclaimed, grabbing the hand of his sibling.

Nikolaos turned his head to see if he could see her nearby, but it looked as empty as before. “How about you ride with me for a while until you find your mama? Did you know that my horse is named after a queen? Her name is Kristina, just like Her Highness the Queen.”

Eyeing her wide-eyed and somberly, the blonder of the two bowed and pretended to remove a hat from his head.

Nikolaos laughed at the antics, relieved they didn’t seem afraid. It would get dark in a couple of hours, and he couldn’t well leave two little babes by themselves.

“No crown. Queens have crowns,” the child added.

“Ah, you talk, I hear.” That was a relief, too. “Where’s your mama? Can you show me where you live?”

“No, we lost.” It sounded very-matter-of fact, as if there was no concern at all. Maybe they were used to romping around in the woods by themselves.

"How old are you?" Nikolaos asked.

"Twenty-three and my bother is sixteen," the little tot said, not quite managing the word brother, holding up three fingers.

"Ah, grown up and all I see," Nikolaos said, trying not to laugh. "I'll put you both on Kristina's back and then I'll climb up behind you. What do you say to that?" He had been right. At least the youngest was a boy. "What are your names?"

Neither of them replied.

Nikolaos shrugged, then carefully picked them up one at a time. It made him think of how he used to lift his grandchildren. Babies who had all lived full lives and were long since dead.

Nikolaos followed the path ahead, figuring it would lead to people eventually. The boys, if that's what they both were, sat resting between his arms and felt so round and warm that he was tempted to kiss their heads.

After a while, he heard a door slam somewhere and a rooster crowing. Then the forest thinned, and dark freshly plowed fields appeared near a cluster of smaller farms. A lake glittered behind a barn on the far right. It was beautiful. And empty, no one seemed to be running around frantically looking for lost children.

"Do you live in there?" Nikolaos tried, pointing to the first homestead they approached. It was a cottage with a nice garden in front, full of blue flowers and thriving herbs.

The babes shook their heads. But as they approached the second house, the oldest pointed eagerly and started to squirm. They were clearly home. Nikolaos slowed Kristina and steered her into the courtyard. A pig was resting in the corner, gazing at them lazily as a group of geese came running, flapping their wings and squawking loudly. Then the door opened and a woman with flushed skin and sweaty uncovered hair peered out, eyes widening in recognition.

She hurried out and quickly closed the door behind her. "You're on horseback? Didn't you go over to Gunnel's like you were told? You have a sister. A brand-new little sister!"

"Good day," Nikolaos said, dismounting. A birth, that explained why their mother wasn't with them. He helped the children down, and as soon as they were on the ground, they ran off. "Found them in the woods, all alone. They told me they were lost." He wasn't able to keep the scolding from his voice.

The woman shrugged. "Not my responsibility, their mother told them to run over to Gunnel so she could labor in peace."

"I understand, but there are wolves and bears out there. Couldn't their father have taken them there?"

"Their father is dead."

Nikolaos inclined his head, mortified. He shouldn't have made presumptions. "My sincere condolences. May he rest in peace."

She gave a tired smile and nodded. "I thank you for helping us. Is there anything I could get you to show our gratitude?"

"No need but thank you kindly just the same. How old are they? Both boys?"

The woman looked around for them, but they were nowhere to be seen. "Yes, both boys, Tobias is two and a winter, Tyge will be four, come harvest time."

"Tyge knows the words for high numbers already," Nikolaos said with a smile as he put his left foot in the stirrup.

"Yes, he says he's twenty-three like his father was when he died. He's heard it mentioned, and I gather it's a child's way to want to be like his father." A shadow crossed her face.

Nikolaos swung his right leg across Kristina's back and sat down in the saddle. "My condolences again to the family." He crossed himself. How heartbreaking, he had just thought the boy had his numbers mixed up.

"I thank you. Why don't I go in and get you a couple of eggs for the trouble? I don't want to hear you say no again," she said firmly, wagging a finger in the air.

Nikolaos stayed where he was, smiling at both her and the thought of eggs, watching as she carefully closed the door behind her. Only a moment later she came back out and closed the door just as carefully again. Maybe she was afraid a troll would come and swap the baby for its own like Karin had spoken of.

"Pray take it, there is plenty here. Neighbors have been generous since she became a widow," she said, gesturing at the geese and a group of chickens behind the house. "We all take our catechism to heart here." She held up the eggs, wrapped in a frayed piece of sack.

"I thank you kindly," Nikolaos said and bent down, grabbing the parcel from her. It felt heavy. She had been generous. "It was a delight to help them. They remind me of my own," he added without thinking.

"Oh, no wonder. You're a father yourself then?"

Nikolaos nodded and quickly turned Kristina around, leaving before she could ask him for more details. It was a stupid slip. He had to remember to be ready with an explanation. Best would be to pretend he had misheard and had answered the wrong question.

Once out on the road again, he let the reins go and rested the parcel on his thigh while he opened it. There were two peeled, boiled eggs and a sausage. Nikolaos grabbed one of the eggs and put the whole thing straight into his mouth, devouring it with barely a chew, grabbing the second one before he finished it. He was going to save the sausage but ate that too, albeit a bite at a time. It was salty and greasy and delicious. The food in Stockholm hadn't even been that good. What had he been thinking, hiding in his cave all those years, living only on fish and whatever meat he managed to hunt for? Nikolaos shook his head at himself, imagining all the meals he would eat in the future.

The boys and the food put him in a gloriously good mood, and he decided to ride down to the edge of the village to look at the lake. Perhaps he could ask someone for something to drink as a way of introduction. The sausage had made him very thirsty.

But every farm he passed lay deserted with only animals milling about. Where was everyone? It seemed unusually quiet for a village this time of day? Maybe they were all resting after their midday meal.

As he approached the lake, he spotted a brewhouse on the beach. It was right below the last farm which was up on a small hill on the right. Just seeing it intensified his thirst. He urged Kristina into a gallop. The brewhouse protruded over the water, supported on strong poles, and there was a three-step staircase on the beachside. The door above it was wide open. It couldn't hurt to pay it a visit; Maybe they had a pitcher in there for tasting.

Casting a glance around and not seeing anyone, he got off Kristina, tied her to a tree, and hurried up the little steps. A woman was standing there with her back at him, scrubbing the inside of an ale tub so ferociously she didn't hear him and leaning so deeply into the tub that her skirts lifted well above her ankles. Attractive ankles. Nikolaos hoped the rest of her was as beautiful.

He gave the doorsill three quick raps with the back of his hand.

The woman straightened and turned to look at him, looking surprised but not frightened. "Pray, can I help you?"

"Afternoon to you," Nikolaos said and removed his hat, feeling his own smile widen at the sight of her. She was gorgeous. Her thick wheat-colored braids were coming apart from atop her head, her eyes were blue, her cheeks rosy, and her breasts full and barely covered by her bodice. It truly had been a mistake living up in his cave for so long. "I was hoping that someone was here. I was gifted a bit to eat earlier after helping two little boys who had managed to get lost in the woods while their mother was in labor. You wouldn't have some ale for me, would you? The meal made me quite thirsty." He hoped it didn't sound like boasting.

"Britt had the baby? Everything went as it should? Bless her. Poor woman, she's a widow now."

"Yes, she did. I didn't stay long, but it seems the baby is fine. It's a girl. Where is everyone? The village seems deserted."

"They've all gone to the funeral, except Britt and her boys then I take it," she said, as if he would know whose funeral it was.

"Ah, that explains why no one noticed the boys getting lost."

She met his eyes without comment, then went to a table full of wooden mugs, took two, and filled them from a small barrel on the floor. "I know I'm not supposed to drink any, but since Mickelsson is away, it'll make no difference. They won't know."

"Who is Mickelsson?"

"He's the farmer here, Lars Mickelsson." There was a tone of surprise in her voice. "It's his cousin who died." She pulled out a stool from under the table and sat on it. "I know I'm not supposed to drink any, but they're away. It's going to be a while yet before they get back," she repeated, looking at him over the rim of her mug. When she finished, she licked her lips and rested her mug on her lap. Her bosom was moving up and down with each breath as if she were winded.

Nikolaos tried not to stare at it, but the water under the brewhouse was pulling at him, and he couldn't help getting aroused. Taking deep breaths to try to calm himself he started for the table so he could put the mug back and go home. Then just as he stood, she looked into his eyes, holding his gaze. Maybe he could have her if there was no husband nearby. It had been so long since he had a woman. Much too long. "Are you married?" he asked, feeling a bit embarrassed, but he had to know.

She giggled and touched her hair as if to remind him her hair wasn't covered. "No, I'm not married. Mickelsson wouldn't let me go to the funeral. He wanted me to stay here and get everything ready."

Nikolaos stepped closer slowly, trying to sense her reaction. She didn't move or seem afraid. Maybe if she walked with him, he could get her to agree. "Would you go outside with me for a bit? Can you show me the lake?"

"Gladly. Who are you? Where are you from?"

"I'm a musician, a fiddler. I'm living up in the forest back there." He gestured toward his cave as best he could. There was no reason to tell her he didn't live in a proper house.

"All alone?" She took his mug and placed it along with hers on the table.

"Yes. May I ask your name?" Nikolaos asked and made his way down the steps, then turned to wait for her.

"Karin," she said, lifting her skirts so as not to step on them as she went down.

He stared at her. Rusty devils, of all the names in the

kingdom, she would have to have the same name just to remind him of what knowing him could do.

"You look upset, what's bothering you?" She reached for his arm, then removed her hand.

"It's nothing. My name is Nikolaos. Pray show me the lake." He smiled, trying to soften what he said. It had come out harsher than he meant.

"Nikolaos." She returned his smile and didn't seem bothered by his tone. She had great teeth, too. "We call it Mickels Pond after the farmer here. There isn't a lot of fish. His cousin wasn't old, but it's been a poor year for most with another long cold winter, and she was weak. Mickelsson says that we don't get a lot of fish in the lake. It freezes to the bottom each year."

"I see." Nikolaos wasn't sure what the cousin had to do with the lake but decided not to ask, following Karin as she made her way around the brewhouse to the beach.

She sat down on the pebbly ground and gestured for him to sit beside her. "I've not been anywhere, so I wouldn't know how it might be in other places or in other lakes. My parents and I have lived here since I was a baby, working for Mickelsson. He's a good farmer, kind to us and fair. It devastated him when he learned that his cousin needed to be laid to her final rest. I've always wondered how things are elsewhere. But chickens lay good eggs here."

Nikolaos nodded uncertainly. She seemed to have trouble staying on topic. "I've learned as much. I just had two from the widow's farm, very good eggs," he said and sat down, ignoring her other comments.

The lake was pretty. It was small, thereof its name, he supposed, with light brown water and a muddy bottom. Gentle waves moved across the surface, enticing him. He averted his eyes and turned towards Karin. She had her eyes closed, and her face turned toward the sun. He smiled, then shifted his attention back to the lake and jerked back with alarm. The water was churning.

He stood abruptly, already feeling the familiar coolness as his blood turned to water. "I should take you back to the brewhouse," he said, holding his hand out to help Karin up.

She took his hand, coming to stand right in front of him. They were so very close. Just one step and he could bring her into the wetness. The water was coming closer rapidly, bubbling upward and covering more and more of the beach. Nikolaos forced his face away from it, then just as the first wave reached his feet, he stepped away, pulling Karin with him. Gasping with restraint, he let go of her and turned away. He had almost pushed her in!

"Nikolaos, what happened? Are you feeling poorly?" She had walked around him and was gazing into his face.

"Pray forgive me. No, I'm not ill. But I should go now. I have to get home, and your people will be getting back soon I assume?"

"Yes, but not yet. Come and have something to eat too. You do look pale," she said and hurried back to the brewhouse. He followed, both relieved and disappointed.

Karin gave him another mug of ale and a piece of smoked herring. It was tasty, but the water beneath their feet was all he could think about. He ate and drank as fast as he could, then bowed in thanks and was out the door, taking the steps in one leap.

Moving out of sight, he went to a bush to relieve himself. The pee came out in a strong stream from all the ale. He had been given enough and should get Kristina, go back to his cave, and never come this way again. Find another village somewhere where he could settle down. He had already befouled his reputation when he told the midwife he had children. But before he even finished the thought, he shook his already stiffening penis dry, put it back in his breeches, and went straight back to Karin.

She was waiting for him, warm and ready, kissing and touching him everywhere, grabbing at his clothes. He laughed. She was not as innocent as he had thought. "We can do it in the tub, it's big enough. I just cleaned it," she whispered.

It was all that was needed. He took her by the hand and helped her lie down in it. They both fit easily, and the tub was wide enough for her legs to spread. He touched her face, kissing her and pulling at her braids to let her hair loose. It was thick and smooth, warm with sweat near her scalp. Then he pulled his breeches down, arranged her skirts, and slipped inside, thanking God that he had been able to wait until they got back indoors.

They stayed in the tub. Karin rested on his chest, chatting about ale production and hops. It wasn't very interesting, and Nikolaos closed his eyes and dozed off. He had been out for a while when he was startled awake by Karin clambering out, clearly panicked.

"Go, you have to go, they're coming back, the dogs are barking. Hurry, I pray you, I can hear the carriage. If you make a right, you can go around the lake and won't have to take the road past the farms. Hurry!"

"Pray forgive me, I fell asleep." Nikolaos got out so quickly he banged his knee on the tub. It hurt, but he swallowed the pain. Karin was staring out the door towards the road as she plaited her hair into two braids, retying them to the top of her head. "I'll be back. Wait for me, I'll be here in a couple of days," he said, ignoring his promise to himself from earlier, then pushed himself past Karin and hurried out.

She barely looked at him.

He didn't see anyone approach but wasn't going to stay to find out if she had been right and was barely sitting in the saddle before Kristina was galloping in the opposite direction from whence they came.

Chapter 23

Nikolaos couldn't stop thinking about Karin. The fine ankles under her skirts when she scrubbed the ale tub, her thick braided hair. She was kind but a little odd. He couldn't quite explain what it was, but she seemed a little too innocent. Or perhaps it was just the age difference. Karin was well over marriageable age but could be no more than seventeen, maybe eighteen. He was over two hundred years old.

If he was ever going to marry again, it would have to be with someone like her, young and giggly. It felt strange to think it, but Karin Persdotter would have been a better choice in some ways. He would have enjoyed the company and have more in common with her. Even so, she would have felt like his great-grandmother. And they would put him in the stocks. Young men didn't marry such old women.

Only three days later, Nikolaos returned to the village and the brewhouse. He took the backroad, coming in from the lakeside instead of riding through the whole village. There wasn't a clear view of the front of the brewhouse from this direction, and he had to double back to try to see it through the trees along the road. The door was firmly closed. He sighed with disappointment. Karin had spoken in such detail about ale making, it sounded like she spent every day in the brewhouse. But it was unlikely she was inside with the door closed; it was too warm.

Staying where he was, Nikolaos stared at it for several moments, then shifted his gaze toward the lake. There was a birch grove on the far side. The trunks were thick with age, and there was knee-high grass growing in the spaces between them. If he sat over there, it would keep him out of sight but give him a clear view of the village and the brewhouse. He urged Kristina into a gallop, making his way around the lake to the spot. Dismounting, he tied her to a bush and walked over to the birch grove.

He found a good tree and sat down. The grass was even taller than it had looked and reached well above his chest, hiding him perfectly while giving him a great view of the village. It was clear that it was a different place from last time. Now people milled about, women hurried between the outbuildings, carrying baskets filled to the brim with linen, laughing and chatting as they passed each other. Toddlers were getting scooped up by adults who ruffled their hair before they put them back down. Older children carried things that looked like gardening tools. It seemed like a friendly sort of place, full of life, reminding him of his own village before they all got suspicious of him.

It was beautiful on this side of the lake, too. There wasn't a beach to speak of, just more grass with vividly blue cornflowers and bright orange poppies along the water's edge. He leaned back and rested his back against the tree, keeping a relaxed gaze on the brewhouse.

The sun had moved a good way across the sky when a door at Mickelson's farm was thrown open, and people dispersed in different directions. Four men disappeared behind the barn, hurrying somewhere, just as two women entered the farmhouse. And then there was Karin, leaving after they stepped inside, and heading straight down to the brewhouse.

Nikolaos got to his feet, pulled his boots and outer shirt off, then ran to the lake and dove straight in, shooting across it. He was already underneath the brewhouse by the time he heard Karin's footsteps on the floor planks.

She was organizing something on the table in the corner, facing the door. Her hand flew to her mouth when she spotted him. "You're soaked, what happened? Did you fall in?"

Nikolaos laughed. "Yes... you could say that. I fell in." He looked down at the floor, finding two puddles around his feet. It had been an idiotic thing to do. What in the world had he been thinking?

"The Lord be praised you didn't drown."

"Indeed." Drown. The Lord wasn't the one praising him.

"Let me see if I can get you something to dry you with. I should have a blanket here somewhere. We cover the hopsacks with it sometimes." Karin went to the corner and moved two smaller sacks aside then pulled out a gray blanket. "Here," she said, wrapping it around his shoulders with a reproaching look. "What were you doing that made you fall into the lake? You wouldn't want to catch a chill. Next time, wait by the road and whistle for me instead. I'll hear you. What if it had been the farmer's wife instead of me? She'd have fainted and called for her husband. He would've thought you a thief. I'll tell you, you don't want his wrath upon you."

"You're right, I should've been careful, but I wanted to see you, and I hurried too much," he said and leaned forward to kiss her cheek, trying not to laugh at her comment. The wife couldn't have called for her husband if she lay unconscious in a faint.

Karin blushed, throwing a glance at the outside to make sure they were alone, then snuck her arms around his waist under the blanket. "Oh, you really are completely soaked. How did you fall?"

"Well.... to tell you the truth, I didn't actually *fall* in. I saw you coming, and I decided that it was quicker to swim than to get around the lake. Riding would have brought too much attention to the fact that I wanted to kiss you, so I just dove in."

She pulled her arms away from him, staring at him with such a shocked expression that he realized he shouldn't have said anything. "You swam?"

"Yes." Nikolaos tried a sheepish smile but to no effect. Karin looked horrified, as if she couldn't understand what was happening, moving backward until her back hit the wall. Did she realize who he was? "I didn't mean to frighten you," he said. "I learned to swim as a young boy, helping my father when his fishing nets got stuck," he said it slowly, using the vicinity of the water to push his power into her, feeling rather pleased with the fishing net story.

She relaxed visibly. "You frightened me. I've never known anyone who's done anything like that before. I thought water was dangerous. It seeps into your body and can make you sick. I don't think you should do that again."

"I'll take your advice," he said, nodding as if he were considering it. "I came because I wanted to see you. I've been thinking of nothing but you and your beautiful face since I first saw you."

She giggled, sounding almost herself again.

Nikolaos planted his hands on the wall on each side of her, ignoring the blanket falling off, then kissed her cheeks, her eyes, and her left ear. He could smell soil and herbs and pictured her pulling a loose strand of hair behind her ear as she was bending over to prune Mickelsson's wife's herbal garden, wherever it was.

Karin leaned into him and put her arms around his waist again, and he pulled her toward the ale tub and made her lie down behind it, kissing her as he pulled up her skirts. She was slippery and ready, her breasts pushing on his chest. He climaxed earlier than he wanted.

"You're so beautiful. I've been alone for so long. Could you come with me? Pray come and stay with me for a little while," he whispered, putting his mouth close to her ear.

Karin shivered and playfully pushed his head away, simultaneously throwing a glance out the door. "I can't just leave here. I have work to do. Maybe after church if I could get away. By the way, why have we never seen you in church?" She sat up and straightened her skirts and bodice.

She was right; he ought to find a church to attend. It would cause suspicion otherwise like it had in Norrköping. "I'm attending a church closer to my home," he lied.

"I see."

Nikolaos climbed out of the tub and glanced down at her. Her skirts were wet from where he had laid on her. "Would you like me to come with you? I could always explain that I fell in, and you helped me," he said with a sideways grin, gesturing toward the wet spots.

"Lord no, you're mad. How would that look?" Karin giggled loudly and clasped her hand in front of her mouth to stop herself. It seemed slightly hysterical. "I have to go back up. I can't stay idle for this long. They'll look for me. I've lost my mind letting you in here soaking wet in the middle of the day on a Thursday like this. Don't do this again, next time go around the lake and wait for me. If you see me, whistle like a bird, and I'll come see you."

"Well, I wouldn't call you idle." He grinned.

She laughed. It didn't sound hysterical this time.

***

They saw each other every week. Nikolaos was astounded how he, yet again, could have lived so close to something, completely unaware of its existence for so long. He had lived one hundred and thirty years without knowing that Norrköping's House was only days away, and now this village was barely half a day from his waterfall. It confirmed what Old Karin, it was how he thought of her now, had said about people knowing of his whereabouts. He ought to be more careful, more aware of who might be watching. People might have seen him walk around in his animal skins. No wonder they had figured out who he was. If he was going to live in the village openly, he would need new clothes, perhaps even tobacco and a pipe. Make it look like he was not only human but a modern man.

Karin had told him that there was a tailor at an old farmstead south of the village. It was high time he paid him a visit.

As soon as Nikolaos entered the yard, he noticed how large the tailor's windows were. The shutters were open and flooded the home with so much light he could see everything inside. There was a table with strips of leather in the middle of the room and chairs next to an equally large window on the opposite side. The tailor must be doing well to be able to afford so much expensive glass.

Nikolaos dismounted and knocked on the door, taking a step back while listening for sounds from inside. It was completely silent. He knocked one more time, then went to look through the windows again but saw nothing. The tailor wasn't at home.

He had his left foot in the stirrup and was about to get back in the saddle when he felt the scent of tobacco in the air. Moments later a dog barked, and then three hound dogs tore into the yard at full speed. He quickly pulled his foot out of the stirrup and grabbed a stronger hold of Kristina's reins to keep her steady. The dogs stopped in their tracks a few paces in front of them, barking ferociously, creating sharp flashes of orange and icy pale blue. Kristina's hooves moved nervously.

"Hush!" Nikolaos said both to the hounds and to Kristina.

Someone whistled, and the dogs scampered off as a man came running toward him. "My sincere apologies, pray forgive the dogs. They're a bit enthusiastic sometimes."

Nikolaos stared at him, forgetting all about the dogs. It was Karl from Norrköping's House! He couldn't believe it. "Karl, what in the world are you doing here?"

Karl shook his head with an amused look on his face. "You knew my father?"

"Pardon me?" Nikolaos frowned with confusion. Then he understood, feeling silly. It couldn't be Karl obviously. He would have been at least seventy-five years old by now. But the tailor looked just like him, except he had a full head of hair. Could it truly be his son?

"My father, did you know him?" the tailor asked again. "He passed on, some years back."

Nikolaos hesitated, feeling disoriented. "No, I must be mistaken," he said after much too long a pause. "You look very much like someone I used to know a few years ago named Karl. Was your father's name Karl as well? That's rather uncanny."

He laughed. "I'm Jon. Indeed uncanny, I thought you must have known him. We look alike, everyone says. Could you have known him when you were a child?"

"Probably not. I'm new to the area," Nikolaos said, noticing now that Jon was stocky and was probably taller than Karl had been.

Jon looked at him silently, then shrugged and shifted his gaze to Nikolaos' clothes, scanning up and down the length of his body. "How can I help you? I take it you're here for my tailoring and not in need of my healing herbs. Breeches are mostly done differently now. You're wearing your older brother's?"

"My cousin's," Nikolaos lied. "And yes, tailoring services is what I need."

"Tie your horse to the pole there, then come with me and we'll take a look, shall we?" Jon said, pointing to a tall stick attached to the corner of the house.

Nikolaos nodded, grateful to have a moment to sort out his thoughts.

Jon's home was organized in minute details. Everything had its own proper place depending on its use. Shelves with leather and linen, trays with buttons in different colors and sizes, sewing needles and thread, and baskets full of dried herbs. There was a strong scent of something bitter, but not unpleasant.

Jon made Nikolaos stand in front of the window facing the back of the house and brought over a strip of leather with numbers etched into it. "Tell me what you need, and I'll take your measurements. I can do everything. There's no limit to my skills," he said, eyes glinting impishly. He looked just like Karl.

"It depends," Nikolaos said, hiding an overwhelming sense of nostalgia. "I'd like to have another set of breeches, a linen shirt, a warm jacket or a frock, perhaps a waistcoat. The question is your price and if you'd be willing to trade?" He held his breath. If Jon wouldn't trade, he could only pray his ignorance didn't show too much, not knowing what kind of cost to expect or how much coins were worth these days.

"Trade?" Jon's smile faded, and he threw Nikolaos a look of surprise. "Well, people usually pay me for it, but what can you do to get me to reconsider?"

"Good question, I can always hunt or fish for you, and I play the fiddle," Nikolaos said, hoping for the best.

Jon's face lit up again. "My father did too! Played for me and my mother every night, bagpipe mostly though. He used to play in a castle when he was young. Even entertained her Royal Highness Princess Elisabet Vasa." Jon's eyes widened as he spoke. "My mother was a kitchen maid there, cooked for the royals every day," he said proudly.

Nikolaos met his gaze, feeling something warm in his chest. There was no doubt then, it was Karl's son. "Princess Vasa? That's something," he said. Sinful as it was, he was glad Karl was dead. What would he have said, had he seen him?

"Yes, isn't it? They were both very fond of that time," Jon said, placing the measuring strip against Nikolaos' hip, then letting one end fall to his feet. "My mother especially took a lot of pride in it."

"I can imagine. What was her name?"

"Herdis."

Nikolaos nodded. He didn't recognize it but didn't remember if he was ever told what the maids' names were. Besides, she may have worked there long after he left, Karl had been quite resistant to marriage when he knew him.

When Jon had finished his calculations, he picked up a piece of coal from a small shelf and wrote down the numbers directly on the wall behind them. Then he replaced the coal on its shelf and lifted his chin in the direction of a jug on the table. "Want to wet your lips a bit?"

"Why not? I thank you kindly. I take it you were born there then, at the castle."

"No, my parents moved here after it burnt down. I was born here," he said, while grabbing two goblets from another shelf. He poured ale for them both and handed one of the goblets to Nikolaos.

"The castle burnt down?" Nikolaos asked incredulously.

"Indeed, it did, and not only that, but the King was to hold his council meeting there, which obviously never happened."

"Ohhh," he crossed himself, "Was it Gustav the II?"

"I believe it was the one before," Jon said, scratching his head and taking a large sip of ale at the same time. "I never remember his name, Karl the...? To tell you the truth, I'm not sure."

"Karl IX," Nikolaos said and sipped as well. It tasted very good, better than what Karin had given him. Hadn't the previous castle burned, too? Yes, it had been done on purpose to prevent the Danes from taking it. That man who had invited him into his home and told him to look for work at Norrköping's House had told him. He couldn't remember his name anymore.

"That's who they said! Yes, that's him," Jon exclaimed, interrupting Nikolaos' memories. "My father told me of the fire, said it was awful. A terrible day. He wasn't one that became afraid easily, but this... he became visibly shaken each time he spoke of it. The fire started on one of the upper floors. A tapestry had come off the wall, and a corner of it ended up in a fireplace. Whoever saw it called for help and ran to get water, but by the time they got back with buckets, the whole room was lit."

"Did they save the birds?" Nikolaos asked without thinking, picturing their tiny, colorful wings flapping in panic.

"Hmm," Jon frowned, "I've not heard of any birds. What do you mean?"

"It was just an assumption. I heard someone talking about castles always having large cages with birds in them. It might not be true of course," Nikolaos said, trying to play it off.

"Never knew that, how odd."

Nikolaos shrugged, then quickly changed the subject. "Would you consider trading? I'd be most grateful."

Jon pursed his lips, humming a bit before he answered. "You mentioned fishing and hunting. It's reasonable. I actually do get chickens and eggs in exchange for smaller jobs like buttons or broken seams, so why not? I thank you kindly."

Nikolaos smiled with relief. Then they shook hands on it.

Absorbed in his memories on his way back from the tailor, Nikolaos jumped at a sudden sound ahead. It was Karin, sitting on a log at the crossroad between the village and the tailor, crying softly with her face in her hands.

"Karin, what are you doing here? And what ails you? Has something happened?"

Karin gazed up at him with a tearstained face. "Oh Nikolaos, I'm so glad to see you. I was hoping you had gone to visit the tailor today. I don't know what to do! I don't know what to doo..." The last came out as a drawn-out sob, and she rocked back and forth, clutching her stomach.

Nikolaos put his right leg over Kristina's neck and then

jumped straight down, tossing the reins over a branch.

"Karin, what's happened?"

She didn't answer.

He sat down beside her and tried to grab her hands, but she was holding her stomach too tightly. "Pray tell me, why are you crying?"

"There's something very wrong with me. I can't eat." She turned to look at him with an unfocused and flickering gaze. Her eyes were red and swollen. She must have cried for a long time.

"You can't eat? Do you have pains in your stomach?"

"No, but something isn't right. I'm sure of it." She burst out laughing hysterically.

Startled, Nikolaos slid sideways, away from her. "Take a breath of air, deep breath. You're scaring my horse. Try to calm down," he said, flicking Kristina an eye, dismissing a fleeting thought that he could just get up and leave.

Then Karin stopped and took a shuttering breath.

He smiled encouragingly. "There, that's good. Pray tell me what's wrong.

"You mightn't know of things like this, but women… We… every so often, very often actually. We have… there's blood. Blood in a very private part of ourselves."

He almost laughed. Did she expect him to be this ignorant? "I'm aware of what it is."

At that, she threw herself into his arms, sobbing violently again, grabbing his arms so hard it hurt. He gently removed them and pulled her up so that she was sitting again.

"Now, you must calm down, take another deep breath, and tell me. I implore you."

Nodding, she sucked air into herself and wiped tears from her cheeks with the back of her hand. "I know something is wrong because no longer do I get the bleedings and I can't eat in the mornings. I throw up. It's why I can't eat."

Nikolaos stared at her, shocked at her ignorance. Then, the reality of her words sank in, and something cold settled in his stomach. She was with child. Of course! He was an idiot. A real idiot. He should never have gone back to the brewhouse.

"Nikolaos?"

"Pray forgive me. Karin, surely you see what's happening. There's nothing wrong, you're expecting. We're to have a baby," he said, trying to keep his voice neutral.

"A baby? No, Nikolaos, that can't be. We're not betrothed. You know that."

He looked at her silently. Maybe it was the new way to keep your daughters ignorant of these things. Still, he was surprised. Karin seemed too intense, too unaware. "Yes," he said, nodding for emphasis, "I do know that, but we've been lying together several times now. It oughtn't be a surprise."

"What does that have to do with it?"

Nikolaos had to look away to hide his disbelief. "Karin," he said, turning back to her, "it's laying together that makes babies. It doesn't have to do with marriage or betrothals. It's just that most people who do, *are* married or at least promised. We should have waited. Forgive me."

Her eyes widened. "You know a lot. How do you know all this? How old are you? I thought you were my age, but from your words I think differently. Yes, I think differently now. I think you're much older, maybe twenty-three already. Are you married? Is that how you know all this?"

He smiled sadly, grateful for her unintentional suggestion. "I'm twenty-four, but no, I haven't had the opportunity to meet a lovely girl before. I suggest that we start planning for our betrothal."

"You do? Why would we do that?"

Rusty devils. He leaned backward, letting his back rest on the tree behind the log they were sitting on, and closed his eyes briefly. She was dimwitted. It couldn't just be age. What had happened to him? He had been a father, grandfather, and a great-grandfather. A responsible farmer. Lately, it seemed as if life was spinning too fast and he could barely control it. Johannes had drowned. Old sweet Karin, they hung mercilessly, and now he had made a young girl pregnant who didn't seem to understand the implications. Could he start a new family, have children, grandchildren, and great-grandchildren with someone like her? It seemed an unbearable undertaking.

He opened his eyes and noticed Karin looking at him. She sat still now, quiet and thoughtful. She looked so vulnerable, and he felt ashamed of his thoughts about her.

"Nikolaos, I don't understand everything. I know I ought to be married at this age, but seventeen is still young and I have a lot to learn. Had I been married, I would have known more. Pray don't be angry with me."

Nikolaos patted her shoulder, wondering at her ability to be surprised at his proposal yet ruminating that she ought to be married and apologizing that she wasn't. "This is what I suggest, Karin," he said. "Dry your tears now, and then go back home. I'll think of a good time for our betrothal. My home isn't suitable, and we'd need to find somewhere else to live, so it may be good to wait a while before you say something. Maybe we should move to a town where I can provide for us. I've lived well on my music before. I'll have to wait for my clothes to finish. Jon up here," he pointed in the direction he had come, "is having several items done for me. Then we'll see. I'll speak to your father and…"

"My parents are both gone, they died," she interrupted. "I didn't want to tell you, but it's true. You'll have to ask Mickelsson."

"Dead? Why didn't you want to tell me?"

"I'm sad. It makes me sad to talk about them."

Nikolaos nodded and pulled her closer. He couldn't quite put into words how he felt. One thing after the other surprised him about her, and he didn't like it. Still, he felt his attraction stirring when he sat with her, felt his heart open at her innocence.

Nikolaos played his violin for hours that night, playing until the roaring waterfall became his strings, bursting with color. When night came, he climbed up to his stream and swam upriver in the dark water.

Chapter 24

Nikolaos figured that he would need some kind of explanation for why there was so much he didn't know. Pondering it for a couple of days, he decided to confide in Jon and tell him the truth. A very small version of it, anyway.

"Aww, they look mighty fine!" Jon hollered when he saw Nikolaos approach with two freshly killed hares in front of the saddle. Jon was sitting on a small rock by his house wall, feet stretched out on the ground. He stood up and hurried toward him. His dogs were watching Nikolaos' arrival lazily in stark contrast to their first introduction.

"I think so too. This may be a bit forward of me, but I thought to invite myself in for dinner. I'll of course present these hares as a dinner gift and not as part of your payment. There's more where this came from."

Jon smiled with genuine pleasure. "How kind of you. Pray do. Hand them over and tie your horse up in the same place as last. Let me skin these here hares and fry them for us, eh? You go behind the house. I have benches and a table set up near the hops. There's good shade. Sit a while when I get this ready, eh?"

"I'm glad to, I thank you." Nikolaos drew a sigh of relief. It was boding well so far.

He made his way round back, finding the table and the benches. The hop bushes shaded nicely, just like Jon said. There was a stone enclosure abounding with several different herbs in neat rows. Little wooden placards were placed in front of every row, each with pictures of body parts, like eyes and ears, stomach and throat, head and neck. Others were for only eyes, only teeth, or even for the left hand, while another was for the right hand. Jon clearly knew medicines. It could be helpful when he told him of his dilemma.

Jon came back, carrying a tray with a plate heaping with meat, mugs of ale, goblets, and a pitcher of dark red wine.

"What a feast!" Nikolaos said, his mouth watering. "Wine

too, I thank you kindly."

Jon acknowledged him with a nod and placed the meat between them, then poured him a goblet full. "We have a seller who comes here twice a year. He ought to be back at harvest time, if not before."

Nikolaos sipped slowly, letting it sit in his mouth before he swallowed. It was a bit dryer than he liked but had a nice fruity aftertaste. "It's very good," he said.

They ate in silence for a while, both enjoying the meal. It was delicious, perfectly flavored with Jon's herbs and spices.

"I'm impressed with your cooking, or is your wife at home?" Nikolaos asked. He had just assumed Jon was a widower, but maybe his wife was inside.

Jon shook his head. "No wife. I do it all myself. I had a woman come help me a few years back, but I've not married. I've wanted to, but God saw otherwise." A fleeting shadow of sadness passed across his face.

"I see, I'm sorry to hear that." Ironic, living alone was what Karl had wanted for himself, at least while he knew him. He wished he could tell Jon that. Nikolaos put his knife down. "To tell you the truth, I invited myself to dinner to ask you for some advice, can I?"

"Of course. I suspected as much."

Nikolaos took a breath, nodding. "I want to ask you first if you can kindly keep what I'm telling you private. It's a bit of a delicate situation and troublesome as well. I'd appreciate your discretion."

Jon nodded gravely. "Yes. I can keep a confidence. It's something I take very seriously as a matter of fact. People often tell me private things when they want me to cure them of their ills."

"I figured," Nikolaos said, tilting his head towards Jon's herbs.

"Good. Then you know you can trust in my silence. What ails you."

Nikolaos did his best to seem both concerned and nervous, taking a couple of visible breaths. "I've lost my memory. I don't know who I am. I don't know where I'm from or how old I am, and

I'm not sure who my parents are or if I have siblings, though I think I have sisters for some reason." He added that, just then remembering that he had told Karin he had a sister when he had actually been talking about one of his daughters. "I'm confused by things. Once, I ran into a post-runner but didn't know what he was doing. I thought he was a musician. I remember nothing… I don't even know how to explain this. I…" Nikolaos paused for effect, watching Jon's face closely. His expression was calm. "I know that my name is Nikolaos and that the stuff I found in my bundle and satchels are mine, like my fiddle and my catechism. My clothes are not my cousin's like I said. It was a lie. I assume they're mine, but…" Nikolaos trailed off, picking up a tiny piece of meat from the plate with his thumb, and licked it.

Jon remained silent.

"I don't know if I'm married, which is a bit of a… actually it's a big problem because I'm planning my betrothal."

"You are?" Jon grinned, but then his smile faded. "I see, well, one thing at a time. Go on."

"Another matter is that I don't, as far as I know at least, have a place to live. I found a cave half a day's ride from here where I've been camping. There is a wat…"

"You don't live in the cave by the waterfall, do you?" Jon interrupted, eyes widening. "Pray tell me you don't, dear lord!"

"Yes, that's the very place. Why shouldn't I?"

"I don't advise living there. Näcken has been seen in those parts." He swallowed visibly.

"Who?" Nikolaos made sure he didn't avert his eyes. Jon knew. He should have expected this.

"Näcken… he, ah you don't remember naturally. It's quite the tale…" He trailed off, pursing his lips. "I'll explain who Näcken is, but first, what happened? Did you hit your head?"

Nikolaos shrugged and patted his head as if he were feeling for a bump.

"I didn't hit my head as far as I know. It's hard to describe. I just found myself sitting by a tree. Kristina was tied up next to me, my belongings in a bundle behind her saddle. I didn't know where to go, where I had been, or anything. I still don't. I felt cold and hungry. In fact, that's all I thought at first, that I was thirsty especially. I found a stream and drank from it, and then I thought to look through the satchel and found some salted pork. It's odd. I didn't realize that I didn't know anything. I just felt thirsty and hungry like I said, but I felt myself and wasn't thinking much. But then when I got back on my horse, I realized I didn't know where to go, where I'd been or anything. Anyway, I told you already."

"I see, pray continue."

Nikolaos reached for his leather pouch under his shirt and pulled out two small coins, pushing them across the table to Jon. When he lived in Stockholm, he could get a decent meal for them. "I found these, but I'm not sure what they're worth. I don't recognize them. It's why I offered to hunt for you because I wasn't sure if I had enough."

Jon smiled at that and picked them up, weighing them in his hands. Then he carefully bit into one and then licked it. "Hmmm… they look older than I usually see, but they seem to weigh about the same, taste like they should, too. I say they they'll do. Six or seven more of these and it would cover it. But I'm still happy with you hunting."

"I thank you kindly."

"Did Kristina seem to know you?"

"Yes, she did. She was looking at me as if she had been waiting for me to wake up for a long time. And her name came to me as well."

"It might be why you thought I was someone else that first day. Or maybe you did know my father when you were a child, after all."

Nikolaos looked at him, nodding slowly. He hadn't thought of that. It added nicely to his lie, but if Jon asked how he could remember someone named Karl who looked just like his father, he might ask too many questions. Nikolaos tried to think of something to say to change the subject, but then Jon started talking again.

"And then just like that, you decided to live behind the waterfall. How did you come up with that idea?"

"The weather, I was walking to and fro along the lake trying to figure out what I was doing there, and suddenly the heavens opened up. It rained and hailed, and by a stroke of luck I happened to spot the cave behind the fall." It wasn't visible from down below, but he said it anyway. "There's a path along the side of the fall. It continues all the way up to the stream and to the cave. I was cold already and desperate to get my bearings. Have you been there? It's beautiful and quite comfortable. But to bring a woman, that's another story." Nikolaos stopped talking and looked down into his lap, hoping that he still sounded convincing and wasn't overdoing it. He was probably talking too much.

"I see. No, I've never been there. I've heard of it though." Jon leaned across the table and grabbed Nikolaos' arm, squeezing it. "But don't fret. I'll help you. Let us take this one thing at a time, shall we? Maybe wait on the marriage just a bit, just to see if your memories come back. There's no need to rush things, is there?" He let go of his arm, giving him a look.

"I'm afraid there is. There'll be a baby come winter."

Jon whistled.

"Indeed, it puts me in quite the predicament should I already be married." It sounded so convincing Nikolaos couldn't help but feel proud of himself.

Jon narrowed his eyes. "I'm going to give you some herbs to strengthen your constitution. Let us pray you'll get your memory back and realize you don't already have a family. If you do, then God will still provide somehow. Who's the maiden?"

"It's Karin down at Mickelsson's farm. She's a farm maid." Nikolaos braced himself for Jon's reaction. He wasn't wrong. Jon's eyebrows shot up, and his face made it clear that he had no idea how to respond.

"I know, I know, not the wisest girl there is, I realize that." To his own surprise, he felt himself get hot, eager to defend her.

Jon rubbed his chin with his left hand and pulled on his hair with the other. He still looked taken aback. "Eh…" he said finally, "I must admit it's a bit of a surprise. She's known to… well, she *is* a beauty, a stunning beauty, I see that. I don't know her too well myself. I've seen her in church from time to time. Although I don't venture down to the village enough to go regularly as I should, the pastor is on me about it."

"Yes, that she is." Nikolaos sighed, feeling troubled for real now and embarrassed. "I didn't realize at first. I thought she was just young. It's strange, sometimes she acts as if she's perfectly normal, but other times she appears confused and too intense."

"Yes, yes, it's what people say. One can't always tell with women though. They sometimes act in ways that you can't wrap your head around."

Nikolaos laughed, relaxing a little.

"Nikolaos, how did you come upon Karin Svensdotter," Jon asked, looking concerned again.

"It was a day when I was thirsty. Not that day that I mentioned before, much later. I had just eaten and was desperate for something to drink."

"Did she give you an apple?"

"An apple? No."

"I was asking because if a woman sleeps with an apple near her body and gives it to a man the next day, he's incapable of withstanding her charms."

"She gave me ale and fish. Does that have the same effect?"

"Fish, eh? Maybe. You're sure there's to be a baby? You've... Have you?"

"Yes, more than once. I believe her."

"Well then," Jon narrowed his eyes, "we need to get you out of that cave. There's plenty of land back here where you'd be able to build a home. I'll help. We'll start there and then when your memory comes back, we'll deal with whatever comes then. I don't want you staying in that cave. What if Näcken comes back one night when you're sleeping?"

"I doubt it. He'd run off, don't you think? Kristina would stir and wake me. I've been there for some time already and haven't seen anything."

"No, Nikolaos. Näcken is too dangerous. I wouldn't feel safe up in that old cave. People have seen him there and in the water near it, too. And once I heard that he looked like a bear or maybe it was a wolf."

"If I see him, I'll invite him in and ask him which one he takes after," Nikolaos said with a crooked smile but felt a chill. People must have seen him in his animal skins then.

"Don't joke about this, Nikolaos, it's serious. He lures people into the water and drowns them. Or he bewitches them with spells." Jon crossed himself.

Nikolaos widened his eyes, hoping he looked afraid. For some reason, he was reminded of one of the women who had come to him some time after Abluna died. She had dark red hair and the most voluptuous body he had ever seen. They spent a long time together before she floated away. May God forgive him. He was a monster.

As if God himself had heard Nikolaos' thoughts, Jon added, "I advise you to pray. Go to church often. Ask for forgiveness for your sins to make sure that the Devil doesn't get a hold of you living in that cave. Jon leaned forward, putting his elbows on the table to rest his chin on his crossed fingers. "Nikolaos, I know you said you found the cave after you came to, that day when it started to rain, but I have to ask, is there any way you had gone in that cave before you lost your memory?"

"Why?"

"Well, I just want to make sure that it isn't Näcken who's bewitched you. I hope not, but I wouldn't be surprised if *he* is the cause of your memory loss."

Nikolaos felt his jaw slack and quickly closed his mouth, then he almost laughed. What a brilliant excuse.

"I know, I know, pray forgive me for scaring you," Jon said, his face full of compassion.

Chapter 25

It seemed ridiculous to hide behind the brewhouse when they were planning a betrothal, so Nikolaos decided to ride past the farms instead of taking his usual shortcut. He was just entering the yard, readying himself for an introduction, when he spotted Karin walking by the lake. Just then, someone by the barn noticed him and lifted a hand in a wave. Nikolaos waved back but decided to wait for an introduction until Karin was with him and turned right around again.

"Good morrow to you, beautiful!" he shouted when he caught up with Karin.

She started, but then her face split into a broad smile. "Good morrow, Nikolaos. I was just thinking of you! I wanted to talk to you, tell you that I thought it over and that I want to say yes, I want to be promised to you. If you'll still have me?" She sounded completely reasonable as if she had never been confused about anything.

"Of course I do, sweetheart." He dismounted and brought her into his arms. She pressed herself against him, making him feel guilty for how he had spoken about her the night before. He would learn to love her. "Why don't you ride with me a bit?"

She nodded, and he helped her into the saddle, then climbed up behind her. She smelled of sweat and lake water. There was a slight thickening where his arms touched her sides, and he felt a tinge of excitement at the pit of his stomach.

"I think it's a girl, Karin," he said, feeling very sure that it was for some reason.

"What? What's a girl?"

"The baby, I think our baby will be a girl."

"One can't know that, Nikolaos," she said and put both her hands over his. They felt warm.

Nikolaos smiled to himself at the gesture. She was young, that's all. It was silly to expect her to be like him who had lived the age of several grown men already. Karin left her hands where they were, and it felt so nice to feel the touch of someone again. He stayed quiet, steering Kristina toward the brook behind her farm, deciding to check on the trap he had set there last night on the way to see Jon. It was the same waterway that formed his fall and lake. At first, he had thought it connected to Mickelsson's pond, but it didn't. It widened down here and turned at an angle in the opposite direction.

Nikolaos pulled his right hand out from under Karin's and pointed. "I have a fish trap over there. It should have a fish or two by now, I think. We can make a fire, and you can cook. Why don't you wait right here? I'll go and clear it, and then we'll eat. Are you able to make a fire? Or can you gather wood for it?" he asked, dismounting. As soon as he put his feet on the ground, he felt the nearness of the water. They were too close.

"Of course, I can," Karin said while getting down by herself without difficulty. She went to him, putting her arms around his waist to kiss him.

Nikolaos pushed her away and leaped upon Kristina's back, setting off in a fast trot. "Set up over there," he shouted, gesturing at a patch of sand a good distance from the water. Karin's smile vanished, replaced by an expression of hurt and perplexity. He had to calm down. What was wrong with him?

There were three large fish in the trap. Removing his shoes and stockings, he waded in, pulling out the fish and wringing their necks. The water was churning, leaping up his bare calves. He abruptly stepped out. It was stronger today than usual, and all he could think about was that he wanted to drop the fish and submerge, float over to Karin and pull her in with him, have her in the water. But instead, he put the dead fish under his arm and stared at her. He knew how that would go. It wouldn't be an accident but a conscious choice. Murder.

Ashamed, he walked back, staying as far from the brook as he could. Karin had gathered sticks and piled them on the ground. She gave an uncertain smile, then hurried toward him to take the fish.

He pulled her close, thanking God for protecting them both. "Pray forgive me for rushing before, and for shoving you like that.

I'm just hungry. I'll make the fire, and then we'll talk, shall we?"

"Yes, I'd like that, Nikolaos," she said and squeezed his hand, looking relieved.

Once the fire died down, Karin tended the fish as it cooked over the embers. She expertly deboned them and handed him two, keeping the third one for herself. It tasted wonderful, and the urge to grab her and push her into the water dissipated with each bite. She was with child. With his baby. He was losing his mind.

Nikolaos finished the last piece of his fish, threw the bones on the fire, and turned to her. "I haven't been honest with you. As I mentioned, my home isn't suitable for both of us to live, but the truth is that it isn't a home at all. I've been staying in a cave by a waterfall. It's why it's better for us to wait a month or two before we tell Mickelsson." He searched her eyes, hoping she had never heard the rumors of who lived there. "It would be better if I built something proper for us, a real house."

But Karin looked back at him calmly without the slightest hint of fear. Her lips were moist with fish grease. "You live in a cave? Why? Did you have problems with bears where you lived before?"

"Bears?" He tried not to get distracted by her lips.

"Yes, bears cause a lot of havoc. I thought maybe that's why you chose to live in a cave. Thick walls."

Nikolaos coughed, hiding a laugh. "No, it's not that." There it was again, a disconnect that wasn't entirely illogical. Bears could certainly cause havoc, getting into food stores and even killing people, but usually, they were the ones who lived in caves.

"Maybe we could both live there. And the baby," she added.

"No, living there with a baby wouldn't be wise."

"Why?"

"Well, it's a sort of a temporary home for me, and I think it would be rather dark for a child."

"I see." She narrowed her eyes and looked as if she was about to disagree but then decided against it.

He shrugged and got to his feet to help her up. They stood close for a moment, just holding each other. Suddenly his blood started shifting to water within him, each breath a wave, pulling the water in the brook toward them. Then somehow, he stopped it.

"We ought to leave," he said hoarsely, letting go of her, then turned to the fire pit and kicked dirt on it. It made a sizzling sound. He frowned. The ground was saturated with water, circling them as if they were standing inside a fairy ring. The hem of Karin's dress was soaked. God help him, what was happening to him?

With one sweeping motion, he grabbed Karin around the waist and threw her on Kristina's back, jumped up behind her, and urged Kristina into a gallop, steering toward his cave. It was stupid, of course it was, especially when he was so affected already. He did it anyway, keeping his arms tightly around her waist as they tore through the woods at breakneck speed.

When they neared his lake, he let Kristina ease down to a slow trot, pointing toward it to show Karin, but she stayed silent. Even when the fall became visible, she didn't react. Did she finally understand after all? Maybe she had heard the talk just like Jon had. Nikolaos continued, going all the way to the water's edge. Most of the danger was above the fall where the water was rapid as it rushed down the cliff, he knew that, but given his reaction earlier, it was irresponsible and careless to bring Karin here. It didn't matter that Old Karin had been perfectly safe. Today was different.

He reached for her hand, feeling torn. "Isn't it beautiful, Karin? You see how strong the fall is?"

She didn't answer.

Pulling Kristina back from the water's edge, he let Karin be, staring toward the woods while he considered what to do. There was something at the tree line. A rider approaching steadily. Had someone managed to follow them? Then the rider came out from under the tree shade and rode into the sunlight, and a rush of both relief and disappointment filled his eyes with tears. It was Jon.

Nikolaos swallowed hard, turning Kristina around to face him. By the time Jon reached them, Nikolaos had collected himself enough to sound normal. "Jon! What are you doing here?"

"Good afternoon, Fiddler Nikolaos," Jon said, greeting Karin with a nod. He gave Nikolaos a sharp look, adding a slight shake of his head. It was clear he didn't want to say too much with her there. "I thought of what we spoke of yesterday, and I thought I should come see for myself."

"It's right up there," Nikolaos said, pointing. "I just brought Karin here to show her. I wasn't going to take her up." He paused, feeling ridiculous. It sounded like he was making excuses for himself.

Jon's eyes went to the cave, then shifted back to Nikolaos. "But I'm tempted to see it. You said you hadn't seen," he flashed a look at Karin, "*him* there."

"You want to go up?" Nikolaos asked, surprised, then hesitated. Could he really bring her so close to his river after what just happened? But he felt better now. It had probably just been some kind of temporary confusion before. Old Karin had been perfectly safe, and Jon was there. "Well, why not? Come up, and I'll show you."

"Yes, let's head up," Jon said, looking both nervous and eager. Then he looked at Karin again. "Pleased to see you, Mickelsson's Karin."

She eyed him, then looked down at her lap and didn't return his greeting. It was embarrassing.

Jon shrugged, then pointed to his saddlebags. "I have some wine that I traded for earlier. Was enquiring about the wine merchant I told you about yesterday, but he's not coming for some time yet. Can we drink it up there?"

"I don't see why not," Nikolaos said.

When they climbed the narrow path to the cave entrance, Karin held so tightly to Kristina's mane that the skin whitened around her fingers.

"Do the horses go in the cave as well? Will we all fit in there? I don't like mushrooms," she whispered. "Who is he? He's so large. I'm afraid of him."

"Who? Jon? I was under the impression that you knew each other. It's the tailor, Tailor Jon. Don't you recognize him?" Nikolaos helped her down, not sure what mushrooms had to do with anything.

She didn't answer, just stared at everything with a childish look in her eyes. It irritated him, but he swallowed the urge to comment on it and turned to Jon, who was coming up behind them. He had dismounted already.

"This is remarkable, it's bigger than my farmhouse," he said, touching the wall with his left hand as he looked around. "Do you have a torch? I want to see what's in the back. There's even furniture in here. It's astonishing. Who put them here do you think? I hope it's not Näcken's!"

"You never know, but I doubt it." Nikolaos raised an eyebrow mockingly, getting a fearful look from Jon. He changed his tactic. "Someone must have lived here once. It's very comfortable. There's even a pallet. It's still covered with animal skins. Whoever did must have been here for a while, then left for some reason." He lit his lantern and handed it to Jon, wishing he could tell him he had made the furniture himself.

"I gather you're right, but I wouldn't be so sure it wasn't Näcken who scared him off," Jon said and carefully walked into the back of the cave, holding the lantern up so he could see. His fear seemed gone for the moment. "It's quite something, this cave. Wouldn't you say, Karin?" He handed the lantern back to Nikolaos. "How are you faring these days? It's been a time since you came with mending from Mickelsson's."

Nikolaos followed their conversation, interested to see how she would respond. But Karin just looked at him, then moved closer to Nikolaos' side, pressing against him. He exchanged a glance with Jon, who didn't look all too surprised.

"Let's have some of that wine, Nikolaos, shall we?" Jon said, clapping him on the back.

But after a couple of goblets, the tension disappeared. The wine loosened Karin's tongue, and she seemed just like anyone else. Nikolaos played the fiddle, and they even danced for a while. Karin was a strange young woman, but he decided to enjoy it for what it was.

Chapter 26

After a surprisingly quick interview with the village pastor and a sixman, during which all they asked was if he knew his catechism and the Ten Commandments, Nikolaos was given permission to build a house near Jon's property. He set to work on it immediately.

Jon and Nikolaos were on the roof, adding thatch to it, when Nikolaos remembered he wanted to send a letter to a young fiddle maker in Stockholm he used to know. Not that he would be young now, but he might still be alive.

He pressed down the thatch with both hands and flattened an uneven part near the ridge, then straightened and looked at Jon. "Pray tell me, how do people send letters? I made a fool of myself last I spoke with a post-runner, and now I'm too embarrassed to ask the one here."

Jon gave a half-sided smile. "You did mention something about that."

"Uh-hum, like I probably told you, I assumed he was a musician, and he thought I must be a Finn since I didn't know what a post horn was." Nikolaos laughed. It did seem funny now.

Jon chuckled, then grew serious. "Maybe my telling you will remind you. The postal service came about when I was a boy. I remember it well because people talked of nothing else. It was decided that farmers would be responsible for the mail, with two to three miles between each farmer participating. Those farmers must have two farmhands to take care of it, meaning they're required to bring the mail to the next farm, then hand it over to the farmhand there, and so on. They're the ones you see with the post horn and the plaque. Doesn't it sound familiar to you?"

Nikolaos shook his head. "No, I can't say it does."

Jon looked disappointed. "Anyway. If you have a letter, you just give it to the post-runner, and it'll get there in no time. It was one of those first post-runners who told us about Näcken as a matter of fact." Jon swung his right leg over the roof and hooked it around the cross beam, letting his other leg hang loose. "He had met a group of people who had been looking for him up by Large Lake. Someone had found a dead man floating in the water, not in Large Lake but in one of the smaller lakes near there. It was a farmhand who had been on his way to a trial for a woman who'd been fornicating with Näcken." He raised his eyebrows and shook his head emphatically. "An old woman, too. They said Näcken did what he does to both the old woman and the farmhand. Strangely enough, she didn't drown." He pressed his lips into a fine line and shook his head. "But they hung her, so she must have had relations with him in some way." He shook his head again, a look of disgust on his face.

Nikolaos stared at him, hearing a faint buzzing in his ears. It was Johannes! Somehow no matter where he went, people always knew what he had done. He felt dizzy.

Jon continued, oblivious. "We had all heard it said that Näcken was living in the cave and had been for years and years. No one had ever dared to look. But when they learned what happened, people decided to investigate. They found some of his things there. Probably the furniture you showed me. It's why I was scared of going there first and why I'm suspecting that Näcken might be the cause of your memory loss. Maybe you encountered him that day and forgot that too."

"Rusty devils," Nikolaos whispered, his heart picking up speed. He must have been in Jönköping still when those men went into his cave. If they knew that they had hung Old Karin, he would already have been on his way home. What if he had come home when they were still there? He grabbed the crossbeam with both hands as images of Old Karin's dead body swaying as she hung from that noose, and Johannes' body lying lifeless in the dark water, flashed before him. His beautiful face had been white as marble in the starlight.

Without noticing how he got there, Jon was suddenly sitting right in front of him. He looked Nikolaos square in the face and grabbed his arms. "Calm down, you're shaking. I know it's frightening. Pray forgive me, I shouldn't have said all that. Let's take a break now, shall we?"

Nikolaos managed a nod.

"I'll get down first and steady you a bit. You should drink something. It's hot today." With another searching look into Nikolaos' face, Jon climbed down, using the corner logs as a ladder.

Nikolaos didn't have to pretend anything. Jon was convinced he was shaken up because of what he said about Näcken being the cause of his memory loss and the death of two people. All he needed to do was play along.

While Jon rummaged around in his satchel for his water skin, Nikolaos' thundering heart slowed, and the images of Johannes' and Karin's bodies subsided. He was who he was. It was in the past now. He had to stop feeling so guilty. Humans lived such short lives anyway.

Jon found the water and they sat down on the ground, leaning their backs against the new wall.

Nikolaos drank and returned the skin. "Thank you kindly."

"Ah, you sound better now. I didn't mean to scare you. I understand it's frightening with you living in that cave. I should've insisted that you left."

"It's fine, Jon. And you did, I'm leaving now. Who was the man they found in the water? Did they find his family? They're sure it was Näcken who did it?" His stomach clenched.

"Yes. There was no doubt. I don't think they found his family. But I know he had been a farmhand on a farm not far from where that woman lived, the old woman they hung. It's how they figured it was Näcken who had done it. Had he just been found drowned, they'd probably have thought he did away with himself. In some ways he was lucky, at least they buried him in hallowed ground."

"They did?"

"Why, yes, since it wasn't suicide, I believe so."

Nikolaos had trouble believing that. Old Karin wasn't buried in the graveyard, so why would they bury Johannes there if they knew he had killed him? Still, tears of relief filled his eyes. He looked away to hide them from Jon.

Chapter 27

They had made love on a blanket Karin had spread under the trees behind the village crops. She lay tight against his side as he held her, her round, hard stomach pushing into him.

Nikolaos kissed her forehead. "The baby is growing. Has anyone noticed yet?"

"No, no one has said anything to me. Marja and I walked all the way to the shoemaker yesterday, and she said nothing."

"That's good. But it'll be time for us to speak to Mickelsson soon. I think another week and then the house will be mostly ready. After that, I want us to tell him." He sat up and gently pulled himself out of Karin's grasp.

She rolled over on her back and closed her eyes. "Yes."

Nikolaos pulled up a blade of grass growing next to their blanket, folding it in half and twisting the pieces so it formed a small ring. One of his daughters had shown him how to do it when she was little. Anna, he thought, but wasn't entirely sure anymore.

Smiling to himself, he hid it in his hand, then bent over and kissed Karin gently on the mouth. "Stay here, I'm just going behind the tree for a bit."

After he peed, he went deeper into the woods, scanning the ground as he walked. And just as he had hoped, a patch of forget me nots was growing in the moist earth under a fallen tree. He crouched down and picked a nice bunch of the tiny flowers. It was easier than he remembered to twist them around the grass ring, and soon it covered it fully, making a beautiful blue ring with yellow dots. It was very small, but hopefully it would fit Karin's finger. Placing the ring on the ground, he went to work on a bracelet, using several long and flat blades of grass, twisting forget me nots around it the same way as he did with the ring. He spaced the flowers evenly and left the grass exposed. It contrasted nicely with blue against the green, and it looked beautiful. Anna and Abluna would be proud of him if they could see him from their place in heaven.

Karin was sitting up when he went back and was watching him approach. He tried to hide the gifts behind his back when he sat down, but she saw anyway.

"What do you have, Nikolaos?" she asked, smiling from ear to ear.

He laughed. "Ah, and here I was trying to keep it secret. Kiss me, and I'll give it to you," he said, leaning in. Then he felt her arms go around his back to search for it, and he gave up, handing them to her.

Karin's eyes widened. "Oh Nikolaos, where did you get these? They're beautiful, so beautiful. Thank you kindly!" She slipped the little grass bracelet over her hand and then the ring on her ring finger. It fit, and she looked so sweet, it melted his heart.

"You're welcome. I'm glad you like it," Nikolaos said, watching her angle her arm towards the sun as if she thought the flowers would sparkle.

"I'll wear this on our betrothal day, and on the way to the wedding bed, Nikolaos," she said, pulling herself up to stand.

Nikolaos was just about to tell her that he doubted the flowers would last for that long and assure her he would make new ones, when she called out, clutching her stomach. Her face had drained of color. "I think you should sit back down for a moment, Karin," he said, reaching for her elbow.

But she didn't hear him. She let out another moan, a slow keening sound. It must be the baby. She was losing the baby.

"Karin, I insist that you sit, the baby isn't feeling good. You need to rest, or it'll come too early."

She stared at him and looked as though she was about to ignore his suggestion, but then she nodded and let him lead her back to the blanket to help her sit down. He put his arm around her and felt her sweat through her dress. She was shaking.

"Pray Karin, tell me what's hurting you."

"My stomach, I think I need to go to the outhouse, it's rushing." She got on all fours and clumsily stood, then stumbled toward a tree, holding onto its rough bark with one hand and clutching her stomach with the other. Then she doubled over. Screaming now. Blood, water, and something thicker fell between her legs, making a splattering sound as it hit the ground.

In the short time it took for Nikolaos to reach her, he had time to wonder if he no longer needed to marry her, feeling both relief and heartrending grief that she was losing the baby. A sob rose in his throat, and he gently pushed Karin to the side, falling to his knees in front of the puddle on the ground. It was mostly a red mass with clumps, some whitish and some thick and red. Then tears obscured his vision, and he couldn't see anymore.

"There are seven babies, seven little babies," Karin cried and clumsily sat down beside him, trailing what looked like the afterbirth between her legs.

Nikolaos pulled her close. "No, Karin, I don't think so… this is just the way it looks sometimes when…" He trailed off.

Karin shook her head vigorously. "No there are seven, look!" She took his hand and pushed it into the mass on the ground, moving it and pressing it into each lump as she counted aloud. "You see, Nikolaos, seven babies, we would've had seven little ones."

"No, sweetheart. Women never have that many at one time." He wiped his hand on the ground, suppressing a wave of fear. One should never touch death with one's own hands.

"Yes, I've seen kittens, they often have at least six."

Stunned, Nikolaos met her earnest eyes and slowly breathed out. There was no sense in arguing about it. Karin was not like other women; he was sure of it now, and ought to be thankful it ended like this even if it was a sin to wish for it. He crossed himself and mumbled a prayer for forgiveness.

"We should bury them. Let me go see if I can get a shovel somewhere," he said.

"No!" She grabbed his arm. "Don't go. We must get them to the pastor and have him bury them in the graveyard." She began to sob uncontrollably, clutching her stomach as if it still hurt. It probably did. He remembered Abluna staying in bed after they lost babies but didn't remember if it was because she had been sad or in pain.

He reached for her hand. "Now, just think on that for a moment. No witnesses have walked us to our wedding bed or seen us shake hands at our betrothal. Do you understand what that means?"

She shook her head.

Nikolaos sighed, allowing the relief that they no longer needed to marry wash over him. He didn't even feel guilty anymore. "Karin, it's a sin to lie together like we have without having had a proper betrothal. The church even wants people to wait until witnesses have walked couples to their wedding bed in some places. They could decide to punish us even if they let us marry after."

"We aren't betrothed? But you gave me a handfasting gift. We'll just show it to the pastor, he'll know."

He eyed her, confused. Which gift was she thinking of? The only thing he had given her was a dress Jon had made for her.

She sniveled and looked tearfully at the heap on the ground. It didn't resemble a baby at all.

Nikolaos tried to recall how Abluna's losses had looked, but he didn't remember ever seeing them. The neighbor woman had always helped her. He forced the thoughts away and focused on Karin, pulling her a little closer while making sure her bloodstained skirts didn't touch him.

"Forgive me, pray forgive me. I didn't mean it." Her chin quivered.

"Mean it? Of course you didn't. These things happen. It's not your fault."

She didn't seem to hear and changed the subject. "Isn't the gold bracelet enough for a handfasting gift? Wouldn't the pastor believe us? I want the babies buried properly."

"The gold bracelet? I never gave you…"

She interrupted him by waving her arm in front of him so the flower bracelet slid up and down over her wrist.

Shocked, he grabbed her arm to get it out of his face. Did she have trouble with her eyes? He had never noticed it before. "This? It's grass and flowers, Karin."

"Can we just bury them here? My seven little babies, they never got to be held by their mother," Karin sobbed, again ignoring what he said.

Exasperated, he shook his head. She truly seemed to think that there would have been seven children. "You rest, Karin. Sit here, I'm not leaving. I'll just get something to cover this with. Then we'll say our own prayer to our baby."

"Our *babies*," she said, sounding indignant.

Nikolaos nodded. There was no point in contradicting her anymore.

He took her back to Mickelsson's farm. It was late, and everything was still and quiet. Helping her dismount, she slid off Kristina and fell into his arms, clinging to him and crying softly. He wasn't sure if bringing her there had been the wisest decision. Letting her get over the shock on a blanket on the floor of his unfinished house might have been wiser, but they were here now, and he better follow through with it.

He gently loosened her arms from around his waist and urged her forward. "There, you go inside now, try to rest. Make an excuse tomorrow to stay in bed. I'll visit you the day after that. How does that sound?"

Karin kissed him, then walked away without protest, her shoulders slumping and her neck bent.

She looked incredibly sad, but all Nikolaos felt was relief.

Chapter 28

Nikolaos had spent all day in the water, gliding along the bottom and letting the cool current comfort his troubled mind. Afterward, he sat a while on his rock above the cave, playing his saddest melodies and praying that God would find the baby on the day of judgment. The relief he felt yesterday was still there, but now he felt guilty and worried, and sorry for Karin.

He had just returned to his cave when he heard an urgent voice calling from the lake below.

"Nikolaos, Nikolaos, are you there? Come quickly!" Jon's voice.

Nikolaos placed his fiddle on the table and ran back out, finding Jon halfway up the path already.

"Evening, is something the matter? What are you doing here?" Then he noticed Jon's startled look at the sight of his wet breeches. "Fishing. Didn't work so well, trap was empty," he lied, patting his thigh. His breeches were so wet it caused water droplets to disperse in the air.

"I see," Jon said, looking relieved. "Nikolaos, I'm not sure how to tell you this, but Karin was found screaming last night, declaring she needed to get to her children. She was so hysterical that Mickelsson had to restrain her."

"What?" Something cold settled in his stomach.

Jon nodded. "At first, they found her sitting on a rock near the alehouse. She was lethargic and was holding something in her hands, which she tried to hide under her skirts when they came near. She didn't want to show it to them because she feared they'd accuse her of having stolen it. They think anyway. Mickelsson insisted, as you can imagine, but all she had was braided grass, something a child would make."

"Rusty devils! Wait for me, I'll get my saddle and come with you."

"I don't think it'll help anymore," Jon said in a tone that made Nikolaos turn back around and look at him more closely. "As I mentioned, they had to restrain her. Karin grew more hysterical, screaming that she needed to get to her children again. Then she claimed that *you* took them from her. And that…" He stopped, body language screaming discomfort. "Well, I'm not sure how to say this, Nikolaos, but she's to have said that you…" He stopped again.

"Pray, tell me."

"She's to have said that you ate the afterbirth."

"I did what?" He fought the urge to cross himself.

Jon folded his hands in front of his chest. "She said you ate it," he repeated, looking embarrassed. "But Nikolaos, it's worse than that. They called for the lawman, and then two of the sixmen came with the pastor. I heard all this from Helge from Borakulle, who saw it all. He said they're saying it's Näcken she's been involved with."

So, they knew, well, it was only a matter of time. Nikolaos' heart started thumbing out of control.

"I told you that you shouldn't have lived in this cave here. It's dangerous. Helge from Borakulle said that Karin screamed about a large man in here, and I can only assume it's me. She said as much to me then," Jon said, looking both angry and scared. He remained where he stood, halfway up the path, one leg higher than the other.

Nikolaos gave an exasperated sigh. "Pray forgive me for getting you involved with this. She's worse off than I had imagined then. I should never have lain with her. I can't believe I was so stupid, all this because I was horny," Nikolaos admitted. "Pray come in here, I'll tell you exactly what happened."

Jon eyed his breeches, then glanced into the cave behind him and shook his head. "I'd rather stay out here if you don't mind it, Nikolaos. The fall," he cleared his throat, "it seems a bit noisy today."

"I see," Nikolaos said, hoping Jon had not seen him climb down with the fiddle. He had called for him only moments later. "Very well, let me tell you on the way over then." Nikolaos tried his friendliest and what he hoped was his most human smile.

Jon nodded with obvious relief, then turned around and walked down ahead of him, quickly.

Nikolaos felt something tighten in the pit of his stomach.

Once they were both horse-borne, Nikolaos went right to it.

"Karin is a lot more dimwitted than we thought. I truly had no idea how bad it was. And I'm not talking about what you told me just now."

"No?"

"No. Those grass things she was holding that you were telling me about, I gave them to her yesterday. We had just made love, and I made her a little ring and a bracelet out of blades of grass that I stuck forget me nots into. I was just trying to be sweet, but she acted as if it were gold. Held it up to the sun as if it sparkled."

Jon gave a sad whistle and reigned in his horse so he was right beside Nikolaos. He seemed less tense now.

"Then Karin lost the baby," Nikolaos added.

"Oh, my lord." Jon crossed himself. "Did it live? I mean at first?"

"No," Nikolaos said and met his eyes. "It didn't look like much. It was just a lump of flesh and blood, not a pleasant sight. She thought she needed to relieve herself, but before she got to a spot, the baby just fell out of her. It made this splatting sound when it landed on the ground. I'll never forget it. For some reason, she thought there were seven babies. She wanted the pastor to bury them in the graveyard, and she didn't seem to understand the difference between cats and women."

"Cats?"

"Yes." Nikolaos nodded for emphasis. "I told her that women never have seven babies at one time, but she said that they do because she'd seen cats have at least six."

Jon tut-tutted. "You must tell them this, Nikolaos, or they'll go around looking for Näcken. People will panic. Cats! Yes, Karin has lost her mind. Does it get worse when they're expecting? I think I've heard that."

"It might."

"You needn't walk to the wedding bed with her now. You'd never be happy with her. I was thinking that when you first told me, but I didn't think it was my place to bring it up. Especially since she was in the family way. But like you said yourself, it's worse than we both thought. Don't feel obligated now when there's no baby."

Nikolaos absently noticed that his breeches were finally drying somewhat. "I don't know, it's what I was thinking yesterday, too. But now I feel responsible. Everyone will know she isn't untouched anymore and no one will ever marry her."

Jon reached over and patted him on the shoulder. "Nikolaos, no one will marry her anyway, especially not after seeing her this distraught and confused. I think the best thing to do is for us to ride down to the village. Maybe you shouldn't tell them you're the father after all. You never know what people will think. Best not mentioning that you've lived in the cave up there either." He gestured behind them. "At least let's see what's happening, and then you can decide."

"Maybe you're right, but I'm not sure yet. I feel responsible."

"Well, if you have to think about it, do. But be careful," Jon said, then increased his speed. Nikolaos let him take the lead, glad of the time to think.

Jon was right. He should go to the village and find out what they were doing with Karin, make sure that they hadn't figured out who he was.

When they reached the village border, Jon pulled his horse to a halt. "I feel that I ought to go home. Why don't you head down first," he said, pointing toward the road. "I'll catch up. I have to finish up a coat for a customer, he's picking it up today. I forgot, I forgot with everything, you know."

Nikolaos tried to catch his gaze, but Jon avoided it and was already turning his horse around. He seemed tense again. Had he seen him play, after all? Or was he just worried that he would be accused himself?

Nikolaos rode around so he was ahead of him, blocking the way just enough so he couldn't pass without seeming threatening. "You sure, Jon? I'll explain everything to them. You needn't worry about her silly fear of you. She's not in her right mind."

Jon gave him a scrutinizing look. For a moment he seemed to be hesitating, but then he shook his head. "No, you go. And don't say anything. It's for the best. By the way, they'll likely keep her either at church or in the barn at the farm behind it. I really ought to ride on now, Nikolaos." He kicked his heels, and his horse pushed itself past Kristina and broke into a fast trot that sent clumps of pine flying behind its hooves.

Nikolaos shrugged. If Jon didn't come down to the village, he would talk to him later.

As soon as Nikolaos approached the road, it became apparent that this would not be handled discreetly. A large group of people were standing in the middle of it and the way they were gesticulating made it clear it was no ordinary conversation.

One husband was hugging his crying wife, and another stood behind his, arms wrapped around her as if to protect her. A group of younger men even had clubs and large sticks in their hands.

Nikolaos urged Kristina into a trot and rode over. They barely looked at him when he stopped, keeping their eyes glued to a man who was speaking animatedly. Nikolaos coughed twice to get their attention and a couple of people glanced in his direction but immediately turned back toward the speaker.

"I'm very, very concerned," the man said. "We must be cautious. Keep your daughters inside. In fact, no one should go outside at dusk anymore. Näcken comes when the sun is beginning to set," the man said.

"What's happened? What are you all talking about?" Nikolaos interrupted loudly, regretting it as soon as he spoke. He should have kept listening to see what they were saying about him.

Finally, everyone turned to him. He saw fear, if not utter terror, in their expressions.

"Who are you?" one of the young men with the sticks asked. It was birch, Nikolaos noticed now, a whole trunk with the branches cut off. Would he die if he was hit in the head with it?

"Good evening to you, I'm Nikolaos. Has something happened?" He forced himself to look away from the sticks, swallowing a rush of anger. They were fools. Clueless fools.

"Indeed, indeed it has," another one of the stick-carrying youths said, casting an eye at the others as if making sure that it was all right that he was the one who broke the news. "We have a menacing situation. One of our own, a sweet young maid working for Mickelsson here," he touched the shoulder of a barrel-chested man with reddish hair, "was lured in by Näcken!"

"I see," Nikolaos said, hesitating. Mickelsson looked much younger than he had imagined, someone who wouldn't be easy to fool. Now would be the time to introduce himself, tell him that it was he, not Näcken, who got her pregnant, even though of course it was. Tell them the same story he told Jon and admit that he had been living in the cave. But then he would have to marry her. He cleared his throat. "You're sure it's Näcken?" he said instead.

"Yes, unfortunately. As he said, the young maid works for me, been a good worker her whole life, a lovely girl. Now she's lost her mind entirely," Mickelsson said, sounding very sure of himself.

Nikolaos pursed his lips slightly at that. "Did she lose her mind, or was she lured in by that fella you're talking about?"

"Fella? Näcken isn't a fella, he's a dangerous manifestation of the Devil himself. A black dog-like being with long ears he lifted her skirts with! She had seven children with him, and he took each one of them to his cave behind the waterfall, but not before he saw fit to eat the afterbirth, lapped it up like a dog he did, then ran off with the babies in his claw-like paws. He gave her gold and a dress, but it turned into grass."

"A ragged black dog with long ears?" Nikolaos asked, trying not to scoff. Rusty devils, did Karin tell them that?

An older woman stepped closer to him, pulling a young married woman wearing a white headscarf with her. "It sounds a tale, doesn't it? But true it is, Näcken has been known in these here parts for years, living behind a waterfall in the woods, never ventured down here, until now. Several of our strong men, these young folks," she said, indicating toward them with her arm, "have volunteered to go look for him tonight. Could you help? You look strong and have a horse."

Everyone shouted out their approval and those holding sticks lifted them. It looked threatening.

"What do we do if we catch him? I thought the Devil was vapor-made during these manifestations. Wouldn't your clubs go right through him?" Nikolaos asked, glad he remembered what Abraham Lövcrantz had spoken of at that lecture. Maybe this would stop them from looking.

Someone gasped. One of the men dropped his stick, and a woman pressed herself between the others and promptly fell to her knees with a cry.

A heavyset man who looked like he was in his fifties cast a quick glance at the others, then pushed himself through the crowd, stepping around the woman on the ground as he gestured for Nikolaos to get off his horse.

He did cautiously, taking a strong hold of Kristina's bit.

"I'm Helge," the heavyset man said. "I live in Borakulle and happened by when they found Karin trying to get to her babes. May I ask how you know this? You an expert on the underworld?"

Taken aback, Nikolaos first thought he was chiding him, but the man looked completely sincere.

"Well, as a matter of fact, I do have experience. Quite a bit, you could say."

"You've seen him?" several people asked simultaneously, moving closer to him and Helge.

"Näcken? No, not exactly. I can't say that I've done that." Nikolaos couldn't stop a chuckle from escaping.

"I've heard that he turns into a horse," Helge from Borakulle said. "And that he drowns people, drowns them by pushing them down under, you know under the surface in the river. He keeps them there for weeks, playing with them, and then they float up when he's done with them. By then their bodies are always bloated and white. A young man was found like that only some years ago up at one of the smaller lakes near the big one up there, up north near Wätter Lacus." Helge pointed diffusely behind him, getting the crowd's worried attention as they followed his finger. One of the men helped the woman on the ground get up, then pointed in the same direction to make sure she hadn't missed it.

"So, how is it that you have experience then?" A woman asked.

"I studied with Abraham Lövcrantz for a time, a short while only, but I learned a lot." Nikolaos lied, suppressing the image of Johannes' strong body under his fingers.

"Oh, Lövcrantz!" Helge said, clearly pretending to know who he was. He looked ridiculous, exaggeratingly knowing, and important.

Nikolaos smiled. "What I learned from him is that it's the Devil who manifests into different shapes, using vapor to do so. He has to do it with natural substances, such as vapor. I've not learned that he would turn himself into a dog or a horse."

"Oh." Helge looked surprised.

"Where's the young woman in question?"

"She's safe, sir. She was taken this morning to be held near church."

"I see," Nikolaos said, amused at being addressed as sir. "Well, I should be on my way. I thank you for your courtesy in telling me what happened." He put his left foot in the stirrup, but by the time his right leg was in midair, there was a tug on the bottom of his coat. Glancing down as he swung his leg over, he found the young married woman looking up at him.

"Dear sir, pray don't go yet. We're very worried here, if there's anything you can tell us about what to do, we'd appreciate it very much. We're …" she stopped, distracted as it suddenly became eerily dark.

Thick dark clouds had collected in the west out of sight and were now rolling in with incredible speed, obscuring the sun. There was rumbling, and then the air lit up with a loud crack, exposing new terror in their faces.

Nikolaos shifted his attention back to the woman still tugging at his coat and shook his head. "I can't stay. You should all go home. Stay inside.

Then he turned Kristina around and urged her into a gallop, leaving the frightened people behind. Thank God for sending the rain so he would have a little time to empty his cave before the search party set out again.

Chapter 29

The latch for Nikolaos' new door had come loose from the wall and was rattling in the wind, catching the door and slamming it against the wall, bursting with green. Kristina's ears pinned back flat against her head.

"It's fine, Nikolaos will fasten it, Queen Kristina," he whispered, patting her neck.

Tying her to the hitching post Jon had made, he pulled his bags and bundles with the things from his cave off the saddle, brought them inside, and then hurried back out. He put a log in front of the door to keep it closed. It would have to do for now. He wanted to go speak to Jon and tell him what the villagers told him, ask him what to do. The latch he could fix later.

As soon as Nikolaos approached Jon's homestead, he sensed he wasn't there. The dogs weren't there, and the shutters were closed. The pigpen was empty, and the cow was gone too, its hobble thrown carelessly on the ground. Disappointed, he went to check on the barn and peeked through a window. Empty.

It worried him. Jon had seemed fine the whole way to the crossroads. Why had he panicked there? As far as Nikolaos could tell, he hadn't said anything that would cause the sudden escape. But Jon must have been more scared than it seemed unless he was just afraid of getting accused himself. He *had* seemed upset about that. It was understandable, but Nikolaos still felt uneasy. He turned Kristina around, setting off in a gallop toward the village, and Karin.

Thunder was rumbling in the distance, and it was drizzling again when he reached the road. A man was walking there, heading in the direction of the village at a fast pace. He looked up with a start as if he hadn't heard the hooves and looked sideways at Nikolaos under a wide-brimmed hat. It was one of the men from the crowd earlier.

"Evening to you," Nikolaos said, slowing down so he was right beside him.

"Evening, sir," the man said.

"Are you on your way to the pastor by chance? Is the girl with him?" Nikolaos asked, amused again to be addressed as sir.

The man shook his head, "No, sir. I'm not. I'm going to go home. I've some more animals to take care of, Tailer Jon brought me his today. I'm to take them for a month or two for him. He left, said he might actually have seen Näcken and was scared he'd come after him. I'd be careful if I were you, riding along here all alone, not knowing anybody. It's getting late.

Nikolaos pushed down a wave of dejection. Jon had been afraid then, after all. "This is terrible news. He saw him?" He exaggerated the tone of his voice. It sounded utterly false, but the man nodded gravely and stopped walking, forcing Nikolaos to bring Kristina to a halt.

"Indeed, he did, more than once. Jon confirmed he lives behind the waterfall up there in the woods." He stared Nikolaos squarely in the face while gesturing in the correct direction. "Näcken had been playing his fiddle in the stream. It's what brought this horrible weather we've had today. Made the world go completely dark as you noticed. A dangerous creature, disgusting too, eating the afterbirth," he spit on the ground. A thick gooey blob.

"What else did Tailor Jon tell you about Näcken? And did he say where he was going?" Nikolaos asked, ignoring the insult. It must have been the change in the weather that got Jon to suddenly become afraid. He had probably heard the rumbling in the distance, it wasn't long after they said goodbye that the thunderstorm was on top of them.

"Away from here, didn't say where. But I'd leave too, had it been me. And Karin, poor woman." The man shook his head slowly. "On the other hand, you don't know," he said, changing his tone. "Womenfolk you know, she might have wanted him. They hear him play that fiddle of his and see him stand there in the water. He lures them, you know. With his music and his looks." The man spit on the ground again. This time it was even thicker, landing with a splat.

Nikolaos looked away, disgusted, then rode on, leaving without saying goodbye.

Right by the first farm of the village was a narrow road leading to the church. It stayed narrow until it turned toward a hill where it widened enough for two carriages to drive side by side. Reaching the top, he could see the church a short distance away. And just like Jon had told him, there was a farm with a large barn right next to it. It was probably where Karin was held. He pressed his feet into Kristina's sides and flew down the hill toward the barn.

There were no windows, just a barn door that was locked from the outside with a thick wooden beam. It should be easy enough to open.

Nikolaos threw a quick look around the outbuildings and adjacent fields, seeing no one. "Karin, are you in there?" he called, just a little louder than a speaking voice, and rode over. He heard movement, but there was no answer. Maybe livestock were moving around, startled by his voice. "Karin, is it you? Sweetheart, it's me, Nikolaos," he tried again, yet a little louder. "I want to help you." Then he heard footsteps.

"Oh dear, you came!" Karin's voice. Strong and clear. "I knew you'd rescue me. I knew it right away when I saw the rat. It looked at me and scurried away so fast. I always sweep the floor."

Nikolaos frowned, not sure what she was talking about. He scanned the area again to make sure he was alone, dismounted, and walked closer to the spot where her voice came from. "Pray, can you repeat that, Karin?"

There was a shuffling from her feet. "They took the gold. Nikolaos, they took it from me, said it was nothing but grass!"

Sudden tears filled his eyes. Even though Jon had told him, it was startling to hear her say it herself. "Now Karin, you must listen to me. Try to focus on my words and take it slow. Can you do that for me?"

"Yes."

"Good. Now, if I open the door, you must be ready to sneak out as quietly as you can. I'll try to open it. Stay where you are, right here by the door. Do you understand?"

"Will you give me gold? They took the gold from me. Where's your dog?"

"My dog?" Nikolaos asked, ignoring her question about gold. Had there only been cloisters these days, he could have brought her to the sisters so they could take her in as a novice. He lifted the beam and tried the handle. It was locked. He saw the keyhole now too. The beam had covered it.

Suddenly, Karin screamed, "Help! Help, Näcken is heeeere, help!"

He jumped and lost his grip on the beam. It fell straight down, hitting his foot with a colorless thump. It hurt, and he called out just as loud as she did.

All at once, Kristina bolted and disappeared into the trees, doors slammed, and then footsteps came at him from two directions while faint flashes of red accompanied the loud sounds. He stood as if struck. If he ran, they would find him guilty, but if he stayed, they might believe her. Either way, he would be found out. Then Helge and Mickelsson came running toward him, accompanied by someone trying to keep up.

Just then, he heard Kristina's hooves, and out of the corner of his left eye, he saw her come back. It broke the spell, and he reached for her and caught her bit. Blessed, blessed Kristina. He remained where he was, trying to look confident.

Helge and Mickelsson waved. The other man, heavy set, wearing a long coat that almost dragged on the ground, nodded in greeting. It was the pastor who had interviewed him; he hadn't recognized him at first.

"Nikolaos," the pastor said, "what are you doing here?"

"Talking with the woman in there," he said with a head tilt toward the barn.

"This is the man we met on the road, the expert," Mickelsson said.

"*You're* him?"

"Yes, I had the pleasure of meeting these gentlemen earlier."

"Ah, very good. Helge was just telling me about it. I wish you had asked me first, though. You can't speak with her without me present."

"Pray forgive me."

The pastor waved a dismissive hand in the air. "I've sent men out to gather the sixmen, and once we get them all here, we're going to question her. Might be as soon as tomorrow. Why was Karin Svensdotter screaming?"

"I don't know. At first, it was as if she thought she knew me. And then she started screaming all of a sudden. It scared both me and my horse, which made me drop the beam on my foot and call out. Kristina here," Nikolaos added while patting her neck, "bolted in fear. It wasn't my intention to disturb you this evening."

"Oh, oh, no matter. No matter at all, the door is locked. But let's put the beam back for safety." The pastor nodded at Mickelsson who hurried over to pick it up. As soon as he reached the door, they heard another shout from inside, "It's Näcken you're speaking to. Watch it, watch it! He said he'd give me gold. I want to see him, open the door!"

Nikolaos felt his throat thicken. He felt for her. This was all his fault. Why couldn't he have left it alone after that first time in the ale tub? And here he was, pretending to not even know her. It wasn't right.

Mickelsson rolled his eyes, but Nikolaos caught Helge looking at him curiously.

"Come with me, good sir," the pastor said. "Helge just invited me to have supper. You shall come as well. I hope your foot isn't badly hurt?"

"It's not too bad. It scared me, but my boot took most of the weight." Nikolaos wiggled his toes. They were a bit sore but would heal by morning.

Helge's home was warm and inviting, full of blankets, furs, and embroidered wall hangings. The dining table was covered by a beautiful tablecloth with intricate patterns in red, black, and blue. A large Bible lay open at the head.

The pastor noted his gaze and nodded knowingly. "We were

searching the scriptures for an answer. Pray don't drink tobacco near it. You can sit over there if you want some," he said, pointing toward the other end of the table where Helge and Mickelsson had already readied their pipes.

"Come here and have some of mine. It'll calm you. Heard how she screamed at you. Poor girl, Näcken has turned her head completely," Helge said and handed him his pipe.

Nikolaos took it and sucked on it dutifully, hoping it looked convincing. "Are you certain she's really been in contact with Näcken? She seems quite insane," he said and handed the pipe back.

"Oh, absolutely. She worked for me you see, a resourceful lovely girl. Not insane at all. It's Näcken. I'm certain," Mickelsson said.

Nikolaos looked at him, unsure of how he ought to react. The way she had acted with him didn't make it seem as if she had ever been of sound mind. It had gotten worse, surely, but even Jon had indicated that she wasn't the wisest of girls. Mickelsson must be hiding the truth.

Helge leaned back in his chair and hollered into a dark room behind them. A moment later his wife appeared. She nodded at the guests and went directly to the hearth, scooping stew into a large bowl.

"My wife is a great cook. Pray enjoy, eat!" Helge said when she brought the bowl to the table, lifting his spoon in the air.

The pastor shot him a sharp look.

"Oh, of course." Helge bristled and put his spoon down, exchanging an embarrassed look with his wife as the pastor bowed his head in prayer.

Nikolaos' fingers had just looked for his new fork in his pocket, realizing he had neither that nor a spoon, and clasped his hands instead. "You have a beautiful home, but I was under the impression you lived in Borakulle," he said when they had finished praying.

The pastor and Mickelsson grinned, and then Helge burst out laughing. Even his wife chuckled as she went to sit by the hearth. "You're *in* Borakulle, young man, this is indeed my farm."

"Oh, of course!" Nikolaos said with an embarrassed smile, feeling ridiculous. Borakulle, it should have been obvious when he climbed the kulle getting here. The church wasn't visible from the road because it was blocked by it. He should have known. "Pray forgive me for my ignorance."

"No need for apologies, you're not from here, we knew that. I should have told you when we met the other week," the pastor said, returning his smile. "I expect to see you at church come Sunday, then someone will take you around and show you."

"I appreciate that." It was a good reminder he would have to go to church now.

"Will you tell us some of what you've learned from your studies with Lövbrandt?" Mickelsson asked, digging his fork into a big piece of meat and a root vegetable from the bowl. They must have slaughtered a piglet just to impress the pastor.

"Lövcrantz is his name, Abraham Lövcrantz."

"Oh, Lövcrantz!" Helge broke in, saying it in the same exact way as he had on the road while motioning to his wife to come sit beside him. She did, handing Nikolaos a spoon as she sat down.

Nikolaos cleared his throat. All their eyes were on him, full of excitement, even glee. Had they no compassion for Karin at all? "Lövcrantz explained that Näcken is known to appear to people in the evenings or mornings when there's a lot of moisture in the air. He uses vapor from clouds or fog to manifest. He can't conquer it up from nothing."

Helge's eyes widened, and Mickelsson and the pastor were staring at him, their gleeful expressions fading.

"This is why you often see him near water. He uses the spray you see. He's old too, older than any man you have ever known, but you can't tell. He looks as young as I do," Nikolaos said and couldn't help but grin. No one saw any humor in it.

Helge's wife promptly burst into tears, and the pastor stared in horror at something right behind Nikolaos as if he thought Näcken might stand there. Helge put his arm around his wife.

Nikolaos kept his eyes on Mickelsson and Helge, avoiding

the pastor to keep himself from laughing. Clueless fools!

"He drowns people," Mickelsson said. "He pulls them under and swims with them there for a day or two. That's why you often find the bodies in a different place from where they went in. Karin is lucky she survived."

"Don't the water people see him?" the pastor asked, glancing nervously at Nikolaos.

"The water people?"

"Yes, surely you've heard of them?"

"Can't say I have, no."

The pastor smiled slightly, looking pleased he knew something Nikolaos didn't. "It's another race of people. They're just like us. They have everything we have, farms, horses, churches even, but they live under the surface at the bottom of lakes and streams and such."

"In the water? Surely you jest."

"No, not at all. They're as real as you and I. The only reason we don't see them is because we can't breathe down there, and they can't breathe up here."

"Of course, that's a logical explanation, no wonder," Mickelsson said.

Helge looked doubtful.

Nikolaos resisted rolling his eyes. There were no people living among the fish. It was ridiculous. He looked around for something to drink to distract himself.

Helge's wife must have guessed what he was looking for and pulled her husband's arm off her shoulder, and stood up. "Pray forgive me, you must be thirsty. I'll get you all some ale."

"No!" Helge grabbed her hand to stop her. "Don't go to the alehouse, woman. Get the wine from the cupboard. I don't want you out there alone. Näcken was out there just now."

The pastor looked at him questioningly.

"I've been sitting here pondering it while Nikolaos talked," Helge added. "When Karin screamed, she said it was him. That Näcken was with her. We didn't believe her, but I think she might have been right!"

Nikolaos felt his leg muscles tense, ready to push him out of his chair on their own accord. He grabbed the edge of the table.

The pastor looked at Nikolaos for a long moment as if to gather who he was, then turned to Helge who was still holding his wife's hand. She stood pale and silent beside him. "What do you mean? Explain yourself. I'm not sure I like what you're implying here, Helge."

"I will, I will…," he coughed and let go of his wife's hand. "Dear, get that wine will you. We're all thirsty here."

But she didn't obey and stood stock still, staring at the pastor.

Nikolaos' heart picked up speed, and he shifted forward on his seat.

"Ida, get the wine, I said," Helge repeated.

"Forget the wine, out with it!" the pastor thundered so loudly that Ida jumped across the floor to get the wine before she realized he had said the exact opposite. Her arm, already in midair, moved to the edge of her worktable, shaking.

"As I said, I've been listening here to him," Helge said, indicating Nikolaos with a nod. "Näcken is conniving you see. He was waiting out there in the dark to play a trick on us. I know it." Helge paused and looked at them, briefly resting his gaze on each person. "He didn't want us to hear him talk to anyone, so he waited until someone came by, and *then* he spoke so only Karin could hear it. Only to us, it looked as if she were talking to Nikolaos here. But it was Näcken she was talking to while he was hiding behind Nikolaos."

Nikolaos let out a slow breath. His legs relaxed.

The room became silent.

Then the pastor cleared his throat. "Now I think we'll have that wine. You may be right, Helge, but we're far from water here, I don't know if…? What do you say, Nikolaos?"

He pretended to consider the question for a moment and waited until Helge's wife had given them each a goblet of wine, then took a sip. "Well, it's a good thought." Nikolaos placed his goblet on the table. "But I doubt it. Näcken wouldn't need to wait, he'd just go inside and talk to her."

"He can go through looked barn doors?" Mickelsson looked horrified.

"He's known to, yes," Nikolaos said, remembering throwing the stable key in the moat at Norrköping's House.

The pastor scratched his chin, leaning backward and letting the chair rest on the wall behind him. "So then, you're saying you don't believe Helge's hypothesis? She was in fact talking to you, and only you."

"I believe so. She might have thought that I was Näcken though. No offense to your maid, Mickelsson, but she sounded confused and dimwitted. She spoke of rats and sweeping the floor without context. I wasn't sure what she meant."

Mickelsson shrugged and Helge looked uncomfortable. Nikolaos got the sense that they all knew how confused she was but didn't want to say anything so as not to disrespect Mickelsson.

The pastor took a long swig from his goblet and said, "Well, that's for the courts to determine. As I said, the sixmen are gathering, and we may need to get it to the twelvemen as well. We'll see."

"Would you like me to try to speak to her? I'm not afraid. I can go sit with her, see if she tells me the truth," Nikolaos said. If they let him in alone, he could just let her out, pretend she overpowered him with the help of the Devil himself.

"Won't work, we can't get in, I gave the key to Jöns. I wanted to be absolutely sure that she couldn't get out. Jöns will come with the rest of the sixmen tomorrow," Helge said.

The pastor nodded approvingly.

They had locked her in and hid the key. There was nothing he could do.

Chapter 30

Nikolaos knew he ought to leave. He was getting dangerously involved, and very close to exposure. But he couldn't just leave Karin. He had bedded her, made her with child. Her fate was his fault.

The pastor was already there when he arrived at Helge's farm the next morning, as were Mickelsson, Helge, and another man he didn't recognize, all relaxing on a bench along the house wall.

"Blessed morning to you, Nikolaos. How's the foot?" the pastor asked.

"Oh, my foot!" He had forgotten entirely. "It's a little tender, but that's all." It was a lie, it didn't hurt. But it would probably have hurt everyone else for a long time, so it was better to pretend.

"Good, good. Mighty fine to hear. Come here and taste this. You must try, it's called sugar. Have you ever had it before?" The pastor picked up a small tray and extended it toward Nikolaos, gently waving the tray. He looked very enthusiastic.

When he stopped waving, Nikolaos could see what appeared to be four tiny rocks. Kristina sniffed at it, and Mickelsson hurried to his feet and grabbed her bridle.

"Pray forgive my horse. What is it did you say?" Nikolaos asked, dismounting.

"Sugar. You should have a piece. It tastes like honey in a way, but not really, or like a pear, a very ripe pear. Lick it first, just a little with the tip of your tongue, then put the piece in your mouth and let it melt. It's like manna from heaven."

Nikolaos chuckled, plucking one of the pieces from the little tray. He licked it, and an immediate, intense sweetness filled his mouth. It did remind him of honey, like crystalized honey that had been left too long in its pot, but it wasn't quite the same. He met the pastor's eyes, then put the piece into his mouth, feeling it melt into a slightly crunchy liquid. It was delicious.

"You like it?" Mickelsson asked with a broad grin, then

pointed to the man Nikolaos hadn't met before. "Jöns brought it."

"Yes, very much. I thank you. What is it exactly?"

Jöns smiled proudly. "It's from cane."

"Cane?"

"Yes, cane. It's a long stick, like a thick kind of grass. It grows in the New World. They have people picking it for us," Helge said and looked at Jöns, who nodded in agreement.

"Not people," the pastor said, "they're negroes, and they plant and pick the cane and make this sugar out of it."

"Oh, interesting." Nikolaos narrowed his eyes, not sure who those pickers were who weren't people. It seemed an odd thing to say.

"The King is to have ordered a shipload of it, I heard. He really likes it," Mickelsson said, sounding both important and impressed.

"The King? Did Queen Kristina marry?"

They all stared at him.

The pastor placed the tray on his lap and carefully put his hand over the sugar so it wouldn't fall off. "Eh, what do you mean son? Surely you know that the Queen left and converted?"

Nikolaos did a quick calculation in his head. It was three years ago now that he met Old Karin, and as far as he knew, Queen Kristina had been reigning at that time. Karin had spoken at length about the fact that they had a woman ruling the country. That the Queen was a rather manly sort for a Queen as well.

"I thought that someone like you would know, you a scholar and everything. How have you missed this?" the pastor asked, shock and disappointment evident on his face.

Mickelsson and Jöns exchanged a glance. Helge's eyebrows were tightening.

"When was this?" Nikolaos asked and frantically tried to come up with an excuse. He wished he could tell them he had memory loss like he told Jon, but it was too late now, or they would question his demonology expertise.

"In the year of our Lord 1654, I believe. June sixth. She abdicated so she could convert, went to Brussels, and became

Catholic. Heretic is what she is! A big scandal, big scandal. Karl X Gustav took her place. How is it that you haven't heard this? Everyone was talking about it," the pastor said.

Catholic. Wise lady. Nikolaos scratched his chin and nodded as if to himself. "That would be a bit over two years ago then, yes?" Nodding again, he said, "That explains it. I was deep in my studies. Spent months on end with my books, reading so much people were getting suspicious because I went through too much tallow and too many candles. The year after that I stayed on my cousin's farm for a bit. My cousin and his wife… Eh well, let's just say that they aren't aware of much. That'd be the nice way to put it."

Mickelsson and Helge both laughed.

"Oh, I see. So that's where you lived before you came here, then? I never thought to ask you," the pastor said.

"Pray don't tell anyone that I didn't know," Nikolaos said, giving them an imploring look. "Did the Queen truly convert to Catholicism? And left the country, that's…" He stopped, feeling idiotic suddenly. It was not a very good lie. Had he been around people who provided him with candlewax and tallow, someone would have been talking about what the Queen did.

"Not to worry yourself, young man. You should be proud that you dedicate so much time to studying that you forget everything else. Good on you. Yes, convert she did. It's just as well that she left the country," the pastor said, shaking his head.

Nikolaos tsk-tsked, then purposely changed the subject. "Where's Karin? What's happening now?"

"We've spoken to the sixmen and two of the twelvemen as well. We have much to discuss. It'll take a while, so there isn't much to do for now. We'll have a hearing and then we'll see. It'll be in two days time, maybe three," Jöns said.

"I see. How is she fairing now? Is she eating?"

"We gave her ale and bread, spread lard on it for her. She needs to keep her strength to handle the questioning. She seems a bit weak," Jöns said.

"Would this be a good time for me to speak with her?"

Jöns turned to the pastor who shook his head and said,

"Let's wait, why don't you go home. How's your new house coming?"

"It's almost finished, I thank you for asking. I can come by here each morning and see if there's any news."

"Very well, doubt anything will happen tomorrow, but come just the same. I enjoy speaking with you."

Chapter 31

Thor had been on his way for days. Rå heard his wagon rumble and saw his hammer glisten in the dark clouds. The animals scurried away, and the air became thick and still. Thor brought rain, but he could also bring destruction, and she understood why the animals were afraid.

But she loved it when he came, that moment just before the rain arrived and everything was waiting with anticipation and a little fear. Standing naked in the open field, she pulled her hair to the side to expose her back. Then Thor's powerful arm sent a flash of lightning across the sky. Rå opened her back hole just as the heavens opened, pelting her with rain.

He banged his hammer until late that evening, sating her well before he finished. She felt wonderful and headed back to her treehouse, hammer-flashes lighting her way.

Then something startled her. A sudden shuffle of human feet somewhere behind her. Rå froze, then reflexively covered her back with most of her hair, leaving some covering her breasts. She slowly turned toward the sound, blinking to keep the rain out of her eyes, aware that the rain glued her hair over her breasts and didn't conceal them much at all. But everything was silent except for the splashing sound of the heavy rain on the trees and Thor's wagon rumbling on the clouds as he turned back home, his hammer safely on his lap now.

Thinking she had been mistaken, Rå continued walking and was almost home when she heard someone cough. Twice. Someone was spying on her.

She stopped, planting her feet deep on the ground, ready to do what she might have to. There was a man there, standing under a tree only a few paces from her. He was shivering, and his clothes were soaked through, hair flattened to his skull from the rain. And he was trying not to look at her naked form.

Rå smiled and spoke clearly, "No need to be afraid, come closer, you're cold. What are you doing all the way in the woods here? No one comes here. You came on foot?"

The man shook his head and indicated to something behind him, and then she saw a small brown horse concealed behind branches and the heavy rain.

"Come, walk ahead of me to the big tree over there," she said, pointing.

The man remained where he was.

"You're cold," she repeated. "You need to come inside to get warm. Get your horse. I'll follow right behind you." Rå needed him to be ahead of her so he wasn't drawn by her back. She didn't like using her power on men she hadn't chosen herself. He would think it was so that he wouldn't see her naked.

"I thank you, mistress," he said, looking relieved, then went to get his horse.

Rå smiled again, watching him walk. He was handsome, with well-built shoulders and strong hands. His hair was long and untied and hung in wet ringlets down his back.

When they reached her tree, she told him to wait and went inside and got dressed. "There," she said as she crawled back out from under the branches, "you can look at me now. I'm dressed."

He threw her a quick sidelong glance, then looked her fully in the face, grinning. "I've never seen someone walk in the rain without clothes. Why did you do that?" He had a dark, pleasant voice.

"I like the rain and Thor's work. My dress would take too long to dry."

"Thor's work, eh? It's God, not Thor who brings the weather."

Rå saw no point in contradicting him and lifted the branches and gestured for him to go first.

As soon as he had crawled under, he stopped with surprise. "There's as much space under here as if you were standing in a church!" He approached her treehouse. "You must have a skilled husband. I'd like to meet him, is he here? I've never seen anyone living like this."

"No husband," she said and grabbed his horse, tying it to one of the pillars supporting her house. "A friend built it for me, a

Dane. We're close to the Danish side here, you see. You must know this already. Who are you, and where are you coming from?"

"I'm Jon," he said, pulling off his wet coat, and finding a branch to hang it on. His undershirt was soaked as well.

"Come up. It's warm inside. You can also take that off and hang it indoors, bring your coat too, it isn't as dry as you'd think under here, the leaves drip a lot after a storm like this. I'm Magda," she said and climbed the stairs, holding the door open for him.

"Magda, I thank you." He pulled off his shirt, expertly wringing it, then got his coat from the branch and wrung that, too. He climbed her stairs, smiling in thanks as he passed her.

Rå pointed to her bench by the heating chest. "Have a seat there. I'll hang your clothes to dry," she said and took them from him, hanging them on her hooks by the door. Jon was so cold, he was shivering. She was glad she had added hot stones before the rain. "I'll get you a blanket, and then you can tell me why you're traveling out here."

She retrieved the blanket from her bed. Her house was no bigger than she could reach across to him from her bedroom, handing it to him. It seemed smaller with him there, too. Maybe because he was a lot bigger than Rasmus.

He wrapped it around himself, looking relieved. "That feels wonderful, thank you kindly." Fingering the edges of the blanket, he nodded approvingly. "It's nicely made. I'm a tailor. Anyway, I decided to leave my home for a month or so, possibly longer. There are... well, we have..." He trailed off, looking at her as if he wasn't sure he could go on. "It's a bit complicated to explain to tell you the truth, and I don't want to frighten you, living here alone with no husband."

Rå lit a couple of lanterns and closed her window shutters to get more warmth for him, then sat on the floor, leaning her back on the bedroom wall. "I don't scare easily, pray tell me."

He looked at her for a long moment, then nodded. "Very well, I live near Borakulle. It's just a half day's ride east from here if you hurry. A few months ago, I befriended a man who had lost his memory from some kind of accident. He insisted on living in a cave behind a waterfall, said that he found it in a rainstorm and would stay there until he remembered who he was."

"He didn't know who he was? What happened?"

"I don't know. He didn't either, so he couldn't tell me. I tried to help him the best I could, but his memory never came back. Then he met a young girl who he spent a bit too much time with. She got in the family way, but she lost both the baby and her mind. Didn't have much to begin with in that head of hers." Jon shrugged. "But she accused him of things that made everyone think that he was Näcken himself. Said he pulled her into the mountain and that there was a large man in there." He paused and looked uncomfortably at Rå. "That would be me. I was in that cave with the two of them. And now I'm afraid I'll be accused as well."

Rå narrowed her eyes, a little confused. "What would you be accused of?"

"That I've been in Näcken's company as well," he said, sounding surprised as though it was obvious.

"I see." Näcken was accustomed to more comfort than a cave. It probably wasn't him.

"There's a part of me that's afraid he isn't who he says he is. It's just too convenient to say you don't remember anything and can't answer questions. But I believed him at first at least. He seemed nice enough and all. But then, that last day before I left, I saw his breeches. They were wet all the way up to his thighs, and he had his fiddle on the table in his cave. You see, I think he had played it in the water, then he tried to persuade me to come into his cave again, but I managed to get him to come out instead." Jon took a deep breath and wrapped the blanket tighter around himself. "It's well known that Näcken is supposed to live in that cave. I even told him that, will you believe it? I thought he was just a man, a man who couldn't know about Näcken because of his memory loss. Now in hindsight, given everything that happened, I wonder. Lord, I wonder if it's Näcken himself that I've been spending time with."

"What did he call himself?"

"Nikolaos, a strange old name, wouldn't you say? Sounds like Näcken when you think about it. I made clothes for him and even ate with him. I'm terrified to think about what could have happened, especially when I was stupid enough to go into his cave."

Rå's eyes briefly flicked away from Jon's face. It was Näcken then, after all. It must have been Thor himself that sent this man to her.

"Pray forgive me, I can see I'm frightening you."

"No, no, I'm not afraid. But I think you may still be mistaken. I don't think a water creature eats like a person," Rå said, even though she knew he did. He had quite a hefty appetite for someone who didn't need to eat that much.

"Nah, I don't agree, I'm sure he can. He ate the afterbirth."

"He did what?"

Jon nodded but looked uncertain. "*He* told me the girl had a miscarriage and became confused, but Karin, that's the girl, told other people that he ate the… well, as I said already. I don't wish to scare you with such terrible details. I might be wrong, maybe everything Nikolaos said is true, and I have just gotten worked up. But I'm afraid I'll be accused of being part of it because she told the lawman that there was a large man in the cave with Nikolaos. I'm certainly a big man." He patted his rounded stomach.

"I see." Rå looked down to hide her excitement, feeling a tingle of warmth in her chest. Borakulle wasn't far at all. She would visit Nikolaos. In the meantime, she should offer Jon a place to sleep for a couple of days. It would be nice to have some company, and she could find out more about Nikolaos, learn where his cave was.

***

Jon was very shy at first. It was obvious that he had never been near a woman before. He didn't seem to be aware that she wasn't human either, for he ate and drank whatever she offered him. Men who suspected who she was never did. They refused, thinking there was power in the food as if that would make a difference.

They lay close together on her blankets in her little bedroom. The moon had found a path between the branches and shone straight into her window. Rå could see Jon's face clearly. His mustache looked a little unkempt, making him very handsome. She grabbed him and took him again.

When she felt sated, she pushed him off and moved to sit against the wall. "Come up here and talk to me, sit with me."

He yawned and sat up reluctantly.

"I want you to go to church for me tomorrow, find the mass wafers, and bring them to me."

"The wafers from the holy eucharist?"

"Pray, yes. I need some. They're good for many things. I'll show you. Your luck in hunting will increase as well."

"Ah, I see. Yes, I can see that. I always pray over my herbs and ask people to do the same."

Rå smiled. Jon had told her that he wasn't only a tailor but also helped people with their aches, as she did. She used wafers just to build trust. Humans thought there was power in whatever had been inside a church. "I'll show you tomorrow once you bring them to me. Leave as soon as the sun rises so you'll be back by nightfall. I've heard church bells to the west, it's not far. Go in that direction, and you'll find people to ask. I need you to do this for me," Rå said, snuggling close to him. She kissed his chin, letting her hand slide down to his penis. It lay relaxed between his thighs, spent and moist. "Now we'll sleep. I'll wake you at sunrise."

Jon shook his head. "I'll get the wafers for you. But let's not sleep yet. I'm suddenly awake again." He smiled but moved her hand away from his penis. "I've been using rosemary for memory loss. Is there anything else you're using? And how much rosemary?"

She put her hand on his stomach. "Just a pinch or two is what I recommend. You're going to give it to Nikolaos?" He *was* old, at least if one compared him to humans. Maybe he actually had memory loss.

Jon crossed himself. "Lord, woman, no. I'm curious about your skills and usage, that's all."

"Might be wise." She paused, pushing Nikolaos out of her

mind. "I've not had too many people come to me for a poor memory, but lemon balm is good. It's calming, which helps with memory as well, I find."

"Yes, lemon balm seems to help. I've also used a climbing vine. It's a kind that likes to grow in the shade."

"Shadow vine? Thick leaved, pushing itself up rockfaces?"

Jon sat up straighter, peering at her in the now disappearing moonlight. "Yes, I've found it thus, but it grows naturally up the wall in front of my barn. I never planted it there. Eaten fresh, it keeps me up at night if I'm sewing."

"Fresh?" Rå made a mental note to try that for herself. She usually dried her herbs and then crushed them, making them into tinctures and poultices. "I'd like to visit you and see your garden, Jon. Will you tell me how to get there, and when you'll be back from your long trip away?" She cheered silently. It was a great way to get him to tell her how to find Nikolaos. He was building a house right behind Jon's. No wonder he was scared.

"Happily, I'll draw you a map in the morning. But perhaps I'll visit you on the way back and bring you with me."

"I'd like that." Rå laid down and pulled the blanket up to her chin and closed her eyes, wondering why Jon thought it would be safe to go back. Whatever the case, Thor had indeed sent him to her, maybe with some assistance from Eir, the Goddess of healing. If she brought Jon mushrooms and lichens, he could give her herbs from his garden.

Chapter 32

Nikolaos wanted to see Karin when they brought her in for the hearing, at least get a glimpse to make sure they hadn't hurt her. He arrived early. The church was impressive, painted white with a tall clock tower that he had heard ring yellow and orange far across the land. Now only the birds were awake, sitting in the linden trees surrounding the church, chirping with that piercingly loud sound birds wake each other up with.

He walked around the perimeter to investigate. The big stained-glass window in front had a small windowpane with hinges on one side and a latch on the other. Throwing a quick look over his shoulder, he carefully lifted the latch. It opened without so much as a squeak, and he peeked inside, ready to duck down if someone was there. There was a clear view of the front row and pulpit through it. The church looked empty and quiet. It was a curious thing to place a peephole there. Maybe someone thought the pastor would need watching over, or perhaps it was the other way around. A way for the pastor to see if someone approached or snuck away from the service. Either way, it served his purpose perfectly.

Thanking God for his incredible luck, he left the little window open and walked across the lawn to one of the trees, climbed up and sat on the thickest branch he could find, and waited for Karin and the sixmen.

***

Three of them came galloping down the hill just as Jöns and the pastor arrived on foot from the other direction. Jöns was leaning in, listening to something the pastor was saying. The three on horseback dismounted, tied their horses to a post, and joined the others at the main entrance. It was obvious from their mannerism that they were having a tense conversation.

Then Helge and Mickelsson arrived in a carriage. Karin was sitting in the back. Helge got down first, then helped her down. As soon as she put her feet on the ground, Mickelsson was by her side, and then he and Helge hurried across the yard with Karin between them.

Nikolaos' heart lurched at the sight. She walked stiffly, braids askew, head downcast. He was a coward; it wasn't right to let them question her without doing anything. Uncertain, he shifted on the branch, then began to descend, keeping one eye on Helge and Mickelsson as they painstakingly dragged Karin toward the other men. He should tell them everything. Say he had memory loss and had stayed in the cave even though Jon had warned him about it. Apologize for lying, pretend it was because he was afraid of what they would think. He was just putting his foot on the lowest branch before jumping down when a thought made him hesitate. What if they got angry and made him marry her? Or hang him for spending time in Näcken's cave. He should never have left Karin that night after she lost the baby. That was his biggest mistake. Had he only taken her with him they wouldn't have found her in that state, grieving and hysterical, and none of this would have happened.

Just then, Karin shrieked. Loud. He could hear every word. "I need to speak to Näcken!! He took my babies, all my babies!"

A wave of both relief and guilt washed over him. He stayed where he was.

When the men and Karin had gone in, Nikolaos finally jumped down, making a wide berth to the right so as not to be seen from the inside. Then crouching low, he ran to the open windowpane and positioned himself so he had his back toward the wall and his right ear close to the window.

"She drank the water at least and ate some of the bread. Spoke about rats, not sure…" someone said, his voice trailing off. Nikolaos turned around and carefully looked through the open pane. He saw the edge of the pastor's coat in the middle of the aisle. There was no other movement. Everything was quiet, except the birds now calmer chirping, and cows mooing in the distance.

Then the pastor moved abruptly, and Jöns and another man appeared, bringing chairs that they placed in front of the pews on the far side of the aisle from where Nikolaos stood. That was good. He wouldn't have been able to see anything had they put them by the nearer aisle. As it was now, he could see all the chairs and the first three pews but was hopefully far enough away to avoid being noticed.

The men filed in, dividing themselves between the first pew and the chairs, facing each other. Karin was nowhere to be seen.

The pastor coughed to clear his throat. "Mickelsson, I pray you, tell everyone what happened, then you, Helge can add what you witnessed." He paused for a moment, pulling on his beard. "No, actually, Helge, why don't you tell them what you told me first?"

Helge slid forward on the pew, nodding with a serious expression. "It was when I had visited Mickelsson. We like to meet in the evenings to drink tobacco and talk for a bit. I was on my way home, had just opened the door to leave in fact, when Karin came walking toward the house to go into her room where she and the other maids live. She walked slowly, then stopped and clutched her stomach. She didn't see me and had to support herself on the wall. It looked as though she was going to faint. I was on my way to help her, but then she straightened and went inside. I didn't understand it then, but she must have had one of the babies. I should have known. I've seen how tired my wife is afterward. The baby wasn't with her, so Näcken must have taken it."

Nikolaos shook his head, resisting the urge to run in there to defend himself.

"Indeed, indeed," the pastor said, then mumbled something. It may have been a prayer.

Mickelsson lifted a hand, indicating he wanted to speak. "It was my wife who saw Karin first. She tried to speak to her, but Karin seemed as if she didn't hear her at all. Crying and carrying on and trying to hide something under her skirts and bodice. Said we'd think she had stolen it if we saw it. That, as you can imagine, got me suspicious." He looked up for a moment, nodding gravely. "I grabbed it by force. It was a little grass ring for her finger and a bracelet or the like, you know, the things little girls play with to entertain themselves."

Jöns' hand flew to his mouth. The other men looked stunned.

Mickelsson stood silent, watching their reaction, then added, "I laughed at that and handed it back to her. But she started to scream hysterically as if Näcken was biting her then and there. Maybe he was?"

"Let's not get ahead of ourselves, shall we? Just tell them what you told me earlier," the pastor said, trying to sound calm. It was clear he wasn't.

Mickelsson didn't look convinced but gave a quick nod. "Karin said, hollered really, that she had had seven children with a man who lives in a cave, a very kind man who'd given her gold. When she said that, she kissed the grass things in her hands and put the grass ring on her finger. Then she explained they'd be betrothed soon and have a wedding. The father lives in a green mountain, she said, and I'm assuming she meant the cave, but I don't know. Anyway, she spent time there with him and with a large man. A very…"

"A man? Another creature? Or an actual man? Involved with this, with Näcken?" someone asked, interrupting. Nikolaos couldn't see who it was.

Mickelsson threw his hands up in exacerbation. "I don't know. Karin only said the man was very large and that she was terrified of him. They were dancing, but she didn't want to dance with him and ran home. There was a huge black dog following her too. She also mentioned that Näcken didn't want her to take care of their children and took them from her and put them in the dirt."

Nikolaos crossed himself. He had buried whatever was left of the baby. Had Karin truly not understood that? The path up to his cave was a bit mossy, and he supposed it could be considered a green mountain. But he had taken her home afterward. She certainly didn't run; she could barely walk. And he never saw a dog.

"It's clear this isn't an ordinary man she's speaking of here," the sixman closest to the middle aisle said, interrupting Nikolaos' thoughts. "The cave is known. Näcken is known to live behind the waterfall there. So, surely it's him. Näcken is the father. There's furniture and everything in that cave, it's Näcken's." He nodded knowingly, boring his eyes into the others.

"I thought Näcken spent most of his time in the river and wouldn't use such things," a man sitting beside him said.

"I'm surprised as well," Helge said. "We spoke to an expert the other day, a man who studied with someone who…"

"Lövcrantz," the pastor reminded him.

"Yes, Lövcrantz, that's the name. Nikolaos, the expert, said Näcken is vapor and uses fog to materialize, but I assume if his vaporized body is strong enough to drown people, it's good enough to sit in those chairs of his."

The pastor and Jöns chuckled, but the other men looked horrified, and it became eerily quiet.

Nikolaos was tempted to move closer to get a better look but resisted the temptation. He saw well enough as it was.

The pastor got to his feet, gesturing to Jöns and Mickelsson, who stood, then disappeared out of view. The rest of the men were looking nervous. One of them kept moving his knee up and down rhythmically.

Karin came into view an eyeblink later, walking alone with the men behind her. Jöns pointed to the chair Mickelsson had sat in previously, and all the men moved to the pews to face her, squeezing together to fit.

Nikolaos' eyes moistened. He couldn't see her face, but her shoulders and upper back slumped forward, and she looked defeated and sad.

The pastor was silent, reading his Bible for several moments before he looked at her. "We'd like you to tell us everything that's happened. I know you're upset, but pray try to stay focused and tell us everything."

Karin straightened. "It began on a Thursday. I was in the alehouse cleaning out one of the tubs. He just stood there suddenly." Her voice was hoarse and congested.

"Inside the alehouse?"

"Yes, he was thirsty, and he wanted ale. I gave him some."

"You're saying Näcken was in *my* alehouse, drinking my

ale?" Mickelsson shouted. He looked scared.

The pastor shot him a glance but continued to question Karin. "What else did you do?"

"He…. we… We did it… in the tub."

All the men gasped. It was so loud that Nikolaos feared he had been spotted, but their eyes hadn't left Karin.

"Just to be clear here, you're saying that you fornicated? Committed ungodly acts only a husband and wife should engage in?" one of the sixmen asked but kept his eyes on the pastor next to him.

She nodded.

"Did you do this more than once?" he asked in a tone as if he were asking if she had gone to fetch a forgotten pair of clogs.

"Yes, once more. He came again the next Thursday and was soaking wet. Said he'd fallen in the lake first, but then he said he swam in it."

At that, Mickelsson got up and began to pace around the floor. Nikolaos moved back slightly. "He lives in my lake? In my lake!" Mickelsson sounded both angry and terrified and sat down in the pew again, unable to continue.

Jöns put his arm around him. "Calm yourself, this doesn't mean he lives there. He may have stayed there temporarily."

Nikolaos scoffed.

Karin stayed silent. Her hands were clasped tightly on her lap.

The pastor went on with his questioning. "Karin Svensdotter, pray tell me, after you spent time in the brewhouse, did you fornicate again?"

"Yes, in his bed. He had made a bed for me in the grass in the woods. That's where I had my babies. I had seven beautiful babies, but he took them all." She burst into tears, sobbing loudly.

The men exchanged glances.

Nikolaos looked away, swallowing something cold building in his throat.

"I went to his cave one time," Karen said, banging her foot on the floor for some reason. "There was another man in there too.

A scary man. I didn't want to go near him. I knew because my aunt had a green dress, a beautiful, beautiful dress. There are so many kinds of fruits, I prefer pears."

The men glanced at each other again, looking confused.

Nikolaos sighed in recognition. It was rats the other day, now fruit.

"I'm not sure what you mean Karin. Can you explain in more detail?" one of the sixmen asked, leaning forward with his elbows on his knees.

"What?"

"You spoke of a dress and pears. Could you elaborate?"

"I mean that there was a man in the cave with Nikolaos. I didn't want to dance with him. He scared me. And I said that I prefer pears. They're so sweet."

She told them! Nikolaos' heart started beating fast, and he watched their faces for a reaction, readying himself to run.

But the pastor just looked at the other men, then sighed. "I believe you might be a bit tired. It's been a couple of long days for you here, and you just gave birth as well. Let me ask you some questions about that. Answer them truthfully and remember that you're in a holy place here, God is present."

Nikolaos exhaled, his heart slowing down. Maybe he misheard then. Or maybe the men thought she said Nikolaos by mistake.

Karin nodded several times. "I know we are, we're in church."

"Thank you kindly, Karin," the pastor said, then turned to Mickelsson. "She's worked for you her whole life, is that correct?"

"Yes, her whole family has, I've known her since she was a babe."

"Did she live loosely and impiously?

Mickelsson shook his head. "No, wouldn't say so. She's always been a sweet girl."

The pastor nodded, then turned back to Karin. "Were you involved with Näcken at night, or was it at daytime?"

"It was usually at... in the evenings, when I was finished with my work."

"Were you awake?"

"I… hm, I was awake… I'm not sure if I understand."

"No, need, no need, you answered the question." The pastor waved his hand toward Jöns who moved closer to her and then asked the next question.

"Did Näcken force you to do this?"

Karin shifted uneasily on her chair but didn't answer.

"Did you want it yourself then?" Jöns asked.

She nodded.

Nikolaos couldn't hear it but saw the men's lips form tsk-tsks.

"Did you go to the alehouse on an errand for Mickelsson, or did Näcken bring you there?" Jöns added.

Karin answered something, but in such a low voice, Nikolaos couldn't hear that either. Moving closer to the window, he placed his right ear as close to it as he dared. He couldn't see anymore but heard much better. Even their breathing.

"In other words, you did your work for Mickelsson and was already in the alehouse when Näcken came for you?"

"Yes."

"And you went there on your own? By yourself?"

"Yes, everyone had gone to the funeral. I wasn't allowed to go. I had to get everything ready."

Nikolaos wished he could see Mickelsson's face when she told them that.

"I had ale to put out, people eat a lot after a funeral. Mickelsson was very sad, did you know it's important to get all the hay inside before it rains?" Her voice had changed, and she spoke faster than before.

"Let's not think of that now, Karin. I'm not sure how it relates to the question. I'd like you to be quiet for a moment when I ask Helge something," the pastor said, taking over the questioning himself again.

Nikolaos crouched down and went back to the spot where he stood before so he could look inside again.

The scene had changed somewhat. The pastor and Jöns had switched places, and one of the sixmen was standing behind Karin's chair. She wasn't sitting properly on it anymore but was laying sideways halfway off with her legs splayed out in front of her while holding on to the armrest on the left side with both hands.

"Helge, you said you saw her when you were visiting Mickelsson. And that she appeared weak. It's what you said, isn't it?" the pastor asked loudly, as if Karin's position made it harder to hear.

"Yes, I did. I'd been talking with Mickelsson for a while and was heading home. It was getting a bit late, and yes, it's correct, I saw her."

"I thank you kindly. Can you take a moment and think on it. See if you remember anything else. You mentioned that she was holding onto the wall earlier. Was Näcken there then? Did you see him? He might have been fornicating with her right then and there."

Jöns' and Mickelsson's jaws dropped.

Nikolaos clasped a hand over his mouth to stifle a laugh. What idiots, how in the world would he have managed that?

Helge scratched his arm, looking nervous. The rest of the men began to shift in their seats.

"Think carefully on this now, Helge, it's important."

Helge's eyes went upward and then he shook his head. "No, I didn't see him there. Karin was alone. As I said, she looked weak. I was going to help her, but then she went in on her own."

The pastor turned back to Karin. "I have more questions for you. Karin, sit up properly, this won't do!"

Jöns sprang to the back of her chair, put both hands under her armpits, and lifted her into a sitting position.

"There, thank you," the pastor said, his face blotchy and red as if it were he who had exerted himself. "Tell me, did Näcken fornicate with you there? Was he there when you felt faint?"

"Yes."

Nikolaos almost laughed again. It was becoming completely ridiculous. She was not right in the head. And the men, they didn't seem wiser than her.

"I suspected as much." The pastor got to his feet and turned so Nikolaos could only see his back. Then he asked the question again. "He was right there on the grounds with you? On the farm, fornicating with you?"

"No, he took me home, after... He just took me home."

Nikolaos lifted an eyebrow. Hadn't she just told them they had done it in front of her maids-quarters?

"Did you enjoy your coitus?" the pastor asked.

"Yes."

Nikolaos exhaled, realizing he had held his breath. It was too personal a question, she shouldn't have had to answer that.

"Thank you for your honesty, Karin. I have only a few more questions, and then we're done here." He cleared his throat twice. "Did you notice if you became pregnant each time you fornicated with him? Or did you fornicate several times for it to take?"

"I don't know."

"Hmm, very well. "Did your pregnancies feel like regular pregnancies?"

"No, they didn't. I felt sick in the mornings, and I threw up. I couldn't eat anything. I threw up so much. Nik... Näcken he... I didn't bleed suddenly. It stopped up in me. and it wanted to get out, so I puked instead. Nikolaos, he said that that I..."

"Nikolaos? Who are you talking about now?" The pastor didn't seem alarmed, just annoyed.

"Näcken, I said. I said Näcken." She sounded irritated. "He said that women stop bleeding when there's to be a baby. He wanted us betrothed and have a proper wedding night with witnesses. Näcken was mad at me, and he hit my cheek when I tried to leave."

Nikolaos frowned. He certainly had never hit her. Why would she claim that?

"It's a serious case we have here," someone out of Nikolaos' sight said. "Näcken really tricked her if he said he wanted to marry her. He wants her down in the river with him then. A water wedding."

Karin leaned forward on the chair, her legs wide like a man in breeches. "He took my children! He took them all, hid them from me. I want my babies."

Jöns stood up and reached over and patted her hand, a quick touch, then sat back again. "Did he take your children without your permission, Karin?" he asked.

She started sobbing and pulling on her ears. It looked as if it hurt. "I want my children! I want my babies. There were seven children."

"Karin, you must focus," Jöns said. "Did Näcken take your children without your permission?"

"Yes. Yes, he did." She looked at the pastor. "I wanted to ask you to baptize them and bury them properly. But Näcken said that since we weren't married or even promised, you wouldn't approve, so he took them."

The pastor narrowed his eyes. "Are you saying that the babies died? I thought you said that the children," he sighed, "that Näcken took them, and you wanted to see them. I'm not sure I understand."

"They died, all of them died, and he said that I couldn't have that many, but I can!" She burst into tears, rocking back and forth.

The men exchanged confused glances again. Helge whispered something in the pastor's ear. His head moved up and down in agreement as he listened.

"Karin, pray try to calm down. We're almost done, then you can sit and rest for a while. I have only a few more questions. You mentioned he gave you gifts. Gold, you said?" the pastor asked.

Karin stopped sobbing and looked at him, then whispered something. Nikolaos couldn't hear it.

The pastor smiled slightly. "A bracelet and a ring, I see. Are you sure they're not something ethereal? Did someone else see them?"

"Yes." She sounded distraught, offended. "Mickelsson took them. He ought to know, his wife saw them too, I want them back."

"I told you already, it was just grass," Mickelsson interjected. "And I did give them back to you."

"I see, we're done here, I think. What do you say? Do we have anyth...."

Nikolaos' attention was interrupted by the sound of a wagon on the road. It was coming down the hill fast, disturbing a flock of geese that ran angrily toward it, flapping their wings and screeching. The horses didn't react, and the wagon sped past the church toward Helge's farm, then disappeared around the bend. When Nikolaos shifted his gaze back to the window, the pews were empty.

He froze, afraid he had been spotted. But everything looked as deserted as before. It was odd that people hadn't gathered to hear how the hearing had been going. The sixmen must be good at keeping things quiet if they needed to. Nikolaos cautiously walked all the way to the window, and as he put his face in the open windowpane, the men came back, sauntering down the aisle, and went to stand informally under the pulpit. He slowly moved back out of view.

Jöns sat down on one of the chairs, resting a leg on the chair next to it. "Karin isn't aware of what happened. She's weak-minded. This isn't a clear Näcken case, and I'm not sure what we should do," he said.

The pastor shrugged.

"Mickelsson, that night Karin claimed she was in the mountain with Näcken and that man, was she truly not at home? And I assume she means the cave behind the waterfall. That large man, who's he?" Jöns asked.

"I couldn't say, if she says she wasn't home, she probably wasn't. I don't check on them, we've never had any issues like this. And no, I don't know who the man is."

A sixman came into view momentarily and then disappeared down the aisle again, talking while he paced. "I don't know who he is either. Nor am I sure what to do. Had we been certain Karin has been fornicating with Näcken and had children with him, it would be another thing altogether," he said and came back and sat down next to Jöns.

"You don't believe her then?" Mickelsson asked.

The sixman didn't reply, but the pastor did. "I think she might be imagining things. She's too confused to understand what's going on. Clearly weak and not fully aware of what's happened. She said her children were with Näcken, but then she said she wanted to bury them. I'm not comfortable dealing with this case on my own. I say we write to the Royal Court and ask for advice."

"Can we do that?" Jöns asked.

"Yes of course. We ought to tell the twelvemen first, but let's not. I say we don't bother them with this. I don't want any more trouble. We'll handle it."

"I agree, I'd like it taken off our hands," Mickelsson said. "Let the Royal Court decide what to do. But it angers me to think that Karin has been with Näcken in my alehouse! I almost want to strangle the girl. And what if Näcken is still in my lake?"

Nikolaos felt his cheeks redden. He had acted like a horny boy. Abluna must be waking from her peaceful rest, chiding him from her grave. He, a married father and grandfather, taking a young girl in an ale tub.

"We ought to watch your lake just in case, Mickelsson," Helge said from somewhere in the back of the church. "We'll go home now and eat and rest for a bit, then this evening we'll look for clues, both in the alehouse and in the lake. You oughtn't drink the ale anymore."

"All my ale? I'm not getting rid of perfectly good ale." Mickelsson said, sounding indignant.

Nikolaos grinned.

Then the men stood to leave, filing out of view, one after the other.

Chapter 33

The need for water became painfully urgent. Nikolaos couldn't concentrate, his limbs didn't move properly, and he felt the loss of his voice, even his thoughts. It was years since it's been this insistent. He wanted to go to his spot above his cave but didn't dare and forced himself to look for another place upriver. It took a painfully long time, but he found a place so dense with overgrowth it would be unpassable by people. It was perfect.

With shaking hands, he tore his clothes and boots off, then with one fluid motion as if he were already waterborne, he dove in and sank to the bottom.

***

Someone had moved the log he had put in front of the door and had placed it off to the side, standing up.

Nikolaos froze, instantly on guard. The sixmen must have figured out who he was then and understood that Karin hadn't confused the names. Thank God he had been in the water so he could deal with it.

In the span it took for him to dismount, tie Kristina up, and tiptoe to the door, he was prepared to either kill the intruders or sweet talk them out of the truth.

He flung the door open, then stopped in his tracks.

A woman was sitting there. Right in front of the door, her hair spread around her in a wide circle. He did such a double take that she laughed. It was Rå.

"Didn't expect to find me here, did you? That log of yours doesn't do much to keep even humans out."

"Rå?" He stared at her, utterly dumbstruck.

She stood, trailing her hair along the floor as she moved. It was longer than when he saw her last, almost down to her feet. She reached for him and cupped his face in her hands. Her eyes were moist, and he felt his own tear up in response. "I didn't find you," she said. "Thor did, or rather, he brought Jon to me who then told me about you and explained how to find you."

He grabbed her hands, touched by the gesture, and then realized what she said. "You know Jon, Tailor Jon? I can't believe it."

"Yes, Jon. He ran from you and came upon me. I've been hoping to see you again for years, but Thor didn't find it seemly until now. But it's clear that you need help again."

Nikolaos shook his head with a bewildered smile. "You believe in those old Gods, Rå? I thought I was the odd one, still Catholic."

"I know." She pulled her hands out of his. "Let's go sit somewhere. I'm hungry. I traded herbs for bread and eggs down at the farms. How can I not believe in Thor? He bangs his hammer in the clouds quite frequently. People used to give him his proper respect."

"Have you lived so long that you spent time with his believers?" Her eyes met his, and he kept her gaze, waiting for what felt like a long time, but she didn't answer him. "We can sit there if you want," Nikolaos said, disappointed, pointing to his blanket in the corner. "I haven't made any new furniture yet. The ones I have, I left in a cave. Everyone thinks they're Näcken's, so I can't bring them here." He grinned; he had fooled them all.

Rå reached for a basket that she had placed on his windowsill and brought it to the blanket. "I heard about your cave. You ought to watch yourself and not find such humor in things that could hurt you."

"I know, Rå," he said and sat down, crossing his legs like a tailor.

They sat silently after that. He watched her eat. She ate every morsel and crumb, licking her fingers each time they got sticky with the raw egg she cracked and poured over the bread. She was so beautiful.

When she finished her last bite, she looked up, gazed at him warmly, and moved closer to him. "How can I help you, Näcken?"

"Please call me Nikolaos, that's my name."

She patted his cheek, her eyes crinkling with warmth, but

she didn't answer.

"Before I tell you, Rå, you must tell me where Jon is. Is he back home?"

"No, he's gone to Norrköping. Did you lose your memory, Nikolaos, or was that something you told Jon?"

"I see." What if Jon had understood that he had known his father? "No, I didn't, not really. I told Jon that so he could explain things. I lost time when I lived in my cave. A lot of time." He reached around Rå, grabbing his wine and mugs which he kept on a log in the corner. "I want some of this, then I'll tell you everything."

Nikolaos handed her a mug and poured wine for them both. Then he started talking. Rå listened intently, sipping her wine with the same enjoyment as when she ate. When he finished, he had told her of how Old Karin found him and made him understand how much time had passed, his time in jail with her, her hanging, the lecture, and of Karin and her hearing, even how he found her in the brewhouse.

Rå reached out and squeezed his hand. "Now you feel guilty and think you're the cause of this and want to help her. But you don't want to wed her because she is weak-minded?"

"Keenly observed."

"And you've snared yourself into your own spiderweb of lies that doesn't match up with the ones you told Jon?"

"Yes."

"As for you being losing all that time, I don't know. You shouldn't live so close to waterfalls. It's likely affecting you too much."

He poured them some more wine. "I think so too. It's the only way I can explain it to myself." She hadn't commented on him looking younger, but he decided not to ask. It bothered him so much he didn't even want to think about it.

Rå got up to stretch. The movement made her hair move sideways, and he sensed that the hole in her back was opening. Without a word, she left the room and went outside.

Curious, Nikolaos kept his eyes on her through the still glassless window. She had stopped in the middle of the front yard.

The wind pushed her long hair sideways, and he noticed that she was wearing a brown shift that split in two below her shoulder blades, revealing her now open back hole and smooth, firm buttocks. He felt a rush of attraction mixed with fear and a sudden thought that he should marry her. Then Rå reached around with both hands and pulled off her shift, standing completely naked. She was as beautiful as he remembered from that day in the forest.

"Don't look, you're distracting me!" she shouted without turning her head toward him.

Nikolaos took a sip of wine, then put the glass away and lay flat on his back, staring at the rafters, embarrassed and surprised at his sudden feelings.

The next thing he knew, Kristina was sniffing his face, and it was already dark. "Kristina," he mumbled, disoriented, "what are you doing inside?" He heard a chuckle behind her and the sound of his firestarter as Rå lit a candle. He closed his eyes against the sudden light. When he opened them again, she was smiling at him.

"I brought Kristina in," Rå said. "She seemed lonely, and Thor was driving around again. She was very happy to come with me, but she barely fits through your door."

Nikolaos pushed Kristina's large head aside and sat up, yawning. "I fell asleep. I must have been sleeping for a while. It's dark. The last thing I thought was that we should wed, you and I," he said, only half joking.

Rå put the candle on the floor. "Me and you? It would never work."

"It won't? Why not?"

"Nikolaos, I'm flattered, but no. We're not human and need not follow their folly traditions. And it's not what Freyja would want."

Nikolaos quickly looked away. He had overstepped. She deserved his reverence like Mother Mary. "Pray forgive me, Rå. I didn't mean to offend," he said. But when he faced her again, she was smiling warmly.

"I know. Let me tell you what I felt when you were sleeping.

I was outside for a while before Thor arrived to confirm everything. The pastor and those sixmen are wondering where you are. They expected you to come and ask about the hearing. You should go for a visit as soon as you can, then you ought to leave here. Go start that life of yours that you wanted, find yourself a wife, and be a farmer again."

"Another wife than you." He gave a lopsided smile, still feeling embarrassed. But she was right. It was what he had thought himself anyway. Still, it saddened him to leave his brand-new house. He had been looking forward to putting glass in the windows and getting new and proper furniture.

Chapter 34

The following morning, Rå went to Jon's deserted farm to look at his herbs. She could barely believe what she saw. Rows upon rows, neatly labeled according to use and ailment, spread before her inside a sizable stone enclosure. She had never seen anything like it. Not even the cloister gardens she had visited during the time of the nuns and monks had been as lovely or with so much variety. Jon must have spent years cultivating it. Stepping carefully on the little paths between bushes and plants, she inhaled the heady scent and slowly made her way around, taking everything in. Belladonna and mandrake were growing separately from the other herbs, along with a pale-leafed small bush she didn't recognize. She rubbed her fingers against its leaves and sniffed. Pungent and sharp with an almost sickening sweetness. Her fingers tingled from the touch. The leaves were probably deadly with improper use but might induce visions of the dead if used correctly. Herbs like it were a comfort for many. Jon knew what he was doing, growing them off to the side like this. All three had a sign with a head in front of it too, indicating their effect on someone's mind. Mandrake was said to shriek when pulled from the earth, but she had never noticed it.

Moving forward, she recognized lavender, celandine, blistering nettle, and Saint John's Wort. Interestingly, the Saint John's Wort was growing near his juniper, which she knew was sometimes used religiously. She never sorted her herbs according to what the Gods did. Perhaps she should. One thing was clear, Eir made Thor send Jon to her, there was no longer any doubt about it.

Rå sent Eir and Thor a prayer of thanks, then left the garden. For now, she would trade with the villagers. Jon would come back when Eir willed it.

***

Nikolaos arrived at the church at the same time as the pastor. "Morning, reverend," he said, bowing.

"Ah, I'm glad you're here. I want to tell you what happened

at the hearing and see what you think. Come in for a bit. Care for a mug of ale? I even have a small piece of sugar left." He walked to a side door off the main entrance, looking over his shoulder to make sure Nikolaos was following. Then he opened the door and pointed into a dark corridor. "Make a left and make yourself comfortable in my study, I'll be with you in one moment."

"I thank you," Nikolaos said, waiting for his eyes to adjust to the darkness, seeing a faint light under the study's door.

The room was small but had a nice large window with a wide windowsill. There was a desk and chair, the Bible he had seen at Helge's lay open on the desk, and there was a celestial globe, a quill, an inkwell, and an actual clock! He inhaled sharply. It was as tall as a hand's length, as wide as two handsbreadths, and covered in gold. There were Roman numbers under the glass. An arrow pointed to VIII, which must mean it was eight in the morning. Nikolaos started to reach for it, but just then, he heard the pastor approach and quickly pulled his hand back, turning toward the door.

The pastor entered, pushing the door with his elbow as he brought full ale mugs and a plate with two tiny pieces of sugar.

"I came at the right time. I thank you kindly," Nikolaos said, smiling as he said time but thinking of the clock, not the sugar.

"Take it!" The pastor looked at Nikolaos expectantly.

Nikolaos grabbed one between his forefinger and thumb. It was no bigger than a fingernail, and he licked the surface with the tip of his tongue. He was surprised the pastor had saved such a small piece for so long. It was incredibly good. He would give almost anything to see Rå eat it.

"And... what do you think of it? Better than manna from heaven, wouldn't you say? Blasphemy it may be, but just the same, this must be better."

Nikolaos laughed. "I wouldn't know, I've never had manna. What is it?"

The pastor looked at him silently, and then he laughed too. "To tell you the truth, I don't know. But sit, take my chair, I'll sit on the windowsill here," he said, pointing to the window but keeping his eyes on Nikolaos' face.

Nikolaos placed the sugar on his tongue and let it melt, enjoying the sweetness. It was so tiny, still the flavor remained in his mouth after he swallowed. "It's remarkable."

The pastor nodded with satisfaction and crossed the floor, seating himself on the windowsill. "Remarkable indeed. Well, anyway, I wanted to tell you about Karin. We didn't come to a conclusion about it. It was an odd hearing." He stopped, looking at the Bible on his desk as if he thought it might have an answer for him. "She seems to switch from being lucid and able to answer any question we ask to someone who's confused and speaking about things that have nothing to do with what we're talking about."

Indeed, that was precisely what she did. "I'm not too surprised to hear that," Nikolaos said. "The way she sounded that night in the barn, I got the feeling that she wasn't completely sane."

"Is it common in these cases?"

For a moment, Nikolaos forgot that the pastor thought him an expert and almost told him he didn't know, then caught himself. "It can be, but not quite like this. I'd say most often the victims are no more confused than you or I."

The pastor hummed in response, pursing his lips as his eyes darted around the room. He looked as if there was something he couldn't remember, but then he shrugged. "We sent a letter to the courts. I just got it out last night, was going to send it with the post-runner, but decided last minute to have it brought there personally. Thomas is delivering it."

"Who's Thomas?"

"One of the sixmen, I wanted to make sure it got there directly, no delays. You never know what can happen on route."

"I see, I assume you're speaking of Göta Royal Court?"

"Oh, I didn't say? Yes, Göta Court, they've dealt with these things before. It's all too common. God isn't happy with us. People fornicate too much, don't take heed of His word, and then He allows these creatures free rein to test us."

Nikolaos looked down to hide a chuckle, thinking of how Rå was probably trading her herbs with his congregants at this very moment. For a pastor who was so sure of God's will, he sure was gullible, inviting him in here. He should play with him a little. See if he could get him to give him the clock from his desk. He had brought his fiddle and still felt strong after his time in the river yesterday. It wouldn't hurt to try.

"Hmm…" Nikolaos pretended to absently pick up the fiddle which he had placed next to his chair, then slowly began tapping on it as if he didn't think of what he was doing. "I'm not so sure about that, pastor," he said, reaching for his bow. Concentrating on the feeling of water still remnant in his body, he began to play. Slow and haunting. His own music.

The pastor threw him a surprised look. Then his eyes lost focus, and he slumped backward, putting pressure on the window behind him. There was a crack as one of the panes broke into pieces.

"You're going to stay very calm when we speak here. I'll stay here just a short while longer. Take your boots off," Nikolaos prompted just to see how he would respond.

The pastor did what he said without any inclination of it being an odd suggestion. Nikolaos almost laughed but kept his expression calm. "There, very good. I'd like another piece of sugar. Can I have some?"

"Pray forgive me, there isn't any left. I took the last piece, and we ate it already." The pastor's voice sounded innocent as if he were a boy.

"No need to apologize. Give me that clock there instead," Nikolaos said, putting the fiddle back down by his chair.

The pastor nodded, got up, and walked on bootless feet across the floor. They stunk. He picked up the clock with both hands and handed it to Nikolaos.

"Thank you, I thank you kindly. You can sit now. Sit and rest for a moment," Nikolaos said.

The clock felt cool and smooth in his hands. There was a vibration from the cogs inside it. A true automaton, ticking loudly to its own rhythm but not loud enough to create colors. A shame, he would have liked to see that. Still, it was incredible. What if he took it, hid it under his shirt and walked out? Nikolaos shot an eye at the pastor. He was sleeping soundly, his face expressionless. But as tempting as it was, he wasn't a thief. He looked back at the clock, touching the smooth gold with his fingertips, then carefully stood up, deciding to hide it under the desk instead. It would be enough to confuse the pastor a bit and maybe remind him of who had visited. By then he would be gone. Placing it in the far corner under the desk, he moved his chair to block the spot where the clock used to stand on the desk, then sat down and waited for the pastor to come to.

When he did, he looked bewildered and confused. "Oh, where was I?" I feel a bit sleepy suddenly. My boot, my boot is off, how strange!" He bent to pick one up and put it on, leaving the other on the floor, oblivious.

"You spoke of Göta Royal Court and how they're used to cases like these," Nikolaos said as if they were still in the middle of the conversation.

"Yes... yes, of course. Pray forgive me, it's been a long couple of days here."

"I understand. I'll need to leave soon but wanted to ask about Karin first. Where is she now? Would it be possible for me to speak with her?"

"I don't see why not. She's in the barn still. We haven't decided what to do with her yet. A letter can take a while. Unless the courts read it right away and send a reply with Thomas, but I doubt that. We may have to let her go. Mickelsson will have to keep a close eye on her. We're very cautious, and we have guards at the lake and by his ale house. So far there hasn't been a trace of Näcken anywhere. We even got hold of a harper who played for him, but it was to no avail. Näcken didn't appear."

"A harper?"

"Yes, if you play the harp near water, you'll lure him out. We stood at the ready with our muskets, but as I said, to no avail."

Nikolaos silently thanked him for the warning. "Pastor, how do you know if you see a trace of him? What are the signs that he's been there?"

"I'm not certain, maybe you can tell me, Nikolaos. As I understand it, you'd see strands of his hair near the water or wet footprints that don't dry like other footprints."

"I see. Make sure you don't step in those footprints, they'll burn, you know," Nikolaos said, managing to keep his face straight.

"They do?" The pastor's eyes widened.

"Yes, watch where you're going," Nikolaos said. It was a lie, but it served the pastor right. "I must take my leave if I'm going to have time to speak with Karin. Is Helge home? Does he have the key now?"

The pastor looked at him and blinked, still somewhat confused.

"The key," Nikolaos repeated. "The other day, Helge mentioned that Jöns had the key. Does he still have it, or did he give it to Helge?"

"Oh? Eh… I'm not sure."

"No need. I'll leave you to your work now. I'll visit Helge and see what he says. I thank you again for sharing the sugar with me. It was delicious."

"Of course, I was happy to." The pastor beamed, seeming almost himself, but walked across the floor to see him out without noticing that he was still wearing only one boot.

***

Nikolaos rode past the barn and went straight to Helge's front door, gently kicking it with his foot from where he sat in the saddle. There was no movement inside, and he kicked again, a little harder. No one responded.

Backing up and shielding his eyes from the sun with his hand, he looked across to the herbal garden, the hops, and the woodshed. All was still, no sounds indicating that someone was home. The outbuildings were deserted too. He called out but heard nothing. Maybe Helge's wife and daughters had taken their animals to graze in the woods.

He urged Kristina into a gallop, and headed to the barn,

dismounting before she had come to a complete stop and calling out, "Karin! Karin?"

She didn't answer. All he heard was Kristina's breathing and the wind. He walked around to see if there was a hole or a crack in the wood to peer through but found none and was just about to give up when there was a shuffling sound inside.

"Näcken, is it you?" Karin's voice sounded weak and dry, as if she had just woken up. She probably had.

"Well, it's Nikolaos, Näcken I'm not sure about."

"Oh, you're here, I thank you. Thank you. Pray, let me out, take me with you. I… they asked me all kinds of questions. I'm afraid I got confused. I wasn't sure what I was telling them, I was so nervous."

"I understand, Karin. I heard about it. You did the best you could." He pushed down a burst of guilt and lifted the beam, then tried to open the door. It was locked. Of course. "Karin, I'm going to have to leave to see if I can find the key or something else to try to pry the door open with. I'll try to think of something."

"I understand, Näcken, I do. I thank you kindly for trying."

"Karin, I'm…" he started, then stopped. She kept calling him Näcken. It couldn't just be confusion, she sounded lucid now. He took a deep breath and slowly let it out, then spoke the words that would change both their fates, "I see you understand who I am now, Karin. I wish you good fortune. May God be with you."

He wouldn't come back for her, but at least he hadn't killed her.

Nikolaos was halfway down the road when he spotted Rå leaving one of the farms. Jöns' farm, he thought but wasn't sure. She wore a long, wide skirt that concealed her shape and ankles, a thick blue shawl wrapped over her shoulders, hair tied up and covered by a scarf like a married woman, and a basket on her right arm. She looked very much the farmwife.

He urged Kristina into a trot and caught up. "Good day, to you, mistress. A nice day, isn't it?" He grinned.

"Indeed, it is. Are you in need of any medicinal herbs? Taken with the host, it'll heal you of many ailments," she said, winking conspiratorially and pulling out several communion wafers.

Nikolaos laughed, wondering how she got a hold of them and hoping she hadn't stolen them from a church. "No, but I see a couple of women down there. They'll be impressed with such a holy addition." He pointed to the farm where the little boys lived. A pair of women were already heading in their direction. One was the same woman who gave him eggs that very first day. "I'll be on my way. I'll see you at home," he said and lifted his hat.

Chapter 35

Rå watched Nikolaos ride away. Kristina's rump was strong-muscled, and she trotted down the road with a speed unnatural to most horses. Nikolaos probably hadn't realized she was absorbing his power. But that was no ordinary horse anymore. Just like men not to notice something like that.

The women from the farm were hurrying along the side of the road now. They looked beside themselves with excitement, eager for news and the opportunity to share what was on everyone's minds.

"Good day to you, goodwives," Rå said. "I have herbs if you should be interested? I'll be happy to trade. I'm in need of eggs and bread, as well as thread and yarn if you're able?"

"I've some newly spun. I could spare some happily," one of them said, peeking into Rå's basket. She was so skinny her chest was flat like a man's and her collarbones protruded visibly under her dress. "And I've good eggs and plenty of fresh bread. We had our spring baking just a few weeks ago. Our village bakes it down at Mickelsson's by the lake. Have you passed by it?"

Rå shook her head. "No, I didn't pass a lake, I walked through the woods. "I did get some of that bread from a goodwife yesterday though, but I ate it all. It was very good."

"I'm glad. But as I was saying, we got our share and more. You're welcome to a bit of it with some lard, should you want to come in and sit by the hearth for a bit? We live just back there," she said, pointing behind her.

"We have ale as well if you're thirsty?" the other woman said. She was younger and slim but not as malnourished. There was a roundness to her bosom and her cheeks. She had bright blue eyes and blond hair escaping from her scarf. A nursing mother, Rå sensed.

"Thank you kindly, I'd be delighted. My name is Magda. I've traveled a bit to get here."

"Oh, you must be weary," said the older of the two. "I'm Ida, and this is my daughter, Britt."

Rå curtsied, then followed behind them as they turned around and walked back to their farm.

It looked a little dilapidated, but a pig was sleeping in front, and at least fifteen hens, a rooster and too many chicks to count, were scurrying about. And a flock of geese came running from behind the house, stopping when they saw Rå.

She laughed. "You have a nice brood here. Then I feel good about trading with you and won't take food from your little ones. I'd rather have eggs than yarn then if you're willing?"

"Of course," Britt said, nodding for emphasis.

"How many children do you have?"

"Only three, my husband is gone. I have two boys and a girl who's barely a year."

"Our neighbors have been very generous in her time of grief. They've each given her chickens from their own flocks. That's why you see so many here," Ida said, gesturing toward four fuzzy ones sitting tightly together on the ground, sound asleep.

"I see," Rå said, smiling at the chicks. Then she straightened her face and looked at Britt. "My condolences for your husband, Britt."

"I thank you." She answered without emotion, then changed the subject. "My boys are running around somewhere as usual, and my daughter is wrapped and safe in her cradle indoors."

Ida opened the door and stepped aside so Rå could walk in first. The hearth was blazing, and the heat felt pleasant on her cheeks. The earthen floors were well swept, there was a table with benches by the window, and the room behind the front room had a wool rug that looked neat and clean. She could see the edge of the cradle where the baby must be sleeping. They were doing very well. Why was Ida so skinny?

"Sit," Britt said, pointing to the table. "My mother will get the bread. Would you like some broth or some ale?

"Thank you kindly. Broth would be nice."

Britt got a mug for her and dipped it in a cauldron hanging on the warming hook at the hearthside. "It's still warm. Enjoy it and rest a bit," she said, smiling warmly at Rå.

Ida opened a corner-cupboard and retrieved a pot of lard and a perfectly round piece of hard dense bread from a tall stack. She broke it into pieces, handing Rå the largest. "There, pray take a generous portion of lard, don't be shy."

Britt put Rå's mug on the table. "What do you have?" she asked and sat down. "Do you have something to help a mother's milk? Anything for aches? I get headaches. And Mother gets toothaches."

Ida nodded, touching her cheeks with a grimace.

"Yes," Rå said. "I have caraway which will freshen your breath and help with toothaches. For your milk, Britt, I recommend you eat more than usual and have more ale and wine. Drinking always prevents your milk from drying up. I also have hound's tongue. It'll heal you, Ida, if your sore tooth is festering. And feverfew will cure any headache. I brought a good amount of it as many people use it. I'd be happy to give you several bunches."

"Thank you kindly. I'd like that," Britt said.

"You're welcome. They'll stay potent if you grind them up and keep them dry in a tightly lidded clay pot. I'll add a blessed host as well for safekeeping if you give me a good laying hen and a few more eggs. I only have one host left, but I feel you shall have it," she added, looking closely at Ida. Her bad teeth might account for her malnourishment.

"I thank you kindly as well," Ida said, joining them at the table. "A laying hen we can spare easily." She got up again and brought back an egg basket. "And eggs, take as many as you'd like."

"I appreciate it. May God bless you," Rå said.

It became quiet and Ida and Britt exchanged a glance. Then Britt asked, "Do you have something to ward off evil?"

"Evil?" Rå lifted her eyebrows, pretending she didn't know who they were referring to. "I like to use thyme, it's a powerful protective." She plucked six eggs from the basket and put them in her own basket. Then she waited.

Ida threw Britt another glance, then cleared her throat. "I'll tell her." She patted the top of her daughter's hand, then turned back to Rå. "I should warn you, and pray forgive, I already forgot your name, M...?"

"Magda."

"Magda, that's what it was. I should've remembered. It was my cousin's name as well. My cousin was a wonderful woman. She died years ago, was always poorly, unfortunately."

"Mother, get to the point. We need to tell her what we're dealing with here. Magda should know if she walks around here by herself," Britt said.

"Yes, yes, you're right. We've had Näcken among us, you see, Magda. Got a young maid with child and took her children. She's mad with grief for them now. They're keeping her in the barn near the church."

Britt gave her mother a sharp look. "You make it sound as if Näcken left. But no one knows if that's true. He might still be here."

"Näcken? You mean the waterman? Are you sure of this?" Rå asked.

"As sure as you're sitting right here, Magda," Ida said. "They found his cave behind a waterfall. You wouldn't believe what was in it! There was a table and a bench and pieces of horsetail. The waterman turns into a horse on Thursdays, you see."

"No, Mother, he can turn into a horse on any day, but Thursday is especially dangerous," Britt said, sounding proud of her knowledge.

"Well anyway, Magda, it's true. I spoke with Algot, he's watching Tailor Jon's cattle, even his dogs. Jon left, thought that Näcken was after him. Algot said the tailor had spoken with Näcken, thinking him just a regular man first, but then suddenly he noticed that his breeches were wet." Ida paused, then her eyes widened. "And he dissolved right in front of him. Just like that, as if he were made of water. Just disappeared, he did! Right in front of him," she repeated, losing breath as she spoke.

Rå maintained eye contact with Ida but said nothing. Had Jon told Algot this? Or had Algot made it up? Tales were spun into more lies when new people got hold of them.

Britt stood up abruptly, then went to the door and called for her boys. And then she went into the other room and retrieved the baby. A round-cheeked little head with thick white-blond tufts of hair stuck straight up out of the swaddling. She was grinning happily, showing two little teeth in the lower gums.

"What a darling, such a sweet little girl," Rå said.

Britt smiled. "A good baby she is. She lies calm in her cradle, unlike the other two, who carried on even though I wrapped them good. Here they come," she said, lifting her chin at the window. Two little boys were running at high speed toward the house. The relief on Britt's face was immense.

The boys were chattering with each other when they entered but stopped talking when they saw Rå.

"Who are you?" the oldest asked. He was just a little taller than the other but skinnier and had lost the roundness of childhood. Both boys were dirty from playing or perhaps helping in the fields and the barns.

"I'm Magda," Rå said. "Who are you?"

"Tyge," the older boy said.

"And your brother?"

"Tobias," Tyge said politely. "Näckla stole the pastor's clock."

Ida and Britt gasped so loud that Tobias started wailing and ran to his mother. She hoisted him up on her lap next to the baby.

"Tyge, sit. Sit down beside Magda and tell us what you mean? Who told you that Näcken stole the pastor's clock?" Ida asked, pointing to the bench where Rå sat.

"Yes, Näckla. Helge said it."

"You've been all the way up the hill? I told you not to go too far!" Britt scolded.

"Yes, we met him by the turch. Helge said Näckla took his boots too, and his clock," Tyge said in his sweet child's voice, mispronouncing the words and ignoring the scolding.

Britt caught Rå's eye and then Ida's. "Dear Lord in heaven."

Rå sighed. She could imagine it. Nikolaos had looked somewhat mischievous when she saw him on the road. It was only a matter of time until they figured out who he was. She was glad she had told him to leave yesterday.

"Britt, I'd be glad to get that laying hen now. I ought to go."

"Yes, you ought, it's better. Do go straight home. Don't linger here anymore," Ida said.

"I shall," Rå said, pulling out three large bunches of herbs and explaining what each meant. Then she handed them both a small bunch of thyme. "This is for your protection, keep it in your pocket or under your bodice in a piece of cloth."

"Thank you kindly from the bottom of our hearts. You came at the right time, Magda. Perhaps you want to stay a bit longer, instead? Or maybe stay here tonight? You're welcome to. It isn't safe out there. Should you really be wandering on your own?" Britt asked, putting the thyme in her handkerchief and stuffing it under her blouse.

Rå reached for her arm and squeezed it. "It's kind of you, but I should be going. I appreciate your kindness. Leave some of my thyme out for safety, and silver if you have it, it'll protect you. Oh, and here, take another host," she added, forgetting that she had told them she only had one left until she said it.

"Bless you! Thank you, I'll get the hen now for you," Britt said and didn't seem to notice the error. She went to the door and waited until Rå was right next to her before she opened it. Letting Rå out, she followed close behind and quickly closed it again.

Britt's face was drawn in fear while she clicked her tongue to gather the hens. She grabbed the first one she could reach and handed it to Rå. "She's a good one. Hurry now Magda. Get away from here to a safe place. I must go inside to my children."

"I will, and you as well." She curtsied. But Britt didn't see it. She had already turned away.

Rå walked cautiously at first to calm the bewildered hen in her arms. On the road, she loosened her shawls and opened her back, and the hen settled, nuzzling her head in Rå's armpit. She didn't even react when there was a sudden bang from a shutter closing and a woman's voice calling out in surprise at something.

Chapter 36

Rå hurried up the path Nikolaos and Jon had created by shuttling construction materials between the trees. Nikolaos was playing. She heard his vaporous music reverberating through the air, getting stronger the closer she came.

He was sitting on a piece of wood, playing like he had no care in the world. Didn't he understand that the music would alert people to where he lived? Clearly, he didn't, for his eyes were closed and his neck tilted to the side as his strong right arm moved the bow across the strings. His dark hair was long now, reaching just below his shoulders, not short and stubby like it had been when he visited her in her boulder home all those summers ago. He didn't have a beard, but a slight stubble colored his chin. It made him very handsome. Maybe she should have said yes to his halfhearted proposal the night before. She laughed. What a thought!

Nikolaos stopped playing when he heard her laugh, looking up with a grin. "You're bringing me a hen? Where's your head covering? I was so impressed by your disguise on the road."

Rå set the hen on the ground and touched her head, feeling her tied up plaits under her fingers. Her scarf had slid down and wrapped around her shoulders, and her thick shawl was gone, leaving her back hole open and exposed through her split shift. "Oh, I never noticed losing it." She pointed to the hen, which was already picking at the ground. "I traded for it. You, I heard, stole from the pastor. What were you thinking? How could you be so careless, especially when I'm here?" It was irritating. She was having such a nice chat with Britt and Ida until they found out what he had done. "That you put yourself in danger is one thing, but I don't want to be caught in it."

"How did you hear that?" Nikolaos asked, looking slightly shamefaced. It didn't last long, then his face split into another one of his handsome grins. "I didn't steal anything. I just put it under his table and had him pull his boot off. I couldn't help myself. They're so gullible sometimes. I was rather enjoying myself. I'd give anything to see his face when he finds it and learns that it wasn't stolen, after all," he said, eyes glinting.

Rå tried not to smile. She had to admit it was funny. "Britt's boys told me. Everyone is talking about you and is afraid. It isn't safe here."

"The pastor told them this?"

"Someone named Algot did, and Helge. Nikolaos, you should gather your things. You should leave now. I'll go with you part of the way. I want to ask you something."

He didn't reply but got to his feet, put his fiddle under his arm, and disappeared into the house. It was too bad he had to leave it. It was a nice house he had built for himself.

Rå was sitting in front of Nikolaos on his otherworldly horse. She could feel from his posture behind her that he was nervous about being so close. While other men became beside themselves with lust, Näcken seemed in awe, afraid of touching her. He hid it well, but she noticed. His arms, wrapped around her to reach the reins, were tense, and he was trying to hold them away from her so as not to touch her waist. They did anyway, and she felt the strong muscle under his shirt. Part of her didn't want him to go, but it was time.

"I'll send you on your way now." She turned in the saddle, looking him in the eye. "Näcken," she said, ignoring his request to never call him that. "Why didn't Karin drown?"

He stared at her, and she thought he would get upset, but then his eyes softened. "I managed to keep her safe because we were never in moving water."

"And the waterfall?"

"It's different, it doesn't seem to cause danger."

"I see." It was strange, but clearly he was right since they had all been in the cave with him. Part of her wanted to see it for herself, but she didn't want to intrude on the Mountain Rå's domain. The mountains were hers alone.

"I never do it on purpose, and I never mean to hurt anyone," Nikolaos said, bringing her back to the present.

"I thought so." Rå cupped his chin in her hand, then kissed

him gently on the mouth, "Bye, Nikolaos Näcken, pray be safe. We may meet again."

He looked utterly stunned.

Rå smiled, lifted her left leg over Kristina's neck, then jumped down and waited until Näcken had turned Kristina around. Then she headed home with the hen safely tucked under her arm.

PART THREE
Anno 1674

Chapter 37

Rå had enjoyed the company and the conversation with the women of Jon's village. It reminded her of when she used to be part of a community. Nikolaos had been surprised that she worshipped Thor, wondering if she had really lived among people who still believed in those old Gods, as he called them. He would be shocked if he learned how old she was. It shocked her too, when she thought about it. But time moved on its own, and everything changed so slowly that she was already used to the new by the time it had.

She had been just a baby when the woman who was to be her mother found her crawling around in the moss underneath the Ash Tree. Only moons old, old enough to crawl but not yet able to pull herself up to stand. She had been very hungry, and her new mother had let her suckle from her own breasts which were full of the milk she fed her own baby with. Then she sent her man back to the tree, leaving a rune for the baby's family to find so they would know where she was. But no one came. Though they sent word in many directions, there was never anyone to claim her. Her new family named her Rå, and she was taught the rituals, offerings, and blood sacrifice for Thor and Freyja. Never to Odin, he wouldn't approve of her, Mother said. Rå was too wild and too intuitive for his liking.

They lived in longhouses then, large homes with plenty of space for several families and fires in the middle aisles keeping everyone warm. Those fires had been their gathering place. In the evenings when it was dark and cold outside, too cold to do anything of use, they used to drink and laugh, share stories, or sing together. It had been a good time. People were calm and loving. They were sure of themselves and had a sense of gratitude that permeated everything in a way she had never experienced since. It all changed when the men with the crosses around their necks came. At first, people were interested and happy to meet new folk with exotic ideas. But then one after the other began to change. Just a little at first, most still laughed if someone warned them of the hellfire they would encounter if they didn't pray to the man hanging on that stick. Jesus, their lord and savior, she knew that now. But then, most thought it odd. Odin had already hung himself to get knowledge from the well of wisdom by the roots of Yggdrasil. He had offered an eye for it. Why would they need another?

As if to help her remember those old days, a large crow landed on a branch before her. It stared at her with its large black eyes, reminding her to never forget. Then it took off, its large black wings flapping only inches from her face and fanning her hair as it flew off.

***

Rå named the hen Soft after her soft feathers. She was such a personable little bird that Rå was grateful Ida and Britt hadn't offered her more than one that day. If they had, Soft would have preferred hen company instead of hers.

Rå was sitting on the floor of her porch with Soft on her lap when a sudden rustle in the leaves got her attention. She lowered her head to see under the thick porch railing and spotted a hand being pushed through the leaves. Soon after, Jon's face appeared and then the rest of his body.

"Jon!" She stood up and Soft jumped off her lap with a start, fluttering her wings and cackling in protest. "What a pleasant surprise. I didn't expect you back yet for a while."

He stretched, breaking into a broad smile. "Eh, I had planned to stay longer, but then I thought it silly to stay away so long for the sake of Näcken. Didn't want him to scare me away like this. Once the summer ended, I decided to get home before it got cold."

"You're not frightened of Näcken anymore?"

Jon shrugged. "Well..." He shrugged again. "Let me bring my horse inside here first. You don't mind, do you?" he asked, disappearing under the leavened skirt without waiting to see what she would say.

Soft flew up and sat on the railing, staring at Jon as he reemerged with his horse behind him. He left it untied and hurried up her stairs, standing so close she could feel his breath. He reached for her waist but left his arm in the air in an unspoken question.

"Tell me what happened. You're not scared, you said," she prompted, ignoring his want and taking a step back.

He looked disappointed. "I wouldn't say that, but it seems the panic has left people."

"It has? The villagers seemed awfully panicked when I visited. They said he had stolen a clock and a boot from the pastor."

Jon's eyes rounded with surprise. "You visited?"

"Yes, you drew me a map, remember? I have to admit, I went and looked at your herbs. You have an astonishing collection."

He looked momentarily taken aback with excitement, then he shook his head and gazed up at the canopy for a moment, laughing. "Well, will you believe it? It seems the pastor himself had misplaced that clock unless it was the young girl who cleans for him. Apparently, he found it under his desk. And his boot lay next to the windowsill. I'm surprised he admitted as much, but everyone is talking about it and laughing at him. Nikolaos is gone. In fact, I got a letter from him just last week."

"What did it say?"

He smiled knowingly. "I thought you might ask. I brought it. Do you read?" He pulled a well-thumbed letter from the pocket of his waistcoat and handed it to her.

"Yes, I do." She shot him a glance, then opened it and started reading.

Dear Jon,

I had hoped to speak to you in person, but you were gone, as were your animals which indicated a longer journey. I hope this letter reaches you on your return.

I decided to leave. I know it is cowardly of me to abandon a woman I promised to wed, but like we spoke of, she is of weak mind, and I cannot spend my life with her. Pray forgive me for all the work on my house that came to naught. Take it to use as you wish.

My memory is coming back to me in bits and pieces. I thank you kindly for all the help you offered me when I was troubled.

With affection, Nikolaos.

She kept her eyes on the letter to have some privacy to think. Nikolaos was wise, she had to give him that. Blaming everything on the woman gave him an excellent excuse. She just wished he had been more careful in the first place. He should have kept his distance instead of getting so involved. It was foolish and caused too many rumors. Rå looked back up and gave a small headshake. "Cowardly and cruel, I'd say," she said, even though she of course couldn't blame him for leaving. "Have you heard of the girl? How is she faring now?"

"I'll tell you. I found out just yesterday," Jon said, taking the letter back and putting it in the same pocket as before. "I spoke to Mickelsson."

"Mickelsson?"

"That's the farmer who she works for. He…"

"I see." Rå interrupted him and touched his shoulder. "Let's go inside for some ale, shall we?"

"Gladly." He looked pleased.

She gestured for him to go ahead of her, then let her hair down to cover her back.

"Ale is a treat. I don't always have it, but I happened upon a merchant recently who was kind enough to give me two small kegs," Rå said when she came in, motioning to the corner where they stood stacked on top of each other next to her mugs. "Would you mind filling those for us?" she asked, reaching for her shawl on her bed and wrapping it over her back.

"Mickelsson told me there was a hearing," Jon said and grabbed a mug. "The pastor and his men questioned Karin but concluded that she didn't fully understand what was happening. They sent a letter to the courts, and they replied, saying they agreed with the sixmen's conclusion. That's Göta Royal Court we are talking about here by the way." He nodded for effect and sat down next to Rå, handing her the ale. "The Royal Courts are of a mind that the Devil has influenced her to believe in her own stories. It was the Devil who got her to think she was expecting a baby and everything."

Rå resisted a scoff. "So, Nikolaos didn't get her pregnant then?"

"I'm not sure. According to Nikolaos, she was. And he told me he was there that day when she supposedly lost the baby. But Mickelsson thinks Karin might have just imagined it. She didn't recognize me that time in the cave, so there's no doubt she confuses things."

Rå sipped her ale, nodding. "Are you still suspecting Nikolaos might be Näcken?"

"I don't know that either. Maybe not. Especially after reading his letter and speaking to Mickelsson. I might have panicked a bit." Jon looked embarrassed.

"It certainly sounds like it." Rå smiled broadly, not bothering to hide her amusement, then felt bad. Nikolaos killed people. It was nothing to laugh at. He was a dastard.

Jon's cheeks reddened. "Mickelsson told me that even though there are laws. Karin's case isn't clear enough for them to implement them."

"There are laws for this?"

"Yes, there are. Mickelsson told me. He said there's a law from the year of our Lord 1643, which states that anyone who has anything to do with Satan and the occult shall be punished. It's in chapter six. It says women should be burned, and men should be thrown on the rack." Jon touched her arm apologetically. "I know this isn't fit for women's ears. It's mighty gruesome." He removed his hand. "There was a new law added recently which says that suspicions of involvement with Satan *have* to lead to a trial."

"Hmm," Rå said, sipping more ale.

"But the court letter stated that since the village tried Karin and found that she didn't fully understand what the Devil had done, they recommended that we all pray for her. Satan and the Devil are the same, you know that don't you?"

"Yes."

Jon nodded. "They'll call for another hearing, but Mickelsson thinks she'll be too weak still and they'll have to send witnesses," he said, looking exasperated, finishing his ale in one gulp.

"Have another," Rå said, gesturing toward the keg.

He went to refill his mug, but remained standing, looking out her window.

Rå let her shawl slide off her back and opened her back, waiting for Jon to turn around. She was glad he had come back. She could use a friend.

Chapter 38

Water flowed through Nikolaos, spreading through his arms as blues, greens, and pinks, exploded around him, vibrating with every note. When he finally stopped, he no longer felt solid, but as though every part of him was made of water, coupling with the misty air. It made him cry, or perhaps it was only moisture.

He had just put his right foot on dry ground when there was a sudden movement in front of him. It was a woman, standing right there on the bank. The euphoria instantly left him, and his heart started beating out of control. Had she arrived only moments earlier, it might have been too late.

"Did I startle you Lord Näcken? For it's you, isn't it? I've never heard music so beautiful."

Nikolaos tried to still the panic while eying his breeches and shirt on the ground. There was no point in denying it. "Yes."

"Here," she said and bent to pick up his clothes.

He jumped forward, realizing he still had a foot in the water. "Don't come closer!"

"I won't." She was looking at him confidently and didn't seem bothered by his nakedness or appear afraid of him. She was young and strong, with lovely round cheeks and arms. Her hair was light brown, tied into a thick braid and fastened on her head, and her dress was well made but looked dirty as if she had walked through mud more than once.

"I thank you." Nikolaos grabbed his clothes from her and slipped into his breeches, holding onto his shirt so he could dry more before putting it on. Then he climbed up the bank to flat dry ground.

She followed him as if it was a perfectly normal thing to do, then curtsied and held her hand out. "I'm Stina Andersdotter, from Marstrand."

Surprised, he took it and kissed it. Her hand felt solid and warm under his lips, and he was able to squeeze it despite the watery feeling still lingering in his fingers. "A pleasure," he said, feeling awkward. What was he supposed to do now? What if she told people in the village? He pushed down yet another wave of panic at how close it had been, regretting that he had admitted who he was.

She must have seen it on his face. "You don't have to be nervous about me saying anything. I'm keeping to myself these days. I'm frightened about the witches."

"The witches?"

"Yes, Anna in Holta and old Malin." She looked at him expectantly. "Haven't you heard? Everyone is talking about them."

He put his shirt on. "No, I haven't. What happened?"

"Do you mind if we sit?" She gestured toward a rock behind a group of trees. I think we'll be out of the wind there."

"Certainly."

Stina let him take her arm. "You truly haven't heard?" she asked once she was seated.

"No. I've also been keeping to myself, don't spend much time among people. I only go to Nykungälv now and then to buy necessities and go to church." He took a step back so as not to stand too close.

She gave him an astonished look. "You go to church?"

"Yes, I do. I try anyway. Most people do."

"But," she started but stopped again and just looked at him.

He ignored her questioning look. "I haven't been to church recently, so I've heard nothing."

"If you had, you'd have heard that Anna in Holta made the weather change and sank a boat. And heard that she went to her neighbor Söfren's house at night when he was sleeping. First, she touched his chest, and then down and down it went, and she took it. You know his manhood." She blushed.

"Did she?" He tried not to laugh. Stina looked so serious it was clear it wasn't a joke.

"Yes. Later Anna is to have met Söfren's wife at the door and admitted that she took it. Söfren's wife got mad and told her she should be ashamed of herself. But then, when Anna left, Söfren developed horrible pains in his gut because Anna had made it feel as though it was full of kittens."

"Kittens?" He swallowed, his mind immediately going to Karin's miscarriage.

"Yes. I know it sounds outrageous, but I'm just telling you what people are saying. Söfren is a mason, so you'd think he wouldn't be so weak as that, but he felt he lost his manhood, so he went to Anna's house to get it back. Anna had first insisted that she never took it and that he was lying. But when he threatened to call on the lawman, she touched him again, and he could see for himself she had given it back to him."

"He saw it himself, I bet he did!" Nikolaos put his fiddle on the ground and leaned against a birch for support, laughing. "His wife must have found them together, and then they made excuses. It's not a very good excuse though, is it?"

Stina smiled a little. "I thought so too, at first. As did everyone else. They were all laughing at them too. But then Anna was taken to jail. They claimed she had actually pulled it off of Söfren's body and brought it home, then put it back again."

Nikolaos scoffed. "How did she do that?"

"I don't know." Stina made a face. "Not long after that, my neighbor came to tell me that Anna had once wanted to borrow some yeast from Signe Larsdotter. But Signe didn't have any, and then Anna is to have said three times that nothing good would come of it. Signe's daughter got sick, and lay as a baitworm, wizening away. Still does I suppose if she's alive."

"You mean she threatened her?" It sounded like what Old Karin had told him about being accused of putting the disease on people.

"Yes, precisely. Anna was taken to the courts and was tried and given the water test. Three times they tried, and she floated."

"Pray slow down a moment, Stina. What are you talking about? What's the water test?"

"You don't know about the water test either?"

"I don't."

Stina seemed momentarily taken aback, looking at him as if to see if he was joking or testing her. Then she said, "They tie the hands and feet of whoever they think is a witch and push her into a lake or a river. If she floats, she's a witch. If not, she isn't. Only witches float."

"Lord have mercy."

Stina nodded and crossed herself. "Well, it's what they say. And they said it was the Devil who gave Anna the power to float. Anna hung herself in jail afterward. But before she died, she confessed to her witchery and claimed that old Malin, eighty years she is Malin, had been with her, learning all matter of witchery. They…"

Nikolaos held up a hand to get her to slow down again. "Can you take one thing at a time?"

"I apologize. I'll try." She took a breath. "Where was I? Yes, Anna told them that old Malin had flown to the Blue Hill to be with the Devil," Stina lowered her voice, "to fornicate with him! So they gave Malin the water test, and she floated too." She looked down at her feet, clearly disturbed. "The butcher's wife and his daughter are also witches. His daughter lived with the Devil for three months to study with him."

Nikolaos gave her a doubtful look. "This sounds a bit too dramatic. How could someone do that? Are you sure these aren't just rumors?"

Stina shrugged a shoulder in a gesture of uncertainty. "The butcher's daughter didn't admit it first, but then she's to have mentioned that the Devil is very slimy. How could she have known that if she hadn't been with him? At the same time, I wonder. It seems to me that it can't *all* be true. I hardly think the Devil would spend this much time in our little village, would he?"

"Probably not."

"It's what I thought. But both the butcher's wife and daughter admitted to spending time with Anna in Holta. They had been to her house and eaten butter she had fried in her frying pan apparently." She inhaled sharply. "I believe about the butcher's wife and daughter, but old Malin? I don't know, not her. She's just too old." Stina shook her head. "People are so afraid they're becoming suspicious of each other. That scares me almost as much as the witches themselves. Lord Näcken, I'm afraid. Afraid of what my neighbors think of me and afraid the Devil is trying to get at me." She made the sign of the cross again. "It's why I haven't been home for a long time."

Nikolaos nodded. He could certainly understand her fear of both. "Stina, you obviously know who I am, but there's no need to call me that. My name is Nikolaos."

"Nikolaos? I didn't realize."

"It's no bother, now you do. I understand why you haven't been home. It sounds frightening."

"There's more." She looked at a spot behind him while gathering her thoughts. "One Sunday a young woman fainted during service. Her body shook as she lay there, flailing hither and thither. They said it was the Devil doing things to her, right then and there in church!" Stina's eyes widened. "After that, I packed and left. I've been wandering ever since, sleeping under trees and other places. If the Devil is in church, then no one is safe. I never thought he'd ever enter sacred ground."

"That's terrible."

A mourning dove cooed, distracting them. Stina wrapped her arms around herself for warmth.

"You're cold, Stina. I can take you home. Where are you staying now you said?"

"I'm staying in an abandoned hut, it's up the hill back here."

"Come with me and sit by the fire a while first," he said, noticing how she was shivering. "I can bring you home after. I have a horse. It'll be quick."

"Fire? Doesn't it get wet?" Her eyes shifted toward the river.

Nikolaos chuckled. "I have a small farm. As far as I can tell, my roof doesn't leak." He pointed in the opposite direction from the river.

"I didn't know that. Then I'd gladly sit by the fire for a bit," she said, looking relieved, then slid down from the rock and started walking up the path.

Amused, Nikolaos caught up to her. "I'm not what everyone thinks of me. I've been married, had children and grandchildren, even great-grandchildren," he said, feeling a need to explain. For some reason his voice caught in his throat, and he had to blink away tears.

"I didn't know that, Nikolaos."

He swallowed the catch in his throat.

His farm was at the edge of the woods with no neighbors within shouting distance. A small main house and a small shed had been the only structures still standing when he first found it. The house had only four walls, no roof or floors, but intact openings where the windows and the door had been. He spent months building on it, creating a beautiful little home with a strong dirt roof, a new door and windows filled with glass panes, and a chimney that two men from the village helped him build. There was a rectangular enclosure below the farm, but it had crumbled and fallen apart in several places. At one time, there might have been another village that had grown crops within that wall, but now only trees and scrubs grew there. There were three crumbled stone structures back in the woods, attesting to that theory.

Approaching his farm now, Nikolaos felt proud and happy to show it to someone. The sun was getting lower in the sky, and the grass growing on his roof shone brilliant green in its light. His grain was growing strong too. It was just a small square, but he grew it all by himself instead of joining the village plot, which wasn't close.

"There, you see, right there across the field, that's my little home," Nikolaos said, pointing to it. Kristina, grazing alongside his cow, lifted her head at that movement and looked at them.

"It's beautiful! Your horse is as well. Is it true that it can lengthen its back to fit ten people? And run forever until people fall off starved?"

"It sounds convenient, but I assure you she's a regular horse. Her name is Kristina." His eyes flashed to hers, and he couldn't keep the annoyance from his voice.

"I see. I meant no offense," Stina said, keeping her eyes on his, looking calm and unafraid.

He gave a nod, and her smile widened. When she lifted her

arm, he thought she would touch him, but instead, she pointed to the stacks of hay in front of the house.

"If you find clover, add that to your stacks. Your cow will thank you for it and will be generous with her milk for you. Especially the flowers, they love those, but they're hard to find this late in the summer."

"Really?" he asked, noticing the bees swarming around the stacks. "Maybe I accidentally got some flowers already, look how the bees are hovering over them?"

"From here? Nah, I can't see that far. Can you really see bees?"

"Yes, absolutely."

She nodded, then fell silent.

Nikolaos kept stealing glances at her while they walked. He couldn't describe his feelings. Maybe it was just because he had been in the water for so long, but he felt so content, and there was something that reminded him of Abluna. The way she walked and the way she smiled. He couldn't put his finger on it, but it was as if she belonged.

Stina had stopped shivering once they made it inside, but he added two logs to the fire and invited her to sit in front of it anyway.

She held her hands out toward the flames and sighed with satisfaction. "I've missed a proper hearth. Mine is still standing I hope." A shadow of fear came across her face. "I don't understand it. From one day to the next, people who were good, friendly neighbors became angry and scared of each other. Have you ever experienced anything like it?" She nodded in thanks when he handed her a mug of wine.

"I have, yes. I've been known to cause all kinds of trouble. Stealing babies, turn into a horse or a dog with long ragged ears that lift women' skirts."

She started, almost spilling her wine, but then she laughed. "Oh, Nikolaos, I… for a moment I actually thought you… How silly of me. Pray forgive me, of course, you of all people would understand. I can only imagine how people treat you and what they accuse you of.”

"They don't always get close enough for me to hear it directly. But I've heard rumors and seen their panic."

"I understand. People say all kinds of things when they don't know you."

He nodded at that, and then they drank their wine in silence. A light rain began to fall, smattering gently against the windowpanes.

"I'm scared people will think *I've* been to the Blue Hill since I have been gone so long," Stina said, interrupting the silence. "But I have some things I want to get from home and must decide if I should stay there or move somewhere else. It scares me, I don't know how people will react. Would you be willing to come with me?" She looked at him so earnestly and again something stirred him that reminded him of Abluna. That naked hopeful look.

"Me? I don't know if that's wise. If you're afraid they'll accuse you of things, bringing me along would be the last thing you'd want to do. As I mentioned, I've seen what that can do."

She hesitated but then shook her head. "I'm not scared of that. What I'm scared of is going back alone, not knowing how people will receive me. I'm young, eighteen years of age only. My older brothers perished in the war, and my parents died the year before I left. I've stayed away for a long time now, and I fear they'll use this as proof of my traveling to the Blue Hill. I'd feel much better if a man went with me."

Nikolaos stood up and walked across the floor to look out the window while he thought about it. The rain was coming down hard now. Kristina and the cow were huddling together under a tree. He would have to ted the hay to get it to dry properly. If he could just do that first, the farm should be fine to leave on its own for a few days. With his eyes still on the outside, he said, "I'll go with you, but we must use caution, and I must get a few things done before we leave." He turned back toward her.

Stina was sipping her wine and swallowed quickly, looking relieved. "I'm so glad, thank you. And I'll tell no one who you are."

"Good. I appreciate that." He smiled. "Can you just tell me

where this blue hill is that you've been talking about. It's not near where we're going, I hope."

"No. It's supposed to be up north somewhere, or maybe it was east. Even children are lured away to it. They fly there. Witches bring them, and then they come back and tell horrific tales of the place." She shuddered. "What worries me is that he's taken so many in such a short time. The pastor said it's because of our sin, but I have seen no more sin than usual."

Nikolaos sat back down beside her, spinning his mug in his hands. Pastors always blamed everything on people's sins. "Can the Devil really make them do that?"

"It's what they say. They fly on brooms."

He nodded uncertainly. People said a lot about him that weren't true, either. It also struck him that maybe he ought to treat what she said like lunacy, like Karin's ramblings. But he could sense it wasn't the case. She was too calm and collected, just retelling confusing information. Something was happening.

They sat in silence again after that, looking out the window at the rain. It was so heavy now it was turning the summer evening dark. He couldn't in good conscience let her leave, but neither could he suggest that a young unmarried woman should stay overnight. Turning in her direction to ask what she wanted to do, he found her slumped, chin touching her chest, sound asleep.

Abluna used to do that too.

Maybe he was finally getting old and sentimental, but it was uncanny how many things reminded him of her.

He found a blanket and covered her with it, then left her as she was and went to bed.

Chapter 39

By the next morning the weather had cleared. Nikolaos found Stina outside, sitting on his bench in the sun. She had placed a bucket of milk in the shade under the table.

At the sound of the door opening, she broke into a smile. "Good morrow to you," she said, pointing to the bucket. "I took the liberty of milking her. She gives good milk for an older cow."

"She does, though I've tried to make butter, but it just bubbles, and nothing happens. She's too old and skinny now, I think. My wife used to make it, took only a couple of turns with the churn."

"A couple of turns with the churn." She playfully slapped his knee with the back of her hand. "Menfolk! Making butter takes a lot of work. A couple of turns," she repeated, making him chuckle. "I can make you butter. I'll help you around here while we collect a couple of days' worth of milk and let it settle. That's the least I can do for your help."

"It has to settle?"

She shook her head, grinning. "Yes, it must sit in a flattened bowl so the cream can float to the top. It takes a bit of time. It's the cream you make the butter out of. Do you have a churn? Any settling dishes?"

"Yes, and I might. I found this place abandoned, and it had many things left out in the shed. I'll show you." He hurried down the flat stone which formed a step below the front door and went around the corner, reaching the shed long before she had gathered her skirts and caught up with him. When she did, he opened the rickety old door, indicating what was inside with a wave of his hand. "It smells, I apologize," he said, glancing with horror at the dust and spiderwebs.

Stina stepped inside without hesitation and found the churn in the corner. Brushing a thick web off the plunger, she angled it toward the door so the light would make it easier to see the bottom. "This is a good churn, it isn't cracked, just a bit dry and dusty. It ought to do fine, I think. This would be a fine place for the milk to cool as well," she said and looked around for a dish. Her gaze fell on three shallow bowls stacked on top of each other on the shed's only shelf. "Pray, will you get them for me, I want to look to see which one is best," she said, pointing.

Moving across the floor in the narrow space to give him space, her skirts tickled his legs. It aroused him so immediately that he took an involuntary step backward, feeling embarrassed.

If she noticed, she didn't say anything. Looking carefully at each one, she handed back the top two and wiped the dust off the third with her sleeve. "This one will do. Will you get the bucket with milk for me, Nikolaos?"

He nodded and pressed past her, noticing her body's warmth and scent. The short way back to get the bucket suddenly felt too long, and he wished he could have asked her to come with him.

When he returned, Stina had put the churn outside and stood in the door waiting for him. "I'll leave it here to air out a bit until we have enough cream. The butter might taste like dust otherwise."

Handing her the bucket, he hoped his fingers would touch hers, but they didn't. She disappeared into the shed, and he heard the milk splash into the settling bowl.

"There," she said and smiled at him from inside. "That's all for now. What else do you need help with? Have you had anyone else here to help you with women's work?"

"No."

"You've had no baking-woman here to help with spring baking?"

He shook his head.

"I see. Well, you can also make fresh bread on the hearth if you have a flat baking stone. You have flour? Yeast?"

"Not yeast, but I have flour. My crop was good last year, and I got some milled but haven't used much. I use heavy grain for porridge."

"You did that all yourself. I mean, you cut it, got the grain ready for milling and everything, all by yourself?"

"Yes." He gestured outward with both hands. A vivid memory of Abluna with a group of women and their children in tow, bringing in the newly cut grain to thrash, came before him. It had been sunny all day and warm, his youngest sweating and wiping himself constantly, getting tiny sticks stuck to his cheeks. Nikolaos smiled at the memory.

"I'll find a baking stone and make you flatbread to go with the butter. It'll do without yeast," Stina said.

"That's very kind of you, but I'm not sure what I've done to deserve all this."

"You have, your music moved me, and you're going to help me."

***

Four days later, they were on their way. Stina had made butter and helped him salt meat and fish for his winter stores. He was impressed. She was capable and strong, used to handling fish from the island where she had lived. Not only that, but so tall she had to sit behind him in the saddle, or he wouldn't see properly. It felt unusual, but after a while, he relaxed. They stopped by her little hut first, a dank old place without a proper door. It couldn't have been comfortable during the two winters she had stayed away. It was an incredibly long time to live all alone, but she claimed it hadn't been as hard as she had expected.

Once they settled into a steady pace, Nikolaos' mind became occupied by the strange tidings Stina spoke of. He hadn't thought of it when she first told him, but thinking back on it now, he remembered a merchant from one of the weddings he had played at who claimed that some women were acting strangely and disappearing at night. Nikolaos had listened as politely as he could for as short a time as he thought would seem polite, before he purposely changed the subject, thinking that the merchant had been referring to *him*. Now he wondered if it wasn't witches the man had been talking about instead.

285

***

When they arrived at the coast, Nikolaos' heart sank. There was no harbor or ferryboats like he had foolishly assumed, just a beach. He hadn't even thought to ask her before they left.

"Do you have a boat?" he asked now, dreading her answer. A small personal boat would never be safe. And he didn't like leaving Kristina.

Stina gave him a surprised look, then burst out laughing. "You're funny. If I didn't know who you were, I might actually believe you," she said, eyes twinkling.

"What?" Nikolaos felt his own lips curl into a smile in response to her hearty laughter but didn't understand.

"Your horse of course!" She looked at him expectantly but when he didn't respond, she added, "Even if she isn't able to take ten people on her back at once, it's clear she's not a regular horse, that much is obvious. I asked for you for a reason, you know."

"Eh… I thought I told you she's just a horse."

"You said, yes. But I'm not stupid." Stina looked at him pointedly, then grabbed Kristina's bridle and opened her mouth. "I can tell from looking here that although the teeth are strong, they're not like the teeth of a young horse. She looks as if she's at least… let me guess, thirty, maybe even thirty-five years old. Are you telling me that your old mare here can get two people to the coast in such a short time? This isn't a regular horse, Nikolaos."

"She looks like a regular old horse to me," he said and shrugged.

Stina scoffed. "She isn't. But if you insist, I left my boat under some brambles over there." She pointed to a cluster of bushes growing near a boulder further down the beach. "I'm sure it isn't there anymore though. Someone probably took it. Can't we just try to get Kristina to take us?"

Nikolaos shaded his eyes with his hand and looked at the sea, feeling uncomfortable. "Stina, do you realize what you're asking of me?"

"Of course. But if you'd rather sail, we can. I just thought it would be convenient if we didn't have to walk once we're on the island. My house isn't near the harbor. And I don't want to wait around for someone to take us and then…"

"Stina," he interrupted, "you're not thinking this through. You know who I am. I can't take you into the water. I might kill you." His words were harsh, but he had no choice. It was the truth.

"Oh." She gave a startled look, color rising on her cheeks.

"This is what we'll do," he said, already regretting telling her. The only other person he had ever been as candid with was Rå. "Go look to see if your boat is there after all. If it is, you take it, and I'll see how Kristina does in the water. I'll get there one way or the other."

Stina nodded, her eyes teary from embarrassment. "Can't you sail with me?"

He looked toward the bushes. "I'm assuming from what I see that it's not a big boat you have?"

Stina's head jerked back with realization, then she turned on her heels without a word.

Nikolaos watched her walk across the beach, feeling sorry for her. She must feel like an idiot, having brought him all the way here just to realize how stupid her plan had been.

Stina pulled the branches aside, and he saw her bend down and peer inside. When she straightened, one of the branches slapped her across the cheek. She winced and pushed it away, leaving a streak of blood on her cheek.

He ran over. "Did you get hurt? Did it catch you in the eye?"

"Not my eye, but it hurts. Got my cheek it did." She wiped her face again, and the blood smeared and mixed with the dirt on her hands. "But I found it. The boat is still here, look!" She pointed into the bushes at a small boat overgrown with thorns.

The sail was stuck in the upper brambles. It looked like it had survived the thorns, but it would take some doing to get it out.

"You were wise to put it here. People aren't likely to search for it in something that would hurt them," he said and touched her cheek, getting a smudge of blood on his finger. A moment passed between them. Nikolaos could feel her wanting to reach for his hand but didn't. Then he wiped his finger on his breeches and the moment was gone.

"Yes, I was, it seems," she said, flushing.

"How long do you think it'll take you to get to Marstrand from here?"

"A good long while if there isn't enough wind, I've gone in the morning for just a quick round trip, and by the time I'm back on the island again the sun is high in the sky already. My island is the second largest. If you see the fort, you've gone too far."

"Good to know."

"Yes, you want to stay away from there. It's on the next island. They're using thieves to build it. Stay away. A scary, scary place," she said, crawling into the bushes to untangle the sail.

It was easier than it had looked, for only a moment later she came back out, grabbed hold of the stern, and pulled, getting it quite far by herself. Nikolaos grabbed it with his right hand and pushed it to the water.

"You're very strong, Nikolaos," she said and went and stood next to him.

He grinned, then realized he was much too close to the shore and took several quick steps back, trying not to look at the blues and greens forming from the crashing waves. "Stina, you should go. I'll find it."

Her face fell, but she seemed to understand and clambered into the boat and started rowing. "Meet me behind the fishnets to the left of the harbor. They're a good distance from it, and you should be able to get there unseen at this time of day," she hollered over the waves.

"I will!" he hollered back as the wind caught in the sail, pushing Stina further out.

Nikolaos drew a deep breath of relief. This was the sea, a completely different body of water than the rivers and streams he was used to. It pulled at him, but it felt thicker somehow, almost sluggish. For a moment, he considered abandoning the whole idea, leaving Stina to her own fate and going back home. But what kind of man would he be if he didn't help a woman in need? He had enough on his conscience as it was. He pulled Kristina's saddle off and stuffed it where the boat had been, then walked straight into the sea. As soon as they were deep enough, Kristina swam as if it were an everyday occurrence. He never knew that horses could do that.

Stina was well ahead of him still, staying close to the islands she passed. There were several boats, none too near but he was probably not out of sight. What if people recognized him and tried to shoot at him from their boats or take him to the fort? There was a smaller boat only a stone's throw away from him with two men, but they had their backs to him and their faces glued forward. A larger boat, however, was coming in his direction and from the look of it, there were people at the railing looking in his direction. He slid off Kristina's back and slipped under the surface. The seawater went into his lungs effortlessly, and he pushed forward with one hand, holding Kristina's bridle with the other. It was as easy as it was in the river and Kristina seemed just as comfortable as he was.

Nikolaos kept going until he was sure he was out of sight, and when he resurfaced, the harbor Stina spoke of was already in view. It had gone incredibly fast. The fishnet poles were empty, and no one was there just like she had thought. He went under again, swimming until it became shallow enough to stand up. When he did, his lungs didn't transition to air right away, and for a moment he couldn't breathe, but then as quickly as it came, air rushed into him.

There was no beach, just large boulders covered in bird poop and what looked like some kind of moss, like lichen or something. Kristina got out easily, sliding just a little on the slick surface. But he had a harder time. His lungs and throat burned from the salty water, and he had to let go of her bridle to get his bearings and spit out some residual seawater. Kristina looked at him and exposed her teeth as if she were laughing at him.

"Ah, Queen, you have four legs," Nikolaos said and went to her, scratching her on that warm spot behind her jaw. "I only have two, be kind to me. How did you keep up with me? We moved so fast, I think Stina might be right. Maybe you're not a regular horse."

Kristina gently bit him on his ears with her lips in response.

Nikolaos patted her neck under the mane. It was hard to say what she was, but he loved her either way. She had been his only companion for a long time now.

He sat down on the stone, careful to find a spot without too much bird poop. Kristina wandered around on her own as he scanned the water for Stina's approach. She had been moving rather fast at first, but he must have passed her. While he sat there, the clouds parted, and moisture evaporated in the warm sunlight, creating a low fog on the wet rocks. He chuckled to himself. According to that Näcken expert he listened to years ago, he was made of the stuff.

When Stina arrived, she expertly stepped out of her boat and anchored it. "I told you, you'd get here first," she shouted when she spotted him.

"So you did, and you might have been right about Kristina after all," Nikolaos admitted when she got closer.

"I knew it!" Her face split into a wide grin as she easily made her way up the now dry boulders. Then she took a couple of steps to the side, and for the first time, she looked nervous around him.

"Stina, I appreciate your caution."

She nodded.

They continued on foot and found a path, a road really, wide enough for both wagons and horses.

Nikolaos could sense the hesitation in her steps, and when he turned to look at her, she barely met his eyes. "Stina, you're fine now. We're far enough from the sea that you have nothing to worry about."

She let out a visible breath and finally looked him in the face. He smiled and leaned forward and kissed her cheek. It was just a quick peck, but enough for her to blush. Then, with one move, he grabbed her by the waist and hoisted her up on Kristina's saddleless back. He found a tree stump to use for support and took his seat in front of her. She wrapped her arms around his waist, and they set off in a trot.

"My village is straight ahead, and my house is north of it," Stina said. "It's the only house standing off on its own. My parents said they preferred to live a bit more privately. Most of the other fishing families live in the fishing village. They'd feel lonely otherwise you know."

He hum-hummed distractedly, not paying attention to Stina talking about details and people he didn't know.

"Nikolaos, look," Stina prompted suddenly, getting his full attention. "That's the fort straight ahead."

He whistled when his eyes fell on it. Just like she had said, it was on the next island. It had a big tower which was looming large over the land. "It's huge. It's for defense?"

"Yes, they added the top part with the windows a few years ago. It's so they can stand inside and shoot. There was a lot of fighting there when I was a child. It still scares me looking at it. And as I mentioned, they have thieves and other scoundrels building it. Let's hurry so we don't have to look at it. Do you see how the path divides down there on the left? Just cross it. If we ride through the grass, you'll see the roof soon." She pointed ahead. Her hand was shaking.

Nikolaos stopped. Shifting his weight sideways, he turned around to look at her. Her face was swollen with tears, and they had made streaks through the blood still visible on her right cheek. She was breathing erratically. "Stina, what ails you? Can I do anything?"

"I don't have a good feeling, Nikolaos. I think, well, I don't know, but it's not good. I'm so very glad you're here even if you…" She stopped and sniveled loudly. "I feel stupid for not realizing the danger. I'm still very glad you're here, even if I'm a bit scared of you too. It's too late now though obviously," she said, managing to laugh through her tears.

He smiled. "I'm happy to be of help. It's the least I can do. And again, here you have nothing to fear. I promise."

She took a deep breath and wiped her nose on her sleeve. "I thank you, Nikolaos, you're very kind. We can go now I think."

He was just about to kick his heels in Kristina's sides when a rider followed by two wagons loaded with empty fishing baskets, came thundering toward them at high speed.

The rider nodded. "How do you fare?" Then seeing Stina behind Nikolaos, he repeated, "How do you fare, goodwife?" He slowed down his horse, tipping his hat.

"I'm faring fine, thank you kindly," Stina said. If he wondered about her red, tear-stricken face, he was too polite to ask and continued on his way. The first fishing wagon did the same, but the second one stopped.

"What ails you, goodwife?" the driver asked, looking suspiciously at them, eyeing Nikolaos' wet clothes and Stina's face. "There's something wrong?"

Nikolaos looked the man straight in the eye. There were dark circles under them, and he didn't look too well himself. "I thank you for your care. We're well. My wife here is feeling a bit poorly, is all." Hopefully, the man would think her courses had come.

"You ride in fine clothes but don't own a saddle? Why aren't they dry, your clothes? It didn't rain, did it?" The fisherman driver motioned to the now completely cloudless sky.

"No, just some wet grass. We better be going. Good day to you," Nikolaos said and couldn't quite hide his irritation. He felt Stina's heart race through his shirt as she clung to his back.

The fisherman made no indication he had heard and continued with his many questions. "But I don't understand how wet grass can get both you and your horse wet. Have you been trying a witch?"

"Pray pardon me?" Nikolaos felt more than heard Stina gasp behind him.

"Eh, well, one could easily make that assumption given the state of things. We live in dangerous times. Where are you headed then?"

"Indeed, we are," Nikolaos said, avoiding his question.

"Careful if you pass the Witch House down there. The witch has been on the Blue Hill for several years now. Stay as far as you can from it, for it might be cursed," the driver said, then clicked his tongue to get his horse moving. The fishing baskets rattled and slid from side to side as he hurried away.

Nikolaos was so stunned he just sat there, but Kristina started trotting on her own, sure it was what her master wanted once the odd conversation was over.

"I knew it, Nikolaos, didn't I tell you?" Stina said, grabbing his waist tightly. "They think I'm a witch. I recognize him now, it's the wife of Fishing Karl. I mean it's Fishing Karl, his wife's name is Lina. I told you they'd think I'm a witch," she repeated. "I should never have left."

Nikolaos shook his head. "I'm beginning to see what you've been talking about. He seemed quite suspicious. Could there really be no other reason for being wet, especially in a fishing village?"

"You'd think, you might have gone in to retrieve a net. Why did you say I was your wife?"

"Seemed the most plausible explanation given that you're sitting on my horse. Now let's go look at your house, shall we? We don't know for sure that it's your house he's referring to."

"I hope you're right," she mumbled but didn't sound convinced.

"What did he mean? Trying a witch, what does that have to do with my clothes?"

"I supposed he wondered if you had to go in and fish her up again after she sank, but I'm not sure. I thought they used a rope to haul them up."

"Rusty devils!" He tried to recall what she had told him the other day but couldn't remember the details. "Pray, explain this method again, Stina," he said, pressing his heels in Kristina's sides to get her into a faster trot.

"They tie them up and throw them in the water. If they sink, they're innocent, if they float, they're guilty. That's how you know."

Nikolaos shook his head with discomfort. People who floated usually sank after a while and didn't come back up for a long time. But they always did in the end. It's how people figured out it was his fault.

They rode in silence the rest of the way. Birds chirped

around them, and seagulls called out on their way to the fishing boats, looking for spills, unaware of what the humans on their island thought of each other. The ground was flat and soft, well stomped by feet and hooves. There was a cluster of low bushes ahead, and behind that, he spotted what must be Stina's house. It was small, its wood grayed from the salty winds. It looked undisturbed. The shutters were tightly closed, as was the door.

Nikolaos swung his leg over Kristina's neck and jumped to the ground, then reached for Stina and helped her down. She collapsed for a moment from the emotion. Why did she trust him so? She didn't know him.

"Nikolaos, pray come with me. I'm scared of what I might find, pray come inside with me."

"Of course, I'll go first and look," he said and resolutely walked up to the door, unhinged it, and pulled it open. "You have no lock?"

"Nay, never have I needed it."

It was just a one-room cottage. It smelled dank and dusty, but he couldn't sense anything amiss. "There's no one here, everything is fine," he said and motioned for her to follow. "It's just dark."

"We can push the shutters open from inside. I don't have glass in them," Stina said, cautiously squeezing past him, then walked over to a small window on the shorter wall and pushed open the shutters. Her face looked pale in the sudden light.

Nikolaos stood on the threshold, giving her some privacy while she opened her shutters and went around to check everything, opening cupboards and lifting pots and bowls.

"It looks like everything is here," Stina said, slapping a lid closed and wrinkling up her nose. "I might have been overreacting after all. Maybe Fishing Karl wasn't talking about my house. It *is* possible."

"Of course. Is there another house he may have meant?" Nikolaos stepped inside and walked over to the little table. He didn't sit, leaving the chair for Stina.

She sighed. "No, I'm the only one near here."

"I see." Maybe it would be best if he stayed a few days. The way Fishing Karl had reacted, he couldn't in good conscience leave her there alone. And he had claimed she was his wife; they would ask where he was. In hindsight, that might not have been the best thing to say. He was considering what to do when Stina suddenly called out and ran to the door, then bent down and picked something up off the floor. A letter. It wasn't sealed.

She unfolded it, crossing the floor to the bigger window for more light. Then her hand went to her mouth. "I'm not sure who wrote this. It says that if I'm not here for another reason than what everyone thinks, I should leave, or they'll come for me." She grabbed hold of the wall. "They hung Hanna and her daughters, and Anjalena drowned during the water test. People think I'm in special favor with the Devil because I don't have to travel back and forth, she says." Stina fell into the chair beside Nikolaos and waved the letter in his direction.

Nikolaos took it and read, assuming it was what she wanted. When he was done, he shook his head in disbelief, anger surging through him while simultaneously feeling like a hypocrite. It was what he did too, drowning women.

"You mention she, who do you think it is?" he asked when he finished, glad to have something practical to talk about.

"Pray, pardon me?"

"You said first that you didn't know who wrote it, but just now you said that *she* says… Do you think you know who wrote it?"

"Oh." Stina shook her head. "I don't know, it might be Gunnel or Inger. They're the only ones I know that write, so I think," she inhaled sharply, "it's one of them. Whoever of the two it was didn't want to be implicated writing to the witch and didn't sign it."

"I wouldn't leave the letter here, just in case. You don't want anyone to find it. I want you to come back with me, Stina. You shouldn't stay here anymore."

Her eyes flashed to his with both surprise and resignation. "This is my home. I've lived here all my life. I lost my parents here and my brothers." Her chin quivered, her eyes taking stock of her belongings.

"I understand. Take your time in here, Stina. I'll go out a while. Collect the things you want to bring with you. I'll stay here with you tonight, then we'll leave just before the day breaks tomorrow." Nikolaos handed her back the letter and walked to the door, then turned to her just before he opened it. "If you want to, I'm happy to have you in my home or help you with whatever you decide to do. But I do advise you not to remain here. Not after reading that," he added, pointing to the letter which she had opened again and put in her lap.

She didn't respond.

Nikolaos closed the door, then sat down on the flat stone that functioned as a step under the door. It was just like the step he had at home. The fort loomed large on the horizon. Maybe it was where they had tried the witches with that water test of theirs. Were they really witches? Rumors spread quickly, but there was usually some kind of truth to them, however small. He *had* spoken to Old Karin and suggested an herbal cure, he *had* played his fiddle in the Motala River, the King *had* seen him on that pole outside of his castle in Stockholm, and he *had* been with Karin and helped her bury the dead baby, even if it wasn't much of a baby yet. Maybe the women had communed with the Devil for some reason, and then the truth became exaggerated because no one had all the facts. He shivered at the thought.

The Devil used to terrify him when he was a boy. Many a night he had laid awake, scared the Devil might be lurking by the bed curtains his mother always pulled closed so she and his father could have privacy. He hated it. If they were left open, he would at least see the Devil come across the floor. Instead, he lay awake, afraid the Devil was standing on the other side of the closed curtains, waiting to pounce on him if he needed to get up to go to the outhouse.

The island seemed an odd place for him to unleash his evil. Nothing in the little garden around Stina's house reflected his power. The bushes were green and lush. Gooseberry, it looked like, tuberoses, and several others Nikolaos didn't recognize. In the harbor, fishing boats were coming back full of fish, and seagulls were flocking around them, contrasting starkly with the clear grey-blue water. It was a gorgeous sight and seemed entirely peaceful. Stina was nice and had been so warm and helpful. She seemed eager to get things done on the farm without being pushy. Maybe Saint Nikolaos had sent her to him. Saint Nikolaos, the seafaring saint, was his namesake after all, and it was fitting he would send him a woman from an island. Something warm came into his chest, making him smile, and he admitted to himself what had been on his mind since they brushed against each other in his shed. He wanted her. Smiling wider, his gaze stayed on the sea and the boats bobbing gently over the waves.

Moments later, he felt the door bump into his back when Stina tried to open it. "Wait a moment," he said and started to get up.

Stina pushed herself past his back and went to stand in front of him. She looked determined. "If you still want to, I'd be grateful to go with you."

"I'd be delighted to have you, Stina." He smiled, warmth creeping up in his chest again. "Had this been ordinary circumstances, I'd ask your father, but he's no longer with us you mentioned?"

"Oh, you would?" She looked perplexed. "He... it was years ago now."

"Do you have uncles?"

She shook her head. "My mother had two brothers just as I did, but I don't know where they are. They fought in the war with Poland. No one has heard from them. My father's sisters live on the mainland with their families. We're not close."

"I see. I was thinking when you were inside, and I'd like to ask you if you would consider becoming my wife?" Nikolaos asked carefully, suddenly knowing how much he wanted her to say yes.

She stared at him with a look of complete astonishment, then she laughed. "I believed you for a moment. You told Fishing Karl that I was your wife, and I can see how that was a good idea. It wouldn't be seemly otherwise, people might talk. Yes, certainly. I'll tell people that I'm your wife."

"No, no, Stina, not like that. I mean it. Nothing would give me more joy." He reached for her hand.

"Oh." Her face lit up in a smile, but then her expression changed, and instead of letting him take her hand, she walked away, not stopping until she got to a tree in the corner of the garden.

He cautiously went after her, uncertain. "Stina, pray if I have offended you, I apologize. I have nothing but honorable intentions, but if you don't want to, I'll understand and respect it."
She kept her back to him, scraping at the tree's bark with her fingers. Piece by piece fell off and stuck to her blouse and skirts. He walked around to face her.

"Nikolaos," she stopped scraping and looked at him, "I don't know how that would work. I'm honored that you're asking me, but I can't live in the water. It's frightening me, and I don't know how I'd breathe down there."

"Of course not." He frowned, feeling confused. "What makes you think you would?"

She laughed nervously and reached for the tree again, pulling off a large piece of bark, then tossed it to the ground. "Nikolaos, I know who you are. I can't live down there with you."

"Down there? You've seen my farm. I thought I made it clear that that's where I live."

"Nikolaos, pray don't make it worse by mocking me."

"I'm not trying to mock you. Are you really saying that you think you have to live in the river with me?"

She nodded.

He tried not to smile. "I see, I didn't realize that I needed to explain this. The river is not where I live. It's just that I have a need to spend a lot of time there." Deciding to leave it at that, he thought carefully about what to say next. Stina already knew almost as much as Rå. "Other than that, I'm an ordinary man except that I've been alive for a very long time. And I was married, remember? My wife's name was Abluna, and we loved each other. She died a long time ago. We had several children, and I saw them all die, too, most of old age. I've not had a wife since then." Nikolaos stopped talking, embarrassed. He had probably told her too much and was speaking too fast, sounding desperate. There was no way to explain it, but he didn't want her to leave and would do anything to make her stay so he could wed her. "Pray forgive me if I'm scaring you. I don't mean to. I'll go back to the step and sit for a while. I'll help you any way I can. Just tell me what to do."

"How old are you?" she asked, ignoring his comment.

"Oh." He paused, not sure if he heard right. "I'm not quite sure. They didn't keep track of time too well in the past. At least not where I grew up, but I calculate I'm around two hundred and ten, something like that."

Her eyes widened. "In all that time you've only been married once?"

"Yes."

"You don't look it, like you're that old, I mean."

He chuckled. "I know."

She caught his eyes, then moved her gaze to his throat, standing still and silent. When she looked at him again, she said, "I thought maybe you only spent time at the farm, but your real home was in the river. You looked so at home there, and it's what everyone says. Do you truly live on that farm?"

"Yes, I live there. I do need water, but unless you come closer than you did that day when we first met, you won't need to worry. I'll never bring you. It's just something I need to do in private."

She looked searchingly into his eyes. Then she nodded. "I will do it. But we must find a good church to witness our betrothal."

He smiled and finally dared to move close enough to embrace her.

Stina let him kiss her, warm and shy under his hands. They stood together, close and without words until she pulled herself out of his arms. "I only have a few things inside. Wait here while I fetch them," she mumbled, hurrying back to the house with spring in her step.

Waiting for her, Nikolaos walked around and inspected what

was growing, feeling exceedingly happy. He pulled off a couple of branches from one of the gooseberry bushes. Maybe Stina knew how to get it to sprout to plant it. The tart berries would thrive in the sun behind the house at home. He smiled at the thought, picturing her there.

He put the branches in his pocket just as he heard the door open, and Stina came outside with a small sack thrown over her shoulder. "Is that all?" he asked and walked toward her.

Stina opened her mouth to answer, then closed it abruptly and gestured to the road with her chin. Two riders were approaching, and it was not to be a friendly visit, made obvious by their stern facial expressions and the rigid way they held themselves.

Instinctively, Nikolaos hurried to her side and put his arm around her shoulder. "Do you recognize them?"

She nodded. "I think it's Jesper, the first one is, he's a sixman. The other one might be Povel, Fishing Karl's oldest. He always gets his nose in everyone's affairs. Fishing Karl must have mentioned he saw us, and now he wants to investigate." Stina put her hand up to shield her eyes from the sun, then took a sharp breath in. "Yes, it's them."

"Just stay calm, Stina, I'll deal with them," Nikolaos whispered.

When the horses trotted through the opening in the bushes, Nikolaos lifted his hat. "Evening, gentlemen. Such luck, you just caught us before we were on our way to leave again. You must be Povel and Jesper. My wife here has spoken so much of you."

The men glanced at each other, and then Povel turned his gaze toward Stina without acknowledging Nikolaos. "You look more or less the same, Stina. It's a surprise wouldn't you say, Jesper?"

Jesper made his horse back up several steps before he answered. He looked scared, Nikolaos thought. "Yes, but she's skinnier, much skinnier. It's often a sign that they've been with the Devil."

"Pardon me?" Nikolaos asked, trying to sound appropriately offended. Not that he wasn't. They looked ridiculous, like children, plumb and rosy-cheeked.

"It's the fornication," Povel said. "If they do it often and wildly enough, they get skinny even if they feast up there on the Blue Hill."

"No, the more they do it, the rounder and the more voluptuous they become, their bosoms grow, and then the Devil drinks the milk. You clearly see the Devil's mark on her cheek. He might have suckled her for blood," Jesper said.

Stina covered her mouth with her hand to hide a gasp, pressing closer to Nikolaos.

"Rusty devils," Nikolaos hissed. He gave Stina's shoulder another squeeze, then let go and marched up to Jesper's horse, grabbed his leg and pulled him down. "There, now I can look you in the face when I introduce myself. My name is Nikolaos. It's *my* wife you're insulting. And for your information, she scratched herself on a thornbush. Is this your usual manner of greeting someone you've not seen for several years?"

"Sir, pray forgive me," Jesper stammered, blushing like a woman. Then he turned to Stina, who was looking somewhat relieved. "I didn't know you were wedded. You disappeared. Everyone assumed you had been traveling with the witches."

"Don't listen to them, Jesper," Povel said. "Get back on your horse. They aren't telling you the truth. I spoke to my father. He saw them both on the road before, and they're not to be trusted." He pulled his horse around and got it into a slow gallop, circling around them while keeping a wide berth between him and them.

But Jesper stayed where he was. "No, Povel, I think you're wrong. Stina, it's nice to see you. I'm delighted that you're wedded," he said and smiled sheepishly at Nikolaos.

Stina finally got over her shock. "Jesper, it's quite the surprise to come here with my husband excited to introduce him to everyone and instead get a greeting full of accusations. It wounds, I tell you, it wounds me. But I do thank you for your well wishes."

Jesper's face flushed again.

"You spoke to your father, you said?" Stina asked and looked at Povel who was still galloping around in circles. "Didn't he tell you he thought my husband had been *trying* a witch, not that *I* was a witch?"

Nikolaos flicked her a look of approval.

"Yes, he did. At first, that is. But then he got to thinking that it didn't seem right. Why would he have gone in if he had tried one? They're too dangerous to get in the water with. Your husband claimed to be wet from the grass, but no one gets that wet from dew. Besides it's too late in the day for it. He looked as if he had been submerged. Maybe your husband floats?"

Nikolaos scoffed. "Now this is enough. You're insulting my wife again. I'll have no more of this. You both need to leave. Now." He bored his eyes into Povel's, trying to feel the power of the seawater in his body, but it had no effect at all. But Povel looked scared enough as it was. They were no more than little plumb boys showing off to each other. Nikolaos nodded at Jesper. "Nice to meet you, young man. Now get on with it. We'll see you another day when we're all in a better mood for it."

"Thank you kindly," Jesper said and got back in the saddle. "We'll go now," he added, motioning for Povel to follow him as he got his horse into a trot.

At first, it seemed like he might protest, but then Povel kicked his feet in the stirrups and galloped after him.

When they were through the bushes, Stina sank to her knees. "Dear lord in heaven, dear Jesus, thank you, thank you."

Nikolaos put a hand on her shoulder but kept his eyes on the riders, willing them to keep going. They were galloping fast, hooves pounding the flat soft ground. Once they reached the road, they made a left and sped toward the village. Were they getting help? Or just going home? Whatever they were doing, they should get off the island as soon as possible. "I think we should leave now, Stina," he said quietly.

She scrambled to her feet. "I was right to ask for your help."

"I am glad you did. I'll get Kristina," Nikolaos said. The cut on Stina's cheek seemed bigger somehow. What were the odds that she had cut herself just as they arrived? They noticed immediately.

Once they were on Kristina's back, she ran so fast the wind made his eyes tear and his hat fall off. There was no time to stop for it.

The beach was no longer empty. Fishermen were hanging their nets on the poles, a woman was fixing a broken fishing net as her husband waited, others were dividing up fish into smaller baskets that women hoisted to their hips and walked off with. None paid them any mind.

Nikolaos stopped at a safe distance from the water and in view of Stina's boat. Dismounting, he reached for Stina and helped her down. They were both quiet, moving as fast as they could.

"Get in your boat and go. I'll get in further down the beach and keep my eyes on you. May God be with you, but I must keep my distance. He made the sign of the cross on her forehead, wondering if it would appear Catholic and blasphemous. But she smiled, left his embracing arms, and ran to her boat. The fisherman and his wife stared after her but gave no indication that they thought it was an odd time to leave.

Nikolaos waited until she had pushed her boat out, then walked off along the water's edge to get out of sight. It was flat and empty here, with no bushes or trees. With a quick look around, seeing no one staring in his direction, he stripped, rolled everything into a bundle, and tied it to Kristina's bridle on top of her head. She looked ridiculous, but this way no one on the other side would get suspicious of his clothes being wet.

Stina's boat was far out already, and it looked like the wind was at her back. "Thank you, Saint Nikolaos," he whispered and rushed into the water. He followed at a safe distance as her boat moved steadily forward, past other boats and the smaller islands. No one saw him.

Once Stina was closer to the mainland, he made a wide berth around her, reaching the beach ahead of her. He dressed and stepped back to a safer distance, watching her pull the boat in. Her hair was coming loose from her braid in the wind. She should have covered it since they said that they were married. They made an odd married couple, he with his wet clothes and she bareheaded. No wonder people were suspicious.

Stina took one last look across the sea and left the boat at the water's edge, walking toward Nikolaos with a determined look on her face. "I'm ready to leave. I'm done with this place."

He touched her shoulder. "Come with me instead," he said and kissed her on the mouth.

They had just gotten back on Kristina's back when a lonely fisherman hurried toward the beach with a thick net thrown over his shoulder, smiling at them and wishing them a pleasant evening. Nikolaos was glad that his clothes were dry.

Chapter 40

They set out to Saint Halvard's church in the early morning of the third day home to speak with the pastor. It was at least a half a day's ride away in Ytterby. Nikolaos had conflicting feelings about it. A lot had changed since he and Abluna wed in what he thought was back in 1469. At that time, weddings had been a simple affair. They had shaken hands before their friends and family and then feasted together until their guests walked him and Abluna to their wedding bed. That had been that.

Now it would be different. The pastor would ask them questions and might announce their upcoming wedding in church to see if anyone was against it. Apparently, this was to make sure they weren't related. It was no longer enough to shake hands in front of witnesses at wedding feasts either, the pastors wanted couples to do so on the church steps. Sometimes people even had a second church ceremony inside the church afterwards. Stina had told him all about it. She loved weddings. And she said that the pastor in her church always asked for someone to represent each couple and to speak for them. Hopefully, the Ytterby pastor would accept them coming on their own. He might have heard that Nikolaos had been restoring the old, abandoned farm in the woods. Nikolaos hoped he wouldn't be scolded for his lack of attendance. He would blame the distance, but it was a poor excuse.

"You're quiet, husband," Stina said, interrupting his musings. "You haven't changed your mind on me now, have you?"

"No, I haven't." He could actually tell her the truth. The thought of it made him smile. "I was thinking of how the church has changed since I wedded my first wife. We ought to explain to the pastor that your family is dead and how you come from far away. No, need to tell him from where I take it, just to be on the safe side. We'll tell him we're both alone and hope for the best. Not much else we can do."

"That'll have to do, Nikolaos." Stina squeezed his stomach from where she sat behind him.

"We should get you your own horse, darling, even though I

admit liking the feeling of you behind me. But when the babies come, it won't work," Nikolaos said, patting her hand.

"Babies? There will be babies?"

"What?" Nikolaos pushed himself sideways in the saddle so he could look at her. "What do you mean, don't you know how babies…?" He stopped talking when he saw her grin.

"Yes. I know how people do it, but you're not…"

"Not people."

"No." She looked embarrassed.

"It works, it's the same as for everyone else," he said, smiling so broadly he felt his cheeks tighten. "Abluna and I had seven children. I've told you. What did you think I meant?"

"I know you did. But still, is it the same when you, you know what I mean." She blushed.

"Yes, exactly the same!" he exclaimed, his lips curling into a wicked grin, partly intentional and partly due to his own amusement. When he turned forward again, he heard her laugh behind him. His grin widened on its own.

The little church stood in a green meadow surrounded by old, gnarled oaks. A big river ran right past it. That was another reason Nikolaos hadn't gone to church there much. The river was too distracting. Today, there was a dock with several boats moored at its side. A crowd had clustered at the church entrance, and Nikolaos counted twelve wagons parked on the side. It seemed like a lot for such a small church. People were craning their necks to see inside but didn't enter. Was it full? Something didn't feel right. He pulled Kristina to a halt.

"Is it Sunday today? I thought it was Friday. It's so crowded. Is it a feast day?" Nikolaos whispered, feeling embarrassed he had lost track.

"No. I don't believe it is. I thought it was Friday too."

"Odd then," Nikolaos said, urging Kristina back into a slow trot.

When they reached the back of the crowd, an older man turned his head to see who they were and then quickly looked back at the entrance. He had an odd expression on his face.

Following his gaze, Nikolaos instinctively readied his heels to kick Kristina into a gallop. It was too dark to see all the way inside, but from the look of it, the church was so full, people were standing in the aisles. There was a palpable tension in the air. This was no ordinary service.

"What's happening?" Stina whispered.

Nikolaos made Kristina back up slowly, heels still at the ready. "I don't know, but we're leaving," he whispered back, then turned Kristina around and put his heels in her sides. She was almost at a gallop when two riders hurried toward them from the opposite direction, blocking their escape.

"Did they hang the witch yet?" the first one hollered.

A collective hush went through the crowd, and several people turned angrily at the sound of the man's voice. He was heavyset and sweating profusely, wiping his forehead as he leered at the crowd, not bothered in the least that they had shouted at him.

"Witches, there are three of them now!" someone in the crowd shouted, immediately followed by another angry hush.

Nikolaos urged Kristina forward, steering around the men on the horses. "What's happening? May I speak to you for a moment?" He gestured toward the road. "In private."

The heavyset man looked to the crowd with pursed lips and made a tsk-tsk sound, but then he nodded.

"I can't see why not. No need to try to get to church now, we can't get through."

"Thank you kindly."

"Certainly. You hadn't heard, eh?" he asked as his companion lifted his hat and rode off to join the crowd.

Nikolaos shook his head.

They followed the man as he made a straight line toward the cemetery, stopping when there was a view of the crowd from the other side of the church. Nikolaos positioned himself so the river was at his back.

"As you can see, we have a lot of worried people here. You

ought to know that we have a witch among us, three it seems now if that man is correct up there," the man said gravely.

"Are you certain?" Stina asked.

"Yes, unfortunately so, mistress. It began when Anne's daughter, Trine, was herding their cows in the woods. She was taking them to her usual place, but suddenly, the cows wouldn't walk. No matter what Trine did, they wouldn't budge and just stood stock still. She feared leaving them and stayed with them until her father worried and came to look for her. But by then she couldn't move either. He had to pick her up and carry her all the way home, leaving the cows where they were until the next day. Then it was revealed that Medicine Gunnel had been seen in those woods and must have put a curse on the cows and Trine. Medicine Gunnel has been arrested, thankfully."

"That's very serious," Nikolaos said, feeling Stina's arms tighten around his waist.

"Yes, it's a frightening time, but I'm afraid I don't know more than that. Seems to me that Medicine Gunnel has admitted the truth though since there is such a crowd. Stay and wait until they come out to find out. It's what I'm planning to do. Where are you from? I've not seen you here. Are you traveling through the area?"

"We live about half a day from here. We were hoping to speak to the pastor and plan our betrothal," Nikolaos said. "We don't know many here, but I wanted to invite people to a small wedding feast to witness us going to our marriage bed. But if Medicine Gunnel is a witch, I'm not so sure it would be wise to do it. I thought we lived in a safe and God-fearing land."

"So, you would think. It always has been. But now, I'm not sure." The man pulled his hat off to cool off, exposing hair soaked with sweat. Then he put it back on and turned to Stina. "Pray forgive me, I'm being impolite. I'm Eskil, Farrier Eskil, most call me. Should your horse need shoeing, I'm down by the road behind the lake here. It's the same road the post-runner takes. Everyone knows my place," he said proudly.

"That's very good to know. I'm Fiddler Nikolaos, and my woman here is Stina. As I said, we want to be promised in front of witnesses. We have no family to speak of."

"No family at all?"

Nikolaos shook his head. "Stina's parents passed on, and her brothers died in the war. I've been an orphan since I was a child. A pestilence took my whole family." He felt Stina stiffen behind him, but she would have to get used to his lies. It wasn't like he could tell the truth.

"I see, I'm sorry to hear. Life can be harsh. If God sees fit, he'll take from us. You may have to come back another day. Today isn't the best day for it," Eskil said.

"Yes, I can see that," Nikolaos said. "I don't like it. As I mentioned, I thought people were God-fearing good people. How do we suffer a witch here?"

Eskil wiped sweat off his face with his sleeve. He looked scared. "I don't know." Just when he said that there was a stirring in the crowd. Then it split in two as people shifted to the sides when someone was pushed outside from one of the church's side buildings.

"There she is, that's Medicine Gunnel!" Eskil shouted. Then with a shake of his reins, he set off in a gallop toward the church.

Nikolaos watched in horror as two other women were pushed outside. Their left arms hung loose and bobbed around without control when they were forced forward. Their skirts were bloody, and one of them had all her hair sheared off.

"We need to go find out what's happening," Nikolaos said, swallowing what felt like bile in his throat, remembering the sound of Old Karin's bones when she was pulled out of their jail cell.

"I don't know. I'm scared, Nikolaos. I don't understand how the Devil can be involved here too, we're far from Marstrand."

"You'd think, but..." he started but stopped again, not sure of what to say. It wasn't actually that far.

Riding closer to the crowd, he could feel fear and excitement in the air. People were staring almost gleefully at the women, and several people spit at them. The accused looked beside themselves with fear. And the bald woman kept falling to her knees and was roughly pulled up again by a large-muscled man who had joined in to help.

"Hang them! Hang the witches!" people shouted. A man with his arm around his wife threw a rotten apple at them.

Then the pastor came out from the chapel. He stopped on the church steps and looked ominously at the sky.

The crowd grew silent, staring at him with rapt attention. Something about their expressions scared Nikolaos. There was more than fear in their eyes, something fierce. It was similar to the people waiting for Old Karin at the courthouse in Uppvidinge.

The pastor lowered his head and looked at the crowd. "We have witches among us!" he shouted. "These three women here have admitted to everything. They've traveled to the Blue Hill every night. Not only did they commune with the Devil himself, but they also brought your children. At night, when you're sleeping, they creep in through holes in the walls and take your children." His voice lost some of its strength as he spoke and became hoarse, tinged with fear.

The woman whose husband had thrown a rotten apple earlier started to scream hysterically. Her husband did nothing to stop it. He just stood there staring at the pastor. Several people looked around themselves nervously.

The pastor cleared his throat and continued with renewed strength. "This is dangerous. I implore you to keep watch over your children. There can be no more cases of innocent children taken at night. No more. You hear me? No more." He grabbed hold of the church wall for support. "The witches didn't admit to it initially, and we could have let them loose. God have mercy on all our souls had we done that. But not to fear, we saw reason to question them further. And with the proper amount of pain, we got them to finally admit to the truth. They have indeed taken children at night, and they're not the only ones." He paused as a gasp of shock went through the crowd. Then he lifted his arm and pointed to a woman standing toward the back by herself. "Get her! She's the one who put the disease on Potter Matz's pigs, making him drop the bowl in the kiln, and then his pigs got sick. Medicine Gunnel told me herself just this morning. Arrest the witch."

The woman he pointed to didn't say a word. She just turned around, lifted her skirts high enough to expose her ankles, and bolted. Nikolaos' mouth fell open as the crowd dispersed in several directions. Four men grabbed the three witches while two others ran after the newly accused witch who was running faster than he had ever seen a woman run, while others ran screaming into the church in total panic.

Stina was sobbing behind him, and he felt her tears wetting his shirt as she pressed his face to his shoulder.

The witches were dragged to a large tree behind the church and made to stand on pieces of wood. With a start, he noticed nooses attached to one of the branches. They were going to hang them right there, so close to the church. That surely couldn't be seemly, could it? They were on sacred ground.

The women seemed apathetic, staring into nothingness as the men attached the noose around their necks. The bald woman pissed herself. The pee splattered on the dry ground, hitting one of the men's feet. He screamed with an expression full of disgust, and then he slapped her across the face with the back of his hand.

They had to get out of there. With his heart pounding, Nikolaos turned Kristina around and urged her forward through the throngs of people, aware of everyone around them and ready to sprint if needed. No one paid them any mind.

When they reached the road, he heard the wood pieces kicked aside, followed by necks snapping. At least he thought that's what he heard. It was a surprisingly loud snapping sound. He urged Kristina into a gallop, wondering if they had caught the one who ran.

They were back home before the sun had moved past afternoon.

Stina went inside without a word. Nikolaos took care of Kristina and brushed her until she was dry and clean, then gave her a little water and attached her hobble so she could stay outside.

Stina was sitting at the edge of the hearth poking in the fire when he came inside.

He sat down on the bench in front of it, leaning forward and resting his elbows on his knees. "You should add another log on that, or the fire will go out."

Stina nodded and grabbed one from the basket but placed it on her lap, looking drained. "Nikolaos," she began, then stopped, staring unseeingly at him. Then her gaze focused. "I'm scared of the witches. What if they come here at night?"

"Well," he said, uncertain.

"I feel sorry for them too, the witches. I can't believe they hung them. Do you really think they deserved it? Are they truly witches, or were they accused just like I was, for no reason at all?"

"But they admitted to it. People can't hide the truth if they're tortured. Did you see the arms? They must have crushed the bones and pulled them out of their sockets. No one can keep the truth hidden after that. I wouldn't have lasted long."

She gave him a long scrutinizing glance. "You're strong, Nikolaos. You'd be able to."

He doubted it but didn't contradict her.

They sat in silence after that. He really didn't know what to think. But one thing was for certain, they should stay away from people.

***

Nikolaos went to the river before Stina woke up, calming himself from all the tumultuous things that had happened in the short span of time since Stina found him.

Afterward, back home, he brought his fiddle to the apple tree and sat down in the shade, feeling relaxed and sure of what to do.

When he stopped, he found Stina watching him from the table outside, a bowl of porridge set out.

"That was so beautiful it brought tears to my eyes," she said.

"I thank you," he said, left his instrument on the ground, and went to sit beside her. "I didn't notice you come out, I'm glad to eat."

They each picked up their spoons and stuck them in the bowl at the same time, their hands bumping into each other. Stina laughed, and he knew he loved her already.

"Stina, I've been thinking. I know you want the pastor to witness our hand shaking and promise to each other on the church steps. But we have no one to speak for us, no one to witness it."

"But in the village where you traded to get your cow, can't they do it?"

"I was thinking that too." He paused, waiting for her to get another spoonful of porridge. "But they don't have their own church. They usually worship south of there, forget what the church is called, or at Saint Halvard's."

"Were they there yesterday?"

"Don't think so, I didn't recognize anyone."

Stina looked relieved. "Then let's ask them."

Nikolaos hesitated, thinking of what to say. "But then they'll probably suggest we'll go to Saint Halvard's, don't you think? Let's not go back there, Stina. What if they find out who I am? Imagine what they'd do to me." And to Stina, but there was no need to tell her that.

Her hand went to her mouth. "Dear lord!"

He put his spoon down and put his arm around her. "I suggest we give each other our promises right here by ourselves. God will see it. He's present everywhere and because of the circumstances, I believe he'd forgive us our trespass. It wouldn't be much different than when I married my first wife."

Stina stared at him silently for a long moment before she answered. "Yes, but then you had people follow you to make sure you got into your marriage bed. Someone must do that, so people know we're really married."

"God will," he said and stroked her back. "He'll know, Stina."

"Can I think on it?"

"Of course, I wasn't suggesting we do it now. I'd be too tired anyway," he said, winking.

She laughed.

They continued eating, watching the sun get higher in the sky behind the trees. If it hadn't been for the terrifying events yesterday, it would have been one of the happiest moments of his long life.

Chapter 41

They went to the river. Standing close enough for Nikolaos to feel the power of the water without losing control. It felt sacred as if God used the river as a witness. Looking into each other's eyes they shook hands and solemnly promised that they would be together as man and wife until the end of her days. Then they walked side by side to the marriage bed, which Stina had covered with the linen she had washed in the river and covered with sweet-smelling grasses and herbs.

***

Nikolaos carefully pulled Stina's shawl off her shoulders and untied her bodice, watching her chest heave with each breath and her cheeks redden with shyness. Her blue eyes reminded him of cornflowers. When she stood in only her shift, he gently picked her up and laid her on the bed.

"We're almost married now," he whispered, stroking her arms, neck, and breasts. She smiled, but he could feel her fear as well as longing. Was she afraid because of who he was? Or because it was her first time? Putting his nose in the crook of her neck, he drew in the wonderful scent of her and whispered, "Don't be afraid, my dear wife, I'll be very gentle."

"I'm afraid, but I want to," she whispered and wrapped her round arms around his neck.

It made him want her, but he waited, taking long deep breaths and tracing kisses across her face until he felt her body relax between his. He slipped inside, feeling her wetness and only a fleeting sense of obstruction. Tears came to her eyes, and he slowed down, kissing the tears away.

Afterward with his head propped on his arm, Nikolaos smiled into Stina's face. "We're married now. Bishop Angermannus would have frowned upon it, but I'm very happy, and I dare say that God is surely happy for us too."

"Who's Bishop Anger Magnus?"

"Angermannus," Nikolaos said, the corners of his mouth twitching before he succumbed to a bout of snorting laughter. "Anger Magnus! Rusty devils that's good." He shot an apologetic glance at Stina's surprised face, trying to stifle his laughter, but it kept bubbling.

"What Nikolaos? Explain."

Nikolaos took a deep breath and was finally able to stop. "Anger Magnus," he said, grinning again, "is how I'll think of him from now on. But Angermannus was his name, pronounced aehnger and mannus, Bishop Angermannus. He *was* angry, a dogmatist who traveled around the country to ensure people lived moral lives and followed what he deemed God wanted. He was relentless and cruel, disapproving of the way we lived. People didn't care much if people were intimate before they married. It was enough just to say that you were planning a betrothal for people to respect your relationship," Nikolaos said, letting his finger slide across the inside of her arm. "Angermannus hated it and claimed it was indecent."

"People really didn't care? What if someone became with child?"

"It made no difference other than that you'd have your wedding feast sooner than you planned."

"Oh well then, if God blessed your marriages back then without the church, I'm going to have faith that God is happy with our marriage today," she said, looking content.

"Just what I'm thinking too. I'm sure he will." Nikolaos pushed a lock of hair from her forehead. "It was an easier time in some respects then. Freer in many ways. Our churches used to be full of saints. I loved praying to them. But Angermannus did away with our Catholic rituals. We weren't even allowed to keep our saints even at home and were forbidden to wear a crucifix." Nikolaos shifted in the bed and put his hand on Stina's chest where a crucifix would sit if she had worn one. "Angermannus wasn't well liked. He was harsh and cruel and had people punished for not being what he considered properly married. There were still some people who regularly spoke of Thor and Freyja, and he hated that too." Nikolaos slid his hand downward and rested his hand on her stomach. "I'm not sure I remember exactly, but he had to flee to Germany for some reason and stayed away for thirteen years. I think." He narrowed his eyes. "Despite this, once Johan the III died, he was made Bishop. Pray forgive me. This is a horrible subject today of all days," he said and kissed her on the lips.

"No," she said under his kiss, "I like to hear you talk of it. You know so much. I've never heard of him and knew nothing of this. Did you meet this Bishop?"

"Thankfully, no," he said and sat up. "Let me go light our candle so it's not so dark in here." Nikolaos crawled out of bed and brought the bedside candle to the hearth to light it. When he came back, she sat leaning on her pillows, her long hair spread out around her shoulders. She was so beautiful he felt his breath catch in his throat. "My lady, you're beautiful. I'm a very fortunate man to have you right here in my bed with me." He crawled back into bed and kissed her again.

She kissed him back and looked at him shyly. "You really are like a person, a regular kind and sweet person, and it works just the same like you said!"

"How would you know?"

"Well, I've seen horses and cows and I…" She stopped when she saw his mischievous expression.

Chapter 42

A woman's hand made all the difference, and Nikolaos' farm was thriving. Buttersweet, the name Stina had given his cow, gave them so much milk Stina set aside butter to trade. She was hoping for a couple of chickens, but they were still nervous about meeting people after what happened at Saint Halvard's and decided to wait.

They avoided the subject.

Nikolaos had mended the old wall around his little crop field so they could use the whole enclosure and plant more in the spring. It would be nice to plant more wheat and leave a spot where Stina could have vegetables and berries.

Having spent the whole morning harvesting what was already growing, Nikolaos put his sickle down and took everything in, shielding his eyes from the sun with his hand. Their animals were resting in the shade, and their rye was thick and healthy. Stina was all the way down by the woods, gathering it into a large basket. She looked beautiful in the scarf she proudly covered her hair with since their wedding night. It was light gray with tiny, embroidered blue and red flowers, and had long ends trailing down her back. His beautiful wife.

He smiled to himself and went back to work. The cut rye lay like a thick mat on the ground. A few more cuts and it would be finished. His sickle was in mid-air when, out of the corner of his eye, he saw Stina drop her basket. For a moment she stood still and stared into the woods. Then she screamed.

Nikolaos threw the sickle on the ground and hurried toward her just as she lifted her skirts, kicked her clogs off, and ran, her clogs smashing into each other in the air with a blue clap before they fell to the ground.

Her face contorted into a grimace of fear, and she was sobbing by the time they caught up with each other.

"What is it? Were you bit by a snake?" He pushed her away from him and held her at arm's length to get a good look. Her hand was covered with red marks, but it looked like scratches from the rye. "Did it get your hand? Your legs?"

Stina shook her head between sobs. "No. It wasn't a snake. A witch!"

"A witch bit you?" he asked, astonished.

Her eyes widened, but she shook her head again. "No, no, there was a witch in the woods. I saw her fly."

"What?" Shock and fear as well as relief made him break out in a sweat. He pulled her close.

"I saw her! I was just about to put a pile in the basket when I saw her. She was right there, flying between the trees as if it were nothing unusual. I heard the flapping of her arms and everything."

"Where?"

Stina looked scared but grabbed his hand and pointed into the trees. "There, do you see that large pine there?"

"Yes," he said, frowning. Everything looked normal. There was a slight breeze. Birds chirped in the distance, and there was rustling in the bushes from small animals but nothing large enough to be a witch. The only sign of something out of the ordinary was Stina's basket toppled on the ground with the rye spilled out. He breathed a little calmer.

"The witch sat on that branch, and then, from one moment to the next, she flew to the other tree. I heard the wings flap. I told you. I mean her arms."

"Stay here," Nikolaos said and climbed over the wall before she could stop him.

The ground on the other side was full of brambles and thornbushes. If it was a witch, he certainly could understand why she had chosen to fly. It was next to impossible for a woman to walk there, her skirts would get stuck. But there were no broken branches in the trees, nothing was bent out of shape, nor was anything scraped off the trunks. If something as large as a witch had flown from one tree to the other, there would be signs of it.

He let out a breath of relief and climbed back over the wall, pulling thorns off his breeches and shirt. "Stina, I think it was a bird you saw. An owl perhaps. There's nothing amiss out there."

She didn't look convinced. He grabbed her around the waist and kissed her head. "I thought you said you weren't sure about these witches."

"I know, but I know what I saw. That was no owl, it was a witch."

***

Stina made Nikolaos go out every morning and every evening to make sure the witch wasn't lurking in the trees. He never saw any sign of her.

Life continued peacefully without incident, and after a few weeks, Nikolaos decided that the time had come for them to visit their neighbors despite his initial feelings about wanting to stay away from people. It was better to know what people around them were saying than to hide.

After some discussion, they decided to go to the farm where Nikolaos had played his fiddle in exchange for Buttersweet. Stina would bring butter from their former cow as a gift, and he would ask if he could buy a couple of chickens or perhaps play again. Additionally, Stina hoped to find out if a baking-woman was expected in the area soon.

The farm was in a small village with just three other farms surrounded by a green, bordered by a brook and a sizable crop field. If their visit went well, Nikolaos wanted to ask them for a furlong on it for the future. Their own harvests wouldn't be enough when they had more mouths to feed.

When Stina and Nikolaos arrived, two men were drinking tobacco in the shade of the barn at the first farm.

"Afternoon, gentlemen," Nikolaos called, slowing Kristina down to a walk.

"Fiddler Nikolaos! What a nice surprise," one of the men exclaimed. It was Alf, Nikolaos realized. It was his brother's cow he had taken home.

"It's nice to see you too, Alf. This is my wife," Nikolaos said proudly.

"Wife? Dear Fiddler Nikolaos, what manner of nonsense is this? You play at our weddings but don't invite us to yours?" He shook his finger at him in mock anger, then laughed, poking the other man with his elbow. "Congratulations!"

"I thank you." Nikolaos chuckled, nodding as he met the other man's welcoming gaze. "Stina and I were promised and wed just a few weeks ago," he said as he dismounted. Maybe it had been a mistake not to have a proper wedding after all. The men were so nice.

"A pleasure, goodwife. Fiddler Nikolaos is a good man," Alf said.

Stina dismounted on her own, exchanging a merry look with Nikolaos. "I think so too, Alf. And thank you."

"We're glad to see him happy. We felt for him living all alone on that old ruin of a farm. This is my son, Knud," he said, gesturing.

"Congratulations!" Knud came forward, lifting his hat. "I wasn't here when you played that time, Nikolaos, but my father has spoken of you. Can I offer you tobacco? Did you bring your pipe?"

"Nah, I haven't developed a taste for it."

Knud gave him a surprised look. "You haven't? You really ought to start. It's very good for you, especially for dry scalps. I had a lot of white flakes in my hair, but almost none now, I recommend it."

"As do I," Alf said. "It helps with all kinds of pain. My teeth for example are giving me a lot of trouble." He pulled on his lip, exposing red swollen gums and several teeth missing. "But if I drink tobacco throughout the day, I feel much better. It soothes the gums. How old are you, Nikolaos? You lost any teeth yet?"

"Only one in the back," he lied, aware of how perfect his teeth were. He closed his mouth.

"Eh, you're young yet. Once you get closer to thirty your body changes," Alf said, but didn't press on about his age.

Nikolaos met Stina's eyes and grinned. She smiled but quickly looked down at her skirts, clearly uncomfortable.

"How's your cow?" Alf asked, oblivious. "I hope my brother gave you a good one."

"He did. In fact, she's doing so well Stina brought a tub of her butter. In truth, I was also hoping I could buy a couple of chickens from you. Or play a bit for them?" Nikolaos asked, looking at Stina who had grabbed the tub and was holding it out with the lid removed for the men to see.

Alf leaned forward and sniffed, then nodded approvingly. "How thoughtful of you, Stina!" he said, then turned to Nikolaos. "Why don't you let Knud bring Stina in to see my wife? Then you and I can talk for a bit."

Walking next to Alf with Kristina behind him, Nikolaos patted Alf's shoulder and went straight to the point. "I thank you for this. I was fine on my own, living on my fishing and hunting and the few crops I have. But Stina longs for eggs and bread. She wants to ask your wife if there'll be a baking-woman coming through here soon."

"Actually, we do all our baking here ourselves. Kajsa down in the last farm there," Alf pointed toward the farm on the far side of the green, "has two large ovens outside. They baked some last week, but if you bring your flour in a day or two, I'm sure Kajsa can get talked into baking some more. After that, she'll be traveling to help out in other villages, not sure where she goes exactly."

"I appreciate it."

"It's always nice with visitors. Good to get some news and hear of your marriage. Who *is* Stina? Where's she from?"

As they had agreed upon, Nikolaos grew serious. "Stina's an orphan, and she lost her brothers in the war. Lived near Kungälv." Stina hadn't liked it, but it was what they decided sounded the most plausible. People knew Nikolaos went to Kungälv now and then, and it wasn't Marstrand, which they had decided not to tell anyone in case rumors had preceded her.

"I'm saddened to hear it. Those many wars with Poland bring more ill than good." He tsk tsked.

"Yes."

"But I'm glad you're here and that our area will grow more families. As a matter of fact, we've been thinking of building a church. Just talk as of yet, but when the time comes, would you be able to help?"

"That's very good to hear. Stina worries about how far the churches are from our farm. She'll be delighted. And yes, of course. I'll do whatever I can." It wasn't untrue despite their current feelings about attending church.

Alf looked pleased and hummed in response.

Nikolaos walked alongside him in silence, letting the moment pass, then changed the subject. "I have something else I wanted to speak with you about if you don't mind?"

"Not at all."

Nikolaos took a deep breath. "What are your thoughts on the witches everyone is talking about?"

Alf gave him a startled look. "I've heard rumors, but we haven't seen any in these parts. We had a wiseboy looking around here a few months ago, but he left again."

"A wiseboy?"

"You've not heard of them?"

"No, I haven't."

Alf put his arm around Nikolaos' shoulders, then lowered his voice. "Wiseboys are young boys with a special knack for spotting a witch. They sense it somehow and can tell if someone is a witch just by being near them. But as I mentioned, ours mustn't have sensed one here, thankfully."

"Thank the Lord." Nikolaos had wanted to tell Alf about what happened at Saint Halvard's and that Stina thought she had seen a witch in the woods, but what if it drew unnecessary attention to them? Maybe it was best not to mention it lest they sent wiseboys to investigate. "Stina is afraid. She has trouble sleeping at night," he said and left it at that.

"I'm not surprised." Alf shaded his eyes with his free hand and looked at something ahead of them. "I've seen a lot all my years here, but this, this scares me. To think that God-fearing people can get tricked by the Devil and turn to witchery. Little children, too, they say. It's the stuff of nightmares, but all we can do is pray. Advise your wife to go to sleep with a cross by the bedside.

It'll help her relax."

"That's very good advice. I heard that several witches were hung in Ytterby," Nikolaos said, deciding to mention it without telling him that they had actually seen it.

Alf shivered visibly and pulled his arm from Nikolaos' shoulder, crossing his arms over his chest. "We live in terrible, terrible times. I heard too. They burned them afterward, on big pyres."

"They burned them?" Nikolaos turned around to stare at him.

"Yes, they don't want their bodies buried even at the gallows."

Nikolaos crossed himself. They hadn't done that with Old Karin as far as he knew. Maybe he should take it as a compliment, they thought him less dangerous to be with than the Devil.

"Prayer is good. Don't worry, Nikolaos," Alf said. He didn't cross himself.

"Stina says they fly. But between you and I, man to man. Is that truly possible? How would someone without wings fly?"

"I don't know. I've wondered the same. But I think the Devil gives them that power." Alf stopped walking as they neared his house. "Let's not talk of it where the women can hear it. Go join your new wife and have some ale with us. I'll tell everyone you're here, and then we'll plan a nice dance for tonight. We should be merry, don't worry, Nikolaos." He gave a quick wave and set off, running stiffly. It looked like his hip was hurting him.

Nikolaos found Stina and Alf's wife at a table set with ale and a plate with what looked like some kind of sweetmeats. Alf's wife was heavy with child.

"Fiddler Nikolaos!" she exclaimed and stood up, supporting her heavy frame on the table. "You're bringing home five laying hens, and Stina will be baking in a day or two. Baking-Kajsa will be happy to help, I'm sure. We were talking about making another batch in a couple of days when our neighbors from the south are coming, anyway."

"I thank you kindly."

"It's our pleasure. We're glad to part with what we have. God has been good to us, and we have aplenty." She smiled and curtsied clumsily, then sat again, "Pray forgive me, I must rest."

"Of course," Nikolaos said and eyed her belly, smiling ruefully at Stina who promptly blushed.

"Boel has nine other children, all have survived," Stina said once Nikolaos had sat down opposite them.

Boel nodded proudly. "Yes, not a one has succumbed. We're very fortunate. Baking Kajsa lost four of hers to the fever. Our wisewoman wasn't here, or she might have been able to help. And, anyway, the pastor says we oughtn't speak with her anymore." She glanced at Stina who nodded gravely. They must have spoken of the witches just as he and Alf did. How much had Stina told her?

"Poor woman, I'm saddened for her loss," Nikolaos said. "Who's your wisewoman?" He nodded in thanks when Boel handed him a mug of ale.

"Wise-Magda, we call her. She travels here and trades her herbs. We've not seen her for several years now. Can't blame her, I wouldn't travel alone when witches fly overhead."

Wise-Magda, maybe it was Rå. He took a sip of ale.

"I've heard them myself at night. If you listen, you can hear them fly off on their brooms, it makes a special sweeping sound in the air," Boel said, putting a protecting hand over her belly.

"Brooms?" Nikolaos exchanged a shocked glance with Stina.

"Indeed, they smear them with a special salve to get them to fly. Doesn't work without it. Although some fly on their own without brooms, just like the one Stina saw. That I have not seen nor heard myself." She looked relieved.

"I see," Nikolaos said and threw another glance in Stina's direction. "Who's the pastor you mentioned? Alf told me the village might build a church."

Just then, Knud came in. "Fiddler Nikolaos, my father is down at the green. Are you able to go down? Niels is there too. He's probably hoping you'd show him how to play, he has his own fiddle and is learning."

"I'd be glad to," Nikolaos said and rose to stand, giving Boel an apologetic look.

She waved her hand in the air. "You go, Fiddler Nikolaos, I'll tell Stina about our pastor. He lives here, and like Alf said, we're going to build a church to house him. Pastor Otto is his name, but no one ever calls him that, just Pastor."

Niels and Alf were sitting on logs serving as benches along the green, waving as Knud and Nikolaos approached. Niels kept his eyes on Nikolaos the whole time. There was something charming in the way he held the fiddle and bent his head sideways.

"You want me to show you a tune or two?" Nikolaos asked, smiling. Niels' shirt was open, exposing a muscular chest. It was impossible not to notice.

Niels blushed. "I thank you, pray yes."

Knud and his father were oblivious. They said their goodbyes, promising to come back with everyone else once the sun was a bit lower in the sky.

It became chilly that evening, but the dancing made everyone warm. Every resident from the four farms was there, including an old couple seated on the logs wrapped in shawls and blankets, too old to dance but happy to watch. Niels kept up well, and everyone cheered him on, not minding his frequent mistakes.

By the time Nikolaos and Stina left, they had their new hens in a large basket and an appointment to return in two days so Stina could bake with Kajsa and Nikolaos continue his lessons with Niels.

Chapter 43

Rå felt the panic and fear like a disturbance in the air.

Years ago, when Pastor Klint had spoken of Näcken at church, people had been afraid. Still, there was also a sense of curiosity, and even community, as if it brought those who were not involved closer because they had something new to gossip about. This was not the same. No one felt closer to anyone. People feared each other, suspicious of every little thing. Even a bird flying in a different direction might mean someone was a witch. She had never seen anything like it. It frightened her. And nothing ever had.

Rå stayed in her tree, alert and alone, or went deep into the woods and dug her feet into the moss, standing there with her back open and her hair flowing like branches in the wind.

Then she decided to go visit Jon.

"Magda, I had a feeling you were going to visit," Jon said, beaming, and kissing her on both cheeks. "You look beautiful as usual. Come in, come in." He stepped aside to let her pass, still beaming.

"It's nice to see you too, Jon." She pulled him close, reaching under his shirt to pinch his nipples.

"Magda, what if I had a customer in here," he teased, then kissed her on the lips. "Come have dinner with me. I was just about to eat. I went fishing today."

"That sounds delightful," she said, removing her fingers from his nipples. She followed him and sat down at his table, watching as he went to fetch plates and mugs.

Their relationship had been like this for several years, lots of flirting and occasional lovemaking, but not more than that. They were friends more than anything, and neither had romantic feelings for each other. It suited them both fine.

Jon brought a tray with everything, including his fish fried in butter and herbs and two full wine glasses. "I poured wine instead, but if you still want ale I can…" He trailed off, pointing with his chin toward his counter where he had first placed the mugs.

She shook her head. "Wine would be very nice."

"Knowing you, Magda, you came because you wanted to talk to me about everything that's happening. I'm not wrong, am I?" he asked, handing her one of the glasses and a fork.

"No, you're not." She took a sip. It tasted a little sour, but she didn't say anything. Jon must have left it uncorked for too long. "I've been keeping to myself because of it. People seem awkward and tense. I spoke with someone who said they had hung and burned a witch somewhere near here." She took another sip of the wine, deciding it was drinkable. "Is that true? Who was it? I couldn't bring myself to ask."

"The shoemaker's wife in Odala. It's that little place near the mill."

Rå put down her wineglass and stared at him in disbelief.

Jon nodded gravely. "Yes. They said a cat had acted strangely around her house. Apparently, it walked around in circles several times, and then it sat down under her window and stared at her while she mended shoe leather. How that proves she was a witch, I don't know. But several people insisted the cat must have been waiting for her to take it to the Blue Hill and the Devil. Everyone went to the execution except me. I pretended that I didn't know about it. I had heard, of course, but didn't want to watch the... the spectacle."

"The spectacle? You don't think she was a witch?"

"Magda, I don't know," he said, rubbing his chin. "I never noticed anything. I go to Odala now and then, not only for flour but sometimes because I need leather for my tailoring. The suspicions came so suddenly. She always had cats. Why is it strange that it was looking at the window? It probably wanted to see if she'd throw it a scrap of food. It still sits there, looking for her. I've seen it. It breaks my heart."

Rå glanced away from Jon and looked out one of his enormous windows. She could almost feel the cat's disappointment and grief, waiting in vain for someone who never came back. Humans and their ridiculous beliefs and superstitions. They always came up with new things to accuse each other of, hurting both themselves and animals. She was sure the woman wasn't a witch. "I met the shoemaker's wife a couple of times," Rå said, fixing her eyes on Jon again. "She seems, seemed, I mean, kind and caring. A little odd perhaps."

"Yes, she was, didn't talk much. But her husband loved her. He's devastated now. I heard he tried to stop the hanging and managed to run to her and lift her up so her neck wouldn't break… or to stop the suffocation. I'm not sure how it works." Jon clenched his fists, his face etched with horror.

Rå reached across the table and took his hand. "I'm so sorry, Jon."

"Mm." He put his other hand over hers and kept humming, lost in thought. Then he said, "I really don't know. But I don't like it. It reminds me of Nikolaos, you remember him, don't you? It's," he looked upward, calculating, "twenty years ago or something, isn't it?"

"Yes, of course I remember him. What does he have to do with this?" Rå asked even though she had thought about it too.

Jon let go of her hand and poured them more wine, then cut and ate two pieces of fish before he answered. "Nothing, it's just that I remember how sure I was for a while that Nikolaos was, well, I don't want to say it out loud. What if it's the same with the shoemaker's wife? Maybe someone has misunderstood something." He stood. "Let's bring our wine outside. I want to get some air."

Rå hadn't even tried the fish yet and handed Jon her glass and picked up her plate, eating with her hands as they walked out. It tasted incredible. Jon was an excellent cook. It's what happened when men lived alone and had to cook themselves.

"Delicious!" she said when they got to the back of his house, looking down at the valley below them. The village was visible in the distance. She put the plate on the ground and stuck her hand under Jon's shirt, then grabbed her wine glass from him. "This is a bit sour, though."

"It is?"

She gave a one-sided smile and pulled her hand out again.

"Yes, but it's drinkable."

He laughed and kissed her head. "Let's not talk of the shoemaker's wife anymore. I want to enjoy your company instead. It's a nice evening, I'll walk you home, and we'll look for wild herbs on the way. I don't want you visiting the village this time, Magda."

"I wasn't planning to." She smiled, happy about his suggestion. Jon was at least sixty-five if not more, but still had the stamina to walk her all the way home, which at his human pace took more than a day and half a night.

Chapter 44

Nikolaos placed his own fiddle right below the bone of his left shoulder, resting it comfortably and said, "Here, Niels, if you hold it like this, you'll be able to move your bow easily. Don't press just hold it stuck there. If you press too hard, it'll hurt eventually, just rest it. This way you'll be able to play with more feeling. You played well last time, but the notes weren't flowing because both your arms were cramping."

Niels did what he suggested, but each time he put his bow on the strings his instrument slipped and landed on his knee.

"Pray forgive me," he said, looking embarrassed.

"Take your time. There's no rush with this. Try it again." Nikolaos picked up the instrument and positioned it in the right spot, grabbing Niels' fingers and the bow with it, placing it gently on the strings. "Like this, do you feel the difference? The lightness of the touch?"

"Yes." Niels looked straight at him, keeping his hands in the correct position but sitting absolutely still.

Nikolaos swallowed, suddenly aware of how close they were sitting. He could see Niels' tiny eyelashes under his blue eyes. The brook was growing louder. What if he brought Niels down there? Two instruments would color the wavelets in ways he had never seen, and after a while they would both get in. His heart started hammering. Niels blinked and moved closer. Then a puff of wind carried the warmth and scent from the bake ovens, and the sound of women talking.

Nikolaos tore his eyes away from Niels' face. "I need to take a walk," he said hoarsely and stood abruptly. His fingers felt watery.

He felt Niels' eyes on his back and heard Stina laugh in the distance.

***

As soon as Nikolaos was out of sight, he went into the brook, and by the time he stepped back on dry land, it was already dark. He felt like an idiot. They had almost kissed. Right there on the green! Anyone could have seen it, and while he had his wife baking with the other women. Feeling his cheeks burn from shame, he dressed, cursing aloud when he put his breeches on backward. How could he have been so stupid? He didn't even dare to think about what would have happened if he had gone to the brook with him. But pulling his breeches off and putting them back on, Nikolaos realized he also felt relief. He had resisted. The brook wasn't that close either, or he would have suggested they practice somewhere else. And it was Niels who had tried to kiss *him*.

Feeling better, he made his way back to the farm, hoping the women would still be outside. But the front yard lay deserted, and the ovens were empty and cold.

The candlelight from inside the window formed a large square of light on the ground. He stepped into the illuminated patch and looked down at his clothes, brushing them off and making sure his shirt was on correctly.

Then the door opened, and Stina came running out. "Nikolaos, where have you been? I've been worried."

"Pray forgive me." Nikolaos put his arm around her and pulled her close, burying his face in the crook of her neck. She smelled of yeast and bread. "I couldn't resist the water, I had to get to it," he mumbled, overcome with immense relief that he could tell her the truth and thanking God that nothing had happened with Niels.

She laughed softly. "Oh Nikolaos, you had me so very worried. Niels said you didn't feel well and left early to go for a walk."

He smiled, but he had pulled her into the shadows, and she didn't see it. "We'll let them think that. It's best."

"I agree, but we must stay here tonight. They won't let us leave in the dark. Kajsa is nervous about witches. And I agree with her. I don't think we should either. Not now. There's something I've been waiting to tell you." She paused, and he felt her smile against his ear. "I'm with child," she whispered.

Something burst within him, and he pulled her closer still, stifling a sob.

***

The midwife, Nikolaos had already forgotten her name, had been with Stina since sunup, and it was already late afternoon. He was getting anxious. As far as he could remember, it hadn't taken this long the first time Abluna had given birth. It had also been a calmer affair then. Not so here. Boel and her baby had shown up without warning two weeks ago, insisting she should move in to help Stina. Then Baking Kajsa and her two older daughters came to stay. They slept in the barn, which made the house at least feel less crowded, but he still felt intruded upon. He was due for a visit in the river too, but Kajsa's daughters wouldn't leave him out of their sight, claiming they needed to know where he was so they could tell him if Stina's labor was starting. It was driving him mad, but he couldn't well tell them to leave. They did it out of kindness, helping Stina during her first birth. And it was helpful. One of Kajsa's daughters had fetched the midwife last night when Stina's pains had started. Alf had driven them back, getting the midwife there safely in the middle of the night.

Now Alf and Nikolaos were sitting on the ground, leaning their backs against the shed wall, while Nikolaos was keeping a close eye on the house, waiting for one of the many women in there to come out and announce the birth.

"Don't fret, Nikolaos," Alf said. "It's her first time. It always takes longer. You'll get used to it." He nodded for effect, putting a hand on Nikolaos' arm. "You'll be a father any moment now." His face split into a wide contagious smile.

Nikolaos' lips twitched a little in response, but then his smile faded. "It's just that I'm scared for her. I'm not used to having a house full of women either, not used to it," he repeated. "As you know, I lived quite secluded before I found Stina."

Alf chuckled and shook his head at him. "It's how it is around here. Womenfolk always love when new babies come. But to change the subject." He put his hand on Nikolaos' arm again. "Not to worry you even more, but I might as well tell you now when we have time."

Nikolaos' stomach lurched. "What is it?"

"Well, a couple of things. For one, we've had more flybys at night."

"Flybys?"

"It's when a whole group of witches flies over your house at night. Boel says it wakes her up almost every night now. But I've only heard them once myself."

Nikolaos looked at him, trying to think of what to say while remembering Boel talking about the swishing sound of brooms. It had to be birds. It was spring, likely she heard geese flying north. Did geese fly at night?

"I know, I know, it sounds impossible, but they use a salve. It's what makes the brooms flyable," Alf said as if he knew what he was thinking.

"You actually heard this? You sure it was truly witches you heard and not something else?"

"Well..." Alf pursed his lips thoughtfully. "I don't see what else it could be, I've never heard a sound quite like it. It's sweeping like, as if they were sweeping a floor up there in the air."

"Hmmm." Nikolaos glanced briefly at the blue sky above them. "Stina thought she saw a witch in the woods. She hasn't seen it again since, thanks be to the Lord," he said and crossed himself. "That one didn't fly on a broom though. Did Boel tell you?"

"Yes, yes she did." He looked toward the woods with a concerned expression on his face. "And you never saw her?"

Nikolaos shook his head. "No, I went in there to look," he pointed, "but there was no sign of anything amiss. It might have been an owl."

Alf's eyes rounded. "An owl? Could that be what we hear at night?"

Nikolaos whistled, throwing his head back with realization. "I was just wondering to myself if it was geese, but I don't think they fly at night. Owls do."

Alf's eyes lit up, but then darkened again. "But not in groups."

They stayed silent after that. Then Alf smiled and changed the subject. "It's good that your baby is born in the spring. Spring babies always do well."

"They do?"

"Yes, there's more food for the mother all summer, berries, peas, and beans and all that, then in the fall we have the harvest, and if the baby is eating food by then, there's lots to choose from. Haven't you noticed how plumb our little one is?"

"I see, and yes I've noticed." Nikolaos smiled with pleasure, remembering how his and Abluna's babies had all loved apple compote.

"Nice thought, eh? Boel's broad beans are coming along unusually well, she says. Do you have some here?"

"I don't know." Nikolaos pointed to Stina's garden section by their little rye field. "She's planted several things, gooseberries too, but that's over there behind the house," he said with a jerk of his shoulder. His eyes stayed on the door, willing someone to come out, but no one did.

"Don't fret, Nikolaos. Birthing takes time."

Nikolaos nodded and got to his feet. Alf stood up too, and then Nikolaos took him around the property to show him their improvements and everything Stina had planted.

After finishing the tour, they sat on the crumbled wall by their crops to keep an eye on the door again.

"It has to be soon now, don't you think?" Nikolaos asked.

"Yes," Alf said, looking a bit distracted for some reason. "Did you notice anything weird with Niels when you taught him to play back in the fall?"

"Weird? No, he was a fast learner. Why do you ask? Had he seen a witch?" Nikolaos asked, hiding a sigh, annoyed Alf was bringing it up again.

"As I thought!" He shook his head several times. "No, that's not what I meant. But fast, huh? I knew you weren't his first teacher. Näcken got to him first. It's why he learned so quickly. You see, when he plays now, chairs and tables move around by themselves, hopping and sliding across the floor."

Nikolaos laughed, not able to help himself. He had been accused of a lot of things, but that was ridiculous.

"This isn't a laughing matter, Nikolaos," Alf said sharply, looking offended.

"Pray forgive me." He barely managed to seem serious. "Are you certain of this? I noticed nothing odd that day."

"Didn't you leave to go for a walk because you felt ill?"

"I did, but it was probably something I ate. I didn't want to sit there and fart in front of him. I was embarrassed," Nikolaos said, trying to look humorous and convincing at the same time. It was a stupid lie. It just made him feel like laughing more.

Alf looked at him, eyes glinting. "Nikolaos, perhaps you're right. And this is a horrible subject, pray forgive me. Soon you'll have a little baby. This isn't something we should be discussing today. I'm going to go knock on your door and ask Boel for some ale for us. What do you say, eh?"

"Pray yes."

"Good, I'm going." Alf slipped off the wall and walked across the grass, chuckling as he went.

Nikolaos looked after him, relieved he at least saw the humor in some of it. It was also annoying. Not even on the day his wife was laboring could he be free of his own misdoings. He leaped off the wall, deciding not to think about it anymore.

Boel was handing Alf their mugs by the time Nikolaos reached the house, and Alf was smiling at him as he approached. "Here, drink up. The baby is almost here. Boel said Torja can see the head," he said as Boel quickly slammed the door shut.

Torja, that's what the midwife's name was. Nikolaos drank the whole mug down in one long sweep, swallowing his fear along with it. What if it got stuck, strangling itself, the body in and the head out? "She's so quiet in there, I thought women screamed when they gave birth," he said.

Alf lifted an eyebrow. "You didn't hear her?"

"Oh, I did, but I thought she'd be louder." Abluna had been

ear-piercingly loud.

"She sounds pretty loud to me," Alf said.

Just then, the door opened again, and Boel smiled at them from the threshold with Kajsa's daughters looking out from behind her. "You have a son, Nikolaos. You should go in." She handed him a lantern.

Something warm and uncontrollable swelled in Nikolaos' chest, and he pushed himself past the women. Alf called something after him, but he couldn't hear it, and he didn't care.

Stina was leaning on their pillows holding him in her arms, already tightly wrapped, with only his little head sticking up. He looked impossibly small, and Nikolaos remembered thinking exactly the same when his other babies had come. He burst into tears.

Stina looked at him, tears flowing down her cheeks as well. She looked a little pale but not too worn.

"It's a boy," she said, then whispered, "perfectly human."

***

They named him Hindrich. He was a strong, happy baby with fat cheeks, laughing at almost everything he saw. It charmed them, and they kept inventing things to make him laugh even more. Each morning they crawled around on the floor pretending to be animals, making Hindrich belly laugh until he was out of breath. Their neighbors would have thought them lunatics had they seen them. But it made them so happy.

Nikolaos farmed the land and was given a plot for rye at the communal crop field, which meant that they both spent more time in the village. It felt good. People accepted him and never suspected anything. If it hadn't been for his need to visit the river, he almost forgot he wasn't human, refusing to think about the reality of Stina and his children aging while he stayed young.

***

Stina wiped her hands on her towel and pointed at the door. "Nikolaos, you're not listening. Stop wiggling your arms like that. It's annoying. You need to go in the stream for a bit. Come back when I can talk to you," she said and waved a finger in the air.

He laughed, again relishing that he didn't have to lie to his wife. "I will, but I want to finish my work first," he said, looking at the tools on the table. They were rattling. He was indeed shaking both hands and legs where he sat, wiggling as Stina called it. "On second thought, I think I'll leave it for now and go out for a while."

Stina sighed with relief and picked up Hindrich from the floor. "Wave bye-bye to your father, Hindrich," she said, and he waved with his chubby little hand.

When Nikolaos got back home, Hindrich was sleeping, and Stina had dinner ready. She kissed him, pulling at his wet hair as if to check he had truly done what she told him to do.

"Boel and Kajsa came for a visit," she said and sat down, pushing their shared bowl toward him. She had made a stew with fish and root vegetables. It smelled heavenly.

"That's nice," he said, grabbing a heaping spoonful. "And this is too." He smiled with his mouth full, then noticed that Stina looked worried. "What is it?"

"The witches are back," she whispered, glancing out the window as if to make sure the one from the woods was not lurking out there. "Boel said Alf can't sleep now because now he's the one who hears them at night. And Kajsa said her husband and several other men will see if they can find builders to get started on our church. They want you to help too, Nikolaos. We're not protected here without a church. I'd like to worship again anyway. There's a church south of the village. It's where everyone in the village goes, Boel told me. It's far, and even further for us... but. It's important."

Nikolaos took one more bite and then left his spoon in the bowl. "But it was something we decided on after that first time we visited Saint Halvard's. I stand by it, Stina. You saw how it was. Until people stop talking about witches from sunup to sundown, it's safest to stay home."

"Yes, I know, but still, it's not good. One must go to church. I don't want to pretend anymore."

He nodded, hiding his disappointment. It had only been a matter of time before Stina would insist. They had been telling people they traveled all the way to the church near Kungälv where they baptized Hindrich but had stayed home, afraid there would be a wiseboy who might understand who Nikolaos was.

"It's unseemly," Stina added, interrupting his thoughts. "And I'm scared, Nikolaos. What if God sends me to hell for not going?"

"See!" he exclaimed. "*This* is one of the reasons I don't like the new church. It makes people scared instead of giving them comfort."

"Didn't the priests talk of hell in the old church?"

He shrugged. "It was in Latin. I never paid much attention to it. I just prayed to my saints." He took another spoonful, remembering when they came and pulled down every saint in their church. No one ever told anyone what they did with them.

"Do you speak it?"

"Latin? Yes."

She lifted her eyebrows. "I thought you said your family were farmers and you stayed on the farm with Abluna until you went to live in Norrköping. Your family spoke Latin instead of..."

"Swedish," Nikolaos filled in. "No, they spoke Swedish, but a good amount of Latin as well." He smiled, still awed he could tell her everything and feeling energized by his visit to the river. "There was a monastery in our area and two of the monks living there used to walk around the villages and teach, speaking only Latin. Then when they closed the convents and monasteries, Brother Peter who was an old man by then, came to live with me and Abluna. He lived with us for several years."

To his surprise, he felt tears in his eyes. It had been a long time, maybe decades, since he last thought of him. How could he forget like that? Brother Peter had been so kind, always grateful and happy to eat whatever Abluna cooked. He was very skinny after living sparsely for most of his life, and no matter how much she fed him, he stayed exactly the same. He laughed a lot. Come to think of it, Hindrich was a little like him, always happy.

Stina looked at him, eyes wide. "I want you to go speak to Alf tomorrow and see what you can do to help. On Sunday, I want us to go to church with the others. You can ask Alf where it is," she said, changing the subject.

"I'll head to the village tomorrow," Nikolaos said, swallowing the disappointment that she wasn't as interested in his old life as he had hoped. It made him feel so old. And he was.

****

The village not only had its own church but new neighbors as well. A whole settlement of carpenters, stoneworkers, and welders had formed, expanding the village to twice its original size. There was even a pastry chef. An incredible luxury that made all the wives excited as well as nervous about the competition. And the church, built on a hill overlooking their village, was a feast for the eyes. The outside was wooden, with bare unpainted panels and windows with four windowpanes in each. The inside, contrasting with the plain outside, was breathtaking. Warm reds, golds, and blues, resplendent with imagery from the Bible. One scene depicted Jesus' transfiguration, and another had the Devil standing over the flames of hell, torturing souls. Nikolaos tried not to look at that one too much. There were statues too, meticulously carved into angels, even Luke with an ox. He couldn't remember what the ox signified or what it had to do with Luke, but it was well done. The paintings, however, while colorful and descriptive, were crude. The pastor had traveled to Kungälv hoping to hire artisans but had come back declaring that it was something the villagers had to do themselves. No one knew what price he had been quoted, but it was clear from the pastor's mood it had been an outrageous sum.

Nikolaos was surprised that he wanted the church so full of imagery. It seemed very similar to the old church, he felt. But the pastor had explained that it was important to have a visual context to his sermons. It was instruction, not idolatry. No one knew how to read except for him, and his Bible was the only one in the village anyway, he said. Nikolaos decided not to tell him that both he and Stina could read.

He had to give it to the pastor, his sermons were interesting and not tedious in any way. Knowing that Stina was sitting on the women's side with Hindrich and baby Elsebet made him feel less alone, too. That and the fondness for the church they had all helped build together made Sundays a day he looked forward to.

After the service, Nikolaos joined Stina who was standing in the sun, chatting with Baking Kajsa. The women were laughing, and Elsebet, perched on Stina's hip, was turning his way as he approached, hoping for attention. Her nose had a big goo of green snot running down to her lip. It looked disgusting.

"Her nose, Stina," Nikolaos said, annoyed that she hadn't noticed.

"Oh." She quickly pulled out her handkerchief and wiped it off.

"Where's Hindrich?"

"He ran off with the boys."

Nikolaos nodded, touching Elsebet's cheeks and forehead. She wasn't feverish. They lost little Thomas to fever just before Elsebet was born, and he had grown obsessed with checking her for fever. He knew Stina was as well, but they never spoke of it.

"We're heading to the pastry shop. The boys will meet us there later," Stina added, glancing at Baking Kajsa who looked unusually excited for some reason.

"What do you two have planned? Don't you want me to join? You look suspicious," Nikolaos said with a wink, his annoyance forgotten.

Stina laughed, glancing toward the new houses and the little pastry shop, which could be seen down the road. Its sign was newly painted and adorned with yellow buns, shining brightly in the sunlight. "No," she said, then looked at Baking Kajsa again and laughed until she snorted.

"What's so funny?" he asked, smiling at Elsebet who cooed happily at the strange merriment.

"Nikolaos, you ought to know the shop is closed. Did you forget where you just came from?" Baking Kajsa asked.

It was Sunday, of course. They weren't going there then, after all? He met Stina's eyes in question, but she didn't say anything, and now there was a hint of worry in them. He turned back to Kajsa. "Now you must tell me what this is all about."

"He's left us pastries, lots of pastries," Kajsa said, eyes glinting impishly, "out back behind his shop. It's payment for allowing him to use my ovens. Whatever the pastry baker hasn't sold, he'll give us each Sunday to take home. Last week he left me two big tins," she said proudly, glancing at Stina who laughed again.

"I'm going to leave you women to that then," Nikolaos said. I think I'll head home. Today was a good day to visit the river. If Stina spent time with Kajsa he could get away sooner and for longer.

"You go husband, you've been wanting to rest a bit. I'll help Kajsa and will bring something home for us. I'll be gone a while."

He nodded gratefully. Stina knew what he wanted to do.

Leaving them, he retrieved Kristina, wondering why they had to do it on a Sunday and in secret. Couldn't Kajsa just get the pastries when the shop closed on Saturday?

"Fiddler Nikolaos, do you have a moment?"

Nikolaos startled at the voice and turned toward it, stiffening when he saw who it was. It was the pastor, making his way toward him with long, hurried strides. Had he heard of Stina's and Kajsa's plans and disapproved? Maybe getting pastries on a Sunday was a sin since it was a barter payment. Steeling himself, he stopped and waited for him to catch up.

"Lord's peace be upon you. I have a philosophical question for you, will you come back into church with me?"

"A philosophical question for *me*?" Nikolaos asked, surprised and relieved.

"Yes, indeed I do," the pastor said, nodding for emphasis, then turned back to his church. "Pray, come."

Nikolaos threw a glance at the women who were already halfway to the pastry shop, removed his hat and followed him inside.

"Here, come see this," the pastor said, walking up to a statue near one of the windows. "You see this?" He reverently touched a plumb little foot belonging to one of the many golden angels, then at her harp. "Do you think she sees God in her music? Look at her enraptured face."

Surprised, Nikolaos' eyes flicked to the pastor and then back to the angel. He hadn't been sure what to expect, but this wasn't it. "Well... Do you mean this particular angel? Or the angels in heaven?"

"I'm asking about this one, of course. We can be certain God's angels do see Him in their music. If they didn't, He would surely banish them from heaven," the pastor said sternly.

"Oh, pray forgive me," Nikolaos said quickly, embarrassed.

The pastor nodded absently, studying the angel closely. "Has the proper expression been captured? Is this how it feels to play music? Is her enraptured face a true expression of someone feeling God in their music? Or is it a mockery of His gift to us?"

Nervous now, afraid he would say something the pastor would find inappropriate, Nikolaos moved forward and took a closer look. The angel was very small, like a baby really, or a toddler, with folds of fat where her arms bent to hold her harp. Her eyes were looking upward, and there was a faint smile on bright red lips, as if she were looking at someone who loved her. It was almost lustful. Perhaps it was why the pastor was questioning it. It did look out of place.

Nikolaos straightened, deciding it best to keep that observation to himself. "I think it's a fine rendition of God's work and the angel's love for him."

The pastor looked relieved. "Yes indeed, isn't it? It's God she sees, looking at His face while she plays the music of the angels." He put his arm around Nikolaos' shoulder, leading him back outside. "I'm glad to hear it. I thank you for your candor. It's very important to me that our church, in every detail, is pleasing to our Lord. Then when he sends his son back to us, we shall be confident that it's done right."

Nikolaos nodded, shielding his eyes from the bright sun as he stepped out.

"Do you feel close to God, Nikolaos when you play?" the pastor asked, squinting up at him. Outside, he seemed shorter and less imposing than before.

"I do."

"How?

Nikolaos hesitated, wondering how to describe it. He wanted to tell him about colors exploding and cascading through the water with a beauty that was so overwhelming he often cried, but he obviously couldn't tell him that. "I feel grateful," he said finally. "Thankful God gave me a talent which brings happiness to people."

"Yes, it's something to be thankful for indeed," the pastor said, putting his hand on Nikolaos' arm and squeezing it. Where's your wife? Did she leave already?"

"Not yet," Nikolaos said. "Stina and the little ones went for a visit, she'll ride home with them on her own later."

"Ah, good. You have a strong wife Nikolaos." With that, the pastor let go of his arm and hurried down the church steps.

Nikolaos stared after him, feeling awed. Life was good here, and he could relax, let go of the fear of being found out, and hide the truth even from himself. He shifted his gaze to the old village, the green, and the new homes and shops. To think the pastor had even asked him for advice, and his biggest worry was whether it was a sin for Stina to get pastries from the baker on a Sunday.

Chapter 45

Anno 1683

A few summers and winters had come and gone without any rumors of witches or strange happenings.

Rå felt the ease in the trees, in the wind, and even in the soil. A calmer presence and a sense of freedom, making flowers spread their petals wider and trees grow taller.

When winter came again, she decided it would be safe to venture out among humans again and that she would ski all the way to the winter market in Jönköping.

Skiing was new for her since just last year when Jon had taught her. At first, she had used his skis, but they were too big and cumbersome, and the straps didn't fit right. Then, in the spring, Jon had come for a visit and brought her a brand-new pair he had made just for her. They fit perfectly.

Rå packed a satchel full of her baskets, herbs, and poultices and set off. It was much faster on her new skis, and she laughed aloud as she sped across one frozen lake and field after the other, feeling like she was flying. Why had she never tried this before?

Crossing one of the lakes, however, she slowed down as she was accompanied by a sleigh so heavy with wares, she was afraid it would fall through the ice. But the horses pulled everything all the way across without incident. The road on the other side of the lake was full of skiers and other sleighs. It was as though there were a special feast day in church. She must be going in the right direction.

Catching up to a man skiing alone with a big pack on his back, she decided to ask him just to be sure. "Pray pardon me, where does this road lead?"

He lifted his hat, and an open, friendly smile lit up his face. "It goes all the way to Jönköping, my goodwife. If you keep your good speed, you'll get there well before dark. Heading to the market? I heard it's enormous this year. There's a rumor that a clockmaker who makes watches is coming. I'd like to see one."

"Only see? You don't have plans to buy one for yourself?

And yes, I'm heading to the winter market too." She smiled, feeling excited.

"Well, that's a matter of perspective," he said, eyes glinting. "Plans, I have none. I can't see myself being able to afford one. That said, should I ever come across riches I certainly *will* have plans to buy one."

"At a market?" a voice said from somewhere behind them. Rå turned and saw an older man on bright red skis. He had long gray hair under a wool hat, a beard reaching down to his stomach, and was wearing thick gray mittens even though the bright sun made it warm enough to go without. "You won't see watches there, not even in Jönköping. Where did you hear that anyway, son?"

"No? Just round here, everyone's talking about it." He looked disappointed.

The old man shook his head, then pushed his hat upward and sped away without another word, passing a heavy sleigh drawn by two horses.

"I hope he's wrong, but if he's right, maybe it's for the best. I'd just get upset at the price. I'm Sven Andersson from Apple Farm, you may have heard of us? We delivered apples to Karl XI's men some years ago. You heard of it?"

"I'm Magda," Rå said. "No, I haven't."

"You should have," Sven said with a wide smile, pushing off with his ski poles. "Good day to you, Magda!"

Rå moved along, watching his backside as he skied away. It was getting colder, and her breath began to make clouds in front of her face. That old man had been wise to wear mittens. She would invest in a pair at the market if she earned well. Pulling at her sleeves to cover her hands, she pressed on. A large sleigh hauled by two horses, piled high with sacks, rugs, and several cupboards passed her. The driver looked determined and barely threw her a glance.

After a while, she noticed the air growing hazy and the scent of woodsmoke. She was nearing Jönköping already.

It still took a while, and by the time she arrived, it was getting dark. There was a line of people waiting to pass the city toll.

Jon had told her she would have to pay a fee if she was going to sell something, and she had brought coin.

Two men standing toll-guard grinned rudely when she approached.

"How's a lovely woman like you traveling on her own? Whoring is not allowed within the walls," one of them said, tobacco smoke coming out of his mouth as he spoke. It smelled awful.

She smiled her kindest smile despite his terrible rudeness. "I'm a God-fearing woman with Him alone for company. I have herbs for ailments that I was hoping to sell at the market. Would it be possible for someone such as me to get a corner where I can do so?"

Both men shook their heads. She sensed their disappointment in her mention of piety. Then one of them moved a little closer to Rå and said, "I wouldn't know for sure, but you can always try. Show us your passport."

"My passport?"

He shook his head again, tsk-tsking. "You haven't brought it? What were you thinking? It's dark already, you going to run home and get it?" He laughed and sneered merrily at his companion but waved her in. "Go," he said and waved again. "Go before the people behind you want the same treatment."

Rå hurried through, feeling both relieved and angry, then promptly got stuck when her skis slid onto bare ground which had been dirtied by boots, horse dung, and whatever else it might be. She bent down to pull off her skis and heard the men laugh behind her. She forced herself not to respond. The men exuded disdain, and she could only imagine what they did to human women. And what was a passport? Jon had never said anything about it.

Carrying one ski and one ski pole under each arm, Rå found the market and instantly felt a better mood coming on. It was almost completely dark now, and the stalls were closing, but an older couple were standing by a large cauldron hanging over an open fire. Something smelled irresistible.

The woman noticed her approach and smiled a broad toothless smile, visible in the flickering firelight. "Is she hungry, young child? Why won't she come over for a bowl? New in town, is she?"

"Yes, goodwife, I just arrived," Rå said, smiling at the comment of her being a child. "I was hoping to sell some of my herbs and do some shopping of my own. It seems I'm too late tonight, though." Rå pulled her mug from her satchel and held it out for the old woman.

The husband prodded his wife with his elbow as if to tell her to hurry, and she gave Rå a nice helping of a thick soup, adding several large pieces of meat.

"I thank you kindly, goodwife. How much will I owe you for this? I can pay, or trade it for herbs should you need."

She considered it, glancing at her husband. "I'll be glad for herbs. If you have nowhere to stay for the night, I'm glad to take you in as well. We both are," she said and poked her husband the same way he had moments earlier.

Rå smiled at their antics. What a sweet couple. "It's very kind of you. Bless your kindness. I'll gladly take you up on your offer."

The woman nodded, returning her smile with a warm, welcoming expression, then grew serious. "Just don't be afraid. We live close to Hanging Hill, as we call the gallows here. You can see it from our window. They hung an old woman for learning herbal cures from Näcken. Will you believe it? It was so terrifying that the executioner left town afterward. Said Näcken came and took his horse from him in the middle of the night. It's a long time ago now, but I remember. The whole town was talking about it."

Rå's eyes widened. This was too much to be a coincidence. Thor must have sent her to them for a reason. "I'm not afraid. I gratefully accept your hospitality. Can I help you carry anything?" she asked, smiling when she thought of Kristina going home with Nikolaos.

"No need, I've got a wheelbarrow here," the husband said, indicating to the stall behind them where it stood hidden under a blanket.

Without checking if more customers might be coming, the

old couple lifted the cauldron off its hook and gently placed it in on top of the blanket in their wheelbarrow. Then they both kicked dirt over the fire and started pushing the wheelbarrow across the square.

Finishing her soup, Rå plucked out the remaining pieces of meat with her fingers and followed the couple. They carried no lantern but walked quickly and surefooted in the dark.

Their home was a small gray cottage with the roof hanging so low they had to bend down to get through the door. The woman put a finger to her lips. "My mother may have gone to bed, she likes to stay up late and knit, but today I think she's gone to bed for the night," she whispered.

Rå nodded, bending almost double when she entered. There was a table with three chairs, a small hearth, and two beds built into the wall opposite the table. The woman's mother was sound asleep in one of them, her long gray hair escaping from her cap, her wrinkly sunken face still and peaceful on the pillow.

"Your mother is beautiful," Rå whispered and got a quick smile in return. She must be ancient. Her daughter looked to be at least seventy or eighty herself.

"Here, I hope it won't be too hard for her, we would let her have the bed, but our bones are too old, just like Mother mine," she whispered as if she knew what Rå had been thinking, then pulled a folded blanket from the foot of her mother's bed and placed it on the dirt floor.

Rå patted her shoulder and was about to tell her that her name was Magda, and that she didn't know their names. But the woman had already slipped into bed, lying with her back turned toward her. Rå shrugged and lay down on the blanket, covering herself with her coat. Before the husband came inside, she had fallen asleep.

When Rå woke the next morning, the little cottage was empty. She folded her blanket and placed it on a chair, then left a bundle of dried nettle and angelica on the table as a thank you, hoping the women would know to use it as a strengthening tonic.

She went to look for them at the market so she could explain and thank them in person but saw no trace of them. It was as if they had been there just to feed her and get her a safe place to sleep. It felt eerie for some reason, even though there might be many reasons why they hadn't gone back to the market. Whichever it was, she decided to take the night's hospitality as one of Thor's blessings and enjoy the rest of the day.

The market was enormous. The section where the old couple had their stall the night before was in a section clearly meant to cater to the poorer customers. The stalls were simple wood structures, and the ground was trampled and muddy, whereas stalls across a wide avenue of sorts had pine and straw placed on the ground and sturdier stalls lined with colorful wall hangings. Some merchants even had men standing guard.

Rå stared at the finery for a moment, then decided to explore the poorer side first. Knick-knacks, linen, ribbons, dried fruit, and toys lined the unclad shelves. There was even a stall with human bones they claimed came from the lord himself. A throng of people were crowding and shoving each other to pay a hefty viewing fee to see them. Rå hurried past them, smiling politely while shaking her head at a woman trying to get her to queue with her. People were so gullible; surely it couldn't be Jesus' bones. If it had been, they would have been laid out on the expensive side of the market and with guards.

She would take a closer look at everything later, but first, she needed to sell some of her own herbs, or she couldn't afford anything.

A woman behind a small table at the very end of the row in the poorer section was selling dried fruit and wooden necklaces. Each kind of fruit was neatly organized in little wooden boxes.

"Goodwife, pray tell me, do I need permission to sell my medicines here?"

The woman laughed. "Eh, call me Emma. You should have a husband speaking for you if you want permission. It's not seemly for a woman to stay here by herself, but as you can see, no one seems to care much. I've come here five winters now. And without my husband." She grinned widely, exposing her teeth. It didn't appear that she was missing even one, Rå noticed. Her dress was brown with a red bodice, and she wore a thick beige shawl over her shoulders and a gray winter scarf over her hair.

Rå laughed. "Well then, perhaps I can hang my wares in the tree over there. I have good medicine for aches and coughs and a few for earaches. I also have herbs to cure nausea," she said, lifting her satchel strap a thumb's width, then letting it fall back to her shoulder.

"Oh, absolutely. They don't pay too much attention to us down on this side anyway. I'd be interested in what you have for a cough. My husband has been racking for weeks now. Last year he coughed all winter. Coughed up blood too, he did. I'm surprised he survived it!" she said, laughing loudly as if it were amusing. But maybe it was a nervous laugh.

Rå pulled her herbs out and handed Emma a small bundle of dried hound's tongue wrapped in a piece of cloth. "This ought to help. Would you be willing to trade it for some of your dried pears and apples?"

"Glad to. I make a brew of it?" Emma asked as she grabbed a handful of dried pears from her box. "You have a basket to put this?"

"Yes, I do." Rå put her satchel on the driest spot on the muddy ground she could find and pulled one out. She kept them stacked inside each other at the bottom. "And yes, make a brew with hot water and honey, then mix in a small spoon of hound's tongue. It should seep for at least a day first."

"One day," Emma said with a nod, then eyed Rå's basket. "That's a lovely basket. Did you make it yourself?"

"Yes, I did. The winters are long, and I like to keep my hands busy," Rå said proudly.

Emma let the dried pears fall back with the others, took Rå's basket, inspecting it by turning it this way and that, then banged on it with her knuckles. Her nails were cracked and dry and very dirty, Rå noticed.

"Very nice," Emma said, then grabbed a more generous handful of her dried pears, apple rings, and raspberries, placing it all in Rå's basket.

They spent a pleasant morning chatting in between their customers. Emma sent all of hers to Rå each time they finished at her stall. By the time the sun was high in the sky, Rå had a pocket full of coin and no more herbs to sell.

"I thank you for all your help today. It's been a pleasure," Rå said and walked around the table so she could kiss Emma's cheek. Then she pressed several coins into her hand. "Take these. I wouldn't have done this well without you."

"Nonsense, Magda, that's not necessary. You kept me company, that's worth much more." Emma gently pushed Rå's hand away.

"I thank you kindly." Rå looked at her, wondering if she should insist, then decided it would seem rude and put the coins back in its leather purse. She had already turned to leave when it came to her that she could give her a basket. Stopping, she pulled out a tightly woven, lidded basket and handed it to Emma.

"For me?" Her eyes shone with pleasure. "Bless you, Magda. May God keep you safe always."

"And you as well. I thank you for your help today," Rå said and walked off, smiling.

Now it was time to see the rest of the market and buy some things before she left. Rå tied her skis and ski poles to her back, making them point straight up behind her head at shoulder width. Then she cautiously walked into the fancier market. Seeing it up close made the stalls seem even more luxurious than they had from across the way. The colorful blankets gave an impression of people standing inside a real room as they presented their merchandise. One of them sold fancy carved boxes filled with gold and silver bracelets adorned with shiny stones she didn't know the name of. Another had wooden toy animals painted in brilliant colors, not the simple carvings she had seen in her section, but intricately cut with the smallest details, even eyelashes. There were piles of colored fabric in red, golden, yellow, and green so beautiful it was hard to resist touching them. Blue fabric was sold separately and had a stall all to itself. It was darker and brighter than the most bottomless sky and unlike anything she had ever seen.

There was a simpler stall further down the aisle with paler fabric at a much lower price. She bought a good piece of light green linen. And she found thread and new needles at another stall, then a pair of mittens and spices at a stall that sold both.

Men and women strolled with a contented air, stopping here and there to look and to ask about whatever took their fancy. Two men had enormous dark curly hair reaching almost to their waists. Something didn't look right with it, but she couldn't put her finger on what it was. One of the men nodded pleasantly in her direction, but the other gave her a disapproving look, probably wondering what she was doing there alone. She wished she could ask them about their hair, but that would obviously be a very intimate question to ask of someone.

Buying a piece of fish and a small meat pie, Rå walked out of the market as she ate. It had been a good visit. She had found more than she could have hoped for and was ready to go home.

* * *

Rå was skiing across a small lake, deep in the woods already, when she heard the swishing sound of another pair of skies behind her. Slowing down, she glanced over her shoulder, immediately recognizing who it was by the big pack on the skier's back. It was Sven from the day before.

"My mistress on skies, all alone again," he called and sped up to her, sliding to such an abrupt stop the snow swirled around him like a cloud.

She laughed. "I'm used to being on my own, but I'd be glad for some company," she said, watching his muscular legs and wide shoulders as the snow settled around his feet. He would do fine. It had been a while since she saw Jon. "Did you find your watch?"

To her surprise, he looked crestfallen. Then he took one

353

more look at her and fled.

She stared after him, not sure what to make of it.

But when he reached the other side of the lake he stopped, one ski on the ice and the other on the bank. Then, with one quick push with his ski poles, he turned around and came back to her.

"I'm not certain why I'm doing this to tell you the truth. I should keep it to myself, but I won't." Putting his hand inside his thick winter jacket, he pulled out a round object attached to his neck with a chain. "Come close so you can see, I don't want to take it off," he said, tilting it toward her. It was round and somewhat flat, covered in smooth glass with an arrow pointing to one of the numbers beneath it. It looked just like the big clock she had seen in Norrköping some years ago, only this was tiny.

Rå moved so close the glass fogged. "Ah," she closed her lips, trying not to breathe on it, "you did find one. It's so small."

Sven wiped the fog off with his sleeve. "It's indeed a watch, an old one though. Can you keep a secret?"

"Yes of course." She stepped back slightly.

His eyes flashed to hers, then he said, "I went to the inn. I was sitting there having a bite to eat and some ale when a pair of rich merchants came in. They were loud and wore fancy coats and long wigs. I..."

"Wigs?"

"You haven't heard of wigs? It's what they call that thick, loose hair they put on top of their own. It's long and very curly."

"Oh, so *that's* what it was. I saw a couple of men with strange hair. It's truly not their own?"

Sven laughed, shaking his head. "No, it's like a hat made of someone else's hair. In the winter, they leave them out at night so the lice freeze to death."

Rå frowned, picturing it. A hat made of hair, how ridiculous.

"Quite the image, eh?" Sven put his watch back under his shirt and coat and pushed off on his skies, continuing his tale when she fell in beside him. "The merchants sat down right in front of me without taking notice of me. A poor farmer like me might as well have been a chair for all they care. As soon as they were served their wine, one of them pulled his watch off his neck and showed it to his friend." Sven gestured to his own neck with his ski pole. "The merchant said he wanted to replace it with one that showed the minutes. It's supposed to have one more hand, you see."

"A hand?"

"That's what they call the little arrow that moves inside the watch."

"I see."

"After that, they didn't say much more about it. Their food arrived, they ate and drank more wine, and then they left. I finished my meal and was about to leave too, when I noticed the watch still on the table. It was just lying there. No one paid attention to it. I looked around to make sure, but people were eating and talking, and then I just grabbed it, gathered up the chain and the watch in my hand, and walked out. I thought that if I saw them, I'd give it to them, and they'd give me a reward. And there they were, right there outside the inn, arguing about something. I stood for a moment to see if they would stop, but they kept yelling at each other. The one who had the watch was screaming about someone's wife, the other man's maybe? He was red in the face and was waving his finger in his companion's face. It made me think that if they were angry already, they might not have taken well to me having it even if I was returning it, so I left. Kept looking back to see if they would follow me or send someone after me, but no one did. And now I have it." He smiled uncertainly, but with a look of determination.

"I believe I'd have done the same. They didn't appear to be missing it."

"Not at that moment at least. I should've gone back inside and left it with the innkeeper, but I couldn't bring myself to do it," he said with a lopsided grin.

Rå smiled and leaned into him, kissing his cheek. "I think you're meant for it, why don't you come with me. I know a place where we can be alone. I might even take you home," she said and sped off into the trees.

There was a soft crushing of the top icy layer as Sven's skis pushed through the woods. He was following her. Rå waited until he was almost upon her, then pulled her feet out of the ski straps and stuck her poles in the snow, untied her shawls and let them and her coat fall to the ground. Then she loosened her hair and jumped further into the trees, aware that Sven could see her hair sway over the now open hole in her back. It was just for a moment so he would be drawn in, but not long enough to really understand what he had seen.

When he caught up, she watched him pull his feet out of his ski straps. His heavy feet sunk deeply, but he didn't notice, looking astonished and dazed. Just the way she wanted him.

"Come closer, I need you. Come to me." She grabbed his hands and pulled him toward her, then untied his breeches and pushed him down in the snow. "I need you," she whispered into his ear, pulling her skirts up so that she could sit on him.

He blushed with a look of both horror and exaltation.

Rå pressed herself as close to him as she could. He smelled of sweat and tasted of ale and salty fish. "Do you want me?" she asked, and when he nodded, she let the forest engulf them both.

Chapter 46

Anno 1697

It had been snowing for two full days, and the wind was howling with an intensity Nikolaos hadn't heard for years, if ever. It caused clumps of ice and snow to fall down the chimney, making the flames in the hearth sputter so bad it had gone out twice. There wasn't much to do but wait out the storm, and they had all gathered in the middle room, the parlor they called it now, for warmth. Stina and Elsebet were knitting, sitting as close to the hearth as was possible. Hindrich was sound asleep on the daybed, covered by an extra blanket, and snoring loudly. Nikolaos, sitting at the foot of the bed, was just about to give him a shove to get him to turn over when there was a loud knock on the door.

Stina started, dropping her knitting on the floor. "Who'd come on a day like this?"

"Something must be very wrong. Maybe someone in the village has gotten hurt." Nikolaos said, pulling his blanket off his knees and getting to his feet.

"Why ask us? We're too far to travel to for help in a storm," Stina said and followed Nikolaos.

It had snowed so much that even though Hindrich had shoveled so Stina and Elsebet could go to the barn that morning, Nikolaos could barely open the front door. When he finally managed, the snow and wind rushed inside with such force that it took him a moment to see who stood out there. It was a stranger, a man in a thick grey fur coat and a large fur hat. A sleigh with two horses stood parked behind him, another fur-clad man standing by it, musket visible but relaxed. They had come to arrest him. After all these years, they would finally take him.

Nikolaos' first instinct was to close the door and lock it, but instead, he took an involuntary step backward, heart pounding. He felt more than saw Stina's knees buckle beside him. Instinctively, he put his arm around her. From the corner of his eye, he saw Hindrich wake up, glance through a tiny spot in the window that hadn't become covered by snow, and open his mouth in shock.

"Father who's that?" he asked, standing abruptly.

Nikolaos met Hindrich's eyes with a barely perceptible shake of his head, indicating that he didn't know.

The man outside bowed. "Pleasure, it is my honor to make your acquaintance. May I come inside for a bit? God has sent some harsh weather on us."

"Yes, he has," Nikolaos said, heart slowing down a bit. He wouldn't speak of honor or ask for permission to come in on his way to arrest him, would he?

The man banged his boots on the doorsill to get the snow off. It would have gained him a look of approval from Stina if she hadn't been so frightened. "My utmost pleasure to meet you, Fiddler Nikolaos. You are Fiddler Nikolaos, are you not?" he said formally, enunciating every word.

"Pleasure is all mine, sir." Nikolaos swallowed a dizzying sense of bewilderment. "Yes, I'm he, though some of my neighbors call me Nils, thinking Nikolaos sounds too old-fashioned. They also call me Jens' son or Nikolaos Jensson," he said, knowing he was rambling and giving the man way too much information. It wasn't necessary to school him on new customs. Besides, his father's name had been Evergistus, not Jens.

"No, the pleasure is certainly mine, I insist. You are well known all over the land. I have traveled far to call on you. I will call you Nikolaos. It is a fine name."

Nikolaos exchanged a glance with Stina. Elsebet slowly rose from her chair and walked over to stand next to her mother. She looked pale.

Finally, it was Hindrich who spoke up, "Good sir, what can we do for you? What is it you've come to call on my father for? And in a storm like this, of all things."

"My deepest apologies," the man said and finally removed his fur hat, then bowed with a flourish, holding onto his long dark wig with his left hand as if he were afraid it would fall off. "I come in an errand directly from the King's court. The King is ill and would be comforted by your beautiful music, Nikolaos."

Nikolaos opened then closed his mouth, flooded by such surprise, he had to grab onto the doorsill to steady himself.

The man smiled patiently and pointed to the wood sofa by the window. "May I sit?"

"Yes, yes certainly," Stina stammered and curtsied deeply, grabbing Elsebet on her way down to get her to curtsy as well. She did, albeit with a stumble.

Nikolaos finally snapped out of his stupor. He shot a stern glance in Hindrich's direction and bowed as low as he could, hoping that Hindrich would take the hint and do the same. Much to his relief, Hindrich caught on, then straightened up almost at the same moment as Nikolaos.

The man chuckled. "As I said, the pleasure is mine, although I come with the sad news of our King."

"We're deeply saddened by this news!" Nikolaos exclaimed, horrified that he hadn't said something sooner.

The man nodded. He still hadn't introduced himself, and Nikolaos didn't know how to address him.

"It is devastating, the court is distraught, very distraught. The King is extremely ill. That is all I am at liberty to say about it. I take it that you would like some words of explanation of why I am here?" he asked, pinning them with his eyes one by one.

"I'd be grateful for it, good sir," Nikolaos said, hoping 'good sir' wouldn't give offense.

It didn't seem as though it had. "You may have heard that the King travels often, visiting his subjects. The King came around these parts only a few years ago and heard you play," he said, smiling.

Nikolaos stared at him, forgetting his manners. "The King heard me play? Sir, are you certain you have the right man? I mean no offense, but I don't remember the King."

"No, no, no, I know who you are. The King doesn't always make himself known, you see. Sometimes the King travels by horse with just a few of his men. The King took note of you on a day when I believe there was a larger harvest feast near here? You were among several musicians. Two of them played the keyed fiddle. The

King was up in the woods listening for a good while but didn't get the opportunity to introduce His Royal Self. The King prefers smaller gatherings on the advice of his men." He gestured with a flowing motion. "Do seat yourself, there's no need to stand attention for me," he said, sounding a lot less formal. Then he smiled at Stina and added, "goodwife, do sit."

Thank you very kindly, sir." Stina unsteadily crossed the floor, grabbing hold of her chair as she sat down.

"I don't quite know what to say," Nikolaos said and sat down beside her. "I didn't have the slightest inkling we had a royal audience. I remember that day well." He grabbed hold of Stina's hand under the table. He didn't actually remember which of their harvests it might have been. They played together often and had at least one gathering a year where people from the neighboring villages came.

"I understand. It's often how it is with the King as I said. Anyway, you and your wife are to travel with me to Stockholm once the snow stops. I take it this is your wife? And your son and daughter? You may call me Addam, by the way."

Nikolaos flashed a surprised look at Hindrich, clearing his throat nervously. Addam wanted him to travel to *Stockholm?* He had assumed the King would stay somewhere nearby and that he would visit there. It must be serious then, the illness. "Yes, Stina is my wife. And this is our daughter Elsebet and our son Hindrich. He'll be betrothed early this summer," Nikolaos added proudly.

"Very nice, very nice," Addam said and met Hindrich's eyes in acknowledgment. "I'll go out a while and speak with my man at arms, give you and your wife some time to talk it over. We'd both be grateful if we could stay here tonight, get fed, and stable the horses?" He had reverted to a more casual tone again.

"Most certainly," Nikolaos said and smiled at Stina. She looked utterly flabbergasted.

The sound of the wind was so loud it sparkled blue when Addam opened the door.

Nikolaos waited until Addam had closed it behind him, then said, "I don't see how we can say no to this."

"Father, it's the King. There isn't a question of saying no. You've no choice," said Hindrich.

Nikolaos and Stina looked at each other, both reminded of his encounter with another King when Nikolaos lived in Stockholm. They hadn't yet told their children the truth, having decided long ago they would wait. Now Hindrich was twenty-one and Elsebet nineteen and they didn't know if they should tell them at all.

"I suppose you're right, Hindrich," Nikolaos said, letting go of Stina's gaze to look at him. "But who'll take care of the farm?"

"Father, we will of course. How can you even think of anything else?" Elsebet asked.

Touched, Nikolaos reached out and patted her cheek. "I thank you."

"What should we call him? Should we truly just call him Addam?" Stina asked, stroking her dress with the back of her hand. It was dirty and threadbare at the knees. "I have nothing suitable to wear in the royal castle. They'll laugh at me. I can't go. Nikolaos, you must go alone."

"I won't go alone." Nikolaos got up and looked out the window. "He isn't knighted then since he didn't introduce himself as lord. I assume we should call him Addam like he asked, or it won't seem polite. We should say sir as well though, you know, just in case. I might…" He trailed off, turning at the sound of the door opening.

The guard entered. He didn't shake the snow off his boots but walked straight in, tracking the floor with snow, then seated himself at the table. He placed his musket beside him and stared at Elsebet and Stina as if to gather whom to address. "Aww, I'm starved. Can I have some ale? Have you any meat, fish?"

Stina turned anxiously to Nikolaos.

"Pray forgive me. Herring, pottage, bread, winter apples, and cheese is all we have at present," Nikolaos said, answering for her while she confirmed it with a nod. "I'll go out and hunt. I may catch a hare despite the weather."

"Out of the question, Fiddler Nikolaos, there's no need. We'll do fine with what you have here. Hadn't there been a snowstorm I might have let you, but we need to get you sound and healthy to Stockholm. If you let us put our horses with your own, I'll thank you."

The door opened again, and Addam came back in, kicked the snow off his boots same as before, then went up to the fire, holding his hands as close to the flames as he dared.

Nikolaos exhaled with relief. He had felt obligated to suggest hunting but hadn't felt comfortable leaving his family alone with them. One could never be sure, and the guard had a musket. They seemed honest enough, but it bothered him that they hadn't waited for the weather to ease up before visiting. Was the King truly so ill they had to get him there at all costs, in all weather? Hindrich looked nervous too and was shifting his weight from foot to foot.

"Why don't you bring their horses inside Hindrich? Put one in Kristina's stall and the other in the nook," Nikolaos said.

Hindrich got to his feet, gingerly stepping over the puddles from the guard's boots so he wouldn't get his thick wool socks wet, and put his boots on.

They had the space now. Kristina had died just two winters ago, a very old queen by then. Stina insisted the mare had taken on his powers, and maybe she had, living to at least fifty. They still kept her stable empty. Nikolaos couldn't bear putting another horse in there and kept it for hay and buckets of grain. Hindrich would have to make an exception today.

***

The evening proceeded in a nervous flurry of activity. Stina and Elsebet served the men what they had, then made beds for them in their new room in the back, spreading out furs and blankets on the floor. It was the nicest room in the house, but it still felt terribly inhospitable to let the King's men sleep on the floor, of all places. Nikolaos offered them their own beds, but the men refused, insisting they were perfectly comfortable.

They had built the new room, as they all still called it, ten years prior. It was large, made for musicians to play in, with space for dancing when the dining table was pushed aside, and with high ceilings Hindrich and Elsebet thought were for acoustics. It was true enough, but Nikolaos made it that way to keep people from getting entranced. And it worked. There hadn't been any incidents at all.

The storm had stilled somewhat, and when the King's men had settled, Nikolaos brought Stina to the stable with him under the pretext of going to see to the animals.

"What are we going to do? Do you realize where we're going?" Nikolaos asked, feeling a chill as he uttered the words. He went to stand between their two cows, facing the door so he could keep an eye on it. "What if someone painted a picture of me out there? The King tried to shoot me! They could have spoken of this for a long time. What if there's a painting and they recognize me?"

Flower pushed on his left arm, demanding treats. He pushed the cow's head aside and scratched her behind the ear.

Stina glanced at him, grabbing a handful of grain for the animals. "No, Nikolaos, I don't think so. Even if they did, why would they think it's you? It was a very, very long time ago now. They think you'd be long dead. They can't think it's you. You'd be long dead," she repeated."

"That means nothing if they know who I am. They think I'm made of vapor. Vapor doesn't get old."

A shadow of fear came over Stina's face as she fed a small handful to their horse. The men's horses were sound asleep and didn't even stir. Then she shook her head. "Nah, Nikolaos, that's very unlikely. We must go. It wasn't a question. You've been called to serve the King. It's an honor you should be very proud of." She smiled, but then her face fell. "Oh, sweet lord Jesus, I have nothing to wear. What am I to do in a castle? And what shall I do all alone when you're performing? And for the King! You're going to play for him. His Royal Highness." Her voice changed to a whisper.

He chuckled, feeling his worry dissipate a bit. Stina was probably right that there would be no way they could know who he was. "Do you remember I told you that I used to live in Norrköping's

House? You know the castle with the caged birds?"

"Yes, you talk of it often," she said with a lifted eyebrow, handing their cows their share of the grain.

"I had nothing, and they provided me with clothes. I'm quite sure it'll be the case now too. I'll speak with sir Addam about it."

"No, don't suggest it! Lord forbid it, you wouldn't want to seem greedy."

"Oh… You're right." What had he been thinking? Presuming the King would clothe him? "We'll have to see then, I take it. We'll bring the finest we have. It'll have to do."

"Yes, but hopefully you're right, I can imagine you are. Up in Stockholm in the castle, they want people to dress a certain way and probably realize that people might not have the means to." Stina found a milking stool and sat down. "Will our children fare well here on their own?"

"Yes, of course they will." He reached for her hand and squeezed it. "I can't believe this. I truly can't. The fact that the King saw me play at all is astounding enough, but that he asks for me when he's sick?"

"It *is* astounding, Nikolaos but you're a good musician. It's not surprising the King wants to hear it." She beamed at him, wiping a tear from her cheek.

He smiled, then bent down to pat her knee. "Don't worry about your dress. I'll buy you fabric in Stockholm. Just make sure I'm good, I pray you. If I act as if I need water, pray tell me before I get desperate. I can't put us at risk at the King's castle."

Stina's face grew serious. "I will, husband. I promise I will."

Chapter 47

Nikolaos woke up to silence. The wind had died down, and there was no sound of birds. It must be nighttime still. He turned toward Stina and immediately felt her grab for his hand.

"You awake, Nikolaos?" she whispered, so low he could only just hear it.

"Yes," he whispered back just as quietly. "I can't sleep. I keep thinking about the King. What kind of illness does he have, do you think? Is he old?"

"I don't know. And who is he? It's Karl, isn't it?" Stina asked, the bed creaking as she shifted to the side and pulled on the blanket.

Nikolaos nodded, forgetting it was too dark for her to see, then said, "Yes, it's Karl. I think Karl XI." He thought back to that day when he had spoken with the pastor and those men in Borakulle when he had tried sugar for the first time. Yes, they had said Karl X; he was sure of it. Then his son took over the throne, which meant he would be King Karl XI. "I think you're right, but it's some forty years since he came to the throne. He's probably old then. Maybe he's dying of old age? It would explain why he can't travel and why we have to go there."

"Was he already old when he came to the throne, or I mean, not a young man at least?"

"Hmm… I don't know. Could I ask sir Addam? Or would it be rude to ask about a King's age?" Nikolaos got out of bed, stepping on the ice-cold floor with bare feet, thinking back on the pastor in Borakulle again, how surprised he had been when he didn't know who the King was.

Stina followed him out of bed, putting her sock-clad feet straight into her soft indoor shoes.

"Come here," Nikolaos said, pulling her close. They stood together for a moment, then he let her go and went to put logs on the fire. It had gone out again during the night. Stina lit a candle, and then they tiptoed around the house so as not to wake the men, smiling with excitement when they passed each other. Stina packed

Nikolaos' fine coat and breeches and a good linen shirt he wore when he played at larger events. But her own dress for these occasions was not in as good condition. She had lost some weight these few years, and it hung like a sack on her. Although they had done well, food had been sparse after several frigid winters and poor harvests. No matter how much money Nikolaos had saved throughout his long life, if there was nothing to buy, they suffered just like everyone else. He hoped royal life would put meat on her bones.

"I can't appear in front of the King and his court like this. What will the princes and princesses think?" Stina said, folding her dress and carefully placing it in the trunk Nikolaos had brought inside. "And I wish the Queen was still alive. I would've liked to meet her. She was so kind and charitable. I overheard the women speak of it in church just a few weeks ago. A nice, nice woman, Queen Ulrika Eleonora." Stina smiled with a dreamy look on her face.

Nikolaos nodded, distracted. As he remembered it, the castle was enormous. Even if Addam said that the King had asked for him, he wondered if they would actually be allowed to see him. It was more likely that he would be one among many musicians, and the King would sit somewhere and listen from a safe distance. Stina would probably never get near him. "Yes, that's what people say. You'll have a lot to tell the women when we get back. I was just thinking of when I was near the royal castle last time. If they only knew," he said, grinning at the thought even though he was nervous about it.

"Let's not talk of it anymore. It scares me, it really does. It's nothing to smile about Nikolaos. The castle is almost in the water. You told me so yourself!"

"I'll be careful. I promise. I have you to help me."

She didn't look convinced.

***

It was still dark when they were leaving. Addam's man of

arms lit a torch that he attached to the side of the sleigh, giving them just enough light to see their way as they climbed in. There was a step and a small, low door you could open and close so you wouldn't have to climb over the side. Addam took Stina's hand, helping her to her seat as if she were a fine lady. Nikolaos smiled as he saw her blush in the flickering torchlight.

Addam waited until Nikolaos had sat down, then stood at attention as his man at arms reached under the driver seat in front and pulled out two fur blankets. He placed one of them over Nikolaos' and Stina's knees, waited until Addam had sat down opposite them behind the driver's seat, and then put the other blanket over his knees. The man at arms was like a personal servant it seemed, not just a guard. It was odd, but they hadn't been told his name and hadn't heard Addam address him. When he finished with the blankets, he climbed down, picked up the little step and put it on the floor, then closed the door and climbed into the driver's seat. Nikolaos tried to see if there was another step he used to get up but couldn't get a good view from where he sat.

As they drove off, Hindrich and Elsebet were waving from inside, appearing like silhouettes behind the windowpanes. Nikolaos swallowed, hiding a sudden tug at his heart.

Addam was leaning back against his backrest, his fur hat pulled down low, keeping what seemed a scrutinizing stare straight at Nikolaos' face. What if this was not what they said it was, and he would be arrested after all? It could all be a lie. They might not be the King's men, but twelvemen from Stockholm, or even from Borakulle. Maybe after all this time, Karin had convinced them of who he was. Then they would arrest Stina as well, torture her to get her to tell them the truth. He looked away from Addam, glancing at the little door at the side of the sleigh. If he pushed it open with his foot, maybe they could jump off. Even if he had to drag Stina off the seat, he should be able to catch her when they tumbled out. The horses weren't speeding. But where would they run to? They might get shot.

"I'm sorry to be staring," Addam said suddenly.

Nikolaos started, but Addam was smiling warmly, and the

fear dissipated.

"I've been sitting here trying to figure out how old you are? You see, I was told His Highness the King was looking for a young man. I knew you were married, but not that you had grown children. It did surprise me. But given your exceptional talent, it's no surprise that you're not as young as I initially expected." His eyes flicked to Stina, then back to Nikolaos, clearly noticing that she looked much older than him. It wasn't the first time someone had commented on it. Some people assumed he had married an older widow with children.

"I've been told that I look younger than my son. I'll soon send him out to play instead of me. No one will be the wiser," Nikolaos said, trying to make light of it, while feeling Stina stiffen with hurt feelings under their fur blanket.

Addam laughed heartily. "He plays the fiddle as well, your son?"

"To tell you the truth, no, sir Addam, not really. He doesn't have the talent for it, though he plays now and then."

"He's intimidated by his father," Stina broke in.

"Ah, I see. You have a special talent. It's not something that God bestows on us all. I'm assuming you've been playing since you were just this tall?" Addam asked, pulling his hand out and holding it at knee height.

"That'd be about right, sir Addam. I was just a boy."

"I thought so. Your father taught you? Is he alive?"

"No, sir."

Addam nodded slowly, then put his hand back under the fur, leaned back in his seat, and closed his eyes.

Nikolaos grabbed Stina's hand under their fur blanket. They remained thus, watching the world wake up with the sun, not quite sure what lay in store for them.

Chapter 48

They arrived as the sun was setting over a frozen Stockholm. The city looked wider, and there were more buildings than a hundred years ago. The castle sparkled as if lit by its own light, a seagull perched on the three golden crowns on top of the spire of the main tower.

"There," Nikolaos said, touching Stina's shoulder before he pointed to it, "Three Crowns and Saint Nikolaos' church, do you see?"

Addam whistled. "Nikolaos, I didn't realize it wasn't your first time here."

"When I was a boy, I traveled here with my father," Nikolaos said, noticing Stina look away. She hated it when he had to lie.

Addam chuckled. "Too young to take advantage of the Rowing Women's special services then I take it?" he said with a sly smile, then turned to Stina apologetically. "Goodwife, pray forgive my humor."

Nikolaos narrowed his eyes. "Who are they?"

"The Rowing Women? They take travelers between the islands for a fee. They even formed their own group within the Guild. My apologies to you, Stina, but there have been rumors some of them provide…" He trailed off, fidgeting with his fur hat, looking as if he regretted having brought it up. "Let's just say some are selling another type of ride than a rowboat can provide."

Nikolaos laughed. "No, I didn't notice *them*," he said. "Though I do remember some rather colorful ladies, but they weren't in boats." The prostitute who invited him inside when his lantern went out that same day King Karl IX shot at him must have been dead for years.

Addam grinned, then changed the subject. "They've renovated Three Crowns a bit. Keep an eye out for different designs. Nicodemus Tessin wants to rebuild it. He's already rebuilt the north wing. Some disagree with his grand plans and want to keep it as is," he said, turning to his man at arms. "When was it done, a few years ago now?"

"Ninety-two, the Year of our Lord 1692. Since I have your attention, we'll go around the back, sir. Ice is thick enough to drive on."

Addam nodded and turned back to Stina and Nikolaos while the man at arms steered the sleigh onto the ice. "If you remember from when you were a boy, it looks very different now. Tessin, that's the architect, Nicodemus Tessin. He's changed quite a bit with the new wing." Addam's expression didn't foretell whether he approved or not.

"Oh, has he?" Nikolaos shaded his eyes with his hand, trying to see, but couldn't remember anything looking different.

As soon as the sleigh entered the courtyard, doors flew open, and several people came running toward them. Then everything happened very fast. Strong men lifted their trunk with all their belongings off the sled and walked away with it. Two women climbed in, took Stina by her elbows, and whisked her away.

Nikolaos was trying to follow when he felt someone grab at him. A man with massive underarms and impossibly broad shoulders. Nikolaos suppressed a startled yelp.

"Welcome to Three Crowns. I'll take you to get fitted now," he said.

"Fitted?" Nikolaos stiffened, picturing his arms being fitted through the holes in the stocks. It had all been a ruse then. They were arresting him. And they had his wife. His heart started racing.

"You must be fitted for proper attire; the tailors are waiting."

He almost pissed himself with relief. "Oh, I see. Of course. I understand."

"They're very proper here, have to keep up appearances," the man said, rolling his eyes. Nikolaos wasn't sure if he disapproved of what he was wearing or if he thought royal protocols were ridiculous.

"Of course," Nikolaos repeated as he was gently pushed toward the same door Stina had disappeared through.

It opened to a long dark corridor with only a small torch on the wall. The man let go of his arm and walked briskly ahead, stopping in front of a door at the end of the corridor. He waited for Nikolaos to catch up, then opened it and left without a word.

Nikolaos peeked inside and drew another sigh of relief. It truly wasn't a ruse. There were two tailors in the room who both pointed to the corner.

"Come in, come in. Stand there so we can take your measurements. It'll only take a moment, and then someone will escort you to your rooms. You look a bit bewildered, first time here, eh?" one of them asked. He was round as a barrel, with prominent fat folds hanging over his breeches, reaching halfway down his thighs.

"Yes."

"I know how it is. It's a different life here," the other tailor said as he bent down to measure his legs. He was well fed as well but nowhere near as fat as his companion. The fat one measured his upper body at the same time, moving easily despite his bulk.

"There, we have it. You can go."

That was that. The door opened as on cue, and a man in full regalia was standing there, looking important and surprisingly excited to see him. Nikolaos felt his heart pick up speed again. It must be a drabant, one of the castle guards. His uniform was very stylish. A deep blue coat with gilded brass buttons and gold trim at the cuffs and collar, a black hat, that too, trimmed with gold, and with a gilded button on the left side. The breeches looked like moose hide, or maybe it was elk skin, he didn't know. Same with the gloves, and he wore beautiful boots with some kind of folded cuffs or collars just below the knee. Nikolaos looked away, feeling intimidated. He had a saber too, and must have stood outside and listened, ready to use it if needed.

"All clear?" the drabant asked, looking past Nikolaos at the tailors.

"Yes, sir," the slimmer of the tailors said. The drabant stepped to the side and motioned for Nikolaos to come with him. They must have frisked him for weapons in there. It was unbelievably efficient. His head was spinning.

The drabant turned to him and smiled, seemingly unaware

of his intimidating stature. "I've heard that you play more beautifully than anyone else. If it's not too much to ask, would you play for my men during your stay?"

Nikolaos met his eyes. They were gray, and he looked shy, not at all like a guardsman. "It would be my honor. Right now, though, I'd like to find my wife, she was whisked away so fast. I admit I'm a bit overwhelmed by everything."

"Certainly, I'll take you to your rooms. They're in this wing. Some of the servants and non-royal guests stay here, you see. The royal apartments are across the courtyard and in the back. They have better views," he added, eyes gleaming.

"I see." Nikolaos thought of Karl the IX's face in the window. He sure had had a view that night.

They continued through another dark hallway. At the end, they made a left and walked up a flight of stairs that led straight to a door.

"These are the nicest guest apartments in our section. Pray make yourself at home. Food will be sent in a moment. Your wife will be with you soon, too." He smiled and opened the door. "It takes the women longer, but it should still just be a half hour or so, maybe a few minutes more than that. I'll be right downstairs." He gave a quick nod, then left.

Nikolaos nodded back, trying to calculate how long a half hour and a few extra minutes were. He listened for the heavy steps descending the stairs, then entered the room and felt his mouth slack. These were not like the sparse guest apartments of Norrköping's House. It was luxury.

Dark stone walls met high ceilings with thick wooden beams across them, each painted with red flowers and green leaves on a dove-blue background. Pane windows with shiny, green curtains overlooked the courtyard on the right. There was a table covered with a linen tablecloth in front of one of the windows and a five-armed candelabra, lighting the room nicely. One of the table chairs had been pulled out and was facing a fireplace on the opposite wall as if to invite him to sit and warm himself.

He crossed the floor and entered the second room. There

was a huge canopy bed in the middle of the floor. It looked comfortable but seemed odd and exposed. Their own beds at home were attached to the walls with curtains at the open side to keep the heat in and the flies out. Here, it was as if the room was for sleeping only, as if the bed itself was a centerpiece. No candles were lit, and he returned to the front room, noticing a bureau along the wall he hadn't seen at first. It had a large, gilded clock on it. A tower much like Three Crowns' own, guarded by four angels wrapping their arms around it as if to protect it from an unseen danger. Beneath the delicate golden angel arms was a clockface with two hands. The second one must be the minute hand he had heard about. Intrigued, he kept his eyes on it and just as he expected, the larger hand moved. In fact, it was moving in an almost imperceptible, continuous crawl. Nikolaos laughed out loud to himself. He was watching the minutes go by one by one. That's why the drabant had sounded so sure about the half hour and the possible additional minutes. He knew exactly how long that was.

Nikolaos was still standing there when the door opened, and Stina came in, followed by a woman carrying a tray full of food. As enticing as a meal sounded after their long journey, he could barely tear his eyes from the clock. "Stina, look, a clock. A real clock with minutes!"

Chapter 49

One of the tailors, the slimmer of the two, delivered their new clothes to their rooms the following afternoon. He brought two women with him who ushered Stina into the bedroom to help her dress, promising her a tour of the castle once they were done.

The tailor waited until the women had closed their door, then hung Nikolaos' new outfit on a chair. "Here, you should change. The King's page has sent for you. The King is feeling very poorly and wishes to listen to music. I'll wait here, just let me know if I need to help you. A guardsman will take you to the King's apartments as soon as you're ready."

Nikolaos did as bid, feeling self-conscious with the tailor standing right there. Part of him was afraid his true self would become apparent somehow when he saw him undressed. But it was silly. No one ever had.

The tailor expertly adjusted the new breeches without any indication that he thought something was awry. The breeches were light green and tightly woven, almost shiny.

"There, turn around, let me see," he said, pursing his lips while picking off a hair and wiping off some dust on the left shoulder. Then he threw a disdainful look at Nikolaos' feet. "You're still wearing the same shoes you arrived with yesterday? They look like farm shoes. What other shoes do you have?"

"These are the only ones I have."

The tailor lifted an eyebrow, then shook his head several times. "That won't do. You can't see the King in those. Stay here," he said and strode out of the room.

Nikolaos remained where he was, feeling incompetent. It had been so cold when they left it hadn't even crossed his mind to bring the shoes he used for performing or feast days in church. Not even when Stina fretted about her dress did it occur to him. Sighing, he turned his attention to the clock, watching the minute hand's slow crawl. He kept his eyes on it, and it had moved from the II to the V by the time the tailor came back. He was sweating, carrying a large basket that he placed on the floor with a loud thump.

"We have five minutes, hurry and find a pair."

Nikolaos picked out two that looked like the same kind and size and tried them on. The shoes were beige and had square high heels with silky ribbons tied to the front. They fit but made him feel tall and wobbly.

"Ah, nice, you look presentable now. You don't use blush for your cheeks? Powder?"

"No, I usually don't."

The tailor waved a hand in the air. "That's not an issue. The King wants to hear you play, not necessarily see you. You'll be playing in the antechamber by his bedroom. Should the King call for you, someone will brief you on how you should behave. Go on now. The guardsman is waiting downstairs and will escort you." He smiled and caught his gaze. "Don't be nervous, Nikolaos, you'll do well."

"I hope so. I'll do my best, but this is the King, I admit I'm a bit nervous."

"I imagine, please tell me about it should you see the King. I'm curious, I wish I had a chance to meet His Highness."

"You never have?"

"No."

"But you're the tailor. I assumed he… I mean that His Highness the King would need a lot of clothing and alterations."

The tailor's face broke into a wide grin. "I don't tailor to the King. The King has his own private tailor, tending only to His Highness' needs. It's a big castle this," he said, gently pushing Nikolaos toward the stairs. "Pray hurry now, His Highness needs you."

"My apologies," Nikolaos said, feeling stupid. Naturally, he wouldn't have the same tailor as the King. He should have known that. It also felt odd to leave him in their rooms, but he supposed he needed to collect the shoes and everything else.

The same drabant as yesterday was waiting for him below the stairs. "We need to walk quickly. The King wants you by six," he said.

Nikolaos nodded and followed him the best he could in the

new shoes. Everyone referred to the time according to their clocks. It seemed no stranger than speaking of the sun to them.

The courtyard was deserted, windy, and very cold. It was icy as well, and the high heels made it impossible to keep up with the drabant who kept turning around impatiently to see if Nikolaos was coming. Once they finally approached the other side of the courtyard, a door opened by a footman and they were shown into a similar hallway to where they were staying, only this was longer and there were more doors with better wood. He got the sense that there were stately rooms behind those doors and that he was taken through the more private backway to be out of sight of the royal family.

The drabant seemed to know what Nikolaos was thinking. "These are just government offices," he said, "they're all housed here at Three Crowns, as is the royal library. I'll take you to the next wing, where someone will meet you and bring you to the royal apartments. You're fortunate for this opportunity. We're in somewhat of a disarray now due to the beggars."

"Beggars?"

"Yes. You've not heard? Stockholm is full of them. Thousands of people have come because of the cold and hunger. They're housed in the navy barracks on Skeppsholmen." He frowned.

"May our lord have mercy on them."

"Certainly, that's what we hope, but God helps those who help themselves. If they had just been a bit more frugal, they wouldn't have eaten all their stores before the winter," the drabant said with a startling look of disgust on his face.

"Perhaps," Nikolaos said uncertainly. It wasn't just the truth of who he was that needed to be kept from people, but his opinions as well. People certainly weren't starving because they weren't frugal enough.

They stopped by the entrance to a fine room with a floor so polished that the flames from the fireplace reflected on it.

"This is as far as I'll take you. Good day to you," the drabant said with a curt nod.

On cue, a man appeared, wearing a long, curly brown wig. He was heavily rouged and powdered. It looked strange as if he wore a mask that might fall off.

Nikolaos smiled nervously and gave a quick bow. What a difference compared to when he arrived at Norrköping's House and walked straight in through the back door with his horse. Just walking from one place to another was a procedure here.

The man put his index finger over his mouth. "We must be quiet. The physicians are with His Majesty. I'll take you to a room near the King's bed. Pray, play something soothing but loud enough so the King can hear it. His Majesty is not to be disturbed, just soothed. He's very ill." He put his hand on Nikolaos' shoulder and added, "You can call me Antonio."

"I'm very saddened to hear of it. I'll do my best to comfort him… I mean His Majesty, the King."

Antonio nodded, adding a sad smile of acknowledgment. They walked through a room with fireplaces on opposite walls, blazing fires in each. The walls were decorated with enormous portraits of men on horses, pillars encased in what looked like gold in the corners, and large blue and white porcelain vases on the floor. Even the ceiling was ornately painted and molded.

As Nikolaos took it all in, he lost his footing, causing the new shoes to bang loudly.

"Hush! The King is resting just on the other side," Antonio whispered with a horrified expression, lifting his chin toward a closed door ahead of them.

Nikolaos' cheeks burned from embarrassment. He was going to apologize, but Antonio had already turned away, and he was afraid of being too loud.

Then Antonio stopped and pointed to an alcove with a small, cushioned chair, which was placed directly in front of a golden door. "There, you may begin playing now." He gestured to the door with his chin. "Someone will open it and tell you when the King has had enough. I'll be right out here."

Nikolaos bowed. His tongue was so dry it was sticking to his gums, and he was breaking out in cold sweats. Grateful for the chair, he sat down.

There was a painting with four naked baby boys on the wall. Maybe they were the little dead princes. He heard that the royal couple had lost several of their children. Even the rich lost those they loved.

Nikolaos turned away from the painting. It was too much to think of that right now. He felt close to tears from nerves and from knowing that the King lay sick so close to him. Taking a deep breath to steady himself, he began, choosing a calm but what he hoped was an uplifting tune. His left hand shook a little, but his bow hand was steady. One more deep breath. He was playing for the King!

Nikolaos had just finished a fourth piece when the golden door opened, and a man poked his head out. There were tears in his eyes, and he looked at Nikolaos without trying to hide it. "Your music is extraordinary. We thank you. You'll be sent for in the morning," he said, then pulled his head back inside and closed the door.

***

Nikolaos played in the same room almost every day. Each time, he was taken across the courtyard and through all the rooms in the same procedural fashion as the first time. He never heard the King nor saw anyone other than the man who came to tell him when it was time to stop. But the room adjacent to the antechamber had become a theater of sorts. It was now full of chairs where an audience would sit when he played for the King. He didn't know who they were, but the women wore gorgeous, colorful gowns, and most of the men wore wigs.

One evening, about two weeks after they had arrived, the sadness for the King felt especially palpable. The portrait of the four little dead babies reminded him of his own dead children and of the fragility of life for everyone but him, who would always be left alone.

When the door opened, Nikolaos lowered his eyes to hide his emotion. When he finally looked up, the man was smiling at him.

"That was extraordinary," he said, and instead of closing the door as was usual, he entered the antechamber and closed the door behind him instead.

"I thank you," Nikolaos said and stood up, putting his fiddle and bow in his carrying case.

The man smiled, remaining where he was.

Then Antonio entered from the other side. He winked to the King's footman who winked back exaggeratedly, then smiled at Nikolaos again. They were clearly up to something.

Nikolaos looked from one to the other. "Gentlemen?"

"We're not sending you back to your servant wing tonight," Antonio said. "You're to come with us. Everyone wants to speak with you." He put an arm around Nikolaos' shoulder. "A banquet has been arranged for you in Princess Hedvig Sofia's visitor's hall. Her Highness has been sitting with her father listening to you, and she's so moved by your music that she wants to personally thank you. Pray come with me," he said, then started walking, arm still around Nikolaos' shoulder, dragging him along.

This he hadn't expected. "Truly? I don't know what to say. I'm deeply honored."

"The honor is Princess Hedvig Sofia's. No one here has ever heard anyone play with such... such..." He waved his hand in the air as if someone would bring him the forgotten word. "Such incredible beauty. It's as if I were standing in a river with the music flowing around me like water."

The room went still, and the sound of voices seemed to dim all at once. Did Antonio know? He was looking at him strangely.

"Standing in a river?" Nikolaos pulled himself out of Antonio's grip. Somehow after all this time, they were still going to arrest him. Maybe the King's bedroom was too small, and he had entranced them. It had been a worry he hadn't dared to utter even to himself. They would have to run. He started toward the door, praying that Stina was still in their apartments.

Antonio frowned and went around him, placing himself in front of the doorway. "Have I offended you, Nikolaos? Is water… the sound of water, is it not an accurate enough description?"

It was a coincidence. Nikolaos stared at him, pushing down an urge to laugh hysterically. "Pray pardon me, not at all," he said, embarrassed. "It's an excellent description. In fact, it's so accurate you've touched me deeply."

"Oh, thank you, blessed Nikolaos," Antonio said, smiling widely and looking as relieved as he was.

Princess Hedvig Sofia was sitting on a divan with three of her ladies. Her dress barely covered her bosom, exposing long, sloping shoulders with pale, flawless skin. She had dark hair and a fine smooth nose. A thin shawl wrapped around her back and loosely covered her arms and hands. She spotted Nikolaos right away and smiled a brilliant genuine smile. It made her light up with beauty.

Nikolaos glanced nervously at Antonio.

"Bow deeply. She won't extend her hand to you. Wait until she addresses you. Once she does, you may speak. Just remember to call her Your Highness," he said, clapping Nikolaos on the shoulder. "Go, I'll wait here."

Nikolaos exhaled, then started to make his way toward the Princess. It seemed far, and everyone was looking at him. When he was at what seemed a respectful distance, he bowed. Was he supposed to stay in a deep bow until Princess Hedvig Sofia said something or stand again and wait for her to speak? When no words came, he slowly straightened. She was looking at him with a twinkle in her eyes.

"Your music is the most beautiful I have ever heard. How did you learn to play so incredibly, so," Princess Hedvig Sofia paused as if overcome by emotion and lifted a shawl-covered hand to her breast, "full of feeling and beauty? His Majesty the King is deeply comforted. We thank you from the bottom of our hearts."

Touched, Nikolaos bowed again, quicker this time. "It is my utmost honor, Your Highness. I learned to play when I was a boy.

My father taught me."

"Is your father still alive?"

"No, he isn't."

Princess Hedvig Sofia looked pained but didn't comment. Then she put her hands back in her lap under her shawl and said, "Pray enjoy yourself. Enjoy some food and drink. Many are eager to speak with you. Is that your wife I see coming now?" she asked, shifting her gaze to Nikolaos' left.

Stina was escorted by one of the young women who had shown her around that first day. Stina looked nervous, her eyes flickering around the room, looking for him. When she spotted him, her relief was so obvious the Princess laughed.

"You ought to go join your wife and make her comfortable," she said. That was that. The Princess turned her attention to one of her ladies, and he was dismissed.

Antonio reached Stina at the same time as Nikolaos, carrying a goblet of wine. "Ah, this must be your lovely wife. Here, take it," he said, motioning for a footman to bring more. "Your husband is impressing us all. His music goes straight into our hearts, and we'll never be the same again. Nikolaos has forever changed us." He picked up a lace handkerchief from his chest pocket and dabbed at his eyes with it. "Pray forgive me. With His Highness so ill, it cuts your heart in two. The music, I mean your music, Nikolaos, is remarkable."

"I thank you," Nikolaos said, exchanging a glance with Stina, who was smiling shyly.

"I must agree," a man sauntering toward them said. He was wearing a yellow jacket festooned with extravagant embroidery with pearls along the cuffs and a thick reddish wig, like a fox. His face was painted white with splotches of red on his cheeks. "Your music brings the soul to the heavens, as if we could visit for just a moment and see what awaits. It's no wonder that Kepler wrote Harmonices Mundi."

"Jesper!" Antonio exclaimed and embraced the man.

While wondering who Kepler was, Nikolaos drank deeply

from his goblet. The wine was exquisite. This wasn't what they served at the servant wing. "I've not heard of it. What is it?" he asked, finishing the wine.

"No? Harmonices Mundi is the most remarkable work. Kepler discovered that the planets move in elliptical ways around the sun. You see, God harmonizes his heavenly bodies like a sheet of music." Jesper rocked back on his heels, looking proud of himself.

"Remarkable," Nikolaos said, confused.

Antonio nodded enthusiastically. "Indeed, you ought to read it, Nikolaos." He pulled out his lace handkerchief again, dabbing his face with it and staining it with powder. "It's such an incredible thought. If you think about it, obviously God is arranging the planets for a reason, so why not for music?"

"It sounds as though I should read it," Nikolaos said, then turned to Jesper. "Pray, sir, could you clarify what you mean about the planetary movements. I don't quite understand."

"Certainly. As you know, the earth moves around the sun, and Kepler came to understand how."

"Oh." Nikolaos glanced briefly at Stina, but she didn't seem as though she was listening. What did he mean by that? Wasn't it the other way around? The sun moved from one side of the earth to the other each day. "You're saying that *we're* moving, not the sun? Us and the planets?" Nikolaos asked, allowing himself another brief glance away from Jesper, this time around the room. The guests were talking amongst themselves, taking no notice of their strange conversation.

"Yes, of course," Antonio said and grinned at his friend as if Nikolaos wasn't serious. "But Jesper, it *is* quite surprising wouldn't you say? I get confused myself. I admit it."

Nikolaos caught Jesper's eye and he nodded. "I'll take you to my apartments tomorrow and show you," he said. "I have miniature models. It's easier to understand if you can see it. I'll lend you his book as well. Now I must get myself something to eat. A delight to converse with you." Jesper bowed, then walked over to a table by the window. It was full of food, Nikolaos noticed now.

Feeling confused and a bit dazed by the conversation,

Nikolaos took Stina's arm and followed Antonio who was already headed toward it. Nikolaos remembered the conversation he had with Karl in Norrköping's House and how he had asked if the German who had claimed that the sun stood still, was blind. And how they laughed at it. How did it not? He would have to ask Jesper many questions, that was for sure.

Utensils and tiny porcelain plates, along with napkins, were placed on one end of the table. The guests were helping themselves to whatever they wanted. There were meats and birds stuffed with other smaller birds, fresh bread and butter, dried fruits, and pastries shaped like fiddles.

"Will you look at that!" Nikolaos said to Stina and Antonio, forgetting about the sun.

Stina's eyes widened. "These are for you, husband, made especially for you in the King's kitchen."

Antonio eyed them, then smiled at Nikolaos. "I'll be back. I'm going to get more wine."

A man across the table saw their reaction and nodded. "Quite the honor this," he said, picking up one of the little fiddles and bit into it. "Delicious, too."

Nikolaos chuckled and put one on his plate, then reached for some poultry and bread.

"Your instrument is finely crafted, I've noticed. I had wanted to ask, have you heard of Stradivari?"

"No, I haven't."

"Oh, I'm excited to be the one to tell you. Stradivari is known to make the most incredible instruments. The King has a man traveling down to Cremona now to look at some of them. You should speak to Monsieur Pierre Verdier about this." He shifted his gaze to look around the room, then turned back to Nikolaos with a disappointed expression. "I don't see him now."

Nikolaos pursed his lips, pretending to look like he knew where Cremona was or who Pierre Verdier was for that matter. He was out of his league here. How could he compete with all these learned men? He, a farmer and a village fiddle player. A familiar feeling of needing water began to make itself known as well. A diffuse itch in the middle of his head he couldn't quite point to, a pinpoint of irritation that would soon consume him. But the river was still frozen, and they hadn't even left the castle once since they arrived.

He ignored the itch and his feelings of inferiority and said, "Really? I've not heard anything about that."

The man came around the table with his plate, picking up pieces of spiced meat on his way. "Your instrument is quite fine as well. Do you know who crafted it?"

"No, it belonged to my father." An effortless lie, he did get a fiddle from his father once, but it was probably around 1492 or so, give or take ten years. He couldn't remember anymore. The one he used now, he bought when he lived in Stockholm last time, which would make it almost a hundred years old already. A remarkable instrument. He had trouble picturing anything better.

"I see, I'll have a talk with Antonio, and we'll see if we can't get them to bring you one," the man said and smiled broadly, then went back to the other side of the table and added more food to his plate.

Nikolaos took the opportunity to fill his plate as well. It was all very overwhelming. Everyone smelled strongly of perfume too. He hadn't thought of it at first, but now it started to get to him. He didn't even smell the food, just some flowery musky scent. It was nauseating.

Stina waited until the man was out of earshot. "Nikolaos, did you know that Princess Hedvig Sofia has cloven thumbs on both hands?"

"Cloven thumbs?"

"Yes," Stina said, coming closer. "It's why she covers her hands with her shawls."

Nikolaos bent his head back in a slow gesture of recognition. He wasn't the only person in the castle hiding who he really was.

Chapter 50

Rå's treehouse wouldn't make it another winter. The porch had collapsed the previous year, and now the roof was starting to cave in as well. It saddened her, but her home wasn't as private and secluded as it had been when she first moved in, and it would be wise to find something else for that reason alone. People passed by daily. She could see them through the branches while they traveled to and from the village, which now had a mercantile and its own mill, even a shoemaker, people said, although she had never seen him. She ventured into the village now and then, hiding beneath shawls and supporting herself on a cane. She didn't bother to take on the power of an old gnarled tree this time. People took her for an old woman anyway. But soon they would start to wonder how old she really was, question it. It was indeed time for her to leave. She would visit Jon one last time first.

Tobias, Jon's apprentice, was outside repairing something on the barn wall when Rå arrived. She approached slowly, pretending to have aches and pains in her hips and legs.

"Wait, let me lend a hand, Magda. You come here on foot all by yourself?" he called, then put his tools down and hurried toward her.

"I'm not as old as I look. I manage fine. But just now I got a pain right here and would be thankful if I may rest a bit." She rubbed her left hip, leaning heavily on her cane.

"Let me lend a hand," Tobias said again and put his arm through the crook of her elbow. "You may rest for as long as you need. I've been telling Jon he ought to move into the village. People don't come up here. It's too far."

Rå peered at him in the sunlight and smiled in response, hiding her teeth so it appeared as if she had lost most of them. She had wrapped her shawl tightly around her face and pulled it down over her forehead to hide her smooth skin. Putting her hand firmly on his, she stayed silent as if walking were effort enough.

When they reached the house, Jon was standing in the

doorway, smiling at her. "Magda, what a wonderful surprise. Do tell me you didn't walk all the way here?"

Rå gave him a warm one-sided smile in return and let Tobias give her a gentle shove from behind to help her up the steps. "It's just what your young apprentice asked too. I did get a ride by a kind man for part of the way, but I walked through the woods back there," Rå said, gesturing in the direction she had come from. She had hitched a ride for a bit, but it was so short it wouldn't have made a difference had she been as decrepit as she pretended to be.

"Tobias will drive you back. Won't you?" Jon asked him.

"Yes, gladly."

Jon looked searchingly into her eyes, then leaned forward and kissed her on the cheek. "Come in, Magda, sit by the hearth a bit. Tobias will bring us soup." He started to shuffle across the floor in his slippers, then sat down at the table by the fire.

Rå sat down beside him, noticing how his forehead and the skin around his eyes were full of lines from squinting at his work, and his back was a little stopped over. It had been too long since her last visit. She reached for his hand, feeling guilty both for not having visited and for what she was about to say. "Jon, I came to tell you that I'm leaving. I have a niece that I can live with. I'm getting on in years, Jon. My hips bother me and most of all, my treehouse won't survive another winter."

"You and me both. I'll be ninety-seven soon," Jon said, glancing at Tobias who appeared with a large bowl of soup and two spoons. He placed it on the table in front of them, then left them to their own.

"Are you really ninety-seven years old?"

"Yes, born in the winter in the year of our Lord 1600. The pastor tells us what year it is each Sunday. It's how I keep track. Tobias takes me every week."

"I'm sure I'm older than you," Rå said with a crooked smile. She had lived in her tree close to forty-five summers then. Freya must have sent her strength into Rasmus' work, or the treehouse would have fallen apart long ago.

Jon shook his head. "That I doubt, young girl, I take you for no older than eighty."

Rå laughed and tasted the soup. It was hearty and flavorful. Tobias took good care of him.

"Does Tobias cook as well as everything else?" she asked after they had eaten in silence for a while.

"No, his mother comes twice weekly and cleans and does women's work. He…" Jon looked up sharply at the sound of galloping horses and wagon wheels outside. "Was there any commotion on your way here, Magda?"

"No, not at all."

Then they heard the wagon stop and the sound of heavy boots on the dry ground.

"I believe you have company," Rå said and smiled at Jon's surprised face. Maybe someone was sick and needed herbs.

Tobias came in from the other room to get to the door, but before he reached it, it was suddenly pulled open, and four men wearing livery burst inside, shoving him aside. He fell to the floor.

The men ignored him and stared into the room, then all at once threw themselves on top of Jon, right in front of Rå. Two of them grabbed Jon's armpits and the other two one leg each, and then they picked him up and carried him out as if he were a rolled-up carpet. It happened so fast that they were already outside before Tobias was back on his feet.

Rå opened her back and ran past Tobias after the men, her old woman disguise forgotten. "What's the meaning of this?"

They glanced up briefly but turned their backs on her, threw Jon to the wagon floor, and started to shackle his feet to it. A moment later one of them, he was very tall and muscular, she noticed now, and scary looking, jumped off the wagon in one quick leap and went to sit in the driver's seat.

Rå's eyes flew to Jon's, and his gaze locked desperately with hers, but he didn't say a word, and she sensed no explanation from him. It seemed grotesquely wrong. What in Thor and Freya's names was happening?

Then Tobias came running out the door, waving his arms in the air. "I demand to know what you think you're doing!" he screamed.

One of the men in the back checked the shackles, then slowly stood up and looked first at Tobias and then at Rå. "We're taking him to Göta Royal Court for questioning."

"What?" Rå stared at him, dumbfounded. "Why would you do that? He's an old man."

"Jon meddles with the otherworldly. Näcken gave him a book on black arts. Your old man here wrote a pact with him with his own blood! Haven't you, old sinner," he said, turning back to Jon with a look full of revulsion and his voice dripping with anger. "You thought people forgot, didn't you? It's over forty years ago, and you thought you'd get away with it." He slapped Jon across the face with the back of his hand.

Rå staggered, the blow surging through her as if it was she who had been struck. Her back closed itself with a snap.

Tobias reached out to steady her, his face a mask of terror.

Jon was crying silently.

"Black arts? I can assure you, Jon received no such thing," Rå said icily. Nikolaos did a lot, but that was absurd.

"Yes, he did, goodwife," the man in the driver seat said, handing the reins to his companion who was climbing into the seat next to him. "He put the disease on the wife of one of the judges at Göta Royal Court. Not only that, he's also been with the Mountain Rå and the Forest Rå."

Rå took an involuntary step backward. But Jon didn't react to her name. He sat unmoving, back bent forward and head hanging. Of course he didn't know who she was, she would have noticed.

"Don't let his age fool you. Jon is an extreme sinner. He met Näcken and furry troll-like beings in the woods. Some of them wore high hats." He grimaced when he said high hats as if it was an especially significant detail. "That's when Näcken gave him the book with black arts."

"Good sir, there's been a mistake here. I know Jon, he's a tailor. You must have the wrong man. Who has given their authority for this ridiculous debacle? Let him go at once," Rå said, daring to take a step toward the wagon. She felt Tobias follow close behind.

"We're not letting him go." The driver scoffed, then laughed. A cold, harsh sound. With that, he swiveled to face the front, grabbed the reins again, and cracked his whip. Both horses lurched forward, breaking into a gallop as soon as they had momentum.

Finally, Jon was relieved of his stupor. "Let me off, let me off. I've done nothing!"

But the men kept driving, and then the wagon turned the corner and disappeared behind the hill. Rå and Tobias heard Jon scream one more time, then stopped abruptly. The only sound was the horses and the creaking of the wheels.

Rå sat straight down where she stood, forgetting again that an old woman would have stiff old joints.

Tobias sat down beside her. "I don't understand how I could've let this happen. I should've stopped them."

Rå shook her head. "There were four of them, and it happened so fast. There was nothing you could've done, Tobias. The way they carried him off and didn't even say anything. They just took him."

Tobias met her eyes. They were dry but wide with shock. "I don't understand what they were accusing him of. It makes no sense. Troll-like beings in high hats? What's that supposed to mean?"

"I don't know. It's preposterous." She felt weak as the rush of anger dissipated. Her back hole was closed so tight, it hurt.

"I thought Näcken lived in the river. How would he give Jon a book on dry land?" Tobias' hands were shaking.

"Tobias, he can't," Rå said while looking toward the house Nikolaos and Jon had built together. The chimney and some of the roof were visible from where they sat. "The question is why those awful men think he has." She turned back to Tobias, wondering if Jon had told him about Nikolaos and his cave. Tobias' face didn't reveal anything.

"What should we do, Magda? We must help him."

Rå held out her hand, indicating that she wanted Tobias to help her stand. What she needed to do was to find Nikolaos. It was his fault, pretending to have memory loss and bringing Jon and that girl to his cave. Nikolaos should speak to the judges at Göta Royal Court, explain that there was a misunderstanding. She just had to find him. He could be anywhere.

"What are you thinking, Magda?" Tobias asked, noticing her expression. He put his arm around her waist for support. "Where's your cane?"

"Oh, I must have left it inside." Rå touched her hip as if it hurt and leaned into him. "What I was thinking, Tobias, is that Jon used to have a friend named Nikolaos. Did he speak of him?"

"No." He frowned. "Who is it?"

She shrugged, disappointed. "No matter then, I was hoping Jon had mentioned him and that you knew where he lives."

"No, he never has. All he talks about is his plants and how he misses tailoring. I do all the work for him. He can't see fine stitching anymore, or any stitching for that matter. Magda, let me drive you home. Wait here." Tobias let go of her and hurried inside, coming back out a moment later with her cane. "I'm thinking I ought to speak to the pastor," he said, handing it to her.

Rå nodded but hoped it wouldn't make it worse. What if it was the same pastor still? The one whose clock Nikolaos had hidden. "Can you bring me down the road on your way? I'll catch a ride from someone from there."

Tobias looked relieved. "Certainly. I'd insist on driving you all the way home like I promised, but in this case, I should speak with the pastor as soon as possible. I'll go get the horse ready."

***

With her feet deep in the roots and her back open, Rå felt a flicker of Nikolaos' presence northward. It wasn't much to go on, but it was something, and with Thor's help, she hoped she would get to him in time.

Chapter 51

Stina and Nikolaos were walking along the edge of the frozen river below Three Crowns, trying to find a spot where he could get some privacy. Nikolaos was hoping that if there was a way to at least get near water, it might still his restlessness somewhat. The spot in his head was almost hurting now, and he had trouble drawing breaths. Stina was shivering next to him, and he felt guilty dragging her out on this horribly cold day because of his unnatural need.

He pulled her close and put his face near hers under her large hood. "Stina, this is too much. It's too cold, and the water is frozen. I can't handle it anymore. Why is it still frozen? Shouldn't it have melted at this time of year? Make it stop. I need to get to water." Rusty devils he sounded whiny, but he couldn't help himself.

"Nikolaos, you must calm yourself," Stina said and grabbed his face with her mittens. "The ice will melt soon. You have to try to make do, try to think of the water under the ice. It's still flowing under there. Just try to focus on it."

"I can't, I can't feel it." Hot tears fell from his eyes, but it was so cold they froze before reaching his nose. It tickled, irritating him even more. He was losing his mind. "Stina, I can't breathe. Help me, I can't be around people like this," Nikolaos croaked, his voice hoarse from trying to catch his breath in the icy air.

A dog passed them, shivering and walking slowly on sore paws. It turned and looked Nikolaos in the eye as if it understood his desperation.

"Nikolaos, you must," Stina said, ignoring the dog. "Walk ahead to the beach and try. You'll see it'll have helped anyway once we get back inside. You're probably just too cold to notice its effects. I'll wait here and keep watch. You go now."

"I'm not cold, I'm sweating, my need burns like fire, and nothing can cool it but water, you know that!" he snapped, even though he *was* cold, only it didn't bother him the same way as her.

But he obeyed, left her where she was, and walked off. The

place where he had sat that night Karl IX had tried to shoot him was just up ahead. The poles were gone now, or maybe just hidden under the ice. The way the King looked when he opened that window, horrified and disgusted at the mere sight of him. Nikolaos felt a spike of anger and kicked the snow like a child. Then he gave up and went back to Stina.

"I can't, not here. We have to get away from the castle. All I think about is the King."

"I know, it is hard not to. I wonder how he's doing now. They haven't asked you to play for such a long time. What if he…"

He glared at her, incredulous. "You're not even listening. I mean the King who shot me! You're a nasty shrew."

She flinched.

With a scoff, he turned away. She was too sensitive, getting upset with him for the smallest things. Up ahead, a man was pulling a wheelbarrow past two riders who were just standing there, looking at something. Their horses, covered with thick blankets, exhaled clouds of breath that mingled with those of the men. Then they kicked their heels and set off in a gallop, thundering down the main path toward the castle.

Nikolaos waited until they were out of sight, then without a word to Stina, made his way to the water's edge in the opposite direction. The castle was no longer in his direct line of sight, and after a while, he was able to focus his attention on what he imagined was flowing water beneath the ice. To his surprise, there was a faint movement within himself, and then the river picked up speed under the ice. His breathing slowed as his blood responded to the water, and he was flooded with such relief his knees buckled. It worked!

Nikolaos stayed for as long as his conscience let him, only vaguely aware of Stina's shivering form somewhere behind him. When he finished, she was huddling around herself, trying to get some protection from the wind under a tree a safe distance away. She looked sad and was so cold her teeth were chattering. He had been a brute, mean to his own wife. He ran back to her.

"Pray forgive me, pray forgive me, my darling. I wasn't myself. I didn't mean to yell at you," he said when he reached her.

She nodded but looked wary, searching his face for any warning that he would lash out at her again.

He kissed her, pushing down his guilt. He was just like people said, a spawn of the Devil with an unnatural need for water. Not human.

***

Antonio was walking across the courtyard when they came back, giving them a startled look when he saw Stina's huddled form on his arm. "Lord in heaven, what happened?"

"Nothing, thank you kindly, Antonio. She's just freezing. I kept her out too long. We're going in now," Nikolaos said, embarrassed.

Antonio hurried to their side and shook a finger at Nikolaos while looking at Stina. "What was your husband thinking? It's the coldest spring in years and years. You need coffee. It'll warm you right up."

"Coffee?" Nikolaos asked, confused.

"You've not tried it yet?" Antonio asked, looking aghast and excited at the same time.

"No," Nikolaos said and squeezed Stina's shoulders, pulling at her to get her to walk. The short stop to talk had been enough to make her tremble again. "Pray forgive me. I must get my wife in front of the fire."

"Of course, I'll see to it that you get coffee. It's what she needs." Antonio bowed, then hurried away, going in the direction of the offices.

"He's one of the most energetic men I've ever met," Nikolaos said.

Stina, snug and wrapped in her shawls, was sitting with Nikolaos by the fireplace when the door suddenly opened, and Antonio entered, carrying a tray with a blue porcelain pot and small

393

glasses.

"My apologies for not knocking. It was too hard with the tray," he said, striding right in and putting it on the table.

Stina, who had her feet stretched out on a cushion to warm them by the fire, quickly pulled them down. Nikolaos was glad of it, afraid Antonio would think she was insulting the King by resting her feet on his cushions. He really wished Antonio hadn't burst in like that. What if they had been talking about what he did at the river earlier?

"This will warm your feet more than the fire will," Antonio said, oblivious to their discomfort. He sat himself down in the chair next to Nikolaos and began to pour the drink into the little glasses. It was thick and very dark, like wet soot. It looked quite unappetizing. Antonio looked up with a crooked grin. "You'll see, it's something of an acquired taste. His Highness the King has tried it many a time, and His Highness Prince Karl has taken a fine liking to it. Smell it first, then take a very small sip. It's to be drunk hot."

Nikolaos picked up the little glass and sniffed. An overpowering, pleasant, yet too intense scent exploded in his nose. "Rusty devils!"

Antonio laughed. "Wait until you try it, but you first, Stina."

Stina carefully smelled it but put the glass on the table without tasting it. "I'll let my husband try his first."

Nikolaos sipped, letting it sit on the tip of his tongue. It had a bitter yet enticing flavor. He tried to compare it to something, but he couldn't. "This is called coffee?"

"Yes. It's Turkish, very popular there. People drink it day and night instead of ale. Here, it's different. Only apothecaries sell it." He smiled, eyes twinkling with pride. "It's very expensive, but a luxury well worth its price."

"I didn't know that. Thank you for sharing it with us." Nikolaos took another small sip. It was pleasantly warm, which felt odd, but he supposed it wasn't stranger than drinking mulled wine.

Antonio looked pleased. "It's my pleasure. Stina, do tell me what you think."

Stina reached for her glass and sipped carefully, then put the glass down again. "It's too unusual, Antonio, I'll be honest with you." She wrinkled her nose and tried another small sip. Her displeasure was obvious.

Antonio laughed. "Don't force it, Stina. As I mentioned, it's an acquired taste. Nikolaos, would *you* like a little more?"

"I would." Nikolaos leaned back on his chair, watching Antonio pour for him. "Royal life is very different from what we're used to. Here, we try drinks from Turkey and learn about violins from Cremona. At home, Stina and I are simple farmers, living off the land."

"It's why court is so sought after, but you shall not sell yourself short, Nikolaos. It's your outstanding talent that have you with us." He handed Nikolaos his refilled glass.

***

Stina crawled into bed and arranged the pillows so she could lean against them, giving them a hard shove with her palms. They had argued over what happened at the river since the moment Antonio left. As always, when they argued, though it wasn't often, she reminded him of Abluna.

"Nikolaos, you scared me. I realize you're having a hard time here, but for the first time since we met, I was terrified of what you might do. We can't stay here if you can't keep it under control. You frighten me. I've never seen you like this."

He sighed. "You said. Several times now. Your nagging isn't helping."

She ignored it. "I don't understand Nikolaos. You're old and must have been through many winters where you couldn't find water. I've lived through many a winter with you. What's so different here? You're angry all the time, and you can't sit still. Bumping your leg up and down constantly when you sit. When you stand, you shove your fist into your side over and over again. It's distracting. I see it out of the corner of my eye even if I'm not looking at it."

Nikolaos hid his fist in his pocket, trying to hide that he had been doing just that. Then he sighed again. That irritated her too, but he couldn't help it. "Stina, don't insult me. I may be old, but this is different. There's water all around me and guards everywhere. My wits are deserting me."

"You said you lived in Norrköping's House, and there was a moat."

He interrupted her with a wave of his hand. "It was nothing like this, Stina. Besides, it was summer."

"But when you lived here in Stockholm, it wasn't summer the whole time."

"No, but the water wasn't frozen this late in the year, I was able to come and go as I pleased and wasn't surrounded by guards. I told you that. I just told you!" He angrily pulled off his boots and sat down on the edge of the bed, yanking his new watch off his neck and placing it next to his bedside candle. It was a used watch, and he regretted not buying a new one. The reminder served to anger him even more.

"Yes, you did tell me. Pray forgive me, Nikolaos." Tears filled her eyes, and she opened the blankets so he could crawl in beside her.

But he was too frustrated to accept her apology and just pulled the blanket over himself, turning his back on her. After a while, he heard her breathing slow down as she fell asleep. It irked him to admit to it. But she was right; he had never quite felt like this. Even if he did feel better after standing by the ice today, it hadn't been enough. He had no choice. He would have to ask Antonio if he could borrow a horse so he could leave Stockholm for a while and go do what he needed to do.

***

Antonio found him a strong gelding, and in the morning two days later, Nikolaos left Three Crowns.

As if by miracle, the weather had turned. The sun was shining brightly from a cloudless sky, birds were chirping, and there was no wind.

Leaving the town behind, he followed the waterways north and westward. There was still ice, but he could feel and see the water flow in large ice-free patches. Several spots looked suitable, but there were farms and villages everywhere. Maybe it had been like that a hundred years ago too, but he didn't remember. It didn't matter. He had told Antonio he was going to be gone all day, claiming he had to visit a relative. Antonio hadn't suspected anything and assured him he could keep the horse until the next day if needed.

Nikolaos had been riding at a fast trot for over an hour and a half, according to his watch, when he found a path that ended at a vast empty vista stretching toward the water's edge of a large river. It was perfect. There were no farms or homes within shouting distance. Surely it was too cold for people to venture this far from their homes. He urged the horse into a gallop and found a trampled path leading down to a small beach. It was surrounded by thick bushes, giving an additional sense of privacy. Dismounting, he tied the horse to one of the branches, then put a blanket over its back to keep warm. He had asked Antonio for it, telling him that he wasn't sure if his relative had a stable. It had been a wise decision; the gelding's flanks were sweaty now, but he would get cold very quickly, standing still.

The water was rapid and brackish, mostly clear of ice except for large floating sheets, which must have broken off further up. Nikolaos' blood shifted to water just from the sight of it, and he felt weak from want. So weak his hands were shaking when he undid his buttons and reached for the clasp in his belt. It took too long, each piece of clothing an eternity. When he was finally ready, he forgot to take his watch off, remembering just as he put his feet in the water. Almost in tears, he pulled it off his neck, tossing it to a soft spot on the ground, and went in.

Going directly below the surface, Nikolaos swam like a madman, crying with relief as the icy water filled his lungs. It was glorious, each breath loosening that painful itch in the middle of his head. After a while, he stopped swimming and let the rapids take him where they may, just enjoying the flow and the renewed sense of calm. There was no rush, but he wanted to play too, so he turned around, feeling strong and powerful as he pushed himself against the current to get back to where he went in.

The sun was still shining when he surfaced, and he was relieved to see the horse sleeping, looking comfortable under the blanket. Nikolaos reached for his fiddle on the riverbank and started playing right where he stood, watching his colors for a moment before he closed his eyes. He played what he wanted. For himself.

***

When Nikolaos opened his eyes, there was a woman standing waist high in the water. No! He took a step back and stopped playing. But the water was still reverberating with his music, filling the strong current with brilliant purples, blues, and reds. "Pray, no," he shouted, but the roar of the river was too loud, and she didn't hear. Her eyes were large and glossy, and her lips were blue from cold. He had to get her out; humans couldn't withstand icy water like this. She would freeze to death. "No," he pleaded again, but in the back of his mind, he knew it wasn't the cold that would kill her.

Then she came closer, her skirts floating around her, exposing her legs below the surface. Her shawl and scarf had fallen off, and her hair hung in silky red-brown ringlets around her shoulders. There was a scar reaching from below her right ear all the way across to her left collarbone. It was too late.

***

Stina greeted him with a blanket she had warmed by hanging it over a chair in front of the fireplace. "Your restlessness is gone, my love, and you look calm and strong again," she said, helping him get out of his coat and shirt. "Have a seat by the fire, and I'll fetch you some mulled wine from the kitchen."

"Mulled wine would be lovely." Guilt tore at his heart, but he managed to keep a straight face, even smiling at her, until she turned her back to head downstairs.

As soon as Stina closed the door, Nikolaos wrapped himself in the blanket and sunk into the chair. Staring into the flames, a scream forced itself up his throat, and he covered his mouth with his hand so no one would hear. He had promised himself not to do it again. And he hadn't, not since Johannes. It had taken him years not to see the image of Johannes' body in the water every time he closed his eyes at night. Now it would begin again. He would see the woman's hair and bare legs below the surface, see her body bump into the ice and float downstream.

Moaning, he put his head in his hands, wishing he had reacted differently than he had, picturing himself stepping out of the icy water to help her get home. But he hadn't, and no means of willing it would change the past. He had killed her, and he had known he would from the moment he saw her standing there. Still, he hadn't stopped himself; he had reached for her. Racked with anguish, he remained bent over himself until he heard Stina's steps on the stairs, then quickly straightened up, sitting ready with a fake smile.

"Ah, you look so much better," she beamed, oblivious to his actual state of mind as she handed him a large mug of steaming spiced wine.

He nodded and took the mug, pushing the images even further back into that place where he stored his lies, his killings, and the fact that he only pretended to be human.

Chapter 52

Stina was knitting, and Nikolaos was writing a letter to Hindrich and Elsebet.

Nikolaos was dipping his quill to remoisten it when there was a loud knock on the door, startling him so the inkwell almost toppled. "Yes, come in," he called, grabbing the inkwell with his left hand just in time.

The door opened immediately. It was Antonio. His eyes seemed unnaturally wide, and he was swaying, grabbing the doorpost for support. "The King is dead!"

Stina slowly placed her knitting needles on her lap, exchanging a horrified glance with Nikolaos.

"Dead?" Nikolaos and Stina said at the same time. Then Nikolaos stood up and bowed to Antonio. For some reason, it seemed the appropriate thing to do. "What happened?" he asked and sat down again. "I don't understand… of course, I realized he was ill, but I didn't know it was this serious."

Antonio crossed the floor and sat down opposite Nikolaos. He absently wiped his forehead, scratching his head so much his wig loosened and exposed his own hair. It was dirty and plastered to his skull. A big patch of dirt or something other unnamable was stuck to it. Nikolaos looked away.

There was an awkward silence in the room. Then Stina covered her face with her hands and burst into tears. Her knitting fell off her lap and landed on the floor.

Nikolaos looked at her numbly. Should they leave now? Or would they want him to play for the grievers? Was that appropriate?

"I don't know what to do. The whole castle is in disarray and shock. Everyone's crying, and I don't know if I should go home or remain here and help?" Antonio said, putting words to what Nikolaos had been thinking.

Nikolaos nodded. His mouth felt dry.

"Well?"

"Oh, forgive me," Nikolaos said, realizing his questions were not rhetorical. "I don't know how to advise you, Antonio. Will your duties change now when His Highness the King has…" He couldn't get the word dead across his lips. "Pray, what are your duties, if you don't mind me asking?"

Antonio pulled a silk handkerchief from his pocket and handed it to Stina who gratefully took it. He smiled sadly, then turned back to Nikolaos. "My duties lay in escorting some of the guests that come here. It might be good people such as yourself who stay for a longer time, or people who only come for a day or maybe two. It all depends on what's needed. I feel a longing now to seek out my Anna, but I don't know if I should leave or not." He pulled another handkerchief from the same pocket and started wiping at his eyes.

"Of course, your wife. She isn't with you here?"

Antonio shook his head and waved his hand in the air. "Not my wife. She lives out on my farm. Anna, I have set up in her own home in town."

Nikolaos almost asked if it was his daughter before he understood that it must be his mistress he was talking about. He felt Stina's eyes and her shocked disapproval in his side but kept his gaze steadily on Antonio. "I see. Can you not visit?"

"Do you think?" Antonio looked genuinely relieved, as if Nikolaos would be the one who would grant him permission. He put his hands on his face again, rubbing it and smearing his rouge and powder. His wig slipped back down, hiding whatever was stuck on his scalp. He used his handkerchief again, wiping his eyes thoroughly this time, in the corners and eyelids.

"A short visit ought to be fine, wouldn't it?"

"Oh, I don't know, not certain that would be wise, I should be available if I'm needed. I want wine. Can I call for it?"

"Yes, of course."

Antonio went to the door and opened it, then hollered to whoever might hear it down there. "Have someone send wine!" The words echoed in the narrow staircase, making sparks of brown and red bounce off the walls.

Nikolaos closed his eyes to clear it, then noticed that Stina was trying to get his attention.

"What are we to do?" she mouthed.

He shrugged, watching Antonio sit back down. "We're at a loss over this. The King, he was young. Wasn't he? I didn't expect him to die from his illness," Nikolaos said.

"I did," Stina said. "I spoke to the women a few days ago and was told he's been very, very sick and in pain, in severe pain." She blew her nose in Antonio's handkerchief. "He was only forty-two, I think."

"It's a tragedy, such a tragedy. Now his son must take over. He isn't ready. It's too much of a responsibility for such a young boy," Antonio said.

The room felt hot and stuffy. Maybe they could go home now. He had just been describing to Hindrich and Elsebet in the letter how much they missed the farm. He would welcome it, get away from Stockholm, and from his guilt over what he had done here.

There was a knock on the door, and the wine arrived. A woman held the heavy door open as another entered with a tray. Her face was swollen with tears, and she could barely keep from crying as she placed everything on the table. They had brought a bowl with cheese and dried pears as well as wine. Comfort for their loss.

Stina gently touched her arm. "Else, I'll do it. You go and rest a bit."

She looked surprised but nodded gratefully, then both women curtsied and left.

"That's Else. She's the one who told me she thought the King… His Highness the King was getting worse," Stina explained.

Nikolaos nodded absently and waited until Antonio had had some of the wine, then asked, "I assume it would be appropriate for us if we left now, Antonio?"

"Leave? Oh no, no. You must stay. You must stay for the funeral. And your violin. Your Stradivarius should arrive soon. It was months ago now that I wrote to my Cremona-man to ask. I'm certain he's acquired it for you and will return as soon as he hears of our horrid loss. Your fiddle is nice, but someone like you should play on one of Stradivari's instruments."

"I appreciate that," Nikolaos said with a slight smile, self-conscious that even smiling must be inappropriate today, but so excited, he couldn't help it.

That man at the dinner had been true to his word. He wished he had understood the significance of it when he offered. The violins were the finest instruments in Europe according to both Antonio and Monsieur Pierre Verdier. Just like the man at the dinner had explained, Pierre was the right person to speak to about them. A violinist and composer who had come from France with Queen Kristina, he knew not only about Stradivari and his violins but a whole lot about music in general. He was a delight to converse with. Nikolaos had spent several evenings with Pierre, talking about music and violins. He only wished he could share some of his secret melodies with him.

"May God have mercy on the King," Stina said, interrupting Nikolaos' musings. "We'll stay as long as is needed, Antonio. My husband was just writing to our children. He'll explain."

***

A melody full of longing and grief reverberated through the castle walls. People stopped in the middle of their tasks to listen and to try to hear from whence it came.

Although the royal wing wasn't near Nikolaos' apartments, it was said that those sitting vigil for His Highness Karl XI's body could hear faint music so beautiful it brought tears to their eyes. Some said it wasn't Nikolaos at all, but Näcken, sitting out there in the river as he had decades earlier.

Chapter 53

There wasn't much to do other than wait. Nikolaos had been ordered to Three Crowns by the King himself and had not been given leave. Would His Highness King Karl XII let them go? He didn't rule himself yet. His Paternal Grandmother, Her Highness Queen Hedvig Eleonora did, along with five royal advisers, including the esteemed Bengt Gabrielsson Oxenstierna.

The castle was a somber place now. Dignitaries came and went, people hurried back and forth through the halls, determined and busy but conscious of the deep sense of grief permeating the castle. It had been a month since the King's passing. Plans were afoot. But if a date was set for the funeral, Nikolaos and Stina weren't privy to it.

They were breaking their fast in the dining hall with the non-royal guests when the morning peace was disturbed by a young boy hurrying inside, running right up to Nikolaos.

"Fiddler Nikolaos," he said and bowed deeply. "Antonio's waiting for you. Your violin has arrived. You're to go at once and get it."

"It has?" Nikolaos asked, grinning at the boy's serious expression. "That's splendid news. I thank you. Where is it? Did it arrive just now?"

"I don't know, Fiddler Nikolaos. Antonio knows," the boy said, pursing his lips and nodding with an air of utmost importance. "The groom readied the horses for you."

"I see," Nikolaos said, trying not to laugh while he got to his feet and followed the little boy outside.

Antonio was already on horseback with a large brown mare beside him. It wasn't the same horse Nikolaos had borrowed the other day. He was glad. It would have reminded him too much of what he did.

"There you are!" Antonio shouted. "Had we not been grieving with the horrible loss of our dear King or been in wait for our new glorious King to finally honor his father by taking rule, this would have been a joyous occasion."

Nikolaos gave Antonio a surprised glance at the flowery comment, then realized that four men, wearing expensive wigs and big plumed hats, were standing within hearing distance.

"Yes, it would be, had we not been stricken by grief indeed," Nikolaos said, quickly changing his expression to somber.

* * *

It wasn't far, and they could easily have walked had the roads been cleaner and not full of mud and stinking refuse. But what had frozen during the long and cold winter was now rotting in the sun. It stunk something fierce. Nikolaos was grateful for the horse and its height, protecting him from at least some of the stench. Antonio held a small bouquet of tiny blue and white flowers in front of his nose but still looked as if he might throw up at any moment.

"Lord Oxensköld lives in that brick home across the square," Antonio said, letting go of the reins so he could point without having to move the bouquet from his nose.

"Is he a Lord? I thought he was a musician like me," Nikolaos said, wondering if he was appropriately dressed.

"Yes, his Lordship is a musician, a collector of fine instruments, and a lover of music in all forms. He's honored to meet you. He's heard all about you."

"Oh, has he? Honor is mine," Nikolaos said.

Antonio stopped in front of the stately red brick home, then pulled the bouquet from his nose and whistled loudly.

Nikolaos raised an eyebrow. Couldn't he dismount and knock?

Then two dirty ragamuffins came running from around the corner.

"Boys, watch our horses, and I'll give you each a coin," Antonio said and quickly put the bouquet back in front of his nose.

Nikolaos grinned. Wise man, of course, they couldn't leave royal horses unattended.

405

The boys waited until they had dismounted, then solemnly took the reins with bows so deep they almost somersaulted.

Antonio exchanged a merry glance with Nikolaos, then turned his attention to the front door as it was thrown open. A short and portly man, wearing a green silk robe and no shoes, just thick socks, stood there smiling at them.

"Antonio good sir, you brought me my musician! Welcome, welcome," he said, stepping aside so they could enter. It was the Lord himself, opening his own door.

Nikolaos returned his smile, taking a cautious step forward, then stopped, unsure of how to greet him.

Lord Oxensköld waved his hand dismissively. "I'm not much for formalities. Come inside. I have your violin here. I've been looking forward to hearing you play it. I've heard of your exceptional talent," he said, looking genuinely excited.

"I thank you kindly, I'm most grateful, my Lord," Nikolaos said.

Lord Oxensköld nodded impatiently as if even that was too much courtesy and pointed into the hallway.

They were taken through a set of rooms with a ramshackle of furniture, easels, paint brushes, and instruments, including a dusty harpsichord. Clothes and wigs were thrown haphazardly around the room. Lord Oxensköld went to a round table and pushed a black wig to the side. It fell to the floor without him giving it so much as a glance. Nikolaos felt sweaty just thinking about him being responsible for a fine instrument all the way from Cremona. If Lord Oxensköld had traveled himself, he might have had someone else do it for him.

But in contrast to the messy impression, Lord Oxensköld stepped over to a bureau, picked up a long box wrapped in gray fabric, and then carefully placed it on the table. "Come here and unwrap this. I want to see your reaction. I pray you, come," he said, fixing Nikolaos with a stare.

Nikolaos broke into a wide grin and hurried over. It was impossible to hide his excitement. When he touched the fabric, he felt something hard underneath. He pulled back the covering and found yet another piece of cloth. Lifting it away, he allowed himself a quick look at Lord Oxensköld, but he stood unmoving, staring down at what Nikolaos had revealed.

It was a thin wooden box shaped like a violin, covered with what Nikolaos assumed was calfskin with carved patterns and inlaid gold leaf. It was shiny as if the skin was polished somehow. Maybe it was. At the bottom end and along the sides were metal studs. Probably to hold the calfskin in place, but he wasn't sure. The lid was situated on the broader lower section of the case and had a hinge mechanism for secure closure. Nikolaos looked up again, and this time both Antonio and Lord Oxensköld were looking back at him.

"There's a key too," Lord Oxensköld said. "The case was added as a special gift since you played for our late King."

Antonio cleared his throat. "What an incredible piece of art, and to think this is just the case." He shook his head and picked up a small fan to cool himself off.

Nikolaos shook his head uncertainly. What could he say when he had been given such an extraordinary gift because the King had been dying? Bringing his attention back to the case, he opened the lid and put his hand inside, feeling around until his fingers bumped into the violin. Then he pulled it out. It was wrapped in a cloth bag. Removing the bag, he stared at the instrument. The first thing he noticed was how large it was and shiny! The outstanding craftsmanship was evident. Nikolaos let out a slow breath and carefully stroked the smooth surface. Then he picked it up. It felt good in his hand, strong yet delicate.

Lord Oxensköld moved a little closer. "The wood on top is spruce, and the inside is made of willow. If I remember right, the neck and the back are maple. The string... The bow I mean, is also in the case. I hope it's to your liking, my good sir?"

"My Lord, I don't know what to say. It's extraordinary. I can't possibly just take this from you, not a fine instrument like this. I know that Antonio said th..."

"Nonsense!" Antonio interrupted. "It's yours. I told you it's a gift. You've comforted the King during his last days. There's no price too high for that."

"Indeed, there's no question. But I do beg of you one small favor," Lord Oxensköld said. "Pray, play for me. I had Antonio bring you here so I could ask you. It didn't seem appropriate during our time of grief to bring it to Three Crowns. Will you? I hope it's not inconvenient."

As if he would want to wait! "My Lord, it isn't inconvenient. It would be my honor."

Lord Oxensköld laughed heartily and pulled the bow out of the case, handing it to Nikolaos.

Standing back a bit, Nikolaos lifted the Stradivarius, feeling the new smooth surface against his fingers. Then he settled it onto the right spot on his upper chest, took a breath and touched the bow to the strings. The first note came in a little heavy. He relaxed the pressure, and the next note felt so exquisite he gasped. The instrument had a life of its own, and the notes were flowing through his fingers, melting the air in the room, and setting the dust floating in it alight.

Lord Oxensköld staggered backward and sat down heavily on a sofa in the corner, absently pushing aside a pile of letters to give himself enough space.

Antonio remained standing, transfixed.

Nikolaos let himself go. The music soared purple through the room, filling it with a deepness so sweet his breath caught in his throat. Then he made himself stop, watching the purple fade from his fingers.

Antonio and Lord Oxensköld were staring unseeingly.

Embarrassed that he hadn't been more careful, Nikolaos sat down beside Lord Oxensköld. Tears were streaming down the Lord's cheeks, landing on his clasped hands, but he didn't appear to notice.

A moment later, Antonio started blinking rapidly. "Oh…, I was so overcome that…" He stopped talking, looking confused, but then his eyes lit up with realization. "Nikolaos, that was the most beautiful piece I've ever heard. What is it?"

"I thank you," Nikolaos said, surprised that his voice still held and sounded normal. "It's an older piece. My great-grandfather taught it to my father, who then taught me. I don't play it often. It's very bittersweet for me. It seemed fitting today, though."

The truth was different than what he said. He had just been a boy learning to play with his father when a traveling salesman came to live with his family. An unusual man, coming through their parts every year selling magic potions and strange tools no one understood what was for. The monks had disapproved of him. But that summer the salesman had had trouble with his chest and Nikolaos' mother insisted he stay with them no matter what the monks thought. He did, all summer long, teaching Nikolaos how to play songs from the north, melodies unheard by anyone in their parish. He left when the trees began to change colors. After that, they never saw him again.

Lord Oxensköld stirred, looking bewildered, but then he straightened up, seeming himself. "That was indeed extraordinary. Nikolaos, sir. Is the instrument to your liking?"

"To my liking? My Lord, I'm overcome. I don't know how to thank you." Nikolaos slipped off the sofa and went down on one knee, bending his head.

"You're most welcome, Nikolaos, most welcome.

***

The boys were still standing where they left them, holding the reins with steady grips. Antonio mounted and threw them each a coin that would feed their families for at least a month. Their faces lit up, and they quickly scurried away, clearly afraid Antonio might change his mind.

"They deserve it," Antonio said when he noticed Nikolaos' look of surprise. "It's been such a tough winter for many. You'd think spring would come with better tidings, but they found Anna's sister in the river just the other week. No one knows what she was doing, but they're suspecting she may have tried to set fish traps since the ice had finally started to melt."

"A woman setting fish traps?" Nikolaos asked once he was seated in the saddle.

Antonio shrugged, slowing down to ride next to Nikolaos before they headed into the narrow streets. "A sign of desperate times. Her body was found stuck to brambles. Unrecognizable really, her face was swollen and disfigured. She had been missing for weeks." Antonio turned to Nikolaos and met his eyes, shaking his head. "If it hadn't been for a scar, Anna would never know it was her. Augusta had an accident as a young girl, slicing herself on a nail somehow. The scar went from her right ear across to the other side by her shoulder. She was always ashamed of it, but it's how they knew it was her. It's awful. Anna is devastated. As if it wasn't enough that His Highness has passed, now her sister too is gone," Antonio said, staring at him with a horrified expression.

"What?" Nikolaos' heart started racing, and he tasted bile at the back of his throat. He pushed it down, forcing himself not to look away from Antonio's eyes. It was her. Of all people, he had killed a friend of Antonio's. God was punishing him.

"Yes, drowned, floating in the river for days and weeks." Antonio crossed himself, then urged his horse into a trot and went ahead of Nikolaos into a narrow alleyway.

Nikolaos collapsed in the saddle and gagged, staring at Antonio's back and willing him not to turn around. The wig curls bounced over Antonio's shoulders under his hat, and he held himself erect and confident. A man of high standing with the court. What would he do if he found out that he had murdered his lover's sister? Nikolaos followed numbly, dreading getting to a wider street where he would have to ride next to him. It didn't last long. At the next turn, the street was wide again, and Antonio slowed down so he could catch up.

"I'm sorry for her loss," Nikolaos said, nodding, then pretended to focus on riding. He wished he could go straight to the river, a ridiculous thought now of all moments, but the urge was making itself known. He was a monster.

"I thank you," Antonio said, "but let's talk of it no more. I'm tired of grieving. There's so much talk of grief and death I feel I cannot breathe. Instead, let's speak of your glorious new violin. You played so…" Antonio stopped midsentence and stared ahead, then pointed toward Saint Nikolaos' Church and the castle behind it. His horse threw her head from side to side, neighing nervously.

There was smoke billowing over the ceiling and out the windows.

"Lord have mercy, the castle is burning!" Nikolaos exclaimed and crossed himself.

The smoke was unbelievably grey and thick. Flames were spreading across the copper roof with unbelievable speed, thundering loudly. Come to think of it, the sound had been in the background since they left Lord Oxensköld's home. He just hadn't paid attention to it until now.

"We must go at once. Hurry!" Antonio screamed and kicked his heels, setting his horse flying.

They galloped all the way back, dodging people who, like them, were rushing toward the castle to see what was happening. Several men were carrying buckets of water, spilling it as they ran without noticing.

People were streaming out of the castle, bumping into those trying to help. The castle walls and the smoke obscured Nikolaos' view, but it looked like people were leaving from every direction and congregating by the main gate. His heart racing with panic, Nikolaos narrowed his eyes, hoping to see Stina among them. But he was still too far away. What if she was still inside? He hadn't even said goodbye this morning.

The air was now so full of smoke it looked as if it were already evening even though it was only early afternoon. People were coughing and spitting, trying not to choke on the smoke.

By the time Nikolaos and Antonio reached the outer wall, the flames had engulfed the roof and several rooms. They crackled and roared with a life of their own, searing through the castle as if it were just a toy. Then suddenly, a thunderous green sound, unlike anything he had ever heard, echoed through the air. People started screaming uncontrollably, running in sheer panic. Even the men with buckets turned around and ran in the opposite direction.

What was that? He had to find Stina. Vaguely aware that Antonio was still beside him, Nikolaos pushed the horse into the road leading to the main entrance, riding against the tide of bodies escaping the fire and the sudden unexplainable sound.

Some were crying openly and covering their faces with handkerchiefs or shawls to protect themselves from the smoke.

"The library is burning, and the archives. They're throwing the books out the windows!" a man shouted, pointing to one of the windows where books fell like rain.

Nikolaos glanced at it but couldn't take it in and went back to scanning the crowd for Stina. He didn't see her. The flames were dangerously close to their wing. What if she was still inside? He had to get to her. Turning the horse around, he looked for a gap in the crowd. There was none. Throngs of people were closing in from all directions. Fire brigades ran at full speed toward the castle while others were fleeing, running in the opposite direction. He panicked, screaming out his fear. There was no way to get to her. It was too crowded.

"Look!"

The voice startled him, and he was surprised to see Antonio's face right near his. He was leaning awkwardly on his horse to get close and was pointing toward the castle.

"The King, they're moving the King. Look. They're moving the Royal Corpse!"

"What?" Nikolaos followed Antonio's finger with his gaze and saw.

A throng of attendants and guards formed a protective circle around three men who were carrying the body between them and rushing down the entrance road. Then a wind gust blew thick smoke in Nikolaos' face and obscured his view, causing him to cough. When the smoke cleared, the men were lost in the crowd.

"Lord, have mercy on our souls." He crossed himself. "It was the King, wasn't it?"

Antonio nodded numbly, tears streaming down his cheeks from emotion or smoke, or both.

"It's bad then, very bad. If they're moving the King..."

Nikolaos trailed off. "I must find my wife. I must find Stina," he said, hearing the panic in his own voice.

"Give me your instrument, then go find her," Antonio said hoarsely, motioning to the new violin in the satchel thrown over Nikolaos' shoulder. He had forgotten about it.

"I thank you." Nikolaos grabbed the shoulder strap to pull it off, then stopped mid-motion when he heard Stina calling his name from somewhere behind him. Turning toward the sound of her voice but not seeing her, he blinked several times, forcing his eyes to clear some of the smoke. Then he saw her pushing through the crowd. She was running fast, lifting her skirts with both hands, his fiddle and bow under her left arm, her face contorting with tears of relief.

Nikolaos pulled his right leg across the mare's neck and jumped straight down, then ran toward her, catching her as she collapsed into his arms. "Are you unhurt? I was so worried." Out of the corner of his eye, he saw Antonio grab hold of his horse.

Stina clung to him, sobbing.

"We are safe, we're safe, darling. We're not in there. We made it," he shouted over the roar of the fire and the crowds.

$$***$$

Antonio took them back to Lord Oxensköld's home, insisting he would put them up without question.

Lord Oxensköld's footman opened the door this time, shocked to find all three of them covered in soot. He immediately whisked them inside.

Once they had soothed their parched throats with ale, everyone, including the servants and the footman, climbed the stairs to the third floor, where there was a view of the Royal Castle. It was completely engulfed and burning out of control.

Chapter 54

They went home, traveling with the coach system all the way. Antonio had provided them with a letter, ensuring they didn't need to pay a single coin.

The coach system, or the Inn Ordinance as was its proper name, required that there be an inn every two miles that provided fresh horses if needed, horses that farmers nearby had to provide. It also gave the inns exclusive rights to sell wine and alcohol. It wasn't well liked by most, but Nikolaos had to admit it made traveling home easy.

***

It was less than a day's walk from the nearest inn to their farm. Staying close together, Nikolaos and Stina walked in silence, each processing the fire and the King's death. It was a gray day, chilly with occasional rain, which only added to their feelings of despair.

They were passing through Ytterby and Saint Halvard's church when finally, Stina broke the silence. "Nikolaos, what would've happened if you were left in there? Would you have died?"

"I don't know. I hope not."

"No, I mean if you were locked in and *couldn't* get out. Would it kill you?"

Taken aback, he flicked an eye at the church to make sure no one could overhear. "I certainly hope I would. I don't think anyone could survive an inferno like that. Not even me."

"How do you know? You're never sick. You've never had a fever or a broken tooth since I've known you. Never sprained your ankle, never needed to be bled. I'm worried about you. If you had been left in there … no, I don't want to think about it," Stina said, snuggling up to his side. "Have you ever stuck your hand in the fire to see what would happen to you?"

Nikolaos put his arms around her shoulder but picked up the

pace. He didn't want to talk about it so close to Saint Halvard's. "No. And I don't plan to. Stina, I understand your worry, but there's no sense in thinking of what could've happened. I'm not hurt, and I'm not stuck in there."

"How would hell be for you, Nikolaos? Would you burn like the rest of us?"

He let go of her shoulder. "You're assuming God will send me to *hell*?"

"Nikolaos, of course, I don't. But the fire made me think of hell in general. And also, I knew you'd left with Antonio, but thought maybe you'd come back. I was afraid you'd sit there in the flames and suffer for hours but couldn't die. It would just hurt, and I wouldn't be able to help you because I couldn't get to you."

He frowned, then looked away. These were the things he used to obsess over when he was younger. Nightmares of being tortured by someone, never-ending pain that couldn't kill him. A petrifying fear of hell as punishment for who he really was. He had learned to suppress it.

"Nikolaos," she prompted, "say something."

"He turned to her, hurt pushing its way into his voice. "I try to be a good person, but I've made mistakes. You know that, with… with my water needs. There's no need to remind me of hell. I'm aware of it."

Her eyes widened. "Pray forgive me."

He nodded, but it was too late.

Chapter 55

The news that Fiddler Nikolaos and his wife had been present when the King died and when the castle burned spread quickly, and each day they had a steady stream of visiting neighbors wanting to hear about it.

"Here comes another one, Mother," Elsebet said and straightened her back, looking across the garden at a lone woman heading toward them.

"Yes, it appears so. Why don't we stop for the day and get our evening meal settled, Elsebet? We'd leave the men to it, shall we?" Stina suggested, smiling at Nikolaos.

"That's fine, we'll finish up quickly," Nikolaos said, smiling back. Hindrich and he had been bringing cow dung and compost that the women mixed with their soil. It was exhausting work, and he knew Hindrich was getting hungry.

Nikolaos shaded his face with his hand to see who was coming, then almost called out but managed to stifle it. It wasn't one of their neighbors. It was Rå, hair loose and twirling around her knees as she walked, eyes sparkling. There was something so ethereal about her that he felt the need to fall to his knees, but of course, he didn't.

A glance passed between Stina and Elsebet.

"Who's that?" Stina asked, but by then, Rå was too close, and Nikolaos didn't answer.

Rå walked straight up to him and touched his cheek, grinning into his face. "Nikolaos, it's so nice to see you again after all these years. Your wife is here, I see," she said and smiled broadly at Stina, who just stared at her without returning her smile.

"Magda, what are you doing here? How did you know where I live?" Nikolaos asked, bewildered and a little embarrassed, feeling his family's eyes boring into him.

"I have a reason to see you, but little did I know that everyone would be talking about you and the castle."

"You've heard about it then?"

"Yes. It must have been awful."

"It was." Nikolaos relaxed a little. It seemed so normal, and it was, too. Rå was an old friend of his, unbound hair and all. "This is my wife, Stina, our son Hindrich, and Elsebet, our daughter."

"I know." Rå kept her gaze on Stina's face just a moment longer than expected. Then she shifted her eyes to Nikolaos. A quick quizzical look. He couldn't read her intent. "Your father and I met a long time ago when he helped me repair my roof," she said, smiling at Hindrich and Elsebet.

Stina looked somewhat relieved, but Nikolaos could see that she was trying to figure out how much time might have passed. Stina was not a jealous woman, but Rå looked young enough for her to wonder if he had helped her sometime during their marriage.

"Why don't we wait with the rest of the work until tomorrow. It looks like we'll have a nice dry day then too," Nikolaos said, glancing up at the sky. He clapped Hindrich on the shoulder. "Let's go on in and have that evening meal we spoke of earlier."

"I can eat." Hindrich's eyes were bright with mischief.

Nikolaos lifted a warning eyebrow, wishing he could explain what Rå did with men.

Hindrich's smile faded, and Nikolaos chuckled. At least he had the decency to look a little shamefaced.

Rå spoke quietly with Stina as they made their way back, asking her questions about their farm and their animals and gentle questions about the fire.

Rå had a way about her that was very comforting to women.

***

Nikolaos woke just before dawn with a strong feeling that Rå was awake and waiting for him outside. He pulled the bed curtains aside and crawled out, careful not to wake Stina who was snoring softly beside him. Then he got dressed and went outside.

And there she was, standing under the oak, looking up at the lightening sky. A gentle breeze made her hair sway, and she was wearing that shift of hers that was open in the back. He caught a glimpse of her back, rough like the bark of a tree, and with that mysterious hole closed. He shivered.

Then Rå noticed him and turned to face him. "Good morrow. Nice to see you awake, Nikolaos. Can we walk? I want to speak with you a while."

"Gladly." Nikolaos hurried toward her, smiling with pleasure at the thought of spending time with her. He could barely believe she had found him. But she was there, standing in his yard. Something felt warm in his chest.

"You have a beautiful farm, Nikolaos," she said when he reached her, sweeping her arm out to indicate the farm buildings and their animals. The dew made everything glow in the soft morning light. "And it's wonderful to see that you have Abluna with you again."

"Abluna? You mean Stina. Abluna was my first wife. She's been gone for many years now."

Rå wrapped her shawl over her back and started walking. "Nikolaos, I know her name is Stina this time, but it's Abluna who's with you again. It's very touching to see such love." Her eyes moistened.

He felt a chill. "Rå, what are you talking about?" he asked, falling into step with her.

"You heard me. I can see in your face that you know I'm right."

"Rå, Abluna died over a hundred years ago, a lot more than that actually." There was an odd tightness in his stomach.

"Yes, I know that," Rå said patiently. "Nikolaos, you're young. You were born during a time when people had stopped speaking of these things. The monks and priests changed everything when they started coming here with their stories and threats. They lied to people, telling them they'd only live once and that their bodies lay sleeping in their graves until they were sent to hell or heaven on Judgment Day." She gave him a sharp look, her jaw set. "You shouldn't believe in such nonsense. Nothing dies. Just because humans have bodies that don't last long doesn't mean they're not immortal like we are. They're born again, with new families and new lives to live, just like the leaves that fall from Yggdrasil and sprout anew in the spring.”

“I don’t think so, Rå. Before the monks, people thought they’d end up in *Valhöll* with the old Gods, whatever they were called, Odin, Thor and Freeda and such, after they died.”

“Freya is her name, not Freeda, Nikolaos. Yes, but there’s nothing stopping a person from waiting before they head there. Like how Abluna came to be with you, knowing you won’t join her in Valhöll.”

He stared at her, too stunned to reply to that. She stared back, unwavering. Finally, he turned from her and looked back at the house. The sun was rising, and nesting birds flew to and fro between a tree and the bottom of the roof. He wanted to laugh at Rå, tell her she was ridiculous, that she was teasing him. Yet somehow, he knew she was telling the truth. It had been apparent even on that first day when Stina found him in the river. As soon as they had started talking, she had reminded him of Abluna. The way she had looked at him, the feeling of familiarity when they walked home, and the way she had fallen asleep sitting up with her chin to her chest. It had been clear, but he hadn’t understood.

Nikolaos looked back at Rå. She was grinning. “How can you know this? You never met Abluna. Or did you?”

“I saw her, and I recognize her, but no, I never met her.”

Nikolaos laughed nervously. Never met her. It sounded like Rå spoke of someone she had seen at the market.

“Will you prove me wrong?” Rå asked.

He just looked at her.

Her grin widened, eyes alight with warmth. “I’m glad Nikolaos, it’s a blessing not bestowed on everyone. A true blessing.”

“Stina has never said anything.”

“She probably doesn’t remember. It’s rare that people do, Nikolaos. Just be happy she’s with you. If the time arises and it feels right, you can tell her, but she might not believe you.”

Nikolaos nodded slowly, feeling overwhelmed. He would have to see about that.

Rå’s expression grew serious. “I came to look for you because there’s something private I must speak to you about. It’s

Tailor Jon. You remember him, don't you? He lived near the waterfall where you used to live. It's near my treehouse too, by the way."

"Of course. I liked him a lot. I still feel guilty about scaring him."

"Then I don't come with comforting words for you. They arrested him. He's been accused of having had relations with us both."

"What! Now?"

"Yes."

Nikolaos listened with quiet horror as Rå recounted how men had burst into Jon's home, carrying him off as if he were a carpet and shackling him to a cart while she and Jon's apprentice had watched.

"Not Göta Royal Court. Damn them to hell!" he shouted when Rå finished. Horrible dastards. Because of him. Again.

There was a sudden loud bang from the house, and then the south window opened, and Nikolaos saw Hindrich poke his head out. He shouldn't have yelled. "We better get back before we wake the rest of them up," he said, sighing. "By the way, Stina knows who I am. Just so you know. She's known since the day we met."

Rå gave him a pointed look. "Then we can discuss what to do together. It's better." She looked impressed.

Walking back, Nikolaos' head was swimming with thoughts of both Abluna and Jon but wasn't able to form a single coherent question. When they entered the yard, Hindrich was already standing in the doorway. Nikolaos moved sideways so he wasn't so close to Rå, then regretted it. It looked as if he was trying to hide something.

"Father, I heard you shout. Did something happen?"

Elsebet appeared behind him, squeezing herself between him and the doorframe, looking expectantly at them.

"Yes, you could say that. A neighbor of ours, mine and Magda's here, has been arrested."

Elsebet gasped. "Heavens above! Who is it?"

"An older man, you don't know him. They have accused him of black art," Nikolaos said soberly, pointing to their outdoor table in the sun. "Let's have a seat, shall we."

Hindrich looked stunned. "Which neighbor?"

"Someone I used to know a long time ago, Hindrich."

"Where they get these awful notions from, I don't know," Rå said. "Jon is a kind old man and hasn't done any black art."

Elsebet went to sit next to Nikolaos, close, leaning against his side. She waited until Hindrich and Rå were across from them and said, "I thought they stopped looking for witches when we were little."

"Um, so I thought as well. I'll go inside and wake Mother," Nikolaos said and flicked an eye to Rå, warning her not to say too much with a barely perceptible shake of his head. Then he patted Elsebet on the arm and pealed himself from her warm side.

Stina greeted him with a sleepy smile, reaching for him with her eyes halfway closed. She looked so much like Abluna, his heart swelled. He wanted to scream with joy, tell her he recognized her, that she was his long-lost love. But of course, he couldn't, probably never. Instead, he crawled in beside her and pulled her tight against his chest, biting his own hand behind her head to prevent himself from crying out.

Unaware, she let him for a moment, then rolled away and sat up. "Your clothes are wet. Have you been in the river this morning?"

"No, Magda and I just went for a walk. It's dew from the wet grass. Something's happened. I'd like you to come for another walk with me and Magda. We need to tell you something."

A look of surprise, which immediately shifted to anger, shadowed her face. "You may as well tell me now then, Nikolaos. I knew it. I could tell the way you looked at each other. How could you? And right in front of me and your children!" She picked up her pillow and shoved it in his face, then pulled the bed curtain aside and got out so fast she bumped her head on the wood frame. She dressed, jerky angry motions, and looking so much, and so obviously, like Abluna now, he started laughing.

"Stina, darling. It's not what you think at all. I shouldn't laugh, but you look so… never mind. Pray forgive me. I understand what you might be thinking." He reached for her hand, but she pulled it away. "Magda isn't who you think she is, Stina. I'll explain everything later. For now, I'll tell you what we told our children, which is that an old friend of ours has been arrested for meddling with black art, whatever that means. It's me he's accused of being with… and Magda. That I didn't tell the children." He waited for her reaction. It came promptly.

"Magda?"

"Yes. Pray let me tell you once Hindrich and Elsebet can't hear us."

"Who is she? You and her… you're not…?"

He shook his head and got out of bed. "We're more like brother and sister. In a way, we may be." But as he said it, he knew Rå didn't feel like a sister.

Stina narrowed her eyes. It looked as though she wanted to say something, but she turned away from him, peering out the window at the table where Rå sat with Elsebet and Hindrich.

"Let's go join them, and then we'll talk later," Nikolaos said, putting his hand on the small of her back. He couldn't stop touching her. His darling Abluna, his first wife, his love. Could he tell her the truth? Tell her they had known each other before, lived together, and had children. It was a staggering thought. Yet he knew in his heart it was true. His eyes filled with tears, and he quickly wiped them away with the back of his hand.

"I'll heat the porridge for our morning meal," Stina said. She didn't notice his tears.

"Good morrow, how kind of you to let us break our fast this early," Rå said.

"It's my pleasure," Stina said, trying not to stare at her.

"Mother, Magda told me that an old man who Father knows has been arrested for witchery. Magda knows him as well. He's innocent."

Stina scoffed, "His innocence won't help him once the courts get a hold of him. I've seen what happens."

"Yes, I have too," Nikolaos said, exchanging a look with Rå. "Jon is a tailor, a skilled tradesman without a mean bone in his body. He helped me when I needed it, took me in, and helped me build a home."

"When was this?" Hindrich asked.

"It was before you were born," Rå said, then turned to Stina. "I don't know how much Nikolaos has told you, but we both knew Jon back then. We lived in the same parish." Rå took a spoonful of porridge.

"He helped you build a home?" Hindrich asked, frowning. "Here?"

"Hindrich," Nikolaos said, "it was before you were born. No, it wasn't here."

"Really?" Hindrich made a sweeping gesture with his hand. "I thought Mother moved in with you and our grandparents when you married, and then you moved here after the renovations were finished."

"Enough! There's no need for all these questions now, Hindrich." Nikolaos cut him off, embarrassed that Rå overheard how sloppy he was not to have his stories straight. He didn't even remember what they had told them when they were little, but Stina had obviously not met his parents.

***

They pretended to take Rå to see their beehives so they could talk in private. The hives bordered the woods, and there was a path leading to a secluded clearing.

"Your children don't know who you are then, I take it?" Rå asked as soon as they entered it.

"No. Stina and I have spoken about it, but it never seems the right time to tell them," Nikolaos said, looking at Stina, who confirmed what he said with a shake of her head. Her heartbeat was visible in the hollow in her neck. She was nervous. He caught her eye, trying to convey some comfort. "Why don't we sit there," he added, pointing to a thick moss-covered log in the grass.

Rå waited until Stina was seated, then sat down next to her and gave her knee a pat. "My name isn't Magda, it's Rå. I'm the Forest Rå. I've known your husband for many, many years. I met him, well, officially anyway, about a hundred autumns ago."

"Not a hundred Rå, it can't be," Nikolaos said, deciding to remain standing. "You mean the time I fixed your roof for you?"

"You're the Forest Rå?" Stina interrupted, a look of complete disbelief on her face. Her eyes flashed briefly to Rå's back and then to her feet. Then she blushed.

"Indeed I am." Rå pointed to her feet with a smile. "I don't have cloven hoofs or a fox tail. I'm merely the one who has the honor to watch over the forest."

"I see," Stina blushed again, adding to her already red cheeks.

Nikolaos leaned back against a tree and looked down at the seated women. Stina seemed startled and embarrassed but not afraid. She had once told him about someone who had encountered Rå in the woods. A hunter or something who had been doing it with Rå so much, he couldn't give it to his wife afterward. He chuckled. No wonder she was blushing.

"Most of the stories are very exaggerated," Rå said as if she knew what Nikolaos was thinking. "Although there may be some truth to some of them." She craned her neck to look at him and smiled a one-sided smile, then turned her attention back to Stina. "I lived among people once, just like your husband. I had a mother and a family. It was a long time ago before the church came here."

"Before the Lord came and saved people from their heathen ways?" Stina looked incredulous.

Rå's expression changed, and she frowned. "That's how some like to see it. I can assure you that we had a good life and didn't need saving."

"Oh," Stina said, shooting Nikolaos a puzzled look. "Do you need to be near water as well? Like Nikolaos does?"

"No, I don't. He's alone in that regard."

"I see."

It felt awkward after that. Nikolaos could tell that Stina knew she had said something Rå didn't approve of. He didn't understand Rå's fondness for those old ways either, or their strange many Gods. He went to sit next to Stina, reaching for her hand.

"Nikolaos," Rå said, "to get back to what I was saying before. Yes, it's a hundred years since you helped me with my roof. You had been staying in Norrköping's House, and they figured out who you were, remember? That was the first time we spoke. But I had seen you before."

He whistled. "It's that long? Did I ever tell you that I met Jon's father? He was one of the musicians I played with in Norrköping's House."

Rå's eyes widened uncharacteristically. "You knew Jon's father?"

"Yes, I did." He paused, remembering that day when he first met Jon and had mistaken him for Karl. "As you both can imagine, it wasn't something I could tell him. But Rå, you said you had more to tell me about what Jon is accused of."

"I do." She glanced at Stina as if gauging how much she could say. "They said that Jon had written a pact with you in blood."

Nikolaos inhaled to say something but couldn't think of anything and just shook his head, shocked.

"I can only assume it's the letter you wrote him after you left," Rå said.

Nikolaos whistled again. "You know about *that?*"

"Jon showed it to me, Nikolaos. Years ago. If that's what they found, then there is no telling what kind of assumptions they got into their heads."

"They must have connected it to Karin and the babies. She probably said something. Rusty devils! I did nothing. I really didn't. Neither did Jon." Stina was boring her eyes into him. She was probably wondering about the blood. From what he remembered, he hadn't told Jon anything other than that he was feeling bad for not marrying Karin, but that he couldn't go through with it. Maybe they had questioned Karin more. If she had convinced them of who he was, the letter from him would be enough, especially since he had mentioned Karin in it. Rusty devils, he had been an idiot.

"Who's Karin?" Stina asked and stood up, then started pacing back and forth.

"The woman I almost married. She was expecting a baby, but it died. She lost her wits completely after that. I told you about her, remember?"

"Wasn't she old? And they hung her?"

"No, that was someone else. Her name was Karin as well, actually. The young one is the one they questioned in church." He exhaled sharply. "Jon and I were friends, but like Rå said, he was getting suspicious when they questioned Karin, and then he figured out who I am."

"When did all this happen?" Stina asked. Her heartbeat was visible in the hollow of her neck again.

Nikolaos made a quick calculation on his fingers, starting with his thumb. "Fifty years ago, something like that. Wasn't it Rå?"

"I think so," Rå said.

"Well... Kristina had already abdicated by then, and her cousin had taken over. It would make it the Year of our Lord 1656 or 1657, I think. They hanged Old Karin just years before that. Queen Kristina was still reigning then, I know that. So forty years, then."

"Whenever it was, I don't understand how this has come up now after so long," Rå said.

"I don't either. But if Jon is still selling herbs, it might get them suspicious. It's why they were suspicious of Old Karin."

"He *is* selling herbs." Rå looked thoughtful for a moment. "We should go to Göta Court. You can tell them you know him and explain the situation."

"Rå, I can't just walk into the courts and tell them that I didn't write a pact in blood. I haven't aged. If Jon recognizes me, I don't think the court would vote in his favor."

"Pretend you're Hindrich. You look alike. Then you'll tell them your father knew Jon and that he's innocent," Rå said, looking very pleased with herself.

Nikolaos shook his head. "No, we might see someone we

know, and they'd catch us in a lie."

"Göta Court is far from here, all the way in Jönköping. It's only the people in court you have to lie to," Rå said.

"No, Rå. It's too dangerous. One can never assume that. I'm not going to put myself at risk like that. We should just send Hindrich then, might as well tell him the truth too," Nikolaos said, annoyed.

"Näcken! Stop it and get some sense," Rå scolded, getting a surprised look from Stina, who sat back down. "Of course, we can't send him. He wasn't around when everything happened and couldn't defend Jon even if he wanted to. You on the other hand, can tell them the truth. No one is suggesting you tell them who you are, not that they'd believe you anyway." She paused, looking at something in the distance. "What you could do is tell them your father spoke of this. Tell them that Jon certainly couldn't have written a pact in blood because he fled when Karin thought Näcken had taken her children."

"Hmm." Nikolaos tilted his head back in acknowledgment. "You do have a point. But pray call me Nikolaos. I've told you that before."

"Yes, yes. Anyway, then you tell them your father knew Karin and knew that she lost her mind. They should still have the court files for this. The sixmen received word that Karin was free to go, recommending that the congregation pray for her. That should disqualify the case anyway. Hopefully, it already has."

"I never knew that," Nikolaos said and grabbed hold of the moss, suddenly feeling dizzy.

"Yes, Jon told me." Rå reached for him across Stina, squeezing his arm. "Karin was left alone, Nikolaos."

Something loosened in his chest, something that had been sitting there for so long he had forgotten about it. Guilt. "I thank you," he said, his voice barely carrying. It surprised him.

Stina reached for him too. "That's good for you to know, husband. I know it's been bothering you."

Nikolaos let out a breath, holding Stina's gaze for a moment before he turned back to Rå. "You're right, Rå. I take it, we owe it to

Jon to at least try. I'll tell them that my father was a relation, or knew Jon. But I'm not bringing my son into this."

Rå grabbed a branch from a nearby tree and pulled herself up to stand. "I understand, and I'm thankful. I can't live with myself if we don't do something. I just pray it's not too late."

"Yes, may the Lord have mercy on him," Nikolaos said, crossing himself.

***

Hindrich and Nikolaos had made a little rose garden with benches behind the shed a few years ago. It had grown into a beautiful oasis. That evening, Nikolaos was playing his new violin there, enjoying the sunlight streaming through the thorny branches and mixing with his colors.

Stina came and sat next to him. "Beautiful! We were all listening to you from the kitchen. Magda, I mean Rå, and Elsebet will cook. I shall rest, Rå says."

"That's good, Stina, you deserve it. You work hard. Did Rå talk to you about herbs? She said she'll find you something to take that will help you feel stronger."

"She did."

Nikolaos waited for her to say more, but she didn't. He let her be, picking one of Stina's favorite melodies, and started playing again.

"Husband," she said when he finished, a serious tone to her voice. "I've been thinking about quite a few things since the fire. I'm getting old, and people are talking, Nikolaos, I've lost several of my teeth, and you have all of yours. My hair is graying, and my breathing is heavy. Did you know that some of our maids at Three Crowns first thought I was your mother?"

Surprised, he put the violin on his lap and turned to face her. "Surely you misunderstood. I don't look more than a few years younger than you."

"No, that's not true, and you know it."

"No, I don't. You're my wife, and you look as beautiful to me as you did when you came to me that first day by the river."

Her eyes glimmered, but then the warmth faded. "Nikolaos, it isn't really this I want to speak of. Well, it is, but for another reason." She looked down at her hands. "I think we should tell the children who you are. It's unfair to them that people are speaking of us and wondering how you're not aging. Soon, Hindrich and Elsebet will look older than you, and it's time they know the truth."

"Tell them now?"

"Yes, we might as well, Nikolaos. You aren't just a farmer, but a known musician who's the talk of the village because of the fire and the King. Someone will find out what you're doing in Jönköping, then rumors will start, and..." She trailed off and let out a breath, looking across to the goat pen to collect herself. "I think the time has come for us to leave the farm to Hindrich. He'll have his betrothal in a few weeks, and then he and Ekborg can take over. If Elsebet wants, she can come with us or stay here. But I think when we leave for Jönköping tomorrow, we should stay away."

"That's lunacy, Stina. We can't just leave on a moment's notice." After their conversation in the clearing, he thought she would bombard him with questions about Jon and his letter. This he didn't expect. He moved his hand abruptly, forgetting about his violin, which fell to the ground with a loud thump. "Now you're maki..." he began but bit back his words of frustration and bent to retrieve it. The grass had cushioned its fall. "Stina you cannot mean this, last time we were... last time I had children I lived in the same place for a hundred and thirty years. I just got here. We can't move. And we're not telling the children, I never did last time, and everything was fine."

"No, Nikolaos. You've said yourself that people spoke behind your back and feared you, wouldn't help you and ran the other way when they saw you. How you lived all alone and had no one."

"No, it wasn't like that for a long time. I enjoyed my grandchildren for years before anyone became suspicious. We're not leaving our farm. Thanks to my playing in Stockholm and the new goats I bought because of that money, no one will starve this winter. Not only that, Antonio said he'd arrange for us to attend the King's funeral. I'm surprised he hasn't yet."

"I spoke to the pastor the other day, and he said royal funerals take much longer to plan than other funerals. They have to send letters to royals in other countries, and then the royals have to travel here to attend."

"Ah, I see. That's good. I was worried they'd ask for us while we're in Jönköping." Nikolaos placed the violin on the other bench, keeping one eye on Stina's face. She looked sad. Maybe she was jealous of Rå, of her incredible beauty and the long history they had together. It might be why she was worrying about her age instead of his supposed blood pact with Jon. He reached for her hand, stroking it with his thumb. "Stina, you're beautiful. I don't think you look old enough to be my mother." He kissed her lips, tasting tears between their faces.

Chapter 56

When they arrived in Jönköping, the sun was getting low in the sky, and a chilly wind tore at them. It removed some of the town's stench, but compared to how it was in the winters when Rå visited the winter market, something she did every year now, it was awful. She tried to breathe through her mouth, but even then, she smelled it.

As if to illustrate why it was so bad, a man threw a bucketful of poop on the street only paces from them. "Take it to Wätter Lacus like they want!" someone shouted, but the man with the bucket didn't even look up.

"This never happened in Stockholm, Nikolaos," Stina said, pinching her nose.

"It did. We just didn't see it at Three Crowns, they tossed it down the privy holes. If they left it there forever or not, I don't know. I wasn't privy to the information," Nikolaos said, grinning at his own pun.

Rå laughed, watching Stina roll her eyes.

"Antonio told me that they had a lot of issues with the ice since it was so cold last winter," Nikolaos said. "People just put their shit right on the ice instead of making a hole where they would dump it, and it was so full of shit it became too bumpy for the sleds."

"Another excellent reason not to live in a town," Rå said and walked ahead, hurrying past the poop. She wished Nikolaos and Stina would hurry instead of talking so much so they could find out where Jon was held. If he was alive. He might not be. It had been more than two full moons since they took him. She should have gone straight to Jönköping instead of looking for Nikolaos. Her back hole tightened with regret.

There was an inn conveniently located right across from the Court Building, and they went in to inquire about rooms, finding themselves in a vestibule. Windows let in enough evening light that no candles were lit.

A man was sitting behind a desk, writing in what looked like a logbook. He threw a quick glance in their direction and kept writing. But then his expression suddenly changed into a surprised gape, and he stood up abruptly and stared at Nikolaos. "My Lord, I'm most delighted to have you here. I cannot thank you enough for choosing my establishment. Thank you, my Lord, I'm most honored by your distinguished presence. You and your family are most welcome," he said, bowing with a flourish.

Rå stepped aside and grabbed Stina's arm as if she needed her support to stand. Stina let her, but she could feel her discomfort at pretending.

Nikolaos also looked uncomfortable and turned around briefly to make sure the man wasn't addressing someone else who had walked in behind them. "I'm not a lord, good sir. You have me mistaken for someone else."

The innkeeper, whom she supposed was also the owner since he mentioned it was his establishment, held up a hand, indicating that they should wait. Then he went behind his desk and unrolled a piece of paper, holding it up for them to see.
It was a painting depicting Nikolaos playing fiddle in a small room in front of a framed picture of four naked babies. It was a good likeness. He looked calm and a little sad, absorbed in his music.

"It's you, isn't it? You're the royal musician who comforted His Royal Highness the King during his last days," the innkeeper said, his eyes flicking between Nikolaos and the painting.

"It certainly is," Nikolaos said. "Who painted it?"

The innkeeper smiled and gestured for them to follow him through a doorway at the far side of his desk. Linen-clad tables, each with a vase full of blue and purple flowers, came into view as they entered. Rå kept her hand on Stina's arm, walking as slowly as she could. It wasn't easy; Stina kept trying to speed up.

"Sit, seat yourselves. I'll treat you to our finest wine and some tidbits from our kitchen. Who painted it, you asked?" He hurried to a table by the window and pulled the chairs out for them, looking flustered. "Pray sit," he repeated, splaying his arm out dramatically over the chairs. "Lord Oxensköld painted it. He was staying here and spoke of you. Said your music was so extraordinary and beautiful, it brought solace to the court, and His Highness the King himself went to the Lord with comfort because of it. Lord Oxensköld said you visited his home and played for him."

Nikolaos looked genuinely touched. "I took note of his easels, but never would I have guessed he'd paint me." He sat down and exchanged a glance with Stina across the table. "The four babies are from the painting in the King's antechamber that I told you about, Stina."

Stina's eyes widened. "It's the dead royal babies," she whispered.

"Yes, indeed, a very poignant choice now when we know that The King, too, has left the earthly plane," the innkeeper said. "Lord Oxensköld left Stockholm and stayed here at the inn after the fire. Is it true you were performing for Lord Oxensköld the same day the fire broke out?"

"I did, yes. I went to Lord Oxensköld's home because he was incredibly generous and gave me a violin, a Stradivarius." Nikolaos sounded reverent. It must be a special instrument. Rå had never heard of it.

A servant girl interrupted the conversation when she appeared with glasses and a carafe with red wine. The innkeeper grabbed it from her and proceeded to fill their glasses himself. "Mistress," he said, handing Rå a glass.

"Very kind, I thank you," Rå said, grabbing the glass with both hands as if she had achy stiff fingers and was afraid to spill it.

"Lord Oxensköld was eager to hear me play it," Nikolaos continued, "which I did. It was my honor. And yes, it was the same day Three Crowns burned. In fact, my wife and I stayed in Lord Oxensköld's home that night because of the fire." Nikolaos looked at Stina, who nodded.

"My lord, I'm pained to hear you speak of it. It must have been an awful experience." The innkeeper shifted his gaze to Stina, then back to Nikolaos.

"It was," Nikolaos said. "Just to be clear, I'm not a lord. If I may, pray just address me as Nikolaos. Fiddler Nikolaos is what I'm known as at home mostly."

"Fiddler Nikolaos? Bah." The innkeeper waved a hand in the air. "You're certainly more than a fiddler! But forgive me for presuming. Lord Oxensköld spoke so highly of you that I assumed you were a friend of his stature." His cheeks reddened. "I mean no offense, my sincere apologies."

Nikolaos waved a hand in the air just like the innkeeper had. "No offense taken at all." He smiled and leaned back in his chair, looking completely relaxed.

Rå tugged at the scarf she was wearing for her old woman disguise, hiding her annoyance. Nikolaos didn't seem to have a care in the world, talking about his music and who was a lord and who wasn't. She wanted to find out about Jon, not small talk.

The innkeeper motioned to a server boy coming toward them with a tray. "Here, pray eat. We have pheasant that's been cooked to absolute perfection." He licked his lips, making a mm-mm sound. "It's charred on the outside but tender and juicy on the inside. And we have our own jam, very sweet, yet tangy," he said proudly, then started to stand.

"We look forward to tasting it," Rå said, putting her hand on the innkeeper's arm. "Would you sit with us for a moment? I want to ask you something." She looked at Nikolaos, hoping to convey that it was time to change the subject. He gave an imperceptible nod.

"Certainly." The innkeeper sat back down and got the attention of the servant girl who hurried over with a glass, then poured him wine from the carafe.

"You see, good sir," Rå said. "We've come here because we've heard a rumor disturbing us greatly. We're acquaintances of Jon the Tailor. Do you know of whom I speak?"

"Well, I think I do, but I must surely be mistaken. You don't mean Sinners Jon, do you? I doubt such a distinguished group of people like yourselves could be acquainted with such a dangerous person."

Nikolaos grabbed his glass and took a large sip of his wine.

Stina stifled a gasp.

"Jon isn't dangerous," Rå said, unable to stop herself from sounding angry. She took a deep breath. "Forgive me. Jon is a tailor. He's a kind man and certainly not a sinner. Nikolaos, I was afraid of this. It's all due to your uncle after all then, isn't it?"

Nikolaos nodded slowly, eyes gleaming. They hadn't discussed him being Jon's nephew, but it was the first thing that came to her.

"You see Nikolaos' uncle," Rå continued, "was a fiddler just like Nikolaos. As a matter of fact, he's even named after him. Isn't that right?" She threw a warning glance at Stina, then turned to Nikolaos again.

"Yes, that's what they say," Nikolaos agreed. Sipping more of his wine, he leaned forward in his seat. "My uncle was new in the village where Tailor Jon lived, and Tailor Jon helped him get settled. My uncle spoke very highly of him. He, my uncle, became involved with a young woman that..." Nikolaos paused and reached across the table, pulling off a large piece of the wing from the bird, then ate it. "Pray forgive me. It looked so delicious I had to help myself."

"Of course. Eat, all of you," the innkeeper said, looking both pleased and uncomfortable.

Nikolaos pulled off another piece. "Where was I? Oh yes, my uncle fell in love with a farmer's maid. Unfortunately, the woman was confused and not right in the head. And she fell pregnant before they were properly betrothed. Confused as the maid was, she thought it was Näcken who got her in the family way, not my uncle." A shadow of pain came across Nikolaos' face. "The baby was never carried to term."

Rå picked up her glass of wine using both hands. She took a careful sip, and feigning unsteadiness, put it back on the table. "I heard that Tailor Jon had been arrested, and since we know what happened back then, we don't think there are any grounds for his arrest. Tailor Jon is an old man and a kind one at that," she said.

"I'm not sure I follow. Why would they arrest Sinner Jon if it's your uncle who confused a young girl?" the innkeeper asked, looking disturbed.

"Well, the way it seems to us," Nikolaos said, "is that people remember that Jon and he were friends and have made the wrong assumption. If we're right, then he's been unfairly accused. We want to clear up the misunderstanding. I can assure you that my uncle was the father. The woman wasn't right in the head. That's all. Magda here is still a friend of Tailor Jon's, and she was very saddened to hear what is said of him."

The innkeeper stared at Rå, then he shook his head. "I'm afraid you're mistaken. Sinner Jon is," he cleared his throat, "a dangerous, dangerous man. He put the disease on the Royal Court Assessor's wife. This isn't something that has to do with your uncle's relationship with a girl. With all due respect, I must repeat this, as distinguished guests as you are, I must warn you. Our town has been in uproar for weeks now. Sinner Jon is a dangerous man. Did you know he was given a book of black magic from Näcken himself?"

"No, I did not," Nikolaos said, his face expressionless.

The innkeeper drank down his wine and reached for the carafe and poured himself another glass. "He admitted to it, too, said that he was out in the woods and met the Devil and his furry helpers!"

"His furry helpers?" Stina whispered. She looked horrified.

"Indeed, they were wearing high hats and were fuzzy or furry, helped the Devil they did, and sometimes the Devil turned into Näcken, I think." The innkeeper looked confused for a moment. "They were stuck in a mountain, and that's when Jon got the book with black magic from Näcken. Not only that, but he also wrote a pact in blood with him, with Näcken." He pursed his lips with a look of disgust. "I thought it sounded ludicrous myself, but then the Assessor's wife became ill just while they were questioning him." He nodded for emphasis. "It proves it."

Nikolaos frowned. "How did that prove it?"

The innkeeper kept talking, ignoring Nikolaos' question. "Pray forgive me for bringing these horrible tidings to you, especially since you know the man. But I beseech you to stay away. He might put the disease on you too, you know. And those fuzzy helpers may be hovering near town now when Sinner Jon is here.

One of the hunters thought he saw something in the woods."

Nikolaos threw a quick questioning look at Rå, then said, "I thank you, good sir, for your advice, but..."

"Yes," Rå said, taking the hint, "we appreciate your warning. However, like Nikolaos said, I know Jon. He'd never hurt anyone. It might have been a bear the hunters saw."

"Perhaps, but I doubt it. They know the difference between a bear and a…. the otherworldly. I advise you to let the law deal with this, just like we're letting them deal with who torched Three Crowns."

Stina and Nikolaos exchanged a horrified glance.

"Surely you must have heard?"

"No," Nikolaos said. "We left the day after the fire. They think it's arson?"

"Yes, everything is pointing to that. They're saying the fire started in two places. The west wing started burning at the same time as the tower, and not only that but in an area that blocked the way to the fire equipment, including the tubs with rainwater. They had improved the fire safety quite recently and put out axes and pumps in several places where it was deemed necessary. It's suspicious that despite all this, it spread so quickly."

Stina became visibly upset, and her face drained of color.

Rå put a hand on her arm. "Breathe, take a deep breath. Slowly. You're safe."

"If it's true, then it's horrific," Nikolaos said. "Who would do such a thing?" He picked up the carafe and poured more wine for himself, but there wasn't much of it left.

"Indeed. It's not the first time either. Witches threatened to burn the castle down back when Stockholm was plagued by them. There is that, but few think it's the witches this time, besides that's a long time ago. But, you know, Tessin was all too happy to rebuild. He'd been trying to get them to tear down the castle for years. Said it was ugly, old, and disgusting. And now he is to have promised to have the new castle ready in six years."

Stina hid her face behind her hands and burst into tears.

"Rusty devils! The castle is… *was* beautiful. That's an

abhorrent thing to say."

"Yes, I couldn't agree more, even though I never saw it. But Lord Oxensköld said the same thing when he was here. Pray forgive me, I've now given you bad tidings twice." He turned to Stina and Rå. "I don't mean to cause you distress. My apologies to you both. You must be weary from your travel. I can have your meal sent to your rooms. Just give me a moment while I find someone who can take you up."

"I'd be grateful," Rå said, then gave Nikolaos a pleading look and made a move as if she was trying to stand.

Nikolaos hurried to her side. "Here, Aunt Magda," he said, meeting her eyes. She saw compassion and warmth in his expression, and her irritation with him dissipated. He was here, trying his best to help Jon. Tomorrow, he was going to the courthouse.

Chapter 57

There was a chair by the window in their room, and Rå had been looking forward to sitting a while to look out at the bustling town square below. But Stina was sitting on the bed, staring at her from across the room. Each time Rå turned to look back at her, she lowered her gaze to the book of devotions in her lap.

Rå finally decided to say something. "Stina, I see you looking at me. Is there something you're wondering about? Are you afraid of me? You have no reason to."

Stina blushed but didn't avert her eyes this time. "Pray forgive me Rå, I'm a bit nervous to be alone with you. I admit it. I've heard…." She stopped, looking so flustered she seemed close to tears.

"Stina, you can ask me whatever you'd like."

Stina blushed deeper but put her devotions on the bedspread and looked Rå fully in the face. "Who are you really?"

"I'm the forest Rå. I watch over everything that grows within the forest, just like I told you."

"Are you older than Nikolaos is?"

"Yes."

Stina looked as if she had expected Rå to say more but was afraid to ask her to elaborate.

Rå decided to prompt her a little. "Surely, you've heard of me. Tell me what you've heard."

"Oh no, I wouldn't want to embarrass you or hurt your feelings."

"I don't get embarrassed."

Stina looked surprised. "I see. Well, I've heard that men think they see you in the forest but aren't sure if it's you or a tree. Even though they're not sure, they can't resist following you, and then they get lost. And then you find them and lie with them. They don't come home for days and weeks. And afterward none of them remember much. I've heard you make men so tired their wives can no longer get a baby out of them."

Rå laughed. She stood up and went to the bureau and filled

two glasses of the red wine the innkeeper had brought for them. "Men have sated my loneliness many a time," she said, handing Stina a glass. "A few days rest will have them right back in their wives' beds again. The time spent away surely must be worth it. I've never had a man complain about it."

They drank their wine. Stina looked both horrified and impressed.

"I heard that you have a fox tail, horse hoofs, and a tree trunk for a back, but I can see now that none of it's true," Stina said, gesturing toward Rå's back with her wine glass.

"No," Rå said, smiling. She considered showing her how her back looked but decided against it and changed the subject. "Were you not afraid of Nikolaos when you first met?"

"No, not really. He explained everything to me. Nikolaos is a nice, nice man. He's not like other men, doesn't get angry often, hardly ever yells at me or tries to tell me what to do, like other wives always complain about."

"I'm glad to hear it, but surely he gets irritated and angry now and then, especially if he needs his water."

"Oh yes." Stina widened her eyes dramatically, nodding. "But it's not like when other men get angry. They think they know best, and no matter what they say, they always try to turn it around to make it seem as if it's your fault, even your reaction to their accusations. Men always blame everything on your womanly self. Your pregnancies, your moon, or something else. Nikolaos is different. He understands what I think like a woman does."

"Stina, that's the very reason why I don't spend too much time with humans. There's always a man who wants more from me than I can give him, and they're all just as you describe," Rå said, grinning.

Stina laughed.

Rå put her wine on the windowsill. It was already making her feel lightheaded. "You're brave. Not many women would accept Nikolaos for who he is. He appreciates that you do very much. You should know that."

"Yes, he does." Stina paused, drinking more wine. "But I'm

not as brave as you might think. He's always careful around water, makes sure that I or the children are never near when he goes for his needs. He isn't dangerous like they say he is. There are too many rumors about him. That he drowns people simply isn't true."

Rå tried to hide her reaction by pretending to be distracted by a sound outside. Did Stina truly not know how many people he had killed? Then again, why would she? Nikolaos was a good liar and must do everything he could to keep the truth from his wife.

Chapter 58

To make a good impression at the courthouse, Nikolaos had paid a visit to the wigmaker and bought his life's first wig. A periwig the wigmaker called it, or peruke. It was blonde, almost pure white, cascading down his back in curly waves. People were throwing impressed glances his way when he walked across town, making him feel confident and modern. But it soon became clear that wearing it was a hot affair. It was itchy too. He tried to ignore it, unwilling to acknowledge his disappointment.

The door to the courthouse was, as he had expected, closed. He also expected guards outside, but there were none. Knocking, he heard a muffled "come in" from inside, and opened the heavy door cautiously, unsure of what would be on the other side. He found himself in a big mostly empty room. There was a portrait of a man on the wall opposite the window and a desk in the corner. A man with an identical wig to his own sat by it, writing furiously without so much as a glance in his direction.

Nikolaos gave a slight cough and bowed, feeling self-conscious about having the same exact wig and wishing he had picked a dark one. "Pray forgive me for coming unannounced, but I'm hoping you'd grant me an…"

"Sit." Without looking up from his papers, the man pushed a stool out from under his desk with his foot.

Nikolaos sat down and waited. The man kept writing without taking any notice of him. It felt awkward, and he wanted to pull out his watch to see how long it's been but didn't want to imply impatience. When the man finally put the quill down, at least ten minutes must have passed.

"What can I help you with?" he asked, giving Nikolaos an appraising look.

"I'm staying at the inn across the square here. And I want to make an inquiry. I'm a royal musician," he added.

"A royal musician?" His stern face broke into a broad smile. "Delighted, pray can I get you refreshments?"

"I thank you kindly, but no need," Nikolaos said, hiding an irritated scoff at the sudden change in hospitality. "I'm hoping you could clarify why Tailor Jon is in custody. My uncle was acquainted with him, and I think there may have been a misunderstanding."

"Your uncle knew him? Are we speaking of the same person? Sinner Jon?"

"I believe so, yes."

His smile disappeared. Pushing his inkwell and papers aside, he put his elbows on the table and leaned forward. "Is he still alive, your uncle?"

"No, he's gone to his final rest, I'm afraid."

"I see. Well, for his sake, maybe it's better he was spared the truth. Tailor Jon, as you call him, is a dangerous sorcerer. From what I've seen here, I'm surprised your uncle never noticed."

"You're not the first person who's said as much. It's scaring my aunt. We've had no peace since we heard. My aunt goes on and on about how worried she is for Tailor Jon. Wails at night, keeping my wife up." Wailing at night sounded impressive. Nikolaos was glad he thought to say that.

"Assessor Örnevinge isn't here today. I'm Secretary Bödkers," he said as if that would explain something. "Are you quite certain your uncle knew Sinner Jon? Maybe a distinguished man like yourself might be thinking of someone else?"

"I *am* certain. As a matter of fact, if my uncle was alive, he'd be able to tell you that Tailor Jon was not involved with the waterman. What's his name again?" Nikolaos asked, looking Secretary Bödkers straight in the eye.

"Näcken, Rapid Fellow, or the Waterman, like you said. But no, of that there can be no doubt. Näcken taught Sinner Jon how to use magic from a book written by the Devil himself. He wrote a pact in blood with him." Secretary Bödkers nodded for emphasis. "It gave him the power to put the disease on the assessor's wife. She fell down in fits and developed rashes all over her body as soon as Assessor Örnevinge began to question Sinner Jon. Sinner Jon denies it, but we know he's lying."

"I didn't know that Näcken writes pacts. Whose blood is it?

You're sure it wasn't ink?" Nikolaos asked, shifting his eyes from his face to the inkwell on the desk.

Secretary Bödkers followed his gaze and frowned, then he reached for the inkwell and placed it in his desk drawer.

Nikolaos smiled, then quickly rearranged his face before Secretary Bödkers looked back up.

"Do tell me what it is you wish to clarify," he said, closing his drawer with a soft snap. The sound created a pale pink color.

"My uncle said Jon left his home when Näcken was rumored to have been in the area. It scared him, just like it did everyone else. But it turned out that there was no reason for anyone to fear. You see, there was a woman named Karin Svensdotter who became confused and thought Näcken had made her pregnant. The sixmen questioned her and contacted the courts here, and they all concluded that she suffered from insanity. There was no Näcken in the village at all. Karin Svensdotter just imagined it. I'm quite sure you're aware of her case. In fact, the courts here," Nikolaos spread his right hand outward to indicate where they sat, "should have the records of said matter. It should prove that Jon is innocent just like my uncle claimed."

Secretary Bödkers stared at him silently. When he spoke, his voice had turned to ice. "Sinner Jon is already convicted and will be beheaded and quartered. We're just waiting for the assessor to be able to leave his wife who's very ill. As I mentioned, it was Sinner Jon who put the disease on her which just confirms how dangerous he is. And there are *no* such records. Are you insinuating that the Royal Court is fallible?"

"Beheaded and quartered?" Nikolaos cried, ignoring Secretary Bödkers' question and forgetting to hide that he was personally affected.

"It's for everyone's safety," Secretary Bödkers said, giving him a curious look. "It would be dangerous to leave the body intact even if you don't bury him in the sanctified graveyard. We wouldn't want him running around with the Devil when the Lord comes for us on Judgment Day. They'd have done the same with Sven Andersson when he was tried and convicted here. They were going to hang him, but he died out on Älvsborg in the prison."

"Who's this?"

Secretary Bödkers shook his head with disdain. "He was another ungodly fella. He had been spending time with the Forest Rå for years. Will you believe it?"

Nikolaos laughed humorlessly. "The Forest Rå?"

"Indeed, they proved it. His penis hurt from all the fornicating she'd forced upon him. His foreskin moved back and forth easily, just like it does on a married man. At first, Sven said he'd thought she was just a regular woman, albeit a bit horny. But then he noticed that her private womanhood was cold."

Nikolaos decided not to respond to that. It was silly. One didn't need much imagination to understand why an unmarried man's foreskin moved easily.

"First, like I mentioned, he thought she was a woman, but women's undersides are never cold. That too, proves it," Secretary Bödkers added.

"I'm not interested in the undersides of women," Nikolaos said, forcing down another rush of anger. "What I *am* interested in, is you having the execution stopped and Jon released from prison."

Secretary Bödkers lips twitched nervously. "As I said already, Jon is convicted. It's nothing we can change now. Nor would we want to. He's a danger to the public."

"I can assure you he's not," Nikolaos said, remembering Jon's friendly face and kindness. He had to stop it somehow. "Where's the execution going to take place, and when?"

Secretary Bödkers rose from behind the desk and bowed formally. "You're staying at the inn?"

Nikolaos nodded, resisting an urge to scratch his head under his wig. It was itching something fierce.

"I'll send a message when I'm informed. They'll do it at the gallows. You just make a left over by...."

"I know where it is," Nikolaos interrupted, then hurried out, trying not to think about Old Karin hanging from that noose.

***

Rå and Stina looked up expectantly when Nikolaos came back to their rooms. "I don't have good news," he said, pulling his wig off and hanging it on one of the hooks by the door.

Their faces fell.

Nikolaos sighed heavily and started scratching his scalp, wondering if he should return the wig. "Jon is to be executed and drawn and quartered." He went to sit next to Stina on the bed. As the words left his mouth, they felt strangely hollow and not at all the way he expected to feel.

Stina covered her mouth with her hand and cried silently.

Nikolaos numbly put his arm around her and looked at Rå sitting by the window. She appeared like a silhouette, and he couldn't see her expression. "I tried, Rå, pray forgive me, I tried." He swallowed a lump in his throat and pulled Stina closer. She was making him want to cry too.

"Fiends! They're cruel, evil people," Rå said.

"Didn't you tell them about the letter to the sixmen from the courts?" Stina asked between sobs, sniffling loudly. Rå handed her a handkerchief.

"I did, but it did no good. In fact, it might have made it worse because the secretary claimed there were no records of it and accused me of questioning their expertise."

"Humans, Nikolaos, I've always told you they're impossible to reason with." Rå threw Stina an apologetic look.

"Well, you do have a point," Nikolaos said. And that reminds me. Do you know who Sven Andersson is, Rå?"

"I do. Why do you ask?

"Secretary Bödkers, who I spoke to over there," Nikolaos motioned toward the window and in the direction of the courts, "claimed you had spent a lot of time together."

"I met him on my way to the winter markets a few years ago. It was one of the first winters I skied. A nice man. He loves watches, just like you," Rå said, smiling. Then her smile turned to a frown. "How did the Secretary know that?"

"They arrested him for it. He died in prison."

"Oh no, pray no." Rå inhaled sharply. Her usual calm ethereal composure vanished, and she seemed exceedingly human.

Stina slid off the bed and went to her, giving her a hug.

"I'm certain he didn't die in prison of natural causes," Nikolaos said. Karin's broken body in the jail cell and the bobbing arms of the women who were hung at Saint Halvard's flickered through his mind.

"Sven was an apple farmer, a kind, sweet man," Rå said. She leaned into Stina and closed her eyes. When she opened them again, she said, "At least Jon is alive. We have to try to do something, Nikolaos."

Standing up, Nikolaos shrugged helplessly. He felt sorry for Rå, she looked utterly distraught, and he could feel her back hole opening. He didn't know how he knew it but felt sure of it. It was thickening the air somehow. "What though? There's nothing we can do." He shrugged again and went to the window to look outside, staring blindly at the courthouse across the street. Then it came to him. "Assessor Örnevinge," he said, turning back to face the women.

"Who?" Stina asked.

Rå just looked at him.

"Secretary Bödkers, who I spoke to just now, said that Assessor Örnevinge wasn't there because he's at home with his sick wife. Maybe we could find out where he lives and pay him a visit!" Nikolaos exclaimed, feeling a surge of hope.

"Does an assessor have more authority than a secretary?" Stina asked.

"I think so," Rå said, with a questioning glance in Nikolaos' direction.

"Yes, he must. I'm going to head back downstairs and ask the innkeeper. If he knows, we should go at once." Nikolaos crossed the floor in two long strides and reached for his wig, then pulled his hand back before his fingers touched it. There was no need to wear it just to speak with the innkeeper.

He was sitting behind his desk in the vestibule, half asleep.

Nikolaos went right to the point. "Do you know where Assessor Örnevinge lives?"

"Fiddler Nikolaos!" The innkeeper looked up, startled. "I didn't see you come down. Funny you should ask. I don't know where he lives, but I just spoke to him outside. He was heading to the apothecary." He pulled out his watch from where it hung under several layers of lace on his chest and looked at it. "It wasn't more than fifteen minutes ago. He said he was getting medicines for his wife. He should still be there. If not, I'm sure he'll head…"

"He's there *now*?" Nikolaos interrupted impatiently. "I thought, eh, it's of no matter. Where is the apothecary?"

"Just around the corner from here, make a right and then a left, and you'll see it across the square. The sign has a lion on it."

Nikolaos turned on his heels and headed for the door, shouting a quick thank you as he ran. This was an incredible piece of luck. God must have a hand in it.

Making a right and then a left like the innkeeper had explained, he spotted the sign immediately. The lion was bright yellow and impossible to miss. Nikolaos just wished he had worn his wig or at least a hat. But there was nothing to do about it now. He also wished he had asked the innkeeper how the assessor looked. Picking up the pace, he hurried over.

A scent of tobacco and herbs and something sharp he couldn't place overwhelmed him as soon as he stepped inside. It was incredibly intense, and he had to resist an urge to cover his nose with his hand. A heavyset man was standing at the counter, speaking with a man behind it who was putting what looked like tiny envelopes into a cobalt blue jar. Could the customer be Assessor Örnevinge? He was dressed fine and seemed to have an important air about him. There was no one else in the establishment.

Nikolaos decided to interrupt. "Pray forgive my intrusion, gentlemen." He bowed, hoping gentlemen sounded polite enough. "Are you by chance, Assessor Örnevinge?"

The man turned around with a surprised expression. Then he nodded. "Yes, how so? You a witness?" he asked in a slow, drawn-out voice.

For a moment, Nikolaos just stared at him, in awe of his incredible luck. "In a manner of speaking, you could say that I am. Could we talk?"

Assessor Örnevinge glanced at the apothecary who responded with a nod. "I've two more powders to prepare, as well as tablets. Come back in fifteen minutes."

The assessor pulled out a chainless watch from his coat pocket. "Very well. Next time inform me if preparations take this long." He glanced at his watch again, shaking his head. Then he met Nikolaos' eyes. "Come outside with me, then."

Nikolaos held the door open for him as they stepped out into the sunlight. It was warmer today, the wind was gone, and even though he regretted not wearing his new wig earlier, he was glad of it now. It would have been too warm. The assessor was wearing both a wig and a hat, and sweat was already beading on his forehead.

"What can I do for you?" he asked in the same, slow drawn-out voice as before.

Nikolaos swallowed hard once, feeling surprisingly nervous. "I have some information I think you should consider regarding Tailor Jon, the man you have in custody."

Assessor Örnevinge threw a shocked glance at his face. "Do you? That's too late. He's going to the gallows tomorrow. There can't be much more to add to his litany of sins. But do tell me, I'm intrigued."

"Adding to his sins? That's not why I'm here." Nikolaos waited for the assessor to say something, but he stayed quiet, his face blank, so he went on. "My uncle knew Tailor Jon and spoke of him often. You see, he was acquainted with Jon and..." He stopped, suddenly forgetting what they had decided he was supposed to say. "My uncle," Nikolaos cleared his throat, "knew a young woman who became pregnant, and she was so confused she thought Näcken was the father. In fact, you should have the papers still. The courts here had recommended prayers. Jon isn't to blame. There was no Näcken. You have that information in your files." That didn't sound good, just disjointed and desperate. Nikolaos moved closer to the wall to get into the shade, upset with himself. He was getting too flustered about this.

Assessor Örnevinge threw his head back in sudden recognition. "I realize who you are now. You're the musician who spoke to my secretary today." He shook his head. "Bödkers told me about it, but as he informed you, we have all the evidence we need. Jon confessed. He had quite a lot to tell us, and there's no doubt he's guilty. Not only that but as Secretary Bödkers informed you, we have *no* such case among our files." He pursed his lips. "Why are you so concerned about some old friend of your dead uncle, anyway?"

"Because Jon isn't guilty."

"It's awfully hot out here," Assessor Örnevinge said dismissively, turning toward the door. "I'm going back inside for my wife's medication, something she needs because of Sinner Jon's ill will, which Bödkers already explained to you. Maybe your uncle is dead because of him too, did you ever think of that?" he asked, then closed the door. He looked afraid.

***

Later that evening, Rå brought Nikolaos outside so she could talk to him alone, and they went to stand under an old oak behind the inn. It was late, and the early summer night was giving just enough light so there were shapes, but no colors or textures. She felt defeated and sad.

"We failed, Nikolaos. Pray forgive me for dragging you all the way here after you just got back home from Stockholm."

"No, don't think like that. It's better that we tried together, and I'm grateful you told me," Nikolaos said.

"Well, I suppose so, maybe. The courts would never have spoken with me like they did with you. And you found out about Sven."

"Rå, I'm sorry about Sven. How well did you know him?"

"Well enough. I brought him home that winter after we met

at the market. It was here in Jönköping by the way. I don't think I
told you that earlier. We spent several days lying together. I
enjoyed his company. His body was wonderful, and his penis was
hard and perfect. And he was nice." Nikolaos looked so stunned,
she laughed. "Näcken," she said, using his real name even though
he didn't like it, "am I making you uncomfortable? I thought
humans were the only ones who got upset at the mention of lying
together and of body parts."

"No." Nikolaos pulled a hand through his hair. "But rusty
devils, Rå, you're so direct! That said, you're the second person
today who's spoken of them. Secretary Bödkers informed me they
could prove you're not a woman because Sven's penis hurt, and
because his foreskin moved too easily. Apparently, he's also to have
claimed your womanhood was cold." His lips moved in a lopsided
half-smile.

"I assure you it's not cold." Rå frowned. Humans were
obsessed with intimacy. What had they done to Sven to get him to
say that? His penis never seemed to hurt when they lay together.

"Pray forgive me Rå. I shouldn't have told you."

"No, no, I should know what's said about me. Did the
secretary tell you how he died?" They had probably tortured him.
She felt her back close tight around itself at the thought. Sven who
had been so full of life. And kind, feeling guilty for having taken that
discarded old watch. "I feel awful, Nikolaos. Both Jon and Sven have
been arrested because of me then."

"And because of me, Rå, mostly me it seems, at least when
it comes to Jon. You have nothing to feel bad about. Me, they *do*
have a reason to fear, even if Jon has nothing to do with it."
Nikolaos looked genuinely distraught, obvious even in the half light.

"Haven't you been able to stop, Nikolaos?" She put her hand
on his arm. It felt warm, almost hot to the touch.

He drew a deep audible breath and shook his head.

Chapter 59

The gallows were so packed with people that even though they had left the inn early, they had to push themselves through the crowds. People glared at them and squared themselves tighter against each other to block them, protective of their own space and the strangers' space next to them whom they felt a sudden kinship with.

"It won't work, Nikolaos. They'll just get angry. We're too far from the gallows to get safely through. Pray stop Nikolaos, you'll just ensure a fight," Stina said, sounding nervous.

He nodded, then had a sudden thought and touched the shoulder of a man in front of them. "Pray forgive me, good sir. May I speak with you just for a moment?"

The man turned and looked at him. "Eh? You want to speak here?" He had a lined face, darkly tanned after years of working outside.

Nikolaos leaned closer, whispering. "We don't want to cause any trouble, but my aunt here," he gestured to Rå with his chin, "she wants the accused to see her. You see, my uncle knew him."

The man's eyes shot upward in surprise. "Your uncle? Dear God in Heaven!"

"Yes. A horrible shock for our family. If you'd help us through, I'd appreciate it. My aunt is very distraught. She wants him to see her face before his head falls."

The man looked away, staring at the throng of bodies in front of them, then with one more glance at Nikolaos, his gaze slid to Rå behind him, finding her head bent as though in prayer. The man let out an audible breath, then turned around and shouted to a man in a waistcoat, "Let these people through." Then he mouthed discreetly, "Family."

The man ahead gave a small nod, then pushed himself forward and to the side. Somehow, he got people in front to step aside. He must be someone of high standing because no one even tried to protest.

Nikolaos turned toward the man with the lined face. "I thank you. This means a lot. And thank you for your discretion."

"Of course," he said, and let them pass him.

They followed the man in the waistcoat through the newly formed path all the way to the front. Not a single person tried to stop them. Jon wasn't there yet, but the executioner stood at the ready next to the platform.

Stina's face was white as a ghost's. Rå was still as marble under her scarf.

The crowd pressed forward, chanting, "Bring the sorcerer! Kill him! Kill him, burn him. Send him to hell where he belongs." Then they repeated it. "Bring the sorcerer! Kill him! Kill him, burn him. Send him to hell where he belongs."

Nikolaos reached for Stina's hand, wishing he hadn't brought her. They weren't even trying to hide their glee.

"The sins of these people will come back to haunt them," Rå said, her eyes dark with anger.

Then there was a shout and a bustle behind the platform and the executioner stepped forward and turned toward the road below. A wagon approached, followed by two men on horses. Nikolaos' heart sank when he saw the bedraggled form trying to keep balance in the moving cart. It was Jon. They had him shackled to the front in a position that made it impossible for him to sit down. But his old legs weren't strong enough to keep him standing on the bumpy road, and he hung like a rag doll. He was bruised all over and looked impossibly skinny, like a skeleton covered with skin. He was dirty, and his clothes were torn to shreds. As the tailor he was, that must be particularly humiliating. In all of this, there was a peaceful look in Jon's eyes. It caught Nikolaos off guard, and before he realized it, tears were streaming down his face. That calm, almost serene look in a body so broken… it was unsettling. Jon would rather die than stay one more day in that prison.

The wagon reached the platform and stopped abruptly, causing Jon's body to jerk and slam into the front where the shackles were attached. He was grimacing from pain.

The two men on the horses rode forward to opposite sides of the wagon while the executioner took his time walking over. He smiled at the crowd as if he were proud of his task. Maybe he was.

The crowd was quiet now, holding its breath. Men had their arms around their wives' shoulders, and some women closed their eyes while others stared gleefully at Jon.

Stina turned from the horror and buried her face against Nikolaos' chest.

The executioner motioned to someone, and then a young boy, not more than eight or nine, came running forward and took something out of the executioner's hand. Then he scaled the wagon, perching the crossbeam on his haunches while he reached down and unlocked the shackles. Jon's hands fell straight down like ropes.

There was a collective gasp and a rush of prayers. Nikolaos couldn't determine whether they were prayers of mercy or not, but he sensed surprise. At least there was some humanity in their voices now and not only glee. The executioner, however, seemed completely unfazed and grabbed Jon by the shoulder, pulling him down as if he were a sack of potatoes. Nikolaos saw Rå flinch at the sound of bones breaking when they hit the ground. Then Jon was dragged roughly toward the platform, wailing like a child. It was unbearable.

Without thinking, Nikolaos pushed Stina out of his arms and started toward Jon and the executioner. But before he had even taken a step, he felt strong fingers grip his arm. Then a surge of something surrounded him. It was like steam or smoke, yet he didn't see anything, just felt it. He was vaguely aware that Stina was staring at him.

Then Rå leaned close. "No, Nikolaos, no," she whispered into his ear. "You can't do anything. It's too late now. Jon needs to leave the body behind. It functions no longer. Let him go. You'd just draw attention to yourself and put your wife in danger." There was a buzzing in his ears and then Rå let go of her grip on his arm.

Nikolaos nodded, feeling all his strength drain out of him. He reached for Stina, pulling her back to his chest without a word. Rå was right. There was nothing he could do, even though all of this was his fault and even though it hurt. He turned his attention back to the platform, steeling himself.

The executioner threw a glance in their direction as if he sensed a disturbance, then turned back to Jon and addressed him. "You've admitted to sorcery, companionship with both Rå and Näcken. Will you confess and repent?"

Jon didn't answer, instead, he suddenly lifted his head and looked straight at Nikolaos across the empty space between the platform and the crowd. A flicker of recognition lit up his eyes. "There he is!" His right arm twitched, but only his finger moved.

Nikolaos froze. Jon was trying to point at him.

The executioner hesitated, staring first at Jon and then at the crowd, his gaze passing over Nikolaos without stopping. Then he pushed Jon's body forward over the block and lifted his ax.

***

The executioner and his men attached Jon's head to a pole for display.

They left before they saw where they put the other parts.

Stina was shaking so much that Nikolaos had to carry her. He tried to hold her up by the shoulders, but her legs didn't bear any weight at all, and he just picked her up. People stared at them strangely for some reason, and some were whispering. It was odd, but maybe they thought Stina ought to have been able to walk on her own. He dismissed it, concentrating on following Rå while carrying his wife.

Once they managed to leave the square and had more privacy, Stina shifted in his arms and slid out of his grip. As soon as she put her feet on the ground, she retched. The vomit hit a large flat rock on the ground and splattered his face. It stunk of fear and the ale and meat they had ingested earlier. He wiped it off his face with the back of his hand, exchanging a look with Rå. The pain in her eyes was so apparent he let out a sob.

Chapter 60

Stina had fallen into an exhausted sleep, and Rå and Nikolaos were sitting by the window, talking in whispers so as not to wake her when there was a loud knock on the door.

Irritated at the disruption that would surely wake Stina. Nikolaos hurried to the door and opened it with a finger on his lips.

It was the innkeeper. He took no notice of Nikolaos' finger and went straight to the point, aloud. "Fiddler Nikolaos, there's a man downstairs, an old man as a matter of fact. He says you stole his horse."

"What?" Nikolaos stepped out of the room, pointing to the bed where Stina was by miracle still asleep. "My wife is distraught," he whispered. "She didn't take well to the execution. It was a horrendous affair."

The innkeeper peered over his shoulder at Stina's sleeping form on the bed, then grabbed Nikolaos by the arm and pulled him further into the hallway. "My apologies," he said, whispering, "but the old man is downstairs with a very muscular ruffian. He claims you've stolen his horse. Pray come down and show them your horses in the stable so they'll leave. I tried, but they're very insistent. The old man says that he was the executioner here himself several years ago, and like I said, that you stole his horse."

Nikolaos felt a chill. It couldn't be, could it? "Why would he admit to having had such an occupation? They're all former thieves themselves," he said.

"Apparently it's not a concern of his."

"Very well. Hold here a moment. Let me just put my wig on, it may impress the fella," Nikolaos said, hiding his sense of foreboding.

"Good thinking!"

Nikolaos slipped inside, mouthing to Rå that he was in trouble and might need help if he wasn't back right away. She nodded with questioning eyes that he didn't have time to satisfy. Then with his wig in place, he went back out and followed the innkeeper.

Nikolaos' breath caught in his throat. The executioner was very old now, but there was no question, it was him. There he stood, the dastard who had cut off Old Karin's finger. Nikolaos forced himself to stare at him blankly.

The old man gave him one look, then spit on the ground. "That's him just as I thought. I *knew* it. Damn the devil to hell!"

The innkeeper regarded him with an incredulous expression. "Pray get a hold of yourself. He's an esteemed guest of mine. A royal musician who's kind enough to take the time to come down here and clear up this ridiculous misunderstanding. He even offered to show you his horses, so you'll see he doesn't have yours, and you're spitting at him? I guess I shouldn't be too surprised, executioner as you are." He tut-tutted.

Nikolaos threw him a grateful glance.

"Nonsense, that's no ordinary man," the old executioner said, turning to Nikolaos with a look of disgust, seemingly without any sense of shame for his former occupation. "I recognize you. You came and took my horse. I remember it as if it were yesterday. I was collecting blood from some old witch who I had to hang for fornicating and for doing ungodly things with Näcken himself, learned herb lore from him even. You came and tried to interrupt my work. And then suddenly both you and the horse were gone. Take off your wig!"

Before Nikolaos had time to respond, the other man, indeed a muscular ruffian, just like the innkeeper had described, grabbed it and pulled it off.

"See, I told you it's him!" the old executioner shrieked. "That's the man who took my horse. He might be Näcken himself. I remember him joking about it. I suppose it was no joke after all!"

Nikolaos scoffed, adding a headshake for good measure and then a deep sigh. "I truly don't know what you're talking about. This is getting ridiculous. Pray give me back my wig and tell me when this thievery is supposed to have happened. Like the innkeeper here said, I was going to show you my horses, but I think I won't since you've treated me in such a rough fashion. I don't have time for this."

The old man moved closer, the ruffian following close behind. "Oh, I'll remind you. It was about fifty years or so ago. At night. I had just come to collect the blood. Was getting a good pri..."

The innkeeper interrupted him when he broke out in a loud guffaw. "Fifty years ago? Have you looked at his face? Pray leave now. We truly have no time for this nonsense." He shook his head, still laughing.

"I suppose I should be insulted. I must look very old," Nikolaos said. "I've always heard I look *young* for my age, but not anymore, I take it, because never have I been told I stole horses before I was born. Adieu now."

The innkeeper grinned, put his arm around Nikolaos' shoulder, and brought him back inside. He didn't bother to say goodbye. As he closed the door behind them, they heard the old man holler, "I'll get you, Näcken. I know it's you."

The innkeeper looked apologetically at Nikolaos. "Pray forgive me for having brought you down for this." He looked embarrassed.

"I understand, no need to apologize. I must say it was a curious conversation. They're an odd sort, these people, no wonder they're the ones who execute people for a living."

"You do have a point there. They're all ruffians who aren't right in the head."

"Indeed."

"What happened?" Rå whispered, looking up from her seat by the window.

Nikolaos lifted a hand but looked at the floor for a moment to collect himself. He had played it off well but felt panicky now. It was uncanny how things always followed him. Maybe God was punishing him by forcing him to look at what he had caused. He walked over and sat down beside Rå, trying to breathe calmer.

She turned to him, her large eyes full of concern.

"Do you remember Kristina?" Nikolaos asked.

"Your horse? Or are you referring to the Queen?"

"My horse, did I tell you how I got her?"

"I believe so, you took it from an executioner, didn't you?"

"He was here. He's still alive," Nikolaos said, trying to roll his eyes in an attempt at humor, but it wasn't funny, and it came out like a grimace. "That's who I had to go downstairs to talk to. He recognized me, Rå. And why wouldn't he? I stole his horse while he watched. Rusty devils, I can't believe this. How can he still be alive? He knows who I am too, he said as much when he left."

"Freya's strength upon you," Rå said, making an odd hand motion.

"I take all the strength I can get."

Rå put her hand on his thigh. "It would be wise to leave now. We've done what we came here to do."

"He knows you're really Näcken?" Stina asked from across the room, sitting up with the blankets around her and hair askew.

"Shush!" Nikolaos hissed, afraid someone would hear.

"Forgive me," she said, glancing at the door. She lowered her voice. "I think Rå's right. We should leave. I don't want to stay here if they're accusing you of things. There's nothing we can do for poor old Jon anyway. I want to get out of this horrible town."

"But if we leave, it just seems as if I'm guilty."

"Nikolaos, you are," Rå said.

"What?"

"With all due respect Nikolaos, you did spend time with Jon, there's no denying that. He helped you build a house, and he even went to your cave. And you did steal that man's horse."

"Rå, we were friends. As were you. What did you do with Jon? Brought him to bed?" Rå just raised her eyebrows. It infuriated him. "I didn't give him a book of black art. Why the rusty devils would I have given him a book? And you know it was a letter and what I wrote in it!" Nikolaos abruptly stood, then went to the bureau and started pulling out their traveling bags, throwing them on the bed.

"Stina, pack our things, we're going. I'll go speak with the innkeeper."

He stomped to the door and walked out. Anger was making

his heart thump fast, and sweat was forming under his wig, making it itch again and angering him more. He reached to pull it off, but just then the innkeeper peeked around the corner from the dining room, breaking into a broad smile when he spotted him.

"Fiddler Nikolaos, pray come in here. You have another guest, this time a much more distinguished visitor I must say."

"Certainly." He swallowed his irritation and tried to smile, but the innkeeper had already turned around. When Nikolaos entered the dining room, he found a woman wearing a silky blue dress with a décolletage so deep it looked like her breasts would fall out. She collapsed into a deep curtsy and fluttered her eyelids at him, her breasts somehow still staying put. Nikolaos remained where he was, at a loss for words.

The woman tried to rise, but her legs got stuck in her skirts, and she stumbled. The innkeeper rushed to her side to help her, throwing Nikolaos a meaningful glance. Taking his arm, she managed to stand and went straight to Nikolaos without so much as a glance at the innkeeper. "I've come to formally invite you to perform at my home as we celebrate the birth of my sister's son," she said, standing so close she was almost touching him with her near naked chest.

"Oh." Nikolaos glanced at the innkeeper who was grinning widely. "When is this to take place?"

"On Saturday. Do say yes, I beseech you."

He let out a breath. This might be the excuse he needed for why they needed to leave earlier than planned.

"Well, mistress, it's a bit of short notice. "I'll have to think about it before I decide, but I'm honored at the invitation. I thank you." Nikolaos smiled, the irritation from before easing.

The innkeeper caught his eye. "Ah, Fiddler Nikolaos, say yes to this kind gentlewoman. She and her husband would treat you and your family like royalty." Moving closer, he added, "You deserve it after today's debacle. I'm still thinking of ways to compensate you for that horrible man coming here with his awful and ridiculous nonsense!"

"I appreciate your kindness, but there's no need for that. It's certainly nothing you need to feel responsible for."

The innkeeper looked relieved, nodding gratefully. "Why don't I get you a nice wine and you two can have a seat to discuss the invitation?" He motioned toward a small table by the fireplace, then left them.

Nikolaos pulled out a chair for her, and to her credit, even though she looked curious about what the innkeeper had referred to, she didn't say anything. He sat down opposite her. "I don't know your name, mistress, may I ask it?"

"Of course, you may. My name is Esmeralda. My husband is German and is close to Gyllensköld. They hunt together," she said proudly. Nikolaos didn't know who she was talking about, but her expression told him he ought to be impressed. He pretended to pretend *not* to be.

Her eyes gleamed with satisfaction. "We'd compensate you greatly and would very much want you there. We'll set you up in your own suite on our estate, and you may stay as long as you'd like. Perhaps you like to play for me privately when my husband hunts?" She stared deeply into his eyes, slowly licking her lips.

"I rarely do private audiences," he said politely, embarrassed at her obvious flirtations. "As for your event, I'll consider it. Just let me think about it for a moment and speak with my wife. I'd have to take her and my aunt home first."

"Or you could leave them here," the innkeeper interjected, coming back with the wine. "It's Tuesday today, you'd barely make it if you went home first and then traveled there."

"Hmmm," Nikolaos said, reaching for the wine the innkeeper was handing him. "I may do that." Of course, he wouldn't leave Rå and Stina after being recognized but played along for now. He took a sip of wine. It had a nice bouquet with a strong scent that lingered in his nose just the way he liked it.

Esmeralda sipped her wine as well, then put the glass on the table and licked her lips in the same fashion as before. "I beseech you to come. I'll leave directions for you with our innkeeper." She reached across the table and caressed his hand.

Nikolaos pulled it away, embarrassed again. She was

attractive, he had to admit that, but her behavior was daring to the point of being ridiculous. "I thank you. If I'm not able to perform, I'll send word, but I don't see a reas…"

He was interrupted by the front door slamming and a clamoring in the vestibule. "I just had a visit from a man who claims you're harboring Näcken here and that you tried to stop them from arresting him!" someone shouted. He recognized the voice and felt his chest tighten. It was Secretary Bödkers.

Esmeralda fell back into her chair, a shocked expression on her face.

"Has he now?" the innkeeper asked calmly but loud enough for them to hear from the other room. "You may speak to him if you'd like. He's right in there having wine with Mistress Esmeralda from Havets Castle." His voice was dripping with disdain.

Nikolaos excused himself from Esmeralda and walked out into the lobby. "Secretary Bödkers, I see you found out who I am after all," he said, not sure if he ought to be scared or should be enjoying himself, feeling a bit of both.

Secretary Bödkers stared at him, his eyes wide with shock, but then he laughed, "You? Is it you he's talking about?"

"It is. I stole his horse some fifty years ago apparently," Nikolaos said pointedly. "As you must see when looking at me, he's likely telling the truth."

"Oh lord in heaven, um well…"

Nikolaos kept his gaze, staying serious. "I assume he may have heard that my uncle was a friend of Tailor Jon's, which might have made the old man disoriented."

"I see, that explains it. I was afraid Näcken had come here to revenge himself on us after Sinner Jon's death." Secretary Bödkers sat down on a chair next to the desk.

The innkeeper's eyes were narrow with constrained irritation. "I'll tell you, that bedraggled old man came here and insulted my guest. It's unacceptable. He's a royal musician! His wife and aunt are distraught enough as it is today, as I'm sure you can imagine. Not only that, but the bedraggled old man also brought a thug with him, a scary ruffian of a man. They tried to push themselves in here, causing a ruckus. Pulled off Nikolaos' wig too, will you believe it? He's a royal musician," he said again. "It's an outrage!"

"It really was. You should've seen it," Nikolaos said, nodding curtly at Secretary Bödkers before he turned to the innkeeper. "I'm thanking you for your generosity, but I can't cause undue pain to my wife and my aunt. This is terribly unseemly. I understand that man wasn't right in the head, but him going so far as to contact the courts". Nikolaos indicated Secretary Bödkers with his right hand. "I'm not comfortable with it anymore. Pray forgive me, but my family and I will leave today."

The innkeeper exhaled with an audible sigh. For a moment it looked as though he would protest, but then he nodded. "I'm very disappointed. I had hoped you'd play here a few evenings. But of course, I understand. My sincere apologies."

"No need, you've been a most generous host," Nikolaos said, then turned to the secretary. "Secretary Bödkers, why are your former executioners allowed to roam the town like this, causing trouble for my family? First you hang my aunt's friend, and now I'm accused of the vilest things. See over your affairs."

Secretary Bödkers looked startled but didn't try to defend himself.

"Well," Nikolaos said, hoping it was in fact the court's job to keep a town as large as this in order. It might not be. He walked off without another word and went back to the table to say a proper goodbye to Mistress Esmeralda, feeling the men's eyes burning on his back. Nikolaos smiled; Secretary Bödkers was a gullible snob.

Mistress Esmeralda was no longer sitting there. A neatly folded unsealed letter lay next to her empty wine glass. He opened it.

Dear Nikolaos, esteemed Royal Musician,
Do come. I will be waiting.
Celebrations begin on Saturday at six in the evening. Do come the night before.
Havets Castle, Stövelskog

Nikolaos nodded with approval. Stövelskog, he knew where that was, and had even seen what must have been Havets Castle from afar. It was closer to his farm than the inn was, and he would have time to take Stina home and get his new violin.

When he passed the lobby to go back upstairs, the innkeeper and Secretary Bödkers were speaking softly, heads close together.

Chapter 61

When Nikolaos arrived at Havets Castle, there was thick fog wrapping around the walls, diffusing a warm glow from candlelight. From the looks of it, a party had already begun, and every window was alight.

He went around to the front and dismounted, then left his horse untied and approached the front door.

It was opened by a footman before he reached it. "Yes?"

"I'm Nikolaos Nordvatten," Nikolaos said, not knowing where the name Nordvatten came from, but he was suddenly struck by the fact that Mistress Esmeralda thought him a royal musician, and it slipped out of his mouth.

"You're expected, good sir. Pray come inside. We have a suite ready for you, sir. I'll take you to it," the footman said, stepping aside to let him pass.

"I thank you kindly," Nikolaos said, a little taken aback that the footman didn't offer to introduce him to their guests. But maybe he expected him to bring his satchel to his room first and perhaps change his clothes. His satchel was old and torn. He shifted it to hide its most damaged side so the guests wouldn't think him a tatterdemalion and stepped inside, bracing himself for curious eyes.

But the room was empty. That was odd. A chandelier hung from an ornate ceiling, and every candle was lit, but there wasn't a single person present to enjoy its light. Surprised, he tried to glimpse the adjacent rooms, listening for the din of conversations in the distance, but there was nothing.

The footman escorted him to a stairway across from the entrance, then went ahead of him. A small table with a lit lantern decorated each landing. Stopping at the third, he picked up a candle from a box beside it and lit it from the lantern flame. Then he led the way into a dark hallway, opening a door to their right. "Here, sir, are your rooms." His eyes flicked to Nikolaos' satchel, and a slight look of disapproval shadowed his face. It really had been a stupid choice not to bring a better one.

There were two rooms, one with a large canopy bed and a

dressing table, the other with a sofa, a small dining table, and a bureau. Someone had lit candles already and placed them on every surface. They must go through an enormous amount of candle wax. How could they afford it?

"I'll have someone bring you wine," the footman said. "Do you require anything else? A bite to eat, perhaps?"

"Wine would be fine, I thank you."

The footman gave a curt nod, then left, closing the door soundlessly.

Nikolaos had just put his Stradivarius on the bureau when he realized he had left his horse untied outside. Rusty devils, that was stupid. What if she had run off or gone and pooped on the lawn? He ran downstairs, across the empty room with the chandelier, praying he would get to his horse before the footman returned with the wine.

Outside, his horse was of course munching on a perfectly trimmed bush in the shape of a heart. He jumped off the stairs and ran over, grabbing the bit just as she bit into a leaf, which made a whole branch tear in the process.

The footman appeared at the front door looking startled, wine bottle and glass in hand. "My sincere apologies. Did I forget to send someone for your horse? I'm mortified. This usually doesn't happen," he said.

Nikolaos breathed a sigh of relief; at least he wasn't blaming him then. "No need to apologize. But I'm afraid my long-maned friend here enjoyed your bushes."

"It'll grow back. It grows like weeds," the footman said with a smile, looking quite charming suddenly.

Nikolaos drew another sigh of relief.

"Kindly wait here," the footman said, then hurried back inside. Only a moment later, he returned sweaty and out of breath, followed by a man who, with wig askew, looked as though he had been roused out of bed.

The man rushed out and took the reins from Nikolaos. "My apologies, Lord Nordvatten. I'll make sure your girl is comfortable."

"I'm not a lord, I thank you though, just the same."

The man gave him an odd look but didn't comment.

***

The following day, Nikolaos woke to the sound of boots and shoes across bare floors, doors slamming, and wagon wheels outside. He reached for his new watch, feeling a tingle of pleasure as his fingertips reached the cool surface. It was a remarkable piece of craftsmanship. Smooth and thin, it was only a quarter as thick as his old watch. It had a mother-of-pearl cover with a tiny painting of a black horse standing under a leafless oak, a single red leaf on the ground. And inside, beneath both an hour hand and a minute hand, was the same tree now lush and green. Nikolaos had never seen anything so beautiful. He had bought the watch as they left Jönköping, insisting they stop at the shop on their way out, even though Stina and Rå had been nervous at the delay. It had sure been worth it. Opening it now, he looked at the hands; it was exactly eleven minutes after eight in the morning. Time to rise.

Putting his feet on the floor, he met his reflection in the mirror on the dressing table next to the bed. His skin was smooth and plump, his hair shiny and long, albeit flat from having worn his wig yesterday. There was no denying it anymore. He looked younger than his wife, much younger. They would have to devise a plan, or it would only be a matter of time before people got suspicious. He didn't want to think about what they should say to Elsebet and Hindrich.

A loud bang followed by laughter brought his thoughts to a stop, and he walked over to the window and looked outside. Guests were arriving by carriage. Others were walking on the lawn, taking in the view of the sea. He got dressed and tied his hair, then put his wig on and went downstairs.

The same footman from last night greeted him with a smile.

"I hope you had a pleasant night. You're welcome to go sit in the garden. Doctor Döbelius is already seated and most eager to meet you. There are refreshments." He held the front door open, motioning leftward.

"I did, and I'll be delighted," Nikolaos said. From the footman's expression, he gathered the doctor was an important guest. He walked across the lawn and found the doctor sitting at a table under an apple tree. Leaning back in his seat, his eyes were closed, and a half-finished glass of ale was leaning on his belly, moving up and down with the rising and falling of his breathing.

Nikolaos sat down as quietly as he could. The doctor didn't stir. He wore a powdered wig with thick, neat curls barely reaching below his shoulders. The footman also wore a shorter wig. Nikolaos hoped his own long wig wasn't going out of fashion already.

The table was laid out with a spread of cakes, breads, and fresh fruits, complemented by a tankard of ale and delicate crystal glasses. Reaching forward to pour some for himself, a creak from his chair woke the doctor.

"I must have fallen asleep," he said with a sheepish yawn.

"You looked comfortable. Pray forgive me for waking you."

"No harm done." He chuckled. "You must be the musician, Nikolaos Nordvatten? A most unusual name by the way. Northern water. It's beautiful."

"I thank you." Nikolaos was beginning to regret his spontaneous name change. It probably sounded too noble. He should have gone with his usual lie and called himself Jensson. But it was too late now.

"Water is something that interests me by the way."

"Really?" Nikolaos stiffened.

"Yes, as a doctor, I've come to understand that there are many benefits to drinking water. Especially if it comes from natural springs. It's something I'm investigating. I've seen a few cases where people have drunk a lot of water to their great benefit."

"Oh, for drinking! Interesting," Nikolaos said, relieved. "But shouldn't we be careful about that in case the water is spoiled?"

"Yes, yes. But haven't you had water when you've been very thirsty, from a well or even a clear brook? Did you have any ill effects those times?"

"Of course, and no, I was fine." Abluna had become violently ill once after visiting someone who had served them well water instead of ale. It had smelled off, but they still drank it. Naturally, it hadn't affected him.

"There you see! You look strong and healthy. I notice you have strong teeth," Doctor Döbelius said with satisfaction, almost as if he knew what Nikolaos had been thinking. Then he changed the subject. "I know Fleisher from my time in Germany. I was born there and studied medicine in Rostock, you see."

"Mistress Esmeralda mentioned that her husband is German," Nikolaos said, realizing just then that she never told him what his name was.

"That's right, he is. As you can see," Doctor Döbelius splayed his arm out, indicating the stately home behind them, "he's doing very well for himself here. He is a merchant specializing in wax candles."

"Ah, I did notice an abundance of them last night. That explains it," he said, nodding.

"Yes, they're fond of their candles, they get buyers that way too. No one fails to notice. Fleisher deals in tobacco and salt as well, which reminds me that I'd like a pipe after a good morning snooze. I'm going inside to light this," he said, rising to his feet while pulling a pipe out of his pocket. "I wish you a good day. I'm looking forward to your performance tonight."

"Good day," Nikolaos said, staring after him. It seemed brusque to leave like that. He hoped he hadn't offended him with his comment about water being spoilt. And what were the odds that he would meet a doctor interested in water, of all things?

***

A few hours later, after a lavish meal on the terrasse overlooking the lawn and the sea beyond, Mistress Esmeralda and her husband approached Nikolaos. She wore a light green dress with as deep a décolletage as the other day but gave Nikolaos a polite smile without a hint of flirtation.

Nikolaos bowed, hiding a chuckle as he bent down. What a difference. Maybe he should ask her what the matter was, just to see how she would react. "A pleasure to see you again," he said when he straightened, meeting her eyes. He almost winked but decided against it at the last moment. "And a pleasure to finally meet you, Merchant Fleisher."

Merchant Fleisher smiled broadly, appearing pleased to see him. "I've heard much about you, Nikolaos Nordvatten. It means a lot to us to have a royal musician perform here. An honor, sir, an honor," he said in a thick German accent.

"The honor is mine."

"It's indeed nice to see you again, Nikolaos," Mistress Esmeralda said evenly, standing straight and tall. Then she pointed toward a fountain on the lawn. "We'd like you to perform there, Nikolaos."

He froze, pushing down a wave of panic. Thick plumes of water were shooting straight up, creating a fine spray over horsehead-shaped bushes surrounding the fountain. "There? That won't be suitable unfortunately. The spray could destroy my instrument." He had purposely sat with his back toward the lawn so as not to get distracted by it. Playing there was out of the question.

"Ah, I understand your concern," Merchant Fleisher said. "But don't worry, come, let's go down and take a gander. I guarantee it won't get wet." He took Nikolaos by the arm and led him down a set of stone steps leading directly to the lawn. Mistress Esmeralda followed close behind.

Dread sat like a pit in Nikolaos' stomach as they neared the fountain. The sound of the water created aquamarine waves in the air, which made it seem as though the horse heads were moving. He could already feel his blood react.

"You'll see, Nikolaos, the spray won't hit your violin. It's designed that way. The fountain is created to mist the bushes, not the grass," Mistress Esmeralda said, looking immensely proud. She touched his arm, then let go as if remembering how close her husband was.

Nikolaos pretended to consider. Servants were coming from all directions, placing rows of chairs in front of it. He swallowed, then took a deep breath. "It's a lovely place and a beautiful fountain, but I'm not comfortable playing here. I have a very special violin with me, and I cannot risk it even being close to moisture. Pray forgive me."

Mistress Esmeralda exchanged a look with her husband who shook his head. "I'm afraid we can't agree to that. It's how my wife wants it."

"I understand, but surely you could have me sit with a view of the sea instead? I think it would be lovely. People can listen and watch the waves below the cliffs."

Merchant Fleisher frowned, exchanging another look with Mistress Esmeralda, then said, "No, you'll play where arranged."

Nikolaos looked at him, not sure how to respond. Not even at Three Crowns had anyone spoken to him like that, ordering him to do things.

"You see, we've already described this in our invitations. It's too late to change now. People would be disappointed," Mistress Esmeralda said. She smiled with some of the same warmth she had at the inn. Then they both turned their backs on him and walked away. Just before they were out of earshot, Mistress Esmeralda turned around. "You surely see how the movement of the cascading water would add to the effect of your beautiful music."

That it would. May God help him.

***

There were about fifty people seated on the chairs, dressed in fine silks and adorned with wigs of various colors and lengths. The women were more bejeweled here than in Stockholm.

Doing his best to ignore the sound of the water and its movement, which was faintly visible out of the corner of his eye, Nikolaos nodded toward Mistress Esmeralda's sister and husband in the first row. "I thank you for this honor and congratulate you on your son."

They both smiled and inclined their heads. The mother held a tiny porcelain doll on her lap, wrapped in a silver embroidered blanket. Apparently, it represented the baby who was safe at home with his wet nurse. It was very odd. Why would you hold a birth celebration without the guest of honor?

"I'm playing a new instrument today," Nikolaos continued. "A magnificent violin. It came all the way from Cremona, made by a craftsman named Antonio Stradivari." Nikolaos looked straight at Merchant Fleisher, who avoided his gaze. "It was gifted to me after I comforted His Highness King Karl XI during his last days. I'm saddened to tell you that His Highness lost his life before my new instrument had finished its long journey to Stockholm." Nikolaos paused, looking at the audience with what he hoped was an appropriately somber look. He was too irritated by Merchant Fleisher for it to feel genuine. "It's worth noting that this beautiful instrument, which traveled so far to reach me, could have succumbed in Stockholm." He lifted the Stradivarius high in the air, turning it this way and that. "You see, Lord Oxensköld had invited me to his home to gift me with it on the very day…" He paused, deciding to wait with the reveal and hoping Merchant Fleisher was impressed a lord had given it to him. "I was on my way back with a royal courtier when we smelled smoke. As we turned a corner, we saw it with our own eyes, Three Crowns was burning."

"Aww!!" Mistress Esmeralda cried and slumped toward her husband who grabbed her fan and waved it in front of her face.

A man beside Doctor Döbelius blew his nose, and a woman in the back row burst into tears. Nikolaos had a fleeting thought that the proximity of the fountain had already started to entrance people, but he dismissed it.

"It was awful. I've never seen anything like it, but I won't speak of it now," Nikolaos said. "I was safe, my wife got out, and this," he held up the violin again, "is here."

He looked at the audience and saw faces bright with anticipation. If he pulled his chair closer to them, the fountain would be at a safer distance. Surely Merchant Fleisher wouldn't protest in front of everyone, would he? Hesitating, legs twitching as they responded to his internal debate, he ignored the thought and remained where he was, putting his bow to the strings. The music reacted to the water immediately. Blue, red, orange, and purple poured from his strings, bending backward to catch the spray. It floated around him, filling him with color. He closed his eyes to stay in control. He should have moved the chair forward.

After a time, he stilled his bow and opened his eyes halfway. It took time for the colors to dissipate, and he waited until they were completely gone before daring to open them all the way. When he finally looked at the audience, a few appeared moved to tears, but everyone seemed fully aware of their surroundings, sitting calmly on their chairs. With a breath of relief, he started again, daring now to keep his eyes open a bit.

The Stradivarius danced in his hands as if it were alive, colors bounced off the strings, and the evening sun made the spray glow as if by its own light. He loved this instrument! What an incredible piece of art. His fiddle was like a child's toy compared to it. The thought made him laugh, and he rose to his feet. The audience laughed and stood as well. He took no notice.

It was hours later when he stopped. By then it was almost dark, and the chairs lay strewn across the lawn among wigs, fans, and shoes. His audience, sweaty and unkempt from hours of dancing, dropped to the ground unconscious. Nikolaos put the Stradivarius on his lap, feeling spent but incomplete. He needed more.

Without thinking further, he got to his feet and strode across the grass, leaving everyone where they lay. At the allée in front of the estate, he broke into a run, then veered off to the right, following the scent of flowing water somewhere in the woods, sniffing the air like a hound on the scent of prey. Somewhere in the back of his mind, he felt ashamed, aware of how ridiculous he must look. Then he caught a flicker of water in the pale evening light, a brook flowing between thick trunks and lush tall grass. He cried with relief.

Tearing off his clothes and his wig, aware despite his stupor, that they needed to be dry when he returned, he lay down in the shallow water. The effect was immediate, stilling his pounding heart, and releasing the sluggish blood which had tried to shift to water with only the fountain for help. Feeling calmer already, he sat up and reached for his violin, deciding to play just a couple of songs before he headed back to deal with what had happened.

He chose one he had written when he first started to play in water. It was a beautiful song with soaring notes he loved, but which others would find old-fashioned now. He was almost finished playing it when he perceived two human forms wading toward him. A man and a woman walking hand in hand, already much too close. He hadn't heard them. He stopped playing and put the violin on dry ground. And then they were there beside him, sitting in the water.

Nikolaos hesitated for an eyeblink, then with one quick move, he grabbed the man by the neck and kissed him, pulling the woman close at the same time. Her breasts were pushing into his side while the man wrapped his arms around him, unquestioningly willing.

The woman clung to him and enthralled with his power as she was, she kissed his ears and touched him with her hands. Her legs embraced his and her warm moisture felt hot, almost burning his water-cooled skin. He got them down to the bottom of the brook, kissing and holding them both. When he pulled himself out of their embraces, they remained, legs and arms intertwined, hair floating freely in the water, mixing with grasses and floating twigs. Faces just at the surface.

It was darker now, and a pale moon had risen in the east and was gleaming between the dark trees. He stood, strong and filled with power. Sated. Devastated.

Chapter 62

Someone had lit torches and lanterns on the lawn. The guests walked around aimlessly, stepping over people on the ground. It was still and windless, the only sound the shrill chirping of grasshoppers and the thumping of chairs righted and put back on the soft grass.

A man sat up, yawning wide while reaching for his wig, which lay tossed on the grass. He replaced it on his head and looked straight at Nikolaos with a confused frown.

There was no sense in hiding. The summer night wasn't dark enough for him to go unnoticed and his violin made it obvious. Nikolaos took a deep breath and walked toward the man, feigning nonchalance.

"What happened? Did you see it?" the man asked, giving Nikolaos a bewildered look while brushing his breeches free of grass.

"See what?"

"I heard someone say that it was a comet, but I'm not entirely sure I heard right. I just woke up."

"No, I didn't see anything," Nikolaos said.

"Where were you?"

"I took a piss."

"Oh, and you didn't see anything odd?" The man followed Nikolaos, avoiding a chair turned on its side.

"No, I didn't," Nikolaos said again, hoping he sounded normal.

"My memory fails me. I didn't realize that I had drunk that much at the table, did you notice if I seemed inebriated?" the man asked, rolling his shoulders in a stretch.

"No. But I'm pleased that you liked my music. I'm a bit confused about this," Nikolaos said, gesturing at the lawn. It seemed the best strategy to act as surprised as everyone else. "Where are the Fleishers?"

"They're over there," a woman with a dress hoisted halfway up her shins, interjected, pointing to the gazebo where several people huddled together.

Nikolaos left them and walked off in their direction. Guilt and anxiety sat like a weight on his chest. He pushed it down, heading steadily forward.

Mistress Esmeralda greeted him with her hands outstretched. "Nikolaos Nordvatten, that was marvelous, so incredibly beautiful. And the dancing! When you played those tunes, I couldn't stop, the music pulled me with it. You have such a talent. Did you see the comet? Is that why you left? I know they're scary."

"To tell you the truth, I didn't. I took a break to, well…" He pretended to look as though he didn't want to admit it to a woman, then added, "I had to relieve myself, and when I came back several people were on the ground."

Mistress Esmeralda nodded, a serious expression on her face. "It was the comet. Comets have that effect, you see. Coming in from the heavens with such speed, it can cause a rumble and a shaking so strong people fall down." Her gaze was earnest in the torchlight.

"I see, I didn't know that." This was some excuse. How convenient.

"Yes, they're dangerous, always bring ill too. I wouldn't be surprised if the King's death and Three Crowns fire had to do with it." She shook her head for emphasis, putting her hands to her heart.

"The fire and the King's passing? That was a long time ago now. I don't think a comet that hasn't arrived yet can cause something like that."

Mistress Esmeralda shivered and drew her shawl tighter around her shoulders. "But isn't it odd though that this happens only a few months afterward? Don't you think it's an omen?"

"I sure hope not." He frowned.

"We'll sort out what happened. Nikolaos, your music is incredible. I didn't mean to imply that the comet brought ill to your performance. Everyone seems to be fine." She touched his arm, and it seemed as though she would do something flirtatious like she had at the inn, but then her expression changed. "Let me call on my husband a moment. We must pay you for your services." She turned to the gazebo where Merchant Fleisher stood leaning on its doorsill, speaking with Doctor Döbelius.

When he noticed Nikolaos, Merchant Fleisher put his hand in his pocket, pulling out a leather purse and headed toward them. He looked somber. "I thank you for making our celebration something to remember," he said when he reached Nikolaos. "I apologize for whatever it was that happened. I can assure you that no one meant any disrespect to your performance, falling asleep in this way. We're speaking with Doctor Döbelius to see if he thinks it's something that we may have eaten or if the comet caused it all."

Disrespected, now that was a twist he hadn't expected. Nikolaos flicked an eye at the doctor, nodding, but he didn't return the greeting, just gave him a piercing look. Turning back to Merchant Fleisher, Nikolaos said, "I thank you kindly for your generosity. But there's no need to apologize. I didn't notice anything until I came back after my break." He bowed as Merchant Fleisher put the purse in his hands. It was very heavy. Mistress Esmeralda hadn't exaggerated when she said he would be compensated nicely.

Merchant Fleisher stared at him. "I'm surprised you didn't see it. Where were you? Why did you take a break?"

Nikolaos glanced around to see if Mistress Esmeralda was still by his side, but she had left and was standing in the gazebo. "I took a piss."

"Oh!" His eyes lit up with understanding. "I see. Yes of course, of course."

Nikolaos smiled apologetically, and they exchanged a few more words, then he excused himself. Crossing the lawn, he ignored guests wanting to speak with him by pretending not to see them and went straight to his room.

As soon as he closed the door, he sank to his knees on the floor and put his head in his hands, only to clumsily get back to his feet when he saw that someone had placed a jug of wine and a glass on the table. With shaking hands, he drank straight from the jug. There was a pewter of liquor, too, and a big bouquet of flowers with a card that read, 'Thank you.' It was Mistress Esmeralda's handwriting. It felt like mockery. He was a murderer. Turning away, he placed the wine back on the table and filled the wine glass with the liquor. Bringing the pewter and glass with him, he entered the bedroom, drinking as he walked. It burned his throat. Somewhere in the back of his mind, behind the anguish and regret, he realized that he ought to leave. Maybe even go out and look for their bodies and bury them in the woods. But just thinking about it made him nauseous with guilt and horror. He was a murderer. The Devil's spawn, just like everyone said.

Nikolaos kept drinking, refilling his glass again and again, until he fell into a fitful sleep full of lust and death and music. And of two people laying on their backs with their faces just below the surface of the brook.

***

When he woke up, he was still nauseous and frantic with regret and guilt. Having drunk so much didn't help either, even though he wasn't usually very affected by drinking. It felt like it was late, but he hadn't wound his watch and couldn't tell what time it was. Either way, it was high time to leave. Grabbing his clothes and stuffing them in his satchel, he noticed that the pewter was empty. He had drunk the whole thing. A human man would never survive drinking so much alcohol and wine all at once. He froze, wondering if he should lay it on its side as though he had spilled it, then decided against it. The maids would probably just assume he had had guests in his room.

Relaxing somewhat, he looked over at the bureau only to inhale sharply again. The Stradivarius wasn't there. The room seemed to sway. What if he had left it by the brook? He blinked, grabbing hold of the wall to steady himself, heart pounding. Could he really have been so stupid? It was evidence.

With one quick motion, he slung his satchel over his shoulder, praying he could get out unseen to go retrieve it. He swallowed a new wave of nausea at the thought of having to go back and see the death he had caused and ran toward the door. Then he stopped in his tracks. The Stradivarius was lying on the floor where he had sunk to his knees last night.

***

When he made his way downstairs, Mistress Esmeralda was standing on the stairs, right below the first landing. She was pale as a ghost. It was obvious that she had been crying.

"Mistress Esmeralda, are you not well?" He hid a sigh of relief that the footman wasn't at his post by the door so he would have a quick way out if needed.

"No," she said, sniveling, "I'm not. Something terrible has happened. We were expecting a cleaning woman and her husband from the village last night to help us clean up after the celebration, but early this morning, her father came here, worried. They didn't make it home. Their children had been left alone the whole night, with no parents there when they awoke. The little ones had toddled over to their grandfather all by themselves. Then he came here to see if the parents had stayed the night, only to learn that they never arrived." She drew a deep shuddering breath. "They found them by the brook in the woods right here just across our lane. Näck... terrified."

He swallowed hard. Mistress Esmeralda's words lost comprehension as he tried to keep his face neutral. They knew. They found the bodies. He needed to get out, now. Thank God he hadn't left the violin behind.

"We don't know what happened, but they're both cold and frightened. My husband finally got them to admit they had come here at first, but they left again, drawn away by Näcken. They're lucky to be alive."

"They're alive?" Nikolaos staggered from relief, blindly reaching for the banister behind him without finding it.

Mistress Esmeralda pulled out a handkerchief from somewhere among her skirts and handed it to him. "Here, wipe

479

your face and sit down on the stairs for a moment. It's a shock, I know. Yes, they *are* alive." She nodded somberly. "We have the Lord to thank for it. Näcken usually drowns his victims, but they somehow survived." She took several steps down to stand on the floor below the stairs. "They mentioned they saw you leaving with your violin and that they were curious and tried to follow, but you disappeared so fast, and then they heard…" She stopped abruptly. Then her eyes widened, and she stared at him with shock and understanding.

Nikolaos opened his mouth to try to say something, but just then, the front door opened, and Merchant Fleisher and Doctor Döbelius walked in. Both had grim looks on their faces.

Doctor Döbelius was speaking in a low voice. "There's nothing to be done for them. They're confused and scared. They said that he, that Näcken, took advantage of them in ways… well, it's not for a woman's ears." He stopped talking with a cautionary glance at Mistress Esmeralda and waited until Merchant Fleisher was by her side before he continued. "What's unusual is that they were both victims. I didn't know that he did that. With a man."

"How horrific," Nikolaos said, trying to keep his voice steady. It was only a matter of time before Mistress Esmeralda said something. He was surprised she hadn't already, but she stood silent and numb by her husband's side. "I feel awful to leave now in light of this, but I have another engagement and must make haste." Nikolaos bowed to Mistress Esmeralda, then quickly made his way down the last flight of stairs, feeling her eyes on him as he bowed to Merchant Fleisher and Doctor Döbelius, pushed himself past them, and walked out the door.

As soon as he had closed it, he ran, speeding around the castle to the stable behind it, expecting the merchant and the doctor to chase after him with every breath, but didn't hear or see them.

The groom greeted him politely, and by the look on his face, it was clear that he knew what happened last night. He offered to get his horse for him, but Nikolaos shook his head and went into the stall on his own, putting the bridle and saddle on mechanically, feeling out of place and not very human. And his boots and stockings felt wet.

Chapter 63

Rå stayed with Stina for a couple of days when Nikolaos left to play at the celebration he had been invited to. Stina was a strong woman, but she was very distraught by the hanging, and Nikolaos didn't want to leave her alone. Not that she was truly alone. Their children were there, but still. It was good to stay so they could talk about it. Humans were terrified of death, and women especially had a need to process things by talking. Rå understood, but she was beginning to feel restless. And she wanted to be alone to process her own grief. She hadn't told Stina and Nikolaos how close she and Jon had been. It had been too painful.

"Stina," Rå said, gesturing at the woods behind the farm, visible from where they were sitting on the outside benches. "I'm going to leave now." She kept her eyes on the trees. They were calling to her.

Stina whipped her head around to look at her. "Oh, I had thought you'd wait until Nikolaos came back. I wanted to make a special dinner for us."

Rå nodded. "I know Stina. But I need to be alone, sit with my trees." She hesitated, then decided to just tell her. "I regret not going directly to Jönköping. I should've tried to follow those awful men who arrested him. I had thought Nikolaos could help, but now I'm certain it was the wrong decision and a devastating waste of time. Had I only been there early enough, maybe I could somehow have persuaded them to release him."

Stina shivered visibly and pulled her shawl tighter around herself. "No, it wouldn't have made any difference. You saw what they had done to him. It's not something they'd do if they weren't so convinced he was guilty. There was nothing you could've done." A single tear fell down her cheek. She didn't wipe it off.

"Maybe you're right. Nikolaos said the same thing," Rå said, but wondered if she could have visited the prison and opened her back, gotten one of the guards to give her the key.

"How come you need to move? Can't someone build a new house for you?" Stina asked, interrupting her thoughts and

reminding Rå that she had told them why she had visited Jon that
day.

"Someone could, surely. But I need to live alone with the
trees and wildlife keeping me company instead of people." She
smiled to soften what she said. Stina looked a little taken aback and
surprised. She probably thought she needed a man near her all the
time. "The village close to where I live, or lived rather, was
becoming too large. While I loved having Jon near, the village was
crowding me."

"I see, it's the same here. When Nikolaos and I married,
there were only a few farms down there." She pointed behind her.
"Now we have a church and shops, even one for pastries. Nikolaos
says he has never seen a village grow as fast."

Rå stood up, suddenly not able to take Stina's chattiness
anymore. "I thank you for your hospitality and kindness, Stina. Pray
say goodbye to Nikolaos for me and to Hindrich and Elsebet." She
gave a slight curtsy. Stina's eyes widened, but before she could
protest, Rå turned from her and walked away.

***

Three days later, Rå pulled her feet from the roots of a
beech tree, feeling much better. Another few days after that, she
was walking through an old forest, carrying everything she owned
on her back. It was raining, just a soft warm sprinkling, enough to fill
the air with a delicious musky scent of earth and wet leaves. Jon
was gone, hurting no more. He wasn't thinking of her, so why
should she think of him? It was harsh perhaps, but the truth.

It was harder not to think about Nikolaos and his family. A
part of her was envious of the closeness he had with them, while
another part felt restless and frustrated just by the thought of living
in constant proximity with humans. The way they were always
talking, seemingly oblivious to the world around them, got to her. It
was strange that Nikolaos could stand it. Yet, the love in that family
was so sweet to see, and she couldn't help but feel a little lonely.

Continuing forward, she waded across a stream and

climbed up the bank on the other side. It was steep, and she stopped at the crest to catch her breath, scanning the trees ahead. Northward, the trees were less dense, and there was a deer trail leading toward a stone ruin. From where she stood, the stonework looked mostly intact, forming a foundation for what must have been a large home at one time. The hearth looked intact as well, but the chimney was gone, and bushes and several thick tall trees were growing where the floor used to be. About ten paces from the foundation was a round stone hut with only the door missing. It had probably been used for food storage. Rå smiled and hurried toward it, opening her back as she walked, sensing nothing that disturbed the peace. She had had a feeling she would find something, crossing that stream. The deer trail had probably been part of a road back when people lived in this house. She went straight to the stone hut and peeked inside, then entered. It was large enough to stand and stretch her arms wide in all directions. She nodded with satisfaction. It was a fine place to live, and if she found a man who could build another hut right next to it, it would make a fine adjacent room. He could clear the bushes from within the walls of the old foundation, and then she could cook in the hearth. As much as she had wanted to be alone, some lovemaking and help with building was just what she needed.

Pleased with herself, she retrieved her bedroll and her blanket and placed them along the wall on the right side in the little hut, then lay down and went to sleep.

Rå was awakened by a huffing sound outside, followed by what sounded like someone pulling something heavy across the ground. Maybe a group of hunters had set up camp. If they had, Freya had been quick sending her builders. Rå remained under her blanket to decipher how many of them there were. But no voices came, just more huffing and a sound as if someone dumped a sack of grain on the ground, then a slurping sound. What were they doing out there? As silently as she could, she sat up, pushed the blanket aside, and got to her feet. Staying in the shade the sun didn't reach through the opening, she moved her head just enough to see around the corner, then found herself face to face with an enormous black cow. She started, not daring to move.

The cow didn't react, its large eyes unblinking. It remained put, blocking the door. Then it lifted its head and licked her face with a thick wet tongue.

"Did Freya send you to me instead?" Rå asked it with a chuckle and gently shoved the head aside and stepped outside.

Another cow and a small calf were out there, staring at her in the same unblinking way as the first one. The calf was lying down, which probably explained the sound Rå thought was a sack of grain dumped on the ground. They too, were black like a winter's night.

Scratching the head of the one that had licked her, Rå looked around for their herding girl, but saw no one. What were they doing there by themselves? Each cow looked strong and healthy, and she noticed now that the one who had greeted her with a lick had a full udder and must be the mother of the calf.

Rå walked off to the side so she wouldn't scare them, then shouted, "I have your cows here. Come get them, they're up heeere!" Her voice echoed across the land, but there was no answer. No one came running, and there was no sound of kulning, the herding call women used to call their animals. Maybe the girl had been frightened by something and run off without making sure she had all her cows with her. But unless she had a very large herd, two of them and a calf was a lot to lose, and Rå didn't like it. A while ago, she couldn't remember how long, there had been a Royal Decree that only girls, never boys, should herd. The King and the pastors claimed boys were much more likely to copulate with their animals than girls were, and were afraid they would sire monstrous offspring. Supposedly, it was worse with boys who never went to church. As usual, people feared the most foolish things. It was much more likely for a young girl to get raped in the woods than that boys would relieve themselves with a cow or goat. Both scenarios were horrifying, but she had never seen a cow give birth to some kind of human-looking calf. Girls who had been raped by horrid men, she had come upon though. More than once. She hoped whoever the wayward cows belonged to was safe.

The sounds were different from what she was used to in this forest. Birds were chirping much louder and from several directions, mixing with a deafening trilling sound from some kind of insect. If there were other birds and insects, there would be plants and trees she wasn't familiar with, or at least flora she hadn't seen for a long time. Pulling a couple of baskets from her satchels she had yet to unpack, Rå went outside. It was early morning still. The sun was just starting to rise in the east, and it was hazy. The cows eyed her lazily where she stood in the little doorway but made no move to get up. She passed them, half expecting them to come with her, but they stayed put.

The path she had followed when she found the place continued on the other side of the stone ruin, going down a little slope. Looking at the terrain more observantly now, it became clear that she was in a radically different forest than where her treehouse was. For some reason, she hadn't paid enough attention before. There was more underbrush between the trunks here, thickets with bushes sprouting tiny red berries interspersed with young pine trees. Dense and impenetrable. Rå plucked one of the little berries and put it in her mouth, chewing carefully. First there was tartness, then a sharp, bitter flavor, and somehow earthy as well, as if it were a mushroom. She picked a small handful and placed them in her basket. There was a slight trace of poison numbing the tip of her tongue, indicating that it might be good for toothaches and mouth sores. Poisonous berries could cure ills if used correctly.

She kept exploring, making her way through the thicket. Animals had created passable paths that led to open fields and copses with lush fresh grass. Rabbits ran back and forth, and she even saw a moose with two calves grazing. There was no scent from human fire or agriculture. She exhaled and opened her back fully, immediately feeling the trees reaching for her. Home.

***

The cows stayed with Rå, making themselves comfortable and eating the soft grass and bushes around the foundation's walls. They were friendly and a little curious but never got in her way. It was nice to have them there.

Two moons later, she was sitting on the ground in front of her stone hut, sorting through her now sizable collection of berries and herbs, when a man came strolling up the slope. She jumped, dropping her wood sorrel. He was walking confidently, broad shoulders swaying. His hair was thick and light brown and kept out of his eyes with a leather string, just the way she liked it. Perfection.

She stood up, but he didn't notice and kept walking. That was disappointing. She hesitated, wondering if she should run after him, then decided not to. If Freya wanted her to have him, he would come this way again on his way back from wherever he was going.

Rå kept her back open, and when the sun was getting low in the sky, she felt him approach again. Her cows had come back too, and were standing right in his path. All three turned in his direction as if they knew he was on his way. It was a good sign. There was no way he would miss them.

Moments later he came walking much in the same way as before, but from the opposite direction and with five dead rabbits slung over his shoulder. He stopped in his tracks when he saw her. "Evening," he said, tilting his head with concern, then glancing at the sun. "You're still herding them this late?" he asked, gesturing toward her cows.

"I'm not herding them. They found me a few moons ago and have stayed put since." She went closer to him. "You haven't heard if someone lost their cows or if a herding-maid has come to an accident, have you?"

"No." His look of concern deepened. "I haven't."

Rå drew a sigh of relief. "That's good. They're fine with me, but I've worried a bit, wondering what happened."

He nodded, green eyes a bit glazed over, responding to her

open back.

She moved closer again. "Will you come sit with me a while? I've moved in here, but as you can see it's just an old stone ruin and, I'm in need of someone who could help me clear some trees and make this place livable."

He was younger than she first thought, she noticed. Old enough to be married and have a family, but not much more. He didn't have the thinner hair or creases around the eyes that came with wisdom for humans. If he had a new pretty wife, Rå would have to keep her back wide open to get him to stay, or the wife would have too strong a pull on him.

He grinned. "Gladly, I'll sit with you. Those trees there," he pointed, "they're not a problem. I'd just have to go home and get some tools first."

Rå smiled at him, and his grin broadened. He was probably not married then, but her back was pulsing, making him forget everything else. She loved this, the moment when the men were hers, but she hadn't yet touched them. He took a hesitant step toward her, eyes searching her face and body. She stepped even closer then kissed him gently on the mouth. "Hang your rabbits in a tree and come sit with me. You can get your tools later." She stepped back, walking over to her firepit.

"Are you the Forest Rå? I didn't know you were this beautiful." His hot breath reached her cheek as he fell in beside her.

She laughed, surprised. It had been hundreds of years since someone had come straight out and asked her. "Yes."

"I thought you were. It's my honor to make your acquaintance. Many speak of you, but very few are as lucky as I am now," he said, a warm glint in his eyes.

Rå met his gaze, nodding. This sure was a different encounter than what she was used to. "What are they saying?" she asked and sat down, getting into a cross-legged position.

"That you care for our trees and the forest, that it would grow out of control and be impenetrable if it wasn't for you."

Rå smiled. "Most are unaware of this and don't have such nice things to say."

"I know. It's a real shame. But it's something my uncles speak of a lot." He sat down opposite her on the other side of the firepit. "We should never take things for granted, but always be grateful and honor those who help us."

"I thank you," she said, touched by his words.

"How come you want to live here? There are only ruins left."

"Well, it suits me. I'm close to the soil and the trees this way, but like I mentioned, I could sure need your help to expand a bit." Men always had the same reaction, no matter where she lived. Though, come to think of it, she had never lived in a regular house. "Can you help me? And what's your name?"

"Måns. My name is Måns. I'll try. It shouldn't be too hard. Have you any tools for it?"

Rå shook her head, annoyed with herself. It hadn't crossed her mind to bring the ones Rasmus had left her. They were still in the broken wooden box underneath her dilapidated treehouse. She opened her back a bit more. "Could you go get some? Do you live near here?" she asked, both dreading and hoping he did. She had craved privacy but had also asked Freya for a man.

"Yes, of course," he said and got to his feet, his eagerness to help enhanced by her open back. "It's not that close, but yes, I can come back. I'll be here again tomorrow."

She tried her most charming smile, holding out her hand so he could pull her up to stand. Then she grabbed his hips and started kissing him. He smelled delicious, musky with a faint scent of something flowery from soap. She wanted to take him now, but it was better to wait so he had something to look forward to, lest he change his mind. "Go get your tools, Måns," she said and stepped away from him.

"Now?" he asked hoarsely, trying to grab her hand.

"Yes, go now."

Måns looked disappointed, and she thought he was going to protest, but then he nodded. "I'll be back with my tools." An eyeblink later, he set off in a run, heading in the direction he had first come from.

***

Måns came back the next evening, arriving on horseback just as she was heading inside after taking a little milk from the calf's mother. He looked nervous and shy without the effects of her power.

"Måns, I thank you. Pray seat yourself and eat some stew. Then we'll sleep. You can start building tomorrow." She went up to his horse and waited for him to dismount, then she kissed him on the cheek.

"I thank you too, but I ate," he said, tying his horse to a tree.

"How about some fresh milk?" She lifted the mug she had used as a milk pail.

He shook his head again, shifting from foot to foot.

Rå tried not to smile at his shyness. "Just put the tools over there." She pointed to the corner of the foundation where she had stacked some of her own things, watching him put his things away, and drinking the milk herself. In spite of his current shyness, there was a confidence about him when he moved, the same as when she first saw him yesterday. He was not very tall but didn't try to make himself look taller by stretching his head upward and back like shorter men often did. He was wearing a different shirt today, and she could see his arm muscles flexing when he bent to put the tools down. She finished her milk.

"There, where would you like me to sleep, Forest Rå?" he asked, blushing when he saw her lick the milk off her lower lip.

She couldn't help but grin at that, at the same time feeling warmth in her heart, hearing him speak her real name. "Come in with me. We'll share a bed tonight." She grabbed both his hands, deciding not to wait until he had built anything, sensing he would do what she asked anyway.

When she was satisfied with him, she watched his chest rise and fall with each breath as he slept. It was hairless and tanned by hours of work in the sun.

***

Måns set to work, building what was more like a tent made of pine trees than a hut. He wasn't very skilled. The thin pine trees he had cut to make logs out of were unevenly spaced and of different sizes, and unless he managed to tighten the holes, it would surely rain in. Rå chastised herself for asking the first man she came across. But it was what it was, and it would do for now. She could always move if she didn't like it.

"Where are you from, Måns," she asked, watching him place a skinny branch next to a thick one, leaning them against the horizontal beam at the top of the structure. It looked more like a roof than the little hut she had been envisioning. She would be living inside a roof without a home beneath it. Well, why not?

"I'm from Kjugekull, or Kjuge rather, it's right near the hill," he said as if she would know which hill he was talking about. He added another equally skinny branch to the beam.

"I've never heard of it. Where is it?"

He stopped what he was doing to throw her a look of genuine surprise. "You have never? You can see it from here, look!" He pointed toward the meadows in the east, and she spotted a small hill in the distance. She would never have noticed it if he hadn't pointed it out. "The King has a big castle there that the army uses now. It used to be Rutger von Ascheberg's residence back in the day. My grandparents spoke of him all the time. They said he was nice to the farmers even though he was sent by the King to make sure they did everything in the proper Swedish way after Sweden took these parts from Denmark." He frowned, then shrugged. "My grandparents were still Danish in their hearts, but they learned to respect him nonetheless. The castle used to be a monastery before the church changed," he added, sounding proud of his knowledge.

"I see," Rå said. People were impressed by names, often telling her about folk she knew nothing about. "Is it a friendly sort of place?"

"I'd say so. People are kind and helpful to their neighbors if one should need anything." Måns looked as though he wanted to say more but turned back to his work, adding more branches to her tentlike dwelling, and didn't elaborate.

When it was finished, Rå had to admit that it was nicer than she had expected. The triangular structure was dark green, covered with thick moss, which would be enough to keep the rain out, after all. It was uneven in places and lopsided but sturdy and functional. There was a door in front she could open and close, albeit not very windtight, a firepit, and a smoke hole in the roof. It reminded her of the longhouses of her childhood.

"This is nice, Måns. I give many thanks for your help. Pray come inside and have some stew with me," Rå said and put her arm around his waist. It felt warm against her skin, and he smelled of sap and pine.

"Can I? We're not supposed to eat Rå-food. It's dangerous and could bewitch us, and then we'll never be able to eat regular food again. It could, couldn't it?" He met her eyes, standing so close their noses almost touched. He looked utterly genuine and very concerned.

"*That*'s a rumor." She kissed his nose. "You can eat my food."

"Truly?" Måns' eyes widened with surprise, and he stood very still, seeming to think deeply. Then he exhaled. "That's a relief, I'm starved." He grabbed her hand and put it on his stomach. It was growling loud enough to both hear and feel.

She laughed. "You'd really think I'd make you work so hard only to send you home with food that would hurt you?"

"Well, you *could*," he said, eyes glinting, "but then I'd likely not come back. Come here, Rå, Forest Rå." He pulled her tight against his chest, and she felt his heartbeat, strong and human. Not like hers, which beat much slower.

"Most people call me Magda. You may as well if you'd like?" She pulled herself out of his arms and pointed inside. "Let's go in and light a fire." She waited for Måns to enter first, then followed with some of the logs he had left outside for her, handing them to him so he could stack them. "Here," she said and put her firestarter and some kindling on one of the stones surrounding the pit.

"Magda?" He looked up from the logs. "I don't know, I like to call you Rå. It's who you are."

"I know, but I can't tell people that. It scares them. You're the first person in many, *many* years who's come straight out and asked me and who hasn't been afraid." Except for Stina and Nikolaos, but that was different.

"Hmm." Måns grabbed the firestarter and lit the kindling, waving his arm over it for it to take hold. "I understand, I suppose," he said quietly, the flames sending moving shadows across his face. Then he shifted in his seat on the ground and slid toward her, eyes alight. "Rå, Magda mine, pray, can I have something to eat now?"

Something flared in the pit of her stomach, something warm, like an old longing she had forgotten about. "Yes," she said and turned away, reaching for the stew in its cooking pot. Then she closed her back completely. With Måns she didn't need magic.

***

Rå was inside, crushing dried lemon balm and anise, the only herbs she had brought from her old place, mixing it with fresh woods growth. She called it woods growth because she didn't know the proper name for the plant. It was a sturdy bright green herb with frilly leaves that almost looked like lace. It grew abundantly here and tall, taller than she had ever seen anywhere else. It was very potent and cured coughs and stuffy noses if mixed with other herbs. Anise and lemon balm was especially good with it, and she was hoping to trade it for seedlings so she could start a new garden. There was a good spot behind the stone hut which would be ideal. It was sunny there and sheltered from the wind most days. She smushed the poultice into three different earthen pots, depending on strength, then covered each with large oak leaves. Sitting back, leaning on her hands, Rå nodded with satisfaction. There was more than she expected when she first started. She ought to ask Måns where she could trade it. Just as she thought that she realized that the mooing she had been faintly aware of as she worked wasn't stopping. In fact, it was incessant. Something was wrong.

Rå scrambled out, then stopped short. The cows weren't there. Not in the hollow behind the foundation walls, nor inside it, and not hiding in the trees in front. How strange, they never went further than a stone's throw in any direction. She frowned, looking around one more time just to make sure she had seen right, but to no avail. They weren't there. The mooing came from the east, from behind the bilberry moor somewhere. There were no trees, and she ought to see them from where she stood. Were they all lying down? Cupping her hands around her mouth, she started calling the names she had chosen for them, "Abundance! Little One! Wise One!"

Almost at once, she heard an urgent moo in the distance, then another. What if someone had taken them? Someone who would steal all of Abundance's milk, leaving Little One to pine for her mother's udder. Rå opened her back and ran, feeling for them as she tore across the brambly bilberry bushes until she reached the other side of the moor. Then she heard four loud moos in succession right in front of her, but all she saw was a wall of trees. The moor ended at the periphery of a forest so dense it made the trees near her new home seem like an open field by comparison. It was an odd place for them to be. Maybe something smelled especially good in there.

Rå stepped over a fallen tree, shoving branches aside but getting the skin on her legs torn up by sharp twigs from the underbrush. The next moment, she was standing on the precipice of a ravine. Panicked, she took a step backward. A wider step and she would have fallen straight down. She grabbed onto a branch for support, then dared to look again, bracing herself for what she would find down there. And there they were, staring up at her from the bottom of the ravine. Alive.

"You're down *here*?" she called. Why hadn't she left earlier? They had mooed for her for a long time, but she had ignored it.

Abundance and Wise One had sunk into a large mud puddle so deep she couldn't see their legs! And Little One was standing on dry land at the opposite side of the ravine, calling heart-wrenchingly for her mother who could only turn her head toward her and moo in response. It must be this Rå had heard.

"Sweetlings, I'm coming," Rå called, tears springing to her eyes from guilt as she slowly started to make her way down toward them.

Then Little One spotted her and started jumping with joy. Rå froze, bracing her movement with her legs. What if Little One jumped into the mud and got stuck? If her cloven hoofs couldn't reach the bottom, she would drown. Standing absolutely still, Rå opened her back as wide as it went, telling her to calm down and stay where she was. Little One looked up in surprise, then gave a sigh and fell to the ground, curling up and resting her head on one of her cloven hoofs. Good girl! Rå loosened her heels from the dirt and began to move downward again. Little One stayed where she was.

Once Rå was level with the older cows, it became clear it had been fruitless. Even if she could reach their horns, she would just fall in herself. She needed help from strong men with ropes and planks of wood. Thank Freya and Thor that she had already met Måns and knew where to go for help.

It had been dark for several hours when Rå finally arrived at Kjugekull. It was much smaller than she had expected from Måns' description. A few cottages were clustered on each side of a narrow road with a thick strip of grass in the middle. It was too dark to see how many there were, but from the look of it, there were no more than four, maybe five. It was still and quiet. No voices or sounds from pigs or goats moving about, no dogs barking. The only sign that someone was home was a flickering light from a hearth in one of the cottages and the faint light from a candle or two in another. She felt nervous. This was different from when she went to villages disguised as Magda. What had Måns had told people about her? Even if he said that she was known and respected here, he might not take lightly to her coming right into his village to look for him. His neighbors might still panic and chase her away, or even hurt Måns. She hesitated, wondering if it was better to turn back, then shook her head. If she didn't ask for help, her cows would slowly die of thirst and desperation. There was no other choice. Taking a deep breath, making sure that her back was covered by her hair, she continued forward.

The little road made a sharp left, and as she turned, her eyes fell on a brightly lit lantern on a stoop, cottage dark behind it. There was a rustling sound, and a shape was moving toward the light. Rå's back opened, and she stopped walking as a man's legs and trunk appeared in the lantern light. Then another shape approached, accompanied by heavy footsteps. A hand reached down into the light and picked up the lantern, lifting it high and illuminating their faces. Two men with wide toothless smiles in wrinkly faces. They had seen her.

"It's you, the lady of the forest," both said, almost in unison, bowing deeply. "Pray tell us, Rå, what we have done to deserve an honor such as this."

"I thank you for your welcome," she said just as formally. "I'm looking for a man named Måns. I'm in need of help. It's urgent."

"Måns is living right here with us," the one to her left said. He was wearing a blue cap, she noticed now, and had unusually large eyebrows.

"Here? Then I've come to the right place. Your lantern has guided my way." Freya must have helped her then, giving them a reason to go out and walk around in the dark instead of bringing the lantern with them.

"Yes, indeed you have. You need Måns' help? What for?" the blue-capped man asked, opening the door before she could explain. "Måns," he hollered, "the Forest Rå is here. She needs help, she says. Wake up!"

Rå raised an eyebrow, getting a merry look from his companion. It had been a very long time since she had met people who were so completely open and unafraid of who she was. It was as if she were just one of the neighbors who had come to borrow fire.

Måns appeared at the door, his eyes swollen and tight with sleep. "Rå? It really *is* you, isn't it?"

"Yes, it is I. My cows have gotten themselves stuck in the mud in a ravine, and I can't get them out," she said, nodding at the older men.

They exchanged a horrified glance in the lantern light. "Oh, poor creatures. We'll help. We'll leave so we're there at sunup," said the one with the cap, patting the other man's shoulder. They went inside with a quick nod in her direction, handing the lantern to Måns.

He put it on the stoop and rushed toward her with his arms spread wide. "I can't believe you're here with me. I've missed you. I was hoping to go see you in a day or two," Måns whispered, pulling her into his arms, his breath hot on her ear. He seemed to have forgotten why she was there. Or perhaps he hadn't heard properly.

"Who are the two old men? And pray, I don't care if it's dark, I can lead the way. Besides, the sun will rise by the time we get there."

"You don't get a man much time to rest, do you, Rå?" he said, but didn't look upset. "They're my uncles. They've been living together for years as if they were an old couple." He turned toward the cottage, pointing through the darkness. The lantern had gone out, and it looked like a gray boulder from where they were standing. "Per was married once many years ago, but his wife and baby died in childbirth. After that, he came back home to live with Bushbrow, his brother."

"I'm saddened to hear that. But Bushbrow?"

"It was," Måns said, grabbing her again to stand close. "It's what everyone calls him because of those eyebrows of his." He laughed softly.

"I see." Rå leaned into him but started walking toward the cottage so he would follow, impatient to leave. "How did you come to live here?"

"It's some years ago now after my parents died." He stopped, scraping a foot on something on the ground. "My siblings all died too. Same sickness, everyone around these parts all got it. It caused coughing and sneezing and hot, hot fevers and then death. It was an awful time. I grieved a long time for them."

Rå reached for his hand, saying nothing, knowing how it felt to lose one's mother. Still after hundreds of years, she looked for hers in the faces of others, hoping she would see her eyes look back at her, born anew.

"But there were several villages north of here the sickness didn't touch," Måns added. "It was because they had seen you."

"Me?" Her eyes flashed to his face, but it was too dark to see his expression.

"Yes. In one village they gave you eggs and a chicken and after that, no one ever got sick there. Since then, we know that whoever is kind to you won't need to worry about sickness. That's why I was so happy to see you that day. We can give you a chicken if you'd like?"

"Hmm," Rå said. It must have been Britt and Ida. They had been so nice that day but always seemed to avoid her after that. Maybe they hadn't then, after all. Surprised and touched by Måns' words, even though she doubted she could protect people from pestilence, she squeezed his hand. "That's very kind of you, but no need. If we could wake your uncles now so we get to my cows before the sun has risen too high in the sky, I'd be most grateful."

"Of course. I'll get them up. We have two horses. If you ride with me, my uncles can ride together."

Rå remained outside, watching through the window as Måns' uncles were getting ready. They walked back and forth, getting things from shelves and stepping in and out of her view. Then finally, Bushbrow came outside. He waved at her as he hurried to their shed, coming back out with ropes and two axes.

Then they were off. Per and Bushbrow on one horse, and she and Måns on the other, riding through what was now a completely quiet and dark village. Hooves on the soft ground, squeaks from leather, and the occasional snorts from the horses were the only sounds.

"Bäckaskog's Castle is over there," Måns said, breaking the silence and pointing to the right, where there was a faint pinpoint of yellow light. "That's the castle. They always leave a lantern or two lit at night."

"It's so that they can see when they piss. I've heard they have a special room inside the castle just for that. Those army guys won't handle defending us from the Danes if they can't even piss in the dark," Per said disdainfully.

Rå felt Måns' body shake as he tried to still his laugh behind her in the saddle. She laughed.

***

It was dawn when they arrived, and Rå steeled herself, worried about how far they had sunk while she was away. Picturing them with only their heads above the surface and Little One gone, drowned in the mud. But she needn't have worried. They stood pretty much as before. Little One was still resting in the same place she left her even. Rå bowed her head and silently thanked Freya.

"Oh, the poor wretched creatures, thank the Lord, you found them, Rå," Per said, with a respectful nod when he noticed her praying.

"And that Måns had told me you live in Kjugekull so I could ask for your help," she said.

"It was meant to be, Rå," said Måns as he dismounted, reaching to help her down.

Rå went first, carefully making her way down the steep slope so her cows wouldn't panic when the men got close and made noise. Once down, she sat herself at the edge of the muddy bank and opened her back, directing all of it toward the cows but away from the men.

It worked, they didn't move, and the men didn't appear to think anything of their unnatural calmness, even as Little One stayed put. They got to work immediately. Måns and Per felled several small trees, handing them to Bushbrow who stripped them clean, placing them side by side on top of the mud. It took only moments, and then Bushbrow and Måns were crawling across the logs, reaching Abundance first. Bushbrow grabbed hold of his rope, then shoved it straight into the mud under Abundance's belly as

Måns reached in from the other side. She seemed to understand that they were there to help and stayed calm, staring at Rå with her large black cow eyes as Måns was groping for Bushbrow's hand under her belly so he could grab the rope and pull it through.

Once Måns and Bushbrow had the rope around her middle, Per put another log in front of her which he carefully stepped on with one foot, then he reached and grabbed her horns "Now!" he yelled. There was a gurgling sound and then Abundance jumped to dry land. She stood for a short moment then her legs gave way and she lay down on the ground, tired but safe.

Rå inhaled sharply with relief, staying where she was so as not to get in the way. It went very fast. The men repeated what they did with Abundance, and then Wise One was on dry land too, but remained standing.

Bushbrow scratched his mud-stained face and hair and looked at Rå, gesturing to Little One. "You're light and agile and could probably walk across if we put the logs down for you, but do you think you could go around and bring the calf to her mama through the trees over there instead?"

Before Rå had a chance to even answer, Little One bounded over to them at the exact place where Bushbrow had suggested as if she understood what he said. The little calf ran to her mother and started licking her face, then proceeded to try to get to her udder where she lay.

Måns lit up with a broad smile and exchanged a warm glance with Rå.

"Thank you," she said, then turned toward Bushbrow and Per, who were helping Abundance get up. "I cannot thank you enough." Rå's eyes moistened as Abundance managed to stand and Little One jumped to her teats.

Måns' uncles looked teary as well. Then Per walked up to Rå and bowed deeply. "We're happy to help. It's an honor. We've long wanted you here, knowing it brings safety, good growth, and game for our forest."

Rå nodded, surprised how much his comment moved her. She looked down, overwhelmed by a sudden memory. She had been standing on their blót hill, with an earthen bowl full of deer blood in both her hands. Her mother had come to her, proud but tearful, and placed her hands on Rå's upper arms while she gazed into her face. Rå could still hear her voice as she remembered her words; *My child, my daughter, you will marry the forest, the moss, trees, leaves, and the very soil upon which we trample. You will make love to the men who visit your land, and you will live forever as you keep the forest fertile. Now drink my child and go. I will watch from Valhöll.* Rå swallowed audibly. It was as if she could feel her mother's thin yet strong hands on her arms, see her tear-filled eyes, and feel her wrinkly skin beneath her lips when she kissed her. It was the last time she felt her mother's touch. An impossibly long time ago.

When Rå looked up, the men had respectfully moved ahead to give her a moment. "Your own cows will stay healthy and strong. No sickness will ever befall them," she whispered.

Chapter 64

Nikolaos couldn't deny that it was likely they would arrest him. Merchant Fleisher only needed to contact the innkeeper who would then contact Lord Oxensköld, who would contact Antonio and so on. The safest thing to do would be to leave the farm. Either tell the children the truth or make up an excuse for why they needed to go, insist Hindrich leave his woman behind.

But he couldn't get himself to do it. Instead, they celebrated Hindrich's betrothal to Ekborg and watched him take her to the marriage bed in the new addition to their farmhouse he and Hindrich had built together. As time passed and nothing happened, Nikolaos relaxed, pushing down the guilt for having been unfaithful to Stina and hiding the blustering happiness that he hadn't killed anyone.

***

It was Harvest Day, and the five of them stood in front of the barn, watching as their neighbors made their way to their home, carrying pies, fruits, and cakes to be shared by all. At the sight of Peder, Ola's son, striding confidentially next to his sisters, Elsebet became visibly breathless. Nikolaos caught Stina's smiling eyes with a grin. Another betrothal was near.

The pastor was on his horse, riding slowly while gesticulating with Eskil Stonemason walking next to him. Ekborg's parents and her six younger brothers and sisters were eyeing them while they all laughed heartily at something the pastor was saying.

Hindrich's eyes gleamed warmly at the sight of his happy in-laws. Turning to Nikolaos with a gesture in their direction, he said, "I'm very glad we have a nice pastor. He says he wants us to have our union blessed in church on Sunday."

Nikolaos raised an eyebrow. "Inside? But you shook hands on the church steps and were bedded already. Why would you need it?"

"He offered, and a blessing is always nice, don't you think,

Father?" Hindrich put an arm around Ekborg's waist.

"Of course, if that's what he wants." A blessing. Certainly, it was nice, but he had seen the church weasel itself into private affairs too often. It was likely just so the sixmen and the pastors would have another reason to get even more involved with people's lives.

Stina and Ekborg proudly escorted their guests to a long table on the meadow behind the house. The two of them had worked hard for several days, and the table was already laden with apple, pear, and plum compote, fresh butter, cream, honey, a goose, and fresh fish that Hindrich had caught. Nyckelharpa Uffe had stopped by the night before with a whole cooked piglet. Now the guests added their own gifts to it, creating an incredibly abundant fest.

"So much food, so much food!" Stina exclaimed, her cheeks flushing with excitement. "I think this must be the best feast in years."

"Yes," Baking Kajsa said, glancing at Ekborg's mother who was walking around the table, inspecting everything with a look of deep satisfaction. Baking Kajsa chuckled at her expression. "You've done well getting your daughter married into this family. You'll have strong grandbabies."

Ekborg's mother looked up from the cakes. "I was just thinking that. Round lil' babies toddling around."

Nikolaos and Stina exchanged a glance, smiling at each other. It wouldn't be long; they had seen Hindrich and Ekborg's affection when they snuck away, stealing some privacy in the middle of the day.

Nikolaos threw his arm out in a wide gesture. "Have a seat, neighbors, sit." He was feeling proud, too. They truly had done well this season compared to the previous years' meager harvests. The pastor claimed it was because God was happy with the villagers' repentance, but Nikolaos had a feeling Rå had had something to do with it, that she had done something when she visited in the spring. It was only last winter Stockholm had overflowed with beggars due to poverty and starvation and when Stina's dresses were hanging loose on her. It must have been Rå. "Do sit," he said again, a little louder this time. When everyone had found their respective seats, he bent his head and clasped his hands. "I thank you, Lord, for this feast day and the extraordinary bounty we have here today. I believe it's a sign that the tide has turned, and we're thankful for the grace He shines upon us."

"Amen," the pastor said, looking at him so kindly Nikolaos felt guilty for what he thought before about churches meddling in personal lives.

It was quiet for a time when the guests filled their plates. Stina handed Nikolaos his, overfull with pear compote, a hefty slice of pork, and several kinds of eggs and sausages. His mouth watered.

"I heard you have a watch that can tell every hour of the day. Pray can I see it later? This is delicious by the way," Uffe said while chewing on one side of his mouth.

"You can see it right now." Nikolaos wiped his hands on his napkin and pulled the chain off his neck, throwing a warm eye at Stina. She was beaming at Uffe's compliment. "It tells time minute by minute. Watches and clocks have two hands now. Look here," he said, lifting the ornate lid proudly.

Uffe narrowed his eyes and leaned closer to Nikolaos. "Each minute?"

Nikolaos nodded. "Every hour has sixty minutes, and the minute hand moves one tiny step for each."

"I'll be darned. Why would one need to be that specific?" Uffe asked, getting a chuckle from around the table.

"My husband is obsessed with watches and clocks," Stina said.

"I'd gladly give you each one of those if it meant you'd come to services on time. When our church bell rings, some haven't even left their beds yet," the pastor said. Not knowing if he was joking or taking the opportunity to chastise them, no one laughed. He looked almost hurt, but when Nikolaos winked, he grinned. He reached for a goose leg, smiling mischievously at Stina who responded with a chuckle.

They had been eating and drinking for some time when they heard a galloping horse on the road. Nikolaos put his hand on Stina's arm and gave a nod. It had to be Antonio. To coordinate the musicians in the area, they always had the harvest feast at Nikolaos' farm on the same day, rain or shine. Naturally, he had invited Antonio before they left Stockholm.

Nikolaos stood, putting his hand over his eyes to shield them from the afternoon sun. The horse was fast and was whipping up a cloud of dirt, but he recognized the wig and hat. It *was* Antonio. "We're getting a visitor from Stockholm!" he exclaimed, turning his attention back to their other guests while silently praying Antonio wasn't followed by guards who were finally coming for him.

"Antonio's here! He's a friend from Three Crowns," Stina said, her eyes shining with pride.

"Stockholm? From the castle?" Borghild's younger sister asked, giggling.

Borghild threw her a warning glance. "Yes, you heard what Stina said."

"He was our host and guide when we were there, helping us get situated. Royal life is overwhelming, and we were glad to have him," Stina said. Borghild was Eskil Stonemason's wife. A sour woman who never seemed happy.

At that, Nikolaos grabbed Stina's hand, and they left their guests at the table and hurried around front to greet Antonio. He was already tying his horse to the post behind the barn when they approached.

"Antonio, good friend! You're here, what an honor," Nikolaos said, meeting Antonio's eyes. There wasn't a trace of suspicion in his gaze, and when they embraced, all he felt was warmth and the special bond you feel with someone you have been through trying times with. Thank God. He let out a discreet sigh of relief.

It was an odd scene to see their neighbors, including Ekborg's parents, breathlessly greet Antonio as if he were the King himself. Even the pastor was blushing and didn't seem to know what was expected of him, if Antonio ought to bow first or if *he* ought to. After an awkward moment, they both did. Antonio's face broke into a sheepish grin, and he slapped the pastor on the shoulder, who looked almost beside himself with pleasure.

***

The next day, Nikolaos and Antonio were slowly walking arm in arm, taking a tour of the farm, when Antonio stopped, turning toward Nikolaos. He met his gaze with a level stare. "I've been meaning to talk to you about something. I know not what to say other than coming right out with it."

Nikolaos braced himself.

"There are rumors you're Näcken."

"What?" Rusty devils, he had been right then, after all. Nikolaos made sure he looked surprised, then pretended to think he hadn't heard him right. "Pray, can you repeat that, I thought you said something else."

"You heard right, I'm afraid. People think you're Näcken."

Nikolaos laughed harshly, or tried to, it sounded hysterical. "Näcken? That's preposterous."

"I know. I'm sorry to be the one to tell you. But I thought you ought to know what's being said."

Nikolaos scoffed, hoping it looked convincing. "Well then, what *are* they saying?"

"You want the details?"

He nodded.

Antonio held his gaze with narrowed eyes. "That when you played for Merchant Fleisher and Mistress Esmeralda, people were so taken by it, they fainted. And when they lay in a faint, you're to have run into the woods and," he briefly glanced at his feet while taking a breath, "pulled a married couple into the water with you. This is hard to relay." He threw a glance at his feet again, looking very uncomfortable. "People are saying you were having sexual congress with them both. That your... your manhood had... you know… with them both. In intimate places!" Antonio pulled a handkerchief from his pocket and wiped his face with it.

Nikolaos tried to keep his expression neutral. It sounded so crude to hear it said out loud. Embarrassing. Antonio, of all people, who was open about keeping a mistress, thought him sick. But it had been beautiful and passionate. He knew they had wanted to, and he hadn't killed them. They survived. Tears came to his eyes without him being able to stop them.

"Oh, Nikolaos, pray forgive me for upsetting you. I should've insisted not to tell you."

Nikolaos shook his head. "No, don't feel bad. I want to know. What else?" The tears had been in his favor apparently.

"Very well, they're also saying that their stable flooded after you kept your horse there and that it destroyed their ornamental bushes."

"Rusty devils!" He turned his back on Antonio and walked off a few paces, wiping his tears with the back of his hand. His shoes and hose *had* been wet when he left the stable. He must have gotten it wet then. It was odd though; he hadn't been near water. What if he had gotten the steps wet when he was talking to Mistress Esmeralda in the house?

"Nikolaos."

He started, realizing Antonio was right behind him.

"You have every right to be upset," he said, and handed him one of his many handkerchiefs. "But do tell me what really happened. It may help me explain things when I get back to Stockholm."

"You have to explain things to people in Stockholm?"

Antonio looked embarrassed. "I'm afraid so."

Nikolaos stared at him, at a loss for words. "It was a nice event," he said finally. "Mistress Esmeralda and Merchant Fleisher had several overnight guests, served us a lavish meal with delicious and unusual dishes. It didn't rival court, but it was close. After dinner, I performed. I thought it went well. Everyone seemed to like it. Like you said, they were dancing and enjoying themselves."

"Did they faint?"

Nikolaos shrugged. "I took a break, and some of the guests were on the ground when I came back. I assumed they were drunk. I only learned it wasn't that when I was asked if I had seen it."

"Seen what?"

"The comet. They didn't tell you about that?"

"No. There was a comet? Did you see it?"

"No, I didn't. Supposedly it shot through the sky when I stepped away. Mistress Esmeralda and several of the guests claimed it did, anyway, and that it made people fall down in odd faints on the ground."

Antonio tilted his head backward in a slow nod. "Hmmm. And you didn't faint yourself?"

Nikolaos relaxed a little. It always amazed him how much he could get away with as long as he stayed close to the truth. "No, and I noticed nothing out of the ordinary. As I said, they were probably just drunk. I do admit, though, my horse did get hold of one of the bushes when I first arrived and pulled off a big branch. I felt bad, but no one blamed me at the time. In fact, the footman apologized for not having called for a groom when I was invited inside."

Antonio winced. "Oh, no. People are particular about their gardens."

"I know. I felt stupid."

"Eh, don't." He waved his hand in the air. "What I don't understand, why would they think you were *Näcken*," he said his name in a whisper, "if they claimed a comet was to blame?"

"I don't know. But Mistress Esmeralda told me what had happened to their cleaning staff the morning after the party. Why she thinks I had something to do with it, I don't know. It's perverse."

"Oh, she did tell you?"

"Yes, but..."

Antonio shook his head several times. "It's perverse and rude, terribly rude. Could the comet have brought him, the creature? Did you notice the water in the stable?"

Nikolaos walked off again, exasperated. "No! Rusty devils,

why in the world would that have anything to do with it? They obviously need to check to see where the water is coming from if it floods!"

Antonio didn't say anything.

Then suddenly, Nikolaos thought of the executioner. The old man had confronted him just before they left Jönköping. He could use it to his advantage. It probably wasn't even a lie. He spun around and stared dramatically at Antonio. "Wait, I think I know where this is coming from!"

"What?"

"The rumors."

"Oh." Antonio looked bewildered. "Really?"

"Yes. How did you learn of all this?"

"Eh… um, a royal courier who buys candles from Merchant Fleisher for the court told me that everyone spoke of it at the inn he stays at in Jönköping. One of the King's men heard it too. I can only assume it was the courier who told him. But I don't know for certain."

"I thought so," Nikolaos said. Then he told Antonio everything about Jon and the execution and how he had been accused of stealing a horse.

"That doesn't make sense. You're not old enough," Antonio said when Nikolaos finished.

"I know. The innkeeper tried to explain that to them too. But I must look like someone I suppose. The man was old, probably beginning to lose his wits and forget things. We laughed about it afterward, and I just brushed it off. It never crossed my mind that the old man and that ruffian would go around talking about it. Apparently, I was wrong. This is very disturbing. I should confront Mistress Esmeralda and her husband, ask them why they believe in such nonsense." He obviously couldn't, but it seemed the right thing to say.

Antonio pursed his lips, looking thoughtful, then shook his head. "It does explain the rumor then. Yes, it's very disturbing, but no, you shouldn't confront them. It's beneath you. Besides, it's stupid. How could a person be Näcken? Doesn't he live in a river somewhere?"

"I think so." Nikolaos exhaled. He usually enjoyed the irony in conversations like this, but now he just felt nervous and uncomfortable. There was too much at stake, and Antonio was from the Royal Court.

Antonio sighed deeply, narrowing his eyes. "Did your relative really spend time with him?"

"I find it very hard to believe, but the legal courts were convinced of it. It's a terrifying thought to think that my uncle might have known someone who was meddling with the otherworldly, with Näcken himself." He shook his head for good measure. "But that it should lead to this? It's... I have children and a wife to protect."

Antonio patted his back.

They went inside, leaving the uncomfortable subject behind.

Antonio sat down on their sofa in the new room, gratefully accepting the mug of ale Elsebet offered him, and nodding pleasantly at Stina and Ekborg. "I had almost forgotten to tell you, the funeral will be held on the twenty fourth day of November." He took a long sip. "Court has been nothing but mayhem these months. I can't wait for it to be over so we can go back to normal, as normal as it can be that is. Why, with a new King and all."

"Surely the King must have been buried already," Elsebet said and sat herself down next to Antonio, a look of disbelief on her face.

"No, not yet."

"But surely... the body must smell," Elsebet said, blushing deeply. She looked like she was embarrassed to infer the King wouldn't smell good, even after his death.

"They embalm it. There's also incense and oils to hide whatever odor might still be present. One shall not speak too much of this in some company," Antonio added with a smile at Elsebet.

She laughed.

"In fact," Antonio said, "those working on the preparations are nervous they won't finish in time. Tessin has his staff working day and night. But even so, it's worrisome. He has a long list of other responsibilities as well. Like drawing up the blueprints for the new castle, continuing his work with the royal stable, which also had a fire."

"The stable burned too?" Stina exclaimed, exchanging a horrified glance with Nikolaos.

"Yes, but it was about a year before Three Crowns burned," Antonio said. "Anyway, not only that, Tessin is responsible for making Wrangel Palace appropriate for the royal family since they obviously can't live at Three Crowns. And last but not least, he's planning for young Karl's coronation, which will be held only a few weeks after the funeral."

"This seems an enormous undertaking for one person," Nikolaos said. "Why is Tessin the only man responsible?"

Antonio shrugged. "I've wondered the same. There's a lot of talk at court about it, too. But it's what they've decided."

"I see." No wonder the innkeeper had claimed it was arson.

"I'm to bring you back with me. You're to play in church," Antonio said, his expression unreadable.

Ekborg gasped, and Stina fell back on the seat, hands clasped over her heart.

Nikolaos stared at Antonio, ignoring the women's excitement. Antonio had been sent to see if there was any truth to the rumors before he was called to perform, using the perfect opportunity of the invitation to their harvest feast as a ruse for a visit. There had been an ulterior motive for him coming to their harvest feast. He could have been arrested if Antonio hadn't believed him, just as he had feared.

"It's my honor to bring you," Antonio said with an apologetic expression. "Perhaps I should've brought it up at your harvest feast, but I decided to wait until we were alone. Unfortunately, we can't bring you, Stina, this time." He touched her hand. "As you can imagine, the court no longer has as much space."

"Of course, I understand. I wouldn't have been able to go anyway. I have a new daughter-in-law here that I need to help get settled." Stina smiled at Ekborg.

"Antonio, I thank you," Nikolaos said simply, wishing he could convey how much it meant.

Chapter 65

The funeral procession moved solemnly from Wrangel Palace to Riddarholm Church, their path laid with black cloth. Men walked in mantles that trailed to their feet, while the women wore headwear resembling towering white steeples. Among them, young King Karl was escorted by twenty-four personal drabants.

Yet, no one in the procession could have anticipated the splendor that awaited inside. The church was ablaze with luminance, radiating from seven grand crystal domes. Remarkably, the flames within them produced no smoke, casting a pure light onto Karl XI's Royal Coffin. Positioned on an elevated podium, the regalia lay to its right, shrouded in black lace. To the left lay his Knightly Vestments, the blue velvet mantle, the red coat, his chain, and garter. The King had received the honor of the Most Noble Order of The Garter at just fourteen, something only Gustav II Adolf had preceded him with.

The coffin was draped in black velvet adorned with golden crowns that mirrored the funeral crown, resting atop it. Suspended above was Tessin's masterfully crafted canopy encircled by four silver statues representing Svecia, Gothia, Wandalia, and Virtue to express the immense grief of the people. Towering cypresses were carved into steeples, surrounded by leaves and additional crystal lamps. Crowning it all, a cloud hovered with forty angels and cherubs, each as large as a man, made of wax and clothed in golden and silver silks. It was the most amazing display Nikolaos had ever witnessed. A magnificent theatre of death, all put together by Tessin and his men.

Nikolaos sat hidden from view on a simple stool behind it, feeling breathless and taken by the enormity of his task. He was to begin as soon as the choir sang the first note, a soft, solemn piece that would accompany the singing like a wave in the background. Those were the choirmaster's words, not his, fitting as they were.

Then the choir began, a low keening first, and the skin on his arms became gooseflesh as he lifted his bow and put it to the strings. Slow at first, then faster as the singing became louder.

Colors bounced around him, hitting the dazzling crystal domes as the choir voices mournfully tore through the church. Nikolaos couldn't see the young King from his vantage point, but his chest constricted at the thought of him listening. He must be missing his father and fearing the reign that came upon him much too quickly, just as it had his father before him. He was only fifteen years old.

Then the choir stopped, and Nikolaos played alone while Archbishop Svebilius prepared for the eulogy. He had practiced with the choir several times, but now it seemed to take forever, and even though it sounded right, it felt like his hands were shaking. When the archbishop finally approached the podium, Nikolaos only just managed to end on the right note.

Archbishop Svebilius spoke at length, and Nikolaos tried his best to focus on it, but he was too nervous. His thoughts kept wandering in other directions, and he couldn't stop looking at the incredible display, wondering how the candles, or perhaps they were oil lamps, could be so bright but be entirely without smoke. Whatever it was that caused it, his musings calmed him down, and when it was his turn to play again, it felt much easier. His new violin sang, and his colors danced across the church, hitting a higher note as the choir began to sing again, only to stop with a dramatic crescendo. He heard sobs in the nave, and from what he could see from where he sat, it looked like Archbishop Svebilius was wiping tears away.

Shortly thereafter, the five nobilities approached the podium and gently picked up the regalia. They walked ahead of the pallbearers who lifted the royal coffin, then followed the nobilities to the crypt. The choir began to sing again. Nikolaos played along softly for just a short while, as had been arranged, and then the sounds of canons and guns echoed from outside. A final prayer and a blessing were sung by Bishop Haquin Spegel from Linköping. Then the congregation sang together, and it was over. At that point, Nikolaos was sobbing.

Once the procession had left the church, the choirmaster hurried toward Nikolaos. He looked relieved. It must have been days since he slept. "Good sir, that was beautiful. I thank you. I was right to have you hiding in the back, hearing but not seeing made it seem like the music came straight from heaven."

"I thank *you*," Nikolaos said. "I admit I was nervous, but it went well. I've never been part of something as grand as this. It's quite overwhelming. I know it's presumptuous of me, but it feels like it's a personal loss. I was nearby when the King lay sick, playing for his comfort. And even though I never met him, I feel truly moved by this, more than I'd expected." Nikolaos looked to the ceiling to stop the tears from overflowing again.

"Oh, you have every right to feel grief. We all do. The King was taken too young." The choirmaster handed him a purse, patting his hand as he took it. "I thank you again, Nikolaos Jensson," he said and hurried off, leaving Nikolaos alone with the guards.

One of the guards moved toward him. He kept the distance respectfully, but it was clear he didn't want him to linger.

Nikolaos nodded, then shot a parting gaze at the funeral display and walked out. The air felt cold against his face and smelled of gunpowder.

***

The coach Nikolaos traveled with to get home changed horses at Jönköping's Inn. At first, he was going to stay in his seat when they fetched fresh horses, but at the last minute, he changed his mind and scrambled out. It was late, and he was hungry and tired, longing for a proper bed.

The vestibule was empty, but Nikolaos could hear the innkeeper's familiar laugh in the dining hall, and he strode right in, finding him with none other than Lord Oxensköld. "My Lord!" Nikolaos exclaimed, breaking into a broad smile. "I'm surprised to see you here. Aren't you still in Stockholm? I assumed you were at the funeral." As soon as the words were out of his mouth, he felt stupid. It was not for him to question or have opinions of a lord's whereabouts.

"Nikolaos!" Lord Oxensköld exclaimed, turning around to

face him. He rose to his feet and reached for his hand, shaking it as if he were making a deal with him. "I heard *you* were at the funeral. What are you doing here?"

"I was," Nikolaos said, feeling worse than before. If he had been there and was here now, then Lord Oxensköld could have as well. He likely had his own coach too, with strong, fast horses. "Pray forgive me for my intrusive question and my assumptions. I was humbled to see His Highness laid to rest. May God keep His Highness in his hands."

"No offense taken, but you assumed correctly. I wasn't invited to the funeral because I've been arguing with the Royal Court!" He exchanged a glance with the innkeeper.

"Oh," Nikolaos said, surprised.

"Well, I don't believe for a moment that Tessin is innocent," Lord Oxensköld said gravely, exchanging another glance with the innkeeper.

"Indeed, I tend to agree," the innkeeper said, pointing to the chair next to him. "Sit with us." There were several glasses on the table, and he grabbed one and started filling it with red wine. While pouring, he threw a wary eye across the room. Two men were deeply involved in their own conversation but didn't seem to pay attention.

"What isn't he innocent of?" Nikolaos asked, lowering his voice anyway.

Lord Oxensköld's face darkened. "I think he's the one who set the fire, he and his companion Hans Conrad," he said, speaking in a normal tone of voice, clearly not caring if the other guests heard. "I'm quite sure of it, and I'm not the only one either. Tessin pushed himself into court, taking over every project. I think he had the drawings ready long before the castle burned, might even have had the funeral planned as well. And who knows if he didn't poison the King himself!"

Nikolaos stared at him. "Poisoned the King?"

Lord Oxensköld gave Nikolaos a pointed look. "Indeed. They claimed to have found tumors after they performed the corpse opening, which was done after the King's own wishes, but how do we know if it's true? Tessin could have paid them to say that. Or what if the poison caused the tumors? Don't you think it just a bit odd that both Tessin and Hans Conrad were in the attic during the fire?"

Nikolaos opened his mouth to say that it indeed was, then closed it again, feeling nervous about agreeing. It was an insane accusation. Still, the innkeeper had said as much as well, except for the part about the King being poisoned. Nikolaos turned toward him, and the innkeeper gave him an 'I told you so' look.

"I'm certain of it," Lord Oxensköld said. "He managed to get a whole new title while he was at it, Superintendent. It's new. French." Lord Oxensköld tut-tutted, swirling his wine glass in his hand. "Tessin got them to invent a title, then put himself in charge of the drawings for the new castle, stables, Wrangel Palace, and the coronation. And the funeral as well. It was beautiful, wasn't it?"

"Yes, it was. Extraordinary, I've never seen…"

"Bah, as one thought, as one thought," Lord Oxensköld interrupted. "And much too elaborate to have been planned in such a short time with his long list of responsibilities. This, you see, is why I think he and his companion had all of this planned since years back. They had the King poisoned, then swooped in and took it all."

Nikolaos didn't know what to say. No wonder Lord Oxensköld hadn't been invited to the funeral if he harbored theories like that.

Lord Oxensköld finished his glass of wine, refilled it, and drank all of that too, then wiped his lips with a napkin with great care. "Well, I realize it sounds outrageous, but many speak of it. It's too queer that he managed to plan all this so quickly," he said, eyes firm.

Nikolaos nodded. "I must say that I've been thinking it's strange that he took on several projects at once when just one of them, the funeral, for example, would've been quite the undertaking on its own. It's quite unusual to do so much, isn't it?"

"Indeed," the innkeeper said.

"Yes," Lord Oxensköld agreed. "Tessin was already rebuilding the north wing. Everyone knows he found Three Crowns old-fashioned and ugly. And let's not forget that some say Three Crowns was cursed. Näcken was seen there once. One of the older Kings shot at him, King Karl X or IX I believe it was."

Nikolaos felt the innkeeper watching him. It was getting a little too close for comfort. He tried to look nonchalant and picked up his wine glass and took a slow sip.

Lord Oxensköld continued unaware. "I've read Abraham Lövcrantz' work. He describes how the King saw Näcken sitting in the river right outside the castle. He tried to shoot him but Näcken threw the bullet back at him!"

"I met Lövcrantz, and I listened to him speak of it. I forgot until now," Nikolaos burst out without thinking.

"That can't be. Abraham died in fifty-seven," Lord Oxensköld said, looking amused.

The innkeeper's face fell.

Nikolaos feigned ignorance. "Am I misunderstanding something here?"

"Naturally, you must. Who did you say you met?" The innkeeper's voice had gone down several octaves.

Lord Oxensköld cast a confused glance at them both.

"Abraham, what was it? Lövcrantz, I think. He spoke at a church a few years back," Nikolaos said, willing himself to stay calm, making up the part about him speaking in a church, and pretending he hadn't heard what year he died.

"Which church is that?" The innkeeper moved closer to Lord Oxensköld.

Nikolaos ignored it. "Near my home, in Ytterby." A lie of course.

"I see. You're mistaken, my good sir. Abraham Lövcrantz whose book I read, died in fifty-seven as I mentioned. You must have the names confused. Most likely the man you listened to spoke of him," Lord Oxensköld said, picking up his wineglass and winking at Nikolaos.

"Ah, I see." Nikolaos smiled. "My apologies." He narrowed his eyes as if he was trying to remember what his name was. Then he shook his head. "Pray forgive me. I can't remember the man's name now."

"How could Näcken have thrown a bullet? Is that even possible?" the innkeeper asked. He still sounded tense.

"Well, why not? Isn't he also known to play the fiddle? If he can hold a fiddle, why not a bullet? So yes, I'd say it's possible," Lord Oxensköld said, looking important.

Nikolaos kept himself very still, praying that the innkeeper was somehow still ignorant. Then he heard the innkeeper stand up abruptly. His chair crashed to the floor. Nikolaos faced him, feigning concern and surprise.

The innkeeper pointed a shaky finger at Nikolaos. "That's not who it seems. May the lord in heaven forgive me for not believing it until now. Have him arrested and get him out of my inn!" He crossed himself.

"What in the world are you talking about?" Lord Oxensköld asked, eyes flashing between the innkeeper and Nikolaos.

The two men across from them had stopped talking and were staring in their direction.

Nikolaos slowly rose from his chair, ready to fight for it if he had to. "I don't know what's gotten into your head, good sir, but you've clearly had too much wine and you're embarrassing yourself. I'm a royal musician," he said icily.

"No, no more. I've fallen for your lies enough times now. *Fiddler* Nikolaos, indeed. That executioner was correct, I should've seen it then, but I was so blinded by your dangerous charms that I didn't. You did steal his horse, and you came here to rescue Sinner Jon, your prodigy. That's why you spoke to the courts and all that. I see it now. You're not at all who you pretend to be. Mistress Esmeralda told me everything, how you had played for so long that people fainted from exhaustion, blaming it all on a comet. How two young people were lured into the water with you and were forced to do unnamable private things. Sexual things. Even the young man! And there I was defending you. Convincing her that you had just happened to be there at the same time. Oh lord in heaven, forgive my blindness," he cried. Then he crossed himself again, turned abruptly and ran to stand behind the counter.

Lord Oxensköld looked like a deer caught in lantern light.

Nikolaos scanned the room for an open window, but there was none. It was November, and each window was firmly closed, even shuttered. He moved sideways and positioned himself so he could run out the door if needed.

"Innkeeper… Anders, is it not?" Lord Oxensköld asked. "You come with quite the serious accusation. You might want to heed Nikolaos' words and keep in mind that we've had quite a bit to drink. I take responsibility for plying you with it." He pushed his own glass to the middle of the table.

"Indeed, this is ridiculous," Nikolaos said as curtly as he could. "However, I will not tolerate such treatment any longer. It was quite enough that you dragged me from my room when that bedraggled old man came to slander me, Innkeeper *Anders*. Quite enough. I'll take my leave now. Goodnight, gentlemen." He nodded at Lord Oxensköld and gave a quick bow. "My Lord." With that, Nikolaos left the dining room and hurried through the vestibule toward the front door. Shocked voices erupted behind him, belonging to the two other men who had clearly heard every word.

Angry and ashamed, Nikolaos pushed open the door. But before he had even put a foot through, he felt a hand grabbing a strong hold on his shoulder, swinging him around. Lord Oxensköld. Of course.

"Not so fast, *Fiddler* Nikolaos," he said.

Nikolaos sighed, pretending to be annoyed instead of afraid. "My Lord, leave me be. I won't stay here and be humiliated in this way."

"No, Fiddler Nikolaos, you and I need to talk. As your Lord, I demand it."

Could he do that? Nikolaos hesitated, turning his head to look at the street through the open door. Yes, he probably could. It was better to comply. "Very well then," he said, turning back toward him with another sigh. "There's a tavern near the wigmaker. Come with me, and I'll treat you to a bite to eat and tell you everything."

"I pray that you do."

Nikolaos frowned but didn't respond. Then they walked out. He half expected Lord Oxensköld to grab him by the arm, but he didn't.

It had started snowing heavily, and a strong wind was blowing sideways, hitting the lantern by the door, making a colorless sizzling sound as it met the warm glass. The square in front of the inn lay dark. Nikolaos set off at a fast pace, bending forward and pushing his hat down over his face.

"It's cold as the devil's bottom!" Lord Oxensköld cursed behind him.

The tavern wasn't much more than a low-to-the-ground cottage, but the windows were glowing invitingly. Nikolaos let Lord Oxensköld step in ahead of him. He was squinting with his lips drawn tight. It was probably not an establishment that a lord would visit often. Hopefully, the warm air hitting their faces and the smell of cooking would make him comfortable enough. The men around the tables were eating what looked like a hearty soup.

A servant girl motioned to a table in the middle of the establishment. She was a rosy-cheeked woman with thick hair braided and tied to the top of her head. "It's freezing out there, isn't it, gentlemen?"

"It is. The snow is coming down heavily. Can you bring us those large bowls of soup and meat, whichever you have of the best cut."

She grinned, exposing a mouth with two missing front teeth. The girl was too young to have lost them naturally and must have either been in a fight or an accident. A fight, Nikolaos guessed, since she didn't try to hide it.

Returning with a tray, she gave them each their own bowl and put a plate of salted pork on the table.

The soup was too hot, so Nikolaos began with the meat. It was delicious. He hoped it wouldn't be the last meal he ate. Taking another piece and swallowing it whole, he looked Lord Oxensköld straight in the face.

Lord Oxensköld carefully held the bowl in his hands despite

its heat and sipped, meeting Nikolaos' gaze as he drank. Nikolaos tried to stay calm, but it might have been a mistake coming here. What if the innkeeper heard him say where they were going, and was getting the lawmen to come and arrest him? He was an idiot; he should have waited to suggest it until they were outside.

"Well, Fiddler Nikolaos, do explain yourself. What in God's name was he referring to? Who is Sinner Jon and why does he think you stole a horse from an executioner?"

"I can certainly tell you what I know. First, though, I must ask what he said after I left?"

"He said that you're Näcken." Lord Oxensköld's voice was void of feeling.

"He did, did he?" Nikolaos shook his head as if he thought it was stupid. "Doesn't Näcken live in the water somewhere? In a stream or a brook?"

"I'd like to hear you explain how this isn't so, just the same."

Nikolaos' stomach churned, and there was a cold feeling in his chest. "Very well." With a deep sigh to make sure he seemed annoyed, he recounted his visit to the courthouse, Jon's hanging, the executioner's visit, and finally his evening at Merchant Fleisher's and Mistress Esmeralda's home. It didn't even feel like lying anymore. He had told the same version of what happened so many times.

"Did Merchant Fleisher pay you for your services?"

"Of course."

Lord Oxensköld narrowed his eyes, then sat up straight and started eating as if there was nothing wrong.

Nikolaos swallowed his panic and waited until he had finished his last bite, then said, "Why is the innkeeper accusing me of such nonsense? I'm a royal musician and a family man with grown children. He insults me."

Lord Oxensköld looked at him without responding. Time passed, but he kept staring. Then he moved forward in his seat. "Well, you're not actually a royal musician, you've just been given two great opportunities because the King wished it. Don't try to raise above your station, *Fiddler* Nikolaos."

The reprimand caught him off guard. Lord Oxensköld wasn't wrong. He was just a fiddler who was housed among the servants at Three Crowns. His cheeks burned. "My Lord, pray forgive me."

Lord Oxensköld gave a small smile, a slight movement of his lips, and a brief twinkle to his eye. Then he sat as before, looking at Nikolaos as if he was testing him or checking whether he was human or not.

Nikolaos couldn't take it anymore and looked away. The wind was gusting outside, and the windowpanes were already packed with snow. He would have nowhere to go, nowhere to run to, and would be stuck here with his Lord who could bring him straight to the authorities tomorrow when the snow had stopped. They might hang him without trial. This could be the end of his long life. If it killed him, that was. What if it didn't? How long would they let him hang, and what would they do if it didn't work?

When he looked back at Lord Oxensköld, he realized he had been saying something. "Pardon me, my Lord?"

"I'm at a loss here. I'm inclined to believe you. You obviously act like a human made of flesh and blood."

"Inclined?" Nikolaos began.

Lord Oxensköld raised his hand to stop him. "No matter what the truth is. The royal family has enough as it is. A rumor about this too, would destroy them. Even I who's not feeling favorable toward them right now, wouldn't want that."

"Good point, Lord Oxensköld," Nikolaos said, suddenly angry. He had been sitting there humbly like a servant. It was enough. "But Imagine for a moment what a rumor like this would do to *my* family. I'm deeply troubled that you deemed it necessary for me to explain it. I have, as you pointed out, no royals to help protect my family from these rumors."

Lord Oxensköld looked stunned.

Nikolaos suppressed a smile of satisfaction. It had been a good thing to say apparently. He got to his feet, staring down at Lord Oxensköld. "My Lord, I've told you what happened. I've humored you enough." Then he walked away, feeling Lord Oxensköld's eyes on his back. His heart thudded in his chest.

Forcing himself not to turn around, he found the servant girl at the bar disk and paid her.

"You leaving in this?" she asked, gesturing toward the windows. "You sure? We've space in the attic if you want to stay. We've no proper beds nor rooms, unfortunately, but mats on the floor at least. Many of our customers stay if they get stuck here in bad weather."

"I appreciate it, but I must leave."

"Dressed like that?" She pointed to his silk stockings and buckled shoes. "You won't get further than the lane."

"You do have a point there, girl. Is there any other place where I could go? I've reason not to stay at the inn, or here with him," he added in a lower voice, gesturing toward their table with a tilt of his head.

"Do you now?" She kept her eyes on him for several moments, then seemed to decide he was trustworthy. "You can stay with my grandmother. She's home. Just get yourself to the other side of the street here, and you'll recognize the cottage by the large rock near the door. It'll be a huge snow mound by now. Tell her I said so, and I'll keep it between us."

"Thank kindly, I won't forget," Nikolaos said and patted his pocket to indicate his purse.

He threw a quick glance in Lord Oxensköld's direction. He was cleaning his pipe and didn't look up. Nikolaos let out a sigh of relief, opened the door, and stepped out. In the short time they had eaten and talked, the snow had covered everything and lay thick and unshoveled in his path. It already reached halfway up his calves, instantly soaking through his stockings with ice-cold wetness. He should have changed into something warmer before he left Stockholm, but wanting to seem impressive on route, he had stayed in what he wore when he performed. This was what he got for his pride.

Nikolaos found the cottage. The grandmother merely nodded and gestured for him to step inside, then pointed to a ladder leading to a hayloft. It was already occupied by two hens and a cat, and it smelled of cat piss. Lord Oxensköld would probably think it served him right, befitting his station.

***

Twice, Nikolaos woke to the sound of footsteps, ready to fight whoever had come to arrest him. But it was only the young tavern girl coming home and her grandmother getting up to use the chamber pot.

His head was spinning with thoughts and anxiety. It seemed almost ridiculous that a slip of the tongue and a moment of confusion was the last straw for the innkeeper. But it had been. And it was his fault. The risk had been too high for them to try to help Jon. At least he ought to have gone alone, and he should have stayed out of people's way instead of prancing around the inn in a wig like a rooster, pretending to be a relation to someone who was tried at court. He had really mishandled the situation.

Giving up sleeping, he changed into his boots and thick stockings. Then as silently as he could, he climbed the ladder and peeked out the window. Dawn was coming in the east, reflecting faintly in the white snow and making the world gray rather than black. There were three pairs of skis jutting upright from the snow, ski poles beside each. Contemplating for a moment, he placed a coin on the table, slipped out the door, seized the largest pair of skis, and fled Jönköping.

***

As Nikolaos got further west, the snow disappeared, and he walked until he found a farmer willing to let him borrow a horse. He let the farmer have the skis and paid him handsomely.

The next day, the little horse cantered happily toward his farm, picking up the scent of food and other animals when the front door was flung open. Then, Hindrich, Ekborg, and Elsebet pushed themselves outside and ran toward him.

525

"Father, they have Mother. The sixmen are questioning her!" Hindrich cried, getting to Nikolaos before he had even entered the yard.

Nikolaos pulled on the reins and got the horse to a sudden halt. The farm seemed to tilt sideways, and there was a ringing sound in his ears. He grabbed hold of the pommel for support. "Hindrich?"

"They said she's been involved with the otherworldly," Hindrich said, his eyes dark and weary.

Elsebet caught up and took him by the arm. "Thank the lord you're back home, Father. She's been gone for several days. No one will speak with us, and we don't know how she's doing." She burst into tears. Her eyes were red and swollen, and the skin under her nose was rubbed raw. She had been crying for days. What had they done to his family? It was his fault. All of it. He dismounted and wrapped his arms around her.

Behind Elsebet, Hindrich met his eyes. "I'll bring the horse to the stable. Will you help me? Ekborg and Elsebet can get something to eat for you."

"Of course, son," Nikolaos said, giving Elsebet a firm squeeze. "I'll be in as soon as the horse is settled."

Walking in silence the short distance to the stable, Nikolaos tried to still his panic and think of what to say to his children, but his mind was completely blank.

"Whose horse is this?" Hindrich asked, holding the door open.

"I borrowed it from a farmer. I've promised to bring her back in the spring well fattened up. We can afford it. The farmer looked rather relieved, glad that he and his family can eat her grain this winter. It's far though, near Boåker, almost by Jönköping."

"You went to Jönköping again?" Hindrich asked, turning toward him in surprise as he brought the horse into an empty stall.

"I did, yes," Nikolaos said, feeling ashamed. Had he stayed on the coach, he would have been back a lot sooner. "On the way back from Stockholm. What happened?"

Hindrich swallowed, then coughed once. "We were at home,

the women were inside weaving, and I was wintering the stables. I had brought the animals inside already because there was snow in the air, but it never came. I was adding hay and grain for the cows when I heard them galloping down the road, fast as if there was a fire, and shouting. Someone came all the way here, dragging sticks along the wall as they rode by. I don't know who it was. But whoever it was saw fit to frighten the animals." Hindrich stopped, visibly upset, and stepped out of the stall so his mood wouldn't bother the horse.

Nikolaos stepped aside to give him space, shaking his head. He wanted to find out who did that.

"When I ran out to see what it was about, I tripped and twisted my ankle badly. It hurt like you wouldn't believe. I'm still not able to put my full weight on it. Not sure if you noticed?" He sat down on the bench in the back, stretching his leg forward.

He hadn't. It was shameful. That too, was his fault.

"Once I had managed to get up and was hobbling to the house, they were already bringing Mother out. Eskil Stonemason held her arm and pushed her into the pastor's wagon, and then the sixmen surrounded…"

"All the sixmen and the pastor were involved in this?" Nikolaos interrupted. Eskil and Uffe then, who had broken bread at their harvest feast just over a month ago.

"Yes," Hindrich said, nodding.

"When was this?"

"The day after church, so Monday. It's Friday today already."

Nikolaos sat down beside him, trying to think of what he ought to do and what to say. Maybe now was the time to tell Hindrich the truth? But if he did and they arrested him, all they needed to do was torture him, and he would tell them. Then they would execute him just like they did with Jon and Old Karin. The thought made him feel as though someone was sitting on his chest, making it hard to breathe.

"Father, I went after them, got on my horse with my sprained ankle, and hurried after them. But they didn't let me go to her. I waited all day and that night. We've been back every day, but they won't let us talk to her or see her." He looked close to tears but hid it well.

"Where did they take her?"

"To the community hall."

Nikolaos inhaled sharply, forcing air into his lungs. The community hall was a small refurbished storage barn that had been converted into a meeting hall a few years ago. It didn't have a fireplace. Stina would be freezing. She was always cold.

"Who's with her?"

"I'm not sure. I think Anders and Eskil Stonemason stayed. I knocked, but they refused to even acknowledge me. I stayed and listened through the wall to make sure that..." He stopped, unable to say what he was thinking.

Nikolaos clapped him on the shoulder, "I thank you, son."

Hindrich lifted his eyes to his, then immediately looked away again and kept talking. "The next morning the pastor arrived. He told me they had gotten word Mother was involved with the otherworldly and that it was his duty to take it seriously for the safety of the village. He wouldn't tell me the specifics, but he mentioned that Näcken was involved and that it was very serious. Much more than I could ever imagine, he claimed."

"It's rusty outrageous," Nikolaos said, pushing down a surge of anger and shame. He felt like hitting something.

"Yes. The pastor urged me to go home and wait. He swore to me that she would be safe and just questioned. Father, I don't understand. Is there something that I don't know? Pray if there is, tell me. I won't say anything to Elsebet or Ekborg, I promise. Just tell me the truth. I pray you."

Nikolaos hesitated, giving his son a long, scrutinizing look. Now would be the time. The truth felt so close, he could taste it, but then he stopped himself and told Hindrich what he had told Lord Oxensköld and Antonio instead.

Hindrich grew pale as he listened, staring at him with disbelief and terror in his eyes. How would he have taken it if he had told him the truth?

Chapter 66

An hour later, Nikolaos banged on the pastor's door, hitting it so hard it hurt.

He heard quick footsteps from inside, then the pastor's voice. "Yes, yes, I'm coming. Hold on a moment." The pastor opened the door wide, a smile already on his lips which faded as soon as he saw Nikolaos. Then he slammed the door in his face.

It hadn't even crossed Nikolaos' mind that the pastor would be too afraid to let him in. But naturally, he was, now when he knew who he was. The pastor and everyone knew. He had slipped. Forgotten who he was and raised above his station, putting his family in danger.

He knocked again, this time even harder, not caring that it hurt. It made him feel human. "You open your door now, Pastor! Open the door, or I'll break it for you."

Only a moment later, the pastor slowly opened the door, holding up a large cross and his Bible like a shield.

Nikolaos scoffed with irritation, and hurt too, and pushed himself past him, striding into his parlor. There was a lit candle and a mug of mulled wine still steaming on a little side table in the corner beside a comfortable chair.

"Sit!" Nikolaos barked, pointing to it. "Enjoy your warm drink. It's a cold day. When we're finished talking, I need you to get my wife. The community hall is freezing, and here you sit with hot drinks and comfort. You should be ashamed of yourself. I don't think she's given the same comforts as you have here."

The pastor's hands were shaking, and he almost fell when he sat down, busy as his hands were with his cross and Bible.

"Did you hear me?"

"Yes." The pastor's voice was merely a whisper. He had put the Bible in his lap and the cross on top of it. The cross was so tall it blocked his face.

It looked ridiculous. If it had been anything other than holy items, Nikolaos would have flung them from his grasp, but he stayed calm. "Good, then put the holy book and the cross down so we can speak properly."

"Oh no, I most certainly will not," the pastor croaked, just a little louder than before.

"Then at least lie it down so I can look at you. I can't talk to you like this. Tell me what's happened to my wife."

"She's not your wife!"

Nikolaos frowned, something cold settling in his stomach. "Yes, she is."

"No one here witnessed you going to your marriage bed. I've spoken to those who knew you when you first came to our area, and you were alone. Then suddenly you had a wife. Who is she, and where's she from?"

Nikolaos was just about to answer him when it struck him that they might find out what her neighbors in Marstrand had accused her of. He said nothing.

"As a matter of fact, I'm going to start the House Hearings," the pastor said. "I should've done so earlier, but I've been lagging, thinking I knew my congregation well enough. I see now that I was wrong. I should've followed the law, many parishes have done this for years. God is punishing me for my disobedience."

"House Hearings?"

"It's so that I can make sure that everyone in the parish knows their Catechism. The church wants us to have hearings on it. They also want me to make sure I have the correct information on where people are from and when they were born as well. It's done in the congregants' home usually." He stopped, a surprised expression on his face as if he couldn't believe he had said all that with him there.

It was so obvious that Nikolaos laughed. "That's some news indeed. But I must say I agree, if you had, you'd know we're a God-fearing household, that you don't already, is beyond me. And insulting, I was with you from the very beginning, helping with the building of our church." He shook his head. "My son and his wife were blessed in it. I need you to tell me why you have Stina, and then I want you to take me to her. And I need you to tell the sixmen

I'm bringing her home."

The pastor stared at him, looking so scared Nikolaos feared that he would throw up, hugging the Bible to his chest with one hand and the cross with the other. "We thought you were at the King's funeral. Instead, I hear you were performing for Merchant Fleisher and made people faint. Two young people drowned because of you. You had congress with them both!" His voice broke, and he tried to cross himself but the holy objects in his hands got in the way.

"Yes, so I've heard. I made a comet appear too, it seems."

The pastor screamed, startling a flock of birds outside that noisily flew off to settle somewhere else.

Nikolaos laughed coldly. "You must calm yourself. This is ridiculous. I'm done with these insults. I've humored you long enough." He grabbed the pastor and pulled him out of the chair.

The pastor squealed like a child. The cross and Bible slid off his knees and fell to the floor with a clatter.

"Now tell me who told you all of this and who it was that got the mother of my children arrested. Then you bring me to her, you hear? Or I'll contact the King and have you in jail. I, compared to you, have the ear of both the Dowager Queen and our new King!" None of it was true of course, but the pastor didn't know that. It worked. He became soft as clay in his hands.

"I'll tell you, of course I will. Pray forgive me, Lord Näcken."

Lord Näcken. Nikolaos let go of the pastor as if he had burned himself on a log from the fire and walked over to the window, hearing the pastor yelp and fall to the floor. Nikolaos didn't care. His life was slipping from his fingers, and he didn't seem to be able to do anything about it. Out of the water he was just a man, and he didn't know what to do.

When he turned back around, the pastor was getting to his knees with the help of his chair, grabbing his Bible on the way up. Nikolaos resisted the urge to push him down again, but satisfied himself by just grabbing his arm, hard.

"Do not call me Näcken again. Ever. Do you hear?"

"Yes, sir."

"And I'm not a lord. Now do what I asked and tell me who made you believe such vile things of me. I won't ask again."

"Merchant Fleisher and Secretary Bödkers. They told me everything."

Nikolaos flinched. He hadn't expected Secretary Bödkers to get involved. "Well, Pastor, I *did* perform for Merchant Fleisher *and* at the funeral of our late King. As for the rest, you're wrong. Rumors such as these are not worthy of my time and need not my defense. You ought to be ashamed to believe in them and cause my family discomfort. Now you bring me to my wife," Nikolaos said, quite proud of himself. Not needing to defend himself had been a perfect thing to say.

The pastor looked confused and was clearly struggling with what to believe. He remained where he was, patting the surface of the Bible with his hand, his mouth moving in a silent prayer. Then he surprised Nikolaos and put both the cross and the Bible on the table and snuffed out the candle with his fingers. "We'll leave now, Nikolaos. I'll get you your wife."

Too stunned and too relieved to say anything, Nikolaos stepped aside and let him pass. He waited until the pastor got his coat and hat, and then they left. Not another word passed between them.

When they arrived at the community hall, the pastor knocked to announce himself and was promptly let inside. Only a moment later, the door opened again, and Stina was pushed straight into Nikolaos' arms. Someone slammed the door closed behind her.

They clung desperately to each other, and Nikolaos carefully patted her all over to see if she was in one piece. She was, but she felt rigid in his arms.

"Come, we're going home." His voice was raw from emotion, or maybe it was from having screamed at the pastor.

***

He wished he hadn't left his horse at the pastor's. Stina

could walk but was so weak from exhaustion that her legs barely held her, and he had to carry her on his back as if she were a child.

They didn't say a word to each other until they had retrieved the horse and were on the empty stretch of road leading out of the village. Then, sitting behind Nikolaos with her cheek next to his face, Stina started talking. "I was weaving with the girls when we heard them come. They shouted and carried on, and at first, I thought a war had broken out and that they had come to collect Hindrich to make him join the army. I was so afraid of it that I was relieved when it was me they came for. But then it frightened me. Eskil grabbed me by the arm and forced me to walk with them. I tried to talk to him, but he didn't listen. Then Uffe came running in and grabbed my other arm. It hurt. I'm still bruised. Ekborg and Elsebet rushed to help me and ask what was happening, but Eskil pushed them away from me, Nikolaos! They forced me to get into their wagon, and the pastor was sitting there waiting for me."

He squeezed her hand, too numb with anger to answer.

"Nikolaos, I've never seen our pastor like this, angry and cold. He told me I was accused of meddling with the otherworldly. I thought that someone from Marstrand had come looking for me after all these years. But then Uffe told me they found out who you are." She stifled a sob. "Said we've been hiding in plain sight here for too long and would finally be brought to justice. They'd begin with me, who had hidden the truth from my neighbors for so long, hidden the fact that you…" Stina trailed off, then said, "I'm afraid they hurt Hindrich because once he finally came running to help me, he was limping and wincing with pain."

Nikolaos felt her tears against his cheek. It was unbearable. What had they done to her? "No darling, I've spoken to him. He twisted his ankle. They didn't hurt him."

"Praise be God," she said, sobbing.

"He twisted it when he tried to get to you. It was a bad sprain, but he's better."

"God was intervening then. There's no telling what they'd do if he'd caught up," she said, her sobs easing. "They're very angry, Nikolaos. Merchant Fleisher's wife had contacted Secretary Bödkers and told them we had been involved, that you had been involved when Jon was convicted, that you had tried to stop it because it was just the way the courts said it was. You know, about the blood pact and the book of black arts. And that the executioner recognized you and that you had tried to save Jon because he was your prodigy."

Nikolaos let out a breath, turning sideways so he could look at her. "I was afraid of that. Stina, can we take a break and sit on the grass a bit, if you're not too cold? Just so we can talk things through before we see the children."

She nodded.

Nikolaos dismounted and helped her down, bringing her close for a moment before he let her go. He pulled his coat off and wrapped it around her shoulders, wiping the tears from her cheeks with his thumb. He could have lost her.

Together, they walked off the road and sat down in the wintery dry grass. Nikolaos wrapped his arms around Stina inside the coat, warming her freezing, tense body between his arms.

Stina took a deep, steadying breath, then started talking again. "They're saying people fainted at your performance. And that you lured a couple into the water who nearly drowned. They were only saved 'cause the water wasn't deep enough, they said." She looked away, blushing.

He knew what she was afraid of saying. What did one tell a wife after having been unfaithful to her? He had committed a grave sin, made graver since one of them was a man, and graver still because he thought he'd killed them but hadn't even stopped to make sure or to help. It was odd though, that the pastor had accused him of having killed them. What reason did he have for that?

"The pastor," Stina continued, "claimed that you hadn't performed for the King at all and was just putting on airs, even after I told them that we were there, and that I could vouch for you. Still, they wouldn't believe me. Remember when Alma lost two of her babies? Eskil said it was you who pulled them out of her womb and took them into the water with you."

"They said what?" Nikolaos stared at the sky in

exasperation. "Damn them to hell!" He tightened his fists. The right
one smarted from having banged on the pastor's door.

"Yes," Stina said with surprising conviction. "They're awful
men. I'm surprised I never saw it before." She pulled her hand up
from under the coat and touched his cheek. Her fingers felt icy.
"They peppered me with questions, intimate questions about our
life together."

Nikolaos said nothing, just took her hand, warming it
between his. What had they done to her? If they had hurt her, he
would kill them. He pictured sticking a knife through their chests
one after the other. It made his heart race.

"They asked if our bed is made of water and if I need a piece
of wood to sleep on so I don't sink. If we have a second home on
the bottom of the river, and if you show me all the bodies of the
ones you… you." She stopped. "I'm to be taken to Göta Royal Court.
They'll surely hang me for it!" Tears started sliding down her cheeks
again.

"No, Stina, no one will take you to court. I'll make sure of it.
Don't you worry about that." Nikolaos hugged her tighter. They
were in real trouble. What would happen to their children if they
were both arrested? And his in-laws? What did Ekborg's parents
and siblings think? "Stina, we need to decide what to tell Elsebet
and Hindrich, and then I think we should leave."

She looked at him, more tears forming in her eyes. "Where
would we go if, even in Stockholm, they know who you are?"

"We go south, perhaps to Helsingborg. It's all the way in
what used to be Denmark. They might not know of me, and we'd be
able to start anew. We can bring Elsebet at least. Hindrich and
Ekborg, I don't know."

"Elsebet has her heart set on that boy, she'll never leave."

"We'll see." He pulled her up and put his arm around her
waist to support her as they walked, grabbing the horse with his
other hand. It would really surprise him if there would be a
betrothal now. "Stina, I don't think we have much choice. The only
reason they let you go today is because our beloved pastor," he
grimaced, "was so scared of me he did whatever I told him to do.

He knows who I am, Stina."

"How? How can he suddenly see it?"

"I don't know."

"Ekborg is with child, Nikolaos."

"She is?" He grinned, but then it faded. They might never see the baby.

"Yes, she told me just after you left for Stockholm. It's coming in about five months." Stina paused, looking sad. "I suppose you're right. I don't particularly want to see any of them again after what they've done to me."

"We've no choice. It's not safe. I had hoped Hindrich and Ekborg could inherit the farm, but as it is now, it's better if we all leave, isn't it?" His chest constricted at the thought. "You were right, Stina, when you said we ought to leave after Jönköping. It would've been better if we had. I should never have gone to the courts to try to stop the execution. I put you all in danger. And I should never have accepted Mistress Esmeralda's invitation."

She looked at him without answering. The question about what he had done in the river hung between them unanswered.

***

Once Elsebet and Hindrich had assured themselves that their mother truly was unharmed, they sat down by the hearth in the front room. Wrapping Stina in a blanket, they fed her bread with butter dipped in broth to soften, feeding her like a child. She let them for a few minutes, but then waved them away and ate it herself. When she finished, she handed the bowl to Ekborg. "I must go to the outhouse, it's pressing, I haven't pooped the whole time."

"Oh, my lord," Ekborg said, rushing to her side at the same time as Elsebet. They would have laughed if the reason behind it hadn't been so horrific.

As soon as the women were out of hearing, Hindrich turned to Nikolaos, a look of disgust on his face. "To imagine that she hasn't even been allowed to go to the bathroom. It's a disgrace, I'll kill them!"

Nikolaos cocked an eyebrow at him but pictured killing them himself, this time with a twist of the knife as he stabbed them. He would probably be sent to hell for it, should he ever die, but he couldn't think of that now. It gave him a perverse comfort to imagine it. "It's crossed my mind too, Hindrich. But I assume she's been allowed to go somewhere at least. She doesn't usually poop if we travel or if she's scared."

"I see. But they're our neighbors. How can they treat us this way?"

Nikolaos opened his mouth, but no words came out. He wondered the same but also knew why. Then Stina burst through the door, and he was glad he didn't have to answer. "You've already been at the outhouse?" he asked her.

Stina shook her head, looking embarrassed. "No, I never made it. I'm afraid I made a mess outside, not even halfway there. Elsebet is getting a shovel. Ekborg is throwing up."

Hindrich stared between Stina and Nikolaos. Seeing his mother's crocked smile, he laughed.

"You'll have a strong baby, my son," Nikolaos said. Stina's smile instantly turned to tears. He had caused so much pain, he couldn't bear it.

The door opened again, and Elsebet and Ekborg came back inside.

Stina smiled through her tears, turning toward them. "I thank you both. Pray forgive me again."

"Don't mention it," Ekborg said and went to pour herself some broth. Then she made her way back to sit by Hindrich, careful not to spill it or trip over Stina's blanket-covered legs.

"Mother, Father," Hindrich said, a look of deep consternation on his face. "I don't understand. We've known our neighbors our whole life. How can they suddenly suspect you of something like this? I don't understand."

Nikolaos took a deep breath and exhaled slowly. "I found out more, son. The pastor informed me that Secretary Bödkers and Merchant Fleisher were here talking about me. They're the ones who've started all these rumors." He put his head in his hands and rubbed his face. "This is my fault. I owe you all an apology. We should never have gotten involved with the courts, no matter how horrific it was for Jon. God bless his soul, and may he rest peacefully." He made the sign of the cross and exchanged a glance with Stina. "I should've left it alone. We common people can never affect the law. I ought to have known this. All it did was to start rumors. I'm the head of our household, but I've failed you. Pray forgive me."

"No, Nikolaos, you haven't. You haven't failed. You did your best," Stina said.

"Who's Merchant Fleisher? And Secretary Bödkers?" Elsebet asked.

"Merchant Fleisher is Mistress Esmeralda's husband. Secretary Bödkers works for Göta Royal Court. I spoke to him before Jon's trial. The rumors reached them both, it seems."

"I heard people were so entranced by your music that they fainted. The shoemaker and his wife spoke of it, but as soon as I got near, they changed the subject." Ekborg said.

Elsebet looked silently into her lap.

"It's ridiculous, they've all heard me play, and none of them have fainted," Nikolaos said angrily, then purposely changed the subject. "Elsebet, have you seen Peder since your mother was taken?"

"I did, Father, but he wouldn't speak with me."

The chill of the devil's bottom has reached us, Nikolaos thought, reminded of Lord Oxensköld's choice of words the other night. Stina turned to him, and their eyes met. He gave a small nod.

"Elsebet," Stina said, "given what's happened and what your father and I have been accused of, we feel that the best thing to do is to leave. It may be wise for you to come with us. We had wanted Hindrich and Ekborg to take the farm, just like your father and I did when you and Hindrich were little babies. But now, after what they did, it's wiser if we all leave, we believe."

"Leave! But I can't just... my betrothal," Elsebet stopped abruptly and straightened in her chair, looking straight at Nikolaos with an expression he had never seen before.

His stomach twisted. She knew. He didn't know how, but she did. Time stilled as they stared at each other, and he felt his new daughter-in-law's questioning eyes upon him. He braced himself for exposure, wondering if he should deny it or tell them the truth, risking Ekborg panicking and running home to her parents, telling them she was pregnant with Näcken's grandchild.

Then Elsebet looked away, and Hindrich broke the silence.

"Father, this is outrageous. Why would you leave your home for this? I realize it's bad what's happened. But leaving would just make you seem guilty. I'll talk to the pastor, make him apologize publicly on Sunday." Hindrich looked pleased with himself as if he was sure he had talked them to their senses.

"Son, the decision is made. You should know that we've thought about this for a while. Like Mother said, we've wanted you to have the farm. I'm not as young as I look, and I want to spend my last years performing more."

Hindrich stared at him for several moments, then with a quick look at his wife, he said, "We're staying Ekborg and I. And I frankly don't understand why you need to leave. This is your home. You can still perform more and let me do the heavy work. I'll handle the rumors."

"It wouldn't make a difference, Hindrich," Stina said. "It's me who wants to leave. I can't look the pastor or the other men in the eyes again after what they accused me of. I just can't."

Hindrich stared at her, and suddenly he looked so sad, like a little boy. Then he pursed his lips, nodding slowly. "Of course, Mother. I'll speak to Peder and see where his loyalties lay. I'd be surprised if he believes the rumors. He might just be scared to talk to you. But I don't want you going to see him alone, or at all until we know, Elsebet."

"I thank you, Hindrich," Elsebet said. A moment later she lifted her eyes and looked straight at Nikolaos. She looked angry. There was no longer any doubt. How had she found out?

Chapter 67

"I think we should get married Rå, Magda mine," Måns said with a grin that lit up his whole face. He was leaning on an old fence they had come upon in the woods. It must have been protecting someone's crops at one point long ago. Now there was no grain to be seen, just large trees for as far as the eye could reach. It was remarkable that the fence was still there, stretching the span of at least fifty men standing side by side. Parts of it was interlaced with birch and pine trunks that had grown straight through it.

She laughed, "Måns, we can't do that."

"Why not? We already are. We just haven't had our wedding night witnessed."

"Well, Måns," she lifted her skirt and climbed over the fence to stand on the same side as him, "I wouldn't call what we've done a wedding night."

"Then I pray you, let's wed. I want no one else." He put his arms around her neck and kissed her on her ear. His breath tickled her, and he felt so warm in her arms.

"I can't marry you, Måns. I'm the Forest Rå, it's not my destiny," she said, but wasn't sure if it was right anymore. The vow to her mother had been a very long time ago. And their marriage wouldn't last very long, just one human lifetime.

***

"Did you change your mind Rå, Magda mine?" Måns asked a week later.

She smiled at him, pulling her hood off her head and placing her mittens to dry by their hearth. "No, I haven't." But she had. At least in a sense, but she didn't want to tell him that. Strange how she could suddenly waver. Maybe seeing Nikolaos and his family had affected her too much.

"Oh well, at least you're visiting." His eyes were alight with warmth.

"Yes," she said simply, reaching her hands toward the flames to warm them.

"Why are you here then, Rå? It's dark." He brought over a chair from their table so she could sit.

"I came to ask if you and your uncles could help me build a lean-to or a shed for my cows. I'm worried about the winter. Where are they today? Your uncles," she asked as she sat down.

"At Olga's checking on her cow, believe it or not. It's not doing well. Her son's cows are sick as well. And cows died for no reason at Sjömölla a few weeks ago. Olga is worried they have the same sickness."

"What kind of sickness?"

Måns shrugged. "I don't know exactly, but everyone is worried."

"Of course. I understand."

"Our own cows are fine though, which is a relief. Would you come with me to Olga's and see if you can help? I was just about to head over," he said and reached for his coat, hanging on a hook by the front door.

"I will," Rå said, disappointed. She had hoped they would have time in his bed before his uncles were back home. It would have to wait. "Does Olga and her son know who I am?"

"Yes, they do."

"I see." She frowned, putting her cloak over her shoulders as she followed him outside, leaving her mittens where they were. "Måns, I realize *you* knew, but it makes me uneasy that everyone else does. I'm not accustomed to this. You and your uncles are the only people with whom I'm this open, and I'm not sure if it's wise to tell others."

Måns carefully closed the door and bolted it, then took her by the elbow and walked out to the road. "I didn't know that. Everyone here in Kjugekull thinks of you as a saint, Rå. They respect you very much."

She smiled, her heart warmed by his words. "I'm so used to pretending."

"No need for it here, Rå, Magda mine," he said and put his arm around her waist.

Rå leaned into him, then kissed him on the cheek. It had a nice stubble.

They made their way through the village. Olga lived at the end, just where the village crops started. The castle was visible from where they were walking, with candles and lanterns lit in several windows. It looked out of place here in this tiny little village. There should be dark woods around them, not a tall edifice. It felt like a giant had placed it there, then forgotten about it.

Måns held out his lantern so they could see to step around a large puddle. "You're old, Magda mine," he said affectionately. "It must be lonely to never marry."

"Don't call a woman old, Måns."

He laughed, a guffawing sort of laugh. "You're not a woman, Rå."

She chuckled. He was very funny at times. She could let her guard down with him, which felt surprisingly good. "I do get lonely sometimes, but I like to be free, not bound by anything. I'm used to it, Måns. Like you said, I've lived alone for a long time now." He moved closer to her, and she wrapped her arms around him, kissing him. He tasted salty and of some kind of smoked fish. It made her hungry for both him and food. "Måns, I have considered marrying you. Part of me wants to say yes." There she said it. But it would never work, she would get too restless.

"Oh, Rå, Magda mine, have you really? You'd do it?"

"I'm not supposed to, Måns." A gust of icy wind tossed her hair to the side as if to remind her of her hole under it. "But it feels so good to be here with you, and my heart is touched by how everyone here respects me."

He hugged her tightly, and she could feel him wanting to say something, but then they heard a barndoor close, and shortly thereafter, a circle of lantern light made its way toward them.

"That's them," Måns said and pulled out of their embrace.

"They didn't make it. All of them, both Olga's and her son's cows died one after the other," Bushbrow called out as they approached.

"I'm very saddened to hear that. Who else has cows here?"

Rå asked.

"It's just us now."

"I see. I'll go see to your cows. Don't worry about them."

"You could do that?" Per asked. "Pray, thank you. Bless you Mistress Rå."

"Of course, it would be my pleasure. You've already saved mine. And, I almost forgot, I came here to ask you to build a wind shelter for *my* cows. So, it's the least I can do."

Rå pulled open the heavy barn door and was greeted by the smell of cows and fresh hay. Lifting her lantern, she found three cows and two goats in a large enclosure. The fragrant hay was piled high behind them in the corner. Each animal was chewing languidly while slowly moving toward her, looking strong and healthy. There was nothing wrong with these cows. She opened her back wide and let them lick her hands with their slippery yet scratchy tongues, chanting softly to strengthen them against any ills that might befall them. Soon they were resting peacefully, eyes lowered and heads leaning on each other while the goats curled up beside them and fell asleep.

Chapter 68

Hindrich strode in and tossed his coat on Stina's knitting chair. "That dastard is calling off the wedding!" he shouted angrily, shooting an apologetic look at Elsebet. "Pray forgive me. I tried my best to talk him out of it."

"No. Oh, no." Elsebet staggered and grabbed hold of the wall behind her.

Nikolaos hid a sigh of relief. This meant she would come with them.

"He claims the barn is falling apart. Said they have to replace it cause the roof is leaking. When I asked why they need to replace a whole barn just because of a hole in the roof, he said that the entire roof is falling apart and leaking on the walls, which caused them to rot."

"He's lying," Elsebet said quietly.

"I know. Remember when I helped them fix their tool shed? There was nothing wrong with that barn then. And I checked today. I went and slapped and banged on the walls. There's nothing wrong with it. I made a real show of it." He gave a sad one-sided smile. "I know they saw it too. Both Peder and his mother were watching from the window."

Nikolaos raised an eyebrow, smiling back at him. That was well done. Dastards indeed. They deserved it.

Stina walked in from the other room and went to hug Elsebet. She exchanged a grateful look with Nikolaos. Stina was relieved as well.

"It's a breach of contract. We could make him marry her, say we'll hold the wedding feast here." Hindrich went to sit down at the dining table, keeping his eyes on Elsebet, who shook her head but stayed silent.

Nikolaos shook his head as well. "We could, but given what happened at the courts with Jon, only God himself knows what they'll think of next. It's not safe here anymore. Are you sure you and Ekborg don't want to come with us, Hindrich? There's no telling how they'd treat you and Ekborg. Or the baby."

Hindrich had a sour expression on his face. "No, Father. I'm not leaving. It would be outrageous. Scared off from our home and property due to some stupid rumors about you being Näcken." He rolled his eyes. "Again, Father, I can't understand how you can allow for it. I know Mother wants to leave, and I understand her, but why don't you put your foot down and say no? Go demand an apology from our neighbors!" He sounded angry.

"I won't, Hindrich. I can't do that to Mother." Nikolaos turned to Stina, wondering if she regretted not telling Hindrich and Elsebet the truth. "You saw how they were. I'm more concerned that you're staying here," he said, turning back to Hindrich.

"I know, Father, I know. I do understand. It's just that Ekborg could've used the help with the baby. Now she's all alone. I don't like it. It feels like you're abandoning us."

Nikolaos nodded, guilt sitting like a clump in his chest, making it hard to breathe. "I understand, but we'll write when we're settled. Promise me, you'll come south at the first sign of trouble. Head to Helsingborg and leave a message in Lady Maria Church. I'll find you." He went over to the table and pulled Hindrich close and embraced him, clapping him on the shoulder.

***

They left without much more than the clothes on their backs and two horses. Nikolaos felt worse than when he left his and Abluna's farm. Then he had been alone with nothing to lose, but now his heart was breaking, leaving Hindrich and Ekborg to an uncertain future with neighbors they couldn't trust anymore. And it was his fault. He had failed them all.

After three days and nights, a snowstorm hit them. It came as if from nowhere. Large flurries first and then a biting wind full of snow and ice that covered them within minutes.

"It's going to be impossible to find an inn in this weather. We're too far off the main roads," Nikolaos called, shifting sideways in the saddle toward the women. It made the wind blow right into his face. "Did you see any farms or cottages back there? I've not paid as much attention as I should. I'm feeling distracted." He caught Stina's eyes apologetically, knowing that she knew he was getting restless for water. "If we don't find someone who can take us in soon, we'll have to find a pine to stay under. I can cut off branches to make room inside."

"Nikolaos, that'll be too hard. We'll never survive the night. We need to find something. You need to get us to safety. We're cold!" Stina shouted through the wind and urged their horse up next to his. "We've been out for three days now. When are we getting to Helsingborg?" She glared at him. It was obvious that she wasn't feeling compassionate toward his particular need.

"I think we ought to be there by tomorrow or the day after that. Stina, don't be frightened. I'll get us there."

Elsebet pulled her head out from behind her mother's back and shook her head at him as if he could do something about the weather. She even wagged a finger at him like she used to do when she was little.

"We'll find something. I'll get us a safe place somehow," Nikolaos said, turning forward in the saddle again and kicking his heels. They were right though, no matter his mental state, they needed to get inside as soon as possible.

The road was just barely visible through the storm. Each time they lost their path, the horses sank into the ditch beside it, and Nikolaos had to dismount and pull them out.

They pressed on, and after what felt like an eternity, the harsh wind and blinding snow suddenly ceased. The clouds were swept aside, and brilliant moonlight bathed the landscape. And there, as if by magic, a wide road stretched out before them. Nikolaos knew where they were. That road led straight up Halland's Ridge.

He held in his horse to get the women's attention, pointing ahead. "We'll make it. Margarete Inn is just on the other side of that ridge."

Stina nodded, smiling with relief.

It wasn't as close as it looked. Elsebet's and Stina's lips were blue, and their teeth were chattering when they finally arrived. They looked so frozen that the barkeep immediately ushered them inside, inviting them to sit on a bench right in front of the fire, promising them hot soup.

Nikolaos left them and went to bring the horses to the stable, drawing a sigh of relief when he found the stable clean with plenty of room. Someone had put out extra blankets and a good amount of feed, with a sign encouraging him to use it. It would probably cost him a substantial sum, but in this weather, he was grateful to be able to cover their backs and fill their buckets.

Pretending to be as cold as the others, Nikolaos hurried inside, finding them by the fire as promised. There were several tables in the room, but they were all empty and dark, every candle and torch blown out. The only light was from the fireplace and a candelabra on a metal chest.

Nikolaos had only just sat down beside them when Stina excused herself and left to go to sleep. Clearly, she was still angry. Not that he could blame her. He sat back, gazing at the flames, feeling guilty again.

The barkeep came and handed Nikolaos a bowl of steaming hot soup, added logs to the fire, and then left them alone.

The only sound was the crackling of burning wood and Elsebet fidgeting with something on her dress that made a rasping noise when her fingers moved across it. Nikolaos knew she wanted to question him, felt it as if her thoughts were something he could see, like his colors almost. He had some of the soup, waiting.

"Father," she said, only an eyeblink later. But just then, they heard footsteps approaching and the barkeep appeared again.

"Good sir," he said. "Would you like me to send for someone to carry your luggage to your room?"

"I thank you, but there's no need. I can carry it myself. We'll retire now," Nikolaos said and got to his feet. The poor man probably wanted to go to sleep. He grabbed their bags. They weren't heavy, but it was cumbersome to hold them by himself, and he changed his mind. "Actually, I'd be grateful for the help."

"Certainly, good sir, I'll go up with ye, no one's here anyway," he said, taking two of the bags. "It's late. The weather's been too cold, and we had quite the storm earlier this afternoon." He led the way up the stairs and down a corridor. "You travelen' onwards to Helsingborg tomorrow then, I take it? You a merchant?" he asked, turning around to face them once he reached the landing.

"Yes, kind sir, my father is a merchant," Elsebet replied with a wide smile, looking unabashedly straight at the barkeep.

Nikolaos raised an eyebrow, both impressed by her quick tongue and taken aback at the lie.

"Ah, see, I knew it," the barkeep said. "I can tell these things, been here a long time and meet men from all over the country, even other countries. Had a fella here who sold chocolate once even. You, being a merchant n' all, must know about it, I'm sure, but I'd never seen it before. I was offered a sample, but I politely declined. It looked too odd for me, dark and almost black as the night itself."

Nikolaos had no idea what it was he was talking about but nodded and said, "I've thought so myself." He feigned hiding a yawn. "If we could speak more in the morning, I fear exhaustion is taking its toll on me. It's been a long journey."

"Of course, of course, pray forgive my questions. I tend to talk too much. I'll take you to your room. Our maid has warmed the beds for you. Just take care before you lie down. The bed warmer may still be hot."

Nikolaos acknowledged him with a quick nod.

"Ah, very good. I leave you to it then," the barkeep said and briskly walked ahead and placed their bags in front of a door at the end. "This here is your room. May God give you a nice rest." Bowing, he glanced at them both, then left.

Nikolaos sighed with relief. He had been afraid he would follow them inside and insist on showing them everything. The maid, he assumed, had lit a lantern and hung it on a hook right by the door. It was bright enough to reveal a bed lengthwise along the wall on the left. Stina was sleeping in it, two blankets covering her up to her nose. He smiled, hopefully she was warm now. The back of the room was shrouded in darkness. Nikolaos carefully brought the luggage inside, then pulled the lantern from its hook and tiptoed across the floor. There was another bed, also lengthwise along the wall, at the end of the room.

Elsebet followed him and sat down heavily on it.

"Why did you lie and say I was a merchant?" he whispered and sat down next to her. She didn't answer, just sat there, dragging her fingers across her dress like before. There was a stain, he could see now, a dried sticky substance she was trying to scrape off with her nails. He reached for her hand to stop her and to squeeze it. "Elsebet, tell me what's on your mind and why you lied."

She threw a quick glance at her mother's sleeping form, then unlaced her shoes, pulled them off, and slipped under the covers. She winced as she bumped into the bed warmer, then used her shawl as a potholder and pulled it out.

"Father, it's for the best. Don't you see that? You can't be a musician anymore. They'll find you."

They might. She was right about that. "But I don't know anything about being a merchant. Or where to sell things," he said.

"In Helsingborg, of course."

"Yes, I understand, but I know nothing of it. I'm assuming there are regulations."

Elsebet shrugged, pulling the covers higher for warmth. "I don't know. I only meant to protect you."

"I know, but it's not wise to lie like that, especially if you can't back up your claims. Lying is always wrong. But if you're going to lie anyway, you need to plan for it and have a proper story to tell with details that can be checked. I've learned from my own mistakes too many times." What kind of father was he, telling his daughter how to lie? He was glad Stina was asleep.

"What have you lied about, Father?" she asked. Nikolaos could hear the catch in her breath.

"Well, I've told little lies to get out of things that I didn't want to do mainly. More often than not, I was caught in it. Since then, I've learned to at least stay as close to the truth as I can."

"Did you do that with our pastor when you went to get

Mother? What did you tell him?" Elsebet asked, her voice rising. She met his eyes and held them.

"I didn't need to tell him anything. He was convinced that I was Näcken. He was already so scared that he did whatever I told him."

Elsebet inhaled sharply, moving her head to look past him at the sleeping form of Stina.

"Why didn't you deny it?"

"I did, but I don't doubt the only reason he agreed to release her was because he didn't believe me and was scared of me."

"But I don't understand. He's known us for years. Mother hasn't done anything." She began to cry, covering her face with her hands to stifle her tears so as not to wake Stina, who was snoring loudly now.

Nikolaos let her cry. He was cold too, but he didn't want to disturb her by sharing her covers. Carefully, he touched the surface of the bed warmer and found it very warm but not hot and placed it on his lap to warm his hands on it.

Elsebet stopped crying and looked at him. "Isn't it too hot?"

"Not really. We ought to go to sleep. It's getting late. I'm so sorry this is happening to us and that your wedding isn't happening."

"I know who you are, Father. I've known since I was a little girl."

Nikolaos stared at her. His heart started thumping so loud he felt it in his ears. He thought she might have wondered if the rumors were true, might even have understood the truth because of them. But not that she had already known. He blinked, confused. And scared of what she would say.

"I found your old version of Luther's Small Catechism. Why do you keep it under the floorboards and why do you keep women's jewelry there? That ring is too small to fit Mother's hand," she said, face flushing.

"Elsebet, I..."

"Father, I pray you. Just tell me the truth." Suddenly hot, Elsebet pulled her arms out from under the blankets, wiping her sweaty forehead with her right hand. "Father," she repeated, "Answer me."

"I prefer not, beloved daughter."

"I know that they're telling the truth about you. I saw you in the water."

He jerked back as if she had struck him, shame settling like a stone in his chest. Frantically, he searched his mind for when that could have been, but there was nothing. "How long have you known?"

She smiled, a quick smile of satisfaction that he finally admitted to it.

"It was when I was ten. Do you rem…"

"Ten?" he interrupted, stunned.

Elsebet ignored it. "Remember how cold it was? The snow stayed well into the spring that year. Once it was finally warming up, I overheard you and Mother speak of your need for water. You thought I was asleep, but I had woken up to go to the outhouse." She paused, swallowing. "I remember how you said that you couldn't do it anymore, how it was unbearable, and you'd do it even if you had to break the ice with an ax. I thought you meant that we didn't have enough to eat and would fish. I wanted to help you, so that morning I fetched my fish basket and followed. I had to run all the way there to keep up with you. Then I hid behind a tree and wanted to surprise you just at the right moment." She paused again and took a deep, shuttering breath. "I was just going to call out when you pulled your clothes off and walked into the icy water and disappeared. I was… it was horrible. I thought you were going to drown yourself, but the way you walked and disappeared under the ice; as if you belonged."

Nikolaos felt tears slide down his cheeks. He wiped them off with the back of his hand.

Elsebet waited, her face expressionless. "When you reappeared, I was going to run to you. But then I saw how your body looked, how parts of it seemed almost transparent as if it were made of water. You looked so peaceful and didn't seem cold at all. It really frightened me, Father," her eyes flashed to his, "and I started to run home. As I was running, I heard you start to play and almost turned back to ask what you were doing, but I was too afraid." Her voice broke.

Nikolaos looked down at the blanket covering the bed. Had she not been frightened, she might have been drawn in with him. Would he have had the wits about him to even recognize her?

"Father, can you stop pretending now. I pray you."

"Yes."

They silently regarded each other.

"Did you do all those things that they accused you of? Did you kill the couple, and did you cause a comet to come down and make people faint?"

"No, I didn't. A couple did see me in a brook, but they're very much alive. I take it they're the ones who've started these rumors. I need to be more careful." But it was only because it was so shallow, or he would have killed them, too. He had to stop killing people. What if he had killed Elsebet? Lord forgive him and deliver him from evil.

Elsebet exhaled, a long deep sigh. "Don't you get cold? How do you breathe under there? Under the ice?"

"I do get cold, especially if it's icy, like that day when you saw me." He wanted to reach out to touch her, but he didn't. "It doesn't hurt me, Elsebet. It's just not as comfortable as when it's warmer."

"How's it like? How do you hold your breath for so long?"

"It's beautiful, darling." He dared a smile at her. "I wish I could show it to you. It's soft and calm. There's a whole unseen world full of things no one ever sees. Whole forests made of grasses in sharp or dark green, sometimes brown." He tried to catch her eye, but she kept her gaze somewhere below his chin, looking stunned. "The plants move like trees in the wind on land. There are caves full of fish, and beavers with their babies. It's wondrous. I don't need to hold my breath. I can breathe there too."

"You can? How?"

"I don't know Elsebet, but I can."

"What jewelry did you have under the floorboards?" Stina

asked, startling them.

Nikolaos turned around and found her walking across the floor in her shift.

"I've been awake a while," she said, giving Nikolaos a look he couldn't read. "I'd like to see it. I assume it's no longer under the floorboards?"

He shook his head and pointed to the door. "In my violin case, in a pouch inside. Will you bring it? I'll show you."

Stina turned around without a word, grabbed the blanket from their bed, and threw it at him, then went to get his case.

Nikolaos caught the blanket, his heart thumping as he watched her carry his violin case in her arms. Would she recognize her crucifix? Or her other necklace? The necklace she had worn every day since he gave it to her as a Morning Gift when her name had been Abluna. It was a small silver ball covered in roses which had belonged to his grandmother. He had the smith remake it into a pendant before their wedding. Its chain was longer than her crucifix chain, and she wore them both even when crucifixes were frowned upon, hiding it beneath her blouses and shawls. There was a ring too, which he had given her for one of her birthdays. He had wanted to show it to Stina, to see if she would recognize her former favorite things, but he had been afraid of his own feelings, afraid of what he would do if she did.

He held Stina's eyes in his as she handed the case to him, but she was unaware of the deep meaning he was trying to convey. Pulling the pouch out, he opened it and let his fingers slip inside, feeling the bumps in the silver and the sharp edges of the well-worn ring. He held them just for a moment before he handed them to her, holding his breath as her face fell upon them.

"Oh, these are lovely. Did they belong to your wife?"

Nikolaos swallowed his disappointment and a little relief too. "Yes, it was. I mean yes, they did."

"Your wife?" Elsebet sat up straighter, staring at first him, then at Stina.

"Yes, Elsebet, your mother is the second woman I've married." The only one.

"But Father, you're younger than…" She stopped, eyes widening. "That's why the catechism is so old. You wrote those dates in the margins. Anno 1530, Anno 1562, and all the names." She crossed herself, visibly pale.

Nikolaos and Stina exchanged a glance. "Yes, it is. But how is it you've known for so long but never said anything?"

"Well, I assume it's because I didn't really believe my own eyes. When you came home that day, you were my regular sweet father and I thought maybe I had imagined it. I tried to never think of it again. I had never heard of Näcken then. It wasn't until these last few weeks when everything happened that I had to face what I'd seen. Father, are you truly Näcken?"

"Yes."

She startled, the pain so obvious on her face that he almost called out with his own pain.

"Do you fornicate with people in the water and drown them?" Her cheeks burned, but her voice was steady.

"I'm focused on my music or on the water. I'd never hurt someone on purpose," he said, evading her question, hoping she wouldn't ask him to elaborate. It had sounded so harsh, hearing his daughter say it. He didn't even know if Stina knew. She had never asked, but she sure was aware of what people were saying. He felt her eyes boring into his side, but he didn't move.

Elsebet remained silent.

It was still dark outside, but he could hear stirrings of birds and critters through the window. Dawn was coming, and they had been awake all night. Everything felt awkward.

"Elsebet, your father is a good man," Stina said and reached for Elsebet's hand. "He saved my life once, put his own life in danger for me only days after I met him. Your father just has a need to be near flowing water. It's a need in him that he's born with and at no fault of his own."

Chapter 69

Anno 1706, Helsingborg

The freezing air hit Nikolaos in the face when he left Lady Maria Church. It must have snowed while he prayed because his boots made that crunchy squeaky sound that came when new snow changed the surface of old packed snow. Cold as it was, it was beautiful. The moon was reflecting on the white ground, making it light enough not to need a lantern. He decided to take the long way home and visit the tavern for a glass of wine. Tightening his collar, he set off at a brisk pace, enjoying the sound his footsteps made the whole way there.

When he stopped at the entrance, banging the snow off his boots, he realized he could still hear squeaky footsteps. Someone else was out in the cold night too. He spun around, curious, then stood stunned. It was Doctor Döbelius, that water doctor from Mistress Esmeralda's party, and he was coming right up the stairs, smiling at him. Hell's bottoms, how could this be happening?

"I knew it was you. I knew it," Doctor Döbelius said, laughing heartily. "I saw you at prayer, but I wasn't sure if it was really you, so I followed you here to see if I was right." He clapped Nikolaos on the back several times, first on his upper back, then on the shoulders, while gently pushing him toward the torchlight by the door. "Let me take a look at you. It's so nice to see you. Let me buy you a drink, let me buy you a drink."

"Doctor Döbelius, what a coincidence," Nikolaos said, forcing himself to remain where he was and not pull away from the doctor's ministrations. The doctor's eyes were a little puffier, and he wore a new modern wig, but otherwise, he looked the same. It was him, the very Doctor Döbelius who had arrived only moments after Mistress Esmeralda had understood who he was, and the very man who had treated his victims. It was too much. Nikolaos felt trapped and was barely able to hide his panic.

"Isn't it? Isn't it, indeed?" said Doctor Döbelius, then finally let go of him and opened the door. "Come in, let's sit down together."

Nikolaos followed numbly, glancing around just to make sure there were no guardsmen ready to arrest him, brought there by Doctor Döbelius. But nothing of the sort happened. The doctor led him to one of the tables near the windows and was practically beaming at him when he sat down. Maybe Mistress Esmeralda hadn't said anything after all, that day. He exhaled, feeling a little calmer.

"What a nice surprise to meet again. I've never seen you at church. Are you new here in Helsingborg?" Nikolaos asked.

The doctor nodded but then shook his head. "A few months now." He held up a hand, indicating he wanted Nikolaos to wait, turning toward the barmaid heading toward them.

She acknowledged Nikolaos with a nod, then said, "Doctor Döbelius, where have you been? I was worried about you. Scared you'd been set upon by one of those thugs in the robber woods."

Doctor Döbelius chuckled. "Eh, you have a very imaginative mind, always thinking of those robbers." Then he changed his tone. "You shouldn't worry yourself. I'm perfectly safe. Bring my water and a nice wine, I pray you."

She narrowed her eyes. "I will, Doctor Döbelius but do be careful. I've warned you before." At that, she turned on her heels and headed into the kitchen.

"What was that about?" Nikolaos asked, leaning back on the chair to stretch out his back.

"Eh, she knows I spend time in Ramlösa village. It's claimed the woods there are full of robbers."

"I didn't know that."

"Well, I've never seen any, only a fox once or twice. There's a natural spring down there that I'm investigating. Remember the water studies I told you about? When was that? It must almost be ten years ago, isn't it?"

"It is, or nine years, rather. The King died that year, Three Crowns burned, and I performed at His Highness' funeral. A year I'll never forget, it was..." Nikolaos trailed off, regretting bringing it up. Mentioning the King might have been unwise, lest the doctor think he was putting on airs, like Lord Oxensköld had.

"That's right, you were telling me how you played for him. I didn't realize you were to play at his funeral. An honor, albeit sad."

"It was."

Doctor Döbelius regarded him silently, then said, "As I was telling you back then, I've studied the health benefits of water and have learned that the spring in Ramlösa village is quite extraordinary. The military was headquartered there during the war with Denmark."

The barmaid came back with a tray and started placing wine glasses and a bottle on their table, as well as a carafe with water and two small ale glasses. "There, I know you like to pour your water yourself. I'll leave you to it for now," she said and turned from the doctor with an admonishing shake of her head, then put her hand on Nikolaos' shoulder. "Merchant Nikolaos, I want you to speak some sense to Doctor Döbelius for me. Tell him to stay out of the robber woods."

"I'll try my best." Nikolaos raised an eyebrow and got a chuckle in response from Doctor Döbelius.

"Merchant? What happened to your music? It's not joint pain, is it? If it's pain, then you must come with me to the spring and drink regularly. My water will cure you." Doctor Döbelius reached for the carafe, held it high above the glass with an artful pause, then tilted it and poured. The water sparkled with light from their table candle as it slowly flowed into the glass.

Nikolaos averted his eyes from it. "I thank you but have no pains to speak of. Your water can cure aches?"

Doctor Döbelius nodded enthusiastically. "Indeed, it can. It was the military that discovered the spring, you see. All their men suffered from Soldier's Disease, cramping, diarrhea, and weakness. It's all the fighting and bad food. It's common, you know, very common. What's unusual was that when they clenched their thirst from the spring, they were cured. This was back in seventy-seven, and there have been rumors of its potential ever since. I've been testing their claim and have had good results."

"That's remarkable."

"Yes. It also cures shortness of breath, constipation, pains in the joints, hysterics, and other female issues. It's quite extraordinary. I began investigating this in… let me see, it was… six years ago the first time, no, pray forgive me, in 1701, five years. And as I said, the last few months, I've been settled here in town to study it further."

Nikolaos relaxed as he listened to him. Maybe Doctor Döbelius had simply forgotten about the rumors. He picked up the water glass and drank. It tasted wonderful. There was a scent to it as well that he couldn't place.

"It's iron that gives it its distinct flavor," Doctor Döbelius said.

"I see. I like it."

Doctor Döbelius smiled. "Have a bit more, have a bit more, then we ought to have some wine. It's good, she keeps a special bottle for me, you see. They don't sell it here, but my girl, the barmaid," he gestured toward the kitchen, "keeps some for me. She keeps my water here as well. The spring water which comes from the actual spring in Ramlösa village."

"Very nice," Nikolaos said, feeling overwhelmed. He didn't remember the doctor talking this much or repeating himself so often.

Doctor Döbelius' eyes gleamed. "My pleasure. Now tell me everything. It's truly not your joints that have you a merchant instead of a fiddler?"

"No, not at all. I do play still, but I also have a small mercantile on Möllestradet," Nikolaos said, wondering if he should have pretended to have achy joints to seem older. "We sell a little of this and that, as my daughter says. Some smaller samples of fabrics, threads, needles, ink, quills, ribbons, things like that. We try to get what people ask for if they can't find it anywhere else. We also have tallow candles and a small selection of beeswax candles," he added proudly.

Doctor Döbelius nodded slowly but didn't respond.

Nikolaos eyed the wine bottle, hoping for a glass, but the doctor was still sipping his water.

“A family business, I take it. Your mercantile?”

“Well, in the sense that my wife and daughter help with it, yes.” Nikolaos never told anyone how hard it had been to get a permit. It had been denied twice because he didn’t have the proper license for it, nor a father with one. There was a Merchant Society, which he hadn’t known existed with rules on the matter. It wasn’t until he managed to bribe several people with quite a bit of money that he was able to open the little mercantile and start a new life.

The doctor nodded. “I was in your establishment just this week, I believe. Is it your wife and your mother behind the desk?”

Nikolaos hesitated. Stina was almost fifty now, whereas he still looked thirty, even though he tried his best to look older.

“My wife and daughter. Stina is my wife. She’s older than me.”

Doctor Döbelius looked taken aback, but he hid it well and poured another glass of his water for himself. “Ah, I see. Forgive me for presuming.”

“Of course.”

There was an awkward silence. Nikolaos considered reaching for the wine but decided against it.

“Nikolaos,” the doctor said after what felt like several minutes. “I must ask you what happened that night when you played at Merchant Fleisher’s home. People spoke of it for years. If you don’t mind, that is?”

Nikolaos exhaled, then shook his head; they might as well get it over with. “I don’t. But like I told everyone back then, I don’t know what happened. I took a break to relieve myself, and when I came back, several people had fainted. I never saw anything, but people said there had been a comet. That was that, really. I went to sleep and left the next morning. You remember, we ran into each other on my way out.” He forced himself to breathe calmly. “Did *you* see the comet?”

“No, I never saw it either.” Doctor Döbelius looked uncomfortable. “I don’t know if I should even tell you, but I will anyway. Pray forgive me, I mean no offense.”

Nikolaos just gave a slight nod.

"Very well. As soon as you left that morning, Mistress Esmeralda started screaming. Did you not hear her?"

"No."

"I'm surprised. She was practically hysterical, screeching and pointing at the door, saying it was you," he discretely glanced around the room, then moved his water glass to the side and leaned in close, lowering his voice, "who had done it. She said you were *Näcken!*"

Nikolaos widened his eyes, hoping it looked as if he thought it was absurd. Part of him wanted to laugh at this play-acting, it had been a long time now since he had to do it. Should he tell him that he knew of the rumors, that their village council had tried his wife? "Pray, would you repeat that?" he asked instead, deciding not to say anything else for now.

"Forgive me, yes." The doctor leaned closer yet, looking flustered. "She did, Mistress Esmeralda claimed you were, er… um… well," he stammered, avoiding saying it out loud. "It caused quite a ruckus. Mistress Esmeralda was completely distraught and said that when she saw you on her stairs, she finally realized that since you were there to play violin, it was *you* the couple had encountered in the brook. She claimed that there had never been a comet, that it had been you all along, you who caused people to faint."

Nikolaos kept his gaze, pretending he was too surprised to say anything, biding his time to see how much Doctor Döbelius knew. It reminded him of the conversation he had with Lord Oxensköld.

"I had to take her upstairs and bleed her to calm her. It didn't help. She insisted I speak with the couple again so they could confirm that it was you. I'm afraid I had no choice," the doctor said, eyes flickering away for a moment.

"You spoke to them about me?"

Beads of sweat appeared from under Doctor Döbelius' wig, sliding down his forehead and getting stuck at the eyebrows. "Yes, I had no choice. Merchant Fleisher was convinced the couple's description of how Näcken looked proved it was you."

Nikolaos frowned.

"Maybe I shouldn't have said anything. I don't want to offend you."

Nikolaos ignored it. "Do you still see the Fleishers?"

"From time to time, yes, not as often as before. I won't tell them I've met you. They still speak of it."

"Do they?"

"Yes." Doctor Döbelius was looking increasingly uncomfortable.

Nikolaos scoffed. "What's your opinion on the subject? Do you think Näcken was truly in that water?" He didn't lower his voice.

Doctor Döbelius looked surprised and straightened up in his seat. "Oh, he was there. There's no question about that. I could tell. They were completely distraught, confused, and scared as only those who have encountered creatures like that are. Näcken had done whatever it is he does with them, sexual things. Their skin showed clear signs of water exposure, too. The couple survived only because of the low water level in that brook. Had it been deeper they'd either be dead now or still with him down there. There's no question at all. They did encounter Näcken. I'm afraid you got caught in it. I'm truly sorry. Truly sorry. You know how women can get."

Nikolaos exhaled with an immense sense of relief. "It's certainly not your fault."

"Well, still. Still. I heard they visited your pastor as well. Is that true?" Doctor Döbelius asked, looking concerned.

So, he knew then. Nikolaos let out another breath. "Yes, Merchant Fleisher and Mistress Esmeralda had the village council question my wife." He couldn't conceal the anger and disgust in his voice. "They terrified her and caused horrible rumors in our village. And when I wasn't home to defend her. Stina wasn't herself for a long time after that. My daughter's betrothal was canceled. She was heartbroken and hasn't found another. We moved because of them, while my son and his pregnant wife stayed, forced to deal with hostile neighbors. They destroyed our lives." There, he said it. It was the truth.

Doctor Döbelius looked utterly stunned. "Oh, I wish I'd known. I wish I'd known." He shook his head. "Did you try to clear your name?"

"No, I never did. Stina was too afraid. Besides, she didn't particularly want to see our neighbors again after what they put us through, her especially."

Doctor Döbelius tut-tutted, a sad expression on his face. "The accusation was absurd in the first place. I said as much then, but they were too distressed to listen to reason. Again, I'm deeply disturbed by this and how much it has hurt your family." He looked away, staring at something across the room. Then he changed the subject. "By the way, the theories are changing a bit nowadays. Some say that creatures are perhaps not vapor as previously thought but the offspring of a person and an animal."

"That's curious. What do you think then?" Nikolaos asked, forcing his voice to stay neutral. Maybe he had patted him down out there on the steps to make sure.

Doctor Döbelius cocked an eyebrow, then nodded as if to himself. "Well," he said, finally reaching for the wine bottle, filling first Nikolaos' glass and then his own, "*that* I couldn't say. I can only observe the reaction and bodily appearances of my patients."

Nikolaos nodded, relaxing again. Surely, the doctor wouldn't serve him wine if he knew who was, or express sympathy like he had. He took a deep sip of wine.

"Pray forgive me, Nikolaos. I see I'm causing you angst. I mean no offense." Doctor Döbelius looked apologetic, gesturing for Nikolaos to push his glass forward. "Let me refill your glass, then we'll talk of something else."

Nikolaos left the tavern and headed home. Making a right down their narrow street, he went through the gate of the large half-timbered house to the courtyard in which they lived. Three families, theirs included, had homes there. The courtyard was large enough for their own sizable cottage, two other families, and the farrier's workshop. Nikolaos rented space there for the one horse they had left. Many people lived as they did, within the walls of half-timbered houses, built like a square with all sides attached. Barn on one side, carriage house on another, kitchen and storage on a third, and lastly, the manor house across from the gateway. Some rented apartments within the walls of the buildings as well. At first, they had felt it suffocating living within the walls, used as they were to the open air of their farm. But after a while, they began to appreciate the protection from the noise and crowds on the outside and from the wind, which was almost always completely absent within the walls.

They had all been left in peace. Until today.

Chapter 70

Rå put her hand on the trunk and opened her eyes in surprise. There was something urgent in the way the sap greeted her, a quick pulsing, like a peck on the shoulder from an impatient child. Something was wrong. She looked up, searching for signs of trouble in the leafless winter crown. It was an ancient oak, thick branches reaching high and wide, evenly. Everything looked normal. She put her other hand on the trunk too. And there it was again, an urgent pulse from the heartwood. It shouldn't feel like this. The heartwood was always quiet and still. Rå let go with a pat, then walked over to its neighbor. Putting both hands on it, she immediately felt the same thing. It was fainter, but there just the same. The trees were trying to tell her something.

Looking around, Rå noticed several trees surrounded by patches of bare ground amidst the otherwise snow-covered terrain. She smiled. It was no accident; the trees had melted the snow for her. They had softened the soil too, and her feet easily went deep down, reaching their secret network of roots. She opened her back.

There was a faint tickling as the tree roots and sap connected to her toes. She sighed, opening her back further, anticipating the softening and melting sensation she had tried to explain to herself but could never put into words. But this time the sensation rushed through her, growing so intense it hurt. She felt a spike of intense alarm. Then it stopped. And she was told, as clear as if she saw it with her eyes, of dead trees, sour soil, and naked branches in the summer. The roots and sap around her toes receded. Rå's eyes welled with tears. Her tree sisters and brothers in the north were sick. It shouldn't have taken her this long to notice that. She had been spending so much time with Måns that she had neglected the duties she had made a blood vow to keep. Shamefaced, and with her mother's familiar words echoing through her mind, she pulled her feet free. *My child, my daughter, you will marry the forest, the moss, trees, leaves, and the very soil upon which we trample. You will make love to the men who visit your land, and you will live forever as you keep the forest fertile. Now drink my child and go. I will watch from Valhöll.*

She had no choice but to go northward. The trees needed her.

***

The closer to Kjugekull Rå came, the more her chest and throat hurt from unshed tears. Even Little One, a strong adult cow for many years now, and the only one she had left was mooing. It tore at her heart. But Måns was the closest thing to a husband she had ever had, and she couldn't leave without saying goodbye.

He was outside chopping wood, wearing only a shirt despite the sunny but cold winter day. As soon as he saw her with Little One, carrying all of Rå's belongings on her back, his face fell.

Then he dropped his ax on the ground and ran toward her. "No! Rå, Magda mine, no." Slamming into her, he threw his arms around her. "Pray, don't leave, why, why do you need to go?" he asked over and over again like a chant.

She cried softly into his shirt, feeling his hot skin sticking to her cheek as her tears made the fabric wet. It was unbearable.

Måns grabbed her head and held her face between his hands, staring into her eyes. "I can't live without you." The pain was so obvious her back hole tightened. How could she tell him that being with him distracted her, that what she was giving him, she should be giving to the trees?

"Måns, I must go north. There are trees up there that aren't doing well. I have no choice."

"And you won't come back." It wasn't a question.

She shook her head.

"Is it the house? The lean-to? I can rebuild it or build you something new, a proper house. My uncles would help." He started to shiver from the cold. Or maybe it was sadness.

"No, Måns, it's not that. Shall we go inside for a bit? I can see you're freezing." She looked toward the house. "Are your uncles home?" Maybe she could have Måns just one more time before she left.

He gave a quick smile, looking like his normal happy self again. "I know what you're thinking. But, yes, they're at home." He pulled her close and kissed her hard on the lips, and then the sadness was back in his eyes. "I *am* cold. Let's go in. Would you like some soup?"

"That would be nice." She took his hand.

He squeezed her fingers in response, then let go so she could tie Little One to their hitching post.

"Rå is leaving," Måns said to his uncles as soon as they entered.

Bushbrow looked up sharply from where he was sitting at the hearth, stirring the soup Måns had offered. "You're leaving? Why?"

"It's not our business," said Per and gave Rå an apologetic nod. He pulled out a chair for her at the table. "Sit a while, Mistress of the Forest."

But Bushbrow ignored him. "Where are you going, and why?"

Rå sat down, flicking a glance at Måns. He looked close to tears. Maybe it would have been better to just leave a note for them than drawing this out like this. "I have to," she said, nodding in thanks when Måns put a bowl of soup in front of her. "I've been called north to care for my trees up there. There's sickness."

Bushbrow gave a slow upward nod. "You're doing what you're called by the Lord to do. His trees will thank you for it."

She smiled. That was one way to look at it.

Per gestured to the door. "Bushbrow, we shall leave them alone for a bit, allow them some privacy to say their goodbyes." He waited for Bushbrow, who had stiff joints, to get up, then got their coats from the hooks by the door. They left, not a word of goodbye. That was surprising, and she felt unexpectedly hurt by it.

Måns sat down opposite her with his own bowl of soup, glancing at the door as it closed. "Bushbrow is more understanding than I. I just want you for myself," he said, letting out a long audible breath.

"I'll always remember you, Måns. You and your uncles

welcomed me without fear. It's something that will stay with me forever," Rå said, noticing that he had some gray in his hair and lines around his eyes. Funny how she hadn't thought of it until now.

He nodded, eating some of his soup.

People didn't use to have individual bowls or plates when they ate, but now it seemed everyone did. Come to think of it, it had been the same at the inn in Jönköping. She took a spoonful. It was delicious, very rich.

"Rå, what if I come with you?"

She looked up, having expected him to say that. It truly had been a mistake to get so involved. The cottage was starting to feel heavy with sadness. It made her feel panicked and restless. She needed to leave. "We're both getting too attached. It's my fault. I should have left a long time ago, but I enjoyed being with you too much."

"Rå, one can never love too much."

"Yes, Måns, you can." Rå wiped a tear from her left eye and stood up. He was wrong. It was possible. It made everything raw, chafing memories that haunted you for years, like her mother's farewell. She reached for the basket she had brought. It was filled with herbs, neatly wrapped with descriptions for each. "Here, this is for you and your uncles." She tried to smile, but it felt like a silent sob. "There's a small carved box at the bottom with a salve for your musket. Smear the barrel with it, and you'll never miss your target."

"I thank you, Rå." He got to his feet and wrapped his arms around her waist, pulling her close. "Let's go to my bed." He took her by the hand and brought her to the alcove at the back of the house where his bed was.

She crawled in with him and pulled the bed curtains closed. The darkness felt comforting.

Måns lifted his blanket so she could snuggle close. "Rå, Magda mine, will you at least write to me? I can't bear to never hear from you again."

Surprised, something lifted in her chest. He was right. She could write to him and probably find a place where he could send replies. She pictured someone taking Måns' letters from the post-runner and keeping them for her. It was something she had never done before. "I could do that. Then I'd put Kjugekull on the letter and a post-runner would bring it here, wouldn't he?"

"Yes, then when he blows his post horn, I'll go out and ask him. I suppose it would be wise for you to put my name on it as well. Then in the letter, you can write where you are, and I'll send one back. I've never written a letter before, but I'll do my best." He kissed her on the cheek, laughing softly.

"I haven't either. It'll be very nice to try." She grabbed his hand, holding it between both of hers. "Måns, I'm glad to have you. I wish things were different and that I could be a wife to you, but they're not. I have duties, and I must go where I'm called to go."

He didn't answer her, just squeezed her hand.

They stayed like that, sitting side by side in his narrow bed, just holding each other.

Rå was getting ready to leave when there was a knock on the door, and then the door was pulled open a crack. "Can one come in?" Per said, head still outside.

"We're not naked if that's what you thought, Uncle," Måns said, smiling sadly at Rå from where he sat at the table.

She reached for his hand and patted it. They had both stayed fully clothed today, just sitting with each other.

Then Per opened the door wide and poked his head in, smiling broadly. "Rå, you should come out. People are here to say goodbye."

Rå felt a lump in her throat. Bushbrow and Per hadn't left without saying goodbye like she had thought. She exchanged another glance with Måns. His eyes were warm, intense.

Outside, Bushbrow was standing with what looked like most of the village. She did a quick headcount. There were twelve adults and six children, each carrying something. Then a woman, Rå didn't remember her name, stepped forward.

"I thank you, Rå, for your care of our village. It's been an honor to have you. Go in peace," the woman said, pressing a loaf of bread into her hands, then bowed and stepped back. As she did, a man came forward. He bowed as well and gave her a basket full of fresh fish. Behind him, two women and a small girl, each with cheeses, came forward. And so it continued until the villagers left one by one and she was standing there with her hands full of gifts and eyes full of tears.

Bushbrow and Per looked away discreetly, giving her a moment to compose herself. Per went inside and fetched a large sack, handing it to Bushbrow. "Here," he said, "put Måns' Rå's food in this. Then we'll have to let her leave."

Måns' Rå's. It cut right into her heart.

Per kissed her on the cheek. A quick peck. "Go in peace, Forest Rå. I thank you for your kindness to us and to my nephew."

"It's been my pleasure, Per," she said with a voice that barely held. "I've felt accepted and welcomed here, and I'll never forget it."

Per held her gaze as Bushbrow reverently bent down and touched her feet, and then, without a word, they went inside, leaving her and Måns alone.

She could barely keep it together, and the lump in her throat had grown into something that felt impossible to swallow.

Måns took the satchel with all her gifts and attached it to her luggage on Little One's back. He was sobbing now, shaking as he tied it to the rest of Rå's things.

She went to him, pulling his hands from the rope. "Måns, come here."

He put his arms around her, and they stood there, holding each other. There were no words. Nothing she could say.

* * *

Rå disguised herself as if she were a woman herding her cow. Tying up her long hair and hiding it under a white cloth, she wore a long skirt with a short white blouse and a shawl covering her back. She walked northward, sometimes even riding on Little One's back. It startled a man she came upon so much he fell to his knees.

569

Once he calmed down, she told him she had far to walk and that her feet bothered her. It wasn't true, she just felt lazy, but he seemed to understand, or at least pretend to. He too, was hiding something and claimed he was a coal miner on his way home, but his arms were too thin and his shoulders too narrow.

She left him after a time and continued walking through tall forests where all she heard was the wind and the soft thumping of Little One's hooves on the ground.

Chapter 71

Nikolaos was engrossed in the mercantile's inventory list as the late winter sun managed to enter their courtyard. A sudden knock interrupted his calculations. Setting down his quill and leaving the candle alight, he approached the door with the current sum still in mind, half-expecting to see an errand boy with a delivery or the neighbor woman asking for Stina.

But his sums disappeared as soon as he opened the door and stood face to face with Doctor Döbelius, who bowed, elaborately swinging his hat in his right hand. He would have been rather handsome had he only been younger and not so flamboyant, Nikolaos observed.

"Ah, this is where you live!" he exclaimed when he straightened up. "I've been looking for you for days. I came to enquire about you and your well-being. And to make certain I didn't offend? Speaking so frankly about Näcken, a subject you and your family prefer not to discuss, I'm certain, might have been unseemly. Pray forgive me if I did offend or cause discomfort."

Nikolaos regarded him, surprised at his frankness and the emotion it caused. He felt short of breath suddenly. "No, I wasn't offended. But you're correct that I wasn't entirely comfortable." He wanted to close the door on him but obviously couldn't do that. It would be terribly rude. When Doctor Döbelius made no move to leave, he reluctantly stepped aside. "Come inside and have a seat."

"I thank you." Doctor Döbelius looked relieved and perhaps a little embarrassed.

Nikolaos gestured to their modest parlor. "Have a seat here," he said, then picked up his pipe and lit it with one of the sticks he kept for the purpose by the fire. It couldn't hurt to make the doctor think he partook in the beneficial habit if nothing else but to make him seem more human. In reality, he drank it rarely. "Can I offer you tobacco?"

"Later," he said and waved dismissively. "I must offer my humblest apologies. Bringing up these old rumors was insensitive and unnecessary. I admit that I was curious to speak with you after hearing how they questioned your wife. As a doctor with an interest in water…" Doctor Döbelius started to chuckle but stopped himself, probably realizing that he wouldn't find the comparison humorous.

Nikolaos raised an eyebrow.

"Pray forgive me," Doctor Döbelius added. "A doctor's habit to always investigate. It's an occupational hazard. Will you forgive me?"

Nikolaos kept his eyes on him, pretending to consider even though he had already forgiven him. It seemed he was genuine. "I accept."

"Oh, I thank you, I thank you. Now, I pray you, and do say yes, come with me to Ramlösa village and let me show you the spring. They've given me permission to clean up the underbrush and clear paths to make it accessible to the public. I pray you, do say yes," he repeated.

"You want me to come to a spring with you? Is it to prove that you don't think I'll drown you in it?"

Doctor Döbelius looked utterly crestfallen. "I assure you that I have no such ulterior motives."

Nikolaos grinned. "I was jesting, Doctor."

"Oh, my dear," Doctor Döbelius said and wiped his forehead with the back of his hand.

Nikolaos laughed.

***

Town was far behind them when Doctor Döbelius touched Nikolaos' arm, pointing to a large cluster of trees. The sun was shining through the branches, creating ribbons of light on the ground. It was beautiful. "There it is," he said, smiling excitedly. "We're driving in on the old road where the military headquarters used to be, then we'll leave the carriage there and walk down. It's rough terrain, but I find it easier in the winter when the ground is frozen, and the branches aren't entirely overgrown. You don't have any young strapping sons who could help us, do you?"

Nikolaos chuckled. "I do, as a matter of fact, but he and his wife are at home on the farm. It's a bit far." The doctor seemed to have forgotten that he mentioned him yesterday.

"I see. How many children do you have?"

"Only two surviving, Elsebet, who lives here with us, and my son."

Doctor Döbelius threw him a sideways glance. "It's hard to believe that you have two grown children. Must have started young then, eh? You don't look older than I, and mine are barely out of dresses yet."

"That's what people say, but I'm forty-three years old," Nikolaos said and met his eyes evenly.

"Forty-three? Your humors must be exceptionally well balanced."

"They must, I rarely get sick."

"If I may ask, how long does it take you to feel well again once you *do* get sick? How long do you cough and how long do your sniffles and sneezes last?"

"Not long, a few days only. My wife and children suffer longer." A lie, he had never been sick, never had a cough or a stuffy nose, and never once puked because of a sickness. It was only that one time when he injured himself with his ax that he had been sick and had a fever.

"You're fortunate. I have patients your age who are already inhibited by sore joints and chronic coughs."

"So I've realized. My son gets coughs that can last a whole winter." It reminded Nikolaos that he ought to write to him when he got back home, see how they were all faring. It had been a cold winter again.

Doctor Döbelius stopped the carriage and climbed down, tying the horse to a branch before he responded. "It's a common affliction. My water helps with that, too. It loosens the itch in the throat. We can have some of it sent to your son if you'd like?"

"Truly? That's very kind. It's far though, our farm is near Ytterby." Nikolaos still thought of the farm as his, but it wasn't of course, not anymore. He could never go back there again. His youthful appearance would confirm all of their suspicions.

"That's not an issue, I have messengers going that way anyway." Doctor Döbelius looked shamefaced. "Mistress Esmeralda, you know."

"Ah." Nikolaos resisted a grimace. He couldn't dictate who the doctor was associating with. If he wanted to send water to his son through the same messenger, he supposed it was safe enough.

"The cave is just down below," Doctor Döbelius said, motioning to a trampled path in the bushes.

"There's a cave here?" Nikolaos asked, ignoring the awkwardness.

"Yes, I call it that. It's deep enough for you to stand protected from the elements in it."

Doctor Döbelius led the way, walking steadily downward until they were standing under an outcropping filled with bushes, grass, and smaller plants, browned now by the season. It was swampy, and their boots sunk to their ankles. Large trees surrounded them on all sides, and Nikolaos felt moving water nearby but couldn't see it.

"This is remarkable. So much growth down here."

"You should've seen it before. I've had people from the neighboring farms help clear some already. Look through the branches there. You see the brook?" He grabbed Nikolaos' arm and pointed to a spot where water flickered in a ray of sunlight. "I'd like this whole area all the way down to the brook cleared of debris and growth."

Nikolaos nodded, looking at it with relief. It was very shallow and not very rapid. If he didn't get too close, he should be able to ignore it.

"Then we can place chairs and tables and build a shed or some kind of structure here," Doctor Döbelius continued. "We'll have something that looks nice. A place where people can stand dry-footed if it rains or is windy. Come, I'll show you the spring."

Doctor Döbelius kept his grip on Nikolaos' arm and turned him around, pushing through branches and dead winter leaves with his other hand. And there it was. A cliff wall with water that was moist and red like rust, dripping slowly into a puddle beneath.

Nikolaos had never seen anything like it.

"This is the water we drank the other day?"

"Indeed, it is!" Doctor Döbelius grinned. "Do taste it. It's even better here."

Nikolaos sank to his haunches on the moist, swampy ground and cupped his hands under the drip, filling it until he had a mouthful. It tasted fresh, with a strong scent of iron and a subtle earthiness. It was more intense than it had been at the inn. He drank two more mouthfuls before he pulled himself up to stand, finding Doctor Döbelius looking at him expectantly. "It's extraordinary. I expected us to get the water from the brook. I didn't realize it would come directly from the cliff wall like this. Why is it so red?"

"From the brook? No, no." Doctor Döbelius gestured toward the cliff wall. "Therein lies its power, right in the red rocks there. As you see for yourself, it's no regular water. Those soldiers were very ill when they arrived here, and every one of them was cured. All they needed to do was drink this for a few weeks." He paused to loosen his cravat and clear his throat. "Some villagers have been getting water here too, and they're all strong and sturdy people. But many are still scared of coming here. I want to change that, I want to change that," he repeated. "There's something to this water that's strengthening and curing for the body. As a businessman such as yourself, you surely agree it's an opportunity. Don't you?"

"Yes. I'd say so."

Doctor Döbelius met his eyes, a searching look. "Let's take a little walk and I'll show you what I have in mind." He moved the branches and waited for Nikolaos to step through before he let them snap back. "I want to clear this whole area but leave clusters of bushes to create private sections where we can put tables and chairs. A finer area where the long-term residents can sit and converse while they drink."

"Long-term residents?"

"Yes, I'm working on that just now. I have spoken to the farmers about it. Some are willing to take in residents for a few weeks."

Nikolaos raised an eyebrow, nodding with approval. The doctor was quite the businessman himself.

"It'll bring income to the families, and the sicker patients don't need to travel. I want the villagers and poor to drink for free you see. Those with means can pay for it. What I'm hoping is to open a clinic here." He pointed to a path on the left that led up the slope directly from the spring. "It's not swampy up there. It may be a good place for it. The view is extraordinary too."

Nikolaos nodded approvingly again. "It sounds very nice. I'll help you with this. Whatever you need. I have a horse and can ride out to speak with people, help you find builders for your clinic, and find farmers that can help if you wish?"

"A kind offer, Merchant Nikolaos, but no need. What I was hoping is that you could offer small water samples in your mercantile to spread the word. And provide a pamphlet. And then, would you play your music here in the evenings? When the time comes?"

Nikolaos smiled. Clearly, he was redeemed from all suspicion. "It would be my honor."

"I thank you." Doctor Döbelius solemnly placed his hand in his. They had a deal.

Chapter 72

When Nikolaos approached the corner by Lady Maria Church, he heard agitated voices. Surprised, he cautiously turned the corner and then stopped in his tracks. A crowd was pushing itself toward the church door, eager to read a new placard fastened there. He hurried forward, recognizing the town's wigmaker and the butcher as he pressed himself through to get close enough to see what it said.

Written in thick black ink that had already started to smudge, it read:

Soldier in Skara has admitted to fornication with the Forest Rå. Both the courts and the military tribunal may get involved if he is tried. The soldier says the Forest Rå had short black hair, human eyes albeit large like a cow's, woolly horse legs and a horsetail, black lips, and teeth like a foal. She wore a dirty white kerchief on her head, and her breasts were so long her dirty blouse didn't cover them. The Rå tried to feed the soldier bread and cheese, and when he refused, she made him do lustful things with her.

Nikolaos burst out laughing.

The din silenced abruptly as several people stopped talking to stare at him. "My good sir, this isn't a laughing matter," said the wigmaker.

"It is if she's described as that. It isn't how she looks," Nikolaos said.

All eyes were on him now.

"How would you know, Merchant Nikolaos? Have you seen her?"

"Not I," he lied. "Though I've met a fella who has. He described nothing like that. In fact, he said her hair is long, so long it reaches below her knees, and it's brown, not black. Large eyes but regular legs like any woman. Her back is rough like the bark of a tree." He regretted it as soon as he said it, feeling like he had betrayed her trust. He shouldn't have said that.

"I've heard the same," a woman said. "And that she helps men hunt. The Forest Rå has a salve she puts on their muskets, and they never miss a target."

Nikolaos nodded at her, noticing her red and chafed hands, likely from the cold and handling fish. She must be one of the fishermen's wives. "That's what the fella said as well," he said as the crowd tightened around him.

"Was it near these parts? Or was it further north where you're from?" the wigmaker asked, getting close enough to touch him.

"It was in Stockholm, right after the castle burned. After the fire, a few of us clenched our thirst and came to talk about it," Nikolaos said, lying again.

The wigmaker and another man exchanged a glance and nodded in agreement. "It's common to confide in each other after a traumatic experience," the man said. "You heard the truth then, I'm sure of it. But if the military tribunal and the courts are involved, I can only assume she does have those long breasts as well. The military doesn't get involved in mere rumors. Unless she's a shapeshifter of course. She might be." He nodded for effect, causing several people to gasp.

"Seems like it. The Devil can change her appearance. I believe it," said the wigmaker.

It resulted in a debate between him, two other men, and the fisherman's wife. She waved her chafed hands in the air and said she knew with certainty that Rå had legs like a horse and never changed.

Nikolaos took the opportunity to get away and gently elbowed himself through the now even denser crowd. There was no sense in arguing with them. He had done all he could.

***

Stina pulled a blanket over her legs and her indoor shawl tighter around her back. "I don't like it," she said. "It's too much of a coincidence that they're placarding about Rå just days after you've suddenly come upon Doctor Döbelius after all these years. And he's asking about Fleisher too. It's scaring me. I think there's a connection. Especially since he knew I was questioned by the sixmen. There are mysterious forces afoot. I feel it. They're coming for us again."

Nikolaos left his place by the fireplace and sat beside her, reaching for her hand under the blanket. He wished he hadn't told her what Doctor Döbelius said. Now she wouldn't stop worrying about it. "It's an odd coincidence is all. We've lived down here in Skåne for almost ten years now and haven't heard a word. There have been no suspicions. I've been careful and stayed out of people's way. No one has seen me in the water. I swear it. You needn't worry about it. Besides, that's not Rå, she doesn't look like that. Skara isn't near here or even near Jönköping. And no one knows we know her, so how could there be a connection?"

"I don't know Nikolaos, but we've become too comfortable, almost forgetting who you are. That's what worries me. That year the castle burned, you forgot your true self, and things went out of control. You were pulled into things, and you had no time for your need. It confuses you and makes you forgetful. You know I can't go through it again. I can't. We don't know if someone has learned that we know her. What if Rå told the man in Skara about us? Then he might have told someone, and now they're looking for us. Maybe that's the real reason why you just happened to come upon Doctor Döbelius in church that day. Maybe he was sent here to investigate."

Nikolaos looked at her sharply. Doctor Döbelius *had* patted him down out there on those steps. It had been his first thought too. And then he offered to send Hindrich water. Nikolaos felt a pang of fear, then dismissed it. "Stina, Rå looks nothing like it. That man hasn't seen her at all." Pulling his hand from hers, he got up and went back to the fireplace. "This is what we need to do. I've been thinking on it for a while anyway but never found the right way to say it. Elsebet has to marry. She's many, many years past marriageable age now, and we've let it go too long. The plan all along was to set the mercantile up here, then she'd marry someone who'd take care of it and then you and I were going to move again. When we do, we can pretend you're my aunt or mother."

Stina flinched. "I look so old to you already that you'll put me away?"

"Darling, of course I won't. And no, you don't, but I do look younger now."

Stina was forty-nine years old. Her hair was gray and hung in a thick braid around her left shoulder like a snake peering at him from behind a tree. She had grown nice and round again in the last few years, and her face was still smooth with only the faintest lines around her eyes and forehead. It made her beautiful.

She nodded, making the tears welling in her eyes spill down her cheeks. "I suppose us moving somewhere and pretending that I'm your aunt or mother once Elsebet is settled is the best option."

"Yes, I think so, darling." He joined her again, gazing out the window as he sat. It was raining now, heavy spring rain that would wash all the snow away and make the town muddy and dirty. It made him miss his farm. "It won't be for a while yet. Let me help Doctor Döbelius like he asked. I promise to be cautious. If I start to suspect that he's here for any other reason than he says, I'll tell you immediately, and we'll think of what to do."

She reached for his hand and squeezed it. "You do that. Maybe it isn't as I fear."

He put his hand over hers and patted it in response, feeling better about it. "I forgot that I spoke to Arne Shoemaker. I meant to tell you last week, but I forgot. His brother was widowed last year and is looking to marry again. He has two young daughters who'd be a delight for Elsebet. Not only that, but he also has experience with a shop. Had his own mercantile in Malmö, but it burned down at no fault of his own."

"How dreadful! What happened?"

"Arne said it burned along with two other storefronts, but no one knew where it started."

She nodded. "I do like Arne. If his brother is as sweet as he is, I'm happy."

"I feel the same. Arne says that Fredrik, that's his name, is very kind and respectful and willing to marry an older woman."

"Older? To you, she's but an infant." Stina put both her

hands on his cheeks and kissed him on the lips. "You, my young handsome strap of a husband," she said, exactly like she used to say when she was Abluna.

***

Nikolaos and Elsebet were walking arm in arm through the silent town. As always, when passing Helsingborg Castle, Nikolaos was reminded of the day they arrived almost ten years ago. His first reaction to seeing it again was that they had gone too far and had ended up in another town. Then he had realized that it was in fact, the same tower, but that the outbuildings and the wall encircling it were all gone. Someone told him that there had originally been plans to even tear down the tower, but it never happened. Now torches were placed at the entrance, and their light made the fog above it look thick and yellow against the brown brick walls.

Elsebet tugged on his arm, interrupting his musings. "I know marriage is expected of me, Father, but I don't want to. I like my life with you and Mother. Can't I stay here and take care of you when you and Mother grow old. Most women my age who aren't married do so."

"You know that's not possible in our case. You won't have an old father who'll need your help."

"Yes, but then I could pretend to be your mother. I mean, once Mother has passed on."

Nikolaos hushed her and scanned the street ahead of them. The street was empty, but he lowered his voice just to be sure. "It's complicated, Elsebet. I did that before, even pretending that I had died and that my grandson had come to help my unmarried daughter. It wasn't easy to keep that charade going for so long, Elsebet. It was too hard to keep up appearances, and I was always on my guard. Frankly, Elsebet, I won't do it again."

"I understand," she said, but he could hear the hurt in her voice.

"Arne says that Fredrik is a kind, gentle man. And he tells me he's very nice to his daughters. From that, I gather that he'd make a

581

good husband. You'll have two little girls to love until you get your own. They need a mother." He touched her cheek, removing a strand of hair that had come loose from her braid. "Fredrik is interested in taking on the mercantile as well. You'd be settled Elsebet. Mother and I could move in a few years before our age difference becomes too noticeable. No one will know us. I'll pretend to be her nephew or someone like it, and we can live our life together until the day comes," he said, immediately feeling guilty. It was essentially what he just told Elsebet he wouldn't do. But it was different. Stina was his wife.

"But I'd miss you, Father. I'll grow old, and you won't be with me."

He stopped walking and lifted his lantern so he could see her face. Her eyes were dry, but she looked so sad. "Darling, I know. But we'll write to each other." He touched her cheek again. "Say that you'll meet him at least. You can take a walk and talk amongst yourself and see if he's as nice as Arne says."

"How can I live with someone else and get to be an old woman with grandchildren, knowing that you're still somewhere hiding from me?" she asked, tears brimming in her eyes now.

He pulled her close, grabbing her shawl which was sliding off her shoulders, and rewrapping it around her with his other hand. "Sometimes I wonder if it was wise for me to have a family, R..." Nikolaos stopped himself, he had almost told her that Rå always advised against it, but he had never told her that Magda was Rå.

Elsebet didn't reply. If she was offended that he wondered at his decision to have her, she didn't show it. Letting go of his arm, she walked ahead and stopped to look at Merchant Svend Phil's farm.

It had four half-timbered structures forming a square with a courtyard inside just like the courtyard where their own little house was built, only much, much larger. The farm had been built by Merchant Jacob Hansen back in 1641, Nikolaos learned recently. It was one of the few farms that survived the war with the Danes and certainly the wealthiest. Helsingborg had become almost decimated after the war. In fact, the town had been so ravaged by the Danes that it still didn't do well. He often wondered if it had been the right choice to come here. Their mercantile only just sustained them.

"This is quite another merchant family here. They're rich," Nikolaos said, wondering why they were still in town even after the war.

"We do well enough father." Elsebet turned to face him. "Perhaps you're right. I'll meet Fredrik and his daughters. If they're nice I'll say yes."

"Thank you," he said simply.

Chapter 73

They had an early summer wedding, and as the church recommended these days, Elsebet and Fredrik sealed their marriage with a handshake on the steps of Lady Maria Church and then went inside to listen to the pastor read from the scriptures. Stina and Nikolaos held the feast in their courtyard, and then they walked the newlyweds to their wedding bed at Fredrik's house on the other side of town.

***

Nikolaos stood naked at the edge of the Råå River. Råå village was to his right by the coast, but he was well hidden here among trees and shrubs. Despite the names, neither the village nor the river had a connection to Rå herself. Even so, he always felt like the river was his because of it, as if she had blessed it for him. It was still and smooth now, with a slight ripple on the surface pulling at him. He stepped in slowly, savoring how his skin prickled just where it met the surface, moving upward as he went deeper. When it reached his waist, he fell forward, kicking his legs out behind him and shooting through the water like an arrow.

The water was cold and refreshing, and he took his first watery breath as his ears closed and his eyes stopped needing to blink. Small schools of fish separated and veered off on each side of him as he swam. He was in his element here. Alone and free. It was unusually deep today; the bottom was far below him, and he couldn't reach the surface when he stretched an arm upward. He smiled, sending a stream of bubbles through his nose and mouth, left over from breathing on land. The snow and rain must have added much more water than usual because he didn't remember it ever being this deep.

Pushing his arms forward and back in a strong arm stroke, he glided between two boulders above a broken chair that someone had thrown in. On the other side, the bottom of the river started slanting upward, narrowing his swimming space. He stopped moving his arms, allowing himself to sink lower. Something sparkled in the sand in front of him. A coin? He reached out and grabbed it, turning it over in his hand. It wasn't a coin but a gold locket, worn and not larger than his thumb. Without thinking, he opened it, and then a miniature of a young boy with dark long hair fluttered out and was swept away by the current. He tried to reach for it, but it was gone. Alas, it would have been nice to see who the little boy was. He snapped the locket close and clutched it in his hand. It would make a nice gift for Stina. She could put her own miniature in there.

Afterward, he relaxed on a rock on the beach to let his hair dry. It had been a while since he wore his wig. His own hair was thick and long, and he didn't see the need for it.

Råå village looked peaceful. Chimney smoke moved straight up in the windless evening, and he heard someone laugh at something. It was hard to imagine the horror that had taken place there thirty years ago. General Carl Hårdh resided at Helsingborg Castle at the time, a nasty man whom people still spoke ill of. The New Swedes, as people in Skåne were called back then, were not as loyal to Sweden as they were supposed to be. One day, some women had crossed over the sound to Denmark to shop there without having proper permission. They were fined by the twelvemen, but Hårdh was angry at what he thought was too mild a punishment and ordered the whole village burned. Just for shopping in the wrong place!

Nikolaos looked away from the village and reached for his violin. Starting gently, he let his bow rest on each note as gravity moved his hand, keeping his eyes on the slow ripples in the river. Time escaped him until he was startled to attention by loud, shocked voices. He got to his feet, his heart racing in his chest. But there was no one. Whoever had seen him must have run off.

Rusty devils! It would only be a matter of time before new rumors started. Then Stina would assume that Doctor Döbelius had been sent to get him. Just like she said, they had become too comfortable, and he was getting careless.

Chapter 74

It was Stina's and Nikolaos' turn to host the House Hearing. Stina had spent the whole morning and the evening before cleaning and baking.

"I wish Elsebet were here to help me with everything. Since they live in town, shouldn't they still be questioned here?"

"No, I told you yesterday Helsingborg is too large of a town for everyone to be questioned on the same day." Nikolaos hid a sigh and went outside to wait on the stoop. Stina had been fretting for several days, and she was getting on his nerves. They both knew their scriptures, and he saw no reason to be insecure about it. He looked forward to it. It would be interesting to see how well their neighbors knew theirs this time; last time, several of them had been told to go home and study.

A door opened across the courtyard, and Nikolaos automatically slumped and grabbed hold of the doorpost to seem older. Moments later, Beata Lybecker appeared. She walked briskly but, as always, cradled each elbow in the opposite hand in front of her chest.

"Orvar is on his way. He had to use the outhouse. I hope he makes it back before Pastor Troilius gets here. I don't want to have him lecture Orvar on the importance of promptness, especially not after having to poop," she said and raised her eyebrows dramatically.

Nikolaos chuckled. "We shall have to hope not."

He brought her inside and went back out, finding Orvar arriving with their eldest son. Pastor Troilius, Farrier Nils, and his wife were approaching as well. Beata would be relieved.

Pastor Troilius' eyes fell on their catechism as soon as he sat down. "I see that you have Luther's Small Catechism in place, Nikolaos. Do you not know it well and see the need to practice before I arrive?" he asked sharply.

"It's not that, but we thought it might be good to have on hand in case you wanted to read from it."

"Good, but I won't be reading from it today."

Nikolaos felt Stina's eyes on him but didn't dare to turn in her direction. They had discussed exactly that yesterday, hoping Pastor Troilius would be later than everyone else so those who needed it could look it over before he arrived. Stina hadn't wanted to do it, afraid Pastor Troilius would get mad. Nikolaos reached across the table and picked it up, placing it on a shelf behind him, wishing he had listened to her.

Pastor Troilius looked around the table, making eye contact with everyone. Then, he asked each of them to pick one of the Ten Commandments and explain what it meant, skipping the catechism altogether. Everyone was able to give him a satisfactory answer, and the pastor didn't chastise them. Nikolaos felt relieved for their neighbors. Pastor Troilius was kind, but he could be stern at times.

After that, he turned to Stina and Nikolaos. "Your daughter married last year, didn't she?" he asked.

"Yes, she did, last summer," Stina said.

Pastor Troilius smiled a little as he wrote it down. Then, he methodically put his notes away. The House Hearing was over.

Everyone breathed a sigh of relief.

"Let's eat, then I want to learn more about the water you speak so highly of, Nikolaos. Fredrik told me when I visited your mercantile yesterday. What is it for? Why does the doctor want us to drink it?" Pastor Troilius asked.

"Good to hear," Nikolaos said. "I'll tell Doctor Döbelius. He's bringing a whole group of us to the spring next week to show us. If you're interested, do come. Didn't Fredrik give you a sample?"

"What is this you're speaking of?" Beata asked, leaning forward on her chair to hear better.

Pastor Troilius held his hand up, indicating that she ought to wait until he had finished. "He had none left. I saw the cups and the pamphlet with information about it. It's supposed to help with gout. If God has provided me with a way to find some relief, I can't tell you how I'd appreciate it. My legs, they give me such pains."

Beata's eyes widened, and she looked as though she wanted to say something but stayed silent, waiting for Nikolaos to respond.

"Already gone? Doctor Döbelius left several jugs only days ago. I'll ride out and tell him," Nikolaos said, then turned to Beata. "There's a spring in Ramlösa Woods near the village. The water is full of healthy substances, and Doctor Döbelius is prescribing many glasses of water of it daily. It cures almost anything, even Soldier's Disease."

"Doctor Döbelius," Beata stated, looking impressed. "Pray Nikolaos, pray let me come and try it. My arms hurt. I can barely move them, never get things from shelves, nor brush my hair. Orvar has to help me with everything, don't you, Orvar?"

"Yes." He nodded gravely. "She can't lift her arms above her head. Not even behind her back, I have to tie her aprons for her. It gets worse every year. Especially when it's cold. If the doctor could help her, it would indeed be a gift from God."

"You should try it. I have a better time with my stomach now. I used to have trouble in the morning and couldn't do what I needed to do," Stina said without a hint of embarrassment.

"My husband has the opposite problem!" Beata exclaimed, getting an annoyed look from Orvar, which made Stina and Beata laugh and shake their heads at him.

***

Nikolaos couldn't believe his eyes when he and Stina arrived in Ramlösa Woods with Elsebet, Fredrik, and his little girls.

It was as if everyone in the villages and the whole town of Helsingborg were present. Every path between the trees, every open space on the sloping ravine, was packed with spectators. There were even men perched in trees.

"There must be at least four hundred people here, Nikolaos!" Fredrik said, pulling Elsebet closer to his side as four people pushed themselves past them on the steep trail.

"I say at least the double," Nikolaos said, glancing at a crowd of people standing in a now open space, which had been full of bushes and trees just a few weeks ago.

"You're right. Should have charged a fee for our samples,

shouldn't we?" Fredrik said, deadpan.

Stina and Nikolaos looked at each other and laughed. The waterman charging for water that would be something.

They carefully made their way to flatter ground among the throngs of visitors. Some were dressed in their finest wigs and silks, whereas others came straight from the fields or from fishing. One man was carrying a large fishing net over his left shoulder. A powdered and rouged woman stared at him with a handkerchief over her nose, clearly bothered by the smell.

Doctor Döbelius was standing in front of the spring, now cleared of underbrush and bushes, giving everyone a good view of the rust-colored wall. An upside-down box beside him served as a table. A boy was placing small glasses on it, filling it as close to the top as he dared, then stacking some of them on top of each other. Still there were nowhere near enough glasses for the crowd.

With a tilt of his head, Fredrik indicated an empty spot not yet filled with people near the brook. "Let's go stand there," he said and took his daughters by the hand and walked over, turning around to make sure the rest were following.

Elsebet did as bid with an anxious glance at Nikolaos as Stina pretended to stumble to slow them down. "Is it safe? It's so very near the water. Can you handle it?" she whispered as Nikolaos came to her aid.

"They're standing a bit close, yes. I'll go see if Doctor Döbelius needs anything. When I get back, the crowd might have filled up, and then I'll stand over here. I thank you."

Stina nodded, but the anxiety didn't leave her face.

But Doctor Döbelius was getting the crowd's attention by clapping his hands and it didn't look like Nikolaos could use him as an excuse. He remained for a moment, then went back to Stina. She was standing off to the side, as far from the brook as she could without seeming rude to the others. He joined her, grateful, putting her between him and the brook.

Then Doctor Döbelius began. "Esteemed guests, I'm pleased to see that so many of you have come here to learn of the blessing this spring will provide. I'm a Medicinae Doctorem. I studied at the esteemed medical establishments in Rostock, and I'm the Provincial Medicinae Doctorem here in Skåne and Bohuslän," he said, sounding very proper and impressive.

"He's a doctor, a provincial doctor!" someone in the crowd shouted as several people murmured eagerly.

Doctor Döbelius waited for them to quiet down, smiling at all the faces. "Some of the older folk here may remember the war, especially the last months of Anno Domini 1679 when King Karl XI had his troops here. Some of you may even have had some of them staying with you and can confirm that many soldiers were very ill when they arrived. Very ill. It happens to quite a lot of our armed forces. Their insides empty out, and they can't keep anything down. But staying here cured their ailments! They drank this very water and were *cured*." He paused, nodding for effect. "It's rich with what strengthens the body and balances the humors. I found that it not only cures male ailments, but female ailments too, shaky joints, melancholy, and even dizzy spells."

The crowd gasped and exclaimed almost in unison.

Doctor Döbelius smiled with satisfaction, waving to the boy who hurriedly brought him a glass filled to the rim, somehow without spilling. Doctor Döbelius lifted it high and moved it from left to right to show the audience. A group of older people pushed each other to get closer, but the boy held his arms out, stopping them. "You'll get to drink as much as you want shortly," Doctor Döbelius said, throwing a grateful eye at the boy. "Let me continue. The list of betterments is so long it'll impress you yet more. Shortness of breath will no longer bother you, nor red eyes, or...."

"It can't all be true," a man called out suddenly, interrupting. "Sounds like something only God could take care of. Man has no power over these things. What prayers are needed for it to work?"

Doctor Döbelius didn't hesitate. "God has sure provided us with the knowledge to find this spring. I advise you to try it for yourself. Do form a line and sample the water. Once you've done so, share the cups with your neighbors and come to me, and I'll give you recommendations."

He turned around and scanned the crowd, and once his eyes fell on Nikolaos and Stina, he gestured for them to come forward.

"Would you mind helping me, Merchant Nikolaos? Pray refill the glasses to half. Stina, will you wipe them after they've been used a few times? Some people may have dirty hands or too much rouge on their lips, and it won't look good. If you could wipe off the glasses, I'd be thankful."

"I'm happy to help Doctor Döbelius," Stina said, her cheeks burning with pride.

They set to work with two other men, wearing new wigs. It made them look stylish, Nikolaos thought and decided to buy a new one for himself.

One after the other, people came forward and described in great, intimate detail what bothered them. Nikolaos had never known that people could have so many ailments, but Doctor Döbelius listened carefully to everyone, seeming to think nothing of it. He explained to each one of them that they needed to drink about eleven glasses per day for several weeks.

After a while, Nikolaos found it hard to focus on what was being said as three people, himself included, dipped their ladles in bowls full of water and poured it into glasses over and over again. He had to use all his concentration to remain standing normally, trying to think of the mercantile inventory instead of the sound of water all around him. He was surprised Stina didn't seem worried about it, but she was cleaning the glasses and smiling at all the guests, looking like she was enjoying herself. He kept pouring, ignoring the gurgling water.

Suddenly everyone stopped. Relieved, Nikolaos put his ladle down, then noticed that people sounded upset, even angry.

"Several weeks!" a man shouted. "How much time do you think we have? You said it would cure us of our ailments, not that we'd have to spend all our time here. You lie."

Nikolaos stood frozen until he spotted the man, who was shaking his head and walking away, pulling his wife by the arm.

Then people in the crowd started shouting and dispersing. Moments later, they walked off, climbing up the slopes of the ravine on both sides and filing up the little path to what Doctor Döbelius called the view mountain. They looked like ants running away from water in a sandbank.

Doctor Döbelius was staring after them, a look of shock on his face. He opened and closed his mouth several times, then cleared his throat once and said, "Dear visitors, do come back. You ought to try it first. Do come back and try it." The end of the sentence was no more than a whisper and Nikolaos thought he would cry. But then he smiled at the ones who were still in line.

About a half hour later, they had a crowd of about forty people left. Nikolaos had stepped to the side, leaving the others to continue pouring. To his relief, no one seemed to think anything of it.

Beata Lybecker was talking to the doctor now, manipulating her own arms while explaining about her pain. "I want to try it," she said. "Merchant Nikolaos was telling me about it the other day, and if you can help me, I'd owe you my life. My pain is so bad sometimes. I can't sleep. I'll come here and drink every day. I have a friend that lives nearby. I can stay with her and her husband."

"That's good. Good indeed. Do come. I want you here in the morning, midday, and evening. I have a remedy as well I want you to try."

Beata curtsied. "I thank you, Doctor Döbelius, thank you kindly."

"Yes, yes, you're welcome," he said, then turned when the man with the fishnet over his shoulder approached.

"My son and I and a few others can help you build a structure to protect people from the rain," the man said. "I overheard you speak of it earlier. I'd be glad to do it. I heard that you're planning to let the poorer folk come as well. If my father can come and drink for free, I'd be grateful. He pains so from achy joints."

"Yes, he can. I've spoken to Governor Stenbock about providing water for everyone, so yes, certainly your father can take the water here. Certainly he can. And I'd be most grateful for your help."

"Governor Stenbock himself?" a man asked, looking impressed and meeting his wife's eyes with an astonished nod.

Nikolaos couldn't stay out of the conversation any longer and walked over. "Doctor Döbelius, do tell them about your thoughts on the…"

"To inaugurate the spring on his Highness' Birthday my friend?" he interrupted and put his arm around Nikolaos' shoulder. "Yes, yes, as his birthday is on June seventeenth, I thought it would be a perfect day for it. My friend Merchant Nikolaos here is a musician, and he's promised to play for us. He has a Stradivari, played for the King's father when he lay ill."

The man's wife unfolded her fan with a snap. "Oh, it must have been so sad," she said and put the open fan over her heart.

"It was. I tried to stay professional about it, but it was hard not to feel overcome. I sat in a small antechamber behind his sickbed, didn't see the King, but just knowing he lay sick in a bed, lay dying in the bed, we know now. Well, it was hard to take. It made me very emotional." Nikolaos swallowed hard, noticing Stina and Elsebet giving him a curious look. He was surprised himself. He wasn't usually this affected by it.

The woman let out a sob, hiding her face behind her fan.

Nikolaos met her husband's gaze. "Pray forgive me, I didn't mean to cause distress."

"No need, no need. We're honored that you chose to confide in us. I think it'll be wonderful if you play here on our new King's birthday. It seems very fitting that you of all people, should do so after playing for his father. A continuing of life itself and a celebration of life-giving water."

"Yes, yes! Indeed," Doctor Döbelius broke in, "that's a very metaphorical way of looking at it. I'm touched. Deeply touched. To tell you the truth, I hadn't thought of it. I thank you." He grabbed the man around the shoulders and kissed him loudly on the cheek.

Life giving water, how ironic was that. Nikolaos looked at Stina, but she was averting her eyes.

Chapter 75

Karl XII's birthday, Seventeenth of June 1707

They were standing in the courtyard, dressed and ready. Stina was wearing a new dress made of pale blue silk, flowing generously to the floor from her waist. Doctor Döbelius had surprised her and Elsebet with the silky fabric last week, which he said came from his clothing factory near Sege River. It was the first Nikolaos had heard of the factory, and the doctor explained that it was a business venture. They usually made coats for Skåne's army, but he claimed there was a stash of fine silks hidden away which would never be of use. No soldier would ever wear it to battle, he had told him, handing it to Stina with ceremony. Now Nikolaos could barely take his eyes off her.

"Darling, you look so beautiful. Prettier than when we lived at Three Crowns," he said.

She blushed like a girl and kissed him. "I feel pretty, but it's ten years later. I can't possibly look that good."

"Yes, you do. You're beautiful," Nikolaos said. He suddenly remembered the locket he had found. Pulling away from her, he rushed inside to fetch it. He had completely forgotten about it after hearing those voices. Returning, he pressed it into her hands, excited to give it to her.

"Nikolaos! What's this? It's gold, how could you afford it?"

He leaned close, whispering into her ear, "I found it in the river. It was months ago now. Pray forgive me for forgetting. I had meant to get it polished and bring a ribbon from the mercantile for it, but it slipped my mind."

"Dear lord! She stared at him for a moment, then her face broke into a broad smile. "I have fabric left from this," she said and pinched her sleeve. "Do I have time to run inside and cut a piece?"

Nikolaos pulled out his watch from his shirt and glanced at it. "I think so. Hurry though, it's half past the hour."

When she went in, he looked at his reflection in their window. He had bought a new wig for the occasion with large white-blonde coils. It looked fetching with his beige waistcoat and breeches, like a real gentleman. He gave Stina what he thought was a gentlemanly bow as she hurried past the window inside, the locket now hanging snugly around her neck on a blue silk ribbon, but she didn't notice.

"We ought to go wait for Elsebet and Fredrik. They should be here now," Nikolaos said when she came back out, listening for their carriage wheels on the street.

***

Nikolaos was seated on a stool beside a newly constructed yellow and white gazebo. Elsebet and her stepdaughters were helping some women adorn it with garlands made of ivy, pink asters, and blue cornflowers.

Inside the gazebo was a real table, draped with a tablecloth patterned with golden crowns on a blue background. Fine tall glasses and a decanter full of Döbelius' water were placed on it, and two high-backed chairs cushioned with the same royal pattern as the tablecloth stood to the left.

"It's for those who need to sit. I'll sit beside them and inquire about their health. They'll be calmed by your music, Nikolaos, and will tell me about everything that ails them," Doctor Döbelius said when he noticed Nikolaos eyeing the setup.

"It looks beautiful. When do you want me to begin?"

Doctor Döbelius looked around, pursing his lips. "I think now. There's a group coming. Are you comfortable? Do you need anything before you begin?"

Nikolaos shook his head, getting a quick smile in response, and then Doctor Döbelius went to sit in one of the chairs only to get right up again and walk over to the cliff wall to wait there.

Nikolaos discreetly moved his chair a little closer to the gazebo, but not so close the pouring would bother him, and turned so he would face away from the brook. He could only pray Doctor Döbelius didn't disapprove, but the brook was too close for comfort. Stina caught his eye, and he saw her draw a sigh of relief.

595

As Nikolaos played, a steady trickle of people arrived, strolling down the path leading from the view mountain. Many of them wore wigs and the fine clothing of the Upper Estates.

The Lower Estates and the peasants kept a respectful distance and walked off to the sides, politely letting the more well-to-do down the hill first.

It made Nikolaos think of his own life. He had owned his own farm twice, but even so, had still been considered Estate-less and part of the lower peasant class. Did that change when he was invited to the royal castle or when he became a merchant? He didn't know. All it did was add another layer of otherness to his life.

When Nikolaos took a break, the spring was surrounded by people, and there was a line to get into the gazebo to have a talk with the doctor. He hurried past the line with the Stradivarius under his arm, then set out to look for Stina and the others, only to find himself face to face with Beata who just then came running out of the gazebo.

"Nikolaos," she said, then lifted both arms above her head and spun around. "Look, have you ever seen such a quick recovery? It's a miracle."

"It truly doesn't hurt?" he asked, astonished.

Beata pulled her arms down and hesitated for a moment, then said, "Well, if I claimed that it didn't, I wouldn't be truthful. It still does a little, but the fact that I can move my arms this way is more than I could ever have wished for. I can never thank you enough. It's thanks to you mentioning it at the House Hearing. If you hadn't, I would never have known about any of this."

"I'm very glad to hear," Nikolaos said and smiled, then felt his smile fade when out of the corner of his eye he thought he saw Merchant Fleisher and Mistress Esmeralda waiting in line to see Doctor Döbelius. Nikolaos spun toward them just as they briefly turned their heads in his direction. It *was* them. A spike of anger and fear made his heart pick up speed. Merchant Fleisher looked good, his hair was still long and thick, and he seemed strong and straight-backed. Mistress Esmeralda, on the other hand, looked very thin, which may account for why they were here.

"Are you ill as well? You seem distracted and pale suddenly," Beata said, her face full of concern.

It snapped him back to reality. "I'm not." He couldn't think of what to say and just patted her arm and walked off, leaving her standing there looking after him with consternation.

Had Doctor Döbelius invited them here? How could he do this to him? They would obviously recognize him. Was this why he was asked to play here? Nikolaos stopped walking and turned around to look back at the gazebo. They were inside it now. Merchant Fleisher was standing behind Mistress Esmeralda who was sitting down. She was taking small continuous sips of water from her glass while Doctor Döbelius was talking to her. From where Nikolaos stood, he could only see their faces in profile, but they looked calm and seemed to be conversing pleasantly.

Quickly and with his heart still thundering in his chest, he turned around and headed in the opposite direction, scanning the area for his family. They were all standing by the spring, and Fredrik saw him approach, gesturing at him with a broad grin.

Nikolaos lifted his hand with acknowledgment. Would he ruin their lives now? It might only be a matter of minutes, then everyone here would know. After that, it would reach the whole town. He couldn't put his family through it again.

"That was beautiful, truly extraordinary," Fredrik said and clapped him on the shoulder.

"It's the first time he's heard you play, Father," Elsebet added.

"Nah, didn't I play a bit at your wedding feast, daughter?"

"Nikolaos, you didn't play like this at our wedding. I've never heard anything like it. I now know what Elsebet is talking about." Fredrik said, looking thoroughly impressed.

"I thank you kindly," Nikolaos said, forcing himself to smile, hiding his panic. Then he shifted his gaze to Stina, moving his head slightly to convey he needed to speak with her.

"Fredrik and Elsebet, I want Nikolaos to walk with me a bit. I need to find a private place where…" She stopped, playing the part perfectly as she pretended to be embarrassed that she needed to pee somewhere. Blessed wife.

"Should I go with you, Mother?" Elsebet asked.

"I'll do it. I have a long enough break and could use a walk," Nikolaos said and put his hand on Stina's shoulder. He managed a genuine smile and a nod and then took Stina by the elbow, walking toward the uncleared trees along the newly widened road. As soon as they were out of earshot, he leaned close to her ear. "Mistress Esmeralda and Merchant Fleisher are both here. They might still be talking to Doctor Döbelius," he hissed, the panic getting the better of him.

Her eyes widened. "You don't mean…?"

Nikolaos nodded. Then he pulled her into the trees, out of sight.

"Did they recognize you?"

"I don't think so. Not yet. They probably will."

"You're wearing a new wig."

"It won't help much, Stina. And I must get back before the good doctor wonders where I went."

"I knew it! Didn't I tell you this?" she said, giving him a pointed stare. But her chin was quivering.

"I know. You did. Pray forgive me, Stina."

She kept her eyes in his for another eyeblink, then buried her head in her hands and sobbed silently.

People were walking toward them now, getting uncomfortably close to where they stood. Two women were staring and whispering. It made him angry, and he had a sudden thought that he could just kill Doctor Döbelius. Rusty devils, if he had invited him here to play because he knew that Merchant Fleisher and Mistress Esmeralda would come, he deserved it. Nikolaos was so angry he hadn't noticed that Stina had stopped crying and was walking away from him. The fear was obvious even from behind.

He couldn't do this to her again. With two long steps, he was by her side and wrapped his arm around her waist, looking at her. Her tears had messed up the white powder and rouge she had painted her face with, creating mushy pink lines. "Stina, don't you worry. I'm going to go speak to them."

"That's mad, husband."

He shook his head and slowed down so they wouldn't walk into the crowd, then pulled out a handkerchief. "Let me wipe your cheeks. They're stained," he said and spit on the fabric to wet it a little, then started wiping under her eyes. "No, I'll tell them how much they hurt us when they accused me of being…"

"You *are* Näcken," she interrupted.

Nikolaos stopped wiping abruptly. Even if no one could have heard, he couldn't believe she said that. "Let me take you back," he said icily, gripping her elbow. They walked back to the others in awkward silence, and he left her there without saying goodbye and without acknowledging Elsebet and Fredrik with as much as a nod. It was rude, but he couldn't deal with it.

Then, when he returned to the gazebo, he realized he had left his instrument by one of the trees and had to run back to retrieve it. It seemed everything was going wrong today.

Thankfully his violin was still there at least. He bent to pick it up, slowing his hurried motions a bit. Maybe it was better if they left. He could tell Doctor Döbelius what he thought of him at another time instead of causing a scene. Protect Stina and his family by giving them enough time to get away. He exhaled, looking up into the trees as he considered. But he wouldn't be able to control the situation if they fled. Then if Merchant Fleisher and his wife realized who he was, they might tell others of him, and he wouldn't even be there to see it. Maybe they already had. He took a deep breath. They were human. Weak and petty. He wouldn't let them hurt his family.

He went back to the gazebo, energized by his decision. Doctor Döbelius was sitting in there still, listening to a man who was rubbing his knees. Mistress Esmeralda and Merchant Fleisher were seated outside at one of the tables. Nikolaos pulled out his watch from under his shirt and checked the time. It seemed longer but he had only been on break for about fifteen minutes. There would be time for him to confront them without disturbing Doctor Döbelius.

He could yell at him later.

Grabbing an empty chair from another table, he brought it to where Merchant Fleisher and Mistress Esmeralda were sitting, putting it down opposite them as gently as he could. In his mind, he slammed it.

They both looked up, surprised but smiling, and then their expressions faded. Mistress Esmeralda grabbed her husband's arm and got to her feet so fast the table wobbled. Their glasses toppled over, and the water spilled on the white tablecloth.

"You both stay where you are," Nikolaos said and sat down. "I see you recognize me now, finally. I would've thought you'd notice when I performed a few minutes ago."

They stared open-mouthed as the spilled water soaked through the tablecloth, wetting their legs. Neither of them moved.

Nikolaos waited, biding his time. Then just as Merchant Fleisher began to say something, he interrupted him. "Mistress Esmeralda, Merchant Fleisher, it's not my pleasure to see you again. I hope you've asked God to forgive you, or you surely will be sent straight to Hell on Judgment Day." He leaned back on his chair, pleased that he thought to say it like that.

Mistress Esmeralda's hand on her husband's arm shook.

Merchant Fleisher blinked several times as if he couldn't believe Nikolaos was sitting in front of him. Then he finally spoke. "God's forgiveness? This is too much. You're a murderer who drowns people. And you force people to dance until they faint."

"Hush now, let's not destroy this beautiful day for Doctor Döbelius' sake. Don't you agree?" Nikolaos asked snarkily, glancing around, but no one seemed to have heard anything. "By the way, did he invite you here?"

"Not directly, obviously, since you're here. Why would he insult us by doing that? He knows who you are. I don't understand why you're the one performing," Mistress Esmeralda said, her voice sounding weak as if she had trouble breathing.

Nikolaos exhaled, flooded with relief. It wasn't the doctor's doing then, after all. Thank God he hadn't confronted him.

"Yes indeed. We ought to leave now and call on men to

come and take you to the lawman. It's disgusting to see you here,"
Merchant Fleisher added and slowly rose to his feet.

"You do no such thing. You stay, and you listen to what I
have to say," Nikolaos said, keeping his voice level and what he
hoped was a commanding tone.

They stared at him numbly, then Merchant Fleisher sat back
down.

Nikolaos nodded, relieved it worked. "After I left your home,
I went to Stockholm to play at the late King's funeral. And here we
are, celebrating his son's birthday. Seems fitting." He paused and
laughed coldly, raising his eyebrows. Merchant Fleisher didn't react.
"When I got home, I found my children distraught and my wife
gone. Jailed and questioned for days. All due to your ludicrous
claims," he said, voice dripping with disdain. "My daughter's
betrothal was dissolved because of it. They questioned and abused
my *wife*." He paused at that, swallowing a sudden spike of anguish.
"You destroyed our lives. It took years to build it up again. You owe
my wife and my daughter an apology."

Merchant Fleisher looked utterly stunned.

Nikolaos lowered his voice, aware that people were
watching them now. "I take it that you've never been accused of
the vile things you accused me of and probably don't know how it
feels. It would've been one thing if you had done so when I was still
a guest at your home, however insulting that would've been. But to
contact our pastor! My son still lives at our farm with his family,
living with this ridiculous rumor you started. You've hurt a lot of
people."

Merchant Fleisher blinked, moving backward in his chair.
Mistress Esmeralda lost her grip on his arm, and her hand fell with a
thump to the table. "You're not human," Merchant Fleisher said.
"You almost killed those people, and you made our guests fall into a
stupor. On top of that, you flooded our stables. I'm going to call for
help. Now."

All the guests around them were staring at them, and it had
become utterly silent, except for the chirping birds. Nikolaos looked
at the crowd, pretending to seem as shocked and exasperated as

them.

Merchant Fleisher lifted his hand and pointed at Nikolaos. "Arrest him," he said, but it was only a hoarse croak.

As if by miracle, Doctor Döbelius came running across the grass with a big fake smile on his lips. "Merchant Fleisher, Mistress Esmeralda, I do apologize. I see now what you may be thinking. Pray forgive me." He lowered his voice and smiled at the bystanders who were now circling their table. Then he put his arm around Nikolaos' back and gave him an exaggerated squeeze. "Mistress Esmeralda and Merchant Fleisher, you two need not fear. I assure you. Things are not the way you thought. Now calm yourselves. A misunderstanding is all," he added, nodding encouragingly at the bystanders.

Merchant Fleisher frowned, seeming as though he was about to disagree with him but couldn't think of what to say. Mistress Esmeralda's eyes flickered between Doctor Döbelius and her husband. She was pale and silent.

Nikolaos let out a breath of cautious relief. "You heard the good doctor. Enjoy the water. I'll go perform now as has been arranged. When you're ready to apologize, I'm eager to listen."

He walked away, feeling their eyes on his back, wondering what Doctor Döbelius was thinking. If he was angry at him for causing a scene or if he was relieved that he hadn't been angrier. When he sat down with his violin, he saw Stina look at him across the crowd. As their eyes met, he gave a slight nod. The relief made her face crumble. But he was still upset with her for what she said.

***

Nikolaos played until late. The evening sun was golden and soft when he stopped. People were still milling about, walking back and forth with their glasses in hand, conversing. If Mistress Esmeralda and her husband were still there, he didn't see them. He exhaled and pulled out his watch. It was already two minutes before ten. High time to end the evening. Getting to his feet, he went into the gazebo to retrieve his violin case, then spotted Stina arm in arm with Beata, heading his way. The golden light made Stina's pale blue dress and gray hair shine, and she looked so beautiful. His anger from earlier dissolved completely.

"My ladies," he said and ran out, grinning at them both.

Stina met his eyes and smiled, touching his arm in silent apology.

He kissed her cheek. "I shall speak to Doctor Döbelius, and then we'll go home. We can ride with him. Are you staying with your friend still, Beata?" he asked, turning toward her.

"Yes, Orvar is as well. Did you know he no longer has to rush to the outhouse in the mornings?" Beata asked, letting go of Stina's arm so she and Nikolaos could walk together. "He feels much better. I'm telling everyone about this miraculous water. Anyway, I'll leave you to enjoy it for yourself. You ought to drink some to get some sustenance after entertaining us with your marvelous music all evening, Nikolaos." Beata hugged Stina and hurried over to Orvar who was standing off to the side waiting. She certainly looked stronger; there was no doubt about it.

"Did you see Merchant Fleisher? Did they leave?" Nikolaos asked in a low voice once Orvar and Beata had begun their ascent up the new road.

"I think so, but I'm not certain. They spoke to Doctor Döbelius for just a short while after you left their table. I kept my eyes on them. I was going to keep watch of what they did, but then the girls got my attention, and when I looked back, they were gone. Pray forgive me, Nikolaos. I know I should've tried."

"It's no matter. What about Fredrik and Elsebet?"

"They didn't see. They were talking with someone Fredrik knows."

He let out a breath, then inhaled deeply. "Thank God. We'll see what Doctor Döbelius says. We just have to play along for now. At least he didn't invite him here."

Stina stopped walking as her knees buckled beneath her with relief. It hadn't occurred to him that she must have been worried about it.

"Oh darling, pray forgive me," Nikolaos whispered, putting a hand on her back. "He didn't know, he defended me, Stina. We don't have to worry about him at least." It had certainly seemed that way. Nikolaos pushed down a spark of uncertainty.

"You shall see that a week or two of drinking spring water ought to make you strong again!" a man strolling past them exclaimed when he saw Stina's collapsed form.

Nikolaos gave a small nod in acknowledgment as he helped Stina straighten up.

She chuckled at the man. "If he only knew. I'm so relieved."

"I was too, I realized already when I confronted them. Mistress Esmeralda made it plain," Nikolaos said, feeling better about it again. She *had* made it plain.

They kept walking arm in arm. People smiled at them and commented on his music without a hint of suspicion. When they found Doctor Döbelius, he was pouring water for a group of drinkers.

Handing the decanter to a young girl, he turned toward them, a warm glint in his eye. "Nikolaos, Stina, can I offer you a ride home? We'll talk in my coach. I was about to leave anyway." He put a heavy hand on Nikolaos' shoulder.

"Are you leaving when there are still guests here?" Stina asked, her cheeks reddening when she realized she had spoken out of turn as if she was criticizing him for leaving.

"All part of the strategy, all part of the strategy. I have assistants helping me. It looks better if I'm not last. Better that people ask for me than I'm seen sitting here alone."

Stina nodded and smiled politely, but Nikolaos could see that she was close to tears. Her nerves were fraught still. She kept fidgeting with her locket, and he could tell that her fingers were ice cold. He needed to get her home.

Doctor Döbelius' coach was adorned with thick red cushions and velvet curtains, very lavish. Maybe Governor Stenbock had provided it. As far as Nikolaos knew, the doctor didn't have as much money as one would think. Apparently, being the provincial doctor wasn't well paid.

Doctor Döbelius sat down opposite him and Stina and pulled the curtain aside, looking out through the glass window as the coach pulled up the road to the view mountain. The silence felt awkward.

When they reached flat ground, Nikolaos broke it. "It's outrageous. I'm deeply insulted."

"I understand," Doctor Döbelius said, sighing deeply. "I can't tell you how much it pains me. I…"

"What did they say after I left," Nikolaos interrupted impatiently. "I was waiting for them to come apologize."

"Not much. I made it clear that I didn't want to cause a scene."

"You didn't find out what they had to say?" Nikolaos shouted, louder than he meant, and got a worried look from Stina.

Doctor Döbelius' eyes narrowed. "Calm yourself, Nikolaos, we'll get this sorted. Surely you understand that I couldn't discuss this there?"

"I don't. Not at all. We don't know what rumors they've spread about me. Spreading right now. It could destroy my family, again." His elbows were itching, distracting him. He needed water. "I was forced to play for your guests with no way of knowing what he said about me as I sat there on display. The only reason I didn't leave was *you*. I realize how important this day is, but you must understand that it might be too late already. I'm terrified of what Merchant Fleisher might have said. I should kill the dastard."

"Nikolaos!" Stina reproached, her eyes wide with shock.

But Doctor Döbelius chuckled, and in that moment, Nikolaos understood that he didn't have anything to fear from him. He truly didn't believe what was said of him. "Pray forgive me. I'm reacting too strongly to this."

The doctor kept chuckling and reached over and patted his knee. "I understand. I'm grateful to you for not hitting the dastard as you so fittingly called him. I felt what you said was just perfect. They do owe you an apology. And here you're among friends. Let it off your chest."

"I thank you and appreciate that. But I cursed them to hell.

I'm not sure how good that was. Pray forgive me, I hope no one else heard."

"You cursed them to hell?" Stina exclaimed.

Doctor Döbelius waved it away as if a curse was no more than a fly, then looked out the window, nodding to himself.

When he turned his head back in their direction, they were already approaching town. "I don't want you thinking about it, Nikolaos. We had a beautiful evening. I have several new patients signed up, and many commented on your extraordinary music. No one claimed that you're," he lowered his voice, "*Näcken*. No one would've stayed if they had. You shall rest assured."

"I thank you. I do apologize if this caused any discomfort for you, Doctor Döbelius," Nikolaos said, exchanging a glance of relief with Stina. He was right about that; people would have left in a panic.

"It's no matter, and it's certainly not your fault," Doctor Döbelius said, glancing out the window. "We're almost in town. This is my suggestion. Tomorrow morning, I'll speak to them. I must see Mistress Esmeralda anyway. I'll inform them that I'd like them to formally apologize."

"I ought to challenge him to a duel," Nikolaos said irritably, angry again.

Doctor Döbelius raised an eyebrow. "They're no longer lawful."

"Since when?"

The coach stopped, and they heard the driver get down from his seat.

"A long time now. Since 1682, maybe 1684, I can't remember. There was a royal decree. I know that if you duel once, you'll just pay a fine, but people who do it more face deportation. Although that might have been earlier, I don't know. There were two decrees I heard. One year earlier than the one in 1684 or whenever it was. I'm not certain. In either case, I advise you not to."

Nikolaos shrugged and avoided looking at Stina whose eyes were boring into him. Then the driver knocked on the coach door and pulled it open.

"I'll call on you tomorrow, Fiddler Nikolaos," Doctor Döbelius said and smiled gently.

Nikolaos nodded and helped Stina step out.

***

They hadn't more than come inside before Stina was on him. She pounded his chest with her fists as tears were streaming down her cheeks. Her arms moved so fast it took him three tries to catch them in his hands.

"Stina, what in the world has gotten into you?"

"Gotten into me?" she shrieked.

"Yes, why are you hitting me. Seat yourself, woman."

Stina looked so surprised that she obeyed him, sitting down on the divan in front of the fireplace. Then she said, "Nikolaos, you told him that you were going to kill him. Twice. And a duel! Why would you do something so foolish?"

"It's just a figure of speech. You know I wouldn't do it."

"How would I know that. You've done it before."

"What?"

"Killed people. I know you have. I may be just a human Nikolaos, but I'm no fool." She held his gaze, unyielding and furious. "There's no sense in denying it. I used to think it was all rumors. But I've known since Jon's trial that you have. I could see it in Rå's face when we spoke of it."

At that moment, a blackbird trilled outside; its beautiful song seemed entirely out of place.

"You and Rå have spoken about this?"

"No, not directly. I just mentioned your innocence in passing. It was clear she didn't agree, Nikolaos."

He flinched.

"Nikolaos, I'm tired of this. Tired of having to constantly be on my guard for you. Afraid that someone will find out. Exhausted by the fact that each time I tell you to find your water because, like now, you're impossible to be around, I worry that I'm sending some poor woman to her death. And this! Did you pull it off someone's neck?" She untied the ribbon and threw her locket at him, and he caught it in his hand as the wall of pretense fell between them.

"Stina, I…"

"Don't you deny it, *Lord* Näcken." Stina put both hands on the divan and pushed herself up to stand, glaring at him where he stood leaning against the wall.

"Very well. I won't."

Her cheeks flushed. "How many?"

"I don't know."

"You don't *know!* How can you not know? You murder without thought? I don't believe you. Tell me how many."

"Stina, it's not quite like that." But it was. He was a murderer.

She sat down again but got right back up, turning her back toward him as she pulled at her dress. "Help me with my stays, Nikolaos. I can't breathe."

He did as bid. Loosening one lace after the other while his eyes burned with shame.

When he was done, she left him and walked into the bedroom, throwing her dress and stays on the bed.

Unsure of what to do, he poured them ale and followed her, finding her sitting on the bed wrapped in her robe. "Here, drink some if you're thirsty," he said as he downed his own in one gulp.

She put the mug on the nightstand without touching it.

"Nikolaos, I want you to tell me everything. I can't pretend that I don't know that you've been keeping secrets from me all these years anymore."

It stung. But it was the truth. The room felt silent and heavy. "May I sit next to you?" he asked finally, scared she would say no, but she nodded. "Stina I've told you it's dangerous for people to be near me if I'm near water. I've been very frank about that. How is it that you feel that I've kept secrets from you?"

"You love me. It's different. But the others? How many are there? Do you drag them in while they scream?"

"Stina, pray don't think so evil of me. I don't do that. You know I become absorbed with my colors and the water. I don't notice until they're in the brook with me." He paused, wondering if he should lie now, then told her anyway. "I lose control, and then they float away. I try to find private spots, but they come. They always come."

"It's because they hear your music as I did, Nikolaos. You ought to stop playing in the water like that. Then we need not worry about it."

Silence settled between them.

She looked away, and he could see her heartbeat at the base of her neck. It was too fast, and he knew what she would ask next.

"Is it like they say that you, that you have them before you kill them?"

He couldn't bear to answer.

"Is it? Do you lie with them? Is that why they all drown?"

"Yes."

She screamed.

Rising from the bed, Nikolaos walked out. He was a monster.

Chapter 76

It was early morning when Nikolaos came back. Had it not been for the fact that Doctor Döbelius was going to speak to Merchant Fleisher and Mistress Esmeralda, he didn't think he would have come back at all. The house was empty, the hearth cold, and it didn't look like Stina had bothered to make the pottage she liked to make fresh each morning. Finding some hard bread and herring, he ate it standing up, gazing out the window and wondering if Stina had gone to speak to Elsebet about it. How much would she tell her?

He had never seen Stina as she was last night. The way she screamed when he admitted to the truth. Her face had been utterly grief-stricken. Her eyes empty of love for him, as if she were looking at a stranger. He wished he had at least told her that he hadn't pulled the locket off someone's neck. Just thinking of it made him feel sick to his stomach and he tossed the remaining pieces herring out the window, not caring that Stina would have been angry that he wasted food.

Nikolaos had just pulled all his clothes out of the closet and drawers and was getting to his other belongings when there was a loud knock on the door. Instinctively, he put his hand to his hair to see if it was dry, checked his breeches and shirt, then threw a quick look at his face in the looking glass to make sure there was nothing on his person that would betray where he had been.

When he opened the door, there was a young boy with knobby knees and no shoes outside. He couldn't be more than seven or eight.

"I've got a message for you," the boy said. "A doctor sent me all the way from the robbers' woods in Ramlösa. He said he wants you to meet him and Merchant Flisker in church. He said to tell you that Merchant Flisker is willing to speak with you, and they'll meet you at two o'clock."

"I assume you mean Merchant Fleisher and Doctor Döbelius," Nikolaos said.

The boy nodded. "Yes, that's what I said, Merchant Flisker."

Nikolaos smiled and ruffled the boy's hair. "It's far! You ran all the way from there with that message?"

"I did for part of the way, then I got a ride," he said, holding his hand out, giving him such an earnest look that Nikolaos hurried inside and brought back a much bigger coin than what was seemly.

The boy's face lit up as he clutched the coin in his dirty little hand. Immediately after, he spun around and ran across the courtyard so fast he almost ran into Farrier Nils who was coming in with a large mare that needed shoeing.

"Mercy! Watch yourself, boy," Farrier Nils shouted, but he was already through the gate.

Nikolaos arrived promptly at two o'clock. Merchant Fleisher and Doctor Döbelius were not outside, the little square in front of Lady Maria Church was empty, and he neither saw nor heard anyone approach. Maybe they were inside already.

Throwing one more glance in each direction just to make sure they weren't coming, he went in. And there they were, sitting in a pew on the left near the altar. It struck him that it was no accident and that Merchant Fleisher wanted to see what would happen to him in a holy place. He probably thought he couldn't even enter. It was insulting.

Nikolaos walked right past them and went up to the altar without so much as a glance in their direction, feeling their eyes boring into his back. He kneeled and made the sign of the cross, trying not to think of Stina screaming last night or his own thoughts on being a monster. It was impossible. How would God protect him from Merchant Fleisher's wrath in church of all places when he was exactly as he said? God forgive him. He crossed himself again, pushing the thoughts as far back in his mind as he could, and stood up to face them.

Doctor Döbelius nodded pleasantly. "Morning, I mean good afternoon. Do have a seat with us."

"Good afternoon," Nikolaos said, looking only at the doctor.

"Fiddler Nikolaos, or should I say Merchant Nikolaos, I heard we're in similar business now," Merchant Fleisher said. He frowned.

"Nikolaos will do," Nikolaos said and sat down in the pew behind them, forcing them both to turn around to look at him.

"I'll come right to the point. Doctor Döbelius is insisting that I apologize, but quite frankly I'm not sure what to think," Merchant Fleisher said.

"I'm not either. Your accusations are utter nonsense."

"You're saying that Näcken is nonsense?" His voice was dripping with disdain.

"I don't know. I've not been graced by the creature's presence to tell you if he is or not. As I told you in your home, I never saw him or that comet you described. Maybe you're just making it up to slander me. Was it jealously perhaps, since your wife was all too eager to invite me?"

Merchant Fleisher bristled. "I assure you that Näcken was there. I saw the evidence myself, and everything points to the fact that you're him. I'd like you to explain your innocence to me. Then I'll see for myself if you deserve an apology."

Nikolaos threw an irritated glance at Doctor Döbelius, but he wouldn't meet his eyes. "That's outrageous. I'm not explaining anything at all. You owe me an apology. I made myself very clear yesterday. You destroyed our lives. There's nothing to explain." He thrust his right arm across the pew so close that it almost touched Merchant Fleisher's chest, holding it steady in front of him. "You tell me that I'm not a man. You look me in the eye here in church and tell me I'm something so vile. Here, touch it and squeeze it. Then tell me." Nikolaos splayed and closed his fingers while looking him right in the eye.

Merchant Fleisher gasped and drew back as far as he could without sliding off the pew. He didn't touch him.

Doctor Döbelius shook his head and then grabbed Nikolaos' arm with both hands while turning his head toward Merchant Fleisher. "For the love of God, Fleisher, if you don't apologize now, Nikolaos and I will both leave. I'll still treat your wife, as it's my duty as a doctor. But when she's cured, I never want to see you again. This is becoming annoying now. I'm not taking part in this charade anymore." He abruptly got to his feet and started down the aisle, the sound of his heels on the stone floor echoing blue and red. "I'll leave you two to it. I'll be right outside," he called, then opened the heavy church door and slipped out.

"Do it now, or I'll leave as well. Be grateful that I don't challenge you to a duel for slandering my family," Nikolaos said icily.

Merchant Fleisher stared at him, then his shoulders seemed to sink in on themselves, and he sighed deeply. "Pray forgive me. It's clear that I made a mistake. We panicked. When the couple was found, they were very distraught. Convinced that Näcken had been sitting there with his violin. They said that they heard the music and couldn't... Somehow they were drawn into the water with him. I'm not sure how it happens. Neither of them was fully conscious when they were found. They were cold and wet and terrified. They said that he'd been," he crossed himself, "that Näcken had copulated with them both at the same time! People wouldn't make that up. Then when you took your horse from the stable and it flooded... Well, what did you expect us to think? He's known to do that, you know, wherever he walks, there's water. It trails after him, and we couldn't help but assume. We were frightened. When Doctor Döbelius examined them, he said their skin showed clear signs of having been in the water. There was no doubt of it. Näcken had a violin, and they had followed you when you... when you went..."

Nikolaos held up his hand to stop him. "That's quite enough details, Merchant Fleisher. Do you really think I'd bring my Stradivarius to a brook? Do you know what kind of instrument it is?"

"Um, well..."

"I take it that you hadn't thought of it that way. Next time, think things through before you say things that ruin people's lives. I'll be leaving now. I'll leave you to wipe the floor. We wouldn't want someone to slip now, would we?" he said wickedly and stood up. Merchant Fleisher's eyes flicked to the floor, then back at him. He looked embarrassed.

Nikolaos shook his head. Part of him was relieved that the

floor was dry.

***

Stina was at home when Nikolaos got there, sitting wrapped in a blanket in front of the hearth, watching a pot of stew. It was stifling hot inside.

"Aren't you hot?" he asked and opened the window to let some air in.

She shook her head without looking at him and kept staring at the pot. Her eyelids were thick and swollen. He wondered if Elsebet had seen her like that. He sat down in the chair next to hers, resisting the urge to reach for her, but her hands were hidden in the folds of her blanket anyway.

"Stina," he said quietly. "I've broken my vow to you. It's unacceptable."

She finally looked right at him, tears spilling from her eyes. "I know Nikolaos, I know. I can forgive the intimacy, I'm an old woman, and you're still young in your own way. But not the rest. How can you? They're innocent."

"I know they are. But I never mean to hurt them. I just can't seem to help it. When we're done, they float away."

Stina said nothing.

He hid his face in his hands. The words seemed to echo between the walls. Harsh and raw. Real.

He heard his watch tick inside his shirt in the silence, the sound of the house clock on the bureau, the puttering of the stew, and the flames in the hearth. It all seemed too loud. He waited.

Eighteen minutes passed before either of them stirred.

Then Stina got up, pulled the pot off its hook, and set it to cool on the side.

"We ought to eat. Seat yourself, husband."

All he could do was nod and do as she asked. Like she had done every day since she made their first meal. The only thing that had changed was the fact that they used their own individual bowls now instead of one large bowl like they used to. He missed it. Today it only served to enforce the separation between them.

Finishing all of it in a few minutes, not caring that it was too hot and burned his mouth, he put the spoon back in his bowl and pushed it aside. "Stina, we must talk to each other. You need to tell me what you want me to do."

"Do?"

"Yes, do you want me to leave? I'll leave you money." He wanted to ask her to forgive him, but there was no point. No human would. He deserved the same fate Jon had endured. "Stina, I can turn myself in."

"Did you kill someone last night?"

"No."

"Nikolaos, you can't put such shame on us. Your children's and grandchildren's lives would be ruined if you turned yourself in. You'll have to wait until we're all gone." She stood up, then went into the bedroom and closed the door behind her.

Chapter 77

Having finished helping the trees in the north, Rå and Little One were heading back southward. They had been traveling for months when Little One suddenly stopped walking. She gave Rå a long look, then lay down on the ground and curled up. A moment later, she was dead.

Rå heard a gasp, scaring herself before she realized it was her own voice she had heard. There was no question. Little One had left the body behind. Just like that, as if she had decided she was finished with whatever task she needed to do in that body. Rå smiled through her tears and kneeled beside her, pulling on her horns to get the big head into her lap. It was heavy, a dead weight in her hands. "Little One," she whispered, stroking her soft forehead. It was still warm, but her spirit had clearly flown. It didn't even feel like it was nearby. Little One was already on her way somewhere else.

"Well, my sweetness," Rå said, looking into the distance between the trees, "enjoy your new body. If you can fly, look for me in the woods." Giving Little One another pat on the forehead, she pulled herself out from under the heavy head and got to her feet.

Rå cast a last glance at Little One over her shoulder as she walked away. It was getting darker, and she looked like a stone where she lay. The body could stay where it was. It would rot and become food for wolves and vultures at first, and then worms and crows as well. It was beautiful. The earth took care of itself, and life continued elsewhere.

A few days later, the forest was beginning to thin out, and Rå could see the sea on her right. Whiffs of woodsmoke, manure, and cooking floated on the winds. She was near people. Looking down at her shift, she grimaced with disgust. Her white blouse was so dirty, it looked dark brown. It also seemed to have shrunk somehow and barely covered her back. Her skirt was even worse. It was stained with moss and dirt with long strips of something black that might be soot, then again might not. Rå sighed. She didn't carry much anymore and had nothing to change into. Perhaps she could make up an excuse for why her clothes were so dirty and find a gentlewoman to sell her something new. She had a few coins tucked away in her satchel where she kept her blanket and her firestarter, along with some remaining salves. If she traded with it, she might be able to at least get a new shift.

With new resolve, she kept walking toward the enticing scents. Soon she spotted a church steeple in the distance and then a cluster of buildings. Moments later, she heard faraway voices and faint sounds of hammering. Continuing with more caution, Rå entered a meadow along a small road. At the end of it, two women were walking at a slow pace. One of them had long gray braids coming out from under her headscarf, bouncing freely on her back and reaching all the way down below her buttocks. Rå smiled. It reminded her of her own mother, only she never covered her head. The other woman was younger and bareheaded. Maybe it was a grandmother with her granddaughter.

Rå opened her back and pulled her skirt higher to conceal it, then hurried to catch up to them. "Good day, goodwife, she said, nodding at the older woman and smiling at the girl. She was so startled by her voice she jumped.

The older woman just cocked an eyebrow. "What happened to you? Have someone fared ill with you?"

"No, thank heavens, nothing quite that cruel. I slid down a hill after running from what I thought was a bear, tearing my bodice and shift, which stayed stuck in the brambles," Rå said. It was partly true; she did walk through some thorny bushes a few weeks back.

"A bear, are you sure?" the younger woman asked and stepped closer. She had round cheeks and fine blond hair tied into two round balls on the sides of her head.

"I'm not, but whatever it was set me running too fast. And this is the result." Rå gestured up and down her body and gave what she hoped was an embarrassed grimace. "I'm passing through, and I'm so glad to see you. Would you be able to help me? Sell me something proper to wear."

"That's out of the question," the older woman said firmly.

"You shall come home to us, and I'll find you something. There's no need to pay me anything. We women stick together. Don't we?" she said, putting her arm around the younger girl's shoulders while they exchanged a pointed glance. "This is my granddaughter Marja."

"I thank you very, very much, goodwife." Rå smiled at them, wondering what was passing between them. Maybe Marja had some love trouble she had been confiding to her grandmother. Rå allowed her back to close a bit. Women were less susceptible to her power than men were, so it wouldn't make much difference anyway.

"It's no trouble," the older woman said. "I have clothes no one wears anymore. I never get around to making something new out of them." She grinned, a broad toothless grin. "You can call me Nilsa."

"I thank the good lord I found you then, Nilsa," said Rå while silently thanking Freya. "What village is this?"

"Filbacke," said Marja. "Where did you slip and fall? Was it just now?" She eyed Rå's clothes with a frown as if she didn't believe her.

"You have a sharp eye, Marja. It was several days ago now, and my stains have gotten worse since."

"I thought so." She looked proud of herself in that boastful way young adults behaved when they thought they were all grown up.

Rå smiled at her, resisting a wink.

"Have you walked around dressed like that for several days?" Nilsa asked. "Haven't you been cold? Where did you sleep?"

"Under a tree. And yes, I've been very cold."

Nilsa shook her head, then crossed herself. "We shall hurry home, and I'll see what I can find for you." She glanced over her shoulder toward the tree line as if to check if there was a bear, then started walking at a fast pace.

Rå followed, flanking Nilsa. Even though she had claimed it had been a few days ago and that it may not even have been a bear, both seemed genuinely concerned. She would have to warn the bears later, just in case they sent hunters out after them. Bears were mating around this time and didn't need people chasing after them. She shouldn't have used them as an excuse.

Marja ran off when they reached the village, and Nilsa brought Rå to her home. She lived in a large stone house with two floors. They entered straight into a kitchen where five women of different ages were cooking something together. It smelled incredible. They all turned around and stared in wordless shock when they spotted Rå.

"Marja is my daughter's daughter," Nilsa said, ignoring the stares. "This here is the home of two of my sons. They both live here with their wives and their children. I have my own room on the top floor." She touched Rå's elbow and steered her toward the back where there was a wide staircase.

Once they reached her room, Nilsa went straight to a chest of drawers and pulled out a long dark-brown skirt and a simple linen underskirt. Lastly, she reached for a blue shawl from a different drawer and handed it to Rå.

"I thank you. I'm happy to pay you or trade for these. Are you certain I can't offer you anything?" Rå let the fabric slide between her fingers for a moment and felt the tight stitching of the shawl. It was fine quality.

"No, mistress, I'm happy to help. My sons' daughters and wives have finer clothes than these and aren't interested." She smiled and changed the subject. "I never asked your name."

"It's Magda," Rå said, returning her smile. "We all have names ending with the same sound. Magda, Nilsa, and Marja."

Nilsa laughed. "And Anna and Arjavarja downstairs."

Rå started, feeling the skin on her arms prickle and her back push itself open. Arjavarja had been her mother's nickname, used only with family and only when they felt especially loving toward each other. She hadn't thought of her nickname for more years than she could remember.

"Magda, are you unwell? Sit awhile." Nilsa pointed to a chair by the far wall. "Or would you rather come down to the kitchen? I'll have the girls give you something to eat."

Rå nodded, then shook her head. "I'll gladly eat something. I'm not unwell but struck by the beautiful name Arjavarja." Her throat thickened as she uttered it. "Is it your daughter-in-law's name?"

Nilsa looked at her sharply. "My great-granddaughter. You know the name? It's been in our family for generations. Many, many generations. We have a lineage of strong, strong women." She narrowed her eyes, tilting her head to the side as if to gather what Rå was thinking. "Arjavarja was the first one, a mother who loved the forest so much, she gave her only daughter to it to care for it," Nilsa said in a singsong voice. "We're not sure how she did that, but it's what they say. Every generation we have a girl in the family we name after her, always a little one born with a scar right below the right shoulder, as if she hurt herself in the womb."

Rå's back closed abruptly, sending a spike of pain up her spine. "I think I'll sit now," she said and crossed the floor to the chair. Her knees felt wobbly, and she only just made it without falling. Her mother had had a scar below her right shoulder. A burn from when a piece of wood had popped out of the fire somehow. It attached itself to her dress and remained there while she walked all the way to the table to put down a heavy cauldron with hot soup before she could push it off herself. It burned through her dress and seared her skin badly. Rå put her head between her legs to stop the swaying. Nilsa's family must be a relation. An actual relation. What if the great-granddaughter was her mother who had come back? Rå's throat constricted at the thought. She had wished for it so much.

"I'm putting you to bed, Magda."

Surprised, Rå opened her eyes. Nilsa was sitting cross-legged on the floor in front of her. And looking at her face now, she could even see the resemblance. It wasn't just the braids. There was something about the lines around her eyes.

"Come," Nilsa said and helped her stand, then led her toward her bed, a firm hand on her elbow. "You lie down while I fetch you something to eat. Once you've eaten, we'll talk."

Nilsa's bed felt soft and smelled clean. It was very

comfortable. Rå closed her eyes, allowing herself one moment of rest. Then she snapped them open and sat up. She had given her only daughter to the forest, Nilsa had said. That part wasn't true. There had been eight of them, five sisters and three brothers, but the rest, how did she know that? Rå's eyes filled with tears, dripping down and landing on her dirty blouse. She let them flow freely until she heard steps on the stairs, then quickly wiped her eyes with the edge of the blanket.

Nilsa entered with a big tray with a steaming bowl of something smelling as good as it had in the kitchen, a big piece of bread, and a mug of ale. "You're awake. Good, it's better if you eat first," she said, placing the tray in Rå's lap. Then she went and got the chair from over by the wall and sat down next to the bed, facing Rå.

"I should've changed out of these clothes," Rå said. "I'm dirtying your bed with them. Pray forgive me for the trouble."

Nilsa waved her hand in the air dismissively.

Rå ate. It was a stew made with herbs and a lot of meat, maybe pork. It was delicious. This family was of means, making such rich food and wasting it on strangers.

"I think I may owe you an explanation," Rå said when she finished. She took a breath. "The reason I felt faint earlier is because it struck me that we may be related, Nilsa."

"Related?" Nilsa's eyes widened.

Rå nodded. "My mother also spoke of Arjavarja and had a scar just like you described. In fact, she looked a little like you." The lie about speaking of her instead of *being* Arjavarja came easily. Nikolaos would be proud of her. He always said to stay as close to the truth as possible.

Nilsa stared at her, jaw slack. "Child, I don't know what to say. How can that be? Where are you from? And your mother?"

"From a village northwest of here." Rå looked upward, trying to remember what they called it, but it didn't come to her.

"What's the village called?"

Rå took a bite of the bread to save time. "We lived in Knästa," she said, making up a random name. It might not be a place at all.

"Hmmm... I've never heard of it. Did she have an older brother named Jacob who married Tilda? They had four children, one boy who wasn't right in the head."

"No, she was an only child." It was a lie, but Rå wasn't sure what else to do. The fewer people she pretended to have known her, the less likely it would be for Nilsa to ask questions she wouldn't be able to answer.

"Ah, it must be my cousin's family from Falun then. His sister had only one daughter. They moved away for reasons no one knew. What was your mother's name?"

"Solveig," Rå said without thinking, telling her the truth.

Nilsa's eyes widened dramatically. "Solveig, now that's interesting. My great-grandmother claimed that some called Arjavarja Solveig or Soltru. Have you heard that? When did she pass on, your mother? Did I understand right that she's no longer with us?"

"Yes." Rå drank some of the ale. "My mother passed many years ago now. And yes, I've heard that too." She smiled. "According to my mother, Arjavarja's daughter could talk with the trees." Rå took another sip of ale. She had said way too much now. It was as if it had bubbled out of her on its own.

Nilsa threw her head back and laughed. "That I've never heard, only that there was something with the forest that her daughter had to do." Then her expression grew serious. "I've always been afraid it was some kind of human sacrifice with the giving to the forest. You know how they did it in the old days before the church came."

"That, I have not heard," Rå said with conviction.

"Ah, good to know. It always scared me to wonder about it. Did Solveig, your mother, say where Arjavarja lived back then? We always heard it was in Östra Aros, not sure where that is."

Ostarres is what they used to call it. Rå laughed, something warming her chest as she finally remembered. It's what they used to call Uppsala. The grand temple had been there, not far from where they lived. "My mother called it Ostarres, Arjavarja from

Ostarres." Rå let out a sob, picturing her mother's skinny arms and thin body embracing her, and the beautiful vistas of childhood.

Nilsa reached for her hand and squeezed it. Even though her hand was round and fleshy, it felt as if her mother was there with her.

"Pray forgive me, Nilsa. I'm not usually this emotional. I'm not sure what's gotten into me." It really wasn't like her, but given what she just learned, it wasn't very surprising.

Nilsa patted the top of her hand. "No need for apologies. No matter how long it's been since one lost one's mother, the grief stays forever."

Rå straightened up and exhaled slowly. "Yes, Nilsa, you're right about that. And it's remarkable that we're family, distant as it is."

Nilsa smiled broadly. "Indeed! Are you feeling strong enough to get dressed and come downstairs? I'd like you to meet the rest of your family." She stood up and pushed the chair aside. "If you'd rather sleep first, I understand."

"No, I'd love to meet everyone and Arjavarja." Her voice held at the name, but just barely. "How old is she?"

"Four winters and a spring."

Rå pulled the blanket off her legs and got out of bed. "They're darling at that age."

"Yes, aren't they?" Nilsa stood up. "I'll get you a bowl of warm water and a washcloth."

***

Nilsa and the other women were sitting around a table in the corner of the kitchen when she came down, faces turned toward her with anticipation. Arjavarja wasn't among them.

"Welcome, Magda. Come sit, have something more to eat, and some wine," said the woman sitting next to Nilsa, tilting her head toward a jug of wine and a plate with cheese and berries on the table. "We heard you're one of us. You must be the granddaughter of cousin Victus' niece, we think. Does it sound familiar?"

Rå shook her head, pretending to think. "Possibly," she said as she sat down, acknowledging the other women with a smile.

"I'm Anna, Arjavarja's mother," said a plump woman across from Rå. She poured wine into a glass and pushed it across the table toward her. "Nilsa told me your mother's name was Solveig and that she too, spoke of Arjavarja and the trees. That detail is only passed down between women in our family. Nilsa would never have said something if you hadn't reacted to the name. Would you, Nilsa?" she prompted, pouring a glass of wine for her as well.

"No, it was only because of Magda's obvious knowledge of Arjavarja the First, who loved the forest so much, she gave her only daughter to it to care for it," she said, using the same singsong voice she had used upstairs earlier.

Rå took a sip of the wine. "I'm interested in what you know of her, the first Arjavarja. What happened to her? What did she do after the daughter left?"

Nilsa shrugged, glancing at the others. "I don't think anyone knows. But we have a..." She stopped, giving the other women an uncertain look. There was an awkward silence.

Rå tried to catch her eye, but Nilsa and Anna were still exchanging glances with each other.

Then Nilsa cleared her throat and looked at Rå. "We have a rune. It's to have belonged to her. Not that we can decipher it, but we've been thinking we should take it to someone who can."

"I can read it," Rå blurted out much too quickly. A rune, she had written a rune. Of course, she had, it would be just like her. Rå's back opened then closed again. She pulled her new shawl tighter to hide it, just in case.

"You read runes?" asked Anna, an incredulous expression on her face.

"Lord in heaven, this is meant to be," said Nilsa. "Go fetch it, Adelgund," she added, looking at the woman across from her.

Adelgund nodded, then hastily stood up and disappeared into another room. She was plumb too, and her skirts were thick and wide, making a swishing sound that could be heard from the other room.

"I do," Rå said to Anna and left it at that. She was overwhelmed, forgetting what exactly she had told Nilsa about her family and which details she pretended were more recent. There had been too much talk about her actual mother, Nilsa's cousin, and all the other relatives. It was confusing. And where was Arjavarja?

"You look pale again," said Nilsa. "Could you be with child?"

"I'm not." She swallowed, praying no one would ask if she was married.

Then Adelgund came back and put a piece of bone in front of Rå, runes filling every part of it, which meant there were more on the other side. Adelgund had given it to her upside down. It was her mother's. There was no doubt. She could tell by the placement of the first rune, the jaggedness, and the unusual minuteness of each rune. Her mother was known for it.

Rå made a quick decision. "There's a lot here. It'll take me quite a while to try to read it. Could I go sit outside for a while by myself? I'm feeling a bit faint again. Fresh air might help."

"Oh, of course. Perhaps you hit your head when you slid down that hill," Anna said, picking up a large piece of cheese and a handful of fresh berries and putting them on a plate. "Bring these with you. Take all the time you need."

Rå nodded gratefully and got to her feet while turning her face so they wouldn't see the tears.

Once outside, she sat right down on the steps, too emotional to go anywhere else. Putting the plate beside her, she took one long, deep breath and started reading.

I, Solveig, is the mother of the foundling who speaks with trees, whose back pulses with their sap. Feared much she is by the villagers, too fierce for the men here. Fear for her life I do, by the men and women here who claim Odin disapproves. Feared they are, using Odin's name for their gain. Leave, marry the trees, said I, Solveig.

Rå turned the rune stick over to read on the backside. Her hand was shaking.

A blót I held so Freya and Thor will always care for her. Know this, Rå is good. Protecting her I did, know this. Give this rune to your daughter who shall give it to her daughter, and to her daughter. I Arjavarja will watch from Valhöll. Keep this rune, watch for the one who cares for the trees, for she is safe.

Rå called out, gasping for breath as a sob tore through her chest. Her mother hadn't made her leave because she was ashamed of her or felt she didn't belong. She had sent her away to save her. Save her from the villagers who wanted her ill because they assumed Odin disliked her. It wasn't like Rå had thought at all. Turning the rune in her hands, she heard her mother's voice, the old cadence, and way of speaking as clearly as if she were sitting right there beside her. *Rå is good, protecting her I did... Rå is good, protecting her I did.* She closed her eyes, and it was as if she could see her mother between the longhouses back home. But this time, she looked right at her and lifted her hand toward her.

When Rå opened her eyes, there was a stirring near the tree across the yard. Then a shadow shifted as if someone had stood there.

***

"Could you read it?" Nilsa asked, turning toward Rå, an excited look on her face. "You look better child, the air did you good."

"I do feel a lot better. Some air was just what I needed. And yes, I could read it!" She waved the rune in the air.

"Sit, sit, come here," said Anna, waving her over, grinning at the others who looked beside themselves with curiosity.

Rå smiled, putting the rune stick on the table as she sat down. The women came as close as they could, sitting almost head-to-head.

"It'll be slow. Pray bear with me," Rå said and started reading. "I, Solveig, is the mother..." She hesitated, feeling conflicted, but deciding not to read all of it. It felt too private and too exposing, and she skipped ahead. "... of the girl who speaks with

626

trees. Leave, marry the trees, said I, Solveig."

Nilsa gasped and grabbed her hand. "I told you, Magda. I told you how some say her name was Solveig or Soltru, just like your mother. Her name was Solveig!" Tears sprayed straight out from her eyes as if they were pushed out.

Rå felt her own eyes moisten. "There's more on the other side, see." She turned it over. "It says, A blót I held so Freya and Thor will always care for her. Know this, my daughter is good, protecting her I did, know this. Give this rune to your daughter who will give it to her daughter, and to her daughter. I Arjavarja will watch from *Valhöll*." Her voice shook, tears falling freely now. "Keep this rune. Watch for the one who cares for the trees, for she is safe."

Everyone was quiet.

Then Adelgund broke the silence. "What's a blót?"

"It's what they did back then," said Anna. "It's those blood sacrifices they did. It's the old religion with Thor, Freya, Odin, and," her eyes flickered to Nilsa and Rå, "Balder or something. I don't remember the rest."

Rå didn't say anything, letting the women sort it out themselves.

"*Valhöll* was what they called heaven. Arjavarja is watching us from heaven," Nilsa said breathlessly. "It's what we've been saying, then. Exactly like it. That our daughters should give the rune to their daughters. Arjavarja. The name we've kept in our family for so long. Thousands of years then, isn't it?"

"No, not that long, Nilsa." Adelgund chuckled. "Christianity came here hundreds of years ago, not thousands."

"I see." Nilsa looked annoyed that she had been corrected. "How is it that you know how to read this, Magda?"

"A neighbor of mine knew it and taught me. He traveled around looking for runes everywhere and translated them. He said people wrote runes on stones and trees and all kinds of places. It was a bit of an obsession of his. But he's passed on now." Lies all. It was too easy to lie. It was why Nikolaos always did it.

"God must have had a hand in that," the woman sitting next

to Adelgund said.

"What is your name?" Rå asked.

"Oh, pray forgive us. I'm Ellse and Sine here." She smiled and gestured toward the youngest woman among them, sitting right across from her. She was very thin and pale, wearing a green dress that looked much too nice for the occasion.

Rå nodded. "I'm quite overwhelmed by all this. My mother spoke of Arjavarja often. I didn't realize other people knew of her. And this rune it's…" She stopped. The women were so kind. Her family. Actual relations. It was almost too much to take in.

"Yes, child," Nilsa said. "It's indeed overwhelming for all of us. You're a relation to us, a long-lost family member. You have a home here, should you want it. Where are you headed, Magda? We've not even spoken of it."

Rå looked at her, holding her gaze. "I was just thinking the same thing about us being family. No solid plans to tell you the truth. I like to wander in the summers and was hoping to find some good summer markets."

"Summer markets, that's nice," Nilsa said absently, then changed the subject. "If you're not too tired, can I take you to meet our Arjavarja? She's just outside playing somewhere with the other children."

Rå's breath quickened. "Pray, yes."

Nilsa held the door open for her, then took her arm as they crossed the courtyard in front of their house. There was a barn and a smaller house on the right and a narrow road behind that, Rå noticed now.

Nilsa put her hands beside her mouth, forming a tunnel. "Arjavarja! Children, come here a bit!"

Almost immediately, they heard the patter of bare feet on hard dirt, and then four children came running at full speed around the corner.

"There she is, in the yellow dress," Nilsa said.

Rå's throat tightened as she watched the little girl. A skinny thing with brown braids, piercing blue eyes, and pale skin. It was not her mother born again. Disappointment and relief hit her simultaneously, disorienting her while the children's high voices chattered around her. What would she have done had it been her?

"Who are you?"

"Why are you here?"

"Look, look, I can jump on one leg."

"This is Magda, she's family," Nilsa interrupted, snapping Rå back to attention. "She wanted to meet you, Arjavarja, and say good day. Pray, curtsy politely to acknowledge her."

Arjavarja looked at Rå for a moment, seeming to consider. "Good day, Magda," she said finally, grabbed the hand of the boy standing next to her, then ran off as quickly as she came.

Rå laughed. "She's fast, that one."

***

Rå stayed a whole week. When she left, she had a pair of clogs on her feet and a dress folded in her satchel. She would have to decide what to do. Part of her wanted to stay close to them, but she didn't know if she could handle living a life full of half-truths and then pretending to age. Not again, and not with family. She decided to visit Nikolaos and see what he thought. He was the only one she could talk to who understood how it was.

***

"Do you need a ride, goodwife? Where are you heading on this bright morning?"

Rå started, whipping her head around to see who had spoken. There was a wagon beside her, a smiling man in the driver's seat. She hadn't even heard it. "Oh, how kind. Pray yes. I'm going toward Ytterby."

"Well then, I'll take you. Hop up," the driver said, patting the seat beside him.

Rå hoisted herself up by putting one foot on a piece of wood by the front wheel and her right hand on the seat. It wasn't quite a hop, but it wasn't hard. She had placed her clogs in her satchel, finding them uncomfortable and cumbersome.

"I thank you kindly," she said once she was sitting beside the man. He looked to be in his late fifties and had big cheeks and small blue eyes, which were gleaming merrily at her.

"Glad for the company. Ytterby. You live there?"

Rå shook her head. "I'm visiting friends who live near it. Their farm is between Ytterby and a smaller village. I don't know what it's called."

"You must mean Kyrkby, but it's not so small anymore. Was it a long time since you visited?" He threw her a quick glance as if to see how old she was.

"Yes, it's been a long time." She frowned. "I forget, but yes, it's many years now."

"Time goes faster than one thinks. Who is it you're visiting? Perhaps I know them." He snapped the reins and the horse got into a fast trot.

"Nikolaos and Stina, they have two grown children, Elsebet and Hindrich."

He turned toward her with a grin of recognition. "Ah, you must mean Hindrich and Ekborg. They live up at the old farm between the villages. It's not his sister. Ekborg is Hindrich's wife."

Rå tried to catch his eye, but he was already turning his attention back to the road. "I see. Do you know them?" Where were Nikolaos and Stina? She would be old, but unless something had happened, she ought to be alive still.

"Just from church. We usually talk after service for a bit. They're kind people."

"Doesn't Hindrich's parents join? And his sister. Do you know her?"

"No, I didn't know he had a sister," he said, pursing his lips with a surprised eyelift, turning toward her again.

"Nikolaos and his family lived on a farm at the edge of the woods. His son, Hindrich, was betrothed last time I visited. There's just a small road by them, but if you take it southward, you'll eventually get to a village with a large green in the middle," Rå said, wondering if he was talking about someone else with the same name. She didn't remember the name Ekborg.

"Hmmm." He nodded, snapping the reins. "Does this farm have a little rose garden with benches and a sundial?"

"Yes!"

"That'd be the one then. It's right by the edge of the woods like you described. I delivered new seedlings to that garden a few years back with my wife." He shifted on the seat to give Rå a little more room. "The village does have a green, but it's no longer in the middle. They've expanded quite a bit after the church was built. Or so I hear, I didn't live there before that."

"I see. Stina and Nikolaos must have passed on then," Rå said, thinking it was what sounded the likeliest. She kept her gaze on him until he turned his face back to the road.

The friendly man offered to drive her to Hindrich's farm, but she declined. She wasn't in the mood to visit, not even to find out what happened with Nikolaos and Stina, or where they had gone. She wanted time alone to think about her visit with Nilsa and Arjavarja. Process everything. He dropped her off at Saint Halvard's, which he called Ytterby Church, and drove off with a wave.

Waiting until he was out of sight, Rå turned around and went behind the church to go into the woods on the other side. They had hung witches by the church, Nikolaos had told her. Three of them on the same day. Unless it was four, she couldn't remember which. The yard showed no signs of it now. There was a large oak with a bed of flowers around the trunk and a little bench where one could sit. She walked past it, crossing overgrown grass to get into the woods. No one saw her, and she soon found a suitable tree to connect with. It was old, at least four hundred, if not more, with powerful branches. Pulling off her new skirt and standing only in the underskirt, she wrapped her hair over her chest and leaned back against the trunk. When she opened her back and pushed her feet into the ground, she connected with the roots immediately. The soil was well nourished, and there were no disputes over territories or need for sunlight.

When Rå finished, she felt calm and like herself again, and

sure that there was no rush in deciding what to do with Arjavarja and her family. Instead, and this surprised her, she felt an urgent need to follow the waterways south and that Nikolaos needed *her*. Something was happening.

Only days later, Rå was walking along a tributary late at night and felt something nudging at her. A disturbance and a slight tingling in her back. She stopped, letting her back open, and there it was, the same feeling that Nikolaos needed her. He was in the river somewhere, swimming toward the lake. She could feel it.

Rå sat down to wait at the water's edge, right where the river rushed in to meet the calmer waters of the lake. The contrast made the water ripple black to silver, silver to black on the moonlit surface. It was beautiful. Watching it, her thoughts started drifting. It was strange that they both needed each other at the same time. Even that Little One had decided to leave her earthly life right then seemed meant to be now. Freya must have a hand in it. Rå shifted where she sat and folded her legs like a tailor, then wrapped Nilsa's shawl over her shoulders. She closed her eyes and let herself nod off, waking each time her head jerked downward when her neck relaxed.

The day was breaking when her head jerked her awake again, and she was contemplating laying down when there was a sudden wave in the water.

Before long, Nikolaos emerged. Naked. His hair hung in thick wet ringlets down his back, and water was dripping down his muscular upper body, slithering down his flat stomach until it joined the river again. He was so beautiful Rå almost lost her breath, and she felt the water, or maybe it was him, trying to pull her toward the river. She instinctively scooted back, but his power just swirled around her without force.

"Rå?" Nikolaos stared at her, looking as if he thought he was imagining things.

She laughed. "Yes, it's me."

He was on the beach in two steps, water cascading around him and splashing on her.

"I'm relieved to see you good and well," she said, shaking water off her arms.

"Good and well? I don't know about that. But by God, how is it that you're here?" He shook his head in disbelief, then fell to his knees before her, touching her feet reverently with cold, wet fingers. It tickled.

"Nikolaos, you needn't do that. You know it. I've told you before. Now I pray you, find your clothes so we can talk properly. I can't talk to you like this. It's distracting."

"Oh." He looked genuinely surprised, as if his incredible body wouldn't affect her. "What lake is this?" he asked, standing up.

"Våmb Lake, I think."

"I've been swimming too far then. I've lost myself entirely. I'm afraid my breeches and shirt are at least a day or two from here."

"I see." She grinned, pulling her shawl off her back. "Here, take this."

He smiled at her, fumbling with it until he had managed to wrap it around his hips like a skirt.

She stood up. "Let's walk a bit. What's bothering you, Nikolaos?"

"How do you know?"

"You said just now. Said that you weren't sure that I found you good and well." She decided not to say that the trees had told her that something was wrong.

He whistled.

"But I'm not surprised. The water has practically been boiling with your power." That part, she could admit.

He stopped walking to look at her, then covered his face with his hands and began to moan like a wounded animal.

Rå was so stunned she just stood there watching his bare shoulders heave as he sobbed. Behind him, she noticed a boat skim across the lake in their direction, and she grabbed his arm and pulled him back behind a bush. "Nikolaos, you must tell me what's happened."

When he removed his hands from his face, his eyes were filled with so much pain that her back tightened. "I'm a murderer, Rå. I have killed so many, and I've broken my vow to my wife. I don't deserve to live, and yet, yet I never die."

"Nikolaos, what has gotten into you? Of course, you deserve to live." Rå threw a cautionary glance in the direction of the boat. It was a fisherman, mooring only paces away from them. She put her finger to her lips. "There's a boat. We should move over there," she whispered, pointing to a small cluster of trees further back.

They bent low and ran, then sat down in the shadows. His hair was drying, curling a little over his bare chest. No wonder people died. Talking to him so close to the water made his power obvious. Still, he looked incredibly vulnerable now.

"Why can't I stop?" he asked, sniffling. It sounded desperate and full of hope, as if he really thought she could explain it.

She just shook her head.

"Did you know that the one time I didn't kill, I brought more havoc on myself and my family than when people drown?" He grabbed a dead leaf from the ground and blew his nose in it.

"No, I didn't. When was that?"

"Years ago now. Do you remember the flirtatious woman who wanted me to come play at her sister's baby celebration? Mistress Esmeralda."

"Of course, I stayed with Stina when you went there."

He tilted his head back with realization. "I forgot about that. I was with two people there. They were fine, it was just coupling, but of course it started all these rumors." He grimaced, looking over at the lake. "Stina was questioned. It was horrible, Rå. We had to move. We've been living in Helsingborg for many years now."

"Ugh." She didn't know what else to say. Poor Stina. "So, then you were able to stop that time at least."

"No, it was just that the water wasn't deep enough. I was incredibly careless. It was stupid."

"I see. But why are you so upset now, Nikolaos? I'm not sure I understand."

"Some days ago, Merchant Fleisher and Mistress Esmeralda

confronted me in front of witnesses."

"By Freya's tears!"

"Indeed." He raised an eyebrow. "And at an official inauguration, I was playing at, too. That's not the worst, though. I talked myself out of that. But Stina and I argued, and now she knows everything. You know… what happens when I encounter someone." Nikolaos looked embarrassed, and his eyes filled with tears again.

Rå nodded, hoping she seemed sympathetic. She knew it. Keeping something like that secret from one's wife would never last. "Well, Nikolaos I've told you this before, you shouldn't spend so much time with humans. It always causes problems after a while. We've both seen it time after time. Humans don't understand us. They seem to at first, but after a while, things change. It's better to be on our own. I too, have known people who knew who I am. But it can't go on for long. A group of men helped me with the cows I had, and one of them wanted to marry me."

Nikolaos' tearstained face finally broke into his familiar rueful smile. "Knowing you, you didn't marry him."

"No." She gave a one-sided smile in return, deciding to leave it at that. "Nikolaos, I was hoping to talk to you about something else. I was actually on my way to visit you, but someone told me you weren't living there anymore. It's Hindrich's and Ekborg's farm, he said."

"Yes, it's so. They stayed when we moved to Helsingborg. Elsebet moved with us, but she's married now. Who was it? Did he say anything about me?"

"No, nothing. It was just someone who offered me a ride. He didn't know who you were, but when I explained where your farm is, he knew it. He said he had delivered flowers or bushes or something there once. I forgot which. I did think it was a bit odd that he didn't know you."

"Did you ask for Nikolaos or Nils Jensson?"

"Nikolaos." She frowned.

"It's something that's getting more and more common now. A few of the neighbors used to tease me, saying Nikolaos was old-fashioned, pompous sounding even. Then some started calling me Nils. It never really caught on though. Stina's father was Anders, so sometimes she's called Anders' dotter. Stina Andersdotter. So, I just made Jens up, like I was Jens' son, Jensson. In Helsingborg, Nikolaos seems to be accepted again. Might have been wiser to stick with Nils, but I never did."

"I never knew that." She would have to remember it, maybe she should be someone's daughter too. Magda someone's daughter, Gorm's dotter then. Maybe Magda wasn't right anymore either.

"You always have an uncanny way of finding me when I'm in trouble." Nikolaos moved a little closer to her and patted her hand. "What did you want to talk to me about?"

"Freya must have helped us both, Nikolaos. I met my mother's relations." Her voice almost broke, and she took a deep breath to steady herself. He moved closer still, wrapping her in his arms. Then she told him everything.

"I wanted to ask you if I should go live with them or at least live close to them," Rå said when she finished, still sitting with his arms around her. It felt natural and good.

"Didn't you just tell me not to spend so much time with humans?"

"Yes, but this is my family, it's different."

"Stina is and *was* my family too," Nikolaos said, stroking her arm. "And you're sure it's not your mother coming back like Abluna did?

"Yes, I'm sure. I thought it might be but it's not. I can tell."

Rå felt him nod, and then he pulled himself out of their embrace to face her.

"I say it's worth it. We can't live this long all alone. And finding that rune stick is something you can't just disregard. Things are always connected, and some patterns come back again and again. Just think about how I knew Jon's father and how you also knew Jon."

"You're finally becoming old enough to understand these

things," Rå said, impressed. "It's true. Perhaps I should rethink a few things. I've felt lonelier than I used to lately."

Nikolaos sat still, listening intently. It was as though he was sculpted from marble. A strange creature, so powerful and deadly, yet so sensitive. If she took him, she would be able to withstand his power, and he wouldn't kill anymore. The thought struck her out of nowhere, so powerful that her back was pried open, making the trees sway around them. He met her eyes. They burned like fire.

***

Nikolaos found his clothes neatly folded on the tree branch where he left them.

Getting dressed felt strange, as if he were no longer the same person and was putting on another man's clothes. He could barely put into words what had happened between them. But when the trees started moving, he felt that hole in her back embrace him. It didn't last half a minute, but in that instant, he knew she had changed from Goddess to lover.

And then she was gone.

He had waited for her for two days, but she didn't return.

Now, walking along a country road, wearing his clothes again, he felt exalted but calm.

They were both immortal. There was no rush. For now, he would go home to his wife.

Stina and Elsebet were sitting on the stoop with mugs of ale in their hands. Stina kept her eyes somewhere to the side of his body.

But Elsebet's face lit up when she saw him. "Father, you're home! Mother said you've been traveling for a bit."

Nikolaos hid a sigh of relief. Stina hadn't told her. "Darling daughter, what are you doing here today?" he said and sat down next to her, ignoring Stina while he plucked the ale mug from Elsebet's hands and drank deeply, then gave it back to her with an apologetic shrug. "I couldn't help it. I'm thirsty."

She laughed. "I'll get us both more. Father, I have good news. I told Mother already."

Nikolaos caught Stina's eyes and saw the smile in them before she looked away again.

"A baby, Father. There will be a little one after Christmas."

Chapter 78

It had been over two years since Stina confronted him. They lived side by side, by all appearances still a loving couple. Stina took his arm each Sunday when they went to church. She traveled with him to Ramlösa each time he played, as well as when he played at private gatherings among the long-term water drinkers lodging with the farmers. No one would have thought that they no longer touched, that Stina slept in Elsebet's old bed and he alone.

Then the Danes attacked.

Fredrik sighed and walked around the counter to peer at the book of accounts that Nikolaos was looking at. "We've sold no ribbons, bonbons, mint boxes, nor any fans," Fredrik said and traced his finger down the page. "We ought to concentrate on necessities. Helsingborg is too poor a town. People don't buy things they don't absolutely need."

"I know. It's disappointing. I thought we did well for a time. We had more customers when the Ramlösa drinking began."

"Not anymore. It's not good, Nikolaos. We're behind."

"No, it isn't." Nikolaos straightened his back and looked at him. "I feel responsible, Fredrik. I wanted you and Elsebet to have a good life here. I'd understand if you moved back to Malmö. Especially now when you're having another baby."

"It's crossed our minds. I must be honest. But I have a feeling that Ramlösa will bring more people again sooner or later. We shall not give up yet. What needs to be done is to rethink our inventory. Had it only been easier to get goods across the sound, it wouldn't be such a problem. Have heart. I do like it here." Fredrik clapped him on the back and smiled.

Then the door was thrown open, and Stina, wet from the light rain outside, hurled herself inside and threw herself into Nikolaos' arms. "The Danes are here. They've invaded Råå!" she shrieked.

At first, he was just glad that she wanted his arms around her again, but then he realized what she had said and almost laughed. "Stina, calm yourself. You must have misunderstood. That happened over thirty years ago." He met Fredrik's surprised eyes behind her.

"No, Nikolaos, there are troops at Råå," Stina said. "Thousands of them. They're coming. Beata said she heard people are happy they're finally back to save them from us Swedes."

Something cold churned his stomach. He crossed himself. When he did, Stina began to shake so much that he had to help her to the stool behind the counter.

Fredrik exchanged another glance with him, then squeezed past them in the narrow space and opened the door, only to close it again at the sound of fearful shouting and heavy footfall. "Well, I don't see any Danes, but the fishmonger and the baker are both closing their shop windows," Fredrik said. He closed their shutters and then locked the door. "We're leaving out the back door today." He had an expression of surprised consternation on his face, barely visible in the now darkened mercantile. He stood perfectly still. A moment later he crossed the floor in two long strides. "We need to leave now."

Nikolaos grabbed Stina by the arm and pushed her toward the door leading to the courtyard. "Fredrik, get the safe, then hurry! We don't want them to close the gateway to the courtyard."

"Lord have mercy, you're right!" Fredrik pulled his key from his vest pocket and unlocked the cabinet below the counter. His hand was shaking. There were only five tied leather purses, but the time it took him to properly tie each one and fill a sixth purse from the change box seemed much too long.

Nikolaos' heartbeat was thudding in his ears when they finally squeezed themselves through the back door. A forgotten memory of pressing himself between the walls at Norrköping's House to get to the stable before he fled surfaced. It was over a hundred years ago. It had rained that day too; only then it was late at night.

Cold, moist air hit their faces when they stepped out, and he drew a deep breath of relief when he spotted the open gateway.

Their mercantile was housed in a similar half-timbered, four-walled house like the one whose courtyard they lived in, only here they were in the building itself, facing a side street and with a backdoor leading out to the courtyard. Fredrik and Elsebet lived in a small house on the north side of town. It worried him.

Hurrying across the courtyard, Nikolaos got close to Fredrik. "Do you want us to come with you? It might be better if we're together."

"Thank you. Yes."

Nikolaos nodded and stepped out into the street. It was eerily quiet, contrasting with the shouting and clamoring earlier. "Perhaps it would be better if you get Elsebet and the children and come stay with us. We're at least protected behind a gate," he said, eyes still on the street.

"Or locked in," Fredrik said between clenched teeth.

Stina grabbed Nikolaos' arm so tightly he felt her nails through his sleeve. "Do you think they'll stay in Råå? Maybe they won't come here."

He didn't answer. It could only be a matter of time before they did.

"Maybe the Swedish army will get to them before they reach us, but I doubt it," Fredrik said.

Stina squeezed harder.

They hurried through the empty streets. When they reached Fredrik's and Elsebet's home, it lay dark.

"Where are they?" Stina asked, her voice hoarse and dry with worry.

A shadow crossed Fredrik's face as he strode up to the door and pushed the handle down. It was locked. Just like before, when he opened the safe, his hand shook when he reached for his key and unlocked the door.

The house was still, and the fire had gone out in the hearth. A draft from the chimney made the tablecloth flutter. Fredrik had become pale. Putting a finger on his lips, he slowly crept into their second room and disappeared out of view. A moment later they heard him call out.

Nikolaos let go of Stina and ran after him.

Elsebet, the girls, and the new baby huddled in the corner.

Fredrik fell to the floor, hugging them all at the same time.

Tears spilled out of Elsebet's eyes as she looked at Nikolaos and Stina over Fredrik's shoulder. "We were so afraid. When we heard you enter, we were afraid soldiers had gotten inside."

"Didn't you hear the key in the door?" asked Nikolaos.

Elsebet shook her head. "Is it true? Are the Danes really here?"

"We think so. Everyone is acting as if it is. Town seems to be closing down," he said.

"Beata spoke to someone who saw the soldiers. Said there are thousands of them and that some are glad they're back to get rid of us Swedes," Stina said, sounding matter of fact now.

"Beata said this?" Elsebet pushed herself from Fredrik's and the children's embrace and stood up.

"Yes, but how true it is, I can't vouch for. Skåne has been part of Sweden for longer than she's been alive," Stina said.

"But the Danes tried to take it in seventy-six too. They disembarked at Råå then as well," Nikolaos said and stepped aside to allow Elsebet and Stina to move into the front room, then followed.

Maria went to stand by Stina's skirts, hugging her legs. Fredrik's daughter was eight but snuggled up to Stina as if she were still a babe.

"Pull the curtain, Father," Elsebet said to Nikolaos. "I pray you. I don't want anyone seeing in from outside."

He did as she asked, taking the opportunity to check the outside. The street was empty.

"Grandma Stina, I'm frightened," Maria whispered, her chin quivering and her eyes filling with tears.

"I know, darling, but you need not be. Your father and Grandpa Nikolaos are both here to protect you. Grandpa Nikolaos is exceptionally strong. Did you know that?" Stina said and reached out and took his hand.

Nikolaos squeezed it, moved by the closeness. He hoped it was genuine and not only because she was scared.

"They're here! The Danes are here," Fredrik called from the other room, startling him. "I hear the horses!"

Nikolaos let go of Stina's hand and ran into the other room. Fredrik was standing to the right of the window, carefully peering out at the street. He hadn't pulled the curtains closed. Nikolaos stopped cold at the threshold, then slowly moved out of sight by sliding along the walls until he was by his side and out of direct view.

There were three Danish soldiers on large brown horses out there, riding side by side, wearing pale yellow coats with bright red sleeves and collars. Their hose and robes were red as well. The colorful uniforms were so stark compared to the rain and the muddy street that it felt unreal.

"Look, it's Butcher Arild!" Fredrik gasped, grabbing Nikolaos' wrist under the windowsill.

Nikolaos cautiously moved closer to Fredrik to get a better view. Butcher Arild had run out to greet the soldiers and was waving at them with a broad smile on his face.

But the Danes didn't as much as glance at him. They were calm and purposeful, acting as though they had nothing to fear at all. As if what the townspeople thought was irrelevant. It scared Nikolaos more than if they had shown anger or greeted him politely.

"This is what I get for wishing it would be easier to get goods across the sound," Fredrik said and stared at Nikolaos. He looked as though he might cry.

"Those dastards," whispered Nikolaos, putting a hand on his shoulder."

Darkness fell without incident, and Nikolaos decided to take a walk to check on things. He went to the corner and stopped there. Everything was quiet, a bitter humid wind tearing at his face. Most of their neighbors had lit lamps and candles without closing their shutters. It seemed incredibly foolish. The Danes might force themselves inside and demand things. Surely, the townspeople couldn't all be as happy as the butcher. But maybe they thought it was worse to hide, afraid the soldiers would think their homes empty and force themselves inside for that reason. He turned his head, looking at Elsebet's and Fredrik's home. It lay dark and shuttered, with only a faint glow visible beneath the front room window panels, the only sign someone was home. He hoped it was the right thing to do.

As he stood there, looking at it, two figures suddenly appeared around the corner. They moved fast, crouching like, and were at Fredrik's and Elsebet's door before he would have had time to lift his lantern, had he had one. "Who goes there?" he called, heart racing.

The figures stopped, one of them with a hand to the door already, head whipping toward the sound of Nikolaos' voice.

Without thinking, Nikolaos drew strength from the moisture in the air and tore down the street toward the house, ready to attack them whichever way he could.

"Nikolaos! You frightened us. I thought you were a Danish soldier. You came at us so fast," someone said. Orvar. It was Orvar and Beata.

Nikolaos stopped, all the air rushing out of him at once. Thank God he hadn't done anything. He felt as though he could have killed them with his bare hands. He cleared his throat, rubbing his fingers to make sure they felt solid. They did. "I thought you were too," he said, glad his voice sounded normal. "Is everything the way it should be at home?"

"I don't know, we heard canons in the distance. We were wondering if the army was coming from the north. We heard it's threatening to burn town!"

"The Danish army is setting Helsingborg on fire?" Nikolaos pulled open the door with so much force it slammed into the wall.

"No, not the Danes, the Swedes."

Shocked, Nikolaos stared at Orvar in the faint indoor light as Beata pushed herself past them and hurried inside, ignoring the conversation. Stina and Elsebet called out in surprise, and the women started crying and talking simultaneously.

Orvar waited until their voices had died down. "The Old

Swedes don't want the Danes to take the town and rather burn us to the ground then let the Danes have it," he whispered.

"They'd do that?"

Orvar nodded. "They did it at Råå, didn't they? If General Carl Hårdh could burn Råå Village because he was angry at some poor women who just wanted to buy food for their families over on that side, I wouldn't be surprised." He pulled a hand through his hair. "King Fredrik disembarked with the Queen early this morning."

"The Danish King and Queen?"

Orvar splayed his arms in a that's obvious gesture.

"Devil's bottom!" Nikolaos exclaimed, shaking his head. "Let's go inside to the others." He reached around Orvar and closed the door. Then he locked it.

Stina and Elsebet sat close together, grasping each other's hands as Beata told them everything they had heard. Fredrik was pacing back and forth across the floor.

"Nikolaos." Stina turned toward him. "The Danish King and Queen are here! They've disembarked at Råå village, and Beata says that the Swedes will…"

"I know, I heard," Nikolaos interrupted. It seemed like fire followed him everywhere, from Norrköping's House, Three Crowns, and now here. "We've seen no signs of that. Everything looked normal outside."

Fredrik stopped pacing and gestured to Elsebet, "Get us some wine, will you? Sit down, everyone. Let's try to decide what to do together. I'm glad you're here, Orvar."

Elsebet did as bid and brought a bottle and glasses to the table, filling each glass almost to the rim.

"How did you find out, Orvar?" Fredrik asked.

"The pastor. He said a messenger came to the church early this morning."

"It's true then, all of it. We saw Danish soldiers right out here earlier," Nikolaos said, gratefully taking the wine Elsebet was handing him. "Three of them, on horseback. Acting as if they owned the town."

Everyone became silent, sitting stunned and listening for the sound of hooves or running feet outside. Or, God forbid, flames. But all they heard was their own breathing and the sound of Elsebet's and Fredrik's clock ticking.

"Could we leave town, Fredrik?" Elsebet asked, her voice barely holding.

"I've friends in Malmö, but we don't know how wide the troops have spread or if it's safe to go south," Fredrik said gravely.

Nikolaos and Stina exchanged a glance.

"It might be wise for us to go home for a bit, gather our things. I must get my instruments. Then we'll come back here and decide what to do. Stina, come to think of it, I think you ought to stay here," Nikolaos said, rising slowly from his seat.

Stina's eyes widened, but then she nodded. "Bring my mending basket, the dress in the closet, my shawls... and my locket." Stina held his gaze, and something melted between them. She had thrown it at him the last time he saw it.

His eyes moistened. "Where is it?"

"In my jewelry box."

"Nikolaos, should I help? That's quite a lot to carry on your own," interrupted Fredrik, oblivious to what was taking place between them.

"I thank you, but I'll manage, and won't be long. If they've closed the gate, I'll knock on windows until someone lets me in and can take me through a backdoor." He hesitated and turned to Orvar, having almost forgotten that he and Beata had just come from there. "Was it open when you left?"

"Yes, it was, but come to think of it, I'm not sure if that's good or bad? I presume it's safer," Orvar said.

"Lest we'd be locked in when they set the town on fire!" Stina exclaimed.

"I better go," Nikolaos said, and without another word, he walked out.

He ought to have brought a lantern, but it hadn't even crossed his mind. It was overcast still, with no stars nor moon to light his way. He was grateful that his non-human vision was sufficient for him to at least keep a steady pace through the dark streets. Everything seemed as it always did, but it was quieter than usual. Even Lady Maria Church, which usually had a couple of oil lamps burning, was completely dark.

Nikolaos drew a sigh of relief at the sight of their gateway. It was still wide open, and the lantern hanging on its pole in the middle of the courtyard was lit as usual. But it was silent, with no voices, banging of pots, or smells of cooking. A pretense of normalcy. Entering the courtyard, afraid soldiers were hiding in the corners and scared of looking to see if he was right, he forced himself to calmly walk up to his house.

Once inside, he went around in the dark and gathered everything by feel. His fiddle and his Stradivarius, their Bible, and catechism, their coin purses. He found the locket in Stina's box and went to get the other things she had asked for, placing it all in a large basket and in a satchel. Lastly, he pulled out Abluna's jewelry and his old catechism from under their mattress. He kept the catechism wrapped in animal skins now. The names and the dates in the margins had faded, but they were still there, reminding him of his first family and of who Stina used to be before. Carefully, he put it under his undershirt and felt it slide down to his stomach and lodge itself safely by his belt. Then he found a lantern and managed to light it from the dying embers in their fireplace, quickly covering it with a towel without choking it. Perhaps it was silly. If there were soldiers in the courtyard, they would have seen him go home and would see him leave as well. But it felt important to be as invisible as possible.

Going across the courtyard and out to the street, he sniffed for smoke, but there wasn't any. Helsingborg looked like before. Quiet, but with candles lit and shutters opened as if everything were normal.

Once on the street, he decided it was safe to uncover his lantern, and he picked up the pace and carefully stepped across the muddy carriage tracks by Lady Maria. He was just reaching dryer ground when he heard the church door open, but blinded by his lantern, he couldn't see who it was. His body was ready to sprint when he recognized the voice of their younger minister, Hans Jakobsen.

The tension left his body in a rush that made him sweat, and he ran toward the church. "Minister Jakobsen, it's me, Merchant Nikolaos," he said, lifting the lantern to expose his face. "Are you safe? Have the Swedes arrived?"

Minister Jakobsen cast a glance around him, then grabbed Nikolaos' arm and pulled him inside. The church was completely dark, and the lantern created shadows along the pews and aisles, which made it look as if soldiers were standing there. It sent Nikolaos' heart racing. "Yes," Minister Jakobsen whispered, his low voice reinforcing the feeling of shadowy forms watching from the pews. "I'm certain they have. In fact, a delegation will be sent to Råå in the morning to ask the Danes for protection."

"I see," Nikolaos said, fear coming as fast as it left.

"If they can save us from the Swedes torches, what choice do we have?" Minister Jakobsen said.

"True. Seems odd that's all. I would've thought Stenbock and his army..." Nikolaos paused, rephrasing. "I mean, I would have thought the Swedish army would send troops to protect us, not burn the town down."

Minister Jakobsen shrugged, splaying his arms wide. "They're the old Swedes, most of them. I don't think they truly care about us down here in Skåne."

"You're probably right," Nikolaos said, knowing very well that his own voice sounded more like an old Swede than most of the townspeople. "I must head back to my family. I worry. What do you think we should do?"

"I think we shall wait for now, see where it leads. Go home and may the Lord protect you, Merchant Nikolaos." Minister Jakobsen left the circle of light created by Nikolaos' lantern and went to open the door. A rush of moist cold air rushed in. It seemed ominous.

Chapter 79

The next day, Fredrik's and Elsebet's neighbor told them that men had left Helsingborg for Råå to ask the Danes to protect them from their own countrymen. Shortly thereafter, the town filled with Danish soldiers, splashing the gray November day with red and pale yellow.

Swedish soldiers were nowhere to be seen, and it was as if everything was exactly the same as before, but for the sounds of Danes shouting and speaking amongst themselves as they filled their streets and establishments on foot or by horse. There was no violence, no fighting. The false sense of security was palpable. Nikolaos felt as if everyone had gathered for a harvest, and although it was warm and sunny, thick gray clouds loomed in his peripheral vision.

Even so, after a few days, Nikolaos decided it would be safe to go home.

***

They were sitting at the table in front of the fireplace with small porcelain cups filled with coffee made with beans Doctor Döbelius had given them. Stina had put it aside for a special occasion, but saving it was pointless now.

"Do you remember the first time we tried it?" Stina asked.

"Yes, in Stockholm. You didn't like it."

"I'm not sure I do now either. Don't tell Doctor Döbelius. Where is he, anyway? In town or in Ramlösa?"

"I won't, and I don't know." Nikolaos pictured the Danes drinking Döbelius' water like the soldiers had back when the Swedish military stayed there. They had fought the Danes then, at least. Now they did nothing. He grimaced.

Stina took another sip, then pushed the cup toward him. "You can finish it."

He reached for her before she pulled back, gently wrapping his hands over the cup and her hand. "Pray, talk to me. Let's not leave things unsaid between us anymore." He caught her eyes, but she pulled her hand out from under his, careful not to topple the cup. She got to her feet, then went over to the cabinet and poured herself some ale. She didn't offer him any. He drank the coffee, swallowing all of it at once. It tasted bitter.

"Nikolaos, I just wished you had lied," Stina said and put her ale on the counter, licking the ale off her lips. "Why didn't you? You lie constantly about everything. Your whole life is a big lie. Why, why couldn't you have just said no when I asked?"

He looked at her, shocked. Not once during the uncountable imaginary conversations he had had with her, had he ever thought she would say that.

"Answer me, Nikolaos. Why?"

"It seemed the right thing to do at the time. You're my wife. I don't usually lie to you."

She scoffed. "You might not lie to me, but you avoid telling me all of the truth, which is lying by omission." She drank the rest of her ale and sat back down in front of him. "How many have you killed since that conversation?"

"None."

She narrowed her eyes, looking as if she wasn't sure what to believe.

"It doesn't happen so often, Stina, and I try my best to do it in private. But they come to me sometimes and when they do, then …" He trailed off.

"Like I did."

"Yes."

"Only you had already stepped out to dry land when I found you. If you hadn't, I could have died." She inhaled sharply. "Instead, I married you."

"Yes, you did." He was stunned she brought it up. That unspeakable reality which had always hung between them, like a ghost everyone knew of, but didn't dare to mention. "For goodness sake, Stina, I had to spell it out when you thought we could ride out to your island together. I was never untruthful about it. Never. You knew who I was, knew what would happen if you were near me in the water."

"Only the part where you didn't tell me that you fornicate before you drown them."

He flinched.

Stina looked at him defiantly, but then she sighed deeply, and the warmth came back in her eyes. "Nikolaos, it's no matter anymore. Let's stop this. Let's not fight about all this anymore. Not now. Not when the Danes are here."

Nikolaos nodded silently. She was right. Their fight seemed trivial now when they had cause to fear both the Swedes and the Danes. And they had been avoiding each other for too long. Over two years.

"I forgive you, husband. I know you try." She reached across the table and took his hand. "I understand you have needs. I'm old, my hair is white, my teeth are falling out, and I'm dry down in my privates."

"Darling, it's not like that. I just want to hug you and be near you like we used to. I thank you for forgiving me," Nikolaos said, patting her hand and swallowing a lump in his throat. "I won't be with another if I can help it for as long as you're with me. I promise you that." Then he would find Rå. It felt odd to even think it. He pushed it out of his mind.

Stina nodded, her chin wobbling.

He smiled at her. Tears dripped down his cheeks, landing on the table in front of their clasped hands.

They stayed there, listening to the ticking mantle clock, the crackling from the fireplace in front of them, and the small fireplace in the bedroom. It felt both familiar and new, and neither of them wanted to break the spell by saying something.

Suddenly, they heard a sound like thunder in the distance. They both looked up sharply, staring at each other. Nikolaos' eyes flashed to the window, but the weather was as before, cold and wintry. Then he understood. It was the thumping sound of hooves hitting muddy ground. A lot of hooves, creating one continuous sound. He had heard it before.

He stood up, sending his chair to the floor by the sudden

movement, and raced to the window. Pulling the curtain, he looked across the courtyard at the gate, immediately spotting three soldiers on horses in full military regalia. The Danish cavalry had arrived.

"Rusty devils! Wait here." He was out the door before Stina had time to ask anything, running toward the gateway.

Farrier Nils and Orvar were there already, standing much too close to the street than Nikolaos thought was wise. He decided to join them there anyway and went to stand behind the farrier. Nils was short, and Nikolaos could see over his head. There were hundreds of soldiers on horseback, their hooves echoing between the walls, painting the world with more colors than he could name. It distracted him, and he looked down at his feet, closing his eyes.

Orvar, thinking he was overcome with fear, clapped him on the back. "You shall see it'll be fine. They're here to protect us. No matter how odd that is, at least we need not worry about bloodshed."

"I hope you're right, but I'm not so sure. I don't trust it. Look at them, there are so many, and I'm afraid for my son. What if he gets called in to fight? He'd be on the other side of us," Nikolaos said, looking up and ignoring the colors dancing around him.

"Oh," Orvar said, uncertain. He shifted his gaze back to the soldiers on the street. "How old is he now? Isn't he married with his own family? He's probably too old for it."

"Yes, he's married. And maybe, but we'll still be on opposite sides. A lot of families will be separated from each other this way."

Farrier Nils turned around and hushed at them, looking irritated. As he did, one of the soldiers on foot made a sudden move in their direction. He was grinning from ear to ear but shaking his right arm violently. It looked grotesque, almost demonic. Orvar and Farrier Nils jumped back, bumping into Nikolaos, which caused the soldier to laugh raucously.

Nikolaos kept his eyes on the soldier, watching his every move as his heart raced with fear. But then the soldier looked away and followed his companions and disappeared from sight.

The relief was so intense Nikolaos had to grab the wall for

support. As he did, he spotted Stina and Beata hurrying toward them arm in arm, walking fast and making a lot of noise. Beata was wearing wooden clogs, making him see pale green flashes as they echoed between the walls. It was drawing too much attention to them.

"Tell your wife to take off her clogs," he said to Orvar. "She's being too loud."

Orvar left his side and hurried toward her, gesticulating and pointing at her feet. Beata called out, that too, too loud for comfort, and immediately pulled her feet out, leaving the clogs where they stood.

Stina's face was drawn with worry, and she went straight to him, standing as close as she could. He put his arm around her waist and then they stood there, watching as the soldiers marched past them on foot and by horse.

The five of them remained, huddled in the cold in the tunnel-like gateway between the street and their courtyard, watching until the final soldier had disappeared and the last sound of hooves died out, making it seem unnaturally silent. No one said anything, all keeping their eyes on the spot where the last soldier had been.

"I'm bringing my wife inside for something warm and then to early bed," Nikolaos said after a time.

The others nodded wordlessly. Orvar clapped Nikolaos on the back, took Beata by the hand, and walked home. Then a shrill sound of seagulls broke through the silence.

"Seagulls, all the way here?" Stina exclaimed with surprise.

"It's the boats. There's an uncountable amount of them in the sound. At least forty, maybe even over a hundred! The seagulls are looking for food scraps," Farrier Nils said.

Stina crossed herself.

***

King Fredrik IV of Denmark arrived the next day, moving into Mayor Herman Schyleter's home. Schlyleter himself abandoned his

653

Swedish loyalties and was promptly installed as the new mayor as the now former Mayor Gabriel Löfgren fled.

Nikolaos heard all this when he anxiously walked across town to the mercantile. He tried to put his feelings into words in his mind, but he couldn't. Nothing made sense. Each soldier he passed smiled and nodded at him as if they were old friends. And when he arrived at their mercantile, he couldn't believe his eyes. There was a line out the door with customers. A line with red caped soldiers, unbuttoned mantles flapping in the wind, exposing the pale-yellow Danish coats underneath.

Nikolaos inhaled sharply and strode past them. He was just about to open the door when one of the soldiers lay a heavy arm on his shoulder and said something in Danish he couldn't understand.

"My son-in-law and I own this mercantile. I must speak with him," Nikolaos said, assuming the soldier wondered why he tried to get ahead of the line.

The soldier was a burly man with ruddy cheeks and a cut on his lower right lip that he picked at with his upper teeth as he cocked his head to try to understand what Nikolaos said. Then his face broke into a wide smile. "Oh, it's your establishment! Pray forgive," he said, at least Nikolaos thought he did. Then he bowed, gave another broad smile, and stepped aside.

Nikolaos was so relieved he didn't have the mind to thank him.

Fredrik just glanced at him as he entered, focused on a soldier who was handing him a handful of coins.

Nikolaos went to join him behind the counter, keeping an eye on the soldiers. They all seemed calm and stood in a polite line, waiting for their turn. There were no weapons out. It was surreal.

Fredrik gave him a bewildered smile, pointing at their quills and inkwells on an upper shelf, gesturing for Nikolaos to get them down.

Nikolaos did what he asked. There was nothing else to do.

The soldiers kept coming, one after the other, each paying for everything they bought, chatting and joking with him and Fredrik and amongst themselves.

It made the day even more surreal. Yet he understood. Skåne had been Danish a long time before Sweden claimed it, and after that, Sweden forced the population to not only accept it but to act Swedish, speak the new language, and give up their own Danish ways. It explained why people saw them as long-awaited rescuers, not occupiers.

Two hours before their usual closing time, they had nothing more to sell, and Fredrik shut the door behind the last soldier. Leaning back on the door, he closed his eyes and took several audible breaths before he looked at Nikolaos. "I don't know what to say. They paid for it all, all of it. One person paid double. Another couldn't afford my price, and when I offered to lower it, another came up from the back of the line and bought it for him. And then he bought one for himself too!"

"What was it?"

"The tobacco boxes."

Nikolaos lifted an eyebrow. "The polished ornate ones?"

"Yes! I'm glad I decided to go open the store. Elsebet didn't want me to, but my thinking was that if I didn't, they'd break in and steal it."

"Rusty devils!" Nikolaos exclaimed. "You're right." He looked out the window, considering whether he should tell Fredrik about the soldier who had acted so strangely yesterday, then decided against it. "Do you understand everything they say, Fredrik?" he asked instead.

"Mostly, if they speak slowly, I do," Fredrik said and left his place by the door, going behind the counter. He started to count the money that had come in, sorting it into purses.

"Good. It frightens me that I don't fully understand. They have muskets."

"Yes indeed. It frightens me too. And I'm afraid that our own Swedish countrymen will accuse us of treason for taking enemy money."

Nikolaos' stomach tightened. That hadn't even occurred to him. "I'm of half a mind to go north to my son and his family," he said without thinking. As much as he wanted to, for Hindrich and

Ekborg's sake, it was best he never set foot there.

"North? Are you out of your mind? You can't do that. They're guarding the border. On both sides!"

"Both sides," Nikolaos said, confused, trying to picture where Helsingborg's border was. "Wait, what border?"

"Skåne's border, the Danes want all their old land back," Fredrik said. He looked scared.

Nikolaos sat down heavily on the chair. They were trapped then. There was no choice but to follow the Danes' orders and be grateful that the soldiers weren't violent. He looked at Fredrik. "What should we do tomorrow? We've nothing to sell anymore."

"Well, with your permission, I think we should claim the winnings from what was sold here today, for now anyway," Fredrik said and threw a purse at him.

Not prepared for it, Nikolaos had to duck and pick it up off the floor. The purse was heavy in his left hand. He chuckled half-heartedly. At least the occupation was lucrative. "Why not? There's no sense in leaving it in the safe in a locked, empty store. We don't know what will happen in the future."

"My thoughts exactly," Fredrik said as he put an equally large purse into his own satchel and slung it over his shoulder. "Let's leave through the small door, shall we?"

***

That Sunday, Nikolaos left for church a whole hour before the service, hoping he would find Pastor Troilius and Minster Jakobsen alone and have a chance to speak with them and get some advice. He had barely slept since Fredrik said that they were trapped and wanted to find out if it was indeed the case. Maybe Fredrik was just frightened.

The church was dark and silent. No one had lit any candles yet, and it was an overcast morning without much light penetrating through the windows. The altarpiece lay dark as well, and it didn't look like any candles were lit in the empty spaces behind it either. It felt odd. Shouldn't they be preparing for the service by now? He pulled out his watch, but it was too dark to see what time it was. Putting it back in his pocket, he turned to go sit in the pews, then froze. Someone was whispering behind the altar, sounding agitated.

"It's a decree! What are you talking about? We must do what they say. No, you can't make me do this!" the voice exclaimed, louder now. It was Minister Jakobsen. Nikolaos recognized his slightly hoarse voice.

It went silent and then he heard a scoff, loud enough to echo through the church, creating cobalt blue sparks against the brown brick.

"I'm not going to let these filthy Danes come here and tell me what to do in my own church!" another voice thundered, Pastor Troilius.

Nikolaos tiptoed backward, placing himself behind the pillar to the left side of the aisle.

"Yes, you can, by the grace of God. What have the Swedes ever done for us? They're a harsh pillaging people. Think of the land we lost when they came here. This was one of the grandest churches in the kingdom, all lost," Jakobsen said angrily. It was clear he was referring to the Kingdom of Denmark, not the Kingdom of Sweden. Nikolaos' heart took an extra beat. Minister Jakobsen was not a friend of the Swedes. He knew it! Something had felt off the other night.

"That was years ago. What God has put in place, man shall not tear asunder! God willed us to be Swedish. Surely you see that?" Pastor Trollius said, sounding smug.

"But how do you know, Pastor Troilius? Maybe God wants back what was once stolen from him," Minister Jacobsen said.

Troilius didn't respond; at least Nikolaos couldn't hear it. There was a sound of wood scraping against the floor, and it all went quiet again. Then one of them lit a candle behind the altar. If it was one of them, maybe there were more people back there.

Nikolaos quickly sat down at the pew closest to him, bending his head and clasping his hands as though in deep prayer. After a while, the church door opened, and he heard people enter. Out of the corner of his eye, he could see the pale yellow of the

Danish uniforms with their red cuffs. Daring to turn slightly in their direction, he counted five of them. None wore their red capes. The yellow reminded him of lush crop fields, and it seemed almost perverse that soldiers could remind him of that.

They spread out and sat down in different pews. A clearly deliberate choice. One soldier sat down in Nikolaos' pew but kept a respectful distance, staying as close to the aisle side as possible.

Nikolaos pretended to pray but soon gave up and looked straight at him.

The man nodded and smiled. "Pray forgive..." he said, his voice trailing off into unintelligible murmurs. "Go on, I wish not... May your prayers be blessed."

"I thank you," Nikolaos said, confused.

The soldier responded with another smile. He was young and handsome with large green eyes that had a slanted, sleepy look to them. "You have nothing to be fear about. We'll protect you from the Swedish devils, fear not," he said in a strange mixture of Danish and Swedish.

"I must thank you then," Nikolaos said, not sure what else to say, afraid he would say something the soldier might misunderstand. Swedish devils, would he count him and his family as part of that crowd, coming from up north as they did? He pretended to pray again, and after what felt like a sufficient amount of time, he grabbed the back of the pew in front, pulled himself up to stand, and said, "My wife is coming to service. I'll need to find her."

The soldier threw him an uncertain look but moved his legs so Nikolaos could slide past him.

Pastor Troilius was lighting the candles in the entrance chandelier. He looked up when Nikolaos approached and when their eyes met, they were full of fear.

The service went on as it did every Sunday, but Pastor Troilius and Minister Jakobsen kept themselves apart, avoiding each other.

Then, when the time came to bless King and Kingdom,

Pastor Troilius took a deep breath, stepped slightly forward and away from Minister Jakobsen, lifted his hands, and proclaimed, "The Lord bless thee, King Karl, by the Grace of God King of Sweden, the Goths and the Vends, Grand Prince of Finland, and Duke of Skåne. The Lord bless thee and keep thee: The Lord maketh his face shine upon thee and be gracious unto thee: The Lord lift up his countenance upon thee and give thee peace."

At first. nothing happened, then an uncertain murmur swept through the church as the congregants realized that an extraordinary act of defiance had taken place. Pastor Troilius had blessed the Swedish King when they were under the Danish King's protection.

Nikolaos watched Stina stifle a gasp, from where he sat on the men's side. Fabric rustled as the congregants shifted nervously in their pews. Then one soldier after the other rose to their feet and went to stand along the walls.

It was as if the church itself held its breath.

Minister Jakobsen glared at Pastor Troilius, then with a deliberate cough, he stepped in front of him and with a strong, confident voice, started reciting, "He shall pour the water out of his buckets, and his seed shall be in many waters, and his King shall be higher than Agag, and his kingdom shall be exalted." Minster Jakobsen looked out at the congregation, moving his head across the room, then gave a barely perceptible nod to someone near the window.

Nikolaos readied himself to run and grab Stina if needed.

Minster Jakobsen continued as if there was nothing else going on. "And Balak's anger was kindled against Balaam, and he smote his hands together: and Balak said unto Balaam, I called thee to curse mine enemies, and behold, thou hast altogether blessed them these three times. Therefore, now flee thou to thy place."

Someone laughed, and when Nikolaos turned around to see who it was, every one of the soldiers had broad grins on their faces, as did several of the townspeople. Pastor Troilius was running down the aisle and out the door.

***

Nikolaos and Stina were sitting across from Elsebet and Fredrik at their kitchen table, trying to still the panic they all felt after the service.

"Where do you think he went? Can we help him somehow?" Stina asked, looking close to tears.

Nikolaos shook his head. "It would be too dangerous. I wish we could, but Pastor Troilius is on his own. I just pray he went somewhere safe."

"I've always been a little intimidated by him, but what he did today..." Stina trailed off, wiping her eyes with the back of her hand. "Such bravery."

"I wish there was a way we could get to your farm up by Ytterby, but I take it the whole border is guarded," Fredrik said.

"You tell me, Fredrik, you're the one who told me about it," Nikolaos said, then gave an apologetic smile. He hadn't meant for it to sound so harsh.

"I didn't like the way the soldiers reacted when Pastor Trollius was talking. It felt incredibly tense. I'm surprised they didn't arrest him," Elsebet said.

Nikolaos shot her a surprised glance. They very well might have. It hadn't crossed his mind.

"What are we going to do?" Elsebet asked, glancing behind her into the other room where their children were sleeping.

"There's nothing we can do other than what the Danes tell us. And lie low, not talk with people too much, lest they hear we're speaking in a northern dialect." Nikolaos turned to Fredrik. "You and the children are the only ones speaking like a local. if you can handle all our business from now on, I think we'd be safer."

Fredrik nodded. He looked nervous.

660

Chapter 80

Rå ran on bare feet in a drizzle mixed with snow. Invigorated, she surged forward, the trees blurring past in a streak of green and brown. Then a sudden movement ahead made her halt. Maybe it was a bear woken from her winter slumber or one that hadn't settled yet. Bears were slow to recognize her and could be very dangerous. One had shredded her arm to pieces once. It had taken months to heal, and the scars remained for more seasons than she could count. Instinctively, she grabbed her right arm with the left as if to protect it and slowly backed up.

A moment later, a man emerged from behind a tree, walking awkwardly with his breeches still half-down. As he fumbled with the buttons, he headed straight for her, unaware of her presence.

Rå grinned with pleasant surprise. "You? What are you doing here? You're mining for coal this far south?" It was the skinny man she met seasons ago when she still had Little One.

He froze, flushing when he realized that she must have seen everything. Then his face lit up with recognition. Fear too. "No, can't say I am. I wasn't entirely truthful in Skara. I wanted to avoid soldiering and was staying away," he said, surprising her with his honesty.

"I thought as much."

"You knew I was a soldier?"

"No, but I could tell that you weren't a miner. I've known many, none with skinny arms like you. If anything, I'd take you for a pastor."

"That I'm not," he said, laughing. "Where's your cow? And your feet, are they feeling better, mistress?" His eyes narrowed when he noticed she wasn't wearing shoes or socks.

"Yes. My cow left her body behind a while ago. May Freya keep her."

He flashed her a stunned glance but said nothing.

Not wanting to get into a tiresome conversation about the church, or why she was barefoot, Rå quickly changed the subject. "Would you walk with me a bit? It's cold and wet. Let's seek shelter together."

"Certainly." He looked nervous, but excited.

"Will you tell me your name this time?" she asked and looped her arm around his waist. "I'm glad to see you. I've been without men for quite a while now."

"I'm Sven Jönsson."

***

Lying on her arm, wrapped in her long hair under the thick branches of a pine, Sven began to talk. "I became frightened after I spent time with you those years ago, Rå. For it *is* you, isn't it? You're the Forest Rå."

"Yes."

"As I mentioned, I didn't want to go to war. I had seen you several years before as well. You were but like a spirit in the forest, the way your hair swayed and the way your back seemed to be just one of the tall trees on the mossy ground. I'll never forget it. Then when I saw you on your cow... well, at first, I thought you'd taken the form of a cow or that you were a horse."

She laughed. "How could I have done something like that?"

"I don't know." He joined in her laughter but sounded embarrassed. "I saw later that you were just sitting on it. But I want to explain what happened and make amends and ask for your forgiveness."

Rå pulled herself up to sit. There was just enough space under the branches to lean her back on the trunk. "As I remember, we had a lovely time. There's no need for apologies."

"I know that. But I've spoken ill of you. It was only so they wouldn't send me to war. I didn't want to die, Rå. They sent me to Skara court because of it."

"That I understand. All this horrific killing for land and invisible lines on the ground that dictate where one can and cannot step."

"Some are not invisible. There are wide stretches of water between land sometimes. It's not strange that the people on one side of the sea want to keep all that land. In the south, Denmark is trying to reclaim the land on the other side of the sound. But why can't *we* keep it? It stretches all the way down. And there's water on all three sides," Sven said and sat up beside her, pushing at the pine branches to get more room.

"Water is no border. It's just something people have decided because they're greedy. They send young men to die for imaginary lines," Rå said.

"But they're not imaginary. There are different rulers on each side, other laws, and different languages."

"You're right about that," she said, nodding. It was another reason why humans were so complicated. They had too many rules about things.

"We're forgetting ourselves," Sven said, looking happy she had given him right but nervous as well. "I still want to make amends and tell you what happened at the tribunal."

"Of course."

"Well, I wasn't sure what to do at all, but then it came to me that I could tell them that you were part horse. I kept talking and telling them more and more about how you looked, thinking back on what I had thought that time before I realized that you were just sitting on a cow. They didn't believe me at first and asked me all kinds of questions." Sven shifted to the side, stretching his legs out in front of him. "I made up more and more details. At first, I enjoyed it. They were so gullible, and I admit I enjoyed the ruse. Especially since I suspected it would make them think I'd be unsuitable for the army. But after a while I became anxious. They kept asking me odd questions that I couldn't answer, coming at it from different angles or asking the same question in several ways. Aggressively too. It made me very afraid, and I began to regret what I'd told them. I tried to explain that I had made it up, but they wouldn't listen. They took me to the military for questioning, and there they were worse. They tied me up and locked me in a shed. And barely fed me for weeks, maybe months. Then one day they took me to the courthouse in Skara." He paused to catch his breath. "I was questioned by a Colonel, Anders Sparfeldt. I think he was with the military or maybe Skara court, I can't remember. He believed every word of what I had said at first. I tried to explain that you didn't truly look like a horse, but he wouldn't listen either. He asked if you sometimes looked like other animals. Or if I'd seen the Mountain Rå or the Sea Rå, and if they were also part deer and horse or perhaps something else. He was so insistent that I didn't dare to deny it anymore. Someone even asked my wife, but she said she'd never noticed any Rå's."

Rå shook her head slowly, a bit flabbergasted. "Well, I certainly don't have legs like a horse."

"No, you don't. I beg your forgiveness."

"I forgive you, but never lie like that about me again," she said, keeping her voice stern.

"I won't." He looked shamefaced.

Rå nodded and held her hands out to him, but he didn't see it. Humans had poor eyesight, especially in the dark.

Sven sat silent and unmoving, then shifted to all fours and crawled out without a word. As he pushed the branches aside, moonlight flooded their crawlspace, turning his face into a silhouette so she couldn't see his expression. Once he was out, the branches snapped back, obscuring the moonlight again. Rå heard him rise to his feet, his breathing audible. He was ashamed.

An eyeblink later, he threw himself through the branches, landing right at her feet. "Wolves," he gasped, so close to her that she felt his breath on her face. "They're right here. A large pack of at least ten or twenty, ragged and enormous. Creeping like black ghosts."

"Ah, yes. They like to hunt while the moon shines upon us, but wolves prefer something tastier and juicier than men. Do you have a lantern and a fire striker in your satchel?" she asked, opening her back to draw him closer.

"I do," Sven said, sounding calmer already, her power and the thought of light relaxing him. He pulled out a small lantern with a tallow candle and kindled a flame using a dry branch. A bird took off above them, startled from its slumber by the light or the movement, its wings flapping rapidly as it flew into the night.

"You never did tell me what you're doing down here so far south," Rå said.

"No," he sighed, "I'm fleeing again. I was sent here to fight the Danes, but I don't want to do it. I told you, didn't I? That the Danes are trying to take back their land again. Everyone is furious. We thought there would be no more challenges, but they've taken Helsingborg. Just moved in, kicked out Governor Löfgren and Pastor Troilius, and those cowards did nothing to defend it! Will you believe it? Why would I risk my life for such ungrateful dastards who aren't even trying to save themselves?"

Rå went cold. "Pray no, not Helsingborg."

"Yes, that's the town. Do you know it?"

Her back closed so quickly that the pine shuddered, dropping several of its pinecones. "Yes, I've heard of it. My friends live there. I'm going to go outside for a bit to check on the wolves," Rå said. It was an excuse. She wanted to be alone to think.

It was clear and cold outside, and she inhaled deeply, relaxing the tightness in her back. The wolves were still there, turning their heads toward her when they detected her scent. The alpha female approached with quick confident steps, her tail politely low as her pack cautiously followed behind her. She was so tall she reached Rå's hips. Sticking her muzzle deep into Rå's side, her fur rose slightly when she smelled Sven. Then, by a cue Rå couldn't see, the others gathered around her and started smelling her while they leaned against her and rubbed their fur on her skirts.

"If Nikolaos is forced to fight against the Danes, he might panic and do something stupid which might expose him. Shall I go to him?" Rå asked the alpha male and scratched his neck. A shy female turned at the sound of her voice, cocking her head as if she was trying to understand. "I think I shall," Rå said and gently put her hand on the female's back.

The alphas grinned, and then the male let out a deep grunt and ran off. The whole pack followed, leaving her with a gust of cold air whipped up from their sudden departure. Their visit didn't last longer than two of her own slow heartbeats.

She made her way back to the pine. Snow began to fall, and

big wet flakes clung to the branches, glistening faintly from the lantern light inside.

When she entered, Sven was curled up on his side. He startled awake, but when he saw that it was her and not a wolf, his eyes closed again. "You're going to bring me to Helsingborg. We leave in the morning," she said, but he probably didn't hear it.

***

Sven was afraid that someone would recognize him, not only as a deserter but as the man who had been questioned by Colonel Anders Sparfeldt. Rå assured him that he had no need to be afraid, that she had no intention of getting too close to the troops. Men intent to kill was not the type of men she looked for. She had seen enough. Her own family had done their share of arguing to the death. It solved nothing, and the blood made the men crazy.

Sven told her that Stenbock had gathered thousands of men, he among them. But since there were so many, no one noticed when he just walked away one day. He didn't explain who Stenbock was, and she didn't ask him to elaborate.

They made their way south, staying off roads and choosing trails where no human feet had stepped before. Despite his nerves, Sven was oblivious to the troops. But Rå could feel them, noticed it in the way the trees held themselves unnaturally still, the way birds didn't settle for long and flew off in fright, and the absence of foxes and wolves the further south they got. She kept it to herself.

A week later, they came upon four soldiers on horseback. Rå spotted their odd triangular hats above the bushes the moment they were about to cross the path in front of them. Running off would seem too suspicious, so she grabbed Sven's arm and pulled him close, opening her back to protect him.

The first one to cross was riding a gray horse. It was so small the soldier's legs were reaching far below its stomach. It seemed a strange choice for a war horse. The horses following, however, were muscular beasts, brown with black manes cut short. The men wore blue coats and yellow breeches and stockings.

Sven sank to his knees beside her, almost prostrating, and started wailing. "I thank you. I thank you for saving us from the devils, those Danish swine. I'm but a fool who's weak in the head with a broken foot. But I thank you for your sacrifice."

Rå hid her astonishment and nodded to the men, who were now standing on parade, staring at them. "Good afternoon, gentlemen. Yes, we're grateful to you," she said, deciding to play along.

The soldier on the gray horse pursed his lips, keeping his eyes on hers before he pulled his hat off and bowed the best he could where he sat. "Afternoon, mistress. Have you seen any Red Capes?"

"Red Capes, is that what you call the Danes? No, we haven't, but it frightens me to find you here. If we're in your path, pray forgive us." Rå let her back expand more, focusing on pulling at the trees.

All four soldiers looked up at the treetops. "It's getting windy, we need to head back to camp. May God protect you. Walk in peace. Stay east and you'll not be in anyone's way." With a tip of their hats, the soldiers urged their horses into a gallop. Dirty snow was thrown up behind one of the horses as it stepped in a half-frozen puddle.

"Why did you fall to your knees and leave me to do all the talking?" Rå scolded once they were out of sight.

Sven started to get up, grunting as he slipped on the muddy ground. "It was the only thing I thought to do. I'm wearing the same breeches as they, haven't you noticed? I thank God that I threw their coat away. Now I'll get chilblains. Look at this," he said and pointed to his legs. They were dark with moisture and mud.

"You're wearing your soldier breeches still?"

"Indeed, hose as well. The breeches have lost their fine yellow shine, but they'd see had I not prostrated. You ought to thank me, not chastise me."

She laughed. "Indeed, I do. I thank you." Likely it was her power that had saved him. His breeches were recognizable from behind too, but there was no need to tell him that.

Sven brushed the mud off and grinned.

Rå went to him, touching his wet breeches. "You're too wet, you're right about chilblains. We should stop so I can keep you warm." She moved her hand to his bulge and squeezed it. "We'll rest and continue tomorrow."

Two days later, they reached the coast and spotted Helsingborg Castle in the distance.

***

It was so foggy that had Sven not walked beside her, she wouldn't have been able to see him. They made their way forward slowly, going by feel and the sound of Sven's boots on the hard-packed wagon tracks.

Suddenly, a thunderous scream pierced through the thick air, followed by a sound like a hammer hitting a rotted piece of wood. Then the fog shifted as if it had been physically moved and there was a sudden flash of blue and red.

They froze. But the fog thickened again, obscuring whatever they had seen. The sounds stopped too.

Rå felt Sven search for her right hand and grab it. He pulled her back, one slow step at a time. Then the world exploded in front of them. Shouts filled the air, mingled with the thunderous sound of hundreds of hooves striking damp ground all at once. The shrill ring of musket fire pierced her ears, while somehow, in the midst of it, she still heard the sound of flesh being slashed to pieces.

Brimstone burned her nostrils, competing with the smell of blood. The fog cleared again, and a tunnel of visibility appeared across the land. There were thousands of men and horses. A blur of red, blue, and yellow, mixed with blood staining the ground, faces drawn with anger, fear, and death. She gasped as her bladder emptied and slid down her legs, burning her cold thighs.

"Run!" Sven screamed and squeezed her hand so hard she felt her bones crunch. It hurt, but she couldn't form the words to tell him to loosen his grip.

Time seemed to slow down as if in a dream. They abandoned the road and bound across half-frozen ground on what seemed to be a meadow or an unplanted crop field, praying that they wouldn't get caught in the middle of the battle. Sven's fingers shifted a little, easing the pain in her hand. They tripped, pulled themselves back up, clambered across a stream, and then finally dared to stop. They were surrounded by shrubs and bushes. Not a single bird chirped.

Rå turned slowly and looked back whence they came, and her jaw dropped. The fog had dissipated, replaced by wisps of smoke. There were bodies strewn everywhere as if they were ragdolls thrown about by a child. All around the bodies, and on top of them as well, men were fighting to the death.

"I wouldn't have made it. I would've been one of the ones on the ground. Lord forgive them for they know not what they do," Sven prayed.

"We're safe here, Sven," Rå said, more to herself than to him. We'll wait, and when they stop this folly, you'll leave. I'll find my way, and you can go home to your wife."

Chapter 81

They had stood in formation, hidden by the fog in the early morning before they attacked. Then a staggering number of men fought, sixteen thousand Swedes and fourteen thousand Danes. It lasted only hours before Stenbock declared Sweden the victors. The Danes retreated to Helsingborg Castle. They tried to keep the town but were too weak to defend it against the Swedes. So, they really did lose in the end, the Danes. About five thousand fell in battle, and two thousand five hundred were taken as prisoners. The Swedish army lost only eight hundred.

Nikolaos, for one, was relieved. What had begun in November when the Danes paid for everything they took, didn't last long. Soon they demanded food for themselves and their horses. Tax, they called it. It left almost nothing for the Swedes. They took their horses too, including horses brought in from the surrounding farms. Nikolaos' and Farrier Nils' horses were too old for them to use. They were both grateful for that, but they didn't have much feed for them.

Stina had shadows under her eyes and felt bony when they hugged. He wondered if she had lost all her flesh these three months or during the two years they hadn't touched. He was afraid to ask.

Elsebet refused to eat much at all, feeding the little they had to her family. She looked like a ghost of her former self, Stina said.

No amount of money and gold that Nikolaos had tucked away during his long life could buy what didn't exist.

****

The sound of musket fire jolted them awake. It was deafening, reverberating between the buildings. Nikolaos sat bolt upright, staring at the flickering red and blue colors he saw across their wallpaper. He closed his eyes to get away from it, then reached for his watch on the bedside table and flipped the lid open. It was past ten in the morning, incredibly late. There were more sounds of musket fire, followed by grunts and thumps in rapid succession. It sounded strange, and too close for comfort.

"What's happening, Nikolaos?" Stina asked, eyes wide with fear.

Nikolaos snapped the watch lid closed and slipped the chain over his head, then reached for his breeches. "I don't know. I thought the Danes were leaving. I don't like this. I'm going to go find out what's happening."

A small gasp escaped from Stina's lips, then she nodded. "Get Orvar to go with you. Ask him to bring Beata over. I don't want to be alone, and I don't want you alone either. And don't go far!" she added, putting her bare feet on the cold floor and pulling her robe over her nightdress.

Nikolaos peeked out the window at the courtyard. Farrier Nils' horse lay sleeping on its side near the well. Maybe the fighting started last night already. How had they not heard it if there had been such fighting that Farrier Nils didn't even dare to bring the horse inside? "I'll do that," he said to Stina. "Stay here. I'll be back as soon as I can. Don't go look for Elsebet. We have to assume they're as safe inside as we are."

He left the bedroom and hurried through the kitchen. Bursting out the door, he took the steps in one great leap. As he ran across the courtyard, he forgot to pretend he was an older, achy man. And by the time he knocked on Orvar's and Beata's door, he was out of breath.

There was no answer. He turned around, debating with himself if he ought to ask Farrier Nils, go back and get Stina, or leave the courtyard and go out on the streets himself. People were walking back and forth out there, and he heard more of those strange thumps but no musket fire. It was probably safe enough. Walking as briskly as he dared, remembering now, he went past the sleeping horse and then stopped in his tracks at the gate.

A large group of Danish soldiers had gathered in front of what looked like a large military tent thrown on the ground. Swedish soldiers were watching, paces behind them near Lady Maria Church. They had a look of disgust and anger on their faces.

One of them looked as though he was trying not to cry.

Nikolaos narrowed his eyes in confusion. Something felt wrong. Then a movement to the left caught his attention, and he shifted his gaze back to the Danes. They were dispersing, striding off in the direction of the tavern, leaving what was now clearly not a haphazardly folded military tent. He blinked and grabbed hold of the wall while inching closer, then called out and instinctively made the sound of the cross. It was horses. Dead horses lay bleeding on the ground, steam distorting his vision as the hot blood mixed with the cold air. Farrier Nils' horse was not asleep.

One of the Swedish soldiers turned toward Nikolaos, his face expressionless. None of them were doing anything. They just stood there staring at the pile of death in front of them.

Nikolaos shook his head in horror and disbelief, then squeezed between the wall of the neighboring house and the dead horses, trying not to see their dead eyes staring at him. The blood was collecting into puddles, and he had no choice but to step in it. Once he was through, he ran toward the town square and the tavern just as musket fire rang out again, filling the square with smoke and bursts of color. He slowed down and approached slowly. The ground was rumbling under his feet for some reason. A moment later he understood, the ground was shaking because several murdered horses hit the ground at the same time. He staggered.

A man at the corner was retching into the street, thick clumpy goo, like split pea soup being poured out of a pot. When he finished, he stood up and pointed into the square, wiping his mouth on his sleeve. "There are thousands of them. They've killed thousands, I've counted. The dastards are leaving, and they can't bring the horses across the water. The streets are full of gunpowder, they've set fire to our food stores, and they're slaughtering the horses."

Nikolaos stared at him, entering the square without a word. There was a sea of horses on the ground, and red-clad and yellow-clad Danes were shoving their bayonets into the necks of the ones still standing. Horses with eyes full of panic, whites gleaming. And there was black smoke behind the houses across the square. Nikolaos turned on his heels and ran.

* * *

When he came home, Stina took one look at his face and sank into the nearest chair.

"What happened, husband? What's wrong? You look as if you've seen a hanging."

Nikolaos couldn't answer. He walked straight to the cupboard and pulled out their brännvin, then opened the lid and drank straight from the pewter. Salty tears mixed with the alcohol. His father had called it vinum ardens, he remembered for some reason. It had been a new drink back in his time. He heard Stina's woolen socks slide across the floor, and when her warm hand reached for him, he collapsed into her arms, crying until his breath came in jagged gasps.

"There, husband, you need to seat yourself and tell me what's happened. You're scaring me. I've never seen you cry like this, Nikolaos."

His legs felt unsteady, and he let himself get supported by her arm as she sat him down on the sofa in their little parlor. "The horses... they're killing all th..." his voice broke, and he couldn't continue. Those panicked eyes, the utter horror. It felt as if his chest would burst from sorrow.

Stina pulled one of their cushioned chairs forward and sat down in front of him. "What do you mean?" She didn't look like she believed him.

"The Danes are slaughtering the horses. Every single one. There are twelve dead on the street right outside the gate. Farrier Nils' horse is dead as well. There are thousands of dead in..." his voice broke again, and he leaned forward, burying his face in Stina's skirts.

"Nikolaos, it can't be. You're sure? That's not right. Why would they kill their own horses?"

He sat back up. "They're not all theirs. Many of them are

673

ours. They're burning our food stores as well, I saw it. Damn them all to hell! I want us to move back to our farm. We're too vulnerable here in a town like this. It's too poor, and we're not safe."

"We can't move back, Nikolaos, you know that. Especially now, the age difference would be obvious to them."

Nikolaos nodded. She was right of course, but he wished it; he had wished it a lot lately. Getting to his feet, he walked over to the window. Farrier Nils' horse remained. It was obvious now that it wasn't sleeping. He could see the dried blood beneath its head, and crows were already at it, picking at the stiffened blood and at the eyes. "I must go check on Nils," he said more to himself than to Stina. And their own horse, dear God. It just now crossed his mind. He ran back out, then remembered to walk slowly and to stoop.

The smoke hung heavy in the air as he made his way to the stable. He swallowed hard, dreading what was to come, still hoping.

Before he got there, the stable door opened, and Nils came out. A quick shake of his head confirmed his worst fears. "I'm at a loss for words, Nikolaos, at a loss for words. Murderous dastards! Imagine that I didn't care who won? I can only thank God now that they lost. May they go across the sound and not ever come back. If they come here again. I'll kill them," he snarled and spit on the ground.

"Have them drown, all of them on their crossing," Nikolaos said without thinking.

Nils raised his eyebrows, but then he nodded. "Yes, let them all drown. Orvar told me they've pushed the horses into the wells!"

"Into the wells? It'll spoil the water." Nikolaos held his gaze for several moments. "They've killed thousands, Nils, thousands. I saw it all. Is, is ours... was she...?" He couldn't bear to speak her name out loud."

"Slumped in her stall." He met Nikolaos' eyes briefly. An intense look. "She looks as though it was quick thankfully."

Tears sprung to Nikolaos' eyes again, and he wiped them off with his sleeve, embarrassed.

Nils gave him a sympathetic look, his arm twitching as if he was about to reach for him, but then he didn't. "You don't really mean thousands, do you?" he asked.

"Yes. There are twelve out here and ours in there. In the square at least hundreds... or fifteen hundred or so, maybe two thousand. I was too upset to fully count them, but I spoke to a man who did. He said..." Nikolaos trailed off.

Nils became visibly pale.

"Let's go check on the gate, make sure we can lock it tonight. Would you go with me?" Nikolaos asked.

"Course I will. By the way, how are you feeling now? You look a bit stiff and achy. I noticed how you ran out the door this morning. It's when you heard the shooting, I gather. I didn't recognize you at first. You ran so fast I thought it was your son-in-law."

Nikolaos scoffed as if he were chiding himself. "I was hoping you didn't notice. I can barely put weight on my right foot because of it and both my knees hurt. I threw myself out of bed and out the door. We slept until past ten this morning, if you'll believe it. Hasn't happened since we were newlyweds. I thought the Danes were attacking."

"We sleep late too. It's been a long time since the Danes came to me for shoeing. They didn't pay for it anymore anyway, so..." Nils spat on the ground again. "There isn't much to do other than sleep to stave off the hunger."

Chapter 82

Rå felt the death before she entered town. Swarms of seagulls shrieked in the air, crows and vultures circled. She was too late.

When the full extent of the carnage materialized before her eyes, she became numb with shock. There were dead horses everywhere. Every corner of every street was full of vultures and smaller birds feasting on the dead.

"Woman, don't just stand there," a soldier shouted, striding toward her while stepping over the dead horses as though they were nothing to him. "Get your husband out here to do what needs to be done. Move!" He got right up in her face, so close she could smell his breath. It smelled clean and fresh. Alive. It seemed grotesquely out of place.

She was too afraid to contradict him and just nodded, then headed off into the maze of little streets, stumbling and slipping as she tried not to step on the horses. The stench of death coated the roof of her mouth and made her gag.

A woman opened her front door and hurried down the street, her skirts brushing the dead bodies.

Rå ran after her as she turned a corner and headed toward the church. It seemed large and looming amid the death on the ground in front of it. "I pray you, mistress," Rå called out as she caught up.

The woman turned wide-eyed toward her and took a step back. She didn't say anything.

"Pray forgive me, mistress. I didn't mean to frighten you. I only just arrived. I'm looking for my friend Fiddler Nikolaos and his wife Stina. Would you perhaps know where they live?"

"No, I've not heard of them. An odd time for visiting," the woman said and kept walking. Rå heard her gag as she passed a dog with a large piece of flesh in his mouth. A long string of innards still attached to a horse was trailing behind it.

Rå stared after her then hurried past the dog. The street was emptier here, but two soldiers were talking in front of the church. One was drinking tobacco, the smoke billowing in front of his face. It probably helped with the stench.

"Gentlemen, good sirs, may I ask for your help?" She made her way toward them as best she could. There were so many horse cadavers she couldn't walk in a straight line.

The one with the pipe turned toward her. "Mistress, you oughtn't to be out here alone. There are dogs and vultures everywhere. It's not safe."

"I gather, but I've come for my friend and his wife. Do you know Fiddler Nikolaos and Stina?"

"Can't say I do, no."

"You don't? I thought everyone knew them. He's an extraordinary fiddler, a real musician. You really don't know?"

"No," he said then turned back to his companion, ignoring her.

She walked off and kept going aimlessly, trying not to look at the poor horses. It was at least a comfort to know that their souls must have left and were running in the fields of *Valhöll*. Surely dying in a fierce battle like this must give them entrance.

A couple, a middle-aged man and his wife were hurrying somewhere, coming right at her. The wife was hiding her face in the crock of her husband's arm, trusting him to show the way.

"Pray forgive me for delaying you," Rå said when they were almost upon her, "but do you perhaps know where Fiddler Nikolaos and his wife Stina live?" She heard the desperation in her own voice. If they didn't know, she would have to open her back to search for him. That meant absorbing the sadness and death. Then she remembered that Nikolaos had said that some people called him Nils Jensson these days. "His name is Nils Jensson, I should mention," she added.

"Fiddler Nikolaos... Nils Jensson? You mean Merchant Nikolaos? He's certainly a fiddler as well," the man said. The wife peered at her from under his arm.

"Do you know him?" Rå asked with relief. She had forgotten that he was a merchant now. He had told her so himself.

"Indeed, we do. He lives right here, just down the alley from Lady Maria Church. We share the same courtyard. We're neighbors," the man said. He didn't smile, but his eyes were kind.

"Oh, I thank you. Will you take me to him?"

"We absolutely will. We wish we could show you a nicer town. I'm Orvar Knutsson," he said, saying his name the same way Nikolaos had explained. "My wife, Beata Lybecker." He tilted his head in the direction of his arm, and his wife straightened up to acknowledge Rå. "I'm assuming you're not from here, mistress?" Orvar asked.

"No. What happened? It's awful!"

"The Danes killed the army's horses before they evacuated, said that they couldn't bring them across the sound. They could when they arrived though, the dastards. There aren't enough undertakers and executioners that can deal with all of this."

"These were the Danish army's horses?" She stared at him in disbelief.

"Yes. Come, there's no sense in standing here. Yes, they killed their own horses, including the ones they'd previously stolen from our farmers. Then they dragged them into our wells and basements," he said, his voice unnaturally matter-of-fact.

Rå instinctively put her hands over her back to protect it. "That's horrific."

"Yes, and the Swedish army refuses to take care of it," his wife said, pulling her face out of her husband's arm. "All they did was to push them out into the street."

Rå was too stunned to respond. The thought of how overwhelming the stench would have been had it been warm raised bile in her throat, but she managed not to vomit.

They didn't have to walk far. Soon Orvar Knutsson and his wife stopped in front of a half-timbered house. It was like a farm but taller, with two floors on top of each other. A wide gateway led into a courtyard so wide and spacious that it contained three separate cottages, one with a stable and a work shed attached to it. There was something large in front of the well, covered with blankets. A dead horse.

Orvar noticed her gaze. "Yes, here too, they killed both Nikolaos' and Farrier Nils' horses. The soldiers have promised to put them on the street by tomorrow. It took some doing to even get them to do that much." He grimaced. "Nikolaos and Stina live right over there," he said and pointed to the cottage on the right. It was larger than the other two and had four nice windows, a small staircase leading to the front door, and rose bushes growing on each side. Lights from inside flickered warmly. Rå sighed with relief. They were home.

***

A sudden knock on the door startled them.

"I'll get it," Nikolaos said. For a moment he considered telling Stina to hide in the bedroom. There were rumors that the army was taking women hostage to force the men to get rid of the horses, but it seemed too ridiculous to be true. He opened the door just a crack, just the same, then threw it wide open in surprise. Rå was standing there with Orvar and Beata waiting behind her below the stairs, looking pleased when they saw that she would be let in. "Magda! What in the world are you doing here? Come in. Stina! Come see who's here," he shouted, smiling at Beata and Orvar in thanks.

Rå embraced him, holding him so tight he was glad Beata and Orvar already had their backs turned. Nikolaos brought her inside and closed the door just as Stina came to greet her.

"Rå?" she exclaimed, staring at her with bewilderment. "What are you doing here?"

Rå stood rigid, her satchel slipping to the floor on its own. "How could they do this?" she asked, paying no attention to what Stina asked her. "I've never seen anything like it."

"Stina, bring some soup for her," Nikolaos said and took Rå by the elbow. "I'll get her situated in the parlor and give her a blanket."

The parlor was what they called it, the third room of their little cottage. It was very small, but a nice sitting room. Nikolaos led

679

her to the sofa and wrapped their throw blanket around her shoulders and back. He held his hand out to her, and she took it. When they heard Stina's footsteps, he slid his hand from hers.

Rå, I'm glad to see you," Stina said and sat down next to Nikolaos. "We don't know what to do. Nikolaos was just writing to Doctor Döbelius to ask him for advice."

"Who's he?" Rå asked.

"Oh Rå, you wouldn't know, of course." Stina stopped talking and put her hands in front of her heart, looking first at Nikolaos and then back at Rå. "We haven't seen each other since we went to Jönköping."

"That's so," Nikolaos agreed, not daring to meet Rå's eyes.

"And here she is, showing up at our door in a completely different life, different home. We've been living down here for many years. Did you go to our farm first? Did you see Hindrich?"

Rå smiled and looked straight into Nikolaos' eyes. "I had heard you moved. Someone told me you were living down here. And recently, I accompanied a soldier who told me you were at war. He was supposed to fight but had refused. Sven, that's his name, was still brave enough to take me all the way here. I wanted to warn you, but it seems I'm too late," she said and let go of Nikolaos' eyes.

He turned his head and looked at the flames in the fireplace to hide the overwhelming sense of love he felt for Rå.

***

Rå was standing at the parlor window, looking out at the courtyard and through the open gate. The dead horses on the street were just visible from where she stood. "It's not right," she said without turning toward him.

"No, it isn't. But there aren't enough undertakers to take care of it. The army ought to, but they won't. All they did was shove the bodies into the streets. And barely. We heard them argue over it."

Rå frowned. "Orvar told me about it last night. But surely

they can't be left in the street?"

"No." Nikolaos added a log to the fire and sat down on the sofa. There wasn't much else to say.

She joined him, seating herself by his side. Close. Light was falling on the left side of her face and her long brown hair was pulled forward over her shoulder, leaving her back exposed. He felt it and shivered. She smiled, reaching for his hand. "We're not in a rush. We have forever."

"I know."

"Once this horrid time is over, things will grow calm again. And once your humans have all left, we'll know it's our time."

She was right, of course. He would have to wait for them to pass. It would be years still. But when that time came, he wouldn't be left alone. It was a comfort.

"Rå, what if she comes back again?" he asked after a time.

"Abluna-Stina? If she does, I'll wait. I'm not jealous, Nikolaos." Rå leaned toward him, and he could smell her skin and see how soft and smooth it was.

He moved back a little, feeling guilty. "Did you make a decision on what to do with your newfound family?"

"Yes. I've visited and decided to do so again. They have a little cottage on their property I can stay in. They think I travel around the country to different markets, looking for art pieces for a merchant."

Nikolaos chuckled. "A merchant? Why not? We'd sell it."

She looked at him with a frown. Then her face split into a grin. "You're him! That's a good excuse, Nikolaos. You always tell me to stay close to the truth."

"It's the way to do it." He smiled, then grew serious. "Can I write you there when the time comes?"

"Of course." She looked at him with her large green eyes, and for a moment it felt as though he could see trees in them.

Then they heard the bedroom door open, and he got to his feet to greet his wife.

"Good morning, you're both up. I've been sleeping so late lately, Rå. Pray forgive me. You must be hungry and want to break your fast. Some herring is what I can give you. Food is scarce these days," Stina said, looking as if she might cry, but she held herself erect and didn't spill a tear.

"I'd gladly eat herring, Stina. I don't often. For me, it's a treat."

"Is it really?" Stina visibly relaxed. She turned right around and went into the kitchen, hurrying toward the corner cupboard to get the herring. She picked their fancy jar, Nikolaos noticed, a pang of guilt for his feelings for Rå.

It got quiet. He considered sitting down next to Rå again but remained standing, feeling Stina in the kitchen on his right and Rå on the sofa to his left. It was a strange feeling. He felt awkward, but yet not. Somehow it felt natural and good to have them both there. They were friends, and Rå was right; there was no rush.

Just as he thought that, there was a sudden loud knock on the door, startling him. Heavy, insistent, then again.

Stina put the jar on the table and stared at him.

As they held each other's gaze, there was another knock and a voice, "Open the door. Now. Military orders."

Nikolaos threw a glance in Rå's direction, but she had her face turned away, and he couldn't see her expression. Turning back to Stina, he mouthed, "I'll get it. We're going to be safe. Stay here."

He opened the door. Three Swedish soldiers stood there. Then they strode past him and entered his home. One was so thin it looked as if he were a child dressed in his father's uniform. Nikolaos followed blindly, his heart beating fast.

"Get dressed," the one closest to him said, whipping his head around to look at him. "You're coming with us. Time to clean up the streets." He was tall and muscular, scary.

"What?"

"You heard. You put your best boots and coat on, and then we'll go. All strong men are to help."

"I'm not strong. I'm a merchant and a musician."

"It's not helping you. Now move!"

Nikolaos tried to catch Stina's eye. Rå had joined her in the kitchen, and they were both seated at the table. The skinny soldier was standing wide-legged with his arms crossed in front of them, partly blocking his view. He didn't look like a boy anymore, he looked sinister.

"Get back from my wife!" Nikolaos shouted and immediately felt a firm strong grip on his upper right arm. It was the third soldier. He was of average build and height, a calm authoritative air about him.

"You come with us," he said. "Leave your wife and the other woman be."

Nikolaos was pulled out of his home, a bayonet pressing into his back. The muscular soldier tossed his coat at him, motioning for him to put it on. The skinny soldier was still inside. Thank God Rå was there.

"Shouldn't you have younger men doing this? I'm almost fifty," Nikolaos said while putting on his coat. At least they let him have that; it was cold.

"Fifty? Nice try," the muscular soldier said while the one with the bayonet in Nikolaos' back laughed coldly. "Now go. You're needed, as is everyone else here. The horses need to be removed. You can't have them lying around. Surely you agree with that. Once it gets warm, they'll stink even more and will be infested by flies."

"Very well, I'll go. Just get the soldier to leave. I don't want him in there with my wife and her sister," Nikolaos said, thinking that sister sounded wise.

"He'll leave when he sees fit. Now move." Nikolaos felt the sharp tip of the bayonet push into the space between his shoulder blades, urging him forward. It hurt.

There was an impossible number of dead horses outside now, pulled from stairwells, doorways, and the wells where the Danes had left them after killing them, all to make life miserable for the Swedes.

Nikolaos swallowed hard, at a loss for how they would be able to get it done. Farrier Nils and Orvar were already there, along with two men he recognized from the farms in Ramlösa. They all looked as overwhelmed as he felt.

There was a cart, unhitched and tipped toward the ground. Four men were in the process of shoving and pulling a carcass into it with the help of ropes and a shovel. Some kind of hoisting contraption was attached to the cart that a man was securing to the heavy dead bulk of the horse. Doing so, its head lolled sideways and hit the wheel with a loud thump. Further up the street, men were dragging horses on the ground, one at each of the legs and one at the heads. The men holding the heads were all walking backward while the others pushed forward. It looked incredibly cumbersome and heavy.

"You'll work here," said the soldier who was pointing the bayonet into his back. He pulled it away, stepping around to face Nikolaos. "All *your* horses are to be disposed of in the sound. You're lucky and don't have far to go. The mass graves are over there." He used the bayonet to point toward the castle, then at a pile of horses where four men were waiting. They looked relieved to see Nikolaos.

One of them gave a curt nod and pointed to the back legs of a white gelding. "You and Björn take the back," he said, gesturing to a man standing off to the side. "Pick up the hoof with both hands, and when I've counted to three, you'll pull as hard as you can."

Nikolaos flicked a glance at Björn, noting he was of strong build and probably around thirty years of age, then turned toward the man who had explained what to do. "Pull? Shouldn't we push like the others are doing?" he asked with a head jerk at the men up the street.

The man snickered. "They're doing it wrong. They're clueless. It's much easier for the ones holding the head to walk forward." At that, he bent down and picked it up, holding it so the whole neck and head was off the ground, grabbing the mane with one hand while the head was sort of resting on his arms at the same time. The poor gelding looked as though it were staring at him. "One, two, three, pull!" the man shouted, ignoring the sad dead eyes.

Nikolaos quickly bent down and grabbed the hoof, swallowing a wave of nausea when he felt the cold leg in his hands. Then they moved forward, dragging the carcass. It was not as heavy as he had expected.

They were almost at the harbor when the man behind Björn stopped abruptly and dropped the leg. "I must rest. I can't hold it like this, my arm is cramping." He massaged his left lower arm, looking pained.

The man holding the head said, "It's not far now," as he carefully lowered it to the ground. He seemed to be a leader of sorts. "Let's just dump in the harbor this time. No one will care."

Nikolaos let go of his leg and looked at the harbor, which was still a good distance away. "Isn't there a better way to do this? A strong horse would be able to drag them in half the time. This is hard work," he said, turning toward the man behind Björn. He wished he knew their names but didn't bother finding out.

"Horse?" The man scoffed, getting a chuckle from the others. "Which horse would that be?" He laughed coldly, gesturing to the carcasses all around them.

Nikolaos nodded, feeling stupid.

"Let's get on with it," said the leader at the head. "One, two, three, and pull!"

When they finally reached the harbor, Nikolaos' arms ached too. For a moment he worried about being so close to the water, but he felt nothing, just tired and sick to his stomach.

The men were chattier on the way back, and Björn introduced him to the man who had been walking behind Nikolaos, holding one of the front legs. His name was Jacob, a lean and strong man who wasn't even sweating from the effort.

"Why don't we start back here instead?" Nikolaos asked, pointing at the dead horses they were passing. "They're much closer to the water, and we wouldn't have so far to go."

Jacob shook his head. "We asked the same thing after our first rounds before you arrived. We were told to ignore them, the horses near the church must be removed first."

"It's the miasma you see. It blows away down here by the water, but up there where everyone lives, it stays. The buildings are keeping the wind out and the miasma in," Björn explained.

"I see," Nikolaos said, confused.

"It's the vapors. Bad for you to breathe," Jacob said, shaking his head again. "Those blasted Danes. Their hearts are colder than the devil's bottom."

Nikolaos raised an eyebrow, then looked away to hide an involuntary smile. It had been years since he had heard someone say that.

"That they are. Horses are beautiful animals. They must have been so scared. It's cruel to bring them to war. They'd be scared of all the shooting and shouting, then having to watch their companions get slaughtered one by one right in front of their eyes, just waiting for it to be their turn to die. The Dane's hearts *are* indeed ice cold," Björn said, blinking away angry tears.

Nikolaos put his hand on his shoulder, feeling close to tears himself. He wondered at the logic of it as well. Granted, there were not enough horses still alive to help with the removal, but didn't the Swedish army have them? As far as he had understood, the Danes had only killed their own, including the ones they stole from the residents. It sickened him to think about it. How could you kill a horse you've been riding for months, even years, just because you didn't want to take the trouble to bring it home? It was abominable. He tried not to look at the corpses, but it was impossible. There were dead horses everywhere.

They kept at it, and by the time nightfall came and they were finally allowed to go home, Nikolaos had lost count of how many horses they had moved. Everything hurt. His shoulders, arms, neck, and most of all his lower back. There was no need to pretend to be old; he *looked* old.

Walking through the courtyard, he saw candles and lamps lit inside his home and what looked like the back of Stina's head, standing in the middle of the parlor. He inhaled sharply, relieved. Still, his heart was in his chest when he reached their door, terrified at what the scrawny soldier might have done.

Nikolaos pushed the door handle down and pulled the door, only to realize it was locked. Had the soldier locked it? But he hadn't more than thought it before he heard Rå's voice, and then the door opened a crack. "It's me," he said, surprised at how hoarse he sounded.

Rå opened the door all the way, eyes rounding with concern when she saw him. "Nikolaos, may Thor avenge them all with bolts of lightning."

He should have chuckled at her old-fashioned prayer but was so tired he couldn't even nod.

Rå reached for him and pulled him inside. "Help him get out of his clothes and wash!" she called to Stina. "I'll get him something to eat."

Nikolaos leaned against the wall and closed his eyes, dead horses swimming behind his eyelids. Then he felt Stina's hand on him, and he opened his eyes and met her concerned gaze. "Did the soldier leave? Are you...?" He couldn't bring himself to say it.

"Yes, Nikolaos, he left soon after you did. He stood by the door out here for a bit, but after that we didn't see him again." She unbuttoned his coat and helped him pull it off. "Sit on the chair so I can help you with your boots. They're bloody, and I don't want you trailing death in here."

He sat down on their little hallway chair, looking down at his feet with surprise. He hadn't noticed the blood. There must have been a lot, his boots were full of it and something else, something that looked like mud but wasn't. He gagged, then without control, vomited straight down between his legs. "Pray forgive me." Forming the words made the vomit shift in his mouth, and he gagged again, but there was nothing left in his stomach, and he just dry heaved.

Stina pushed on his right thigh. "It's not your fault, Nikolaos. Move to the side so I can pull your boots off, then stand up so we can pull down your breeches."

He did as bid, then stood naked and cold in the hallway, watching her go get a washcloth and a blanket.

"Here's soup and herring, Nikolaos," Rå said when he was finally able to walk into the kitchen, wearing clean breeches and a warm shirt. "I've got a tincture of herbs too. I can feel that your body is aching."

"You can?" He sat down at the table.

"Yes," she said simply, pushing a mug with something thick and green in it toward him. "Drink this, it'll help."

Nikolaos swallowed it in one gulp, trying not to grimace. It tasted foul. How did the other men feel? If he felt like this, human men must be incredibly sore. Come to think of it, it was very unusual for him to have aches at all. Surprised, he looked up, catching Stina's eyes. "I never react like this. I've not felt achy like this since Abluna was alive, and I cut myself with an ax."

"Never have you had to drag dead horses all day long either, Nikolaos. I've never seen its like. Rå and I went out to look and couldn't believe it, seeing how all the men had to push and shove the poor, poor horses."

"And drag them," Rå added. "I would've thought they use carts for them." She frowned.

Ravenous now, Nikolaos took a couple of spoonfuls of the soup before he answered. "There were a few, but there aren't enough horses alive." Except the army's then, unhelpful devils. He pushed down a surge of anger.

Rå met his eyes, and he felt what he assumed was a flair from her back hole in response. "They should've sent for horses from the countryside. There must be farmers with horses or oxen," she said.

"The Danes had already taken them from the farmers around here," Nikolaos said, glad that Hindrich wasn't there to see it. It would break his heart.

***

It took weeks. Nikolaos would never forget the way the heavy bodies splashed when they were thrown into the water. As each dead horse fell, Nikolaos looked across the sound to Denmark and cursed its soil.

Chapter 83

Anno 1728

It was what they had decided to do. Rå, Nikolaos, and Stina so Nikolaos could stay with his wife until the day she died.

The first thing Rå noticed when she approached Hindrich's farm was that the main house was gone and replaced by a fine two-story house painted in a warm rusty red. There were two barns, one made of stone that she thought was the same as before and a new larger one made of wood beside it. It too, was painted in that warm rusty red. There were chickens and goats in front, laundry drying on a line. Children laughing somewhere.

As she neared the house, the front door opened, and a heavyset woman looked in her direction while shielding her face from the sun with her hand. Ekborg, Hindrich wife? The woman went back inside. Before long, three small children squeezed out the door and ran toward Rå.

"Good day, who are you?" one of them asked politely when they were close enough. A boy, just slightly bigger than the other two. Their little faces were round and healthy, and she saw Nikolaos' warm brown eyes in two of them. The third must take after someone else, scrawny with pale blue eyes and a mop of curly hair. It pained her to even think about what she was about to do.

"My name is Magda. I've come to speak to Hindrich. Is he your father?"

"No," the boy said and laughed, "he's our grandfather, he's inside with grandma."

"I see," Rå said and put her hand on his head.

The little ones took her by the hand and led her toward the house, leaving her at the front door, and then they ran off to go play somewhere. That was good. It would be easier to lie without children present.

She didn't need to knock. Hindrich appeared, strong and healthy looking, peering at her with a face already full of wrinkles.

He broke into a big smile, and she noticed he had all his teeth.

"Is it? Magda, it really *is* you."

She nodded, smiling a little, but made sure not to overdo it.

"Ekborg, come here! An old friend of my parents," Hindrich hollered into a spacious foyer. Then he stepped aside to let Rå enter. "You don't look a day older than last time I saw you, Magda. Are you drinking the doctor's water too?"

"No, but I've heard I age well, though under my scarf here, my hair is all gray. It's why I never take it off. I'm vain you see." A lie of course. She put her hand on his arm as if she needed help, keeping it there when he brought her through the house.

They entered a sunroom with two ornately carved sofas covered with thick blue cushions; even the armrests were covered. The sofas faced each other, and Hindrich helped her sit on the nearest one. She took her time, grabbing his arm firmly as she slowly lowered herself to the cushions. When Hindrich felt she was secure enough, he sat down opposite her, smiling.

"Hindrich, where's your wife? I want to speak to the both of you." She was going to say that she didn't have good news but decided to wait for Ekborg.

"She'll be here in a minute. She was baking, and I imagine she wanted to change her dress."

"I understand. You do very well here, I see. The house is new. Did Nikolaos' and Stina's home get too small?"

"Yes, we've had twelve children."

"Twelve! And three grandchildren as well, I noticed." Rå kept her face neutral, registering the number. Twelve must be tough for Ekborg.

"Only the youngest. The other two are neighbors. But they all call us grandma and grandpa," Hindrich said with a crooked smile exactly like Nikolaos'. He looked as though he was about to say something else but stopped when they heard steps along the wood floors.

Ekborg appeared, wearing a beautiful light blue dress with green trim. Her hair was plaited and tied together in a ball in the back, and she was wearing a thin white scarf covering just the back of her head and the plaits. She was not the woman Rå had seen shielding her eyes from the sun earlier. It must have been one of their maids.

After their introductions and when Ekborg was seated by her husband's side, Rå clasped her hands in front of her and met first Hindrich's eyes, then Ekborg's. "I'm afraid I've come with bad news. Your mother sent me. We have confirmation that Nikolaos… that your father is dead."

"What?" Hindrich slumped into the pillows on the sofa.

Ekborg stared at her, her eyes instantly filling with tears. She looked around for a handkerchief but didn't find one and let the tears fall as they may. Then she grabbed Hindrich's hand. His mouth was moving silently in prayer.

Rå looked down at her lap, giving them a moment of privacy. When she raised her head, Hindrich was looking at her.

"Magda, do tell us what's happened, and how is Mother?"

Rå nodded. "First, my sincere condolences to you." She stopped and looked into her lap again, collecting herself and preparing her lies. She hoped she looked subdued and sad. "Stina is devastated," she said after a time, "but is holding on the best she can. She told me that Nikolaos wrote to you a few months back. We're hoping you received his correspondence?"

"Yes, we received it. The postal service is good here. My father said he was traveling to Cremona with a man named Bendelin."

"Yes, and it was Bendelin who wrote to Stina with the news," Rå said. It was a complete lie. There was no Bendelin. Nikolaos had left on his own. Staying away for weeks so Stina would be seen alone while he looked for Rå so he could send her to give them the news. "Your father collapsed on the street. Bendelin felt it best to have him buried there. He said that he felt it wasn't… I have it here." Rå held up a finger, then opened the embroidered purse Stina had given her for the occasion and pulled out the letter with its broken seal. "Here," she said and handed it to Hindrich. It was Rå's handwriting, but they wouldn't be able to tell, as they had never seen it. "I'm so very sorry to be the one to tell you. I wish I had better news the first time I met you, Ekborg. I've heard so much about you."

Ekborg threw her a glance but quickly shifted her gaze back to the letter Hindrich was holding. She may not have heard or wasn't able to take it in. When they finished reading, Hindrich placed the letter on a side table. It too, was carved in the same ornate style as the sofas.

"He always looked so young," Hindrich said and finally looked directly at Rå. "It's hard to even imagine it. But he was older than Mother, and she's seventy now, I believe. Isn't she Ekborg?" he asked, sniffling and clearing his throat.

"Yes, I believe so. Stina was never truly the same after Elsebet died. She told me she wished that they had moved after the Danish occupation. Elsebet caught a plague because of poisoned air after the Danes killed all those horses. The miasma was awful, awful, for several months." Ekborg squeezed her lips into a thin line.

Rå nodded sympathetically, wondering how much they had learned of the utter horror from those days. "When did you see your parents last?"

"At Elsebet's funeral. No, that's not right. We've visited after that, after they moved to the new house out in Ramlösa. Stina never travels here," Ekborg said.

"Elsebet died in 1711, so it must have five or six years after that. They were well settled by then," Hindrich added, crossing his arms. He looked cold. "Do you think we can get Mother to move in with us? Would she, Magda?"

Rå waited before responding. They had prepared for this, but it was still hard. There was always too much to explain, so many details and arrangements that had been made so Nikolaos and Stina could stay together. They had left Ramlösa a month before Nikolaos' supposed death, settling in a new house in a place called Högestad where no one knew them.

"I don't believe she will. Maybe for short visits if that pastor is no longer here?"

"He's not," Ekborg said.

"And most of the sixmen from then have sons who've taken

over," Hindrich added.

"But not all?"

"No."

"You can always ask, but again, I don't think she will, especially since they just moved again."

"Then my father traveled right after moving to Högestad," Hindrich said, anger creeping into his voice. "No wonder he collapsed. He was old, it's too much to do all that at that age."

Rå nodded, making sure she looked appropriately sympathetic and disturbed by his statement. It had all been a ruse so Nikolaos could disappear right after the move so as not to be seen, leaving the spry old wife to take care of all the moving boxes with only outside help. "Your mother wants me to tell you she's hired a young man named Jonas. He's taking care of the property and the animals. It's the son of a friend of mine, and I can vouch for him. He's also a distant relation to Nikolaos. I forgot how exactly." It was what they had decided she should say. But it was Nikolaos posing as Jonas.

"Might be one of his aunt's great-grandchildren or one of the cousin's children. We never met any of them," Hindrich said.

"Ah, I see," Rå allowed herself a deep exhale. They had been nervous about how Hindrich would react. "You'll have to ask your mother. Will you travel to Högestad now? I'm sure your mother would like to see you."

Hindrich and Ekborg looked at each other. "We'll make arrangements. We'll leave as soon as we can."

"I'm glad to hear that. I shall leave the two of you now," Rå said, hiding her relief. It truly was terrible to lie like this. It was too hard to keep track of all the specifics.

"Don't you want to stay the night? Have supper with us?" Ekborg asked.

"I thank you kindly, but I must leave."

Rå pretended to try to stand, then waited for Hindrich to come and give her a hand. Grabbing it, she straightened up and stood for a moment as if testing her legs. "I'll be good now. But I'd be grateful for a hand going down the stairs at your front door."

Hindrich nodded, and then both he and Ekborg walked her out.

Rå looked into Hindrich's face and saw only earnestness there. It couldn't have been easy for them when Stina was accused. Still, they had stayed, taking care of the farm that Nikolaos loved so much. She wondered if there would be a way for him to get it back one day.

It was done.

Chapter 84

Högestad Anno 1745

"Who was it, Nikolaos?" Stina called from the parlor. She was sitting wrapped in her blankets in front of their new tile stove. They had it installed the year before. A luxury item. It was tall, almost reaching the ceiling, with shiny pale blue tiles painted in a dark blue leaf-like pattern. It had tiny copper doors about two handsbreadths from the floor that opened to a small fireplace.

"A letter, darling. Came by special messenger. It looks like an invitation."

"An invitation?" Stina turned around and held out her hand so she could take the letter from him. Her hand didn't shake much today, he noticed.

"I'll get you your spectacles."

"No, you read it, husband. I'm cold. I want my hands in the warmth," Stina said, handing the letter back and shoving her hand back under the blanket.

Nikolaos kissed her on the forehead and sat down on her footrest, moving her feet to the side to fit, then broke the seal, reading silently at first. It was indeed an invitation. "You've been invited to attend a gathering to honor Doctor Döbelius, Von Döbeln, rather." Nikolaos looked up briefly. "Remember how he was ennobled several years ago, Stina?"

"Yes, of course I do."

He smiled. "Then it says that it's a small... and intimate," he held up his hand and waved his finger in the air in a teasing fashion, making Stina laugh, "gathering to honor his work as a doctor, author, and scientist."

"Is the invitation from one of his children?"

Nikolaos looked at it again, then shook his head. "No, an academic, I think. Perhaps a student. Or a colleague from Lund's university. This is nice, Stina, a nice way to remember him. Appropriate now two years after his passing, isn't it?"

Stina looked at him silently. A single tear slid down her right cheek. "It is, Nikolaos. He was very kind to us when Elsebet was ill, personally bringing his water to her. Had it only helped."

"I know, darling." Nikolaos gently rubbed her hand. It was bony now and spotted with age. But she was strong, didn't have many aches or pains, just tired easily, and rested twice every day.

Stina had received a letter from Fredrik a few weeks earlier as well. But other than that, she didn't get mail often. Fredrik and the girls lived far from them now, up north in Umeå. Fredrik hadn't married again but the girls were doing well, nicely taken care of by a housemaid and an aunt. Nikolaos wondered if the aunt was actually Fredrik's mistress, but he had never mentioned his suspicion to Stina.

"Should we attend?"

Nikolaos looked up sharply, startled from his musings. "It's whatever you wish, Stina. You could ask Arna to go with you," he said, referring to the neighbor girl who helped Stina with the household.

"I want you to go with me, *Jonas*," she said. It wouldn't be appropriate to go with her. I should go with my relative."

"Then it's settled. We'll go together." He gently squeezed her foot.

* * *

Nikolaos leaned close to Stina on the driver's seat. "It's in these situations that I wish we hadn't done it. I don't like it. It would've been better if I had stayed your old man husband instead."

"No. You said yourself that it was too hard on you last time and that people were getting too suspicious. But you are an old man," she said and winked at him. "Older than me."

"Yes," he managed, but their familiar bantering didn't feel as fun as it usually did.

Physically, it was certainly easier. He could walk upright, speak with his normal clear voice, laugh, and smile, and not worry if people noticed his white teeth. He could run if he needed, bend down, and do all those things that young people took for granted. But emotionally it tore at his heart. They thought he was dead. All of them. Everyone they knew, except for Rå. And Stina was very old.

When they arrived, Nikolaos helped Stina down and took her arm, thanking the boy who would park their carriage and bring their horse around once it was over.

Nikolaos had expected a grand home, but they were at an official hall. It looked like a courthouse or a library. There was no sign above the door describing it or numerals dating the building. From the style, it looked like early seventeenth century, but he wasn't sure. People were waiting outside to be let in, standing around in smaller groups and speaking with each other in hushed tones. Most were dressed finely but not overly so, and not all the men wore wigs. Of the ones who did, even the older men were wearing the newer thinner wigs, tied with a bow at the back.

A woman leaning on the arm of her maid nodded at Stina. She must be indisposed in some way, maybe with a babe on the way or something else. Her skirts didn't reveal anything, but she was well covered with shawls. "It's hard to stand. I wish they would let us come inside even if we need to wait in there," the woman said.

"Yes, but I'm stronger than I look," Stina said, smiling.

The woman laughed. "I'm glad to hear it. And you have nice help, I see. Is it your grandson?"

"No, Jonas isn't my grandson. He's a helper of sorts, he drives me places and takes care of my garden and my home. He's a relative."

"I see. Did you know Von Döbeln well?"

"Yes, my husband was a musician, and he played at the inauguration of Ramlösa."

Nikolaos shifted his gaze to the maid. She met his eyes and nodded, acknowledging they were both in servitude.

"A musician!" the maid's employer exclaimed, clasping her hands together in front of her heart. "How lovely."

Then the door opened, and Nikolaos didn't hear Stina's

response. "Let's go inside, shall we," he said and took her by the elbow.

There were pews like in a church, but wider, more spread out, and with comfortable cushions. Up in front was a display that looked like medicinal bottles, crystal glasses filled with water, and books. At least it looked like it from where they were standing. Nikolaos hoped it was his work on the history of Lund's University that von Döbeln had written just a few years before his death. There had been articles about it in several newspapers.

Nikolaos helped Stina to her seat and was just about to sit down beside her when he froze. Lord Oxensköld was heading to a seat two rows up from them with none other than Mistress Esmeralda. A knot of fear tightened his stomach. There would likely be a few others he would recognize too, but there was nothing to do other than play indifferent and avoid bumping into people he knew directly.

Aging had been hard on Lord Oxensköld. He was bent and frail, breathing with his mouth open and grabbing the pew in front of him for support. Mistress Esmeralda's face was completely covered with wrinkles now. Other than that, she seemed healthier than she did at the inauguration. The waters must have done wonders for her.

Nikolaos and Stina settled into their seats, intentionally leaving space between them. Not that anyone would think he had an old woman for a wife, but still.

There were speakers and a musical performance. He tried to concentrate on everything, but his eyes kept wandering across the aisles and pews to see if he recognized anyone else. One of the farmers that had housed those first Ramlösa patients was sitting to their left, and he recognized several of the doctor's patients as well. They looked so old. Time had moved again and left him behind.

"Several people are here that I know just so you're aware," he whispered to Stina when they stood up at the end.

"Good to know, Jonas," she said, patting his arm. Age had shrunk her, and she had to bend her head back to look at his face.

They touched so much now, knowing that soon they'd be apart.

They were ushered into a different room to intake the promised refreshments. Several tables were set up with fine white damask and tableware. Nikolaos spotted Mistress Esmeralda and Lord Oxensköld again and got a better look at her. She supported herself on a cane with a silver top but stood straight and steady. Merchant Fleisher was likely dead then since she was here with the Lord. He tried to recall if Lord Oxensköld had been close to them back then but couldn't remember.

As they made their way forward at Stina's slow but steady pace, Lord Oxensköld and Mistress Esmeralda moved sideways, right into their path. They had no choice but to pass them. Nikolaos steeled himself, making sure he kept his facial expression neutral. It did nothing. Lord Oxensköld looked up sharply and narrowed his eyes. Then he turned to Mistress Esmeralda to say something, but by then they had passed them, and Nikolaos didn't see her reaction. He exhaled, deciding not to say anything to Stina.

Leaning down so she would hear him, he said instead, "Are you able to stand for a bit? I'll go see if I can find out where it would be appropriate for us to sit."

"Of course, Jonas." She nodded to a gentleman who accidentally bumped into her. "I'm quite well. No need to fret," she said, speaking to them both.

Nikolaos quickly made his way through the crowd. A footman was standing by the wall, looking bored. "Good sir, are there specific seating arrangements?" Nikolaos asked him, hoping he was addressing him correctly. The footman just glanced at him, then looked forward again. Nikolaos frowned and was about to ask again when he noticed a guest approaching him.

"May I be of assistance?" the man asked, smiling kindly.

"Thank you. Yes, my relative and I aren't sure where we're supposed to sit, if there are specific seating arrangements."

"I see. Did you know Doctor von Döbeln?"

"No, sir. My relative does, did, I mean."

"Ah, no matter, you and your relative shall come sit with us. We're intellectuals here and don't take conventions so seriously," he said conspiratorially. "I was a colleague. I'm a doctor. Doctor von Döbeln took me under his wing many years ago. I was doing very poorly in the beginning, you see."

"You weren't a good doctor?" Nikolaos asked, trying to sound young and impulsive. He regretted it immediately; it just sounded rude.

"Well," the doctor said, a twinkle in his eye, "I hope I was. Personal loss had me lose focus though. Doctor von Döbeln helped me on my feet."

"My apologies. I didn't mean to disrespect your expertise."

The doctor shook his head. "Eh, I see how I may have contributed to that misunderstanding. Apology accepted." He gestured for Nikolaos to follow him, then stopped, looking over his shoulder. "Walk beside me so you can take me to your companion."

Nikolaos fell into step beside him and gestured discreetly in Stina's direction. She acknowledged them with a smile, looking relieved that he was back. "Here we are. This is Stina Andersdotter," he said to the doctor, taking a polite step back. "Stina, Doctor von Döbeln's colleague has invited you to sit with him."

"Oh, how delightful," Stina said but grabbed Nikolaos' arm nervously. "Can Jonas join me as well?"

"A pleasure," the doctor said, bowing. "And yes, certainly. Follow me, I'll go make sure we hold seats for you." He left brusquely without checking if they were coming.

Nikolaos and Stina followed him as best they could. It was crowded, and people were blocking their view while they crossed the floor. When they arrived, the doctor was already waiting for them, standing with a chair pulled out for Stina, smiling broadly. To Nikolaos' sheer disbelief, Mistress Esmeralda was also sitting there, smiling as sweetly as the doctor. And right across from her sat Lord Oxensköld.

Rusty devils! Nikolaos forced down his shock, standing numb as the doctor resolutely pulled Stina from his grip and helped her sit. He had no choice but to join them, acknowledging everyone with a small bow before sitting down, making sure his eyes didn't stay too long on their faces. They should never have come here. It was stupid. He looked at Stina, trying to somehow convey who they were sitting with, but she was oblivious. He hadn't heard if the doctor introduced Mistress Esmeralda or if she told Stina what her name was, but Stina may have misheard or thought it was someone else by the same name. She had never met her in person, so there was no way she could know.

With his heart in his throat, Nikolaos reached for a linen napkin and placed it in his lap, discreetly watching Mistress Esmeralda pick up a green marzipan ball from a bowl and very unladylike pop the whole piece into her mouth.

"These are delicious. You must try them," Mistress Esmeralda said when she finished chewing, smiling at Stina.

"I'd be delighted," Stina said and grabbed one, taking a small bite.

There was nothing to do but pretend that there was nothing wrong. Nikolaos turned to the doctor who had sat down across from him. "Thank you. I appreciate the help so Stina can sit for a while. I apologize, I never caught your name?"

"Doctor Lindbom."

"I'm Jonas. Again, thank you. A pleasure meeting you, Doctor Lindbom," Nikolaos said.

"Jonas," Lord Oxensköld broke in, "I've been looking at you. You remind me of a fella Doctor von Döbeln hired many years back. It's rather uncanny, I must say."

Nikolaos turned toward him slowly, trying to think of how to respond. Normally he would have gone with their official story and explained that he was a distant relative of Stina's musician husband, but he obviously couldn't do that with him and Mistress Esmeralda there. "Oh, how funny," he said instead, hoping his nerves didn't show. Lord Oxensköld kept staring at his face, scrutinizing him. The silence became awkward.

Then Doctor Lindbom changed the subject. "It's kind of you, Jonas, to bring Stina here. As a good friend and colleague of von Döbeln, it warms my grieving heart. I still miss him."

Nikolaos smiled at him, relieved. "I heard he was a good

man."

Lord Oxensköld finally looked away and started talking to Doctor Lindbom about something else.

Stina was deeply involved in a conversation with Mistress Esmeralda. It would have been delightful to see two old women speaking intimately if it hadn't been for the fact that Stina was unknowingly talking to someone she held responsible for much ill in their life.

Nikolaos decided that enough time had passed. It felt too uncomfortable, and Stina would probably get mad at him when he told her as it was. They should leave before Lord Oxensköld, or Mistress Esmeralda for that matter, said something else. It was discourteous, but it couldn't be helped. He pushed his chair out slowly, then stood as he turned to Stina, "We ought to go look at the display, then we need to get you home."

She looked at him, surprise apparent on her face. He bored his eyes into hers, and she finally understood the urgency in his expression. "Of course, you're right, Jonas."

Nikolaos let out a slow breath, thanking God that her mind was as sharp as the day they met. Pushing his chair back, he noticed Doctor Lindbom giving Stina a strange eye.

"If you don't mind me asking before you leave, could you tell me where you acquired that beautiful locket?" he said, leaning forward slightly.

"Why, thank you. My late husband. It was a gift."

"May I see it?" There was a subdued undertone to his voice.

Stina threw a nervous glance in Nikolaos' direction. But then she smiled. "Of course, you may. Jonas, will you help me?" She pointed to her neck.

Something in the way the doctor sounded told Nikolaos that he ought to get Stina out of there, but he couldn't think of something appropriate to contradict her with. He walked around to stand behind her chair, gently lifted some strands of hair that had come loose from her bun, unclasped the necklace, and handed it to her. He had bought the chain for her about ten years earlier when the ribbon had become worn.

Doctor Lindbom took the locket from her hand without a word, swallowing audibly as he moved the locket this way and that. His hands shook for a moment and then stilled.

Everyone was watching silently.

"May I open it?"

"You may. The drawing is of my late daughter. I've meant to get a proper miniature, but I never have," Stina said. She didn't turn to look at him, but Nikolaos could feel her wanting to. He moved to place a hand on her shoulder but stopped and put it back by his side.

Doctor Lindbom opened it, then quickly closed it again. It snapped loud enough for Nikolaos to see a brief spark of gray around the doctor's hands. When he spoke, his voice was unsteady. "If you don't mind me asking such a personal question, but where and when did you get this?"

"It was a gift from my husband. I can't remember when. It's quite a few years ago now." Stina tried to look at Nikolaos behind her but couldn't turn her head all the way. "Jonas, did I tell you when he gave me this?"

"I couldn't say, I don't think you've mentioned it," Nikolaos said flatly. Now he placed his hand on her shoulder, just for a moment. Something wasn't right.

"I'm not quite sure what to say. But that locket was once my wife's. I recognize the flaw beneath the clasp," Doctor Lindbom said and traced his index finger along a little bump in the gold. "She had a miniature of our son in it. I can't for the life of me understand how you can have it."

Sweat dripped down Nikolaos' face all at once.

"As I said it was a gift. My late husband gave it to me," Stina said. There was a catch in her voice.

Mistress Esmeralda put her hand on her arm and smiled. "It's beautiful. Your husband must have been a kind man to give you such a gift. Who was he, your husband? Are you widowed since long? I lost mine fifteen years ago."

Nikolaos held his breath, ready to pick Stina up and carry her out of there if need be. Any moment now, he would be exposed. He should have made an excuse and refused to sit with them.

"He was a merchant and a musician, we..." Stina stopped herself, and Nikolaos could feel her tension as she realized that she hadn't fully comprehended the situation. "Nikolaos, his name was Nikolaos."

"I threw this in Råå River many, many years ago," Doctor Lindbom interjected. "My wife and son died in an accident, and I couldn't bear looking at it. This is remarkable. Someone must have found it somehow and brought it home. Fishing perhaps. Didn't your husband ever tell you how he found it or where he bought it? And was there a miniature of a little boy in it when he gave it to you?"

Nikolaos stared at him, moving so he was standing next to Stina instead of behind her. How could it be his locket? It was just too much of a coincidence. Maybe God was punishing him. He remembered it well, how the tiny likeness of the round-cheeked boy floated away in the water, how he had tried to reach it.

"No, there wasn't," Stina said, her voice tense now.

Lord Oxensköld was breathing laboriously and grabbed hold of the table for support.

Esmeralda's eyes flashed to him, wide with shock. She let out a small gasp, then turned back to Stina with a look full of disdain. "Did you say your husband's name was Nikolaos, a *musician*? And you have a necklace that Doctor Lindbom lost in a river." It was a statement, not a question. "I knew it! I knew that Doctor von Döbeln was wrong back then. It's her *husband* who dragged our workers into the river with him, and then he flooded our stable!" she shrieked.

Lord Oxensköld stared first at Esmeralda then at Stina. "Are *you* his widow? Näcken's widow? Lord, in heaven have mercy. It was true then after all," he said, voice crackling with age and lack of air.

"Pardon me?" Nikolaos said, expecting Lord Oxensköld and Mistress Esmeralda to recognize him for who he was. But they barely gave him a glance.

Stina looked stunned. Her hand shook, making the china on

the table rattle.

"I don't understand. What are you talking about?" Doctor Lindbom asked, unsuccessfully trying to make eye contact with someone.

Nikolaos took the opportunity to bend down to offer Stina his arm. Once she had a steady grip, she stood up and bored her eyes into Mistress Esmeralda. "It's you then, isn't it? I should've understood when you introduced yourself. But forgive me, for I'm just an old widow like yourself and I forget names easily. You destroyed our lives. It was because of you that I was falsely accused and had to move to Helsingborg, bringing our heartbroken daughter with us, her betrothal broken up. She died you know. Of the plague. Had you not accused my late husband of such vile, vile things she'd be alive today. Shame on you!" Then she reached across the table and snatched her locket from the doctor. "This is mine. Are you accusing an old woman of stealing? Shame on you as well."

Lord Oxensköld's mouth hung wide open.

"Jonas, I need you to take me home," Stina said and walked away, pulling him with her, strong as if she were a young girl.

The last they heard was Doctor Lindbom's questions, "What's happening? I pray you, do explain."

***

Once they were finally seated in their carriage, Nikolaos was so relieved that no one had followed them out that he felt weak in the knees. He wrapped Stina in her blanket, then covered her with his own.

"You'll freeze, Jonas."

"I won't. Let's head home. Rest against my shoulder a while. Or do you want to stay at an inn? We have hours to go."

"No, I can't rest, Nikolaos," she said, forgetting herself for a moment. It didn't matter. The street was empty, and no one heard. The only sounds were the hooves and wheels on hard-packed crusty snow. "Why didn't you tell me. I don't understand. How could you expose me to these vile, vile people? I'm an old woman."

"Stina, I know. I tried to get your attention. Doctor Lindbom was already helping you sit down when I realized who we'd be sitting with. I didn't know what to do, Stina. You had never met them. I was afraid to make it worse. Pray forgive me."

"How could it be his locket? It's unbelievable."

"I don't know." He let go of the reins and threw both hands in the air. "It's like the Devil planned it. At least he seemed to think that someone had fished it up. It could've been worse."

"Worse? How?"

Nikolaos threw a glance over his shoulder to make sure they were alone. There was a carriage behind them, but it was far back. "They seemed to realize that it was Näcken who fished it out of there, but what if they had understood who *I* was?"

***

They worried, expecting sixmen to approach them at church or come knocking on the door of their home. Nothing happened. Soon they stopped talking about it. Nikolaos didn't tell Stina, but he was glad she had told Mistress Esmeralda off.

Chapter 85

Stina was over ninety and was still doing well. There had been no real difference the last few years, and they counted each day as a blessing. Nikolaos had known several very old people in his life. Sometimes he wondered if it had to do with him. Stina mentioned it once too, and both she and Rå were convinced that his horses took on his powers, grew longer, and lived for an abnormally long time. Maybe humans did as well.

It was November. One of those windy and cold, moist days that got into your bones. Nikolaos was chopping wood, and Stina was in the barn feeding the animals when two men on horseback trotted toward the house, stopping right in front. They both wore short wigs under tri-cornered hats and wore long modern coats. They looked comically identical except that one of them was much taller than the other.

"Pardon me, is Stina Andersdotter still alive?" the shorter of the two asked.

"Indeed, she is," Nikolaos said.

Both men dismounted and tied their horses to their newly painted white fence. Neither of them asked for permission. It annoyed him, but he let it be.

"We'd like to speak with her. Is she of sound mind still?" the same man asked and walked into their garden. The other one stayed by the fence.

"She sure is. How can she be of service? I'll fetch her." Nikolaos crossed the short distance to the barn and opened the door, bumping into Stina who was on her way out.

"I'm here. What's this about?" she asked, looking curiously at the approaching man.

"You need to come with us, Stina Andersdotter. The twelvemen have questions for you." He lifted his hat as if coming to say good morning.

"*Pardon* me. What could they possibly want to speak to her about?" Nikolaos asked, shocked. It came so suddenly he was taken completely off guard. Out of the corner of his eye, he saw Stina's knees buckle, and he instinctively reached out and put his arm around her before she stumbled.

"It's not for us to say. But we're under strict orders to bring her to Herrestad. Who are you?"

"The great-grandson of my husband's cousin," Stina said in a clear, steady voice. "I'll go. I can imagine what it's about. You can't scare me anymore. Jonas, would you go pack my things?"

Nikolaos stared at her, shaking his head in warning. "You shouldn't go with them. I'm sure there's been a mistake."

"There's no mistake. Get her things now, then get your horse ready. You can come with her, but only if you don't cause trouble. I advise you to do as we say, or you can stay here."

Stina met Nikolaos' gaze, holding it, then nodded. It was almost as if she had been expecting it.

They could go out through the back door. If he carried her and ran, there was a chance they could make it. "I need Stina to come with me. I don't know where her things are," Nikolaos said, eyes still on Stina's face. He felt awful, it had been incredibly stupid not to ask what they wanted first.

"That's out of the question. Get whatever you think she needs. And do it now, we have to go," the guard said, a veiled threat under his breath. Maybe they weren't guards, but it felt like it.

Nikolaos exchanged another glance with Stina, pleading, then gave up and hurried inside. He didn't know what she meant that she needed. All he could think of was to get her another shawl and her warm blouse. She was already wearing her coat.

When he came back out, the other guard had entered their garden, and both stood wide-legged with their arms crossed in front of her as if they thought his frail old wife could run away. He shook his head in disgust.

They allowed Stina to ride with Nikolaos. It crossed his mind to get into a gallop and escape, but there was no way to get away from them. The two men had them sandwiched between their horses, flank to flank. He tried to ask questions, but they stared straight ahead as if they hadn't heard. Stina didn't say a word either. The silence felt awkward and oppressive.

Finally, they stopped in front of a small stone house. The shorter of them immediately grabbed hold of Nikolaos' horse as they dismounted, then gestured for him to help Stina down.

As he did, the other guard went to open the door. Stina walked stiffly toward him. Nikolaos grabbed her arm to support her, feeling his cheeks flush with shame. It had been years since she had been on horseback. He should have insisted on putting her in their carriage.

"Here, Stina Andersdotter, you'll be questioned in there. Your relative can wait right here," the tall guard said formally, speaking for the first time since he and his companion had arrived at their home.

A small room with a bench preceded a big room with twelve chairs around a rectangular table. A twelveman was seated on the far end with a quill and paper at the ready, wearing an old-fashioned long black wig. A wigless man was standing beside him, wearing a common linen shirt and breeches. Nikolaos got the sense that he wasn't one of the twelvemen. The tall guard pulled Stina away from Nikolaos and gently but firmly pushed her inside, then closed the door.

Nikolaos felt a hot rush of anger. "I want to be present. She's over ninety years old and might need help."

"No, that's never allowed. But you may sit out here if you wish. We're going for dinner. If you want to leave, I don't care. Front door is open and unguarded." At that, he walked out.

Nikolaos stared after him, then took one long step to the closed door, pulled down the handle, and pushed. It didn't give, someone, the wigless man he supposed, was leaning on it. Nikolaos looked at the waiting bench, considering, then decided to stay by the door to be as close to Stina as possible. He heard a chair get dragged across the floor and paper being moved about. Then silence.

When the twelveman began, it had been silent so long it

startled him.

"Stina Andersdotter, I'm Twelveman Gunnar. I'll be asking the questions," he said in a loud voice. Nikolaos heard every word. "Did you live in Helsingborg with a fiddler that called himself Nikolaos? Then in Ramlösa after that? And now in Högestad?"

"Yes."

"Yes? I'm glad to hear you telling me the truth. It'll be better for you this way. Are you aware of who he is?"

"Yes."

Nikolaos frowned.

"I'll try to describe this in a different way, Stina Andersdotter, just to make sure you truly understand what I'm asking you. The man who was posing as your husband isn't just a man, is he?" A pause followed, and when Stina didn't reply, he kept going. "We have witnesses who have sworn that he pushed people into a river and had congress with them, plucked a gold locket from Råå River, flooded a stable, and made a whole group of people fall down unconscious. Can you confirm this, Stina Andersdotter?"

"No."

Nikolaos didn't realize he had been holding his breath until he felt his body gasp for air. The guard by the door shuffled his feet at the sound.

"But you admit that your husband wasn't a man but Näcken himself?" Twelveman Gunnar asked.

"Yes, but we weren't married, good Twelveman Gunnar. Even so, we had several children."

Nikolaos' jaw dropped. What was she doing? Over the beating of his heart, he heard the twelveman continue his questioning.

"Children? You have children with Näcken!" He sounded stunned. "Where are they?"

"Our daughter died of the plague, and some died when they were babes or before they were born."

Nikolaos couldn't stand it anymore. He pushed on the door with all his weight and managed to get it open, shoving both it and the guard all the way to the wall. "I've had enough of this!" he shouted. "You're insulting her, and your questions are ludicrous. She's an old woman, and as you clearly have noticed she's confusing things. I don't approve of your treatment of her."

Twelveman Gunnar actually laughed, and then he shrugged. "Eh, I'm not so sure of that. But you can take her home. We're done here. She'll be called in a month or two. She's admitted it so there's no reason for us to hold her."

Stina calmly got to her feet without assistance. "Let's go home, Jonas," she said, waiting for him to take her by the arm.

Twelveman Gunnar waited for them to get through the door and then followed. Once on the other side, he stopped and patted Nikolaos' shoulder, indicating that he wanted to talk to him. "As I said, she's admitting it. These cases are serious, but this seems to be a long time ago, and your relative here is old. She'll be called again. Then we'll see. Take her home for now." He gave another nod, then walked out, pointing to the front door with his thumb. "Your horse is tied up right outside."

Nikolaos was so angry that he didn't say a word the whole way home, perversely hoping it reminded Stina of the silent treatment from the men earlier. When they arrived, he helped her dismount but let her go inside alone while he put the horse in the stable. He should have helped her with the front stairs, but he didn't care.

She was making eggs when he joined her inside, his almost ninety-five-year-old wife who had been riding for several hours after being questioned by a twelveman. A wave of tenderness and guilt came over him. "Sit, I'll finish it," he said and took her place at the hearth. Turning her eggs, he let them cook while he brought bread and butter to the table, then cut her a winter apple in paper-thin slices. The eggs were brown and crispy at the edges the way she liked it by the time he finished that, and he put them on a plate and sat down opposite her, pushing the food toward her.

"Nikolaos I..."

"What were you thinking?" he interrupted, his earlier tenderness replaced by new anger. "They could have imprisoned you. You've been through it before!" He screamed the last words and abruptly got up and went to get some spring water from the carafe, drinking directly from it and downing it as if it would compensate for rapids.

"Nikolaos, I'm tired. I'm tired of lying, I don't…"

"Tired of lying?" He slammed the carafe to the table, making her jump. It was a good thing it was made of metal and not glass.

"Quiet Nikolaos, if you don't let me speak, you'll never understand. Can you promise to let me finish?"

He shook his head irritably but then nodded and sat back down.

"Nikolaos, I've had a feeling about this ever since Doctor Döbelius', I mean von Döbeln's, memorial. I knew it would be just a matter of time. And I was right." She inhaled sharply. "They could get to Hindrich and his family or to Fredrik and his and Elsebet's children. But if they hang me, then that'll be that. I'm an old woman. A year or two is neither here nor there. This will end with me."

Nikolaos rubbed his hands over his face with exasperation. "Stina you can't…" He shook his head, starting again. "If they found you, they can find Hindrich and the rest of our family. You even admitted that you have children with me. That was incredibly stupid."

"I knew you'd say that, Nikolaos. But I never told them about Hindrich, only of our dead babies and dead daughter. If they're dead, they can't be questioned. I'm the last in the line, and you'll be left alone when I'm gone. And Nikolaos, there are too many horrible rumors about you. I want people to know the truth. That you're a kind and caring man who loves his family. A man who's loyal and takes care of me, sleeps next to me in the bed even though I'm an old ugly woman."

"Lord have mercy, Stina. This is… this is madness. You can't do this."

"Yes, I can. I've always known who you are. I'm tired of hiding it from everyone else. People should learn to accept you,

Nikolaos, and not be so afraid of you. It's not right that you should always have to hide. Besides it's too late. I told them already."

He stared at her, too upset to find the right words. Maybe she was losing her mind a bit, forgetting things even though he had never noticed it. Leaning back in his chair, he stretched his arms over his head, then let his body fall forward, his elbows landing on the table with a thump.

She took a bite of one of her apple slices. "If I admit it, then they won't search for more information, and that would be that. They won't go looking for Hindrich and Ekborg, or for Fredrik, or any of their children. They'll be done. I want to do this for my son and grandchildren, Nikolaos. Especially since you're not here to protect them." She looked determined.

"Not here? Should something happen then I'll of course help."

"You're pretending to be someone else."

"But you said just now that you wanted to tell them so I wouldn't need to hide anymore. Which is it?" he asked, sounding harsher than he intended.

It startled her, and he thought he had finally talked her out of it. "You're right. I did say that. But it doesn't matter. I've decided."

He stood up, shoved his chair under the table and walked out.

***

Nikolaos was wet and cold when he made his way back. Their neighbors' homes lay dark. It must be very late.

Stina was still sitting at the table by the window when he entered. The fire had gone out, and the room felt icy. Ignoring her, he crouched in front of the hearth, lit some kindling, and added two logs. Once the flames engulfed both, he pulled off his wet clothes and hung them to dry on a chair. Then he walked naked across the house and lit the tile stove in the parlor. Leaving the copper door open, he spread a blanket on Stina's chair to warm it, then went upstairs to get dressed.

Stina had been heating milk and honey for them when he came back down to the kitchen. She stood straight and strong, pouring the hot milk with a ladle into their mugs. From her backside like this, she looked no older than fifty.

He went to her, then wrapped his arms around her and kissed her neck. "I love you, Stina. Don't call yourself an old ugly woman ever again. Besides I prefer older women," he mumbled into her ear.

She kissed his cheek and pulled herself out of his embrace, reaching for his mug and handing it to him. "I love you too, darling. Do you feel better?"

"Yes," he said, keeping his gaze on her as they went into the parlor.

"You warmed the blanket for me. I thank you," she said and sat down.

"You sat in the cold the whole time I was gone, Stina. It's not good to catch a chill like that."

Stina scooted over to the side in her chair, patting the narrow space between her and the armrest so he could sit with her.

It was too narrow, and he pulled her into his lap instead. It reminded him of the time he was in the cell with Old Karin, how she curled up in his lap like a cat. They had pulled her off him, and they killed her. He shivered.

"You're cold too, Nikolaos. You walk around naked too much. How did your clothes get so wet? I've told you not to go in dressed."

"I didn't. They fell in when I got out. And I'm not cold. It was more like a shudder. I was remembering when Old Karin was taken from me. They hung her, Stina, and they tortured her. Her being old and a woman didn't stop them one bit. She was ninety-seven." He turned to look at her.

"Jon was as well," Stina said quietly, meeting his eyes.

"I know. Can you blame me for being angry with you? And drink your milk. You're still freezing."

Stina drank a bit but didn't answer. The rims of her eyes

were red, and her eyelids were swollen. She must have been crying when he was out. He swallowed a pang of guilt.

"I can't lose you like that, Stina. That's why I got so angry. You can't possibly understand what torture does to a person. I can't let you willingly walk into something like that. It's madness. You saw what they did to Jon."

"Yes, you've said. Several times." She sighed. "But Nikolaos, I love you and you've helped me since the day I met you. Now it's my turn to reciprocate. I want people to know you're a nice man."

"But I'm not. People die. You know that." Still after all this time, his heart raced when he admitted it to her, reminding him of that horrible fight they had in Ramlösa when she almost left him. It was almost fifty years ago.

"Yes, but it's of no fault of your own. All you do is to get in the water. I've never even seen you kill a rat."

He let out a frustrated gasp, "But they didn't recognize me at von Döbeln's gathering, Stina. What's the point?"

Chapter 86

There was no talking her out of it. Each time they argued about it, Stina pointed out that she had already told the twelveman that she wasn't denying anything.

Then in early March, Nikolaos was sitting at his desk by the south window when he spotted a fine carriage approaching. It stopped in front of the house, and then Twelveman Gunnar climbed down, accompanied by another man. Nikolaos stood up, fear settling itself like a stone in his chest. Stina was asleep, so he hurried through the house to get to the door before they knocked. He just made it.

Twelveman Gunnar, old fashioned wig askew, stood with his hand at the ready when Nikolaos opened the door. Startled, both men retreated a few paces down the front steps.

Seizing the moment, Nikolaos stepped outside. "How can I help you, gentlemen?" he asked, looking pointedly at the twelveman, hoping he seemed confident.

"I have a letter of appointment. Stina Andersdotter shall appear at Göta Royal Court in a week and a half's time. I'm here to offer my service to bring her."

Nikolaos blinked, trying to focus. If they were bringing her to Göta Royal Court, it was serious. He felt like crying, but he looked the twelveman straight in the face. "If you wouldn't mind, good sir, let me speak to you for a moment." He threw a glance at the bedroom window. "In private. Let's speak in the garden." He pointed to it and to Högestad Castle which was just visible through the bare apple tree branches. "We have a nice view of the castle as you see."

"Who are you again?" Twelveman Gunnar asked, ignoring Nikolaos' attempt at small talk.

"My name is Jonas. A relative. She's too old to live alone."

"Yes, yes of course. By the way, Kurt here is my brother."

"I see," Nikolaos glanced at the brother briefly. "Anyway, I don't see why she has to go through with this. Jönköping is far, and Stina is very old. It'll be hard on her."

Twelveman Gunnar looked at him blankly.

Irritated, Nikolaos hid a sigh and continued. "The questions you asked of her in November came, if I understand it correctly, after she attended an Honors Celebration for Doctor von Döbeln. It was a few years ago now, but one of them seemed to think that she was wearing his wife's necklace. Is this correct?"

"Yes," Twelveman Gunnar said." A locket."

Nikolaos gave a cold chuckle, eying both men. "Truly, gentlemen, isn't that quite ridiculous?"

Twelveman Gunnar shrugged. "Well, I don't know about that. But the locket seems to be a secondary issue. There are witnesses claiming that the man she said to be married to wasn't a man at all but Näcken himself. It's said that he dragged people into a stream and had congress with them."

Nikolaos raised an eyebrow, feeling nothing. It was as if he were talking about someone else.

"But as I mentioned when I saw you last. This was a long time ago and the courts need to get the information on this while they still can. Your relative has an opportunity to help. It's important that the courts know the truth. It's for the safety of our citizens. She's already admitted that she was with him. I say that the courts would be grateful for her information so they can get to the bottom of things."

"But her husband is dead. How's this helping?"

"*Is* he dead? Where's he buried?" Kurt asked.

Nikolaos was momentarily thrown. He cleared his throat to get his bearings. "Stina's husband died while traveling. Unfortunately, his body wasn't transferred here. He's buried somewhere in Cremona, I believe."

Twelveman Gunnar and Kurt exchanged a glance.

An awkward silence followed, but Nikolaos held his ground, waiting as if he didn't think anything of it.

Finally, Twelveman Gunnar shrugged. "Well, as for now, get her ready to travel. Kurt has permission for us to borrow one of the carriages from the castle, so she'll be comfortable. It'll take about three days to get there. Something like that, maybe a little faster.

We'll be back in a week to collect her. It should be enough time to get there when they want her," he said and started to leave.

Nikolaos felt anger settle like a stone in his stomach. "Hold on, Twelveman Gunnar," he called after him, grabbing his shoulder. "Are you telling me that the people in the castle know she's going to court? We have our own carriage; you could have asked us first."

Twelveman Gunnar pulled his shoulder out of his grip with obvious irritation. "It's only some servants living there. What is it to you if *they* know?"

Nikolaos almost spit on the ground. "Servants have wicked tongues, same as anyone. You should be ashamed of yourselves, spreading rumors about an old woman like this. Stina is kind, she doesn't deserve this."

"Rumors? That's for the courts to determine. We'll leave now. But know you're being watched. Don't try to take her anywhere!"

Then he and Kurt left, walking out of their garden, not caring that they stepped on the first yellow and blue flowers of the year.

***

It was strange to be back in Jönköping after so many years. Nikolaos was nervous they would bump into someone they had known fifty years earlier. He worried they would be housed at the same inn across from the courthouse, that the innkeeper would still be there, and that Secretary Bödkers would be at the courthouse, no matter how old he was. But he needn't have feared. The inn was gone, replaced by pot makers, a tile stove shop on the corner, and next to that, a doctor. They were taken to a lodging house behind the courthouse. It wasn't very expensive, but Stina had to pay for it herself, and Nikolaos resented it. They would likely charge her for the travel as well.

***

That afternoon, Twelveman Gunnar ushered them through

the courthouse, passing the room where Nikolaos had his meeting with Secretary Bödkers all those years ago. It looked the same, but there were two desks now, and it was messier, full of logbooks and papers lying around in a disorderly fashion, even some on the floor. They hurried past it and entered a smaller room with seating along the walls and a closed door. There were two women there, sitting on opposite sides of the room from each other. One appeared to be in her late forties or early fifties, the other around twenty-five or thirty. The younger one threw a nervous glance at Twelveman Gunnar.

Nikolaos had only just helped Stina sit down when a man opened the door. His wig was short and white, tied with a ribbon in the back, and he wore no coat, just a simple shirt.

"You'll each be questioned in here," the man said, waiving them in. "You can come in together." Then he noticed Nikolaos and narrowed his eyes. "You're her grandson? Family isn't usually part of this."

"I'm not. I'm an assistant of sorts."

The man shrugged. "You can come along and help her to her seat. Once you have, go sit off to the side. You're not to interrupt." He gestured toward a row of chairs in front of a podium.

Once Stina was seated, Nikolaos didn't even have time to say anything to her before a guard appeared behind him, grabbed him by the arm, and led him to a chair diagonally behind Stina. After that, he went to stand by the wall beside him. Nikolaos swallowed his irritation. At least he would be able to keep an eye on her like this. He could see her whole face in profile.

The courtroom, if you could call it that, was quiet. The man with the short wig had gone to stand by the window and remained there with his hands behind his back. He looked calm, more bored than someone full of anticipation. Nikolaos turned around, scanning the room for Twelveman Gunnar, but didn't see him. Had he left? It seemed a strange thing to do after going through all the trouble to bring them.

Then the door opened, and a man strode in. Walking purposely across the floor, he slammed a bunch of papers and a scroll on the podium. He had a similar wig to the man by the window but wore a proper coat and a collar wrapped tightly around his neck with the ends long, covering the front of his chest. It was the judge.

He began to sort through his papers. After a brief glance at the scroll, he tossed it aside and settled on a small sheet of paper. After studying it for a few minutes, he turned to the women and said, "We'll start now. Who is Annika Svensdotter?"

"I am," the woman on Stina's right said.

The judge made a low, acknowledging hum, then went back to the paper, speaking as he read. "You're here because you want your betrothed to be fined. Is this correct?"

"Yes."

"I see, and this is from eight years ago, 1740... You were betrothed to Jacob Månsson, and he accused you of having had relations with Näcken, who made you so ill you couldn't marry?"

"Yes, good sir."

Nikolaos frowned.

The judge looked down at his papers again and walked a few steps to the side. "Jacob Månsson has informed everyone that he saw a gray horse when you were ill and therefore could prove that it was Näcken you'd been with. But you're saying that you didn't. Why is this exactly?"

"Why? Because I didn't. Jacob is lying," Annika Svensdotter said, sounding very sure of herself.

"Explain," the judge said, gesturing for her to approach the podium.

Annika rose from her seat and hurried forward. She almost looked excited, but it was hard to tell from where Nikolaos was sitting. "I was weakened by several bad chills and had coughed for months. Jacob is lying. He claimed Näcken made me sick so he could break his promise to marry me. It's a lie, and I want him to pay. Corporal Anders has supported me in this and agrees that Jacob should pay for what he's done to me. For spreading these awful lies, you see."

"Yes, it says so here, and you've made it very clear that

Jacob Månsson is lying," the judge said, picking up the papers again. "It also says that Jacob was to bring witnesses. Has he?"

Annika Svensdotter shook her head.

"Speak up."

"No, he hasn´t, good sir."

"Case is dismissed."

She gasped aloud, and someone snickered in the back of the room.

"Dismissed. Sit."

Annika Svensdotter started to say something again, but a glowering look from the judge had her back in her seat without a word. She looked crestfallen.

The judge kept reading from his papers, paying her no mind. Then he glanced at the other woman. "You must be Britta's sister then," he said, gesturing for her to approach. "Your sister lived in Hjortåsen and went to visit her sick daughter in Herrstorp. Is that correct?" he said when she was standing before him.

"Yes." She promptly burst into tears, crying in big hulking sobs so loud that Nikolaos expected to see colors but didn't.

Something soft came over the judge's face, and he waited for several minutes until she had calmed down a bit. "Now, tell me what happened. I understand this happened only weeks ago?"

"Yes," she replied nasally. "My niece was ill in bed, so Britta went to help her get back on her feet. When she slept, Britta was knitting. All of a sudden, a large black horse lifted the door clasp and walked right in! Britta threw her knitting on the floor, grabbed a burning log from the fire, and then she hit the horse with it. But it walked straight through the vestibule and out the other door." She stopped talking. Nikolaos got the sense she was looking expectantly at the judge even though he could only see the back of her head. "We know it was Näcken," she added.

"How?"

"The horse, of course. Everyone knows that Näcken can take the form of a horse. And it must be him because Britta got so frightened, she couldn't get back in the house after."

"I thought you said she was inside knitting and hit the horse with a log from the fire."

"Yes, but then she went out to look for it and was so weak that her husband had to help her in. She died just after this, and so did my niece. Our pastor says that Näcken scared them to death."

The judge stared at her for a moment, then went back to his papers.

Nikolaos resisted shaking his head at them. What other information did those papers and parchments have about him? It was ridiculous. Humans were so ignorant. How in the world could they blame him for what a horse did? If they took this nonsense seriously, what would the judge do with Stina? He should never have allowed her to let them question her. They should have fled. Fear made his chest tighten, and he struggled to breathe.

The judge waved his paper in the air then sighed loudly. "Well, I don't see why I have this case here. I have the notes from your pastor, and it seems clear that Näcken scared them to death. My condolences, but there's not much I can do about it."

"Can't people look for him?" the woman asked.

"How would you propose we would do that?"

"I don't know." It came out as a whisper.

"I'm dismissing it," the judge said and waved her away. "Next case is Stina Andersdotter. Your case is more interesting. Stay where you are. You two can leave."

Annika and Britta's sister scrambled out of their seats and headed for the door. Stunned and relieved, Nikolaos kept his eyes on them, simultaneously feeling his own panic increase. Surely the judge wouldn't dismiss Stina's case as well. He had to get her out of there. Nikolaos threw a quick glance at the guard, noting that he wasn't looking at him, then got to his feet and darted forward. But he hadn't taken more than a step before he heard the guard come after him.

"You must stay where you were," he hissed, grabbing his arm.

Nikolaos turned to face him, heart racing. "I understand, sir, but since the other two left, can't I sit by Goodwife Andersdotter in case she needs assistance?"

"Absolutely not," the guard said, making eye contact with the man at the window. He hurried over and planted himself between Nikolaos and the podium.

"Pray forgive me then," Nikolaos said, sitting back down, nearly in tears from worry.

The judge waited for everyone to get back to their places, then faced Stina with a look of consternation. "I've spoken to your twelveman, Stina Andersdotter. I'm going to assume that the Näcken you know, look nothing like these women described?" He pointed to the seats the two other women had occupied.

Nikolaos hid a nervous laugh.

"No, he's not like they said. They got it all wrong. Näcken was a good man. Kind and sweet. He helped me back when I was young when there were witches on my island. He helped me, and then we fell in love."

The judge smiled slightly. "I see. And children you had as well. They lived to adulthood all?"

"Not all, good sir, only my… our daughter. But she died of a plague many years ago."

"I'm sorry to hear of it. And you're certain Näcken was the father?"

"Yes, good sir. And a wonderful father too. Kind and firm. He never grew irritated with them. He was always loving."

Nikolaos stared at her, seeing her profile clearly from where he sat, willing himself to stay in his seat. What if he sentenced her to death?

The judge put his hands on his hips and walked around the podium, gazing up toward the ceiling as if asking God for help. Maybe he was. Once he made a full circle, he placed his elbows on the podium and leaned forward. "I take it then that Näcken never plays fiddle in the river and lures people in with him. Never does he swim there, never does he fish lockets from the bottom, nor fornicate with women and even men? The transcripts I have from witnesses are faulty then." He looked intently into Stina's face. His tone revealed disbelief, disgust, and amusement at the same time.

Nikolaos squirmed uncomfortably. The guard beside him

turned toward him with a grin as if they were sharing a joke.

"My husband had a need for water. It wasn't at a fault of his own. He never hurt anyone on purpose."

"Your husband? So, you *were* married then?" The judge picked up the scroll and another piece of paper. "Says here that you never married."

"We did. God witnessed it, but we had no one walking us to the bridal chamber." Stina's voice was shaking.

"I see, not married then," the judge said and picked up his quill, making a quick note in the scroll. "What can you tell me about your locket, Stina Andersdotter?" he asked, pushing both the scroll and the paper aside.

Her hand instinctively went to her empty neck. "My husband gave it to me many years ago."

"He did, did he? Found it in the river, didn't he?"

"I don't know."

The judge raised an eyebrow at that. Then he turned his head and looked in Nikolaos' direction, let his gaze slide past him, and gave a quick nod to the guard who slowly went to the door and opened it. Nikolaos started to stand up, heart in his throat. Had he sent for more guards to take her away?

"You can come inside now," the guard said and stepped aside. It was just a man, coming in alone.

Tears of relief filled Nikolaos' eyes, along with a sudden flush of sweat. The man wore no wig and kept his own hair tied with a blue ribbon in the back. It was dirty and hung below his shoulders over a faded green coat.

The judge acknowledged him with a nod. "Welcome Jöns Alman. You've studied with both Carl von Linné and Pher Kalm, is that correct?"

"Yes, I have. Pher Kalm was a mentor to me before he traveled to the New World."

"Good." The judge gestured toward him with his quill. "You may begin."

Jöns Alman bowed, then crossed the floor to face Stina. He stared at her, a scrutinizing stare that sent a new spike of fear through Nikolaos.

"Did you live in the water with Näcken?"

"No."

"You didn't?" He looked genuinely surprised. "Interesting. How did you live then?"

"I... we lived like everyone else."

"You lived in a regular house? Not all the time, I gather. How about on Thursdays?"

"We lived in our home." Stina threw a quick exasperated look at the judge. He didn't respond.

Jöns nodded slowly, frowning. "Did Näcken dissolve into water on a regular basis or was he able to sit in a chair?"

Stina now turned around and looked across the room to where Nikolaos sat. He met her eyes, afraid to move in any way that would get her to misunderstand and give the wrong answer. She had seen him become at least somewhat watery on quite a few occasions.

The judge noticed her gaze. "Stina Andersdotter, your assistant cannot answer for you."

Stina turned back forward. "Yes," she said. "Yes, good sir, he can. He sits like a..."

"Can? Sits?" the judge interrupted. "Is he not dead your husband? Näcken."

"My husband never came home from Cremona. We think he's dead. We know he is. I have a letter." Stina's voice was shaking.

He had to stop this; it had gone on long enough. Nikolaos slipped off his chair and hurried across the floor, not caring that the guard would try to stop him. Once the guard caught up, he was prepared, and just pushed him off and kept walking.

"When did he die?" Jöns Alman asked, oblivious to Nikolaos. "Didn't the other woman just a moment ago tell everyone that her sister and niece died because Näcken scared them to death only weeks...?" Jöns Alman stopped talking, finally noticing Nikolaos.

"Get back to where you were or leave my courtroom," the judge interjected. "We're in the middle of a hearing here."

Nikolaos gave an unflinching stare. "My charge is getting

tired. You can surely understand that she couldn't have been married to a horse like Britta and Annika were talking about."

"Britta's sister," the judge said curtly.

"Her sister, that's who I meant. But Stina is over ninety years old. She's obviously a little confused." He threw Stina a warning glance, willing her not to contradict him. "And let me confirm for you, her husband *is* dead. As she said, she has a letter from the man who buried him."

The judge looked at him silently for several moments. Then he nodded. "The man has a point. Not only that. I'm hungry. I'm dismissing this case as well. It's all been a waste of my time. If you want to ask the old woman more questions, it's your prerogative, Alman, but you must do so elsewhere. I'm going home."

"You can't possibly end it now. I've barely begun my questioning," Jöns Alman said.

"Yes, I can. I've heard of those studies that you've done and heard that Linné and Kahlm didn't believe in the claims that other races of people live on farms on the bottom of rivers and lakes and such. Case dismissed."

The judge picked up the papers and scroll from the podium, placed them under his arm, and left. He looked exasperated and exhausted as if he thought the whole thing was ridiculous.

***

Stina stunk of fear and sweat and could barely stand upright.

"We're going to the lodging house. Then as soon as you're rested, we're going home," Nikolaos said, grabbing a steady hold of her waist, supporting her the best he could as they slowly shuffled out of the courthouse. He felt close to tears again, both from relief and from anger at having let it come to this. It was his fault in more than one way, and he should never have allowed them to question her.

They had made it halfway down the street when he suddenly felt a tap on his shoulder. Startled, Nikolaos turned around and found Jöns Alman's face next to his. Uncomfortably

726

close. He couldn't believe it. "What are you doing?" he snapped, moving away from him.

"Good sir, may I speak to her? I've many more questions. The judge said that I may ask them elsewhere."

Nikolaos shook his head, hoping it conveyed how annoyed he felt. "He also said your teachers didn't believe in your ridiculous claims, and no, you may not speak with her," he said and kept walking, ignoring him. But Jöns persisted, refusing to leave their side. Nikolaos couldn't take it and resolutely picked Stina up and carried her off. Fast, the way most humans couldn't.

Stina was so exhausted that she didn't seem to have noticed much at all. By the time they were in their room, she was asleep in his arms like a child. He put her on the bed and covered her with a blanket, then left her there and went back out to see if Jöns Alman had followed them.

And there he was, just like he expected, standing across from the entrance with his eyes fixed on the door. "What do you want? I'm not letting you ask her any questions. There's no point in trying to talk me into it."

Jöns rocked back on his heels. "I understand. I do, but could I ask you a question or two?"

"What for? It's starting to rain," Nikolaos said as a rush of drops landed in his hair. He had left his hat inside.

"Well, we can go stand under the roof over there," Jöns said, pointing to the protruding thatch of the building next to the lodging house. There was just enough space to stand under it and not get wet.

Nikolaos hesitated, then nodded. It was annoying that he was so insistent on it, but this would be an opportunity to learn what people thought of him. Jöns looked immensely pleased.

"Well then, tell me what you want to know," Nikolaos said once they were both standing under the thatch. It was moldy on the underside and didn't smell too good.

Jöns followed Nikolaos' gaze and grimaced. "It ought to be replaced," he said and reached up and scraped at the mold with his fingernail, then held his hand out under the rain to rinse it off. "I have a lot I want to know, but first I'd like to clarify that the reason Linné and Kahlm said that they don't believe in it, is just because they don't have enough evidence to back up those claims. It doesn't necessarily mean that it isn't true. But that's really beside the point. I don't know why the judge dismissed the case. Stina, old as she is, did admit that not only did she know Näcken but that she'd been married to him and had children with him. That he dismissed it when witnesses and other cases confirmed his existence," Jöns lifted his eyebrows and shook his head with displeasure, "is improper. A missed opportunity for important research."

"Hmm," Nikolaos said, hiding a smile. "Research?"

Jöns nodded gravely and pulled out a small pocketbook and a stringed graphite stick. "Have you never noticed anything?"

"Well…"

"Did you ever meet her husband? Did he seem odd to you? Was his skin wet? A smell of river gunk about him? Did he ever turn into a horse? Even partly?" He wrote the word *wet* in his pocketbook.

Nikolaos crossed his arms over his chest. Maybe he should take Stina's advice and tell him that Näcken had been a kind and misunderstood man, someone who liked to spend a lot of time in streams but who wasn't what everyone thought. Jöns Alman was a science man of sorts. He might write a dissertation on it which could change people's opinions. Nikolaos took a breath, then decided it was better to just let it be. "Pray forgive me," he said, noting that Jöns was starting to look impatient. "No, I never met him. And as I said during the hearing, she's old and a little confused about things. They had children, a daughter who lived into adulthood. Surely that should prove that her husband wasn't someone who lived in the river on Thursdays. Why Thursdays, anyway? Everyone talks about that day, but I've never understood why."

Jöns looked disappointed, lowering his pocketbook. "Well, that I can assure you, doesn't disprove anything. People have found races of people living under the surface of waterways. They have farms and taverns and everything else down there. My theory is that it's Näcken who's fathered them all."

Nikolaos laughed.

"This isn't a laughing matter, I assure you," Jöns said, looking offended.

"I disagree," Nikolaos kept laughing, letting out an unseemly snort, then somehow managed to stop. "You ought to listen to Carl von Linné. He does know what he's talking about. There can't be people living under the surface anywhere. It's just old stories from people who've seen discarded old furniture and things like that. People always toss stuff they don't want any longer in the river or in sounds." Like dead horses. He pushed the thought away.

"Oh, no, that's not it. They live much deeper than that."

Nikolaos frowned. "Isn't the refuse on the bottom? How could there be people deeper than that?"

Jöns looked taken aback, staring at him with a blank expression. Then he recovered. "That's what everybody asks, but further out from the banks, it's deeper. As for Thursdays, it's because the day is named after Thor, the old heathen god. It gives creatures like these an opportunity to sneak past God's protection."

Nikolaos didn't understand but decided not to ask for another explanation.

Jöns looked impatient again. "Have you noticed anything odd about Stina Andersdotter? How is it that Näcken didn't do away with her? Did he have to go in the rivers privately? How did he manage that?" he asked, holding his graphite stick at the ready.

Nikolaos exhaled slowly. It was getting too close to the truth for comfort. "Jöns Alman, Stina had a normal husband. He died in Cremona. I can't tell you anything else."

A carriage drove by, sending a spray of puddle water and muck their way, some of which landed on Jöns' papers.

He wiped it off with his hand. "I don't think she'd be called all the way to a hearing here at Göta Court if there's no truth to it. If I were you, I'd keep my eye out for her husband so he doesn't come looking for victims."

"Her husband is dead." Nikolaos suddenly felt incredibly tired, regretting that he had agreed to talk with him. He wanted to be with Stina, not stand here under a moldy roof. "I'm leaving," he said and stepped into the rain. Jöns called out after him, but he didn't bother to turn around.

***

The trip home was uneventful, but traveling for so many days tired Stina immensely, and they didn't talk much. Nikolaos was lost in thought for most of it, thinking about the trial. The judge truly didn't seem to care. How could it be so different from Jon's, Old Karin's, and Karin's trials? It was also strange that Annika, the woman who wanted her betrothed to pay a fine for having slandered her, brought it to trial herself. How was that even possible? No one he had ever known would admit something like that. As ridiculous as the accusations of him being a horse entering houses were, and how frightened he had been when they questioned Stina, he felt an overwhelming sense of relief. It wasn't just that her case had been dismissed. Things were different.

Chapter 87

There were no more trials. No one came to question them. The neighbors hadn't even realized what they had been through, which must mean that Kurt had never explained to the castle servants why he needed to borrow the horse and wagon.

Stina invited Hindrich and Ekborg to come and stay a while. Nikolaos hid outside when they arrived, spying on them. His son. Still strong and tall but walking with a stiffness to his gait, his hair gray. Nikolaos watched until they closed their front door, then left for his river, knowing he would never see him again.

* * *

A year later it was time. Nikolaos could feel it, tell by the way Stina was breathing, her scent and the way she looked at him.

He stayed up that night, watching her sleep, the shallow labored breaths, the calmness of the room.

When the sun rose behind the curtains, he pulled them aside, letting the sun's dusty beams in through the windowpanes. Then he woke her.

"Husband, it's so light in here. Are we back on the farm?"

"No, darling we're not. But I wanted to speak with you. Tell you how much I love you. Can you sit a while?"

She nodded, and he helped her up, feeling her skinny bones under his hands, her thick hair brushing his forearm. He sat down at the side of the bed and took her hand in his. It felt the same as last time. Soft and limp. And cool to the touch. She even looked like Abluna somehow, as if nearing death merged them together.

"I love you too, husband," she said. Her voice was faint, barely a whisper.

He cried.

She closed her eyes. A moment of panic sent his heart racing, but she was still breathing. He patted her hand, then picked it up and kissed it, his tears flowing over their fingers. He wanted to tell her the truth, that she was Abluna and that he would find her

731

again. That he would look for her. But he couldn't, not now, not after all these years keeping it from her. Though she hadn't said it, he knew she was looking forward to seeing Elsebet and their dead babies again. He couldn't take that from her.

He stood up and put his arm under her back, moving the pillow from under her, then lifted her and laid her down again. There wasn't much time now.

She didn't notice being moved, and he sat back down at the edge of the bed, facing her. The clock seemed to tick louder than usual, reminding him that he was expected to stop it at the time of her death and open the window so her soul could find its way to heaven.

"Stina," he whispered.

She didn't answer, breaths far in between. Then there were no more.

Epilogue

"Professor, may I speak to you for a moment?"

Nikolaos turned toward the voice and found his colleague smiling at him, holding a bucket in his right hand as flames and smoke billowed out the windows from Three Crowns behind him. "Elion, I didn't see you or know you were here."

"I couldn't stay away," Elion said, swinging the bucket as he approached. "I brought two of my own students today who both want to change their majors to history. They couldn't stop talking about you, so I decided to tag along. I see why you're so sought after, Nikolaos. Your knowledge is extraordinary. It's as if you spoke of the present, not incidents that happened hundreds of years ago. All the details!" Elion put the bucket down.

"Thank you. That's very nice of you to say."

"Oh, it was fantastic. No wonder you steal my chemistry students from me." He grinned. "Anyway, one of them is sitting outside waiting for you. He's an older student, in his mid-thirties, I believe, who went back to school last year. I hope I'm not putting you on the spot, but he said that he really wants to speak with you."

"Not at all, that's fine," Nikolaos said as he turned off the holo-projector, transforming the room back to its original space.

"I was also wondering if I could invite you and your wife to dinner tonight. We're having a bit of a potluck. Is she back from California yet?" Elion asked.

"No, Råalda won't be back for several months. She's on another field study. I'll be glad to come though if you'll still have me. What should I bring?" Nikolaos grabbed his coffee mug. It was half full but cold.

"Of course. Råalda is a geologist, right?"

"Arborist. She's with a team in the Redwoods right now."

"Ah, that's what it was. Sorry, I'm not sure why I can never remember that. If you bring a dessert, we'll be all set."

Elion let Nikolaos walk ahead of him as they left. "It looks like Maelo is waiting for you," he said, gesturing toward one of the benches in the hallway. Then he gave a quick nod and headed to the nearest stairwell.

"I'll see you tonight," Nikolaos called after him. He took a sip of the cold coffee and grimaced, deciding to go get a fresh cup.

The student got to his feet when he saw Nikolaos. He was not too tall and was muscular and fit, a runner it looked like. His hair was long on one side and short on the other in the latest fashion. It was cute and made him look both unassuming and confident. "Professor Nordvatten, I'm Maelo. I hope Professor Elion Sundkhalid mentioned me?"

"Yes, he did." Nikolaos motioned in the direction of the cafeteria with his mug. "I'm about to get another cup of coffee. Why don't you join me?" Then he met Maelo's gaze and time stopped.

He was staring straight into Abluna's eyes.

APPENDIX

Mythology: followed by real-life characters, events, and places in the order in which they appear. (I recommend not skipping this part; actual events inspire more than you might expect.)

Näcken: A.K.A Nikolaos, as he calls himself in my story, is a mythological creature who lures people—especially women—into rivers where he drowns them.

He is irresistibly handsome and is an exceptional fiddle player who spellbinds people with his music. He often has sex with his victims before they drown.

He can take many forms and is sometimes seen as a horse, a dog, or a wave in the water. My interpretation is that he was generally seen as a frightening character in earlier times rather than a sexual being. In my telling, it's a combination of both throughout. His fiddle and violin are also more prominent later, but in my telling, he plays music from the beginning.

Forest Rå: (Skogsrå in Swedish) is a mythological creature who lures lone men into the woods to have sex with them.

Descriptions of her vary. Sometimes, she has a fox tail, horse eyes, or hooves. In her more humanlike form, she is gorgeous with long brown hair. But under her hair, her back is either a tree trunk, a hole, or a tree trunk with a hole in it. In my telling, she has both. It's my invention that she calls herself Magda and is a wisewoman and an herbalist.

Woodcutters and hunters spot her in the distance but can't always tell if she is a tree or a woman. Once they get a better glimpse, they can't resist her exceptional beauty and will follow her even deeper into the woods. Sometimes they get lost and lose time or get sucked into the hole in her back. When they get home, their penises might hurt after all the sex. Her food is magic, and it's best not to eat it. She smears a salve on her lovers' guns to give them luck in their hunts. Additionally, Rå is known as a caretaker who cares for animals and the forest. In Swedish, rå is also the word for care.

Until the mid-18th century, Näcken and Rå were considered real beings. Having relations with them was illegal. As you've read in my story, people were tried, jailed, and often executed when found guilty.

Norrköping's House: castle in the city of Norrköping. It was built in the same place where a previous castle stood, also called Norrköping's House. It burned down in 1604. The first Norrköping's House was torched by Swedes in 1657 to prevent the enemy from occupying it.

Princess Elisabeth Vasa: King Gustav Vasa's daughter, lived in Norrköping's House with her German court between 1594 and 1597. She was married to Christopher, Duke of Mecklenburg-Gadebusch (now Germany), and was widowed in 1592.

Seven Year War (Northern Seven Year War): 1563-1570 was the first big war between Denmark and Sweden.

Passports: also called road proofs, were used to travel within the country, and if you moved to a new parish, you had to prove you knew Christianity and were a lawful, orderly person.

Synesthesia: that Näcken saw colors when he played music or heard loud sounds is my invention. As far as I know, it's not part of the myth.

Violins and fiddles: the chinrest was invented around 1820. Before that, violinists and fiddle players leaned their instruments on their upper chests.

Sixmen: a sixman was an elected public servant in a parish. They were called Sixmen (sexmän in Swedish), as there were six of them.

Pastor Joen Petri Klint: drew a picture of Näcken standing in the Motala River, wearing an Elizabethan collar, cosmetics, fine clothing, with his head shaved. He reported that in 1599, several people had drowned and that a slimy (yes, slimy) comet had been seen, which always brought ill. Nikolaos' and Karl the Bagpiper's unusual habit of shaving their heads was inspired by Pastor Klint's illustration.

Twelvemen: officials in the local court. They were called twelvemen (tolvmän in Swedish), as there were twelve of them.

King Sigismund: King of Sweden from 1592-1599 and King of Poland from 1587-1632.

Castle Three Crowns - Slottet Tre Kronor: the royal castle in Stockholm.

Duke Erik (King Karl IX) King of Sweden 1604-1611. Protector of the Realm 1599-1604. The King is to have seen Näcken in the waterways outside the castle and tried to shoot him and got the bullet thrown back at him. This was told to the Dutch diplomat Anthonis Goatees in Juli 1616.

St. Nikolaos' Church: Stockholm's Cathedral, also known as Storkyrkan - the Great Church, and St. Nicholas Church. In earlier times it was called St. Nikolai Church. In my telling, I chose to use the same spelling as Nikolaos' name.

St. Göran and the Dragon: a majestic statue of St. George and the Dragon inside St. Nicholas Church.

The Cave behind the waterfall: It was often said that Näcken lived in a cave behind a waterfall.

Karin Persdotter: was 97 years old in 1653 when she was sentenced for having "put the disease" on her sister-in-law, another woman, and cattle. Karin had learned which herbs to use from Näcken many years earlier when she was young. She had looked for him in the river and thrown money in it as an offering. She also asked the Devil for help, which was somewhat common at the time according to some sources.
The fact that she owned a rune stick and was old and ugly helped prove her guilt since it was a sign of collaboration with the Devil and thus Näcken. Karin was tried in the local tribunal in Uppvidinge and was sent to Göta Royal Court, where she was sentenced to death by hanging.

That she was tortured and kept in a dank jail cell in Jönköping is my invention. It's also my invention that she looked for Näcken and asked him for help before the trial in Uppvidinge. She *was* buried at the gallows after the execution, but it's my invention that the executioner cut her finger off and collected the blood. However, this was a relatively common practice. As explained by Dr. Judy Melinek, a Forensic Pathologist, after a hanging, blood pools due to gravity, causing "stocking and glove lividity." It will slowly drip at a steady stream but won't gush since the heart is no longer beating. The body's clotting mechanism ceases after death, but blood will eventually dry out.

Wätter Lacus: Large Lake, older names for lake Vänern.

Queen Kristina: 1632 (regent 1644) – 1654. She abdicated and left the country to convert to Catholicism.

Changelings: people thought that babies with disabilities or babies screaming too much (colic?) might be a baby troll. Trolls were known to sneak in and exchange newborns for their own. Fire would keep them away.

Troll butter: was known to grow in the spot where stolen milk had been spilled. Today, we know it's a species of fungi.

The Vasa ship: sunk in Stockholm harbor 1628. That Näcken was rumored to have something to do with it is my invention.

Göta Royal Court: Göta hovrätt, is one of Sweden's six High Courts. (I will refer to it as Göta hovrätt from here on)

Pastor Prytz: wrote about demonology, describing all those interesting details Abraham Lövcrantz lectured about. Abraham is my invention, but the details described in his lecture are consistent with the times' beliefs.

Post horn: The Swedish Postal Service was founded in 1636 and was unique for using farmers, called Postal Farmers at 2-3 Swedish mile intervals who took care of the mail. It was preferable if they knew how to read. Each farmer should have two farmhands who would walk fast —they were not allowed to run—between the farms. They carried a horn to blow in, a plaque, and a staff for protection from wild animals. Horses were used as well, eventually.

Gustav Horn: military general who attacked Skåne when it belonged to Denmark.

Brömsebo Treaty: August 13, 1645. Just like Rasmus told Rå, a deal between Sweden and Denmark was reached. Denmark got to keep what is now Skåne and the land south of Kalmar. This ended the Danish War, also called Torstensson's War - 1643-1645. In 1658, the Roskilde Treaty was reached, and Skåne became Swedish.

Karin Svensdotter: was tried in 1656 at the local tribunal in Borakulle or Hjälmseryd. The exact place for this hearing isn't entirely clear in the historical documents. I chose to place the hearing in a fictional church in Borakulle. As told in my story, Karin was a maid working for Lars Mickelsson. All the details in the storyline, including the questions she was asked during the hearing, are based on historical documentation. The gory details about Näcken eating the afterbirth and that he looked like a dog are also documented. The local tribunal wasn't sure what to do with her case and felt that she was confused and a bit weak, and wrote to Göta hovrätt to ask for advice. The courts concluded that she was possessed by the Devil, who probably made her imagine she was pregnant. They recommended that the parish pray for her.

That Karin was not executed despite her claims is very unusual for the time. Because of this, my interpretation is that Karin Svensdotter had an intellectual disability and mental illness, which may have become worse after what may have been a miscarriage.

Historical records describe that Karin claimed she went into a green mountain with Näcken and a large man she was afraid of. I made this man Tailor Jon and changed the green mountain into Nikolaos' cave. The flower ring and bracelet are my inventions as well. It was a common belief that gifts from Näcken turned into grass, but in this case, the historical documentation says Karin claimed Näcken gave her a golden ring.

Tailor Jon: Jon Persson from Hallebo was tried and convicted at Göta hovrätt in 1697 and was executed by beheading, followed by quartering at age 90 or 97. (Sources are not consistent regarding his age.) Jon was a known herbalist. He was accused of being an especially terrible sinner and warlord since he had "put the disease" on Court Assessor Örnevinge's wife. The details about furry or fuzzy trolls with hats and getting a book of black magic written in blood from Näcken are also documented. He had looked for Näcken in the river three Thursdays in a row and had placed runes in the river. Näcken showed up with a racket after that. This happened sixty years prior.

In my telling, Jon doesn't live in Hallebo but near Karin Svensdotter's village. I also shifted the time a few years to coincide with Karin Svensdotter's story. That he is a tailor is my invention. It is also my invention that Jon spent so much time with the Forest Rå.

Harp Music: as the pastor in Borakulle told Nikolaos, harp music was known to draw Näcken out. His hot footprints are my invention.

Odin: there is historical documentation stating that Odin was angry with the Forest Rå and was often heard chasing her through the night. Some historians theorize that people heard flocks of geese at night but didn't understand what it was. This inspired me to make Rå old enough to have been born in pre-Christian times. The story about Rå's mother and their love for each other is inspired by my mother, whose name was also Solveig.

Stina Andersdotter: was tried in Herrestad in November 1748. The tribunal forwarded her case to Göta hovrätt, and she was tried there in March 1749. She was unmarried but claimed she had been with Näcken for many years and had children with him. (The records are somewhat ambiguous if it was more than one child.) This inspired me to make her the love of Näcken's life, his human love, anyway. That she was the reincarnated Abluna and then Maelo is my invention.

Anna in Holta: was in 1669 accused of sinking boats, making her neighbor Söfren impotent and feel as though his stomach were full of kittens. As told in my story, soon other people were accused in Anna's community as well, including Signe and her daughter. Anna hung herself in jail, which people took to mean that she was compelled to do so by Satan.

The Blue Hill: was the name of the place where witches were known to congregate and feast with Satan.

Witch Burnings: Contrary to common assumptions, only one woman was burned alive at the stake in Sweden. Her name was Rumpare Malin, and she was burned in Stockholm. The other accused were executed first.

Carlsten's Fortress: Carlstens Fästning on the island of Marstrand is now a historic landmark. Just as Stina described, prisoners helped build and add to it. Its final construction was in 1860.

St. Halvard's - Ytterby Church: was consecrated in the 12th century. It is now a church ruin and a tourist attraction. That witches were hung there is my invention.

Bishop Angermannus: Abrahamus Andreas Angermannus, born ca 1540, died 1607. As Nikolaos explained to Stina, he had very strong opinions on rules and religion.

Drinking tobacco: was how people described smoking when it first became popular. It was indeed considered good for you. People thought it cured everything from dandruff to coughing.

Wiseboys: were young boys who claimed they could tell whether someone was a witch or not.

Sven Andersson: was questioned about Rå for eight days by Pastor Petrus Kellander. At first, Sven described her as nice and warm, but after a while, he changed his mind and said that her vagina was cold. Kellander explained how "devilish" this relationship was. Its "devilishness" was confirmed since Kellander became pale when he first found out. Sven admitted having been with the Forest Rå for at least six or seven years. This was confirmed by the fact that his penis hurt and that his foreskin could be pulled back just like married men's. Vättle häradsrätt (Vättle Local Tribunal) sentenced Sven Andersson to death in 1691. His case was going to be forwarded to Göta hovrätt, but Sven died in prison in Nya Älvsborg. In my telling, Rå meets him on her way to the winter market in Jönköping and again on the way home when he shows her his new watch.

Minute hands: were first added to clocks with the invention and introduction of the pendulum in 1656. The minute hand began to appear on watches in 1675 with the introduction of the balance spring, and its use was firmly established by 1710. Both shelf clocks and standing clocks made after 1656 had minute hands.

The Inn Ordinance: was put in place in 1649 and meant that there should be inns, or farmers, no further than two Swedish miles apart. The inns had exclusive rights to sell alcoholic beverages.

Farmers might be responsible for driving and for offering horses for a fee. Some sources give shorter or longer mileage. In my telling, I chose to go with two miles.

King Karl XI: reigned (as an adult) from 1672-1697. He died of stomach cancer on April 5, 1697. It's my invention that Näcken played for him when he lay ill.

Rowing women: in Stockholm started a group within the guild, and some were rumored to take on some sex work as well.

Nicodemus Tessin (the younger): the architect who, among other things, refurbished parts of Three Crowns and built the new castle, now called, Kungliga Slottet - The Royal Palace. He was just as ambitious as my story tells. There were rumors that he had a part in setting Three Crowns on fire so he could get the contract to rebuild.

Princess Hedvig Sofia: daughter of Karl XI and Ulrika Eleonora. Many sources claim she had cloven thumbs (or two thumbs on each hand.)

Monsieur Pierre Verdier: was an elderly musician living at Three Crowns.

Coffee: it is claimed that the first half kilo came to Sweden in 1685. After that, it was sold only at apothecaries and was very expensive. Some sources claim that Karl XI brought it to Three Crowns and that his son Karl XII was very fond of it.

King Karl XII: his paternal Grandmother, Queen Hedvig Eleonora, ruled with Karl XII until he was crowned, along with five royal advisers, including the esteemed Bengt Gabrielsson Oxenstierna.

Three Crowns Fire: The castle burned down on May 7, 1697. The dead King's body, which had been lying in state, was carried outside. Arson was suspected, and there was a trial. Some also suggested it may have been witches since it was said that they had threatened to burn down the castle 20 years before during the Witch Panic. In short, three men were charged and had to run the gauntlet.

King Karl XI's funeral: was just as elaborate as described. Archbishop Svebilius spoke, and Bishop Haquin Spegel sang a final prayer. That Näcken played during it is my invention.

Assessor Örnevinge: was an assessor during Tailor Jon's trial.

Herding Decree: in 1686, the King made a Royal Decree that it was best that women herded farm animals as they were less likely to perform bestiality.

Bäckaskog's Castle: Rutger von Asheberg stayed there, in charge of "Swedefying" the former Danes who were now living on Swedish land.

Kjugekull and Rå's cows: a group of people in a village called Kjugekull helped the Forest Rå when her cows got stuck in the mud. Years later, when cattle disease swept through the area, only the cows belonging to those who had helped Rå survived.

Documentation from 1666 from the village Tjust near the town of Västervik tells of a case where a man, Sven Månsson, started a religion with the Mountain Rå and held services with her where she sat behind a curtain in bed. She brought angels that only Sven Månsson could see. The case went to the courts, but nothing came of it. I have freely taken inspiration from this case, combined it with the case about Rå's cows, and used it in my telling of Måns and his uncles. And in my story, Rå is the Forest Rå, not the Mountain Rå.

House Hearings: home visits by the local pastor to make sure the congregation knew Luther's Little Catechism and for record keeping. Began around 1686 and continued into the 19th century.

Margarete Inn: is one of Sweden's oldest inns. The spot on Halland's ridge has had an inn there since the 14th century. It's called Margarete Torp now.

Lady Maria Church: in Helsingborg is a 12th-century church. It's now known as Mariakyrkan, Maria Church.

Doctor Johan Jacob Döbelius: (von Döbeln after he was ennobled in 1717) founded Ramlösa Brunnspark - Ramlösa Natural Spring on King Karl XII's birthday on June 17, 1707. All the details of how it was discovered and his work to get it ready were just as I told it, including his descriptions of ailments and the anger from the crowd that first day.

The park is still there, and the water is bottled and carbonated today. It's now a residential area with landmarked 19th-century buildings from what you might call Ramlösa Park's heyday. It is my invention that Näcken played in Ramlösa and my invention that a memorial get-together was held for him after his death. However, he did write a history of Lund's University, which was noted in a couple of newspapers.

Magnus Stenbock: governor of Skåne and military general, leading the battle in Helsingborg.

Beata Lybecker: the pain in her arms was cured by Doctor Döbelius' water.

King Karl XI: issued a decree against duels in 1682. This wasn't followed very strictly, and duels were still held off and on until much later.

Östra Aros: or Ostarres, now Uppsala, was an important political and religious place with an important Asatru temple.

Sven Jönsson: who Näcken was reading about on the poster on the church door in Helsingborg, was a soldier tried by the courts in Skara and by military tribunal in 1707-1708. His descriptions of her were as told in my story, as was Sparfeldt's interest in different types of Rå. Sven Jönsson's wife never noticed him meeting Rå and said he made it all up to escape military service, which Sven eventually admitted to. In my telling, Rå encounters Sven Jönsson with her cow and later again when she is going to Helsingborg during the battle of Helsingborg.

Helsingborg's Castle: now known as Kärnan. Just like Nikolaos knew, outbuildings and the wall around it were torn down, and Helsingborg almost lost the tower too.

Merchant Svend Phil: lived on the farm which was built by Jacob Hansen in 1641. It is now landmarked and known as Jacob Hansens hus - Jacob Hansen's House. Svend Phil was Jacob Hansen's son-in-law.

Church Weddings: became mandatory in 1734. Before this, a wedding was a feast held at the bride's home, followed by a procession through the village to the groom's home to show that they were now a married couple. The church ordinance from 1686 states that a betrothal followed by sex was considered a marriage. Over time, the church gradually moved the ceremony from the bride's home to inside the church. This is a simplified overview of a complex historical shift.

General Carl Hårdh af Segerstad: burned Råå village in October of 1677 as punishment for going across the sound to Denmark to shop without permission.

Råå village: was attacked by Danes on June 29, 1676, just like Nikolaos mentioned when Danes arrived in Råå on November 2, 1709.

Burning of Helsingborg: it is claimed that the Swedish Army was discussing burning Helsingborg down rather than letting Denmark take it. I have not been able to confirm this. It may be hearsay or a rumor circulating during the occupation. Many people in Skåne still felt Danish at heart. It is also true that the Danes were welcomed when they first arrived.

Pastor Jacobsen and Pastor Trollius: didn't see eye to eye; Jacobsen was loyal to the Danes, and Pastor Troilius was forced to flee north during the occupation of Helsingborg. The service with them both is my invention.

The Occupation of Helsingborg: King Fredrik IV of Denmark entered Helsingborg on November 5, 1709, making Mayor Herman Schyleter's home his headquarters. Schlyeter abandoned his Swedish loyalties and was promptly installed as the new mayor as the former (and Swedish born) Mayor Gabriel Löfgren fled.

The battle of Helsingborg: took place on February 28, 1710. The Danes lost. As told in the story, before the Danish military left town, they slaughtered 5000-6000 horses. All the details of this gruesome affair are as described. The specifics of how the deceased horses were removed came from my research, informed by consultations with veterinarians.

Anna Svensdotter: sued Jacob Månsson to pay a fine for slander after he said Näcken had made her too ill to marry him. He could prove this because he had seen a gray horse. He claimed to have witnesses, but they never showed up. The judge asked for more witnesses, but there is no more information. *

Britta from Hjortåsen's sister: (there is no other name in the records.) Her story about Näcken coming into her sister's house in the form of a horse is as told. Their pastor wrote in the parish files that Näcken must have scared them to death.

*Both Annika Svensdotter and Britta were questioned in their local courts, but for dramatic purposes, I had them questioned in the same courtroom as Stina Andersdotter at the same time. Anna sued for slander in 1740, not in 1749.

Per Kahlm and **Carl von Linné:** investigated in the 1740s claims of changelings, underwater civilizations, and sea-human hybrids. While they were skeptical, the fact that a famed botanist took time to investigate claims like that is very revealing of the era's beliefs.

Jöns Alman, who spoke at Stina's trial and with Nikolaos, is my invention.

Glossary:

Blót: Norse religious ritual and sacrifice

Brännvin: alcoholic beverage

Freya: Norse Goddess

Kulle: hill in Swedish

Kulning: herding call

Möllestradet: street in Helsingborg, using the Danish name for it, which was still common at that time.

Skåne: the southernmost province of Sweden, which was in dispute with Denmark several times.

Thor: Norse God

Valhöll: Norse spelling of Valhalla

Resources:

Theses and publications:

Näckens dödliga dop : manliga vattenväsen, död och förbjuden sexualitet i det tidigmoderna Sverige - Mikael Häll, Lund's University.

SKOGSRÅET NÄCKEN OCH DJÄVULEN: Erotiska naturväsen och demonisk sexualitet i 1600 och 1700 talens Sverige - Mikael Häll

BROTT, SYND OCH STRAFF Tidelagsbrottet i Sverige under 1600- och 1700talet - Jonas Liliequist

Historien om Sverige: Från istid till framtid-så blev de första 1400 åren - Herman Lindqvist

Sveriges historia: 1600-1720 - Nils Erik Villstrand

Institutions

Livrustkammaren - The Royal Armory – Sweden

Historiska museet - Swedish History Museum

Landsarkivet - The National Archives - Sweden

Lund's University

Svenska kyrkan - The Church of Sweden

Kungahuset - The Royal Court - Sweden

About the Author

Helen Lundström Erwin is the author of the historical fiction novels Sour Milk in Sheep's Wool and James' Journey. She has also written and illustrated a children's book, Officer Helga Hedgehog Meets the New Neighbors. The Lure of Water and Wood is her first foray into the historical fantasy genre.

Helen was born in Helsingborg, Sweden, and lives in New York City with her husband.

Helen is the first novelist in the Metaverse and has a VR World inspired by Hanna's café from her novel Sour Milk in Sheep's Wool, where she holds monthly meetings with women and allies, just like her character Hanna did in the book.

Helen has been awarded the 2021 Swedish Women's Educational Association (SWEA) New York Scholarship for the artistic promotion of Swedish culture and history in New York, as well as a grant from The Puffin Foundation for her work. Her Foremothers Café Community Discussion Series has been nominated for an Auggie Award, and Helen has been nominated for the XR Women Trailblazer Award.

For updates and to connect with Helen, please follow her on social media through her website at www.helenerwin.com

9 780986 266669